Sizzling, sultry and seductive!

HOT SUMMER NIGHTS

Enjoy these stories of three passionate, independent women finding the love of a lifetime from bestselling authors Dallas Schulze, Maggie Shayne and Lindsay McKenna.

The perfect summer treat.

'Ms Schulze knows just how to tap into our deepest fantasies…'
—*Romantic Times*

'Shayne gives readers a rich, sensual and bewitching adventure of good vs evil, with love as the prize.'
—*Publishers Weekly*

'Lindsay McKenna continues to leave her distinctive mark on the romance genre with…timeless tales about the healing powers of love.'
—*Affaire de Coeur*

DALLAS SCHULZE

is loved the world over as one of romance's premier writers. She is the author of over thirty romance novels, both contemporary and historical, and is the recipient of many awards. Dallas loves a happy ending and hopes her readers have as much fun with her books as she does. She loves to hear from her readers, and you can write to her at PO Box 241, Verdugo City, CA 91046, USA.

MAGGIE SHAYNE

is a bestselling author whom *Romantic Times Magazine* calls 'brilliantly inventive'. She has written more than twenty-five novels for Silhouette, has won numerous awards and is a four-time finalist for the Romance Writers of America's prestigious RITA Award. In her spare time, Maggie enjoys collecting gemstones, reading tarot cards, using the internet and spending time outdoors. She lives in a rural town in central New York with her husband, Rick, five beautiful daughters and two English bulldogs. She is also the proud grandmother of two grandchildren.

LINDSAY McKENNA

A homoeopathic educator, Lindsay teaches at the Desert Institute of Classical Homoeopathy in Phoenix, Arizona. When she isn't teaching alternative medicine, she is writing books about love. She feels love is the single greatest healer in the world and hopes that her books touch her readers on those levels.

HOT SUMMER NIGHTS

Dallas Schulze
Maggie Shayne
Lindsay McKenna

First published in Great Britain 2003
Silhouette Books, Eton House, 18-24 Paradise Road, Richmond, Surrey TW9 1SR

ISBN 0 373 04935 8

081-0703

Printed and bound in Spain
by Litografia Rosés S.A., Barcelona

TESSA'S CHILD

Dallas Schulze

Prologue

Keefe Walker cupped one hand around a match and set the flame to the end of his cigarette. Smoke stung the back of his throat, a reminder that he'd been smoking more than he usually did. A pack normally lasted him a couple of days, but he was halfway through his second since morning. Nothing like a wedding to make a man crave a nicotine fix, he thought.

Nothing like a wedding to remind a man of how alone he was.

He pushed the thought aside. Drawing deeply on the cigarette, he turned away from the house and the wedding reception taking place inside to look out over his sister-in-law's gardens. Kelsey cultivated nearly half an acre of vegetables, selling the produce to restaurants in the Santa Barbara area. The beds of vegetables, neatly separated by bark-covered pathways, stretched out from the rambling farmhouse in a patchwork of early-spring greens, punctuated here and there with brilliant splashes of color. Keefe remembered his brother Gage telling him that Kelsey was now supplying edible flowers to some of her customers. So, while the warm golds and oranges were undoubtedly there because of commercial enterprise rather than aesthetic inspiration, the end result was undeniably lovely.

A burst of laughter drifted through the French doors behind him, and Keefe's mouth curved in a smile. Cole certainly fit the image of a happy bridegroom. When he and Addie exchanged their vows, Cole had looked at her as if the sun rose and set in her eyes. A few months ago, if he was asked to describe the kind of woman his youngest brother was most likely to marry, Addie Smith wouldn't have shown up on the list. Quietly pretty academic types had never been up Cole's alley. But looking at the two of them together, no one could doubt that they were very much in love. He was willing to bet that they were going to beat the odds and make their marriage last.

Which was more than he'd managed to do. And that was the real problem with weddings, he thought as he took one last drag on his cigarette. They made him think of his own marriage, set him to thinking about what had gone wrong, wondering if he could have changed things. Keefe's mouth twisted in a bitter half smile as he stubbed the cigarette out against the top of the low brick wall. There was no bigger waste of time than playing "What if?" He drew his cigarette pack from the inside breast pocket of his suit jacket and tapped another cigarette loose.

The past was past, he reminded himself as he struck a match against the rough side of a brick and lifted the flame to the end of his cigarette. There was no going back to change things, and wondering what might have been was a waste of time.

''Mind a little company?''

Keefe started, his head jerking toward the speaker. He'd been so absorbed in his thoughts that he didn't hear her approach. Tall and elegant, her straight posture belying her seventy-odd years of age, Molly Thorpe moved toward him across the brick patio.

''I don't mind a bit,'' he said, his expression easing into a welcoming smile. He straightened away from the low brick wall he'd been half leaning against.

''Don't get up for me,'' she said, waving one slender hand, the knuckles slightly swollen with arthritis. ''Makes me feel like I'm an old woman. And just because that's what I am, it doesn't mean I like to be reminded.''

''I don't think the word *old* will ever apply to you, Molly.''

''If you're offering me flattery in hopes that I won't tell your mother you're out here smoking, you're wasting your time,'' Molly said as she sank down onto a redwood deck chair. There was a twinkle in her blue eyes as she looked up at him. ''Your mother knows exactly what you're up to. On her behalf, I'll remind you that it's a filthy habit and bound to kill you.''

''Did you come out here to lecture me about my

health?'' Keefe asked, eyeing her through a thin veil of smoke. Actually, he hadn't even been consciously aware that he'd lit another cigarette until she mentioned it. It was a good thing Cole was the last of his brothers to get married. Any more weddings in the family and he was likely to become a chain smoker.

''Certainly not. I figure a man of forty ought to be allowed to live his life without interference from his family and friends.''

''Thirty-seven,'' Keefe corrected her. Forty was creeping up fast enough as it was.

''Thirty-seven,'' Molly said, nodding her head. ''That's certainly old enough to choose your own poison.''

''Thanks. I guess.'' Keefe stubbed the cigarette out against the top of the brick wall before turning a rueful smile in her direction. ''There aren't many people who could make me feel like an antique and about twelve years old in the space of thirty seconds. That's a unique skill, Molly.''

''Thank you.'' She bent her head in regal acceptance of the compliment, her solemn expression at odds with the laughter in her eyes.

She was still a lovely woman. Age had both blurred the edges of her beauty and yet refined it in some mysterious way, drawing the skin over her high cheekbones and revealing the determined angles of her jaw. She must have been hell on wheels when she was a young woman, Keefe thought. She was a force to be reckoned with even now.

He'd known Molly for over a decade. She'd hired him to work on her horse ranch, the Rocking M, near

Solvang when he was in his early twenties. He'd worked there for over a year, and then quit to pursue his dreams of rodeo buckles. When he left, she'd told him he was a damned fool but added that, if he didn't break his neck, he was welcome back whenever he needed a job.

He'd worked for her off and on for the next five years, until the year he turned twenty-eight. Her great-niece had come to spend the summer with her that year, and he'd taken one look at Dana Wyndham and fallen head over heels in love. They'd been married less than a month after they met. Four years later, they'd been divorced. His relationship with Molly had proved more enduring than his marriage.

"Your brother seems very happy." Molly's comment drew Keefe out of his contemplation of the past.

"He is," he said, smiling.

"His little girl seems fond of her new stepmother."

"Mary's crazy about Addie, and the feeling is mutual." Keefe's smile grew soft at the mention of his niece. "Cole and Addie were going to wait to get married, because they wanted to give Mary time to adjust to the idea, but she finally asked them what was taking them so long."

"Children frequently have a great deal more common sense than the adults around them," Molly commented.

"I can't argue with you on that one."

Keefe slid his hands into the pockets of his charcoal-gray slacks and leaned back against the wall. Late-afternoon sunshine warmed his shoulders and slanted across the brick patio. He and his brothers had put the patio in less than a month ago, but the mellow patina of the used brick made it look as if it had been there forever. The herringbone pattern had been a nightmare to lay, but Gage had insisted that, if he could engineer a suspension bridge, even the most elaborate brickwork should be within his grasp. Halfway through the project, it had become obvious that bridges and patios had little in common. The pattern had become hopelessly tangled. Gage had endured his brothers' ruthless teasing in stoic silence, scowling at the bricks as if suspecting them of being possessed by some malevolent force. It was Sam who'd saved the day, hacking bricks in half with a ruthlessness that had made Gage moan faintly in pain. The pattern had been successfully continued, with only a slight deviation in the middle—an artistic touch, Sam had declared.

"You've been blessed when it comes to family," Molly said, as if reading his thoughts.

"I have been," Keefe agreed simply.

She shifted her position on the redwood chair, the sunlight catching in her silver hair. "There's been quite a few weddings in your family this last year or two," she commented.

"Three of them." He pulled one hand out of his pocket and started to reach for his cigarettes, changing his mind when he caught Molly's interested expression. He ran his fingers through his hair instead, but he doubted he'd fooled her. Not much got by Molly Thorpe's sharp blue eyes.

"Must make you think," she said.

''About what?'' With deliberate obtuseness, Keefe raised one dark brow.

Molly arched a brow in return, her expression reminding him that she knew him better than he might like. ''Do not make the mistake of thinking that I'm getting senile, Keefe.''

''I know better than that, Molly,'' he said with a reluctant laugh. ''To answer your question, seeing my brothers get married does make me think, but it *doesn't* make me think about getting married again. For some of us, once is enough.''

She frowned. ''I thought you were too smart to let your experience with Dana make you bitter.''

Keefe shook his head. ''I'm not bitter.'' He took his cigarettes from his pocket and lit one, ignoring the faint disapproval in her eyes. ''I'm just a bit more cautious than I was in my younger days, that's all.''

''It's more than caution, if you've made up your mind that you're never going to marry again.''

''I'd never say never.'' He gave her a lopsided grin. ''That would be tempting fate. And I'm not foolish enough to do that.''

Molly looked doubtful as she pushed herself to her feet. ''Fate has a way of making fools of us all at one time or another, most especially when we think we're fooling it.''

''Not fooling it,'' Keefe corrected her as he stubbed out his half-smoked cigarette. He stepped forward to slip his hand under her elbow as she turned toward the house. ''I think of it as staying out of sight.''

''No one can avoid their fate, Keefe.'' Molly's tone held both affection and warning. ''I doubt fate has any intention of letting you spend the rest of your life alone."

"We'll see," he said.

"So we will."

Tessa Evangeline Wyndham Mallory glanced down into the suitcase she'd just filled. It didn't seem possible that she'd spent four years of her life in this house and yet could leave it now with nothing but the contents of this one suitcase and know that she wasn't leaving anything of importance behind. It wasn't much to show for four years.

Of course, she was taking a great deal more with her than what was in the suitcase. Not just memories, but also a painfully tangible reminder of her marriage.

Her soft mouth tightened, her blue eyes turning to ice. Damn Bobby, anyway. Why couldn't he have managed to get himself killed a little sooner? But there was no point in thinking about what might have been, Tessa reminded herself. She could only deal with what was. She flipped the suitcase lid shut and jerked the zipper closed, the sound harsh as a scream in the quiet room.

She glanced around the luxuriously decorated bedroom one last time. There had been a time when she took a great deal of pleasure in the decor. She'd chosen the warm peach-and-ivory-striped wallpaper and soft blue-gray carpeting herself, haunted antique stores looking for just the right pieces of furniture. The end result was neither feminine nor masculine, but a careful blending of the two.

Too bad she hadn't been able to see into the future,

she thought now, taking no pleasure in the soft warmth of the room. If she'd known what her life was going to be like, she might have chosen more appropriate colors—like black and prison gray.

No. She wasn't going to think that way.

Tessa closed her eyes and drew in a deep breath. She wasn't going to let the past four years color the rest of her life with bitterness. The past was past. She couldn't change it. But she could move forward and try to make the future better.

When she opened her eyes again, they held a look of resolution that would have surprised some people who thought they knew her well. Moving to the dressing table, she tugged the heavy diamond engagement ring and thick gold wedding band off her finger. She weighed them in the palm of her hand, and for just a moment she allowed herself to feel regret for the dreams they'd once represented, for the happiness she'd thought she'd found. But the dreams had died a long time ago, and the happiness had proven no more substantial than a soap bubble. Turning her hand over, she let the rings fall. They clattered as they hit the wooden surface, sounding strangely like the rattle of a key turning in the lock of a prison door.

Tessa flexed her fingers, feeling the lightness of her hand. For the first time in weeks, her mouth curved in a genuine smile. Freedom. She'd forgotten what it felt like. Not that she was completely free, she thought as she caught a glimpse of her reflection in the mirror. But she was closer to it than she had been a few weeks ago. Her smile faded, and her delicate jaw tightened with determination.

For the past four years, she'd paid the price of her own foolish blindness, but fate had seen fit to give her a second chance. She was free—almost. She wasn't going to waste that gift in bitterness. Turning away from the mirror, Tessa lifted the suitcase from the floor. She closed the door behind her without looking back.

Chapter 1

"You expecting a visitor?" Jace Reno asked.

Keefe looked up from the posthole he was digging. He studied the cloud of dust making its way up the long dirt road that led to the Flying Ace's ranch house. "I'm not expecting anyone. Doesn't look big enough for a truck," he said. That eliminated most of the locals. This was ranching country, and trucks outnumbered cars by a fairly wide margin. He squinted a little to try and make out something of the vehicle beneath the dust cloud and then shrugged. "They're probably lost."

"Probably," Jace agreed. Since it would be another minute or two before the car reached them, both men returned their attention to the job at hand. "You planning on digging that hole all the way to China, or just halfway?"

"I don't want to have to do it again next year,"

Keefe said, jabbing the posthole digger into the narrow hole, the muscles in his arms flexing as he lifted out a bite of dirt.

"You dig it much deeper and the posts are going to sink so deep that we'll end up with the only two-foot-high corral fence in the neighborhood. Could have saved ourselves a lot of trouble by just drawing a line in the dirt and telling the horses not to cross it."

Keefe glared at his friend from under the brim of his dusty gray Stetson. "Tell me again why I took you on as a partner."

"My wit and charm?" Jace suggested, grinning.

"If that was the case, I made a lousy bargain," Keefe said dryly. "You want to set that pole in place, or are you planning on leaving it there to see if it will take root?"

"An oak tree might look real nice right about here." Jace lifted the post and began easing it down into the hole.

"It might, but getting an oak tree out of a cedar post would be a pretty neat trick." Keefe knelt to guide the base of the post. "Hold it straight and I'll start filling in around it."

He began scooping dirt into the hole, tamping it down around the post. Behind him, he heard the car pull to a stop in front of the house.

"A Mercedes," Jace commented. "If you've got to get lost, you might as well do it in style."

"Probably makes it easier," Keefe said without looking up. He heard a car door slam, and the crunch of footsteps on the dirt and gravel that passed for a front yard.

"Excuse me. I'm looking for Keefe Walker." The voice was soft, faintly husky, definitely female and oddly familiar.

Keefe felt something clench tight and hard in the pit of his stomach, a quick flare of recognition, followed by disbelief. It couldn't be... He rose and turned toward the visitor. But the woman approaching across the yard was not the ghost from his past he'd half expected to see. She was pretty, rather than stunningly beautiful. Her eyes held more gray than blue, and her hair was dark gold rather than moonlight-pale.

She was also heavily pregnant.

"Something you forgot to tell me about, buddy?" Jace murmured.

"Keefe?" She smiled uncertainly as she moved closer.

Keefe blinked, banishing old memories. Whoever this woman was, she wasn't his ex-wife.

"I know I should have called first," she said, looking even more uncertain. She linked her hands together in front of her, her fingers twisting in a childlike gesture of nervousness that contrasted oddly with the very unchildlike bulge of her stomach. The gesture evoked a new set of memories—a young girl, her hair in pigtails, her thin shoulders squared, her small chin set with determination—and the nervous movements of her hands betraying her bravado.

"Tessa?" The name was half question. Recovering from his surprise, Keefe crossed the distance between them in two long strides. He caught her hands in his. "Tessa."

"Have I changed that much?" she asked, her mouth curving in a smile that didn't quite chase the uneasiness from her eyes.

"It's been at least five years," he said, grinning down at her. "You were a little girl last time I saw you."

"I was eighteen. Not exactly a toddler," she said dryly.

"Not exactly an old woman, either."

"No, but I certainly thought I was filled with the wisdom of the ages," she said, her tone wistful, as if she envied her younger self that confidence.

"Who doesn't think that when they're eighteen?"

"True." Tessa shook her head a little, as if shaking away a memory. She changed the subject. "I hope you don't mind me just showing up like this. I know I should have called first, but I was kind of in the neighborhood."

"It's a pretty big neighborhood," Jace said as he walked up to them.

Keefe felt Tessa's hands tense in his at Jace's approach. Her eyes widened, and something that almost looked like fear flickered through them. He dismissed the thought immediately. In the years he'd known Jace Reno, he'd seen him inspire many emotions in women—lust, frustration, anger, an occasional urge to commit murder—but not fear. But then Tessa was pulling her hands away from his, turning toward Jace with a smile and nothing but friendly curiosity in her expression, and Keefe decided that his imagination had to be working overtime. Too many hours in the sun, he thought as he made the introductions.

"Tessa, this is Jace Reno, my partner on the Flying Ace. Jace, this is Tessa Wyndham— Is it still Wyndham?" he asked, glancing questioningly at her. "I heard you got married a while back."

"Yes, I did." Tessa's smile seemed to congeal, her eyes going empty for a moment, but the expression was gone so quickly that Keefe wasn't sure it had been there at all. "Wyndham is fine," she said, as she took Jace's hand.

"Wyndham?" Jace repeated, glancing at Keefe.

"Dana's sister," Keefe said, answering the question in his friend's eyes.

"Which makes me an ex-in-law," Tessa said brightly.

Too brightly, Keefe found himself thinking. There was something just a little...off in Tessa's smile, in her manner. She was trying too hard, making too much of an effort to seem at ease. Maybe she was uncertain of her welcome. His divorce from her sister had not been the most acrimonious on record, but it hadn't been a "friendly" divorce, either. Except for Molly Thorpe, the last time he saw any of Dana's family had been the day he walked out of the courtroom. But, whatever his feelings for his ex-wife and her parents, he'd always been fond of her little sister.

"You're not an 'ex' anything," he said easily. "Friends aren't part of a divorce settlement."

"Thanks." Tessa's smile seemed more genuine this time, held less forced brightness. But there were still shadows in her eyes, shadows that hadn't been there five years ago.

''I can finish setting the fence post,'' Jace said into the silence. ''Why don't you pretend you have good manners and offer Tessa a drink and a place to sit down.''

''Thank you, Ms. Manners,'' Keefe said dryly.

''Hey, I'm just trying to maintain a facade of civilization in the midst of the howling wilderness.'' His expression of martyrdom drew a genuine, if fleeting, smile from Tessa.

''It must be an uphill battle,'' she said sympathetically.

''It is.'' He shook his head, pulling his mouth down into a solemn expression that was at odds with the laughter in his blue eyes. ''If it wasn't for me, we'd soon revert to savagery.''

''Who was it suggested that we could save water by only washing our plates once a week?'' Keefe asked pointedly.

''Just doing my part for water conservation,'' Jace insisted, looking hurt.

''You're full of nobility,'' Tessa said.

''He's full of something, all right,'' Keefe said dryly. ''Come on up to the house, Tessa, and I'll see what we've got to drink.''

They didn't speak as they started toward the house, and Keefe found himself thinking back to the summer he'd gotten to know Tessa. Right after he and Dana were married, they'd gone to live on her parents' horse ranch in Kentucky. The world of Thoroughbreds and racing was a long way from the rodeos and quarter horses where Keefe had worked, but Dana had persuaded him to try working for her father.

"If Daddy likes you, he might leave the ranch to us someday," she'd said, her sapphire-blue eyes sparkling with excitement.

Keefe hadn't been particularly anxious to spend twenty years or more working for his father-in-law on the chance that he'd someday inherit a Kentucky racing stable he didn't particularly want, but he'd been head over heels in love with his bride. Besides, two days after the wedding, he'd taken a ride on a bronc with the inviting nickname of Bone Buster. In the eight-second battle between man and animal, the horse had lived up to his name, coming out on top—literally—and breaking Keefe's leg in two places. Since Kentucky was as good a place as any to recuperate, he'd let Dana persuade him to accept the job her father was offering.

Keefe and his new in-laws had been a poor match. He'd thought Dana's father was a pompous ass and her mother was a featherbrain. They'd resented the fact that their beloved oldest daughter had married a rodeo cowboy who had neither money nor prospects. Their attitude had been condescending and their arrogance had been such that they never realized that Keefe was every bit as contemptuous of them as they were of him.

It had not been an easy two months.

It hadn't taken Keefe long to find out that the one place his in-laws never spent any time was in the stables. Owning a Thoroughbred ranch suited their image and afforded them with appropriate social opportunities but neither of the Wyndhams had any particular fondness for horses or riding. Keefe had appreciated the fact that their lack of interest provided him with a suitable retreat.

Though he couldn't ride, he'd enjoyed working with the horses, and Tessa had often joined him there. At fourteen, she'd been a pale, thin child with eyes older than her years and a quick smile enhanced by the chrome gleam of braces.

It had soon been apparent that, like him, she didn't fit into the Wyndham household. She'd been a surprise baby—an unwelcome surprise, she'd told him in a matter-of-fact tone that precluded sympathy or protest. If she was pretty and charming like her older sister, her parents might have been able to find a place for her in their lives. But she'd been a thin, contemplative child with none of her sister's sparkle, and Tessa's quiet prettiness had been completely overshadowed by Dana's golden beauty.

He and Tessa had spent a lot of time together that summer, and he remembered that she had, even at fourteen, been comfortable with silences. But the silence between them now was not that of easy companionship. Tension radiated from her. He wondered what had brought her here.

Tessa could feel Keefe glancing at her and knew he had to be wondering why she was here. She'd been crazy to come, crazy to think she could turn to him. She didn't have any right to ask for his help. She'd make a little polite conversation, drink a glass of water, then get in her car and go on her way. He'd probably think she was nuts to have traveled all this way just to say hello, but there was nothing she could do about that.

She became aware that he was adjusting his long stride to her much shorter steps and felt her stomach tighten with sudden tension. Bobby had been a big man, too, and it had been a source of constant irritation to him that she couldn't match his pace. When they were first married, she'd tried to point out that since her legs weren't as long as his, he couldn't expect her to walk as fast. But Bobby hadn't been interested in explanations, only in results. That was a catchphrase he'd picked up from his politician father and liked to apply to any situation where things weren't going his way. Tessa had soon learned that it was easier to give him what he wanted than to try and reason with him. She'd done her best to adjust her stride to his, feeling like a toddler forced to half run to keep up with the adults around her.

Now, realizing that she was slowing Keefe down, she reacted automatically, trying to move more quickly, her throat clogging with a familiar anxiety at the thought of angering the large man walking next to her. *Don't make him mad. Don't make him mad.* The words repeated in her mind, her own personal mantra. *Hurry, hurry, hurry. Don't make him mad.*

"Oh!" The exclamation escaped her as a stone rolled beneath her foot. She would have fallen, but Keefe's hand shot out, catching her upper arm and pulling her toward him so that, instead of hitting the ground, she landed against the solid width of his chest.

''I'm sorry.'' The words tumbled out breathlessly. She brought her hands up to push against his chest, her heart pounding. *He was so big.* ''I didn't mean to be so clumsy. I'm sorry.''

''Hey, you don't owe me an apology.'' Keefe took hold of her upper arms and set her on her feet, releasing her as soon as he saw that she was steady.

''I'm so clumsy,'' Tessa muttered. She didn't look at him, afraid of what she might see in his eyes, even more afraid of what he might read in hers.

''You aren't clumsy,'' he said. ''But you might try slowing down a little. I was getting out of breath trying to keep up with you.''

The humor in his voice brought Tessa's gaze to his face. He didn't look impatient or irritated. He was smiling at her, his dark eyes warm and friendly. She felt the knot in her chest loosen a little. This was Keefe. How could she have forgotten the way he could smile with just his eyes? The way he'd always been able to make her feel as if the world wasn't such a bad place after all?

''I thought I might be slowing you down,'' she said.

''And I thought you were racing me to the house. At the pace you were moving, I was starting to think I was going to have to break into a sprint just to keep up.''

The idea was so ridiculous that Tessa's tense expression relaxed into a smile. ''Sorry.''

''Just keep in mind that, at my age, I'm not as fast as I used to be,'' he told her as they started walking again.

"You're not exactly an old man," Tessa protested.

"I'll be forty in a couple of years. As young as you are, that must seem pretty old."

Tessa didn't answer. Just smiled and shook her head. Inside she was trying to remember the last time she'd felt young.

"I thought bachelors were supposed to be slobs," Tessa commented, glancing around the tidy kitchen.

"I am a slob." Keefe got two glasses out of the refrigerator and set them on the wooden counter. "Lemonade okay? It's from a mix, but it's not half bad."

"Lemonade is fine. This doesn't look like the kitchen of a slob." Tessa pulled a chair out from the big oak table that sat under a window at one end of the room.

"For the first couple of years after I moved in, the place looked like a nuclear-waste dumping site. It got to the point where I was afraid to open the refrigerator unless I was armed, because some of the things growing in it were starting to develop teeth."

Tessa smiled as he set the glass of lemonade in front of her. "So what happened to change you into Mr. Clean?"

"Fear for my life," Keefe said as he sank down into a chair across the table from her. "I figured if one of the creatures in the fridge didn't get me, ptomaine would. And there was always the possibility that I'd open a closet one day and be crushed in the resulting avalanche. I doubt if I'll win any awards from *House Beautiful* but at least the place is no longer in danger of being designated a toxic waste site.''

''It's very nice,'' Tessa said.

''Thanks.''

An uneasy silence followed, or at least it seemed uneasy to Tessa. She tried to think of something casual to say, something light and unimportant to keep the conversational ball rolling, but all she could think of was how tircd she was. Exhaustion had crept into her very bones, weighing her down, draining her spirit.

''When is the baby due?'' Keefe asked, and she was grateful to have the silence broken.

''Three months.'' Tessa heard the flatness of her response and forced herself to smile. ''I can't wait,'' she said, trying to look happy, the way an expectant mother should look.

He smiled, but there was something watchful in his eyes, and Tessa looked away. She was going to have to be careful. Keefe was not someone who was easily fooled.

Silence fell between them again. Tessa turned her lemonade glass between her hands and tried to think of something to say. She should never have come here. She had no claims on Keefe. Whatever ties of family there might have been between them, they'd been severed when he and Dana split up. And even if she did have some family claim to him, she, of all people, knew how little that meant. She should say something pleasant about how nice it had been to see him again and leave. But she was so tired. So very, very tired.

"You want to tell me why you're here?" Keefe asked, his tone so gentle that Tessa felt something tremble inside her. She released her breath on a sigh and lifted her eyes to his face.

"I guess you didn't really buy the story about me being in the neighborhood, huh?"

"Like Jace said, it's a pretty big neighborhood. The High Sierras aren't exactly on the way to anywhere else, unless you're going hiking. All things considered, that doesn't seem likely," he said, nodding to her belly.

"No, I guess it doesn't." She took a sip of lemonade and let the tart, sweet taste of it dissolve in her mouth while she tried to find the words to explain her presence. "I guess I'm looking for sanctuary."

"Sanctuary?" Keefe's dark brows rose. "What are you running from?"

Tessa gave a short, humorless laugh. "My life." She rubbed her fingertips over her forehead, trying to soothe the ache building between her eyes. "I need someplace to stay where no one will think to look for me. Just for a little while."

She paused, trying to gather the words of explanation she'd rehearsed on the long drive from Santa Barbara to his ranch. She'd had hours to perfect her story—not a lie but something considerably less than the whole truth.

"All right."

It took Tessa a moment to register what he'd said. She'd been staring at the table, but now her head came up, her blue eyes wide with shock. It occurred to

Keefe that it was the first totally honest reaction he'd seen since she arrived.

"All right?" she repeated in a tone of stunned disbelief. "What do you mean?"

"I mean you can stay here. There's a spare bedroom. It's not fancy, but it's reasonably comfortable. We'll have to share the bathroom, though."

"That's okay. It's only for a little while."

"You can stay as long as you need to," he said easily. "Jace lives in the ranch foreman's house, but we usually eat meals together. There's not a whole lot by way of entertainment, though. TV reception is pretty shaky and, as you probably noticed, we're a ways from the nearest town."

"I'm not looking for entertainment," she said, feeling almost dizzy with relief. It just couldn't be this easy. Nothing was ever this easy. "Don't you want to know why I need a place to hide out?"

"Anybody likely to come looking for you carrying a gun?"

"A gun?" Tessa stared at him a moment and then shook her head. "No one wants to kill me, if that's what you mean."

"Good."

"Would you...would you let me stay if I'd said someone wanted to kill me?"

"Yes, but it would have been a real pain to have to start carrying a gun every time I left the house."

He smiled when he spoke but there was something in his eyes that made Tessa believe that, if it was necessary, that was exactly what he'd do. She had to be dreaming, she decided. That was the only possible explanation for his easy acceptance of her, for his willingness to take her in without questions.

"Come on." Keefe pushed his chair back from the table and stood up. "I'll show you to your room, and then I can bring your stuff in from the car."

"Don't you want to know why?" she asked again.

He set his glass in the sink and turned to look at her. "Do you want to tell me why?"

No, she didn't want to tell him. She didn't want to tell him anything, especially since she wouldn't—*couldn't*—tell him the whole truth. But perhaps part of the truth was better than none at all. Maybe if she told him a little of the truth, she wouldn't feel quite as guilty about the rest of it.

"You deserve an explanation," she said at last.

"I don't need one but if it will make you feel better, go ahead."

Tessa hesitated. The careful web of half-truths she'd fabricated suddenly seemed tissue-thin. Perhaps it would have been better not to tell him anything at all than to tell him only a portion. But she could hardly change her mind now.

"You know I was married," she began carefully.

"Was?"

"Yes. My…my husband…Bobby… He passed away, almost two months ago."

Keefe felt as if he'd been kicked in the solar plexus. She was a widow? In his mind, she was still a girl, hardly old enough to be a wife. Yet here she was, six months pregnant and telling him she'd lost her husband. His first instinct was to go to her, to hold her, but there was an odd reserve about her—an invisible barrier that kept him at a small distance.

"I'm...sorry, Tessa."

"Thank you." She dragged one finger through the condensation on the side of her glass. "It was... terrible," she said, keeping her eyes on the aimless motion of her finger.

"An understatement," Keefe muttered. He pulled his cigarettes out of his shirt pocket and tapped one free. He was about to light it when his glance fell on the heavy bulge of her stomach. "Sorry." He put the cigarette back and dropped the pack on the counter. "What happened to your husband?"

"It was an accident," Tessa said. She'd repeated the statement so often that she almost believed it. She continued quickly, wanting to avoid any questions about what kind of accident it had been. "Are you familiar with Senator Robert Mallory?"

"I know the name, but not much more than that."

Tessa barely restrained a sigh of relief. She'd hardly dared to hope that he wouldn't have heard the news reports and rumors that followed Bobby's death. "Bobby—my husband—was Senator Mallory's son. Since his death, there have been reporters camped outside the house practically day and night. I just need to get out from under the glare of the spotlight."

She glanced up at him and then quickly looked away from the questions in his eyes. "Senator Mallory is being talked about as a candidate in the next presidential race. I guess that's why the press is focusing so closely on his son's death. You know what reporters are like."

''I don't have much personal experience with them.''

''Lucky you.'' Her mouth tilted in a quick, humorless little smile. ''They can be...difficult.''

''So I've heard,'' he said. Keefe studied her face for a moment. He'd have been willing to bet his best horse that she was lying to him. Or, at the very least, telling him only part of the truth. Sometime in the past five years, she'd learned to lie, but she hadn't learned to do it very well. He pushed away from the counter. ''Well, I doubt anyone is likely to trace you here. Even if they did, Jace and I can run them off.''

''You're sure?'' Tessa looked at him uncertainly.

''About running off a reporter or two?'' Keefe asked, deliberately misunderstanding. ''I think we can manage that. Might even be fun.''

''I mean, are you sure about me staying here? I know, since you and Dana split up, we're not exactly family anymore.''

''Yeah, but we're still friends,'' he said, and in his smile Tessa read the kind of easy welcome she could have expected from no one else she knew. She closed her eyes for an instant, forcing back the quick rush of tears. Funny, how she'd known that, even after five years, she could count on him.

''Thanks,'' she whispered.

''Don't thank me yet. The accommodations aren't exactly luxury class.''

When she moved to stand up, he was suddenly next to her, setting his hand under her elbow to help her up. The casual touch was there and gone so quickly that she didn't have time to react. Exhaustion was rolling over her in a thick, dark wave, but somewhere in the back of her mind, Tessa was surprised to realize that she didn't mind Keefe touching her, helping her. It was something she'd have to think about later, when she didn't feel so completely exhausted.

She followed him into the hallway, half registering what he was telling her about the layout of the house. He stopped long enough to get a clean set of sheets out of the linen closet before pushing open another door.

The bedroom was as plainly furnished as the rest of the house. A double bed with a nightstand beside it and a chest of drawers were the only furnishings. The walls were off-white, as were the simple curtains that covered the windows and the chenille bedspread on the bed. The only color came from an old-fashioned rug, braided in shades of blue and white, that lay on the wooden floor next to the bed.

"It's not fancy, but it's comfortable enough. I don't get much company up here—one of my brothers now and again is about it."

"It looks wonderful," Tessa said with absolute sincerity. At the moment, a hovel would have looked wonderful, as long as it contained a bed. But, aside from a light coating of dust, the room was clean and tidy. She couldn't remember when she'd last seen anything that looked so wonderful, unless, perhaps, it was the solid strength of Keefe's large body when she'd first arrived.

"You look beat," he said as he dropped the sheets on top of the dresser. "I'll make the bed, and then you can lie down for a while."

"No, let me." Tessa moved forward. "I don't expect you to wait on me."

"It's no trouble." He pulled the bedspread toward the foot of the bed.

"No, really." She caught the other side of the spread. "I'd feel better if you'd let me do it myself."

Keefe looked across the bed at her, his hesitation plain. After a moment, he released the spread and straightened. "If you're sure," he said doubtfully.

"I'm sure." She reached into the pocket of the soft rose-colored shirt she wore with her dark gray maternity pants and pulled out her key ring. "If you could bring my suitcase in from the car, I'd really appreciate it."

"Sure." Keefe took the keys from her.

The minute he left the room, Tessa sank down on the bed. Her fingers knotted in the soft chenille bedspread, she looked around the room, dazed with relief. She was safe. For the first time in months—years—she was completely safe. The feeling was so foreign that she felt disoriented. Safe, she repeated to herself. For a precious space of time, she could let Keefe hold the rest of the world at bay.

She let the exhaustion wash over her.

When Keefe entered the room a few minutes later, he wasn't really surprised to find Tessa curled up on the edge of the bed, sound asleep. It was obvious that she'd reached the end of her strength. He set her suitcase down just inside the door and crossed to the bed. The heels of his boots clicked on the wooden floor, but the sound didn't penetrate her deep sleep. She didn't even twitch when he eased her toward the center of the unmade bed and covered her with the bedspread.

He straightened and then stood looking down at her for a moment, his expression brooding. After listening to her careful explanation of why she'd come to him, he had far more questions than answers. He wasn't sure she'd actually lied to him, but he knew she hadn't told him the whole story. How long would it be until she trusted him enough to tell him what she was really hiding from?

Chapter 2

It was the scent of food that woke Tessa. Someone was cooking something that smelled rich and brown and delicious, and her stomach rumbled demandingly even before her eyes were open. The room was dark and unfamiliar, but she didn't feel any sense of disorientation. She knew exactly where she was. She was on the Flying Ace, Keefe's ranch in California, a continent away from her old life. There was a deep sense of comfort in the thought.

The illuminated dial of the alarm clock on the nightstand told her that she'd slept for more than three hours, but there was none of the grogginess that she associated with sleeping heavily during the day. Even so, she'd spent too many sleepless nights lately to feel totally rested. She briefly considered closing her eyes and going back to sleep. But the empty, gnawing feeling in her stomach reminded her that she hadn't eaten anything since the Egg McMuffin she had for breakfast a good ten hours before. And not only was she hungry, she was in urgent need of a bathroom. Just one of the many joys of pregnancy, she thought as she rolled awkwardly from the bed.

When she left the bathroom ten minutes later, she was feeling almost human again. She'd splashed cold water on her face and run a brush through her shoulder-length hair. The nap that had served to refresh her had had a less beneficial impact on her clothes, and she considered—briefly—changing into something else. But anything she pulled out of her suitcase was going to be at least as creased as what she had on, and the scent of whatever Keefe was cooking was making her stomach growl. At the moment, eating was more important than her appearance. Besides, it was just Keefe, and he wasn't going to notice—or care—what she looked like.

It wasn't until she heard the low rumble of masculine voices that Tessa remembered that it wasn't "just Keefe." She stopped abruptly. The partner. She'd forgotten all about him. Keefe had introduced them when she first arrived. What was his name? Surely she couldn't have forgotten it in this short space of time, not after four years of being a politician's daughter-in-law. Remembering names was the most elemental of political skills. Her mind remained blank and she felt her throat clog with a familiar panic.

How could she have been so careless? He'd be so angry. He'd tell her she was an idiot, and she couldn't argue, couldn't defend herself. She was *stupid. Stupid.*

"Tessa?"

She'd half turned away, intending to go back to the safety of her room rather than risk revealing her mistake, but at the sound of Keefe's voice, she turned toward him, her eyes wide, her face devoid of color. For a moment, she saw another man standing in front of her—someone not quite as tall, his shoulders less broad, his handsome features twisted in an expression of contempt.

"Are you okay?"

"I'm…fine," she lied. She blinked, clearing her vision of the odd double image. This was Keefe, she reminded herself. Keefe, who'd given her shelter without asking questions, who'd never shown her anything but patience and kindness.

"Dinner's about ready. Could I interest you in some beef stew?"

Tessa started to say that she wasn't really hungry, but she couldn't forcc the lie out.

"Actually, I'm starving," she admitted.

"You'll have to be, to eat the cooking around here," Keefe said with a grin. "I've been known to burn boiling water, and Jace isn't much better."

"Whatever you're cooking smells wonderful," she said. She felt almost dizzy with relief. *Jace.* His name was Jace.

"Of course it's wonderful," Jace said, catching her comment as she and Keefe entered the kitchen. "It's Reno's bodacious beef stew."

"Bodacious?" Keefe arched one dark brown in question.

"An old family recipe, dating back to my great-

great-grandmother's day,'' Jace said. He was standing at the stove, stirring something in a big cast-iron pot. ''She traveled west on the Oregon Trail, and this stew was a mainstay on the journey.''

''No doubt she was the first one to call it 'bodacious,''' Keefe said. An oak table sat at one end of the big kitchen. He led Tessa to it and pulled out a chair for her. ''I can just hear her now, asking the other members of the wagon train to have a bowl of *bodacious* stew.''

''Each generation has added to the recipe,'' Jace said. ''The name is my personal contribution.''

''It's dumb,'' Keefe said flatly. He took silverware out of a drawer and brought it to the table.

''It's creative,'' Jace corrected him. ''A special name for a special dish.''

''It's a dumb name. Besides, the most 'special' thing about your stew is when you don't burn it.'' Keefe glanced at Tessa as he distributed the silverware around the table. The smile in his eyes reassured her that the conversation really was as nonsensical as it seemed. The little knot of tension that had been building in the pit of her stomach eased away. Humor had played such a small part in her life during the past few years that she'd almost forgotten what it was.

''Tessa likes the name. Don't you?''

Tessa started a little, her gaze jerking toward Jace. He was looking at her, his expression holding a laughing demand. His eyes were blue, a startlingly vivid shade that would have made a summer sky look pale in comparison. ''You think it's a good name, don't you?''

"Well, it does seem a little...well..." She hesitated, her nose wrinkling as she considered the question. "Actually, it makes me think of surfers and tofu and alfalfa sprouts," she admitted in a rush.

Keefe's laugh held a wicked edge of triumph. "So much for images of wagon trains," he said, glancing at his partner. "Unless your great-great-grandmother *surfed* her way across the prairie."

Jace shot him a sour look. "It's clear I'm surrounded by people with no appreciation for creative genius. Pearls before swine," he muttered as he lifted the heavy pan of stew and carried it to the table.

Tessa wondered if her chuckle sounded as rusty to her companions as it did to her.

Keefe contemplated the trail of smoke that drifted upward from the end of his cigarette. It caught the light that spilled onto the porch from the windows behind him, twisting and turning in ghostly wreaths as it drifted upward and dissipated in the cool night air.

He wouldn't be able to smoke in the house as long as Tessa was staying with him, he thought. Probably just as well. He'd been smoking more than he should—especially since Cole's wedding, almost a month ago. Maybe having to go outside every time he wanted a smoke would provide him with some incentive to cut back.

Maybe he'd even quit altogether. He studied the orange glow of the cigarette's tip and considered the possibility. He'd done it before. Dana had hated cigarette smoke, so he'd quit the day they were married.

He'd lit his next cigarette the day he got his final divorce papers. He still wasn't sure why. Maybe out of some misguided desire to show that his ex-wife's likes and dislikes no longer mattered in his life. His mouth twisted in a rueful half smile. Talk about cutting off your nose to spite someone else's face.

Well, maybe it was time to quit again. Having a pregnant woman in the house was as good a reason as any. When he thought about it, it seemed funny that he'd quit eight years ago because of Dana, and now here he was thinking about quitting again because of her little sister.

Dana's little sister. Keefe stared into the darkness, his expression thoughtful. It was difficult to associate the painfully brittle woman who'd appeared on his doorstep this afternoon with the quiet little girl he'd known. Five years was a long time, but not long enough to account for the changes he saw in Tessa.

At dinner, she'd been almost painfully cheerful. She'd smiled frequently, but the expression had almost never moved past a quick, meaningless curve of her mouth. Her eyes had remained still and—

He frowned, the cigarette burning, forgotten, as he considered just what it was he'd seen in her eyes. Nothing. There was simply nothing in her eyes. It was as if she'd learned to show the world a bright smile while the real Tessa hid somewhere inside, behind the carefully blank wall of her eyes.

Once or twice, real emotion had broken through that wall and her smile had been genuine, reminding him of the girl he'd known. But those moments had been fleeting. The only other time he saw real emotion had been toward the end of the meal, when Jace asked her about the baby.

"Are you expecting a girl or a boy?" he asked with friendly interest.

There was a pause before Tessa answered him, and something in the quality of her silence made Keefe look at her. Her smile was gone, and there was a moment when he thought he saw something bleak and cold in her eyes, but it was gone so quickly that he couldn't be sure it wasn't his imagination. And then her mouth curved in a bright, meaningless smile. She glanced at Jace, but Keefe didn't think she'd really seen him.

"I don't know. I decided I'd rather be surprised." The bright enthusiasm in her voice was as false as her smile.

"I'm all for surprises," Jace said. His eyes met Keefe's across the table, full of questions his partner couldn't begin to answer.

Thinking about it now, Keefe wondered if maybe he was making too much of Tessa's behavior. She had been widowed recently. If she seemed not herself, that alone was reason enough. When his older brother's first wife died of cancer, Sam had changed. He'd been quieter, less inclined to smile, and there had been a kind of emptiness in his eyes that didn't go away completely until he met and married Nikki Beauvisage. Everyone coped with pain in their own way. Maybe Tessa's too-cheerful facade was her way of dealing with her grief.

Keefe took one last drag on his cigarette before stubbing it out against the porch railing. Grief might offer a reasonable explanation for Tessa's odd behavior, but he didn't believe it was the right explanation—or at least he didn't believe it was the only one. There was just something about her that didn't ring true. He was willing to bet that she was hiding something, running from something more than a pack of persistent reporters. He straightened away from the post he'd been leaning against and turned back into the house. It was a waste of time to speculate on what was really going on. Tessa would tell him the truth when she was ready. And if she never told him, he could live with that, too.

The phone rang as he stepped through the kitchen door. Keefe glanced down the hall as he walked into the living room to answer it. Tessa's door was closed, and he could see no light beneath it. She'd gone back to her room right after dinner, pleading exhaustion. It was one of the few things she'd said today that he believed without reservations. A good night's sleep would put some color back in her cheeks and erase the smudgy circles of exhaustion under her eyes, but he doubted it would be enough to solve her other problems. Whatever was eating at her, it wasn't something that sleep would cure.

He picked up the phone in the middle of the third ring. "Hello?"

"Keefe?"

"Hello, Molly." It wasn't until he heard her voice that he realized he'd been more than half expecting this call. On some subconscious level, he'd realized that there had to be a connection between Tessa's arrival and his friendship with her great-aunt. "She got here safely."

"Already?" It was typical of Molly Thorpe that she didn't waste time questioning how he knew what she was calling about. "She must have driven straight through. I told her not to. I told her to stop halfway and spend the night."

"She didn't."

"Obviously not," she said, sounding mildly annoyed. "I was calling to tell you to expect her tomorrow."

"I appreciate the thought," Keefe said dryly.

"Well, as long as she got there safely, there's no harm done."

"She's pretty beat but, other than that, she's okay."

"Good." There was a brief pause, which Keefe made no attempt to fill. She cleared her throat. "I suppose I should have called sooner." Another woman might have sounded apologetic, but Molly managed to make the words almost a challenge.

"Doesn't matter." Keefe perched on the arm of the huge old leather armchair that sat next to the table that held the phone.

"You must have been surprised to see her."

"A bit." He thought of the moment when he'd heard Tessa's voice and thought she was Dana. Surprised? *Relieved* might be a better word for what he'd felt when he saw Tessa.

There was another pause, and he knew Molly was waiting for him to elaborate. He said nothing. He was very fond of Molly, but she could be more than a bit arrogant. A little unsatisfied curiosity would do her no harm.

"Aren't you going to ask why I sent my great-niece to you?" she asked finally.

"I figured you'd tell me if you wanted to."

"And if I don't want to?" Her tone made the question a challenge.

"Then I guess I'll just have to spend my life racked with curiosity," he said, sounding more sleepy than racked.

There was another silence, the phone line all but humming with her frustration. "Next time I see your mother, I'm going to have to offer her my condolences. You must have been a great trial to her."

"I did my best," Keefe said modestly. "But I can't take all the credit. My brothers did their part." He grinned at her quick bark of laughter.

"I'll offer her condolences times four, then," she promised.

"You do that."

"Tessa tell you anything about what's going on?" Molly asked, getting back to the subject at hand.

"Just that she needs a place to stay until the media finds something to interest them besides her husband's death."

"That's what she told me," Molly said. She hesitated, and Keefe could picture her fine brows drawing together in a frown. "Do you believe her?"

The question surprised him, and he took his time in answering it. From where he sat, he could look through the living room doorway and catch an angled glimpse of the hallway that led to the bedrooms. He thought about what Tessa had told him. When he spoke, his tone was slow and considering, ''I think it's the truth, as far as it goes.''

''But it's not all of the truth.'' Molly's words fell halfway between statement and question.

''Maybe not,'' he conceded reluctantly. He felt uncomfortable discussing Tessa's veracity—or lack thereof—with someone else, even with Molly. Perhaps she sensed as much, or maybe she felt as uncomfortable with the idea as he did, because she didn't pursue the subject.

''Whatever is going on, she said she needed a place to stay where no one would think to look for her. I figured your ranch pretty much fit the bill.''

''It should,'' Keefe agreed. He hadn't seen any of his ex-wife's family in five years, since nearly a year before the divorce became final. It wasn't likely that anyone would look for Tessa here.

Tessa had been the only one of the Wyndhams he regretted losing contact with, but it had seemed awkward to try and keep in touch with his former wife's younger sister. Since Tessa didn't try to contact him, he'd assumed she felt the same. Now he was sorry he'd let her slip out of his life so easily. Maybe, if he'd kept in touch with her, he'd have some idea of what was going on.

''I told her my ranch was the first place any self-respecting reporter would come if they were looking for her,'' Molly said, interrupting his thoughts. ''I'm her only family, apart from her parents. And that nitwit niece of mine and the fathead she married are off in Europe somewhere, not that they'd be any good to anybody even if they were on the right continent."

Keefe's mouth quirked at her acid-tongued summation of Tessa's parents. Unfortunately, she wasn't exaggerating. His former in-laws weren't particularly intelligent, nor were they in the habit of concerning themselves with much beyond their own comfort.

"What about Dana?" he asked.

"She's in Europe with her parents."

And Tessa wouldn't be likely to turn to Dana for help anyway, Keefe thought. The sisters had never been close. Dana's indifference to her younger sister had puzzled Keefe, who came from a tight-knit family. But it hadn't taken him long to realize that a lack of close ties wasn't the only way the Wyndhams differed from the Walkers.

"Tessa's welcome to stay here as long as she wants," he told Molly.

"I told her you'd feel that way," Molly said, sounding satisfied at having been proven right. "A fellow came by today, asking about her."

Keefe's fingers tightened around the receiver. "A reporter?"

"Could have been."

"But you don't think so?" he asked, picking up on the doubt in her voice.

"I don't know. He didn't say, and when I asked him outright what he wanted with my great-niece, he sidestepped the question very neatly."

"What did you tell him?"

"I told him Tessa had been to see me but she wasn't here now and it was none of his damned business where she'd gone. I also told him that, if I found out he'd been harassing my great-niece, I'd call in favors from Sacramento and he'd find himself so tangled up in government red tape that his life would become a living hell. He immediately remembered that he had business elsewhere,'' she finished modestly.

''I can almost feel sorry for the guy.'' Keefe grinned as he pictured her routing her visitor. Molly and her late husband had been heavily involved in state politics for over thirty years. Half the state legislature owed her favors. If her visitor really was a reporter, there was a good chance he knew that hers was no idle threat. ''I'm sure he got the message.''

''I think so. I have no patience with people who make their living by digging into the lives of private citizens. However, if someone is really determined to find Tessa, they may manage to track her down, even at your place.''

''I'll take care of her,'' Keefe promised.

Molly was quiet for a moment, and then she exhaled softly, as if with relief. ''Yes, I know you will. That's why I sent her to you.''

When Keefe hung up the phone a moment later, his expression was thoughtful. It was all very well to say he'd keep Tessa safe, but it would be nice to know just what it was he was supposed to be keeping her safe from.

''Next time that section of fence goes down, I think we should hire someone to stand guard and just shoot any cow that tries to cross the property line." Jace groaned as he swung down out of the saddle.

"Be a little hard on the cow, don't you think?" Keefe asked. He looped the reins around the top rail of the corral fence.

"Days like this make me think the only good cow is a dead cow," Jace said darkly. He loosened the cinch strap and gave his horse a companionable slap on the neck.

"Maybe, but a dead cow is harder to sell than a live one," Keefe pointed out. He arched his back, stretching the kinks out of his spine. They'd spent the morning repairing fence. It was hot, dusty, muscle-straining work.

"I don't see why anyone should object to buying already-dead cows," Jace argued. "We could call them prekilled and market them as a time-saving innovation."

"Prekilled?" Keefe grinned. "Like preowned cars?"

"Something along those lines. Seems to me there could be an untapped market for them."

"Could be, but I doubt it." Keefe took off his hat and ran his fingers through his thick, dark hair.

"You need to expand your thinking," Jace said. "Look at the guy who invented the Pet Rock."

"*You* look at him. All I want to look at right now is a cold beer and some food. I could eat a grizzly."

"Now *there's* an innovation. Grizzly ranching! We could become the world's first bear ranchers," Jace said, looking struck.

"There's even less of a market for bear meat than there is for prekilled cows," Keefe told him.

"You never know until you try."

"Trust me, the world isn't ready for bear ranching."

Their horses taken care of, they started up to the house. Keefe wondered how Tessa had spent her morning.

"How's your houseguest?" Jace asked, his thoughts following the same lines. It was the first time he'd mentioned Tessa.

"She was asleep when I left this morning."

"Probably the best thing for her. She looked like she'd hit the end of her rope."

Keefe's silence was agreement. If he had to guess, he'd have said Tessa had been running on nothing but nerves for a long time. Jace was right—the best thing for her was plenty of rest.

Tessa stepped back from the window. She didn't want to be caught peering through the curtains like a junior-grade spy. She looked around the kitchen, searching for something she'd forgotten, anything out of place. It was always best to double- and triple-check things, rather than risk a mistake.

Mistakes are caused by carelessness. Stupid people are careless. Are you stupid, Tessa? Stupid, stupid, stupid.

With an effort, she choked off the internal recording, blocking out the hateful echo.

"I'm not stupid," she whispered fiercely. "I'm not."

If she was stupid, she couldn't have learned to be so careful, so very careful. Everything was right. She'd made sure of it. Everything was perfect. But that reassurance didn't stop her heart from pounding like a drum against her breastbone when she heard the sound of booted feet on the porch floorboards. The door was thrust open, and she set one hand against the back of a chair to supplement the somewhat shaky support of her knees.

Keefe and Jace stepped through the door, and the big kitchen seemed to shrink. They didn't immediately see her standing beside the table, and that gave Tessa a moment to observe them. Both were big men, though Keefe was a little taller and broader through the shoulders. Both were dark. Keefe's hair was a brown so dark that it could almost be called black, and his eyes were the color of bittersweet chocolate. Jace's hair was dark, also, but it was a rich, burnished shade of brown, holding hints of red, and his eyes were the purest, deepest blue Tessa had ever seen.

Despite their similarities in coloring and size, no one would ever have mistaken them for brothers. Keefe was all steady strength. There was a feeling of solidity about him—a sense that he would be a rock to cling to in any storm. There was strength in Jace's features, but there was something more mercurial about him, a gleam of mischief in his eyes. They were both strikingly attractive men, Tessa thought, and then was vaguely surprised that she'd even noticed such a thing.

Jace saw her first and smiled. "Hello."

"Hello." Tessa almost winced at the thin sound of

her own voice. *Speak up, for God's sake! You're not in a library. Why do you always whisper?* She cleared her throat and widened her smile a fraction.

"Hi." Keefe's dark eyes went over her in a quick, searching look that missed nothing. "How did you sleep?"

"Very well," Tessa said. It was the truth. It had been a long time since she slept so deeply and dreamlessly. "I overslept, though."

"Overslept for what?" Keefe asked as he turned on the water in the sink and reached for the soap. "Did you have an appointment this morning?"

"I was going to make breakfast."

"For us?" Jace's brows rose in surprise.

"Yes. It seemed the least I could do."

"You don't have to earn your keep." Keefe pulled a blue-and-white plaid towel off the rack and dried his hands.

"I'd like to do something. You've been so kind, letting me stay here—both of you." She was careful to include Jace in her gratitude. "I can help around the house—do the cooking and cleaning, things like that."

"I don't expect you to be my housekeeper," Keefe said. There was an edge of temper in his voice that made Tessa's stomach knot.

"I just...I'd feel better if I could help." Her fingers twisted together in front of her rounded stomach. "I took cooking lessons, and I'm a pretty good cook. Even Bobby said so," she added, unaware of how much her words revealed. "I'd... If you wouldn't mind...I'd like to... But if you'd rather I didn't..." She let the words trail off.

When was she going to learn? Don't argue. Never argue. It would just make him mad, and she didn't want to make him mad.

"Are you kidding? We'd love to have someone else do the cooking," Jace said, filling the silence before it became noticeable. "Like Keefe said last night, neither one of us is much good in the kitchen. I certainly wouldn't mind eating some decent food for a change."

Tessa's gaze was focused on the floor, so she missed seeing the quick warning look Jace gave Keefe. But Keefe saw it. Saw, also, the oddly taut expression on Tessa's face. He didn't like the idea of her cooking for them, but it was obvious that it meant a great deal to her.

"If you really want to cook a meal or two, I have no objection," he said. "As long as you don't feel like you have to do it."

"I'd like to." Tessa's smile was fleeting, but at least she no longer looked as if she expected him to bite. She gestured to the table. "I made lunch for you."

There was something so anxious in her expression that Keefe looked away to conceal the anger in his eyes. What the hell had happened to her in the last five years?

"It looks great," he said automatically. It wasn't until he was sitting down that he really saw what she'd done. It *did* look nice. She'd set the table with the same thick white china plates that he and Jace always used, but the silverware was neatly arranged at each place setting. In the center of the table she'd set a canning jar full of wildflowers and early roses from the bushes that grew alongside the house—remnants of some former owners' attempt to beautify their surroundings. The shrubs had survived hard winters, dry summers and total neglect, and always seemed to have a handful of flowers hidden among their tangled vines.

"I couldn't find any napkins," she said, reaching out to twitch a fork into more precise alignment with a knife. "I hope paper towels are okay."

"It's what we always use," Jace assured her. But they'd never taken the time to fold them into neat little wedges and arrange them beside the plates.

"Oh, good." She seemed relieved, as if she'd thought that the lack of proper linens might give offense. "I'll get the food. I wasn't sure what you'd want to drink."

"Beer," Keefe answered for both of them. "I'll get them."

"No. Just stay there. I'll get them."

He started to argue, but caught Jace's look and settled back into his chair. It went against the grain to sit still while a woman waited on him—particularly a woman who was six months pregnant. But it was obvious that any interference upset Tessa. Maybe after she'd been here a day or two, she'd relax a bit.

"There was some leftover roast beef, so I made sandwiches and soup," Tessa said as she pulled open the refrigerator door.

Keefe's stomach rumbled in anticipation. After

fighting that damned fence all morning, he was hungry enough to eat an entire cow. Thick slices of beef between slabs of bread sounded like pure heaven. And whatever the soup was, it smelled good. Maybe it wouldn't be such a bad thing to let her do the cooking, as long as she enjoyed it.

"I couldn't find exactly the right ingredients for the soup, but I think it turned out fairly well." She set a plate of sandwiches in the center of the table before going back to the stove. A moment later, she carried two bowls of soup back to the table and put one in the center of each of their plates. "I'll get your beer."

Keefe looked at the bowl of soup. A crusty slice of bread floated in the center of a pool of dark, rich broth. French onion soup. He'd had it in restaurants a time or two. If he remembered correctly, it was good but not particularly filling. Jace's boot nudged his ankle. When he glanced up, Jace rolled his eyes in the direction of the sandwiches. Keefe stared at them. Thin slices of bread, with the crusts removed, enclosed slices of beef so thin they appeared to have been shaved from the roast. Each sandwich had been cut into four neat little triangles.

"I made some potato salad," Tessa said as she brought a bowl to the table. "I got the recipe from one of my cooking teachers. She liked to use baby Yukon Gold potatoes, but I thought it would be okay with the boiling potatoes you had in the vegetable bin. The Yukon Gold are a prettier color, though."

"These look just fine," Keefe assured her truthfully. What didn't look so good was the amount of potato salad. Hungry as he was, he could eat the whole bowl himself, polish off the sandwiches and have room left over for dessert.

"There." Tessa set a glass of beer in front of him. A glass? Keefe tried to remember the last time he'd had beer in a glass. "Did I forget anything?"

More food. He looked at her hopeful expression and forced a smile. "I can't think of anything."

"How do you think she got that meat sliced so thin?" Jace asked. They were back in the saddle, heading out to finish the fencing job.

"I don't know." Keefe tugged his hat down against the early-afternoon sun and slouched lower in the saddle, his body adjusting automatically to the rhythm of the horse's gait.

"I don't think I've ever seen meat sliced that thin," Jace continued. "Must have taken a lot of work to get it like that."

"Must have." Keefe didn't want to think about how thin the meat had been sliced, because it reminded him of how empty his stomach still was.

"And that soup. I bet that took a lot of work, too, but there wasn't anything but a slice of bread and a few onions in it." Jace's tone was wondering.

Keefe grunted. He didn't know how much work the soup had been, but he did know that it hadn't been particularly filling. Jace fell silent and Keefe tried to think of something besides food.

"What the hell is a Yukon Gold potato?" Jace asked suddenly.

"Probably some kind of gourmet potato."

"She said they were a prettier color. What color do you figure they are?"

"Yellow, maybe, if the name is a clue." Keefe shrugged. His stomach sent up a polite inquiry about the remainder of lunch, and he tried to ignore it. He'd tried to eat slow, in hopes that it might fool his stomach into thinking it was being filled, but it hadn't worked.

"She looked so anxious."

"Yeah."

"I couldn't bring myself to say anything."

"Me neither."

"What do you think she's going to make for dinner?"

"I don't know." Keefe's voice was heavy with dread.

"Everything tasted good."

"Sure did."

They rode in silence a while longer, and then Jace spoke again, his tone wistful. "What do you think she did with the bread crusts?"

Chapter 3

When Keefe was married to Dana, he'd been riding the rodeo circuit and they'd lived out of trailers and motels—only one of many things she'd hated about the life-style. She hadn't minded being on the road, but she'd hated traveling cheap.

After the divorce, he'd spent a few months riding horses no one else would ride, drinking too much, smoking too much and generally doing a good imitation of a man hell-bent on self-destruction. He might have succeeded, too, if he hadn't gotten into a poker game in Montana. He'd been just drunk enough to bet everything he owned on the chance that he could draw to an inside straight. He'd won a run-down ranch in the High Sierras.

When he looked back on it, he figured drawing that card might have saved his life. The ranch had given him something to focus on besides the mess he'd made of his life. He'd taken what was left of his rodeo winnings and moved to the ranch. In the three years since, he'd worked like a dog to put the ranch back into shape. In his mind, the "ranch" consisted of the land, the stock and the outbuildings. The house was merely a place to eat and sleep and do paperwork. He did what was necessary to make it reasonably comfortable and then gave it no more thought.

And then Tessa had come to stay. He'd forgotten what it was like to have a woman around the house. He couldn't put his finger on what had changed, but everything seemed different. It might have been the way the delicate floral scent of her shampoo lingered in the bathroom after she showered, or the soft sound of her footsteps in the hall. He couldn't describe it, but he knew it was there—some indefinable, unmistakable change in the very air he breathed—something that spoke of woman.

The whole house seemed different. If he'd ever thought about it, he would have dismissed the old cliché about a house needing "a woman's touch." But he couldn't deny that, under Tessa's touch, the old house had seemed to shake itself awake. He'd lived there for three years without making much of an impact. In less than a week, Tessa had made the place look lived-in. The changes were subtle. She certainly hadn't rearranged the furniture or hung new curtains, but the thin layer of dust that had coated every surface was gone, there were flowers on the table and the windows were thrown open, letting in fresh air and sunshine.

Pleasant as the changes were—and he liked them

more than he cared to acknowledge—he didn't want her to feel as if she had to work to earn her keep.

"You're a guest—a *welcome* guest," he told her three days after her arrival. "I don't expect you to cook or clean to earn your keep."

"I don't mind." Tessa continued kneading the mound of bread dough that sat on the flour-dusted table.

"*I* mind." Keefe slapped his hat lightly against the side of his leg and frowned at her. He'd come up to the house in the middle of the afternoon to make a phone call and found her elbow-deep in bread dough. "You don't have to work for room and board, Tessa."

"It probably sounds stupid, but I actually like cooking and cleaning."

"Unbelievable, maybe, but not stupid," Keefe muttered, his eyes drawn to the rhythmic motion of her hands as she worked. Her fingers curled gracefully as she dug the heel of each hand into the dough. It seemed to push back, resisting her movements even as it yielded to them. There was something earthy in the motion, a sensuality that caught him off guard. It took a conscious act of will to look away.

"I really like making bread." Tessa glanced at him, her mouth curved in a soft smile—a real smile, he saw. Not one of the bright, false smiles that had come so frequently—and meaninglessly—when she first arrived.

She looked better, he thought, studying her profile. Not exactly right. Certainly not like the girl he remembered. There were still shadows in her eyes, and when she thought no one was watching, there was a haunted quality to her expression, a deep emptiness that made him want to hold her and promise to take care of whatever was wrong. But she looked better now than she had three days ago. There was color in her face, and the dark circles that had been under her eyes were almost gone. She smiled less often, but they were real smiles, not those bright, meaningless displays that put up walls between her and the rest of the world. He still didn't know what had brought her to him, but it was obvious that she needed more time to heal. He was glad to give her that.

"There's something about kneading bread that's soothing," Tessa continued. "I had an electric mixer back…where I used to live, but I didn't like to use it for bread. I like to feel the dough change under my hands. It starts out sticky and fighting your every move, but as you work it it changes, starts to come alive. It's like creating life, I suppose," she finished, her smile taking on a self-conscious edge.

Keefe had been staring at her hands, almost hypnotized by their movements. But, at her last comment, his eyes shifted to her stomach for an instant before lifting to her face. He smiled. "You seem to be getting quite a bit of experience in that lately."

He could see the exact moment that she realized he was referring to her pregnancy. Her mouth tightened subtly, and the skin seemed to draw taut over her cheekbones. He couldn't see her eyes, but he knew they were empty, hollow.

"I guess I am," she said, her tone devoid of expression, the curve of her mouth perfunctory. There was an uncomfortable little silence, and then Tessa flashed him one of those bright, meaningless smiles that he was coming to hate. "I hope you're not going to insist that I do nothing around the house but sit on my hands all day. That would get tedious pretty quickly."

"You're welcome to do whatever you want," he said slowly. He turned his hat between his fingers, his eyes on her profile. He wished he knew what was going on behind those walls she put up. Even more, he'd like to know what it was that had taught her to build those walls in the first place. "As long as you don't do anything major. I don't want you to hurt yourself."

"I'll be careful," she assured him with another of those smiles that didn't reach her eyes.

"I'll see you at lunch, then," he said. Frustration tugged at him as he left the house. He couldn't shake the feeling that there was something more he should say, something more he should do. But he couldn't help her if he didn't know what was wrong, and it was obvious that she had no intention of confiding in him—not now, maybe not ever.

Tessa had been staying on the Flying Ace a little more than a week when she added the laundry to her list of chores. When Keefe protested, she said that she had to wash her own clothes—washing his wasn't that much more work. He gave in, guiltily aware that he wasn't entirely sorry to rid himself of a job he cordially detested. But when he saw the results of her efforts, it was clear that his moment of weakness was not to go unpunished.

Jace pushed his hat back with his thumb, narrowing his eyes against the brilliance of the morning sun. His clear blue eyes moved over Keefe, widening a little when he got to the sharp creases that marched down each leg of his jeans with military precision.

''You going to a party?'' he asked.

''Shut up.'' Keefe glared at him.

''Must be a party somewhere,'' Jace continued, ignoring the menace in his partner's expression. ''Either that or you figure the cows will appreciate your fashion sense.''

''One more word and I'm going to feed you your teeth.'' Keefe swung up into the saddle.

''I don't know what you're getting so upset about.'' Jace set his heel against his horse's side, sending the big bay after Keefe's mount. ''I think you look real nice,'' he said, but his earnest tone was at odds with the gleam in his eyes.

''You're walking a real thin line,'' Keefe warned as they rode out of the ranch yard. ''I can think of any number of places on this ranch where I could dispose of a body.''

Jace looked hurt. ''Here I am trying to pay you a compliment, and all I get for my trouble is threats against my life. I think you just might set a new trend in ranch wear.'' He frowned thoughtfully at the mountains that loomed ahead of them, his tone becoming philosophical. ''When you think about it, there's no excuse for cowboys to go around looking like something the cat dragged in. A man ought to take pride in his appearance."

"Glad you feel that way," Keefe said, his tone so cordial that Jace felt a quick rush of alarm. "When I left the house, Tessa was just starting in on *your* laundry."

"Oh, no." Jace's expression was horrified.

"Oh, yes." Keefe's grin was pure malice.

"We'll be laughingstocks," Jace said gloomily.

"Nobody's going to see us but the cows."

"They'll never take us seriously."

"The cows?" Keefe's brows rose.

"A cowboy wearing jeans with a crease?" Jace shuddered. "What kind of authority figure is that?"

"You figure the cows are going to notice?"

"They'll ignore us," Jace predicted in a tone of doom. "Pretty soon, they'll start muttering about mutiny. Next thing you know, we'll have a riot on our hands."

Keefe's shout of laughter startled a Stellar's jay out of a nearby tree. The bird took off, a flash of sapphire and black against the pale blue of the morning sky, his squawk expressing his annoyance.

"I figure we should be safe enough as long as we don't let them get hold of weapons," he said, still grinning.

"Probably." Jace shook his head. "There's got to be a way to stop her."

"I don't know what it is." Keefe's smile faded as he considered his houseguest. "I was going to tell her that I didn't want my jeans ironed, but..." A helpless shrug completed the sentence.

''Yeah, I know. She looked at you.'' Jace understood completely.

''Yeah.''

They rode in silence for a moment, each contemplating the impossibility of saying anything even marginally critical to Tessa. Neither of them was willing to risk doing anything that might bring back the haunting emptiness that had marked her expression when she arrived. Military creases in their jeans were a small price to pay to keep that look out of her eyes.

''What did she make for lunch?'' Jace asked after a while.

''Ham sandwiches.''

''No crusts?''

''No crusts.''

''What do you think she does with all those crusts?'' The question had been nagging at Jace for over a week.

''Maybe she used them in that stuffing she made last night.'' Keefe said. He shook his head. ''Littlest damned chickens I've ever seen.''

''They were game hens.''

''I've seen sparrows bigger than that.''

''Tasted good.''

''Tasted great. But half of one of those pigeons wasn't enough to feed a two-year-old.'' He frowned as he thought about the beautifully presented meal Tessa had served the night before. Half a game hen, a spoonful of delicately flavored stuffing and two different vegetables, carefully arranged on each plate. ''What do you suppose she did with the fourth half?''

''She's probably going to make soup out of it,''

Jace suggested. They contemplated that possibility in gloomy silence.

"What did you bring for lunch?" Keefe asked.

"Cold fried chicken, potato salad and some of those apple turnovers from Gleason's."

Keefe's mouth watered in anticipation. When Tessa took over the cooking, it had become immediately apparent that they had a problem. She was an excellent cook, each dish perfectly seasoned and elegantly presented. If they'd been holding down desk jobs rather than running a ranch, there would have been nothing to complain about. As it was, at the end of the first full day of Tessa's reign in the kitchen, Keefe had met with Jace in the foreman's cottage after she went to bed. While they devoured potato chips and dip—the only thing edible Jace had to hand—they'd worked out their strategy.

The next day, when Jace went into town to fill Tessa's grocery list, he'd also bought enough food to stock the kitchen in the tiny foreman's house, enabling them to supplement Tessa's beautifully cooked meals with more rough-and-ready fare. Jace packed their lunch in his saddlebags in the morning, and in the evening Keefe waited until Tessa went to bed and then made his way across the ranch yard to Jace's kitchen to finish filling the hollow in his stomach.

It wasn't the most convenient arrangement, but it was better than trying to explain to Tessa that she was about to starve them to death.

Tessa ran the scrub brush over the floor in brisk little circles. It was obvious that cleaning floors had not been high on Keefe's list of priorities. She was willing to bet that it had been months since the floor was mopped, and probably years since it was thoroughly scrubbed. She'd thought the floor was actually covered in prison-gray linoleum until she discovered a rather pleasant ivory-and-slate-blue pattern underneath the dirt.

At least the floor wasn't covered in layers of old wax, she thought as she dipped the brush in the bucket of soapy water beside her. She didn't have to worry about stripping years of wax away. Not that she could have done that, anyway. An afternoon spent breathing ammonia fumes wasn't on any list of recommended prenatal activities. She wouldn't do anything that would be bad for the baby. That was one thing she'd promised herself when she found out she was pregnant. She would follow every instruction she was given and do everything she could to ensure the baby's health.

And she'd kept her promise, she thought. She'd taken her vitamins. She'd consumed so much milk, it was practically coming out her ears. She'd exercised moderately and tried to eat right. Of course, the doctor had also told her to avoid stress. She'd nearly laughed out loud when he told her that. But even she hadn't guessed just how much stress she'd be called on to endure.

If only there had been some way to know that Bobby was going to die, she might have made other choices.

Tessa shook her head as if physically pushing the thoughts aside. She wasn't going to look back. That was another promise she'd made herself when Bobby died. The past was past, and she wasn't going to waste any of the present on regrets. She was going to move on and make something of her life.

You? Make something of your life? You're even stupider than I thought. The sneering voice was so real that Tessa froze, her fingers clenching around the scrub brush. She was half-afraid to look over her shoulder for fear she'd see him there, his handsome features twisted in contempt, his eyes mocking. *You're not smart enough to make something of your life. You're too stupid, Tessa. Stupid. Stupid. Stupid.*

"No," she whispered. "I'm not stupid."

Are you arguing with me? The low voice held a silky threat that made the hair on the back of her neck stand up.

Imagination, she thought desperately. It was just her imagination replaying unwelcome images on a mental screen. He was gone, and she didn't have to be afraid of him ever again.

"What the hell are you doing!"

The male roar of anger was punctuated by the slam of the screen door. Caught in the nightmare of memory, Tessa felt her heart stop. The thud of boots on the half-washed floor brought her around to face that voice. Made clumsy by the heavy bulk of her stomach, she sat down heavily on the damp floor. The tall male figure striding toward her sent her sliding down a long, dark tunnel into the past.

"Have you gone completely crazy?" Keefe demanded angrily. Three long strides took him across the damp floor. "Dammit all, Tessa! I told you not to do anything heavy. Get up off the damn floor."

He bent over her, one hand outstretched to help her up. Trapped in past nightmares, Tessa saw the tall figure looming over her and saw his hand come out. Her reaction was instinctive.

"Don't!" She cringed back against the cupboard, hunching her shoulders, one hand curling protectively across her belly, the other coming up to shield her head from the expected blow.

Keefe froze. Even his heart seemed to stop beating for a moment. He stared down at Tessa, crouched on the floor in a classic defensive posture, her small body curled up as tightly as possible, considering the bulk of her stomach. He breathed in slowly, the air rasping in his throat.

"My God," he whispered hoarsely. "You thought I was going to *hit* you?"

The stunned disbelief in his tone penetrated the black wall of fear that enclosed her. Keefe. It was Keefe. She slowly lowered her arm, but she didn't look at him. She was too afraid of what he might see in her eyes. Her mind raced frantically. She had to explain, had to tell him... She didn't know what, but if she didn't say something, he might guess the truth, might guess the secret she'd kept so carefully.

"Tessa, I wouldn't..." Feeling as if he'd aged ten years in the past ten seconds, Keefe straightened slowly. He stared at the hand he'd reached out to her, as if he might find an explanation for what had just happened written on its palm. But there was nothing to see but a faint unsteadiness. He let it drop to his side. ''I've never hit a woman in my life,'' he said finally, his voice hoarse and strained.

His dazed tone brought Tessa's head up. He looked as if he'd just taken a hard blow to the solar plexus. The skin across his cheekbones was drawn tight, sharp lines bracketed his mouth and his eyes.... Tessa's breath caught. For the first time in a long time, she was aware of someone else's pain, someone else's anguish.

''I would never hurt you, Tessa.''

''I know,'' she whispered.

''You cringed.'' He lifted one hand and thrust unsteady fingers through his dark hair. ''You cringed as if you thought I was going to— You were *afraid*. Of me.''

''No.'' She couldn't let him think that. ''It wasn't you. It was... I was thinking, remembering, and I thought...for just a second, I thought you were someone else.''

''Who?'' he asked immediately.

''It doesn't matter.''

''Doesn't matter?'' Keefe crouched in front of her, bringing his eyes more on a level with hers. She noticed that he was careful not to reach out to her, not to get too close. His care caused a sharp little pain in her chest. ''You were scared to death, Tessa. You thought I was going to *hit* you. And then you tell me that you thought I was someone else and that it doesn't matter? Like hell it doesn't!''

There was anger in his voice, but it wasn't directed at her. Emotionally battered as she was, she could still recognize that. He wasn't angry *at* her. He was angry *for* her, angry at whoever had frightened her. Tessa stared at him as the difference seeped slowly into her consciousness. It had been so long since anyone took her side in anything, and in her entire life she couldn't remember anyone caring enough to be angry on her behalf. Gratitude welled up inside her. But she'd kept this particular secret for four long years.

"It's over," she said, looking away from him.

"It's not over if it can still make you react like that," he said flatly. She shivered, and his voice gentled. "Sometimes talking can help, Tessa."

"No." She shook her head. Her voice was tight and thin with suppressed emotion. "Talking doesn't change anything. I promised myself that I wouldn't look back. It's over. He's dead and it's over."

"Your husband?" Keefe's tone was gentle, but there was determination there, a quiet warning that he wasn't going to be easily dissuaded. He reached out to take her hand, in a slow, careful movement. "Is that who you thought I was?"

Tessa looked at her hand in his. Her fingers appeared slender and fragile lying against the width of his palm. There was strength in his hand. Bobby had been strong, too. As she remembered that strength, her hand trembled in Keefe's hold, but she didn't draw away. This was Keefe, and she could never be afraid of him.

"Tessa?"

Slowly, almost reluctantly, she lifted her eyes to his—and felt some long-held wall inside her start to crumble. The feeling of vulnerability was frightening. She turned her head away and tried to withdraw her hand from his, but his fingers held hers with gentle implacability.

"Tessa? Did your husband abuse you?"

"No!" The denial was immediate. Her eyes jerked back to his face and she shook her head. "He didn't. He just...sometimes he... But it was my fault," she insisted. "It was always my fault. It was only when I was stupid that he... It was my fault."

Keefe had never known he was capable of such powerful anger. It was a white-hot wave sweeping over him, making him feel as if the top of his head might lift off with the force of it. He drew in a slow breath, struggling to control his rage. Anger wasn't what Tessa needed right now.

"Your fault?" he questioned softly. "He *hit* you and you think it was your fault."

Tessa looked away. "Sometimes I did stupid things and he'd...he'd get upset. I didn't mean to, but I did."

The ticking of the wall clock was clearly audible in the silence that followed. When Keefe broke it, his voice was low, each word distinct.

"That is the biggest load of crap I've ever heard in my life."

Tessa felt the wall tremble again, shaken by his calm assurance. "You don't understand," she whispered. "I was—"

"You didn't do anything." Keefe's fingers tightened over hers. "Look at me, Tessa."

The sheer force of his will brought Tessa's eyes to his face. She felt herself start to come apart inside, as if all the tension that had been holding her together for so long were suddenly dissolving and draining away, leaving her as fragile and vulnerable as a newborn kitten.

"You could never do anything to justify him hitting you. Never."

"But I—"

"Never. It wasn't your fault, Tessa. Not ever."

"But—"

"There are no buts. It wasn't your fault."

Tessa felt the protective wall dissolve forever beneath the impact of the quiet words. During the first two years of her marriage, she'd shed a sea of tears, but after that she'd stopped crying. She'd felt as if she'd given all the tears she had to give, as if something had dried up inside and she'd never cry again. But Keefe's quiet assurance that she hadn't done anything to deserve Bobby's treatment of her brought long-buried emotions shivering to painful life.

She pulled her hand from his and pressed it against her mouth as tears stung her eyes. "I'm sorry." Her whisper was choked. Her face crumpled, and tears began to roll down her cheeks. "I'm sorry."

"It's okay." Keefe gathered her into his arms and stood up, lifting her up off the damp floor as easily as if she were a child. Cradling her against his chest, he carried her from the kitchen.

His experience with a woman's tears was limited to his ex-wife. Dana had cried easily, stormy bouts of sobbing that, in the early days of their marriage, made him feel like the lowest villain on the face of the planet and generally resulted in her getting whatever it was she wanted. Over the years, his concern had become more rote and he'd been less willing to give in to her wishes. By the time their marriage ended, he'd felt nothing but a great weariness when she cried.

In contrast to her sister's dramatic displays, Tessa cried almost silently. Her small body trembled in his arms as slow, painful tears seeped out from under her lashes. He knew, on some deep, visceral level that was beyond questioning, that she'd learned to cry quietly because it was safer not to draw any attention to herself. The thought made his gut knot with anger. His arms tightened around her, as if to shield her from past hurts.

Keefe carried her into the living room and sat down with her on the sofa. The worn springs groaned under their combined weight. He didn't say anything, didn't try to top her tears. He simply held her and let her cry.

"At first, it only happened when he was drinking."

Tessa didn't look at Keefe as she spoke. She wasn't sure she'd ever be able to look at him again. He'd held her while she cried, and when her tears finally stopped, he'd gotten a box of tissues from the bathroom and, pulling a handful loose, proceeded to mop her face as if she were four years old. She'd been too tired, too drained by her emotional storm, to object. Leaning back against the worn fabric of the sofa, she'd let him take care of her.

He hadn't asked her anything, hadn't demanded to know how she'd let herself become a victim of Bobby's abuse. He'd just dried her face and then looked at her, his dark eyes unfathomable. And she found herself talking, offering explanations he hadn't demanded, trying to make him understand something she didn't even begin to understand herself.

"Bobby didn't drink unless he was upset about something, and I thought that, if I were a good enough wife, if I made him happy, then he wouldn't drink and he wouldn't...wouldn't hit me anymore."

Her attention on the tissue she was shredding into fine confetti, Tessa missed seeing the sudden tightness in Keefe's jaw, the rage that flickered in his eyes. If Bobby Mallory hadn't already been dead, no power on earth could have stopped him from tracking the bastard down and tearing his lungs out through his nose.

But his anger wasn't what Tessa needed now. He forced it back, making his voice level and calm.

"He had a problem you couldn't solve, Tessa." Keefe reached out and set his hand over hers, stopping her mutilation of the tissue. "No one can make someone else happy. That's something you have to do for yourself."

The look she gave him was doubtful. "Maybe." She shook her head a little as she looked away. "I don't know. I thought, if I could just be the perfect wife, I could make my marriage work."

"It takes two to make a marriage work. One person can't do it all on their own."

"Is that what happened to you and Dana?" she asked, glancing at him sideways. "Only one of you was willing to work on the marriage?"

Keefe's hand tightened over hers for a moment, and then he pulled it away, sitting back on the sofa. He was surprised by how much the reminder of his failed marriage still stung. He'd thought he'd gotten past all that a long time ago. Catching Tessa's questioning look, he lifted one shoulder in a half shrug.

''Dana and I couldn't make our marriage work because neither of us was willing to give enough.''

Privately Tessa thought that it was unlikely anyone would ever be able to give enough to satisfy her beautiful older sister. Dana had been raised to expect the rest of the world to fall at her feet, and it came close enough to keep her expectations high. But Keefe's marriage to her sister was none of her business.

''Well, I was willing to give enough for two,'' she said with a sigh. ''But it was never enough.''

''Why didn't you leave him?'' Keefe asked quietly.

''I don't know.'' Tessa let her head fall back against the worn green upholstery. ''At first, I kept thinking he'd quit drinking and everything would be okay. And then, later, I was afraid of him, afraid of what he'd do to me if I tried to leave.'' She turned her head and looked at him, her eyes much older than her years. ''It wasn't because he loved me. I realized that a long time ago. It was because he liked having control of me, liked having control of something, even if it was only a wife he despised.'' She sighed and looked away, missing the rage that flickered in Keefe's dark eyes.

''His father—Senator Mallory—is a very powerful man. I don't mean politically. I mean personally. I don't think Bobby ever felt like he had any control over his life. So he married me and I...I let him control me.''

Keefe responded instantly to the shame in her

voice, reaching out to cup her chin in his hand and turn her face back to his. ''It wasn't your fault, Tessa.''

''Wasn't it?'' Her wry smile nearly broke his heart. ''I made the choice to stay with him.''

''You were frightened.''

''I was embarrassed,'' she corrected him.

''Embarrassed?'' Keefe repeated, his brows going up in disbelief. ''Embarrassed about what?''

''I didn't want other people to know what was happening, didn't want them to know what a sham my marriage was, what a mess I'd made of my life.'' She read the blank incomprehension in his eyes and smiled self-deprecatingly. ''I guess it sounds pretty dumb. It *was* dumb. But I felt as if all I had was the facade, and if that was gone, I wouldn't have anything.''

Keefe tried and failed to understand her reasoning. ''What about your family? Didn't they know something was wrong?''

Tessa's laugh held little humor. ''Have you forgotten who we're talking about? My parents were delighted when I married Bobby. He was rich, handsome and, even better, from a good family. I was never as pretty as Dana or as popular, but I married bet—'' She broke off, her eyes widening, when she realized what she'd almost said.

''You married better than she did?'' Keefe finished for her. One corner of his mouth curled in a rueful smile. ''Don't worry about hurting my feelings. Your parents never made any secret of what they thought of me.''

"They were wrong," Tessa said fiercely. "Dana was lucky to have you."

"Yeah? Well, there seem to be some differing opinions about that," he said lightly. He shifted the subject away from his marriage. "So you didn't feel you could go to your parents. What about Dana? I know the two of you weren't close, but under the circumstances..."

"I just couldn't." Tessa couldn't even begin to explain all the reasons she couldn't have told her sister about Bobby's abuse.

"Okay. What about Molly?" Keefe asked. "She would have helped you. I suspect she eats senators for breakfast."

Tessa's smile was shaky but genuine. "I wouldn't be surprised if Aunt Molly could single-handedly take on the entire Senate and have them on their knees by lunch." Her smile faded, and she shook her head. "There were times when I thought of going to her, asking her to help me. But she's so strong."

"And this is a bad thing?" Keefe asked.

"No. No, it's a good thing. But just thinking about her made me feel stupid and helpless—exactly the things Bobby said I was." Her fingers shook as she finished shredding the tissue into tiny pieces. Her voice dropped to a whisper. "I was so ashamed. I didn't want her to know the truth."

Keefe looked away from her, grabbing for his self-control. He wanted to shout that it wasn't her fault, that she was the victim in what had happened. He wanted to put his fist through a wall. But what he wanted most of all was to have Bobby Mallory standing in front of him, alive and well just long enough to give him the pleasure of beating him half to death.

He felt frustrated by Tessa's conviction that she'd somehow been to blame for her husband's abusive behavior. And he felt hopelessly ill-equipped to deal with the situation. She'd spent four years in an abusive marriage. She should probably have professional help, counseling. But all she had was him.

"It doesn't matter anymore why you didn't ask for help," he said, choosing his words with care. He looked at her, his dark eyes serious. "You're here now. And you're safe. You and your baby."

"Thank you." Tessa's eyes filled with tears of gratitude. He'd opened his home to her, taken her into his life as easily as if she had a right to be there. She wondered if he'd be as openly welcoming if she told him the whole truth.

Chapter 4

Tessa hadn't realized how much she needed to talk to someone about the nightmare that had been her marriage. *It wasn't your fault.* Four simple words that she'd desperately needed to hear. There was a part of her that had fiercely denied the blame Bobby heaped on her, a part that had insisted that she wasn't stupid, that she wasn't to blame for everything that went wrong in his life. That small core of belief had been all but suffocated by years of abuse. Hearing Keefe tell her that she wasn't to blame for what happened had lifted a burden of guilt from her.

She'd promised herself that she wouldn't spend time looking back, wouldn't waste a minute of her future in bitterness over the past. But it wasn't possible to close the past four years of her life behind a locked door and simply forget about it. She'd needed to look at what had happened, needed to really *see* it before she could finally start to let go of the pain.

Keefe had helped her do that.

Tessa leaned her forearms on top of a stall door and let her eyes roam over the pretty chestnut mare inside. It had been barely a week since she told Keefe about her marriage, but she felt as if in those few days she'd finally begun the process of moving forward with her life.

She shifted position and her belly bumped against the side of the stall, reminding her that there was one undeniable, unbreakable tie with the past. She frowned. It was just like Bobby to have found a way to control her life even from the grave.

"That's Lady. She generally manages to live up to her name."

Tessa had been occupied with her thoughts and hadn't realized she was no longer alone until Jace spoke from behind her. Startled by the sound of a male voice so unexpectedly close, she swung around to face him.

"Hey," Jace stretched out his hand. She recognized that the gesture was intended to reassure, but too late to stop her instinctive move to step back and put some distance between them.

The big barn was suddenly very quiet, as if even the animals were holding their breath. Jace let his hand drop.

"Sorry. I didn't mean to startle you." He smiled, but there was something watchful in his blue eyes.

"I'm the one who should apologize." Her laugh

sounded brittle, even to her own ears. ''Stupid of me to react that way. I don't know why I did. I'm sorry.''

''Don't apologize,'' Jace said easily. ''I'm used to having women fall back in stunned disbelief when they see me. It's the price I pay for being so incredibly good-looking.''

Tessa laughed, just as he'd intended, but privately she thought it wasn't much of an exaggeration. From the solid angle of his jaw to the sharp slant of his nose and the heavy wave of dark hair that fell onto his forehead, Jace Reno was classically handsome. But the vivid electric blue of his eyes, surrounded by thick black lashes, took him from merely handsome to something approaching pure masculine beauty. The fact that he seemed oblivious to his looks only added to his appeal.

''So, you and Lady were getting acquainted,'' he said as he came forward. He wasn't quite as tall as Keefe, or as broad-shouldered, but he still loomed over Tessa's five-foot-nothing, and she had to make a conscious effort not to edge away from him, to put some distance between herself and the danger represented by his size and masculinity.

''I don't think Lady was terribly interested in getting to know me,'' Tessa admitted, and was pleased by how casual she sounded—how normal. ''She seems supremely disinterested in my presence.''

''She's just being coy,'' Jace said. At the sound of his voice, the mare lifted her nose from the feed box and turned her head toward him. ''She doesn't want to look easy, do you, girl?'' The mare's ears swiveled forward, and she snorted, as if in confirmation.

"But I know her weakness," Jace said as he reached into the pocket of his faded blue work shirt. He pulled out a sugar cube and offered it to the mare. "She's got quite a sweet tooth."

Lady stepped across the stall and took the offered treat, crunching it between her strong teeth with delicate greed. Forgetting her uneasiness, Tessa moved closer, smiling at the mare's obvious enjoyment.

"Here. You feed her the next one." Tessa glanced from the sugar cube Jace was offering to his face. There was something in his eyes that made her wonder if he wasn't using the sugar to coax her closer, much the way he'd done with the mare. Her mouth softened into a rueful smile, and she reached out to take the sugar from him.

Lady snuffled the cube from her hand, and Tessa reached out to rub her forehead as the mare crunched the treat.

"I told you she could be bought," Jace said, leaning his hip against the side of the stall. "Just don't tell Keefe. He has this idea that sugar is bad for their teeth."

Tessa grinned at the furtive look he shot over his shoulder, as if he expected to find Keefe looming up behind him. "How ridiculous. He should know better."

"That's what I think." Jace gave her an approving look. "Nothing that tastes as good as sugar could possibly be bad for you."

"Just as long as you brush after every meal and floss at least once a day." She gave the mare a stern glance. "You do floss, don't you, Lady?"

As if on cue, the mare snorted and shook her head. Tessa and Jace both laughed, but Lady ignored them, more interested in getting her ears scratched than in whatever had amused her human companions.

"You're good with the horses," Jace commented. "I've seen you down here this last week. They like you."

"I like them, too." Tessa said. She heard the wistfulness in her voice and slanted a quick, self-conscious smile in Jace's direction. "I practically lived in the stables when I was a girl. I had all kinds of fantasies about being a horse trainer, or maybe a breeder. Silly stuff."

"Sounds reasonable enough to me," Jace contradicted. "What happened?"

"I...married someone who didn't like horses. He didn't even like me to ride. I kept it up for a little while after we were married, but it was such a hassle to drive to my parents' house every time I wanted to ride." *And Bobby had been furious when he found out I was still riding after he'd expressed his opinion of it.* Though the big barn was pleasantly warm, the memory of his anger was enough to make Tessa shiver. "It was easier to give it up," she finished, pushing the memories away.

"He was probably afraid of horses," Jace said.

"Who? Bobby?" Tessa shook her head. "He wasn't afraid of them. He just didn't like them."

"What's not to like? They're friendly. They'll give you a ride for the price of a bucket of oats." Jace gestured to the chestnut mare, as if to illustrate her finer points. "They're ecologically sound—no ozone depletion here. In my experience, a lot of people who say they don't like horses just don't want to admit that they're afraid of them."

Tessa started to shake her head again and then hesitated. The idea that Bobby had been afraid of horses—afraid of anything, really—seemed ridiculous. In her mind, he was such a looming, threatening figure that she just couldn't imagine him being afraid of something as comparatively harmless as a horse. And yet...

There'd been a time, before they were married, when he came to her parents' house to pick her up. He'd been early, and she'd been in the stables, working one of the horses. When Bobby walked up to the corral, she'd ridden the big gelding up to the fence to greet him. Bobby had stepped back from the railing rather quickly, looking less than happy. She'd never been able to coax him any closer than that to a horse, even in the months when they were dating and he was still pretending that he wanted to make her happy.

Tessa glanced up and caught Jace's questioning look. She shrugged. "I don't know. Maybe Bobby *was* afraid of horses. I never thought of him as being afraid of anything, except maybe his father."

"Does his father look like a horse?"

"What?"

"Well, if his father looks like a horse, then maybe your husband was afraid of horses because they reminded him of his father."

Tessa stared at him blankly for a moment and then burst out laughing. All she could think of was how much Robert Mallory would hate the idea of being compared to a horse—and yet his long, aquiline features might be considered vaguely equine.

Jace smiled, pleased with himself. He had the feeling that there hadn't been enough laughter in Tessa's life lately. It was good to hear her laugh and to see the shadows gone from her eyes, even temporarily. She was usually so quiet and serious that he sometimes forgot how young she really was, but for a moment she didn't look a day more than twenty-three.

"I don't think my father-in-law would appreciate the idea that he resembled a horse," she said when her laughter had subsided.

"I don't know why. I've known some very handsome horses."

"Come to think of it, so have I."

An easy silence fell between them. Jace leaned against the side of the stall and watched Tessa without seeming to watch her. She looked better than she had when she first arrived. The fine lines of tension that had bracketed her mouth were gone, as were the dark circles that had looked like smudgy fingerprints against her pale skin. She'd gained a little weight, which he thought was remarkable, considering the way she cooked. She smiled more often, and they were genuine smiles, not those bright, empty expressions that had no meaning.

But she was too young for the shadows that lurked in the back of her eyes, too young for the quick fear he'd seen in her face earlier. He would have given a great deal to get his hands on whoever had put that fear there. If his guess was right, the responsible party was currently facing a much higher authority. But there might be something else he could do to help Tessa.

"I could teach you self-defense." Jace said it so casually that it took Tessa a moment to realize what he'd said.

"Me?" She turned her head to look at him, her eyes wide with surprise.

"Sure. It wouldn't take long to learn a few basic techniques. A long time ago, in a land far away, I actually taught self-defense."

"*You* did?"

"Guilty." He moved away from the stall and sank into a half crouch, his elbows bent, his hands curved in front of him at chest level.

It was a pose she'd seen many times on television, usually assumed by some mystical-looking guy wearing a cotton robe and no shoes. Jace was standing in the aisle of a dusty barn, wearing jeans and cowboy boots. He should have looked ridiculous. But there was nothing ridiculous about the easy grace of his movements—dangerous grace, Tessa thought, looking at him. He was smiling, but she had the sudden sense that if he stopped smiling he might be rather frightening.

"Behold, the terror of the seamy element of downtown Dubuque."

"Dubuque?" Tessa gaped at him. "You're kidding."

"You think Dubuque doesn't have a seamy side?" Jace straightened and then slid back into what she'd come to think of as a classic cowboy slouch. One corner of his upper lip curled in a superior sneer. "Don't be naive. Evil lurks everywhere."

"In Dubuque?" she repeated.

"Okay, maybe not actual evil," he admitted sullenly. "Maybe more of a cranky element. But they were really scared of me."

"Cranky element?" Tessa giggled helplessly. "Did you subdue them single-handedly?"

He sighed heavily. "It was a tough job, but somebody had to do it."

"I hope the citizens of Dubuque were suitably grateful."

"A job well done is its own reward," he informed her in a superior tone.

"Of course it is." Tessa tried to remember the last time she'd had such a nonsensical conversation. It had been years. Maybe during that first summer after Keefe and Dana were married. Keefe had a similar flair for the ridiculous. She'd laughed more that summer than she had before or since.

"So, now that you know you're dealing with an expert, would you like some lessons in self-defense?"

Tessa's smile wavered. She shrugged. "I don't know that I have much use for self-defense."

"You never know. It's more than just the physical knowledge you gain. Knowing how to protect yourself can really boost your self-confidence."

"Is it so obvious that mine needs boosting?" Tessa asked ruefully.

"I didn't say that." Jace's smile took away any possible sting. "But it never hurts to know a few good moves."

''You're probably right.'' The idea of being able to defend herself held real appeal. She hadn't thought of it before this minute, but she suddenly realized that she didn't ever want to feel small and helpless again. But it wasn't quite that simple. ''I'm not exactly in any condition to be throwing people over my shoulder at the moment,'' she said, brushing her fingers self-consciously over the solid bulge of her belly.

''Maybe not this minute,'' Jace agreed. ''But we could start after the baby's born.''

''That's two and a half months from now,'' she said. ''I have no intention of imposing on you and Keefe for that long.''

''Who says you're imposing? We both like the company. Besides, we like your cooking.'' It wasn't a lie, Jace thought. She was a terrific cook. She just didn't cook *enough.* ''You wouldn't condemn us to endless pots of my stew and Keefe's charred steaks, would you?''

Tessa smiled a little and shook her head. The truth was, she didn't have anywhere to go if she left. She supposed a stronger woman would strike out into the world, make her own way and not use a mere pregnancy as an excuse for imposing on her ex-brother-in-law. But then, a stronger woman wouldn't have spent four years in an abusive marriage, either. She touched the top of her belly and then let her hand fall to her side, her breath escaping her in a soft sigh as she half turned away from Jace. ''A lot can happen in a couple of months,'' she murmured, speaking half to herself.

''It must be hard to separate what you feel about

the baby from what you feel about the father,'' Jace said softly.

Tessa stiffened. ''I don't know what you mean.''

''Don't you?''

Almost unwillingly, Tessa looked at him. There was knowledge in his eyes—knowledge, and a compassion that undermined her already fragile defenses.

''Keefe—''

''Didn't say a word,'' Jace said, answering the question before she could ask it. ''And I haven't asked him anything.''

''Then how could you know?'' she whispered.

''A long time ago, there was someone I cared for very much. You remind me of her a little.''

''What happened to her?''

He looked past her, seeing things visible only to him. ''She didn't get out in time,'' he said slowly. He blinked and seemed to almost physically shake off the memory. ''You did.''

''Circumstances threw me out,'' she corrected him. ''As for the baby...'' She sighed softly and set one hand against her stomach. It was the first time Jace had ever seen her touch her stomach the way pregnant women seemed to do so often, as if in silent communication with the life they carried. ''I've never lost sight of the fact that whatever Bobby was, whatever he did, none of it was the baby's fault.''

''It wasn't yours, either,'' he countered softly, and Tessa felt her eyes fill with quick tears.

For four years, she'd been held to blame for everything, whether it was the dry cleaner putting too much starch in Bobby's shirts or the caterer failing to provide enough glassware for a dinner party. Now, in the space of barely a week, she'd been told by two different people that she wasn't to blame for the abuse she'd endured.

"I wish I was sure of that," she said.

Jace heard the pain in her voice. He reached out and drew her into his arms. Tessa stiffened for an instant and then relaxed against him, allowing herself to draw on the comfort he was offering.

"The hurt will go away," he said. "You just have to give it time."

He bent to brush a kiss over her forehead. As he straightened, he caught a flicker of movement out the corner of his eye. He turned his head and saw Keefe standing a few feet away. The light was at his back, but Jace had no trouble reading the disapproval in his friend's expression.

Keefe leaned over to set down the bucket he was carrying. The soft thud as it hit the ground was enough to alert Tessa to his presence. She stiffened, and Jace let his arms fall away from her as she stepped back.

"Hello, Keefe." She tugged at the hem of the loose shirt she wore and then reached up to smooth back a tendril of wheat-colored hair that had worked its way free of the pins she'd used to pull it back. She was embarrassed that Keefe had caught her practically crying in Jace's arms. He was probably going to think that she made a habit of sobbing on every male shoulder that presented itself.

"Are you all right, Tessa?"

"I'm fine," she said, and then winced at the false brightness of her tone. "I...think I'll go start lunch."

She threw a quick smile in Jace's direction and left the barn as quickly as she could manage, considering that the bulk of her stomach precluded actually running.

Jace waited for Keefe to break the silence that fell after Tessa's departure.

"I don't want to see Tessa get hurt," Keefe said at last.

"Neither do I."

"She's vulnerable right now."

"Are you warning me not to seduce her?" Jace asked with a kind of irritated amusement.

Keefe scowled. That was exactly what he'd been trying to do, but said out loud, it sounded a little ridiculous. "Not exactly," he muttered.

"Because we're friends, I'm not going to ask you to explain 'exactly' what you did mean," Jace said. "But I'd like to point out that, while I may have done my share of catting around, I don't think I ever tried to seduce a woman who was six months pregnant and just starting to recover from an abusive marriage."

"She *told* you about her marriage?" Keefe asked in disbelief. He'd damn near had to pry the truth out of Tessa.

"She didn't deny it when I guessed as much," Jace said. "And it wasn't all that hard to guess. And I'll tell you something else." He jabbed a finger in the direction Tessa had gone. "That girl is running from something more than a bunch of pushy reporters. I don't know what it is, but she's scared to death of something.''

Keefe didn't argue. The same thought had occurred to him. He didn't want to think that Tessa had lied to him, but he had the feeling that she hadn't told him the whole truth.

''Maybe,'' he admitted. ''But whatever she's running from, I'd appreciate it if you'd watch your step while she's here. Like I said, she's vulnerable right now. A kid like her could misinterpret things, get the wrong impression.''

There was a moment's silence. When Jace spoke, his tone was conversational. ''If I didn't know that you're just trying to look out for Tessa, I think I'd probably do my damnedest to feed you a few of your teeth right about now. As it is, I'll consider the source. But let me point out—again—that I'm not in the habit of seducing vulnerable young women.'' He held up one hand to stop Keefe from interrupting. ''And Tessa is hardly a kid. She's a widow, about to become a mother. Even without all that, twenty-three isn't exactly a babe in arms. She's a grown woman, and despite what's she's been through, she doesn't need you to play big brother. Neither do I.'' He brushed past Keefe and walked out of the barn with long, angry strides.

Keefe stood where he was for a moment. The big barn seemed to echo with silence. Using the side of his thumb, he pushed his hat back on his head and stared into the middle distance, contemplating his own capacity for stupidity. He knew Jace well enough to know he didn't need to be warned about Tessa's vulnerability. Jace Reno was about as likely to hurt her as he was to flap his arms and take off flying. It was just that, when he walked into the barn and saw Jace holding Tessa, he'd thought— What the hell *had* he thought?

He reached for his cigarettes. As he set a match to the tip of one, he glanced up and saw Lady watching him, her big eyes seeming to hold a reproach.

"I know I said I'd quit," he muttered defensively as he inhaled smoke. "I'm down to less than half a pack a day, okay?"

She snorted and shook her head in apparent disapproval before turning to go back to her interrupted lunch.

"I must be out of mind," Keefe said out loud. "First I insult my best friend, then I start making excuses to a horse."

He shook his head and watched the slow tendrils of smoke rise from the tip of his cigarette, drifting upward to disappear in a shaft of sunlight that spilled in through a dirty window.

Chapter 5

Keefe caught the phone on the second ring, stretching out one long arm to snag the receiver from the hook while continuing to turn the bacon sizzling in the skillet. On the other side of the stove, Jace was whisking milk into a bowl of pancake mix. Half a dozen eggs sat waiting on the counter, ready to break into the pan of bacon fat as soon as the bacon came out. Breakfast was the one meal Tessa didn't insist on cooking for them, and they made the most of it.

"Yeah?"

"You sound wide awake. I suppose you've been up for a couple of hours," a disgusted voice muttered in his ear.

Keefe grinned. His oldest brother, Sam, was not a morning person. "Barely an hour." He glanced at the clock, raising one brow in surprise. "What drags you out of bed so early? Or are you just getting off work?'' Sam was a police detective, and his hours could be erratic.

''I figured this was the only time of day I could be relatively sure of catching you in the house.''

''Is there a problem?'' Keefe caught Jace's questioning glance, the concern in his eyes. Their brief confrontation over Tessa the day before had blown over and been forgotten.

''No. Last I heard, everyone is okay,'' Sam said, correctly interpreting his brother's question. The Walkers were a tight-knit family. As far as they were concerned, if one member of the family had a problem, they all had a problem.

''So what's up?'' Keefe shook his head at Jace to indicate that there was no immediate emergency.

Jace nodded and reached out to take the fork. ''I got this.''

Keefe nodded and backed away from the stove.

''You got anything going on I should know about?'' Sam asked on the other end of the line.

''What do you mean?''

''Somebody's been making inquiries, asking about us.''

''*Us?* About the Walkers in general, or me in particular?'' Keefe immediately thought of the reporters Tessa had said were bothering her. He'd had his doubts about the truth of that. Maybe he'd done her an injustice.

''According to my sources, someone's been asking around about all of us. Some pretty sophisticated computer inquiries. This computer crap is all a mystery to me but apparently they really know their stuff. I already talked to Gage and Cole, but neither of them has a clue."

"I might know what it's about," Keefe said slowly. "Tessa Wyndham showed up a couple of weeks ago."

"Wyndham? As in Dana?" Sam's voice rose, the last of the morning sluggishness vanishing in surprise.

"Her sister."

"She showed up at the Flying Ace? Why?"

Keefe repeated Tessa's explanation as succinctly as possible, ending with "I guess she figured that, since Dana and I didn't exactly remain friends, this was the last place anyone would look for her."

"I sure as hell wouldn't expect to find any of your ex-in-laws seeking refuge with you."

"Tessa was different," Keefe said, answering the annoyance in Sam's tone, more than his comment. "She's a nice kid."

"Kid? How old is she?"

"Twenty-three."

"Not exactly a little girl," Sam commented, unknowingly echoing Jace's words.

"She's young enough to seem like a kid to me."

"Yeah, thirty-seven makes you practically old enough to be her grandfather."

"Well, I'm damn near old enough to be her father," Keefe snapped.

Sam's snort of laughter was echoed from behind him, and he turned on one heel to glare at Jace's back. "Don't forget who you're talking to," his brother said. "You weren't fathering any children at fourteen."

''I didn't say I was.'' Keefe couldn't figure out how he'd ended up having this discussion. ''All I said was that I was nearly old enough—''

''Yeah, I heard you the first time.'' Sam interrupted with the casual rudeness possible of an older brother. ''I'm older than you are, and I don't feel anywhere near old enough to be the father of a twenty-three-year-old.''

Neither did he, Keefe thought. But this wasn't just any twenty-three-year-old they were talking about. This was Tessa and, for some reason, it felt important to make sure that everyone understood that his relationship with her was strictly familial.

''Speaking of fatherhood, when are you and Nikki going to make me an uncle again?'' he asked, deciding a change of subject was in order. He knew his brother and sister-in-law had been trying to get pregnant for the past few months.

''Not in the next few months.'' It was said casually enough, but something in Sam's tone set off warning bells.

''Problem?''

The silence on the other end of the line spoke volumes. ''Not exactly,'' Sam said finally. ''Nikki's worried that something might be wrong. She's talking about going in for tests.''

''Seems a little soon for that, doesn't it?''

''That's what I said, but she's hell-bent on finding out why she isn't pregnant.''

Keefe could hear the worry in his brother's voice, and he sought to offer reassurance. ''Maybe, once she's had the tests and realizes there's nothing wrong, then she'll be able to relax.''

''Maybe, but from what I can gather, it can take years to pin down an infertility problem—*if* there is one. I don't want Nikki going through one test after another, each one more invasive than the last. Having kids isn't that important to me.''

''But maybe it is to her,'' Keefe said quietly.

''Yeah.'' Sam sighed. ''It is to her.''

They spoke for a moment longer, and Sam promised to let Keefe know if he found out anything more about whoever was making inquiries about the Walkers. Keefe hung up the phone and turned to find Jace scooping the last of the fried eggs out of the bacon fat.

''Everything okay?'' he asked as he set a plate on the table.

''Yeah.'' Keefe pulled out a chair and sat down. ''Sam wanted to let me know that someone's been making some computer inquiries about the family.''

''Tessa's reporters?'' Jace glanced across the table, his expression questioning.

''Could be. Seems odd that they'd be looking at the Walkers, though. Tracking me down might be a long shot, but it makes some sense. But Tessa never even met the rest of my family.'' He stabbed a pancake with his fork and dropped it on his plate.

''Who else has a reason to be looking you guys up?'' Jace slathered butter on his own pancakes.

''Nobody I know of.'' Keefe shrugged. ''We aren't that hard to find.''

''Gotta be somebody looking for Tessa, then.''

"Seems likely."

"You going to mention this to her?" Jace asked as he sprinkled a generous quantity of Tabasco sauce on his eggs.

"I don't think so. It may not have anything to do with her. Even if it is a reporter, she already knows they're looking for her. Why worry her? If they track her down, we'll deal with them."

"*If* it's a reporter," Jace commented. It was a reminder of the doubts they both had on that score.

"We'll deal with whoever it is," Keefe said flatly. Whoever—whatever—Tessa was hiding from, they were going to have to come through him to get to her.

The truth will make you free.

For the first time in Tessa's life, she felt as if she understood the meaning of those words. She'd spent four years thinking that nothing could be more terrible than for someone to find out the truth. That fear had been a part of the reason she never tried to escape her marriage to Bobby. Yet, now that it was out in the open, she felt as if a huge burden had been lifted from her. Perhaps it shouldn't have made as much difference as it did. It wasn't as if her marriage had suddenly become a topic of casual conversation, but there was a tremendous relief in just knowing that she didn't have to pretend anymore.

"Come on, now. You're not really afraid of this saddle. You're just acting skittish to show you've got a sensitive nature, aren't you?" The young horse rolled one eye at the saddle Jace was holding and demonstrated her sensitive nature yet again by shying away when he moved closer. "Come on, now. Show some courage. You don't want everyone to think you're a coward, do you?"

"I don't think she's worried about what we think," Tessa commented as Jace's voice drifted across the corral to where she and Keefe stood watching him try to coax the mare into letting him put a saddle on her back for the first time.

"I doubt it, but Jace claims that appealing to an animal's pride is the best way to get them to do what you want."

"Does it work?"

Keefe shrugged. "I don't know, but I do know Jace is about the best I've ever seen when it comes to talking a balky horse into letting him on its back. Only person I've ever seen that's as good or better is Kel Bryan, a friend of mine who runs a place in Wyoming. Kel works a little different, but they've both got a way with horses that's close to magic."

Tessa leaned her arms on the top rail of the fence as she watched Jace coax the skittish mare to accept the saddle. It was late in the afternoon, the sun was warm on her back, dinner was simmering on the stove, she had nothing she had to do, nowhere she had to be. For the first time in years, her life was hers to do with as she pleased—almost hers, she corrected herself, as her belly bumped against the fence. But today, not even that reminder could spoil her contented mood.

"Did Jace grow up on a ranch?" she asked Keefe.

"Not that I know of." He set one booted foot on

the bottom rail and leaned his elbows on the top. Tipping his hat back on his forehead, he reached for his cigarettes, then glanced at Tessa and slid them back in his pocket.

"I don't mind if you smoke," she said, catching the movement out the corner of her eye.

"I'm trying to quit, anyway. It's a lousy habit, and I've heard rumors it's bad for your health."

"No kidding? I've heard the same rumors." She looked at him, her eyes laughing while her mouth remained serious. "Do you think there's any truth in them?"

"Probably not, but I figure there's no sense in taking a chance."

His lazy grin stirred emotions that Tessa had thought long dead. The years melted away and, for a moment, she was a girl again and deep in the throes of her first—and only—infatuation. The rest of the family might think Dana had married beneath her, but as far as Tessa was concerned, Keefe was as nearly perfect as it was possible for a person to be—a great deal more nearly perfect than her spoiled older sister deserved.

"Do you remember that first summer after you and Dana got married?" she asked.

"What about it?" Keefe's gaze shifted back across the corral to where Jace was still talking, soft and low, to the young horse.

"Did you know that I had the most tremendous crush on you that summer?"

"What?" He jerked his attention back to her.

"You must have guessed," Tessa said, laughing a

little at his startled expression. "I practically lived in the stables that summer. Even my parents commented on it, and they rarely noticed my existence."

"I thought you were horse-crazy."

"I was. But I was even more crazy about you."

"You were just a kid," he protested. "I was twenty-eight."

"I was fourteen—just the right age for a mad infatuation. You were tall, dark and handsome and, best of all, you didn't care that I was skinny and plain and wore braces."

"You weren't plain," he protested.

"Pigtails, braces, freckles, skinned knees and a bra size that read in the negatives?" Tessa shook her head as she listed the physical failings that had made her early teenage years miserable. "I was a disaster. But you didn't seem to notice any of it. That might have been enough to throw me into a state of mild infatuation, even if you hadn't been so gorgeous."

"Gorgeous?" he repeated, sounding appalled. Much to Tessa's amusement, color crept up over his cheekbones.

"Gorgeous," she repeated firmly, taking a mischievous pleasure in his obvious embarrassment.

"I think you needed glasses more than you needed braces," he muttered. He reached up to tug his hat down so that the brim shadowed his face.

Tessa's laugh drew a reluctant smile from him. For a minute, she looked very much like the girl he'd met that summer. Despite what she thought, she'd been far from plain. She'd been too thin and solemn to be truly pretty but, even then, there'd been a sweet, almost fey charm about her. He remembered thinking that, when she was older, it would be a lucky man who captured her affection. Remembering that now, he felt a renewed anger that things had turned out the way they had. Tessa deserved so much more than what she'd gotten.

''Well, I think I've got her just where I want her.'' Jace's comment interrupted Keefe's thoughts as he approached across the corral.

''I must have missed something. I thought the point was to get the saddle *on* the horse, not for you to carry it around,'' Keefe said.

''It's all a matter of strategy,'' Jace said as he swung the saddle up onto the top rail of the fence. ''Now she knows she doesn't have to be afraid of the saddle.''

''Looks to me like she's doing a victory dance,'' Keefe said, nodding toward the mare, who was trotting along the back fence, tossing her head.

''Strategy,'' Jace repeated, ignoring Tessa's laugh. He slid between the fence rails and straightened, his eyes going over Keefe's shoulder. ''Are we expecting company?''

''Not that I know of.'' Keefe and Tessa both turned to look at the cloud of dust making its way toward the ranch. ''Jim Sinclair said he'd stop by sometime this week to take a look at that gelding of his, see how the training is going.''

''It would go better if that horse wasn't the dumbest animal I've ever seen,'' Jace said. ''I'm afraid to leave him out in the rain for fear he'll turn his head up to the sky and drown, like a damned turkey.''

''I think that's an old wives' tale,'' Keefe said as Tessa giggled. ''I don't think turkeys are really that stupid.''

''No? Well, that horse is.'' Jace frowned at the dust cloud. ''Come to think of it, Jim Sinclair ain't much brighter.''

''He doesn't have to be bright. All he has to do is pay us for training his horses.''

''True. Let's hope he doesn't get caught in a rainstorm before he can write us a check.''

Keefe's chuckle was drowned out by the crunching sound of tires on gravel as a car drew to a stop in front of the house. It was a new car, a white, four-door sedan of undistinguished make and model. Dust settled slowly on and around it after it came to a stop.

''Not Jim Sinclair,'' Jace commented.

''Doesn't look like it,'' Keefe said as the doors opened.

The couple who got out of the car were as out of place in the dirt ranch yard as a Waterford vase in a mud hut. Both were in their mid-to-late fifties. The man was tall and lean, with silvery gray hair that gleamed in the sunlight. He wore a conservatively tailored charcoal-colored suit and a pair of shoes that had probably cost more than most people's mortgage payments. The woman was nearly as tall. Her hair was a colorless shade that could have been either very light blonde or gray. She wore a tailored dress made of some nubbly fabric in a shade of red that made Keefe think of cranberries. A black-and-gray scarf was tied around her neck in an elegant bow and she wore black pumps.

The whole outfit—both of them—would have looked right at home in an office or maybe in a fancy restaurant, but plopped down in the middle of the Flying Ace, they looked more than a bit out of place.

''Got to be lost,'' Jace said, taking in their elegant clothing and general air of wealth.

''I figure.'' Keefe started toward the newcomers, but Tessa grabbed his forearm, her fingernails digging through the fabric of his shirt and biting into his skin. Startled, he glanced down. She was looking at the older couple, her face tight and still, her eyes full of fear. She looked as if her worst nightmare had just come to life.

Whatever she was running from, it had just caught up with her.

Chapter 6

"You certainly did manage to bury yourself in the back of beyond, didn't you, Tessa?" It was the man who spoke, his tone pleasant, his expression almost amused. "It's a long drive from here to just about anywhere. I didn't expect it to take us this long to find you."

Tessa didn't move as he approached, but the color drained from her cheeks, leaving her as pale as she'd been when she first arrived, and Keefe had the sense that she was shrinking in on herself, trying to make herself smaller, less noticeable, as if she could somehow vanish from sight. He felt a quick rush of anger directed toward the stranger who had so easily stripped her of the fragile layer of confidence that he'd seen building over the past few weeks.

He took a half step forward, forcing Tessa to release her hold on his arm as he moved in front of her, stepping between her and the newcomers. At the same time, Jace moved forward so that the two men stood nearly shoulder-to-shoulder.

The older man stopped and looked from one to the other, his pale eyes taking in the unmistakably protective posture, the cool warning in two gazes—one brown, one blue. His dark brows rose slightly, but that was the only outward sign that he recognized the message.

"It's nice to see that Tessa has such good friends," he said, his affable smile unwavering. "Which one of you is Keefe Walker?"

"I am," Keefe said, unsmiling.

"I'm pleased to meet you, Keefe. I'm Robert Mallory. Senator Mallory." He put a slight but unmistakable emphasis on the title.

Keefe hesitated an instant before taking the man's hand. *Senator* Mallory? This must be the father-in-law Tessa had told him about, the one she'd said was a powerful man, both politically and personally.

"And you must be Jace Reno," Senator Mallory said, extending his hand to Jace.

Keefe raised one brow. No doubt Mallory intended the casual use of Jace's name to impress, and it succeeded, at least to the extent that it demonstrated how much he knew. He thought of his conversation with Sam three days ago. His brother had said that someone was making inquiries about the entire Walker family. Keefe had no doubt that he was looking at the driving force behind those inquiries. Tessa's former father-in-law had the power to start a search like the one Sam had described. But that didn't explain why he'd wanted to find Tessa or why she should be so terrified of being found by him.

"This is my wife, Anne," Mallory said, completing the round of polite introductions.

"Mrs. Mallory." Good manners dictated acknowledgment of the woman, although, from the look of cool disdain on her patrician features, he doubted she appreciated his consideration.

"I do hope you intend to acknowledge us, Tessa," Robert Mallory said, his falsely pleasant tone laced with a condescension that set Keefe's teeth on edge. "We've come quite a long distance to see you. I hope you don't plan to hide behind Mr. Walker all the time we're here."

"Of course not." Tessa's voice was colorless.

Keefe glanced at her as she moved to stand beside him, and saw that her expression matched the voice. This was how she'd looked those first few days after she came to the ranch, as if she'd put up a wall somewhere inside herself and the real Tessa was crouched behind that wall, hiding—leaving nothing but a shell for the rest of the world to see. His hostility toward the man in front of him increased.

"You're looking well, Tessa. You've been taking care of yourself, I hope." Something in Mallory's tone made Keefe think that there was more to the inquiry than polite concern. Of course, she *was* carrying his grandchild, which gave him something of a vested interest in her well-being, but Keefe had a gut feeling that there was more to it than that.

"I'm fine, thank you," Tessa said in that same colorless little voice.

"I'm glad to hear it. Perhaps there's somewhere we could talk?" He phrased it as a request, but his tone made it a command.

"Do you want to talk to him, Tessa?" It was Jace who spoke, his blue eyes ice-cold. He stood with his legs slightly spread, his hands held loosely at his sides, a subtle threat in the stance. If Tessa didn't want to talk to her former in-laws, he was obviously willing to escort them from the property.

Tessa would have given a great deal to be able to take him up on the unspoken offer. The last thing she wanted to do was talk to Bobby's parents. She didn't want to talk to them or even to see them ever again. She'd run three thousand miles to avoid them, but deep inside, she'd always known that she couldn't run far enough or fast enough to get beyond Robert Mallory's reach.

"I'll...talk to them," she said quietly. *He can't hurt me,* she reminded herself. *He has no hold over me. He can't make me do anything.*

"We can talk up at the house," Keefe said.

"This is a private conversation, Mr. Walker," Senator Mallory said, his tone pleasant but firm. His mouth smiled, but his eyes were cool and watchful.

"Tessa?" Keefe spoke to her, but his gaze remained unwavering on the other man.

"You don't have anything to say that Keefe and Jace can't hear," she said.

"I'm sure you don't mean that." Anne Mallory spoke for the first time, her well-modulated voice revealing the influence of the expensive finishing schools she'd attended. "This is family business, Tessa. We don't need outsiders."

"Keefe and Jace aren't outsiders." Arguing with her mother-in-law took courage. In her four years of marriage, she'd learned the hard way that it was safer to acquiesce. But her fear of dealing with Bobby's parents was enough to overcome years of conditioning.

"Don't be ridiculous—"

"We're staying." Keefe's flat statement ended the discussion and brought a pinched tightness to Anne Mallory's mouth. Her husband was no happier with the arrangement than she, but years in politics had taught him to accept defeat graciously.

"In that case, perhaps we could move this indoors?"

Keefe wondered what the penalty was for punching a United States senator. Was there some law on the books that made that a worse crime than simply decking an ordinary citizen? Mallory's smile tempted him to find out.

No one spoke as they walked up to the house. Keefe and Tessa led the way, his hand resting on the small of her back. He glanced down at her, but could read nothing from her expression. Whatever she was thinking or feeling, she was keeping it hidden—something she'd probably learned to do during her marriage, he thought, and felt angry all over again at what she'd endured.

Five people crowded the living room. Or maybe it was taut emotions that made the room seem filled to overflowing. Anne Mallory sat down on the sofa, her feet, in their expensive black pumps, set side by side with military precision, her hands lightly clasped in her lap. Her husband took a position near the fireplace, well-shod feet slightly apart, suit jacket pushed back to allow him to slide his hands into the pockets of his slacks.

Tessa sank down in the big leather chair. She was grateful for its support, even more grateful that Keefe stood next to her, one hand resting on the back of her chair. Jace took a position a little behind his partner.

Like armies facing each other across a battlefield, she thought.

"I generally offer guests some refreshments," Anne Mallory said, looking at Tessa.

Tessa responded immediately to that familiar tone of quiet reproach. She'd heard it often during the past four years. Bobby had repeatedly told her that she was stupid. His mother never had to say the words out loud. She was able to convey her disappointment in her daughter-in-law with nothing more than her tone of voice.

"I'm sorry," Tessa said automatically. She started to rise, but Keefe set one hand on her shoulder, stopping the motion.

"This obviously isn't a social call. Let's not pretend otherwise," he said flatly.

Anne's mouth tightened, but Robert's smile remained unwavering. Keefe was starting to hate that smile.

"I admire a man who knows how to cut to the chase, Mr. Walker. It's a rare quality in my line of work."

''So, why are you here?'' Jace asked.

''You could say we've come to finish a conversation we'd begun with Tessa shortly before she left home so precipitately.''

''The conversation was finished before I left,'' Tessa said. Inside, she was trembling and scared, but her voice was steady. She was proud of that. It was proof that she'd changed in the weeks since she packed her bags and ran away in the middle of the night.

''I don't believe we had finished it.''

His avuncular tone made Tessa's stomach knot. How many times had she heard him use that same tone with Bobby? How many times had that soft, concerned voice delivered words sharp enough to draw blood and then left her to bear the brunt of her husband's rage at his inability to stand up to his own father?

That's all over now. She drew a shallow breath and forced down the familiar wave of fear. She didn't have to be afraid anymore.

''I gave you my answer.''

''But not your *final* answer, I hope.''

''Does somebody want to fill us in on what the question was?'' Jace asked.

Tessa met her father-in-law's eyes. Beneath the surface expression of false concern she could see contempt. He didn't think she'd answer Jace's question. He thought she was too frightened of him. A few weeks ago, he would have been right. She'd been afraid of her husband, but she'd always known that the real power in the family lay in her father-in-law's grasp. Bobby had known it, too, and it was that knowledge, more than anything else, that had made him what he was, that had fueled his rage.

But Bobby was dead, and she was no longer alone. She had friends, people who cared about her. The knowledge helped ease the knot in her stomach. Tessa lifted her chin and met Robert Mallory's eyes directly.

"They want the baby," she said, in answer to Jace's question. "They want to take it and raise it as their own." She had the satisfaction of seeing a flicker of surprise in her father-in-law's eyes.

"Your baby?" Jace asked.

"Our grandchild," Anne Mallory said, before Tessa could respond. "All that's left to us of our son."

"Tessa's child," Keefe pointed out. "I think a mother's claim has priority."

"Not if she doesn't want it," Anne's tone made the words an accusation. She looked at Tessa with something approaching hatred. "And she doesn't want it. She hates this baby as much as she hated my son."

"I don't hate this baby," Tessa said, the words coming with difficulty. Her feelings toward the life she carried were too complex to be so easily categorized.

"You hated my son," Anne said, her elegant features made ugly by hatred.

"If she hated your son, she had reason." Keefe set his hand on Tessa's shoulder, and she drew strength from that light touch. "Men who abuse their wives rarely inspire much affection."

There was an instant of dead silence. Anne sucked

in an audible breath, her expression shocked. Her husband's features tightened and, for just a moment, Tessa saw the real man, rather than the political façade he took such care to show the world. The glimpse sent a chill down her spine. It was gone immediately. His frown was sorrowful, rather than angry.

"I'm disappointed in you, Tessa," he said, his tone heavy with regret. "I never thought you'd tell that ridiculous story outside the family."

"You knew?" Keefe sounded disbelieving. His hand tightened on Tessa's shoulder. "You knew what was going on and you didn't do anything to stop him?"

Robert shook his head. "I don't know what Tessa has told you, Mr Walker, but—"

"Not nearly as much as she could have," Keefe told him, interrupting ruthlessly. "I know enough to know that your son was a miserable bastard who made himself feel like a man by beating his wife. And if you knew what he was doing and didn't do anything to stop it, you're no better than he was."

"How dare you—"

"Anne!" Her husband's sharp tone cut through Anne Mallory's furious protest. She fell instantly silent, but her hands were clenched in her lap, and her face was flushed with anger.

Robert looked at Keefe. "A small piece of advice, Mr. Walker—don't make judgments until you know all the facts. I appreciate your loyalty to Tessa, but you might want to consider the fact that you haven't seen her in quite some time. Not since your divorce from her sister, I believe. People change in that time."

"If you're suggesting that Tessa is lying about what your son did to her, you can save your breath." Keefe couldn't ever remember feeling such a soul-deep rage.

"I don't think it's fair to say that she's lying," Robert said carefully. "I think Tessa actually believes what she's saying. Her doctor says we shouldn't blame her for these little 'stories' she tells."

"What doctor?" Keefe demanded.

"Why, her psychiatrist, of course." Robert looked surprised. "Didn't she tell you about Dr. Mendham? She's been seeing him for the last three years."

"No!" Tessa gasped out the denial. She twisted around in her chair, looking up at Keefe with panic in her eyes. "It's not true, Keefe. I haven't been seeing him. I swear it!"

"It's all right." He sank down on the arm of the chair. Putting his arm around Tessa's shoulder, he drew her against his side. She was trembling like a leaf in a high wind. He looked across the room at the senator and felt a moment of real regret that murder was not a viable option.

"There's no reason to lie about it, Tessa," Mallory said. "There's no shame in being treated for an illness."

"I'm not ill," she whispered. She pressed her forehead against Keefe's side, the fingers of one hand curling into the faded blue chambray of his shirt.

"Dr. Mendham runs a very fine clinic near our home," Mallory said, ignoring Tessa and addressing his words to Keefe. "Not long after Bobby and Tessa were married, we realized that she had a…problem with the truth. Dr. Mendham has been treating her ever since.''

''Are you saying she's a pathological liar?'' Jace asked incredulously.

''I'm not sure of the exact clinical term for Tessa's illness.'' Mallory shook his head, his expression one of deep regret. ''She'd made a great deal of progress, but then, after Bobby's death, she seemed to get worse. No doubt the stress was just too much for her rather fragile mental state.''

''He's lying,'' Tessa whispered, pressing closer to Keefe. ''I'm not crazy.''

''No one has ever used the word crazy, Tessa. We've told you again and again that no one blames you for your illness. We just want to see you get better. That's why Dr. Mendham has been treating you and keeping such careful records of your visits to him,'' he added in a gentle tone that sent chills down Keefe's spine.

He couldn't have made the threat any more clear if he'd laid it out in plain English. Whoever this Dr. Mendham was, he was willing to produce records that said he'd been treating Tessa for the past three years. Keefe tightened his arm around her, trying to offer wordless reassurance.

''So, your argument is that Tessa isn't mentally stable enough to have care of a baby, and that's how you plan to force her to give the child to you.''

''We don't want to have to *force* her to do anything,'' Mallory said. ''We were hoping that Tessa would see that this is the best thing for all concerned, particularly for the baby.''

''No.'' Tessa straightened in the chair, turning to face her father-in-law. ''No. I won't give this baby to you.''

''You can't possibly think that you could win a court battle,'' Anne said, speaking for the first time in several minutes. ''Robert is a *senator.*''

''Senator or no, I think the courts lean pretty heavily toward the mother in a case like this,'' Jace said.

''Not when she's mentally unstable. What's more natural than for us to want to raise our grandchild? After losing our only son in a tragic accident, we—''

Jace's inelegant snort cut her off in midsentence. ''Tragic accident? That's not the usual term for a drug overdose. Cocaine, wasn't it?'' He caught Keefe's surprised look and shrugged. ''I read the papers.''

''That's a terrible lie. Bobby didn't use drugs.'' Anne's voice was shrill, and her eyes were wild. Keefe realized that, whatever else was false—and almost everything about the Mallorys was false—her grief was real. He supposed that a better man might feel more compassion for her pain, but all he could think of was that she'd known what was happening to Tessa and done nothing to stop it.

''The papers seem to think otherwise,'' Jace said. He shrugged again. ''Of course, a lot of it is probably speculation, but I'd guess the rumors haven't done much to raise your stock in the party's eyes, Senator. A presidential candidate with a drug addict for a son isn't exactly a dream come true. A grieving father shouldering the responsibility for his grandchild—that looks considerably better, doesn't it?''

Not a trace of emotion showed in Mallory's eyes. ''The reasons really don't matter, Mr. Reno. What matters is that my wife and I can provide a much better environment in which to raise a child. If necessary, I can provide proof that Tessa is unstable. I would prefer not to do so, of course, but we *will* get custody of our grandchild.''

The cold threat in his tone seemed to lower the temperature of the room by several degrees. Keefe's arm was still around Tessa's shoulders, and he felt a sharp tremor move through her. That little movement solidified his determination to do whatever he had to do to protect her and the baby she carried.

''There's only one problem with this scenario,'' he said, his tone easy.

''What's that, Mr. Walker?'' Mallory's tone held an impatient edge.

Keefe tightened his grip on Tessa's shoulder. She was stiff as a board, and he knew she was holding herself together with sheer willpower. The knowledge put an edge in his voice. ''This baby you're so hell-bent on taking away from its mother?''

''Our grandchild,'' Ann Mallory reminded him, as if that were all the excuse they needed to ride roughshod over Tessa's rights.

''No, it's not,'' Keefe said.

''Not what?'' Mallory asked.

''Not your grandchild.'' Keefe's fingers tightened on Tessa's shoulder and then relaxed. ''The child Tessa is carrying is mine.''

* * *

Tessa had never before understood what people meant when they said they'd had an out-of-body experience, but the phrase suddenly made perfect sense to her. For a moment, she seemed to see the whole scene from outside herself, as if she were looking at a photograph.

She could see herself, looking small in the big chair. She saw every scuff mark and worn spot on the aged brown leather with perfect clarity. Keefe sat next to her, one foot braced on the floor, his arm around her shoulder. His tanned, work-roughened hand contrasted sharply with the pale blue sand-washed silk of her loose shirt. In his faded jeans, boots and work shirt, he looked as if he'd stepped right out of a western movie. Jace stood on Keefe's left, similarly dressed, his hands held loosely at his sides, like a gunfighter waiting for the right moment to draw his weapon.

On the other side of the room from the three of them were the Mallorys—expensively dressed, perfectly coiffed, their expressions holding equal measures of disbelief and outrage.

That was when Tessa realized that this must all be a dream. Because only in a dream would it be possible to see her former in-laws expressing such honest emotion. In real life, neither of them ever allowed anything to ruffle the surface calm they wore like armor. But anything was possible in a dream, including seeing the Mallorys gape like trouts. Even hearing Keefe claim her baby as his own made sense, if this was a dream.

"That's impossible," Robert Mallory snapped.

"What makes you think so?" Keefe asked.

"We *know* the baby is our son's."

"How do you know?"

"Tessa would never have dared to be unfaithful to Bobby," Anne Mallory said calmly, her usual control back in place.

"She wouldn't have *dared?*" Keefe repeated the phrase in a tone of soft menace. "Because she was afraid of him? Because he was a wife-beating son of a bitch, which you knew and refused to do anything about? Is that why Tessa wouldn't have dared?"

"There was no abuse. We've already made that clear." Mallory shot a warning glance at his wife, who lowered her eyes. "Tessa wouldn't have been unfaithful to our son because she knew it would be wrong. Isn't that right, Tessa?"

Tessa felt herself pinned by his pale gaze. His expression reminded her of the way Bobby would look at her just before he told her how she'd failed yet again, before he— She slammed a door on the memory. That was the past. This was the present, and it was neither dream nor nightmare. But she wasn't alone this time, facing a husband who would express his displeasure with his fists.

For the first time in her life, she had someone to stand with her, friends who believed in her. Keefe's lie would buy her time—time to decide how to combat her in-laws, time to find somewhere else to hide, if she had to. All she had to do was back him up.

"He's telling you the truth. It's not Bobby's baby," she said, astonished by the steadiness of her voice.

"You don't expect us to believe this ridiculous

story?'' Mallory asked, his genial facade slipping fractionally.

''I don't see that you have much choice,'' Keefe said calmly.

''Of course we have a choice. A paternity test would prove, beyond the shadow of a doubt, that this is my son's child.''

''I don't need a paternity test. I know Keefe is the father,'' Tessa said.

''I'm sure I could arrange for a court order requiring you to submit the child for a paternity test,'' Mallory said.

''Now, that would make a nice headline,'' Jace commented, his tone casual. '''Senator forces son's widow to submit to paternity test.' It certainly does have a ring to it, doesn't it? Something like that would probably be just the thing to reignite interest in your son's death.''

''It wouldn't reflect particularly well on Tessa,'' Mallory said tightly.

''But Tessa isn't hoping to be the next president of these United States,'' Jace pointed out almost gently.

Keefe shot his friend an appreciative look. He'd never realized what a good liar Jace was, though, considering what he knew of Jace, maybe he should have guessed.

''I don't have much experience with the press myself,'' Keefe drawled. ''But I'd be willing to bet that they could have a field day with a story like this.''

Mallory's expression told him that the senator was well aware of the damage a scandal like the one they were describing could do to his career. At the very least, it would end his chances of a presidential bid. Rage and frustration warred in his eyes, all traces of false affability disappearing in a rush of genuine emotion. He was trapped and beaten, at least for the moment, and he knew it.

"This isn't finished," he said tightly.

"I disagree." Keefe rose from his seat on the arm of Tessa's chair. "I don't think there's anything left to say, except perhaps to make sure you understand that Tessa isn't alone anymore. She has friends now—family. If you cause her a problem, you'll have us to deal with."

Mallory sneered. "Very noble."

"Just a statement of fact," Keefe said calmly. "I think it's time you left. And perhaps I should warn you that, if you set foot on my property again, I'll call the law and have you hauled off for trespassing."

"Now wouldn't that make a hell of a headline?" Jace commented wickedly.

Mallory ignored him. He glanced at Tessa, and then his gaze locked on Keefe. "This isn't over."

Keefe didn't argue. Tessa had to be nearing the end of her rope, and there was no sense in prolonging the scene. "Jace, do you mind seeing Senator and Mrs. Mallory off the property?"

"My pleasure." Jace stepped back to leave a clear path to the door. "After you."

Anne Mallory rose, her spine stiff as a poker, her expression icy enough to freeze a lava flow. She looked at Tessa with something approaching hatred in her eyes. "You didn't deserve my son," she said in a tone of contempt.

"I agree with you on that one," Keefe said, feeling Tessa flinch away from the venom in the older woman's voice. "She certainly deserved a great deal better than a man who was so weak he had to pound on her just to make himself feel strong."

Anne whitened and, for a moment, he almost regretted his harsh words. Whatever else he was, Bobby Mallory had been her son, and he was willing to believe that his death had genuinely grieved her. But then he remembered that this woman had known what was happening to Tessa and had done nothing to stop it, and his sympathy ebbed.

"Come, Anne." Mallory put a hand beneath his wife's elbow and urged her toward the door. "There's no point in saying anything more."

Jace's eyes met Keefe's as the couple walked past him. "I'll see them to the highway," he promised. He glanced at Tessa, who seemed to be huddled in the big chair. He looked as if he might say something to her, then changed his mind. Without another word, he turned and followed the Mallorys out of the house.

Tessa listened to the silence that followed the closing of the door. She should say something. Something that would show that she was calm and in control. But it was hard to sound in control when what she really wanted to do was collapse in a quivering, sobbing heap.

"Thank you," she said, her voice barely above a whisper.

"My pleasure. Getting rid of obnoxious senators is something of a specialty of mine."

His light tone brought Tessa's head up. He was smiling at her, and she felt the nervous knot in her stomach start to unwind. "You're very good at it," she said, smiling a little shakily.

"Thanks." Keefe's smile faded, and he sank down on the battered ottoman that sat in front of her chair. The position put their eyes on the same level. "You don't have to be afraid of them, Tessa. Even if it came to a court case, no judge would award custody to them. You don't have to be afraid of losing your baby."

Tessa looked away, focusing her gaze on the amateurish painting of a horse that hung on the wall next to the fireplace. The painting had come with the house, along with most of the furniture, Keefe had told her.

"The painting is crooked," she said.

Keefe followed her gaze. "So it is."

"Bobby knocked me across the room once for not straightening a picture properly." She said it almost casually. Keefe felt the hair on the back of his neck rise at the image her words evoked. The idea of someone hitting her because of a crooked picture—or for any other reason—made his stomach knot with anger. He looked back at her, and Tessa's eyes slowly shifted to his face. "I wasn't sorry when he died."

"No one could expect you to be sorry," he said, wondering where this conversation was headed.

"When the police came to tell me he was dead, I didn't feel anything at first. I didn't even feel anything when I had to identify his body. Shock, I guess." She smoothed her fingers over the knee of her stretch pants, her eyes on the aimless movement. "It wasn't until the next day that I really started to feel something, and then it was anger."

"Anger's a natural thing to feel when someone dies," Keefe said cautiously. He felt as if he were tiptoeing through an emotional mine field.

"I wasn't angry because he'd died. I was angry that he hadn't died sooner. I kept thinking that, if he'd died sooner, I'd have been truly free. But as it was, I was still trapped."

"Because of the baby," Keefe guessed.

"Because of the baby." She lifted her eyes to his face, and he felt his heart twist at the stark pain he saw there. "I don't want the baby," she admitted, rushing the words as if that were the only way she could get them out. "It was Bobby who wanted it. He thought it would make his father happy. If I...if there'd been a way to do it without Bobby finding out, I would have...I wouldn't have had this baby."

Keefe caught her hands in his, stilling their restless movements. He held her eyes with his. "Tessa, did he...did he rape you?"

"Oh, no!" Her denial was quick, but she continued before he had a chance to feel relieved. "I didn't want... But then, I never did, not after the first few times. I wasn't very good at...well, at 'it.'" She looked away, color running up under her pale skin. "Bobby said it was like having sex with a plastic blow-up doll—that I didn't *do* anything. But I could never figure out what I was supposed to do." Her shoulders lifted in a helpless little shrug. "After a while, I just stopped trying. He didn't... We didn't sleep together very much after the first few months. At first, I wondered if he...had other women, but I don't think he did. I don't think sex was particularly important to him. Once in a while, he'd come to my room. I didn't... But it was easier to just let him. The last time he... That's when I got pregnant.'' The choppy little sentences trailed off. She kept her gaze focused on their linked hands. ''Then he died, but it was too late.''

Keefe looked at her downbent head and wished, for the hundredth time, that he'd had the chance to meet Tessa's husband and beat him to a bloody pulp. As near as he could tell, the only decent thing the bastard had ever done was kill himself with drugs, and he hadn't even done that soon enough.

''What do you plan to do when the baby's born?'' he asked her.

She shook her head, her fingers tense in his. ''I don't know. I thought I might see about a private adoption. But I don't know. What if, after it's born, I can't give it up? I've made so many mistakes. I don't want to make another one.''

''If you don't want the baby, why not give it to the Mallorys?'' he asked.

''I couldn't do that.'' Tessa raised her head and looked at him as if surprised that he could ask such a question. ''They made Bobby what he was. I know it sounds melodramatic, but I think they're truly evil people. I would never let them get their hands on a child. This baby is the one true innocent in this whole mess.''

Keefe could have pointed out that she was as innocent of wrongdoing as the child she carried, but he doubted she'd hear him.

Keefe was on his way to bed when he saw light gleaming along the bottom edge of Tessa's door. He stopped and stared at that thin streak of gold. He'd been thinking ever since the scene with the Mallorys this afternoon. His common sense said that what he'd been thinking was crazy, but he couldn't shake the idea that had come to him.

Now, looking at the light under Tessa's door, he hesitated. He hadn't planned on talking to her tonight, but there was really no reason to put it off until morning. Tessa had barely spoken all through dinner, and the haunted look had been back in her eyes. Maybe hearing what he had in mind would ease her worry. Of course, maybe it would convince her that he was crazy, he thought ruefully. But, crazy or not, he was going to talk to her about it. He lifted his hand and knocked.

"Come in."

He pushed open the door. A table lamp cast a pale circle of light across the bed and created deep shadows around the edges of the room. Tessa was standing beside the window, staring out into the moonlit darkness. She was wearing a cheap ankle-length blue terry-cloth robe, belted awkwardly above the bulge of her stomach. Beneath it, he could glimpse a plain white cotton nightgown. Her hair was pulled back from her face and held by a gold-toned clip at the base of her neck. She looked young and vulnerable.

"Have you ever noticed the way the snow on the mountaintops catches the moonlight?" she asked without turning. "It looks like someone spilled frosting on them."

"A little bit." He glanced out the window but he had things on his mind besides the natural beauty of the mountain. "I've been thinking, Tessa, and I've got an idea that might solve your problems with the Mallorys and with what to do about the baby."

"I think that would take a miracle," she said softly.

The despair in her voice solidified his determination. It might not be a miracle, but he knew what he had in mind would work. All he had to do was convince her of that. Thrusting his hands in the pockets of his jeans, Keefe sought the best words to tell her what he was thinking. In the end, the best words—the only words—were the simplest.

"I think we should get married."

Chapter 7

"What?" Tessa turned from the window and stared at him, her eyes wide with shock.

"I think we should get married," he repeated.

The words didn't seem any more real the second time he said them than they had the first.

"Why?"

"When you think about it, it's the obvious solution to your problems."

"Obvious?"

"It makes perfect sense."

"It does?" She lifted one hand to her head, wondering if pregnancy caused auditory hallucinations.

"Here." Keefe crossed the room with quick strides and took her by the arm. "Sit down and I'll explain it to you."

"That would be nice," Tessa said, allowing him to lead her over to the bed. She sank down on its edge and waited for him to explain why getting married was so obvious and made such perfect sense.

Seeing her expectant gaze on him, Keefe cleared his throat and took a moment to organize his thoughts.

''If we get married, it will get your former in-laws off your back. They didn't believe for a minute that I'm the father of your baby, which means they're not just going to give up and leave you alone. You could leave, but if they found you here, they could probably find you anywhere you went. Anyway, you can't spend the next couple of months on the run.''

Tessa couldn't argue with that. Her thoughts had been running along just those lines for the past few hours.

''If we get married, it makes my claim to the baby that much stronger. They might still be able to force a paternity test, but my bet is that they won't risk the negative publicity, and I think we convinced them that we would be sure the whole thing was public knowledge. The fact that you're married and can provide a traditional home for the baby is bound to weaken their case, even these days, when single parenting is so common.''

He'd been pacing the room as he spoke, but he turned to look at her now. ''Are you with me so far?''

''I'm with you, but... Oh, Keefe—'' Tessa's voice cracked a little on his name ''—I can't tell you how much it means to me that you'd be willing to do something like this for me, but I can't possibly let you.''

''Why not?''

''Because I'm not a total user.'' Her laughter held

little humor. ''I know it's hard to believe, considering the way I descended on you, but I do have some pride.''

''What does pride have to do with it? You need help. I can provide it.''

''It's not that simple. You'd be putting yourself at risk. I don't think you understand how powerful Senator Mallory is. You don't want him for an enemy.''

Keefe cocked one brow, his mouth twisting in a half smile. ''It's a little late to be worried about that, isn't it? I don't think he was feeling particularly warm and fuzzy toward me when he left here.''

''No, he wasn't.'' Tessa looked distressed. ''I hate it that I've dragged you into the middle of this. He can be a very dangerous man.''

''If you ask me, his wife is more dangerous than he is. Good old Robert is always going to do what's best for his career. I'm not so sure about her. I'm not too sure she has both oars in the water.''

''Anne was devastated by Bobby's death. At the funeral, I had the feeling that she wanted to throw herself into the grave with him.'' A chill slid down her spine at the memory of her mother-in-law's grief. She forced the memory aside and focused on the present. ''The Mallorys may not be crazy about you at the moment, but it's nothing compared to how they'll feel if you get in their way again. They're absolutely determined to get custody of this baby.''

''The best way to see that that doesn't happen is for us to get married,'' Keefe said firmly.

''It's a crazy idea,'' Tessa said. ''Marriages of convenience only happen in books.''

"You might be surprised," Keefe said, smiling a little as he thought of his older brother's marriage. Sam and Nikki had barely been able to stand the sight of each other when they said "I do." They'd married for practical reasons and ended up falling in love. Thinking of them was what had given him this idea in the first place. Not the falling-in-love part of it, of course. *That* certainly wasn't going to happen if he and Tessa got married.

"I wouldn't be surprised. I'd be astonished," Tessa said, interrupting his thoughts. "Marriage isn't something you jump into casually."

"This isn't casual." He ran his fingers through his dark hair, frowning a little as he tried to think of a way to make her see how practical the idea was. "If you strip it of the usual emotional complications, marriage is basically a contract, that's all. Marriage to me will provide you with an extra level of protection. The Walkers may not wield a lot of political leverage, but we're pretty hard to push around."

Tessa felt herself weakening. She had to be even more tired than she'd realized, because what he was suggesting was starting to make sense. Surely, if she was married to Keefe and he was willing to claim this baby as his, Bobby's parents would think twice about forcing her into a custody battle.

"I can't use you like that," she said, and wished she sounded more definite in her refusal. "And don't tell me you'd do this for any friend. Marriage goes way beyond offering hospitality. If marriage is a contract, then there has to be benefits to both people. This 'contract' is completely one-sided. Thank you for your incredibly generous offer, but I just can't accept."

Keefe looked at her, and Tessa thought she read an uncharacteristic indecision in his expression, but it was gone so quickly she thought she might have imagined it.

"Would it make you feel better if you thought I was getting something out of it?"

"What on earth could you possibly get out of marrying me?" Tessa asked blankly.

"You said you've been considering arranging a private adoption after the child is born," he said slowly.

"Y-yes." Tessa's agreement was tentative. She knew adoption was the most practical option, but she wasn't entirely sure she'd be able to go through with it. Her feelings for the child she carried were confused and ambivalent. That was why she hadn't contacted an adoption attorney yet.

"What if you didn't have to arrange an adoption? What if you could just leave the child with your husband?"

"My..." Tessa's voice trailed off, and she stared at him blankly for a moment. "You? You want to adopt my baby?"

"If we were married and I was listed on the birth certificate as the child's father, it wouldn't take an adoption. I could simply have custody of the child."

"But why would you—? You don't want a child!"

"Actually, I think I do." Keefe laughed a little, sounding as if he found the idea almost as astonishing as she did. "I've been thinking about it ever since you told me you wanted to give up the baby. And the more I thought about it, the more right it seemed.''

He was pacing again, his long strides eating up the distance between door and window and then back again. Energy vibrated from him, making Tessa feel almost dizzy. Or maybe it was his suggestion that had set her head spinning.

''It's not the kind of thing you can decide on the spur of the moment,'' she said.

''It's not spur-of-the-moment. I've always wanted children, but after Dana and I got divorced, I kind of gave up on the idea. I thought about adoption a couple of times, but it's still pretty tough for a single man to adopt. And I've been busy with the ranch and all. I'd pretty much decided that fatherhood wasn't in the cards for me.''

''You might remarry,'' Tessa pointed out.

''Anything's possible,'' he said, his tone making it clear that, on the possibility scale, he ranked remarriage somewhere between Sasquatches and little green men from Mars.

''Lots of people get divorced and then remarry. There's no reason you won't do the same.'' It distressed her to think of him giving up on marriage. She didn't like to think of him being alone.

''I'm not saying I'll never marry again.''

Keefe stopped by the window and looked out at the moonlit landscape. Tessa's concern was an echo of what he'd heard in Molly Thorpe's voice at Cole's wedding reception and the worry he sometimes saw in his mother's eyes. He knew they all thought that divorce had made him bitter about marriage, but they were wrong. He thought marriage was a damned fine arrangement when it worked. If he'd ever doubted that, he had only to look at his three brothers, see the difference marriage had made in their lives. He wasn't against marriage in general, and he wasn't bitter about his own marriage. But only a fool failed to learn from his mistakes. And his marriage to Dana Wyndham had been a mistake of epic proportions, one he wasn't anxious to repeat.

"I could get married again," he said, turning to look at Tessa. "Anything's possible." His mouth curved in a half smile. "But some things are highly unlikely."

Tessa looked down to hide the distress she felt. Dana must have hurt him badly. She wondered if he still loved her beautiful older sister.

"Even if it was likely that I'd marry again, that doesn't mean I couldn't adopt this baby," Keefe said, interrupting her thoughts. "I'd be a good father, Tessa."

"I know you would." Tessa pressed two fingers over the ache starting to build behind one temple. It was too much to absorb all at once. She was still reeling from the confrontation with her in-laws, and he was throwing a brand-new twist into the situation. "I just don't know, Keefe. It's… I just don't know," she said helplessly.

"You don't have to make a decision right now," he said. "Think about it as long as you want, but I know it could work."

He sounded so sure. Tessa realized that she wanted to believe him. It would be so easy to agree, so easy to let Keefe take care of everything. But she couldn't just take the easy way out. She had to try and decide what would be best for all of them—herself, Keefe, and the unborn child.

She set one hand against the heavy bulge of her stomach. She rarely let herself think of the child she carried in anything more than the most abstract of terms, yet, in an odd way, all her recent actions had been dictated by the desire to do what was best for the baby—the one complete innocent in the disaster her life had become.

"I don't know," she murmured, speaking more to herself than to him.

"Marrying me wouldn't obligate you to give up your baby," he said quietly, his eyes understanding. "You could take your time, be sure that was what you wanted."

"That's not fair to you," she protested.

"Let me worry about what's fair to me." He slid his hands into his pockets and gave her a smile that made her heart crack a little.

"Oh, Keefe—" Her voice broke on his name, and she felt tears sting the back of her eyes. She lifted her hands and let them fall helplessly. "I don't understand."

"What don't you understand?" He pulled his hands out of his pockets and closed the small distance between them, sinking down on his heels in front of her, putting their eyes nearly on a level.

"Why you're so nice to me." She looked at him with honest confusion, her eyes bright with tears she refused to shed. "No one has ever...cared enough to...to do things for me, and you...just... You can't just marry me to keep me safe, Keefe. You can't.''

''Seems like a pretty good reason to me,'' he said. He caught her restless hands in his. ''Stop worrying about taking advantage of me, Tessa. And stop making me sound like Mother Teresa's nearest competition. This isn't such a big deal.''

''Marriage is a pretty big deal,'' she protested.

''It doesn't have to be. Tessa, I want to do this. I want to help you, take care of you and the baby.'' His tone was coaxing, and she felt herself weakening.

After Bobby died, she'd hadn't been able to imagine herself marrying again, but her imagination had stopped short of the kind of arrangement Keefe was suggesting. It was insane, of course. There was no reason to believe that marrying Keefe would protect her from her former in-laws. Even if it would, she had no right to drag him farther into her problems.

She dragged her eyes from his face and looked down at their joined hands. His palm was hard, callused by work, unmistakably masculine. In contrast, her fingers looked delicate, fragile. Helpless.

Tessa caught back a sigh. She'd been so determined to stand on her own, to never let herself depend on anyone again, to be strong. But maybe there was strength in knowing her own limitations. She couldn't fight the Mallorys by herself. She didn't have the strength. She needed Keefe, needed what he was offering. If she'd had only herself to worry about, it would have been different. But it wasn't her they wanted. It was the baby. She wasn't as sure as Keefe was that marrying him would stop Bobby's parents, but if there was a chance it would work, she had to take it. For the baby's sake.

"All right." Her agreement came so quietly that it took Keefe a moment to realize what she'd said.

"All right?" he repeated. "You'll marry me?"

"If you're sure that's what you want." Her eyes were full of doubt. "Are you sure?"

"I'm sure." Keefe grinned at her, his fingers tightening over hers. "You won't regret it," he said.

Tessa managed a weak smile. She wasn't worried about whether or not *she'd* regret it.

"Walker." Sam's voice was slurred with sleep.

"Did I wake you?"

"Keefe?" Sam was instantly alert. "What's wrong?"

"Nothing. I need to ask a favor." Keefe was well aware that this call could have waited until morning—*should* have waited until morning—but he hadn't been able to resist the urge to call Sam. Though he was close to all his brothers, he was closest to Sam.

Dead silence echoed from the other end of the line. "You called me at—" there was a pause while Sam looked at the clock "—midnight to ask a favor?"

"I need you to arrange a wedding."

"A wedding?" Sam sounded as if he were still half-asleep. "Whose wedding?"

Keefe laughed. He was feeling strangely euphoric for a man who was about to make drastic changes in his life. "*My* wedding. I'm getting married."

"You're doing what?" Sam's voice rose to something just under a bellow, all traces of sleepiness gone.

Keefe heard his sister-in-law's voice in the background, and then Sam's response. "Go back to sleep. It's Keefe and he's drunk."

Keefe laughed again. He hadn't expected to find anything amusing about his decision to marry Tessa, but Sam's reaction struck him as funny. "I'm sober as a judge," he assured his older brother.

"I've known some pretty boozy judges," Sam said darkly. A police officer, he held no illusions about the sobriety of those who ran the legal system. "If you're not drunk, then you must be suffering from a head injury. Did you get thrown on your head?"

"Nope. I'm sober and sane."

"Who are you planning on marrying?"

"Tessa."

There was a moment of silence while Sam considered the name. "Tessa? Tessa who's staying with you? Tessa Wyndham? Dana's kid sister?"

"She's not exactly a kid," Keefe said, his good humor fading a little. Reminded of the fourteen-year gap in their ages, he felt uncomfortably like a cradle robber. But he'd only have to worry about that if this was going to be a real marriage. As things stood, the age difference didn't really matter. Still, the reminder made him feel vaguely defensive. "She's twenty-three."

"What does her age have to do with anything?"

"Nothing."

"Then why are we discussing it?" Sam demanded irritably.

"You brought it up."

"I did not." Sam's voice rose on the denial, and

Keefe heard Nikki say something, her tone concerned. "He's not drunk. He's stark, raving mad," Sam told his wife without bothering to cover the phone.

Keefe grinned. Maybe he was a little crazy. He knew Tessa thought so. But, crazy or not, he wanted this marriage. His smile faded as he considered just how much he wanted it, but he shoved the thought aside. His gut told him this was the right thing to do. He didn't want to look any deeper than that.

Tessa's first wedding had taken six months to plan. There had been three hundred guests in the church and nearly twice that many at the reception. Her gown had been made of ivory silk satin, trimmed with hundreds of seed pearls, each hand stitched in place. Cobweb-fine lace had trimmed the sleeves and neckline. More pearls had been scattered across the floor-length veil, and the gown's train had been longer than she was tall. Selected members of the press had been allowed to attend, and pictures of the bride and groom had been on the society pages of every major newspaper in the country.

Her second wedding bore little resemblance to the first. The arrangements were made in barely a week. The only guests were the groom's family and the bride's great-aunt. This time, her wedding dress was an off-the-rack maternity gown that Molly Thorpe purchased for her in Santa Barbara. It was simply cut and made of pale blue cotton sprinkled with white daisies. There was no church with vaulted ceilings and sunlight gleaming through exquisite stained-glass windows. Instead, the ceremony was held at Keefe's mother's home.

Tessa stood in the bedroom Rachel Walker had shown her to the night before. She was getting married in less than an hour. She remembered back to her first wedding. An hour before the ceremony, a makeup artist had been artfully darkening her brows, lengthening her lashes and adding fullness to her lips. When he was done and she looked in the mirror, she'd felt as if she were seeing another woman's face painted over her own, obliterating all traces of Tessa Wyndham.

Looking back, it seemed his work had been prophetic. The girl she'd been had vanished forever that day. The problem was that she wasn't sure just who she'd become in the four years since then. Looking at her reflection in the mirror over the dresser, Tessa wished she knew who the woman looking back at her really was.

Someone knocked on the door, and she turned, grateful for the interruption. But her gratitude was replaced by uneasiness when she saw who her visitor was.

"I thought you might like some help getting ready," Rachel Walker said as she entered the room and closed the door behind her.

"That would be nice," Tessa lied, wondering why Rachel had really come.

She'd met Keefe's mother for the first time the day before, when she and Keefe and Jace arrived at Rachel's home in Los Olivos, a small town not far from Santa Barbara. Rachel had been pleasant, accepting

Keefe's introduction with unruffled calm, as if finding out her son was marrying a woman who was seven months pregnant with another man's child was an everyday occurrence.

Tessa knew better than to believe that facade. Bobby's mother had been the soul of gracious acceptance when they were introduced. It had been months before Tessa realized how much Anne Mallory resented her. Maybe Rachel Walker preferred to take the gloves off right away, she thought. Maybe she'd come to put a stop to the wedding. Her fingers twisting unconsciously in the belt of her robe, Tessa waited for the older woman to start the conversational ball rolling.

"Perhaps I could help you put your hair up?" Rachel suggested. "If you plan to wear it up, that is."

"I hadn't given it any thought," Tessa admitted. She turned to look at her reflection, but the pale woman in the mirror made her uneasy, and she looked away. "I guess I should do something with it, shouldn't I?"

"It looks very nice down," Rachel said. "But, if you'd like to put it up, I could give you a hand."

"I... Thank you."

"Here. Why don't you sit down, and I'll see what I can do?"

Tessa sat down in the chair Rachel dragged over in front of the mirror.

"You have lovely hair," Rachel said as she began brushing it.

"Thank you."

Tessa knew she should think of some pleasant bit

of chitchat. If there was one thing she'd learned in the four years she was married to a politician's son, it was how to converse with total strangers. If she could exchange pleasantries with the president, she should certainly be able to say a few words to the woman who was about to become her mother-in-law. But her mind remained blank. All she could do was wonder what insanity had possessed her, that she'd agreed to this marriage.

"When is the baby due?" Rachel asked, breaking the silence before it became too obvious.

"Two months." Tessa's response was subdued. She knew Keefe had told his family the truth about why he was marrying her. His mother must surely hate her for the way she was using him, and Tessa couldn't blame her. She could never expect Rachel to understand how desperately she needed the shelter Keefe had offered.

"I always thought those last few weeks were the hardest." Rachel gathered Tessa's hair in one hand and began twisting it into a soft knot.

"Did you?" Tessa couldn't imagine how the last two months of her pregnancy could be any more difficult than the first seven had been.

"It was the waiting, I think," Rachel continued cheerfully. "Wondering if it was a boy or a girl, trying to decide on names. Too much anticipation, I guess."

"Probably." Tessa tried to sound as if she knew exactly how Rachel must have felt. It wasn't hard to understand. Most women probably felt the way Rachel did. Anticipation, excitement, hope—those were normal emotions for a woman about to bring a new life into the world. She wished she could feel that way, wished she could feel something besides— She couldn't even put what she did feel into words. It was as if there were an empty space inside where all that sweet anticipation and eagerness should have been. She felt almost numb.

"Do you know if it's a boy or a girl?" Rachel asked as she slid pins into place, deftly securing Tessa's golden hair into a soft knot on top of her head.

"No, I—" Tessa choked on the lie that she wanted to be surprised. The truth was, she didn't want to know if it was a boy or a girl, didn't want to know anything that might make the child she carried seem more real. "No, I don't know," she said in a flat little voice.

Something made her lift her eyes, and her gaze met Rachel's in the mirror. What she saw there shocked her. There was compassion in Rachel's eyes. Compassion and concern and—most astonishing of all—understanding. Tessa looked away quickly, her eyes stinging. She didn't want to cry. She'd done enough of that to last a lifetime.

"It's all right, you know," Rachel said softly.

"No, it's not." Tessa didn't pretend not to understand. "I should be stronger. It's not right to let Keefe... I don't want to use him."

"Don't underestimate my son." Rachel smiled a little as she teased a few locks of dark gold hair loose from the knot and coaxed them to lie against Tessa's nape. "Keefe is no one's fool."

"I never thought he was," Tessa said quickly. "I

think he's kind and generous. Too kind and too generous."

Rachel's warm chuckle was unexpected enough to bring Tessa's gaze back to the mirror. The older woman's eyes sparkled with humor. She shook her head a little.

"Don't make him out to be a saint, either. He has his share of faults."

Tessa couldn't think of any, but it didn't seem polite to argue with Keefe's mother, so she said nothing. Rachel's smile deepened. She set her hands on Tessa's shoulders and squeezed gently.

"There. I think that looks nice."

Tessa allowed her attention to shift to her hair, relieved at the change of topic. She didn't feel as if she had the right to discuss Keefe with his mother. Her hair did look nice. Rachel had pinned it up in a soft knot, with a scattering of fine curls left loose around the sides. The style was both simple and attractive.

"It looks very pretty. Thank you." It was the first completely natural smile Rachel had seen. It lit Tessa's face, giving her an almost gamine beauty, and Rachel found herself wondering if Keefe was being totally honest with himself about the reasons for this marriage.

"Are you sure you know what you're doing?" Sam asked.

Keefe glanced in the mirror as he slid a tie under his shirt collar. Less than an hour before the wedding, and all three of his brothers were crowded into the small bedroom, offering to help him get ready for the wedding. He could have pointed out that he'd been dressing himself for quite a few years now, but he didn't bother. He knew they weren't here to make sure he buttoned his shirt straight.

"I'm getting married," he said, giving the most obvious answer to Sam's question.

"Yeah, but do you know what you're doing?" Gage asked dryly. Three years younger than Keefe, he shared his brother's dark coloring, but where Keefe's eyes were deep brown, Gage's were a clear, sharp blue.

"I know what I'm doing," Keefe said. He frowned at his reflection in the mirror as he fumbled with the tie. He wore one so seldom that he always had to relearn how to knot it.

"You're getting *married,*" Sam said.

"That's what I just said." Keefe tugged loose a half-tied knot and started over again. "I know exactly what I'm doing. I'm marrying Tessa Wyndham."

In the mirror, he saw his brothers exchange a look among themselves. Caught between exasperation and amusement, he let the ends of the tie fall free and turned to face them.

"Look. I haven't lost my mind, and I'm not under the influence of illegal substances—or legal ones, for that matter. Tessa needs someone to look out for her for a little while. Marriage is the best way to do that. It's no big deal."

"Sure. No big deal." Cole nodded, as if that made perfect sense to him. His usually rumpled dark gold hair was neatly combed for a change. His tone was mocking, but there was real concern in his brown eyes. ''Any friend of mine needs looking after, I'd certainly marry them.''

''Don't you think your wife might object?'' Gage asked dryly.

''Nah. Addie's real understanding.''

''I've always wondered what it would be like to have been born an only child,'' Keefe commented, to no one in particular.

Gage grinned. ''Think of all the fun you'd have missed if we hadn't been around to add excitement to your otherwise dull and uneventful life.''

''You mean if you hadn't been around to make my life hell,'' Keefe said.

''Hey, what are brothers for?'' Cole asked.

Keefe looked at Sam. ''Tell me again why we let them live to grow up.''

''It seemed like the right thing to do at the time,'' Sam said, looking as if he had his doubts now.

''It's too late to change your mind,'' Cole said.

''I suppose so,'' Keefe said wistfully. He turned back to the mirror and tackled his recalcitrant tie again.

''Speaking of changing your mind,'' Sam said. ''You're really sure about this wedding thing?''

''I'm sure.''

''Because it's not too late to call it off. Between the four of us, we ought to be able to keep Tessa's evil in-laws at a distance.''

''*Ex*–evil in-laws,'' Keefe corrected him as he tucked the end of his tie through the knot and pulled it snug. He studied the end result in the mirror for a moment before reaching for his suit jacket. He looked at his brothers as he shrugged into the garment. "Look, you guys, I appreciate the concern. I know you all think I've lost my mind."

"Hell, *that's* been missing for years," Gage murmured.

"But I actually have thought this through," Keefe continued, ignoring the interruption. "This isn't as crazy as it looks."

"It couldn't be." That was Cole, adding his two cents' worth.

"It's not a big deal," Keefe insisted. "All it's cost me is a marriage license, a little time and a lot of harassment from the three of you. Now, if you'll all get out of my way, I've got a wedding to attend."

He knew he hadn't convinced them. Hell, he hadn't even convinced himself. No matter how many times he told himself that a marriage license was nothing but a piece of paper, a simple legal contract that could be interpreted in any way the participating parties wished, he couldn't shake the feeling that he was taking an irrevocable step.

But that was ridiculous. He, of all people, knew just how easy it was to break this particular contract.

"Dearly beloved, we are gathered together in the sight of God and these witnesses..."

Tessa had heard the words before, of course. In movies and on television. She'd attended other people's weddings and listened as ministers of a variety of denominations recited more or less the same service. A lifetime ago, she'd stood in front of an altar, trembling with nerves and filled with hope, as she gave herself into Bobby's keeping. There was nothing she hadn't heard before, yet it all sounded different this time.

For better or worse, for richer or poorer, in sickness and in health. The solemnity of the vows struck her in a way they never had before. *As long as you both shall live.* She was promising to spend the rest of her life with Keefe. Her hand trembled, and she felt his fingers tighten over hers, as if offering her silent reassurance. Almost reluctantly, Tessa lifted her eyes to his face. He was watching her, his dark eyes calm and steady, as he repeated his vows.

Standing here, in his mother's living room, which was filled to overflowing with his family, they were promising that this union would last forever, that they were going to grow old together, that they'd found everything they wanted in each other.

They were playing pretend. But what would it be like to stand here and listen to Keefe promise to love her forever and know that he meant it?

You may kiss the bride.

The words seemed without meaning until she saw Keefe's mouth tilt in a crooked smile as he bent his head to hers. Tessa drew in a quick, startled little breath and her free hand lifted to his chest—whether in protest or for support, she couldn't have said. His mouth settled over hers in a kiss that asked nothing but acceptance. The gentle warmth was as unfamiliar as it was irresistible. Tessa's lips softened beneath his, her body curving subtly toward his as her fingers curled around the lapel of his suit jacket.

The kiss lasted only a few seconds, but that was

long enough for Tessa to feel the world shift beneath her feet. This was what it should have been like the first time, this sense of rightness, of belonging. She'd never felt that with Bobby, never felt her world settle into place just because he was next to her.

Keefe lifted his head slowly, ending the kiss as softly as it had begun. Tessa wished she could read the expression in his eyes, but she looked away, afraid of what he might read in hers. What if her eyes revealed her sudden, desperate wish that this was all real?

Chapter 8

"Okay. Enough of that." Sam's voice broke into the taut little silence that had fallen at the end of the ceremony. "As head of the family, I claim the right to kiss the bride first."

"Head of the family?" Gage repeated the phrase derisively. "What makes you head of the family?"

"If a superior intellect isn't reason enough, how about seniority?" Sam asked. Ignoring the less-than-impressed snorts from his brothers, he took Tessa by the shoulders and bent to kiss her cheek. "Welcome to the family, Tessa."

"Thank you," she murmured. She felt dazed by the realization of what she'd just done. Married. She was married to Keefe. It didn't seem possible.

"My turn," Cole said, elbowing his eldest brother aside. "Seniority or not, you don't get to hog the bride." His dark eyes smiling, he planted a kiss on her cheek. "Welcome to the Walker madhouse, Tessa."

"Out of the way, little brother." Gage smiled down at her. "Try not to judge us all by my brothers' uncouth behavior, Tessa. Some of us are quite civilized."

If she hadn't known otherwise, Tessa would have thought that the Walkers believed this was a real marriage. They welcomed her to the family as if she belonged, as if she were marrying Keefe for love rather than expediency. When she remembered the cool, formal congratulations that had followed her marriage to Bobby—a "love match"—she had to swallow an hysterical urge to laugh. There was something irresistibly ironic about the contrast between the two.

Keefe watched Tessa accept his family's good wishes with shy pleasure and thought back to his first wedding. He and Dana had gotten married in Vegas, in a chapel lit by multicolored neon candles. None of his family had been there—only Jace and Kel Bryan, another friend from the rodeo circuit. He'd worn a pair of almost-new jeans and a crisp western-style shirt, and he'd slapped polish over the worst of the scuffs on his boots. The bride had worn white—a mid-thigh-length knit dress that clung to every curve and exposed an astonishing length of tanned leg. A ceremony stripped of all the traditional trimmings had amused Dana. He remembered being vaguely grateful that they weren't being married by an Elvis imitator.

Funny that, this time around, when he wasn't marrying for love, the ceremony should seem so much more real. He'd found himself listening to the words as if he were hearing them for the first time. When he married Dana, he hadn't felt this need to protect her, to take care of her. But then, Dana hadn't needed anyone to protect her. She'd been well able to take care of herself.

Tessa was so totally unlike Dana that it was hard to believe that they were even related. Despite her cool blond beauty, Dana had radiated a fiery sexuality. A man had only to look at her and his thoughts veered toward cool sheets and hot sex.

Tessa was a completely different story. She was attractive, though her beauty was quieter, less obvious than her older sister's. But she had something more than physical beauty. There was an inner sweetness, a gentle warmth, that Dana had never had. Tessa cared—about other people, about what was right. Tessa was…special. She deserved a great deal more than the hand life had dealt her so far.

Keefe frowned a little as he considered the kiss that had come at the end of the ceremony. That kiss had felt more real than he liked to admit, even to himself. Her mouth had yielded to his so sweetly and she'd leaned into him so trustingly that, for a moment, he'd forgotten that this was all for show, forgotten that he was just doing this to protect her, and almost lost himself in the warm, womanly taste of her. There hadn't been anything avuncular about that kiss.

His frown deepening, Keefe reached for his cigarettes, then remembered where he was and let his hand drop. He'd almost given the habit up, but there were still moments when he craved a nicotine fix. The moment he realized he was attracted to his bride was one of them.

Molly Thorpe hugged her great-niece with a strength that belied her years. The delicate scent of White Shoulders perfume wafted Tessa back to childhood, when visits to her Aunt Molly's California ranch had been the highlight of every summer. She closed her eyes and, for just a moment, allowed herself to pretend that she was that little girl again, looking forward to weeks of California sunshine and horseback riding. Life had been so much simpler then.

"You've got yourself a good man," Molly said as she stepped back and looked at her great-niece. The rest of the wedding party was busy admiring Gage and Kelsey's infant daughter, the youngest member of the family, leaving Tessa and her aunt momentarily alone.

"He's not mine," Tessa reminded her. "You know that. This isn't a real marriage."

"Looked pretty real to me," Molly said.

"Well, it's not. It's just a...temporary arrangement to protect me and the baby. Keefe has been incredibly generous, and he's—"

"Don't make the boy out to be a saint," Molly said, in an acid-toned echo of Rachel Walker's words. "I've known him a good bit longer than you have. He's one of the best but he's not ready for a halo and wings. Truth is, he's as pigheaded as they come. Once he's made up his mind to do something, it's like arguing with a mud fence to try and get him to change course.'' From the irritated tone of her voice, Tessa assumed that Molly was speaking from experience. ''Still, he's a good man. Your sister was a fool to let him go, but you were always a great deal brighter than she was. If you've got half as much sense as I think you have, you'll hang on to him.''

''Hang on to him?'' Tessa gaped at the older woman. ''I can't do that! He's not mine.''

''Nonsense!'' Molly said briskly. ''You're married to him, aren't you? Possession is nine-tenths of the law.''

Before Tessa could think of an appropriate response to that astonishing statement, Keefe came up to them.

''How are you holding up?'' He set one hand against the small of her back, a light touch that offered both comfort and reassurance.

''Just fine.'' Tessa had to resist the urge to lean her head against his shoulder, to let his strength support her completely. If she wasn't careful, she was going to lose what little backbone she had, she thought ruefully. If only Keefe didn't make it so easy for her to lean on him.

''Of course she's fine,'' Molly said impatiently. ''She's having a baby, not coming down with the plague.''

''Thanks for pointing that out.'' Keefe's smile was wryly affectionate. ''Glad you could make it, Molly.''

''I wouldn't have missed it for the world.'' Molly gave him a speculative look, her sharp blue eyes smiling wickedly. ''I was just telling Tessa that I hope she's smarter than her sister and has the good sense to hang on to you.''

"Aunt Molly!" Tessa's horrified exclamation was nearly drowned out by Keefe's chuckle.

"You must have made your husband's life a living nightmare, Molly," he said, apparently not in the least disconcerted by her outrageous remark.

"He was lucky to have me," she said briskly. "And I made sure he knew it."

"I bet you did."

"I think everything went very well." Tessa rushed into speech, afraid of what Molly might say next.

"It went just fine." He smiled down at her, his eyes full of amused understanding.

"Your family has been so welcoming," she said wonderingly.

"Why shouldn't they be?" Molly demanded, before Keefe could respond. "He's lucky to get you, and they know it."

"You're right," Keefe agreed promptly.

"Aunt Molly!" Tessa had always admired her aunt's plainspokenness—until today.

"Well, he is," Molly said, ignoring both Keefe's amusement and Tessa's embarrassment. "There's good blood in your veins. Of course, you have to skip a generation to find any evidence of it. Your mother doesn't have the sense God gave a turnip, and your father is the biggest nitwit I've ever known. But the Walkers aren't the sort to hold that against you."

Keefe's laughter was so genuine that Tessa found herself smiling, albeit reluctantly. She supposed she should be offended on behalf of her parents. Unfortunately, there was more truth than otherwise in Molly's words.

"Lunch is about ready," Rachel Walker announced, and Tessa turned, grateful for the interruption. Heaven only knew what outrageous comments Molly might have ready to spring on them next.

He really was going to have to quit smoking completely, Keefe thought as he stepped onto the back porch and let the kitchen door close behind him. He was getting too old to be sneaking around like this. He slid the cigarettes out of his pocket and tapped one free of the pack.

"I've heard rumors that those are bad for you."

The voice, coming from somewhere off to his left, made him start guiltily. Turning, he saw Nikki sitting in one corner of the porch swing. She smiled when she saw his guilty expression. "Caught you."

"I've heard that same rumor," Keefe said, relaxing. He put the cigarette in his mouth. "But I figure it's a filthy lie."

"Like the rumor that fudge ripple ice cream is fattening?" she asked.

"Probably started by the same guy." He lit a match and held the flame to the tip of his cigarette. "I figure there's a government agency somewhere, whose only purpose is to tell the people that everything they like is bad for them."

"Paid for by our tax dollars." Nikki shook her head at the waste of it all.

"Exactly." Keefe shook out the match. "It doesn't matter, though, because I'm quitting."

She arched her brows. "So I see."

Keefe grinned at her through a thin veil of smoke. "I don't believe in rushing into things."

She nodded. "Very wise."

The silence that fell between them was comfortable. Keefe smoked his cigarette and looked out over his mother's casually landscaped backyard. Her huge dog, an enormous animal of uncertain parentage, lolled on his side in the middle of lawn.

"Looks like Mary and Danny wore Hippo out," Nikki commented. Cole's daughter and Gage and Kelsey's son had spent most of the morning playing with the dog.

"Maybe. Then again, Hippo doesn't seem to believe in expending any unnecessary energy."

"He's pretty energetic around half-cooked turkeys," Nikki said.

The first Thanksgiving after she and Sam were married, Hippo had stolen the turkey from the counter, leaving the rest of the family to dine on roast chicken and grilled hamburgers.

"He does show some speed around food," Keefe conceded, smiling at the memory.

There was another little silence, and then Nikki spoke again.

"Tessa seems very nice."

"She is." Sensing there was more to come, he waited.

"I didn't want to like her." The words seemed to come against her will.

Keefe's hand froze in midair, the cigarette halfway to his mouth. His brows rose in surprise. "Why not?"

"Because of the baby. Sam says she may give it

up.'' Nikki's hands lay on her thighs, her fingers clenched in the fabric of her jade-colored silk skirt. ''I wanted to hate her for that.''

Keefe took his time responding. He remembered his brother telling him that Nikki was going in for tests to find out why she wasn't pregnant yet. Sam hadn't mentioned it since, but Keefe had the feeling that he was treading on some dangerous emotional ground.

''Tessa has her reasons,'' he said finally.

''I know she does.'' Nikki exhaled a shuddering breath. ''I know she does.'' She repeated the words, her voice hardly above a whisper. ''It just seemed so unfair that...'' She stopped and looked up at him, her expression bleak. ''We found out last week that I can't have children.''

Keefe read the depth of the pain in her eyes and, for one cowardly moment, wished he hadn't given in to the urge to have a cigarette. He pushed it aside and groped for something to say, but there really wasn't much that could be said, beyond the obvious.

''I'm sorry. I know the two of you wanted children. Is there any hope that things might change?'' He crushed his cigarette out against the porch railing, concentrating on the movement as a way to avoid seeing the pain in her face.

''No.'' She shook her head. ''There's no hope at all. No question that it's my fault.''

''Fault?'' He looked at her, his brows raised questioningly. ''You didn't choose to have this happen, Nikki. It just did.''

''Semantics.'' She rejected his attempt at reason with a sharp movement of her hand. ''Because there's something wrong with me, Sam won't be able to have children.''

Feeling as if he were tiptoeing through a mine field, Keefe reached for his cigarettes, but let his hand drop before it got to his pocket. Some situations were beyond the power of nicotine. The swing rocked gently, chains creaking, as he sat down next to his sister-in-law.

''If you're afraid that Sam is going to blame you, you can forget it.''

''No, he'd never blame me.'' The knowledge didn't seem to give her any comfort. ''But if it wasn't for me—''

He interrupted her firmly. ''If it wasn't for you, Sam would be miserable. Listen to me. My brother is crazy about you. I don't know how much Sam wants kids, but I do know how much he loves you.''

''But—''

''No buts,'' he said firmly. ''I've never seen Sam as happy as he has been since he met you.''

''What about years from now?'' Nikki whispered.

''What about it?''

''What if he starts to think about what he missed out on?''

Keefe set his hand under her chin and lifted her face to his. Steeling himself against the tears swimming in her green eyes, he gave her a hard look.

''If you think there could ever come a time when Sam would resent you for something like this, then you don't know him at all.''

She flushed and lowered her eyes. ''I suppose you're right.''

"I know I'm right," he said flatly. He released his hold on her, letting his hand drop. "Don't sell him short, Nikki."

"I won't." She sighed, and when she looked up at him, her expression was less bleak than it had been. "Thanks for listening, and thanks for pointing out what an idiot I'm being."

"I didn't say you were an idiot," he protested.

"Well, you could have, and I would have deserved it." She shook her head. "I don't think I've been rowing with both oars in the water the last few weeks. When Sam told me why you were getting married, I made up my mind to hate Tessa."

"Why?" he asked blankly, caught off guard by the blunt declaration.

"Because of the baby. Because she has something I can't ever have and she doesn't even want it."

Keefe was caught between a desperate craving for a cigarette and the equally desperate wish that he'd never heard of the damned things. If he hadn't slipped out here to have a smoke, he could have avoided a conversation for which he felt woefully inadequate.

Perhaps Nikki read something of his near panic, because her mouth curved in a half smile and a touch of humor lit her eyes. "Poor Keefe. I bet you're wishing you'd quit smoking completely. Don't worry. I'm not going to dump any more emotional baggage in your lap. I just wanted to tell you that I really think Tessa is very sweet and I think you're very sweet to be doing this for her. And I've got a feeling that everything is going to work out really well for both of you."

''Thanks.''

''You're welcome.'' She smiled again, and the shadows seemed to recede a little farther. ''Now, maybe you should go in and rescue her. You may not realize it, but the Walker family can be just a little overwhelming to the uninitiated.''

''Are you coming in?''

''In a minute. I'm all right,'' she added, seeing his concern.

Keefe hesitated a moment longer before he rose from the swing. She spoke again as he was reaching for the screen door.

''Keefe?''

''Yeah?'' He turned to look at her, his brows raised questioningly.

''Thanks,'' she said softly. ''Thanks for listening.''

''That's what family's for.''

Chapter 9

It was long after dark when Keefe pulled the truck up in front of the ranch house. When he shut off the engine, the abrupt silence was startling. Tessa thought that she had never seen anything more lovely than the golden glow of the porch light.

"I have never understood why riding in a car is more tiring than running a marathon," Jace said as he reached for the door handle. The two of them had traded off driving duties, and the last leg of the journey had been Keefe's.

"One of the great mysteries of life." Keefe opened his own door and slid out from behind the wheel, sighing with pleasure as his feet hit solid ground.

"What we need is a transporter, like they have on the *Enterprise*." Jace got out and then turned to offer Tessa a helping hand down out of the truck. "*That's* where our tax dollars should be going. Talk about an improvement in the country's infrastructure."

"You should write your congressman about it," Keefe suggested. He leaned over the side of the pickup and lifted their luggage out. "I'm sure the government just hasn't thought of it. A letter from you, pointing out the error of their ways, is bound to get them moving in the right direction."

"Wasn't there an episode where the signal got scrambled and somebody ended up trading personalities with a dog?" Tessa asked sleepily.

"They didn't trade personalities with the dog," Jace said. "The transporter split the dog into two dogs—only it wasn't really a dog. It had a horn. It died. But then it turned out that the transporter had split Kirk into two people, one good and one evil."

"You're a Trekkie," Tessa said, amazed.

"I believe the politically correct term is Trekker," Jace corrected her with exaggerated dignity.

"He's a 'Star Trek' nut," Keefe said dryly. "He's got every episode on tape, but he doesn't need to watch them, because he can recite the dialogue by heart."

"'Star Trek' is a genuine classic of American literature," Jace reminded him.

"Yeah, it's right up there with Steinbeck and Hemingway."

"Actually, I never much cared for Hemingway," Tessa said. "But I do like 'Star Trek.'"

"You have genuine class," Jace said. She caught the gleam of his teeth in the darkness as he grinned at her. "You can borrow my tapes anytime."

''I'm impressed,'' Keefe said as he handed Jace his overnight case. ''He wouldn't loan those tapes to just anyone.''

''Well, I certainly wouldn't loan them to someone who thinks 'Bonanza' is the epitome of American television art.''

''You don't get much better than Ben and the boys,'' Keefe said, with an exaggerated western drawl.

Tessa's chuckle ended abruptly on a yawn. ''Sorry.''

''You're beat,'' Jace said. ''We can discuss the relative merits of old television shows some other time. I'll see you guys in the morning.'' He lifted one hand in salute and turned toward the foreman's house.

Watching him walk away, Tessa was abruptly aware that his departure left her alone with Keefe. And Keefe was no longer just Keefe—he was also her husband.

''You know, I've always wondered why Jace doesn't stay up at the house,'' she said, anxious to fill the silence. ''I mean, he didn't, even before I took over the guest room.''

''We both like our privacy,'' Keefe said as he picked up their bags and started toward the house. ''Besides, not only does he have lousy taste in television, he has lousy taste in music. There's a limit to the number of hours I can listen to Tchaikovsky.''

''Jace likes classical music?'' Tessa was momentarily distracted by this piece of information. '''Star Trek' and Tchaikovsky. He doesn't exactly fit the stereotype of the cowboy, does he?''

"Not exactly."

She hesitated at the bottom of the steps. It was silly to be nervous. It wasn't as if they were really married. Keefe set the bags down and reached into his pocket for the keys. Tessa's teeth worried her lower lip. *Husband.* The word had layers of meaning—companion, protector, lover. That was what the word should mean. But overlying those images was the reality of her marriage to Bobby. He'd used the word to control, to dominate, to assert his will and make her feel less of a person. *Husband.* There was power in the word. The thought made her uneasy.

"Tessa?" Keefe turned to look at her, his brows raised questioningly. "Something wrong?"

"No." *Nothing but the fact that I think I've lost my mind.* "I was just thinking of how many stars there are here," she said, blurting out the first thing that popped into her head. "I don't remember ever seeing skies like this before."

Keefe let the screen door close and crossed the porch toward her. Tessa tilted back her head to look at the sky as he walked down the steps, the click of his boot heels against the wood loud in the late-night stillness.

"I'd never realized you could actually see the Milky Way," she said, vividly aware of his size as he stopped in front of her. He was so big, bigger even than Bobby. She wouldn't be able to stop him if he—*Stop it. This is Keefe. He would never hurt me.* But you couldn't stop him if he did, a sly voice whispered. He's your husband now.

"It's because there isn't a lot of ambient light messing up the view,'' Keefe said, responding to her comment. He glanced up at the sky—black velvet scattered with countless glittering jewels. ''One advantage of living so far away from the city.''

''It's hard to imagine why anyone would live in the city if it meant missing out on a view like this,'' Tessa said, trying to look as if she had nothing more than the view on her mind.

''But if everyone left the city and moved to the country, they'd spoil the view with their cars and their porch lights.''

''I suppose.'' Her neck was starting to ache. She lowered her head and focused on the crisp rectangle of light that marked a window in the foreman's house. ''Jace made it home,'' she said inanely.

''Looks like.'' There was a brief silence, and then he spoke again, his voice gentle. ''Tessa, I'm not going to turn into a monster just because we signed a piece of paper that says we're married.''

''I know that.'' She sighed, relieved to have her fears out in the open, embarrassed that he'd read her so easily. ''I'm sorry to be such a fool.''

''You're not a fool. You've got reason to be leery.''

''No, I don't. Not with you.'' She kept her gaze focused on the light in Jace's window, speaking slowly, thinking out what she wanted to say. ''I'd like to be able to say that Bobby changed after we got married, but if I'm honest with myself, I've got to admit that the signs were there all along. I just didn't want to see them. I thought he'd change after we were married.'' She sighed. ''I guess that was pretty stupid.''

"Not stupid. Just human." Keefe slid his arm around her shoulders and pulled her against his side. "When you love someone, it's natural to blind yourself to their faults."

Something in his tone made her wonder if he spoke from experience. Was he thinking of Dana?

"You don't have to worry about anything," he said, giving her shoulders a quick, affectionate squeeze. "I'm not going to change because we signed a piece of paper that says we're married. Nothing's going to change between us."

Tessa allowed him to shepherd her into the house. He'd made her see how foolish her fears had been. It had been silly to think, even for a moment, that she had anything to worry about. Keefe wasn't going to change.

Nothing's going to change between us.

Strange, but she found the reassurance oddly depressing.

It took Keefe a few days to realize just how wrong he'd been. No matter how much he told himself—and Tessa—that a marriage license was nothing but a piece of paper, holding only as much meaning as they chose to give it, he soon realized that that wasn't particularly accurate. Their marriage was like a move in a high-stakes poker game, with the Mallorys as their opponents. They were betting that fear of bad publicity would prevent the good senator and his wife from calling their bluff.

But whatever the reasons behind it, they *were* married and, when Keefe looked at Tessa now, he saw her in a different light. She wasn't the quiet little girl he'd known years ago. She was a woman who had survived an abusive marriage, a woman struggling to put her life back in order. She was his wife.

Keefe reached in his pocket and pulled out his cigarettes. One hand holding the reins, he worked a cigarette free and slid the pack back into his shirt pocket. Pulling out a book of matches, he sighed at the difficulty of lighting up with only one hand.

"I am quitting," he muttered as he drew his horse up. The bay flicked one ear back. Keefe struck the match and cupped his hands around the cigarette to light it. Drawing smoke into his lungs, he shook out the match. "This is my first cigarette today."

The bay's ears twitched, and Keefe frowned. "You don't have to sneer about it. I've practically quit. A few cigarettes a day hardly even counts."

The big gelding snorted his opinion of that rationalization.

"Easy for you to say," Keefe muttered as he nudged the horse into a walk. He narrowed his eyes against the smoke as he drew on the cigarette. He was supposed to be checking on the stock tanks, making sure the cattle had plenty of water. It was an undemanding task, giving him time to think—more than he wanted, really.

His eyes shadowed by the brim of his hat, he looked at the land around him. His land. His ranch. It was the fulfillment of a childhood dream. He'd been born and raised in the Los Angeles basin, in a small suburban house with a small suburban backyard—not a horse or a corral in sight. His father had been a police officer and, as far as he knew, there wasn't a single cowboy in the family tree. Yet he couldn't remember a time when he hadn't wanted to be a cowboy.

He'd been ten the first time he rode a horse. His parents had given in to his pleas and purchased riding lessons from a stable located in nearby Tujunga Canyon. From the moment he sat in the saddle, he'd known what he wanted to be when he grew up.

And here he was, riding across his own land. In the years since he won the Flying Ace in a poker game, he'd worked his butt off to turn it into a paying proposition. And it was happening. Very slowly, and not exactly surely, but it was happening. It was the fulfillment of a lifelong dream. A few weeks ago, he'd have said he had pretty much everything he'd ever wanted.

That had been before Tessa came back into his life. When he told her she was welcome to stay as long as she liked, he hadn't been thinking any farther than giving her the shelter she needed. It hadn't occurred to him that Tessa's presence would change his own life in any significant way.

Keefe's mouth twisted in a self-mocking smile. He doubted there was a crystal ball on the planet that could have foreseen how his invitation to Tessa to stay on the ranch would lead to marriage and potential fatherhood, not to mention facing down a United States senator. But what bothered him more than all of that was that Tessa's presence had made him aware that something was lacking in his life.

He drew deeply on the cigarette, narrowing his eyes

against the smoke. It had taken him a while to get past the divorce. He'd done a lot of drinking and spent a few months trying to break his neck on the back of a bucking horse. But winning the Flying Ace in a poker game had given his life a new focus, and he'd pulled himself together. The past couple of years had been pretty good, and if anyone asked, he'd have said that he had his life pretty well in order.

Then Tessa had shown up, with her soft voice and sweet feminine scent. She'd thrown open the windows, swept the dust from the house, done her innocent best to starve him to death. And, in the process, she'd made him see just how damned empty his life had been before she arrived.

Keefe swung down out of the saddle at the first stock tank. Dropping the end of his cigarette, he ground it into the dirt with the toe of his boot. If Tessa hadn't come back into his life, he might have gone on for years without realizing how lonely he was. Now he was acutely aware of the gap she was going to leave in his life when she left. It was ironic that it had taken a pretend marriage to make him realize how much he missed having a real one.

Tessa caught the end of her tongue between her teeth as she looped the yarn over the right hand knitting needle, slid the tip of the needle under the stitch on the left-hand needle and attempted to transfer it from left to right. When the stitch was successfully completed, she allowed herself to breathe again. *Knitting is a relaxing hobby.* She remembered the woman in the yarn store telling her that, describing all the hours of pleasure that lay ahead of her, soothed by the rhythmic click of her knitting needles.

It had sounded like a good idea at the time, but six months after she'd bought the yarn to make a baby sweater, she had yet to find anything relaxing about knitting. She had a few inches of scruffy-looking blue fabric marked by tiny holes where she'd dropped half a dozen stitches. A sane woman would have thrown the whole mess in the trash and moved on to a simpler hobby—designing nuclear power plants maybe—but she continued to struggle.

She'd started the sweater when Bobby was still alive. She'd kept working on it after his death, though she'd already begun to think of giving the baby up for adoption. She wasn't sure why. Heaven knew, no new parent—adoptive or otherwise—was going to dress a child in a sweater that looked as if it had been knitted for an alien species. She sighed faintly as she tackled the next stitch.

''Problems?'' Keefe asked, looking up from the magazine he was reading.

''Not really.'' She looked up from the wadded mass in her hands and smiled ruefully. ''I'm starting to think that, to be really good at knitting, you need to be double-jointed.''

''Don't they mention that in the instructions?''

''No. Do you suppose that constitutes false advertising? Maybe I could sue someone for misleading me.''

''Emotional cruelty?''

''I think I could make a case for it.'' She held up her needles. ''It's *supposed* to be a baby sweater.''

Keefe looked at the lumpy, uneven swatch. His brows climbed a notch. ''What kind of baby?'' he asked finally.

''That was very cruel,'' Tessa said, her dignified tone at odds with the laughter in her eyes.

''I'm sure it's going to look just fine when you get it done,'' he said reassuringly.

''Well, I guess it can't get any worse than it is.'' Her tone was philosophical.

''It will be fine,'' Keefe said as he returned his attention to the magazine.

Tessa began working the needles again, struggling to transfer each stitch neatly. It occurred to her that, if anyone happened to look in through a window, she and Keefe must look like a stereotypical married couple. The two of them sitting together, her with her knitting and him with his magazine. All they needed was a fire in the fireplace and a shaggy dog sleeping on the hearth and they could have stepped right out of an advertisement for domestic bliss. Of course, it was July, which made a fire a little impractical, and Keefe didn't happen to own a dog, but even without those finishing touches, they presented a picture-perfect image.

Talk about false advertising. There was an edge of pain to her half smile. The problem was that she found herself wishing that this was real. The more time she spent with Keefe, the more she'd come to see all the things she'd missed in her first marriage. There had been no companionship, no affection. Looking back, she found it difficult to remember why she'd married Bobby. She'd been so dazzled by his looks and by the idea of showing her parents that someone eligible—a senator's son, no less—would want to marry her that she hadn't stopped to consider what she really felt for him. She'd certainly paid a high price for her foolishness, she thought. She touched the heavy swell of her stomach. She was still paying it, in a way.

The baby kicked unexpectedly, and Tessa sucked in a quick, startled breath.

Keefe's head came up immediately, his dark eyes concerned. "What's wrong?"

"Nothing. The baby moved, that's all."

His gaze dropped to her stomach, his expression shifting from concern to curiosity. "Does it hurt?"

"Not really. It's more of a kind of quick pressure." She lifted her shoulders in a light shrug. "It's hard to describe."

"Does he kick often?"

"Often enough for an entire football team. Or maybe a chorus line, if it's a girl." It felt odd to be discussing the baby so casually with him. As if they were a normal married couple, anticipating the birth of their child. "Would you like to feel it?" she asked impulsively.

She immediately wanted to recall the words. She'd spent almost eight months trying not to think about this baby any more than she had to, afraid to let it become real to her. Inviting Keefe to feel the baby kick was stepping beyond the barriers she'd set for herself. But he was already sitting down next to her, the sofa cushion dipping beneath his weight.

"Are you sure?" he asked, as if sensing her hesitation.

"Of course," she said lightly. "Give me your hand."

She pressed his fingers against the side of her belly, feeling the warmth of his hand through the layers of her clothing.

"Once he gets started, he usually keeps it up for a while," she said. As if on cue, the baby kicked vigorously. She felt Keefe jerk in surprise.

"A placekicker," he said positively. The baby kicked again, and his smile widened into a grin. Tessa saw the wonder in his eyes and felt her heart twist. Her feelings about the child she carried were so ambivalent. She would have given almost anything to be able to share Keefe's uncomplicated pleasure in the moment.

"Feels like a healthy little guy—or girl," he said, still smiling.

"So the doctor tells me." Keefe had driven her into town the week before to see the doctor, and he had pronounced her and the baby to be in perfect health.

"Think he's through for now?" Keefe asked.

"Could be." Tessa was suddenly aware of the intimacy of the moment. Keefe's large hand was spread against her stomach. He was close enough that she could see the gold flecks that lightened the deep brown of his eyes. A thick lock of dark hair had fallen onto his forehead. She curled her fingers against the foolish urge to push it back into place, and she looked away, afraid of what her expression might reveal.

"Tessa?"

The husky sound of his voice sent a small shiver of awareness down her spine.

"Y-yes?" She had to clear her throat before she could get the word out.

"What would you say if I told you I wanted to kiss you?"

"Me?" She looked at him, her eyes widened into startled blue pools.

"What would you say?" he asked, leaning closer.

"O-okay," she whispered, a heartbeat before his mouth touched hers.

His lips were warm and firm, asking her response rather than demanding it. Tessa felt herself melting against him. His tongue skimmed her lower lip, and she opened her mouth, inviting him inside.

She'd forgotten what a kiss could be, she thought dazedly as his tongue fenced gently with hers. No, she hadn't forgotten. She'd never *known* a kiss could be like this—warm and tender and sensuous all at the same time. Her hand came up, settling against his chest, feeling the steady beat of his heart beneath her palm.

Keefe felt her surrender and lifted one hand, sliding his fingers beneath the silky dark gold weight of her hair, cupping the back of her neck. He tilted her head back and deepened the kiss. Somewhere in the back of his mind, he knew he shouldn't be doing this, had known even before it began. He was supposed to be taking care of Tessa, not kissing her. But she tasted so good, felt so right.

One kiss, he thought. *What harm could there be in one kiss?* Only he didn't want to stop at one kiss. He felt as if he could go on kissing her and holding her forever. But forever hadn't ever been part of their bargain.

Chapter 10

The shrill ring of the telephone shattered the moment as thoroughly as a hammer smashing through a pane of glass. Tessa's breath escaped her in a soft exhalation of regret as Keefe ended the kiss. Her eyelids felt weighted as she forced them open. Looking up into Keefe's eyes, she thought she saw a reflection of her own startled wonder. But the expression was gone in an instant, leaving her to wonder if it had been there at all.

"Tessa, I—" The phone rang again, cutting off whatever he'd started to say. He cast an irritated glance over his shoulder and then looked back at her.

"You'd better get that," she said, her eyes focused somewhere near his collarbone.

"Let it ring."

"It might be important." The phone rang again, a harsh jangle that held overtones of impatience. "Go on,'' she urged, her calm tone revealing none of the turmoil she felt inside. She even managed to curve her mouth into something resembling a smile.

Keefe did not find the expression particularly reassuring, but the phone rang a fourth time, the sound scraping across his nerves like fingernails on a chalkboard. With a muttered curse, he pushed up from the sofa and strode to answer it.

It was a brief call, questions from a neighboring rancher who was interested in boarding a mare on the Flying Ace, in hopes that Jace could soothe her fractious temper. A date for the animal's arrival was agreed upon, as was a price for Jace's work. Keefe hung up the phone, and the conversation vanished instantly from his mind.

He couldn't believe what he'd done. Kissing Tessa, for God's sake! Had he lost his mind? It had seemed so right at the time—inevitable, as if it were meant to happen. But no matter how it had felt, the reality was that he'd promised to take care of her, to protect her. Kissing her had never been a part of their bargain.

She responded, a sly voice whispered. Keefe slapped aside the attempt at justification. Considering all she'd gone through, she might have been afraid of what he'd do if she *didn't* respond. The idea that her gentle yielding might have been prompted by fear made his stomach knot. He spun away from the table, determined to make her understand that what happened had been a momentary madness.

But the room was empty behind him. She'd slipped away while he was on the phone. Whatever he wanted to say would have to wait. He was ashamed to admit that his primary feeling was one of relief. Given a little time, maybe he could come up with an explanation for what had happened tonight—one that would satisfy Tessa, if not himself.

Tessa spent most of a restless night telling herself not to read too much into what had happened. It had only been a kiss, after all. Just because it had sent shock waves through her, that didn't mean that Keefe had felt the same way. Apart from her disastrous marriage, she didn't have much experience with men. She was hardly qualified to judge whether his kiss had held any emotion deeper than comfort.

If it hadn't meant anything to him, she didn't want to know about it. And if it had? Tessa wasn't sure she was ready to know that, either. If her life was tangled, then her emotions were snarled beyond all hope of understanding. The idea that Keefe might feel something more than friendship toward her was enough to terrify, even as it delighted. She needed time to sort out her own feelings before she could even begin to think about Keefe's.

In the end, all her speculation and confusion boiled down to one simple question: How was she supposed to act when she saw him again?

Tessa closed her bedroom door and turned to find a broad expanse of naked male chest only inches from her nose.

"Oh!" Startled, she took a quick step back.

"Sorry. I didn't mean to sneak up on you," Keefe said.

"That's okay." With an effort, she dragged her eyes from the muscled width of his chest and met his gaze. "I thought you were taking a shower."

She'd counted on it actually. They hadn't been alone together since the kiss they'd shared the night before. Since it was now dinnertime, she'd had hopes of being able to avoid him until time for bed. Maybe by tomorrow, she'd have figured out what to say to him.

"Just finished," he said, sliding the fingers of one hand through his damp hair.

The movement drew her eyes back to his chest. His shirt hung open, revealing a solidly muscled expanse covered by a heavy dusting of almost black curls, tapering to a thin line that sliced across the flat plane of his stomach to disappear beneath the waistband of his jeans. She jerked her eyes back up, aware that her cheeks felt warm and hoping the light was too poor for him to notice.

"Have you got a minute?" he asked. There was nothing ominous in his tone, but Tessa felt her heartbeat suddenly accelerate.

"I need to set the table and put out salads and...things," she said hastily.

"This will only take a minute."

"All right." There was no sense in trying to put it off. She might as well hear whatever it was he wanted to say and get it over with.

Now that he had her acceptance, Keefe seemed hesitant about where to start. As if stalling for time, he drew the edges of his shirt together and began to button it. Tessa suppressed a sigh of mixed relief and regret.

"What happened last night..." Keefe began finally. "I don't want you to think..." He stopped, hesitated, and then spoke bluntly. "You don't have to be afraid that it will happen again."

"Afraid?" Tessa was startled into lifting her eyes to his face. "What do you mean?"

"That wasn't part of our bargain. You don't have to feel as if you're...obligated to me in any way."

It took her a moment to realize what he meant. "You think I kissed you because I *owe* you?"

"I don't know." His eyes were bleak.

Tessa felt as if she was out of her depth and floundering badly. None of her fevered imaginings had conjured up this scenario. "I didn't kiss you because I thought I had to. I...I wanted you to kiss me." Her face felt as if it were on fire, but she couldn't let him think that he'd coerced her into anything. "And I enjoyed it very much," she added, with an uncharacteristic touch of bravado.

Keefe stared at her in silence for a moment, as if weighing her sincerity. Apparently he was satisfied, because his mouth curved in a slow smile, his eyes warming in a way that made Tessa's heart thump against her breastbone.

"Actually, I liked it quite a bit myself."

"Well. Then there's nothing to worry about, is there?" she said briskly. He looked as if he might say something else, but Tessa's courage abruptly ran out. "I've got to check on dinner."

She was aware of Keefe's eyes on her as she

walked down the hall. She would have given a great deal to know what he was thinking.

Tessa picked her way carefully across the rough surface of the ranch yard. She carried a flashlight, but she'd turned it off a few yards from the house, finding the sharp patches of darkness beyond the flashlight's beam more deceptive than the softer, less angular shadows created by the light of the full moon that floated just over the mountains to the east.

"Why didn't I just write him a note?" she muttered as she detoured around a fist-size rock. That would certainly have been the easiest thing to do, but when the phone call came in for Keefe, it had seemed to make perfect sense to deliver the message in person. So here she was, traipsing across the yard in the moonlight and wondering if pregnancy might have affected her sanity.

She sighed with relief as she climbed the two steps to the narrow concrete porch that stretched across the front of the foreman's house. Now that she thought about it, it seemed odd that, in all the weeks she'd been here, this was the first time she'd been here. She'd come to think of Jace as a good friend, yet she'd never seen where he lived.

It was a warm night, and Jace had left his front door open. Tessa tapped on the screen door and waited. Somewhere in the back of the house, she could hear the rumble of masculine voices, the sound too low for her to make out words. She heard Keefe say something. Jace's answering laughter was cut off by a metallic rattle, like the sound of a pan dropped carelessly into a sink.

Obviously, they hadn't heard her knock. She lifted her hand to knock again. Her nose twitched. What was that smell? She inhaled, trying to identify the scent that wafted through the screen door. Onions? And... frying hamburger? Ridiculous. Why would Jace and Keefe be cooking hamburgers and onions? Not more than an hour ago, she'd sat in the kitchen at the big house and watched them polish off bowls of vegetable soup and crisp croissants. They couldn't possibly be eating again. Could they?

Tessa let her hand drop to her side. Her teeth worrying her lower lip, she wrestled with her conscience. The right thing to do was to simply knock on the door—loudly and firmly. When Keefe or Jace responded, she could pass on the message about the horse that was arriving tomorrow morning and then go back to the house. It was not only the right thing to do, it was the *only* thing to do. She certainly couldn't just open the screen door and walk into Jace's home uninvited.

The door opened without so much as a squeak of protest. Feeling both guilty and consumed by curiosity, Tessa stepped inside. The house had been built for use by the ranch foreman in the days when the Flying Ace boasted a full complement of hands. Outside, the house was plain as a cardboard box, unadorned by any attempt at embellishment. The interior followed the same pattern. The front door opened directly into the living room, which was square and plainly furnished with items that appeared to have been chosen for comfort rather than style.

Glancing at the sofa, Tessa decided that it might have originally been upholstered in a crisp black-and-tan plaid. Time had faded the colors to a blur of undecided grays. Sitting at right angles to it was a big overstuffed chair covered in a fabric that defied description. Across from both sofa and chair was an aluminum stand with crooked legs that held a television and VCR. A boxy wooden coffee table sat in front of the sofa, and sitting on top of it was a laptop computer, a kaleidoscopic pattern drifting across the opened screen. Its sleek high-tech lines were at odds with the Spartan simplicity of its surroundings. Tessa stared at it curiously for a moment, but there were other things tugging for her attention.

The kitchen wasn't hard to find. Even had the house been large, she would have had only to follow her nose and the unmistakable scent of frying onions. Like the rest of the house, the room was small. The two men seemed to fill all the available free space as they worked companionably. Jace stood at the stove, watching over a pair of skillets, while Keefe stood in front of a narrow slice of counter, his back to her, blocking her view of his task.

''I think we should—'' Jace broke off in midword as he looked up and saw her standing in the doorway. ''Tessa!''

His partner's startled exclamation made Keefe turn abruptly. He stared at his bride in disbelief, his fingers tightening over the thin-bladed knife he'd been using to cut thick slices of tomato.

"Tessa! What are you doing here?"

"There was a phone call," she answered automatically. "Pete Rutherford wanted you to know that the new mare is arriving tomorrow morning. It sounded important, so I thought I'd let you know."

"It wasn't *that* important." Keefe set the knife on the counter.

"You didn't have to come all the way over here," Jace added.

"I knocked," Tessa said, as if it were significant. "You didn't answer, and I thought I smelled something cooking...." Her voice trailed off as she looked around the kitchen.

"We...ah...thought we'd have a little snack," Jace said weakly.

"You just ate dinner," she said, staring in disbelief at the thick hamburgers sizzling on the stove. "You said you liked my soup."

"It was great soup," Keefe said instantly. "The chicken broth and all those vegetables and...and stuff." He stumbled over the description, aware that there hadn't been much in the way of "stuff" in the bowls.

"And those were just about the best rolls I've ever eaten," Jace added, coming to his partner's aid.

"Croissants," Tessa said absently as she looked around the tiny kitchen. A bag of hamburger buns lay open on the counter, puffy rounds of cheap white bread.

"Croissants. That's what I meant to say. They were great croissants." Jace rolled panicked eyes in Keefe's direction.

"And the salad was real good," Keefe said, rising to the occasion. "I bet you could make a fortune with that dressing. It was...real good."

His voice trailed off as Tessa finished inventorying the kitchen and looked at him. The bewilderment in those big blue eyes made him feel as guilty as a kid caught shoplifting candy bars at the local market.

"If you liked everything so much, why are you here, less than half an hour later, making hamburgers?"

"I..." He looked at Jace, but Jace only shrugged. He was all out of clever explanations. "We were sort of still hungry," Keefe admitted finally.

"There was more soup," Tessa said.

"Yeah, and it was great soup," Jace said earnestly. "But there wasn't much stuff in it."

"Stuff? What kind of stuff?"

"Meat," Keefe said.

"Macaroni, maybe," Jace added helpfully.

"It was a vegetable soup. You don't put meat and macaroni in a vegetable soup."

It was best to make a clean breast of it, Keefe decided. He drew a deep breath and then let it out slowly. "The thing is, Tessa, vegetables just don't seem to keep you filled up when you're chasing down a balky cow or digging a posthole."

Tessa looked around the kitchen while she digested his words. She thought about all the times Keefe had left the house after supper, saying he wanted to check something in the barn or needed to talk to Jace about something.

"Have you been doing this all along? Eating at the house and then coming over here to eat more?"

Their guilty expressions answered the question without words.

"I haven't been cooking enough all along?"

"You cook plenty," Keefe assured her, throwing logic to the winds. "It's just that, working outside the way we do, we burn a lot of calories."

Of course they did, she thought, staring at the enormous hamburgers still sizzling on the stove. They spent their days doing hard physical labor. It was natural that they'd need more calories than someone who sat at a desk all day. She should have thought of that. *Why didn't you think of that? Are you stupid, Tessa? Stupid, stupid, stupid.* She seemed to hear the mocking echo of Bobby's voice, telling her she was worthless, belittling her, making her feel as stupid as he said she was.

"Why didn't you say something?" she asked.

There was a moment of silence, and then Keefe sighed. "We were afraid of you."

"Afraid?" It was the last answer she'd have expected. She gaped at him in disbelief, missing the startled look Jace shot in his direction. "Of me?"

"It was the knife," he admitted.

"Knife? What knife?"

"That butcher knife. I've seen what you can do to a carrot with that thing." He shook his head. "I wasn't about to cross you."

"Cross me?" Tessa felt as if she'd just stumbled into a scene in a movie and her script was different from everyone else's.

''Any woman who can handle a knife like that is someone to walk lightly around,'' Jace said solemnly, following Keefe's lead. ''And the scissors.'' He shuddered. ''I saw you lop one of those little chickens in half without even flinching.''

''Little chickens?'' Tessa stared at him, scrambling to keep up with the conversation. ''The game hens?''

''Yeah. One minute, they were whole. The next, you had 'em hacked in two. It made my blood run cold.''

''A woman who can do that to a chicken demands a certain amount of respect from a man,'' Keefe added. ''It takes a braver man than I am to risk provoking someone like that.''

''That's ridiculous!''

''Easy for you to say,'' Jace said indignantly ''You were holding the scissors. It's easy to be brave when you're armed.''

''Armed? With poultry shears?'' Tessa gaped at him.

''I've heard that there are states where you have to register to buy a pair,'' Keefe said darkly.

She looked from Keefe to Jace and back again. They couldn't be serious. ''*Register* poultry shears?''

''In Nebraska, you have to a have a license to carry them,'' Jace said, deadpan. ''And if you're caught dueling with them, you go straight to the big house.''

''Dueling with poultry shears?'' Tessa felt laughter bubble up in her throat.

''Sure.'' Keefe's expression remained solemn, but his eyes gave him away. ''Many a promising young life has ended in tragedy.''

''Snipped in the bud?'' Tessa asked.

''That's awful.'' Jace's pained expression was the final straw.

''Sorry.'' But she spoiled the apology by giggling. Laughter drowned out the last echoes of Bobby's ugly words. The knowledge that, for weeks, Keefe and Jace had been cooking behind her back, like a pair of children sneaking cookies from a forbidden jar, all to avoid the risk of hurting her feelings, left no room for old hurts and insecurities. Looking at Keefe and Jace, she felt a warm rush of affection. And if her feelings for Keefe ran much deeper, that secret was hers alone.

Chapter 11

In a more merciful world, no woman would have to endure the heat of summer while eight and a half months pregnant. Tessa contemplated the injustice of it as she walked across the ranch yard underneath a blazing July sun. Of course, she could save herself a considerable amount of discomfort by staying in the house, sitting in the path of the cooling breeze created by the fan Keefe had set up for her. But reading or watching TV or working on her mauled attempt at knitting provided too much time for thinking. Considering the tangled state of her life, thinking was the last thing she wanted to have time for.

So, here she was, aching back, swollen feet and all, risking heat prostration in the hope of finding something to distract her from the confused circle of her own thoughts. Keefe had ridden out right after lunch to check a section of fencing, but she'd seen Jace enter the barn a few minutes ago. Though no one had said anything, she knew that the two men were careful to arrange things so that she was never left alone. When she realized what they were doing, she'd considered telling them it wasn't necessary, but she'd been too grateful for their consideration to let pride get in the way.

Tessa sighed with relief as she stepped out of the sunlight and into the shadowy interior of the barn. It probably wasn't much cooler inside than it was outside, but the dim light lent the illusion of a lower temperature, and illusion was better than nothing. Her mouth twisted in a sudden, rueful half smile. At the moment, her whole life was a tissue of illusions.

Moving to the far end of the barn, Tessa paused on the threshold of the large, dusty room that served as storage room and workshop. Her nose twitched at the mingled scents of leather, axle grease and sawdust. Jace stood next to a scarred workbench, studying a length of wood he held. He glanced up as Tessa stepped into the room.

"I brought you a snack," she said by way of greeting.

Jace's smile faded into a grimace of mock pain. "I couldn't eat another bite. I'm still full from lunch."

"I just want to be sure you don't go hungry," she said, all wide-eyed innocence. Meals lately had been distinguished by quantity, as well as quality. There was no chance of anyone getting up from the table hungry.

"I'm going to get fat as a house," Jace complained.

But when she set down a plate of cookies, he reached for one anyway.

''I thought it was supposed to be cool in the mountains,'' Tessa said, reaching up to brush damp tendrils of hair off the back of her neck.

''Not in July.'' Jace finished the cookie and dusted his fingers against the sides of his jeans. He glanced at her, blue eyes full of understanding, as if he recognized her need for distraction. ''If you're not in the midst of something else, why don't you hang around for a while? Too much time in my own company and I start talking to myself.''

''If you don't mind.'' Tessa hoped she didn't look too pathetically grateful for the invitation. She didn't believe for an instant that Jace needed her company. Like Keefe, he was a man who was content to be alone. She shifted restlessly, pushing her thoughts in another direction. She spent more time than was wise thinking about Keefe.

''What are you working on?'' she asked, looking for distraction.

''Replacing some slats in a gate. During a portion of my misspent youth, I worked as a carpenter in Spokane,'' he said as he used a soft brush to clean sawdust off the surface he'd just sanded.

''Was that before or after you terrorized Dubuque's dark underbelly?'' Tessa perched herself on the stool that sat in front of the workbench and watched him work.

Jace frowned as if it trying to remember the correct order. ''After Dubuque, before Houston.''

''What did you do in Houston?''

"I worked in the oil fields for a few months. It was the filthiest job I ever had, but the money was good. And it was better than being a short-order cook, which is what I did immediately after Dubuque."

"From crime fighter to cook? That was a bit of a comedown, wasn't it?"

"A bit. But my car died halfway across Kansas, in a little town in the middle of a cornfield. I was flat broke and the demand for martial arts instructors was pretty low, so I took what was available."

"How long did you spend behind the grill?" She picked up a sanding block and tested the roughness of its surface with her fingertips.

"The three longest months of my life," Jace said with a shudder of remembered horror. "Trust me, compared to grilling burgers and frying eggs, working in the oil fields was a walk in the park."

"So you went to Spokane when you left Houston?"

"No." Jace shook his head. He set the brush aside and picked up a tack cloth. "After Houston, I moved to Hollywood."

"California?" Tessa gave him a surprised look as she set the sanding block down.

"The one and only."

"Were you trying to break into the movies?"

"Nope." Jace shot her an amused look. "I'll bet you've never been to Hollywood. You probably have this idea that there are movie stars sauntering down Hollywood Boulevard and casting agents lurking behind every tree."

"I'm not quite that naive," Tessa protested.

"Good, because Hollywood ain't what it used to

be.'' He stroked the tack cloth over the board, lifting the last traces of sawdust from the oak. ''I worked as a mechanic at a service station not far from the Cinerama Dome, practically in the heart of Hollywood, but the closest I ever got to the glamorous world of the silver screen was when I changed a tire for a guy who knew someone who worked as a stuntman on a Stallone film.''

Tessa giggled. ''A real brush with stardom.''

''Yeah. It had my heart doing double time,'' he said dryly. He set the tack cloth aside and ran his palm over the cleaned surface.

''So you've taught self-defense, flipped hamburgers, worked on oil rigs, been a mechanic and a carpenter, and now you're half owner of a ranch.'' Tessa ticked the occupations off on her fingers. ''Is there anything you haven't done?''

Jace appeared to give the suggestion serious consideration. ''Well, I've never hunted giant squid with a blowgun,'' he said after a moment.

''I don't think you hunt giant squid with blowguns,'' Tessa said, laughing.

He shrugged. ''Must be why I've never done it.''

''You've moved around a lot, lived in a lot of different places.''

''A few.'' He set the sanded board aside. Picking up another, shorter piece of wood, he reached for the sanding block Tessa had looked at earlier. Laying the board on the workbench, he began sanding it. ''The thing about moving on is that it can become a kind of goal in itself. You don't think much about where you're going, only that you're going somewhere.''

"The call of the road?" Tessa asked, watching him work.

"Yeah. It's almost an addiction, always wanting to find out what's over the next hill."

"Where did you meet Keefe?" she asked idly.

"At a rodeo in Santa Fe about eight years ago."

"Eight years ago? Then you knew him when he and my sister were married." Tessa hadn't even considered that possibility.

"I did."

"You knew Dana?"

"I knew her." Jace kept his attention on the sanding block, concentrating on the back-and-forth motion, sanding along the grain of the wood.

Tessa waited, but he didn't add anything to the flat statement. "I didn't see much of them the last couple of years they were married."

Jace stopped working and looked at her. "If you're wondering what happened between them, you'll have to ask Keefe."

Tessa flushed, embarrassed that she'd been so obvious. "I wasn't hinting." He arched one brow, and her flush deepened. "All right, maybe I *was* asking—kind of—but I shouldn't have been. Their marriage is none of my business."

"Well, I don't know that I'd go so far as to say it's *none* of your business, but it certainly isn't any of my business to tell you what happened. Besides, the only people who really know what happens in a marriage are the two involved in it."

"I'll bet you have a pretty good idea of what made them get a divorce," Tessa said.

Jace shrugged, his blue eyes shuttered. "I know some of it."

"Did Keefe... Do you think he loved her a great deal?" she asked.

Jace winced at her wistful tone, but he answered her honestly. "I don't think he'd have married her if he hadn't been crazy about her."

"No, he wouldn't have." She focused her attention on arranging a handful of stray nails into a precise row on the workbench. "When I was growing up, I would have sold my soul to be half as beautiful as Dana."

"At the risk of sounding like someone's maiden aunt—beauty is only skin-deep."

"Yeah, but that's as deep as men look, at least at first," Tessa pointed out without rancor. "And when a woman is as beautiful as my sister, a lot of them never look any farther."

Jace straightened away from the workbench and looked directly at her. "If you're worried that Keefe is still in love with Dana, forget it."

"I don't have any right to be worried." But the unsteadiness of her fingers as she continued tidying the nails belied her dismissive tone.

"I don't know that feelings and rights have much to do with one another."

"Maybe not." She sighed and lifted her gaze to his. "I remember the way Keefe used to look at Dana, as if she lit up a room just by entering it. He's not the kind of man who loves casually. Feelings like that aren't just going to be there one day and then gone the next."

No, but, given enough reason, they could die a slow, painful death. Jace didn't voice the thought out loud. Keefe wouldn't thank him for that kind of interference.

"Keefe and Dana have been divorced for a long time" was all he said.

Tessa forced herself to nod, as if the statement meant something. Divorce severed the legal ties, but divorce papers didn't mean an end to the emotional ties any more than a marriage license made a real marriage.

"It's none of my business," she said. "It's not like Keefe and I are really married. *Then,* I might have a right to wonder if he still loved her. But we aren't and I don't. I only wondered because I consider Keefe a good friend and I'd hate to think of him unhappy. About Dana, I mean."

She eased down from the stool, settling one hand against the swollen mound of her stomach when her feet were on solid ground again. She gave a Jace a bright smile. "Thanks for the company."

Tessa seemed unaware of the unshed tears that shimmered in her eyes, but Jace couldn't pretend not to see them. Damn Keefe for a fool, he thought as he set down the board he'd been sanding and went to her.

"Hey, what's this? I know I'm a little rough around the edges, but I don't usually drive pretty women to tears."

His chiding tone drew a watery chuckle, even as a single tear slid down the curve of her cheek. Tessa leaned her forehead against his shoulder, allowing herself a moment to grab for her rapidly dissolving self-control. Jace's gentle teasing reminded her of the way Keefe had treated her when they first met. To a lonely little girl, accustomed to being ignored, Keefe's freely given attention and ready laughter had been a revelation. She'd blossomed under his easy smile and given her heart to him with the abandon of a child.

It was a pity it had taken her so long to realize that she'd forgotten to get it back.

"Am I interrupting something?" Keefe spoke from the doorway behind Tessa, his voice coolly polite.

"Not a thing," Jace said. If Tessa was oblivious to the threat behind Keefe's cordial tone, Jace was not so unaware, but he released her in a leisurely fashion, ignoring the muscle that flexed in his partner's jaw.

"I was just being silly," Tessa said, wiping her eyes self-consciously. "Hormones, I guess. I'm sorry I sniveled on your shoulder, Jace."

"*Mi* shoulder *es su* shoulder." His words drew a watery giggle from Tessa, but Keefe's eyes remained cool.

"I should go start dinner," Tessa said, moving toward the door.

"If you don't feel like cooking, we can manage with potluck," Keefe said, the chill in his eyes replaced by concern.

"I feel fine," she said. With a quick smile, she brushed past Keefe and out the door.

He waited until the sound of her footsteps had faded away before speaking. "You want to tell me what was going on?"

Jace appeared to consider for a moment and then shook his head. "I don't think so."

A muscle twitched in Keefe's jaw and his eyes darkened with temper. "This is the second time I've found you holding Tessa."

Jace raised one eyebrow. "You keeping score?"

"I don't want to see her get hurt."

"And you think I do?"

"No, but it could happen without you meaning for it to."

Jace shook his head in disgust and reached for the board he'd been working on. "I couldn't break Tessa's heart if I wanted to."

"Meaning?"

"You figure it out."

Keefe gritted his teeth. "She's been through a lot."

One hand wrapped around the board, Jace looked across the crowded workroom at his partner. Keefe stood with his feet braced lightly apart, his hands held loosely at his sides. He looked like a man ready for a fight. Caught between amusement and irritation, Jace shook his head.

"I don't know what the hell you think is going on here. If I was planning a seduction, I'm not likely to try it with a woman who's damn near nine months pregnant. And even without that, I don't screw around with a friend's wife. You ought to remember that."

The tension eased from Keefe's shoulders as he met Jace's steady look. He *did* remember. It wasn't something he was likely to forget. He reached for his cigarettes and swallowed a curse when he remembered that he'd left them on the bureau in his room—the latest step in his attempt to give the damned things up.

"I was out of line," he said, offering the apology that was due.

"Yeah, you were," Jace agreed, without anger. He tucked a box of nails in his shirt pocket, slid a hammer into the back pocket of his jeans and lifted the boards he'd cut and sanded. "I'm going to finish up repairs on the gate. See you at supper."

Keefe nodded. He knew that, as far as Jace was concerned, the subject was closed, the brief moment of tension forgotten as if it had never occurred. It was easy enough for Jace to forget—he wasn't the one who'd made a fool of himself.

He jammed his hat on as he left the workroom and stalked the length of the barn. *Jace making a play for Tessa.* How could he have been so double-damned stupid as to think it might happen? If he'd stopped to think, even for a minute, he'd have known better. But he hadn't stopped to think. He'd seen Jace holding her and he'd bridled like a bull moose defending his harem. His first thought had been that Jace had no business putting his arms around *his* wife.

And even now, when he knew the embrace—if you could even call it that—had been perfectly innocent, there was a part of him that still resented it. He recognized the emotion roiling in the pit of his stomach for what it was—jealousy, plain and simple. Only there was nothing *simple* about it. Keefe narrowed his eyes against the glare of the late-afternoon sun as he stepped out of the barn. Where Tessa was concerned, he had no right to be jealous. No right at all.

He scowled. Damn. He'd give his right arm for a cigarette.

Keefe was lying on his back under the kitchen sink when the phone rang. Tessa had mentioned that there was a leak in the pipes under there over a week ago. He was willing to admit to himself that it was sheer guilt that was driving him to look at it tonight. He'd been way out of line this afternoon and the fact that she hadn't noticed didn't alleviate his guilt. Since he'd rather wrestle a porcupine with his bare hands than work on plumbing, he figured it was good a way as any to soothe his guilty conscience.

But that didn't keep him from feeling a definite surge of relief when the phone rang. Even talking to someone who wanted to sell him magazine subscriptions was better than confronting the mysteries of forty-year-old plumbing.

"Do you want me to get that?" Tessa asked as he scooted out from under the sink.

"You stay put. I'll get it." Gripping the edge of the counter, he levered himself to his feet. He glanced at Tessa as the phone rang a second time. She was sitting at the kitchen table, working on a grocery list. Over dinner, Jace had offered to make the drive into town the next day and pick up supplies.

"Walker," Keefe said into the receiver.

"How's life in the great outdoors?"

At the sound of his older brother's voice, Keefe's mouth curved in a smile. "Better than a poke in the eye with a sharp stick,'' he drawled. ''How's life among the criminal element?''

''Tolerable.''

Sam caught Keefe up on family news: Cole's little girl was going to camp for a week, giving Cole and Addie a chance for a delayed honeymoon; Gage and Kelsey were planning on putting up another greenhouse in the fall and hiring full-time help for Kelsey's small-scale farming enterprise; the baby was growing like a weed; and their six-year-old son had decided that he definitely wanted to be professional hang glider when he grew up.

''I didn't know there were *professional* hang gliders,'' Keefe said, grinning.

''Danny may be the first.'' Sam's laughter died away, and silence hummed along the phone lines for a moment. Keefe waited. Out the corner of his eye, he saw Tessa press her hand against the small of her back, a faint move of discomfort flickering across her face. He frowned. It wasn't the first time tonight that he'd seen her do that.

''Nikki says she told you that she can't have children.''

''She told me.''

''We haven't said anything to anyone else in the family.''

''No one's going to blame her,'' Keefe said.

''Nikki knows that. She *says* she knows it.'' There was a short silence, and when Sam spoke again, frustration put an edge in his voice. ''She just needs some time, I guess.''

Keefe's fingers tightened over the receiver. He

wondered if Sam had considered how *he* felt about not having children, but he knew his older brother well enough to know that he'd probably focused himself completely on what Nikki was going through. Sam's instinct was to protect those he loved. It would be hell for him to find himself virtually helpless to alleviate his wife's pain.

"If there's anything I can do..." he said, knowing there wasn't a damned thing anyone could do. This was something Sam and Nikki were going to have to work out together.

"Thanks." Sam changed the topic abruptly. "Have you heard anything lately from Tessa's in-laws?"

"*Former* in-laws," Keefe corrected, his tone sharp enough to catch Tessa's attention. She looked at him, her eyes questioning. He shook his head and wished he'd thought to take this call in his office. If the Mallorys were up to something, he didn't want Tessa to worry about it.

"Former in-laws," Sam agreed. "Have you heard from them?"

"No." Keefe half turned away from Tessa, but unless he wanted to whisper into the phone, there was no way to keep her from hearing his end of the conversation. "I wrote and told them about our marriage. I figured that might head any trouble off at the pass."

"Did they contact you?" Sam asked, sounding more like a cop than a brother.

"No. But I didn't exactly expect them to send a card wishing her luck. What's this about?"

"Remember me telling you that someone was making inquiries about the family, poking into old records?''

''I remember.''

''When you told me what was going on with Tessa, it seemed pretty obvious that it was the senator trying to track her down. But there's still somebody digging into old files, asking questions.''

''The Mallorys know where she is.'' Keefe frowned at a hairline crack in the wall in front of him, courtesy of one of California's many fault lines. Behind him, he could feel Tessa's anxious gaze, but he didn't have any reassurances to offer her. ''Why would they be asking about her?''

''The inquiries don't seem to have anything to do with Tessa. I only thought of her because of the problems she's had with the senator and his wife.''

''Then who are they about?'' Worry put an edge on the question.

''It's weird,'' Sam said slowly. ''Whoever it is, they're digging up old records on Shannon.''

''Shannon?'' Shock made Keefe's voice louder than he'd intended. Out the corner of his eye, he saw Tessa start, but he was too distracted to offer her reassurance. ''Why would anyone be making inquiries about Shannon?''

''I don't know.''

''Hell, it's been more than twenty years since—'' Keefe broke off, his throat suddenly tight. After all these years, it still hurt to think about it. ''Why? After all these years?''

''I don't know,'' Sam said again.

Neither of them spoke as they considered the implications.

"Do you think it could be Shannon herself?" Keefe said, the words all but dragged from him.

"She was just a baby. She wouldn't remember enough." Sam spoke roughly, to conceal how much he wanted to believe.

"She was four. That's old enough to remember."

Sam didn't argue, but he didn't agree, either. Silence hummed between them.

"Have you said anything to Mom?" Keefe asked finally.

"I haven't said anything to anyone but you. There's no point in opening up old wounds without reason."

Especially when those wounds had never really healed. But Keefe didn't say that out loud. Sam knew as well as he did what this could mean—if it meant anything at all.

"Keep me posted," Keefe said, aware that there was nothing more to say. Whatever was happening, there was nothing to do but wait and see how it all unfolded. He hung up the phone and turned around. The cupboard doors beneath the sink still gaped open, and tools were still spread out on the floor. It had been only a few minutes since he abandoned the leaky sink, but it seemed much longer than that.

"Is something wrong?" Tessa asked, when he didn't say anything. "Are the Mallorys causing problems for your family?"

"No." He was glad he could reassure her on that. "I think you've heard the last of them."

She looked doubtful but didn't contradict him. He

looked at the mess under the sink again, but he wasn't really seeing it. His mind had gone back two decades, memories flooding past barriers that had been in place so long that he rarely noticed their existence.

"Who's Shannon?"

"What?" Startled by the question, he jerked his eyes in her direction, pinning her where she sat.

"I'm sorry." Tessa flinched at his sharp tone. "I didn't mean to pry. It's none of my business." She struggled to rise, a simple task that had grown ridiculously difficult in recent weeks.

"I didn't mean to snap." Two quick strides brought him to her chair. He set one hand on her shoulder, pressing her down. "I'm sorry, Tessa."

"I shouldn't have asked—" she began, still disconcerted by his readiness to apologize when he found himself in the wrong.

"It's not a secret," he said. He leaned his hips back against the edge of the counter and slid his hands into his pockets. "Shannon was—is—my little sister."

"Your sister?" she repeated, staring at him. "I didn't know you had a sister. Where is she?"

"She was kidnapped when she was four years old. We haven't seen her in over twenty years." He made it a dry recitation of fact, as if it meant nothing to him, but Tessa saw the look in his eyes and knew the pain was still sharp and hard.

"Kidnapped?" Unconsciously she spread one hand across the heavy bulge of her stomach, as if to protect the child she carried. "Why would someone kidnap her?"

Keefe told the story in that same clipped tone,

speaking rapidly, as if he needed to get through it quickly, without giving himself time to think about it.

"About a year after my father was killed, Mom remarried. I'll spare you the gory details, but the guy was a royal bastard. He resented the hell out of the four of us, and we felt the same way about him. The marriage didn't last very long, but Mom was pregnant by then. I was thirteen and I remember resenting the baby she was carrying. I figured the kid would be a reminder of Harlan, a reminder none of us needed. But then Mom brought Shannon home from the hospital and she was…she was the most incredible thing I'd ever seen."

His smile was soft with memory, and Tessa found herself thinking about the child she carried, about what a good father Keefe would be to that child, if she decided to give it up.

"We all fell in love with her. She could wind any of us around her little finger and she knew it. We spoiled her rotten. It's a miracle she didn't turn into a brat, but she had the sweetest temperament."

"She was lucky to have all of you," Tessa said, thinking of her lonely childhood.

"We were lucky to have her. The only real fly in the ointment was that Harlan—her father—had visitation rights. He took sporadic advantage of them. He used spending time with Shannon as an excuse to see Mom. He kept trying to persuade her to let him come back but she wanted nothing to do with him. I guess he must have finally believed her. Shannon was four when he showed up unexpectedly to take her for the weekend. Gage was the only one of us home. He let Harlan take her. Hell, Harlan had the legal right to take her, and even if he hadn't, Gage was just a kid, only fifteen years old. Harlan never brought her back."

In the silence that followed, Tessa heard the soft *plink* of water dripping into the pan set to catch the drips from the leaky pipe under the sink. Somewhere outside, an owl hooted, a note of lonely inquiry in the sound.

"Didn't you… Wasn't there anything the police could do?"

"They did what they could." He lifted one shoulder in a half shrug. "It's just not that hard for a man to disappear with a child. Harlan was a bastard but he wasn't stupid. And he was a cop. He knew exactly how to go about disappearing."

"I can't imagine how hard it must have been on your mother—on all of you," Tessa said, her hand still cradling the child she had not yet made up her mind to accept into her heart.

"It was about as rough as it gets," Keefe admitted. "For a long time, our lives revolved around finding Shannon. But time goes by and life continues and you learn to put all the questions and fear in a compartment somewhere in your head and lock them away there. Otherwise, you go crazy."

"Yes, I imagine you would," she murmured, thinking of how terrible it would be not to know if your child was safe—or even still alive. Her fingers shifted against her stomach as it occurred to her that, if she gave up this baby, she'd be putting herself in exactly that position. She wondered, yet again, if she could do it.

Keefe's sleep that night was restless, punctuated by tangled dreams of Tessa, Shannon, and an endlessly dripping pipe that couldn't be fixed, no matter what he did. He woke abruptly, a headache pounding at his temples and his heart beating much too quickly. For an instant, he didn't know what had awakened him, but then the sound came again.

"Keefe?" It was Tessa's voice, high and thin.

He sat up in bed. She was standing in the doorway, and for a moment he wondered if he was still asleep and this was part of some new dream.

"What's wrong?" His voice was raspy with sleep.

"I'm sorry to wake you," Tessa said apologetically. "But I think it's time."

"Time?" He blinked at her. "Time for what?"

"For the baby to be born."

"It can't be," he protested blankly. "It's not due for two weeks."

"Tell that to the baby. My water just broke."

"Oh, my God." The words were more prayer than exclamation.

Chapter 12

"It's going to be all right," Keefe said, taking his eyes off the road long enough to give Tessa a reassuring smile. "You're going to be fine."

It was, by conservative estimate, the tenth time he'd told her that in the twenty minutes since she told him the baby was on the way. His initial reaction had been denial. Once convinced that the baby not only *could* be on the way but actually *was* on the way, he'd immediately told her not to worry, she was going to be fine. And he'd kept telling her that as he dragged on his clothes, grabbed the overnight case she'd packed a few days before and herded her out to the truck. He'd all but lifted her into the cab and then asked if she'd be okay while he let Jace know what was happening. He hadn't even cracked a smile when Tessa told him that she didn't think she was likely to give birth in the next two or three minutes.

She'd never seen Keefe thrown so completely off balance. At another time, she might have enjoyed seeing such a classic example of male panic. As it was, she had other things on her mind. Tessa dug her fingernails into the unyielding plastic of the truck's armrest and breathed her way through a contraction.

''We're almost there,'' he said as the contraction eased and she drew a deep breath.

In fact, they were still quite a ways from the hospital, but she decided it would be unkind to point that out. He was trying so hard to reassure her. The funny thing was, she didn't really need to be reassured. Now that the moment was here, she felt remarkably calm. The same could not be said of Keefe.

''It's going to be all right,'' he said again. Keefe knew he was repeating himself. His hand tightened over the steering wheel and he resisted the urge to push the gas pedal down even farther. He was already driving as fast as was safe. He glanced at the illuminated dial of the clock on the dashboard.

''How far apart are the contractions?''

''There's plenty of time,'' Tessa said, sounding ridiculously cool. ''I'm not going to have the baby in your truck.''

''God, no!'' The exclamation popped out, his tone horrified.

Tessa's chuckle was a little ragged around the edges, but the fact that she could laugh at all astonished him so much that he hardly noticed. ''Not in the mood to deliver a baby tonight?''

''Don't even joke about it,'' he pleaded, but his

hands relaxed their death grip on the steering wheel. He shot her a quick look. "How are you, really?"

"I'm fine. Really," she added, when he looked doubtful. "I'm just anxious to get this over with." She stared out the windshield at the night-dark road, frowning a little as she tried to sort out what she was feeling. "In a way, my life has been on hold for the last few months. I haven't been able to make any plans or decisions until the baby was born."

"What kind of plans and decisions?" Talking might help to distract her, he thought. And he wouldn't mind if it did the same for him.

"I don't know." She shot him a quick, self-conscious smile. "I guess I should have some idea of what I want to do, but I don't, really."

"You don't have to decide anything right away."

Tessa knew he was referring to the agreement they'd made when he asked her to marry him—that he would take the baby if she decided to give it up. When they made that bargain, she'd been more than half-sure that she knew what her decision would be. No child could hope for a better father than Keefe, so her conscience would be clear. She could walk away, finally put her marriage to Bobby behind her and pick up the pieces of her life.

Funny, that idea didn't hold as much appeal as it once had.

From the moment she realized that she was pregnant, Tessa had done her best to avoid thinking about how she might feel when the baby was born. She'd considered, in a detached sort of way, whether or not she should give the child up for adoption, she'd even allowed herself to wonder whether or not she'd be *able* to give it up, but she hadn't allowed herself to really *think* about how she was going to feel about the child she'd carried under her heart for nine months.

But no amount of thinking could have prepared her for the moment when she held her child for the first time. Looking down at him, she was awed by his tiny perfection, frightened by his fragility, terrified of his dependence on her. Everything he would be, all he would become—it all began this minute. And the decisions she made in the next few weeks would impact the rest of his life.

The weight of responsibility settled on her like a band around her chest, slowly tightening, threatening to cut off her air. She actually felt light-headed. She wasn't ready for this. She would never be ready for this. After the mess she'd made of her own life, it was a terrible, frightening joke that she should find herself responsible for this new, perfect life.

Tessa lifted her head and stared around the sterile hospital room with eyes that saw nothing but the yawning emptiness that had opened up in front of her. She couldn't do this. It was mistake, a huge mistake. Someone had to do something, had to—

"Tessa?"

Keefe's deep voice sliced through the choking layers of panic. Her head jerked toward him, her heart thumping against her breastbone, sheer terror in her eyes.

''Keefe.'' His name came out on a gasp. The hand she extended to him was unsteady. In her panic, she'd forgotten that she wasn't alone.

''Hey.'' His fingers closed, warm and strong, over hers. ''It's okay.''

Tessa wanted to tell him that it wasn't okay, that she didn't think it would ever be okay again. She opened her mouth to say as much—or maybe just to whimper in terror—and then her eyes met his. His gaze was calm and steady, offering a quiet reassurance that dampened her rising panic.

''It's okay,'' he said again.

It occurred to her that he might have used the same tone to soothe a fractious mare. The idea struck her as funny, and the fear receded another notch. Leaning back against the pillows, she closed her eyes for a moment, still shaky but starting to regain her balance. When she looked at him again, she was able to smile a little.

''I'm all right,'' she said, and hoped she wasn't lying.

''A little overwhelming, isn't he?'' Keefe said. Tessa followed his gaze and looked down at the baby. A wave of fear surged through her, but the steady feel of Keefe's hand on hers made it easier to control. He stroked the baby's cheek with the tip of one finger. Next to the baby's head, his hand seemed massive.

''He's so helpless,'' she whispered. It was as close as she could come to articulating her fear. ''What if I do something wrong?''

''You won't.''

She didn't know whether to be flattered or appalled by his easy confidence. She only wished she could share it.

If Keefe had ever believed in love at first sight, his first marriage had served to drum that foolishness out of him. Love—real love—was something that grew from familiarity.

And then he held Tessa's child for the first time.

A sleepy, frowning, red-faced infant with a few wisps of pale hair perched on top of a head misshapen from the birthing process, the newborn had all the beauty of a wizened old man. Keefe looked down at the boy, felt the fragility of a life that fit in his two hands, and the world shifted around him. Unfocused, vague blue eyes peered up at him, and one hand escaped the soft yellow blanket to wave aimlessly in the air.

"Hey, how you doin'?" He spoke softly, his voice husky with unexpected emotion. The baby immediately stopped squirming and stared up at him, his gaze intent. "So, what do you think of the world so far?"

He continued to talk, carrying on a nonsensical one-sided conversation that would have made him feel faintly embarrassed if he overheard it from someone else, but the baby stared up at him as if fascinated by every word, and Keefe's heart dropped right into his fingers.

They named the baby David Tyler. David for Keefe's father and Tyler because Tessa liked the sound of it. She was startled when Keefe suggested his father's name—startled and a little uneasy.

"I'm not trying to push you into any decisions," Keefe said, reading her hesitation. "I just kind of liked the idea. But if you'd rather not, that's okay."

"No, I think David is a good name." It was a straightforward name, a solid name, reflecting the kind of person she hoped he'd become. She gave Keefe an uncertain look. "What if... I mean, you might have a son of your own someday."

Something flickered in his eyes, an emotion there and gone too quickly for her to identify. Hurt? Anger? Whatever it was, it was gone in less than a heartbeat, leaving his expression unreadable.

"Whatever happens, whatever you decide, I'd like him to have my father's name."

What have I done? Tessa wondered. The bargain they'd made a few weeks ago suddenly seemed full of pitfalls. If she decided to keep the baby, Keefe was going to get the short end of the stick. And if she decided to give him up? Her fingers curled into the soft blanket that swaddled him. She wasn't ready to think about that. One thing at a time.

She smiled at Keefe and hoped her eyes didn't reveal the turmoil she felt. "I'd like to name him David, if you're sure."

"I'm sure."

So, the name David Tyler Walker was put on the birth certificate. Keefe was listed as his father, and the lie he'd told the Mallorys became legal.

The truck rattled across the cattle guard, the wheels kicking up a cloud of dust on the dirt road beyond. Tessa leaned forward, anxious for the first glimpse of the ranch house. It seemed like weeks since Keefe had driven her to the hospital.

"Not much has changed in the last couple of days," Keefe said, smiling at her eagerness.

She laughed and sat back against the seat. "I didn't think it would have. I'm just anxious to get home."

Home. Tessa was surprised at how easily the word came to her. Looking out at the land and the mountains that rose up on every side, she realized that, though she'd lived on the Flying Ace for just a few weeks, it already felt more like home than the house she'd shared with Bobby for four years. For that matter, it felt more like home than the pseudo-southern Gothic mansion in which she'd been raised.

The realization was a little frightening. This wasn't her home, she reminded herself. She was likely to get hurt if she let herself forget that.

But the sobering reminder was not enough to dampen the pleasure she felt when the house came into sight. There was nothing elegant or refined about it, but its almost stark simplicity was more than half its charm, as far as she was concerned. There was something reassuring about the plain lines of it.

"Home at last," Keefe said as he stopped the truck in front of the house.

"Home at last," Tessa echoed, her heart in the words.

You've got to make a choice soon, she told herself as she saw Jace loping toward them. She had no claim on this place, on these two men. Forever had never been part of the bargain, and the longer she dragged things out, the harder it was going to be on all of them.

And then Jace was pulling open the door of the truck and smiling at her. "Welcome home."

Soon, she promised. *I'll make a decision soon.*

Chapter 13

Keefe paused in the doorway to Tessa's room. He was hot and dirty, but the crib was a more powerful lure than the prospect of a shower. He crossed the room quietly and peered over the rail of the crib. His face creased in a smile when he saw that David was awake.

"Hey, kid. How you doin'?" The baby's round face lit up, his blue eyes sparkling. Keefe reached in to take one little hand between his thumb and forefinger and shake it gently. "I guess your mom thinks you're asleep, huh?"

David babbled a response, his legs pumping. Clad only in a diaper, his whole body seemed to quiver with excitement. His mother might remain firm about not picking him up, but he knew Keefe couldn't resist temptation. At almost two months old, he had a pretty good handle on the people who formed his small world. His mother's hands were the softest, but she was more likely to insist on nap time being used for napping. The two men, on the other hand, could be counted on to pick him up.

''Figure me for a sucker, don't you?'' Keefe murmured. His smile became a grin when David's legs pumped harder and his mouth widened in a damp, toothless smile. He gurgled with pleasure when Keefe's big hands slid under him. He waved his arms to show his approval as he was lifted from his crib and cradled against a broad chest.

Keefe held him with easy confidence. He'd always been fairly comfortable around babies. He and his brothers had helped take care of their infant sister, and when Cole's wife left him with a newborn daughter, the whole family had pitched in to help care for Mary. Those experiences had helped prepare him for the practical aspects of taking care of a baby. He could change a diaper, warm a bottle or manage a bath. None of that had prepared him for what it would be like to hold a child and think of him as your own. And whatever happened in the future, he considered this child his.

David gurgled happily, one hand waving as if to emphasize some point he was making.

''Hey, don't make too much noise,'' Keefe cautioned. ''If your mom catches us, she'll have my head.'' David chuckled—a fat baby sound of contentment that made Keefe grin. He bounced the child gently in his arms. ''I bet you think it would be funny to see your Mom come after me with a frying pan. You'd like that, wouldn't you?''

To Tessa, standing in the doorway, the two of them were a picture-perfect image of father and son. She'd been on her way in to check on David when she heard Keefe talking. She had tiptoed closer, smiling at Keefe's easy conversational tone. He never talked baby talk. Instead, he talked to David much the same way he would have talked to another adult. And David always seemed to watch and listen so carefully that there were times when Tessa half believed he understood every word.

Her smile slowly faded as she watched them together. Keefe held the baby so easily, his big hands cradling him with gentle care. He was a natural father. What was more, he was *David's* father, in every way that mattered. From the moment David was put in his arms, there had seemed to be a connection between them, a bond that had nothing to do with blood ties and everything to do with ties of the heart. She didn't pretend to understand it, but she knew it was real and true.

She backed away from the door, leaving the two of them their privacy.

Shaken by the sweet scene, Tessa went back to the kitchen. Seeing Keefe with the baby had forced her to face something she'd been trying to avoid. Since David's birth, she'd been letting time drift by, not thinking about the past or the future, just living from day to day. It had been so easy to do, so easy to think only of the moment. For the first few weeks, just taking care of David had absorbed all her time and energy. But that excuse only went so far. The truth was, she hadn't thought about the future because she didn't *want* to think about it.

Tessa opened the refrigerator and stared blankly at its contents. Keefe loved David, and David adored him. It shamed her to admit but Keefe had fallen in love with her child before she had. It had taken her a little while to work her way past old memories and old anger. Gradually she'd stopped thinking of Bobby when she looked at her baby and she'd begun to see him as a person in his own right. It seemed impossible that this perfect, happy baby had come out of the unhappiness of her marriage. And yet here he was, and she loved him.

Tessa shut the refrigerator without having taken anything from it. She turned and looked around the tidy kitchen without seeing it. Keefe loved David, too. How could she possibly separate them? But she couldn't give up her child. It seemed incredible that she'd ever thought she could.

She couldn't give him up, but she couldn't take him away from Keefe. She couldn't go, but she couldn't stay. That hadn't been a part of their bargain.

Hearing the shower come on, she knew Keefe must have put David back down. It was almost time for dinner. She lifted the lid off the slow cooker and poked a fork into a piece of beef, checking it for tenderness. It seemed incredible to her that, with the weather as hot as it was, Jace and Keefe could still want meat-and-potatoes meals, but they did. Her one venture into the world of pasta salads had been greeted with almost comical dismay. They'd eaten it, pronounced it delicious and then asked where the meat was.

Remembering that, Tessa smiled a little. At least they had been able to tell her the truth. She took that as a sign that she was a different person from the frightened woman who had arrived here all those months ago. Her smile faded as she set the lid back on the slow cooker and went to check the rolls she had warming in the oven. She was different. She had gained confidence, grown as a person. She had changed. Maybe it was time her bargain with Keefe changed, too.

Her teeth worried her lower lip as she considered the possibility. Though she'd hardly been aware of it, the idea had been floating around in the back of her head for the past couple of weeks. What if they changed the bargain, made a new one? Did she have the courage to suggest it?

Tessa sighed as she eased her hand through the mass of thorny canes and slid the blades of the pruning shears around the base of a dead cane. A quick snip and it was cut. She released her breath on a sigh of relief. One down and approximately a zillion to go, she thought as she started backing out of the shrub.

It didn't take a person with a green thumb to know that the roses hadn't been pruned since sometime before the Flood. The bushes were huge, unruly masses of thorns and flowers. Her knowledge of gardening was minimal, but it was enough to suggest that the dead canes should be removed before any attempt was made to tame the rest of the bush.

With that in mind, she'd put David in his carrier and settled him in a patch of shade, where he'd promptly gone to sleep, leaving her free to tackle the roses. Her attempts to cut the canes from above had been only marginally successful. She'd finally thrown dignity to the winds and crawled underneath the bush so that she could cut the dead canes out right at the base of the plant.

Tessa was halfway out from under the bush when she felt something catch at the back of her T-shirt. She twisted her body, trying to dislodge it, but it clung with a tenacity possible only in thorns and small children with sticky fingers. Lying on her belly, she tried to reach her hand around to get hold of the offending cane, but she couldn't get to it, no matter how she twisted and turned. It seemed as if, the more she tried to get loose, the tighter the cane gripped her shirt. She was just starting to think that she was going to become living mulch for the shrub when rescue arrived.

"I've heard of people getting caught up in their work, but I've never seen anyone put quite such a literal interpretation on it."

"Jace! Thank heavens. I'm stuck."

"No kidding."

She could tell by the tone of his voice that he was grinning at her predicament, but he was welcome to laugh all he wanted as long as he untangled her. He crouched down beside her, and she felt a tug against her shirt as he loosened the cane's hold.

"I think you can make a break for it now," he said after a moment.

"Thanks," Tessa said as she slid the rest of the

way out from under the bush. "I was starting to think I was going to become a permanent part of the landscape."

"And a lovely addition you'd make," Jace said. He released the offending cane and rose to his feet, reaching down to give her a hand up.

"What are you doing home?" Tessa asked as she brushed herself off. "I thought you were supposed to be doing something with the cattle."

"Something with the cattle?" Jace grinned. "That leaves a lot of room for interpretation. Could you be more specific?"

"No," she admitted with a sheepish smile. "I wasn't really paying much attention when Keefe told me you were going to be gone most of the day."

"You're forgiven," he said generously. "We were going to be gone, but my horse pulled up lame, so I brought him home."

"Are you going back out?"

"Nope." He moved over to the baby's carrier and crouched down beside it. "By the time I got there, it would be time to start back. Keefe said he'd finish up what he could and then head in."

Tessa brushed a lock of hair back from her damp forehead and looked at the pile of prunings with satisfaction. There was still a lot of work that needed to be done, but she'd made a start. Maybe in the spring she could— She cut the thought short. *In the spring.* As if she'd still be here then.

"Hey, look who's waking up!" Jace said, and she turned, grateful for the distraction. David blinked sleepy blue eyes and gave Jace a friendly smile, acknowledging the presence of one of his favorite slaves.

"He sure is growing fast," Jace commented, grinning down at the him. "Pretty soon, he'll be ready for his own pony."

If we're here long enough, Tessa thought.

"You're very good with him," she said aloud, trying to distract herself from thinking too much about the future. "That doesn't exactly fit in with the bachelor image."

"I was married once." Jace poked David's stomach with one gentle finger and was rewarded by a gurgle of laughter. "We had a child."

"What?" Tessa stared at him, her eyes wide with shock. "You have a child?"

"Had," he corrected quietly. He brushed his finger against the baby's cheek and then stood up. He looked at Tessa, and she had the distinct impression that he wished his words had gone unsaid, but she couldn't simply pretend she hadn't heard him.

"Had?" Tessa repeated faintly.

"There was a car accident. A blowout, the car went out of control. It wasn't anybody's fault." He looked past her, his expression uncharacteristically grim. "She was two."

Tessa stared at him, at a loss for words. There didn't seem to be anything that could be said. "I'm sorry" seemed hopelessly banal but, in the end, it was all she had to offer.

"I'm sorry, Jace."

"Me, too," he whispered, speaking more to himself

than to her. He shook his head, as if physically shaking off the memories. "It was a long time ago."

But Tessa saw the shadows behind his smile. "What about your wife? Was she—" She broke off, uncertain how to phrase the question. But Jace answered without forcing her to find the right words.

"Her injuries were minor—the physical ones, anyway. We were divorced a few months after the accident, and I haven't seen her since. Like I said, it was a long time ago." He glanced down at David, who was contentedly waving one hand in front of his face. "I haven't told anyone about that in a long time," he said, sounding surprised that he'd done so now.

"I don't know what I'd do if anything happened to him," Tessa said, looking at David. She shivered, suddenly cool, despite the late-afternoon warmth.

"At first you wish you'd died with them." Jace spoke slowly, almost as if talking to himself. "After a while, you figure out that a part of you *did* die. And then you start picking up the pieces and going on with your life." He looked at her and smiled, and Tessa thought the shadows had receded a little further. "There's not much point in doing anything else. You can't just stop loving people. You have to take chances. You might as well be dead if you don't."

Tessa thought about what he'd said long after he'd gone. She thought about it while she combed bits of leaves and pine needles out of her hair and changed into clean clothes. She thought about it while she gave David his bath and she considered it while she cooked dinner. *You can't just stop loving people.* Jace's words replayed themselves in her mind. *You have to take chances.*

She looked at Keefe as he came in for dinner, saw the strength in him, the gentleness. She thought of the way he'd opened his home to her, of the way he'd accepted David as his own. She thought of the way he'd held her when she cried, of the times he'd kissed her, of the way he'd helped her regain her confidence, her self-respect.

"Dinner smells good," Keefe said as he walked through the kitchen.

Tessa murmured some response and watched him disappear through the opposite door, on his way to take a shower.

You have to take chances.

Jace was right—but did she have the courage to take this particular chance?

"Could I talk to you?"

There was a tense edge in Tessa's voice that had Keefe's fingers tightening around the edges of the magazine he was reading. He didn't have to look at her to know that her eyes were anxious. He'd caught that look in her eyes often enough in the past few days. He knew what she wanted to talk about. She was going to tell him that their bargain was coming to an end. She was ready to take David and leave.

It took a conscious effort to loosen his grip on the magazine and look at her. He thought of all the reasons he could give her that she should stay, all the logical arguments about why it would be best for her and the baby, but he didn't say anything. He could probably persuade her to stay, but he wouldn't. He would stick to the bargain they'd made, and deal with the emptiness in his own life after she was gone.

"What's on your mind?" he asked, his easy tone revealing nothing of what he was thinking.

Tessa bit her lip and looked away. Why had she started this? There was no reason they couldn't go on just the way they had been. Everybody was happy with the arrangement, weren't they? But she knew it wasn't that simple.

"David is two months old now," she said, her carefully thought-out speech forgotten.

"He's growing like a weed," Keefe said, smiling a little. But his eyes were dark and watchful, and Tessa felt the knot in her stomach twist a little tighter.

"We... I don't think either of us planned to just let things go this long without coming to some sort of decision. About what to do about...David. I mean." Her voice trailed off. She was making a mess of it, she thought.

"I don't remember setting any schedules," Keefe said slowly.

"No, but you know we didn't plan this." She twisted her fingers together in front of her.

At another time, the familiar gesture might have made Keefe smile. Right now, all it did was make him think of how much he was going to miss her when she left—how much he was going to miss both of them.

"I didn't mean to let things go this long," she continued without looking at him. "I thought, when the baby was born, that I'd know right away...how I felt and what to do. But there seemed to be so much to do and so much to learn and time just drifted by and now it's been two months and you love David and he adores you. Any fool can see that. And I know I haven't been fair to you."

Keefe stood up and crossed the living room with long, restless strides, stopping next to a window to look out into the darkness. He'd seen this coming, but damned if it wasn't hurting even more than he'd expected. How the hell was he supposed to let the two of them go?

"Let me worry about what's fair to me," he said, turning to look at her. "If you're thinking you have to take David and leave to protect my feelings, you're wrong."

"That's not it. Well, that *is* it. In a way. Kind of." Tessa caught herself and stopped. Another thirty seconds and she was going to be babbling like an idiot. She'd thought this out so carefully, but it wasn't going the way she'd planned. Drawing a deep breath, she started over. "I thought that—this arrangement has been working pretty well so far, hasn't it?"

"Yes." Keefe left the window and moved toward her. The conversation wasn't going the way he'd expected. He sank down on the arm of the chair, putting himself at eye level with her, and waited for her to continue.

"You're good with David. It doesn't seem to make any difference to you that he's not...yours."

"I think of him as mine."

"You said that you didn't think it was likely that you'd marry again. Is that still true?"

"I guess so," he said slowly. *Where was she going with this?*

"I don't think I am, either—likely to marry again, that is."

"Okay." Keefe waited. Obviously, she had some reason for starting this discussion other than a desire to reconfirm their future marital prospects. But if she did, she didn't seem in any hurry to tell him what it was. She stood there, her fingers twisted together, her eyes fixed somewhere around his collarbone, and looked as if she wished she were somewhere else.

"Tessa?" He waited until she lifted her eyes reluctantly to his. "What are you getting at?"

She stared at him a moment, her blue eyes so big and scared that she made him think of a rabbit mesmerized by a rattlesnake. Just when he thought she was never going to speak again, she drew in a short, choppy breath and then released the words so rapidly that they nearly tumbled over each other.

"I thought, since *you* don't want to get married and *I* don't want to get married but we already are—married, that is—that maybe we could stay that way. Married, I mean."

Chapter 14

Keefe stared at her blankly while he tried to sort through what she'd said to come up with what she'd *meant.* Because she couldn't have meant what he thought she'd said. But no matter how he turned it over, it came down to the same thing.

"You're suggesting that we make our marriage permanent?"

Tessa nodded. Now that it was out in the open, she'd run out of words.

"For David's sake?" he asked.

"Yes. Well, mostly." She flushed and looked away. "For me, too, I guess. I...like it here. For the first time in my life, I feel at home. I suppose that sounds stupid, considering this isn't my home."

"No. This is your home for as long as you want it to be."

"Thank you." She reached up to smooth an invisible strand of hair back from her face and then let her hand drop to her side, wishing she'd had the foresight to wear something with pockets. Pockets would have provided her with a place to put her hands. As it was, they just seemed to hang at the end of her arms, with nothing to do. She linked her fingers together in front of her and drew a deep breath.

"It seems to me that we've all rubbed along pretty well together these last few months—you and me and Jace."

"Let's leave Jace out of it." He made a sharp gesture of dismissal. "This is between you and me."

"Okay." Tessa swallowed and reformulated her thoughts. She'd half thought of leaning on the idea that the four of them—Keefe and Jace and David and herself—formed a family of sorts. She began again.

"Well, it seems to me that we've done pretty well together. I don't know much about ranching, but I do know how to take care of a house. The cooking and cleaning and things." She waved one hand in a vague gesture to indicate what went into taking care of a house.

"We're not talking about me hiring you as a housekeeper," Keefe said gently.

"No, I know. But I'm just trying to point out some of the reasons we might consider... And there's David," she added, feeling on firm ground at last. "You love him."

"Very much," Keefe agreed. He shifted position, bracing his feet on the floor in front of the chair as he reached for her hands. "Come here."

Her movements stiff, Tessa let him draw her forward until she stood between his knees. She kept her eyes down, focusing on their joined hands. He had strong hands, she thought, with long fingers and broad palms, callused by hard work. They were the kind of hands that made a woman feel as if he could take care of her, keep her safe.

"Tessa?" He waited until she reluctantly lifted her eyes to his face. "Are you talking about a real marriage?"

"Real?" Her eyes widened, and her fingers jerked in his. "You mean, we would—"

"Share a room. Sleep together. Make love. Maybe even have another child someday." Keefe filled in the words she couldn't seem to get out. "Is that the kind of marriage you were talking about?"

Tessa stared at him, her expression blank with shock, her mind reeling at the images he'd created. Sharing a room with Keefe, making love with him, having his child.

Oh, my.

"You're thinking of this as being a permanent marriage, as in forever?" he prompted.

"Y-yes."

"Did you plan on both of us spending the rest of our lives celibate?" he asked gently.

"Of course not." The truth was, she hadn't given it any thought at all. She'd been so busy thinking of other things that she hadn't even thought about...that. She cleared her throat and tried to look casual. "I... Of course, I assumed it would be a real marriage."

"Did you?" His rueful smile called her a liar, and Tessa blushed.

"I didn't really think much about that part of it," she admitted.

"Well, think about it now. There's a lot more to a marriage than taking care of a house or even loving a child."

"I know that."

"Would it be so hard to think about sharing a bed with me?" he asked softly. His thumbs brushed across the backs of her hands, raising goose bumps all the way up her arms.

"It's not that. I just haven't thought about...*that.*"

"That?" He repeated the word with her emphasis, and his gently mocking tone dragged a faint smile from her. But it faded as old anxieties washed over her.

"Actually, I'm not very good at...at it," she admitted in a rush.

"How do you know?"

"How do I know?" *What kind of question was that? How did he think she knew?* "I just know. That's all."

Keefe nodded, his expression thoughtful. "I don't suppose your late husband might have anything to do with you knowing that you're not good at 'it'?" Her guilty start gave him the answer. He nodded. "And, of course, we've already established that he was never wrong about anything."

"It's not just what he said," Tessa protested, goaded by his dry tone of voice. "It's not something that you need someone else to tell you. I'm just not very good at...at sex. All right?"

"All right." He nodded agreeably. "We can worry

about that later. Let's see what we have so far. I'd be a good father to David. You would take good care of the house. And we would share a bed, even though you're not very good at sex.'' He tightened his fingers over hers to prevent her convulsive attempt to pull away. ''Am I forgetting something?''

Summed up like that, it seemed like a pretty flimsy basis for a marriage, and Tessa felt her heart sink.

''We could make it work,'' she said, a thread of desperation in her voice. ''I know it doesn't sound like a lot, but I know we could make it work.''

It was Keefe's turn to look down at their linked hands. ''It sounds like quite a bit,'' he said slowly, but before she could feel hopeful, he shook his head. When he looked at her again, his expression was somber, the gentle humor gone, as if it never been. ''I don't want to go through another divorce, Tessa, especially one where a child is involved. Have you even thought about the difference in our ages? You're only twenty-three.''

''I'll be twenty-four in November,'' she offered.

Keefe's mouth quirked in a half smile. ''And I'll be thirty-eight in January. Fourteen years is quite an age gap.''

''It's not that much.''

''When you're my age, I'll be fifty-two. That's not ancient, but it's not exactly a spring chicken, either.''

''It doesn't matter. No, listen to me,'' she said, when he started to interrupt. ''Fourteen years isn't that much. And the older we get, the less of a gap it will seem. When I'm seventy, you'll only be eighty-four. That doesn't sound so bad.''

Keefe laughed reluctantly and shook his head. "I just don't want you to have any regrets later."

"I won't. Not about that. I didn't just come up with this idea, Keefe. I've been thinking about it for a while now, and I'm not just thinking about David."

"No?" He shifted his hold on her hands so that his fingers rested against the fragile skin of her inner wrists. Tessa knew he must be able to feel the erratic beat of her pulse.

"I want this for myself, too." Her cheeks felt as if they were on fire, but she kept her eyes steady. "I'm not an...independent kind of woman. I know it's not politically correct to admit that, but it's the truth. I don't want to strike out on my own and cut a swath through the world. I don't have any career plans. What I want is to make a home—for David and me. For you. I'm good at that." She swallowed and continued more slowly. "And I trust you. I know you'd never do anything to hurt either of us."

"Tessa, I—" Keefe broke off and stared at her helplessly. He knew her trust wasn't given lightly, and she was offering it to him without reservation.

He didn't know what to say to her. He knew what he *wanted* to say, but he had to think of what was best—not just for him, but for all of them. A few minutes ago, he'd thought she was going to take the baby and leave. He'd braced himself to deal with that. Now, she was suggesting that they take their pretend family and turn it into the real thing. It was something he hadn't dared to suggest himself, for fear she might agree out of some misplaced sense of gratitude. But the idea had been hers. Did she have any idea how much he wanted to accept what she was offering?

"Tessa, there's more to marriage than trust."

"I know." Her eyes were more gray than blue as she looked at him intently. "I...care for you. And I think you care for me. That's a start, and we can build the rest of it, can't we?"

"I don't know."

He wanted to tell her that they could. He didn't want to lose her or David. He'd been content enough before they came into his life, but that had been because he didn't realize how empty his life was, how lonely he was. If they left now, he didn't know how he'd ever manage to fill the void that would open up inside him.

He wanted to jump at her suggestion that they make their marriage permanent. *Care* for her? The bland word didn't begin to describe what he felt. But he couldn't—or wouldn't—put another word to it. Not now. Not yet. He wanted the baby. And he wanted Tessa, more than he'd have believed possible a few months ago. But wanting her didn't make it right for him to take what she was offering.

Tessa read refusal in his lengthy silence, and her heart thumped in sudden fear. He couldn't say no. This was right. She *knew* it was right. She just had to make him see it, too. She twisted her hands free from his and, stepping forward, slid her arms around his neck. Surprised, Keefe let his hands settle on her waist.

"We can make this work, Keefe. I'm sure of it."

She was close enough to see the flecks of gold scattered through the chocolate brown of his eyes.

"Are you?" His fingers shifted lightly against her waist, and Tessa's pulse jumped in response.

"I could learn to be good at…at things," she said, hardly aware that her voice had dropped to a whisper.

"Tessa, I'm not worried about our sex life." His laugh was pained. "No matter what you think, good old Bobby was not the voice of authority. Trust me on this one—sex is the least of our worries."

"It is?" Intrigued, she edged closer. "How do you know?"

"I just do." Keefe's hands tightened on her waist, and she thought he might push her away. But then she saw the look in his eyes and realized that he couldn't. Her experience with men might be limited, but even she recognized the way he was looking at her.

He wants me. The idea was both startling and novel—that Keefe Walker should find her desirable! Of course, he had kissed her before and had even said that he enjoyed it. Tessa considered the possibility that she'd been going about this whole thing the wrong way. She'd been trying to appeal to his practical, reasonable side, but maybe there was a better way. She found herself wondering what her sister would do in this situation. Certainly, Dana would never waste her time with reason if there was a more direct method.

She shifted a little closer, her hips brushing against the inside of his knees. Keefe reaction was almost infinitesimal, but she felt him shift, saw the awareness flare in his eyes. Her eyes dropped to his mouth. It was one thing to recognize that he desired her. It was something else to know what to do with that desire. Then again, maybe that was obvious. True, she wasn't particularly good at sex and, no matter what he said, she didn't expect much from it, but at least with him she wouldn't *mind* it, either.

Gathering her courage in both hands, she leaned forward and set her mouth to his.

For an instant, surprise kept Keefe frozen. Feeling his stillness and mistaking the cause, Tessa nearly panicked. She had to convince him, had to make him see that she was right about this. She pressed her mouth harder to his, as if she could force him to respond. Keefe's fingers were suddenly twined in her hair, pulling her head back so that her mouth left his. Reluctantly she lifted her lashes, half-afraid of what she might see in his expression. There was an oddly gentle laughter in his eyes, but there was something else there, too—a spark of something warm and masculine, something…hungry.

"Sexy is soft," he whispered. And then proceeded to demonstrate.

He'd kissed her before, but it hadn't been like this. No one had *ever* kissed her like this. His mouth touched hers lightly. Once, twice, and then again—quick butterfly kisses that offered a tantalizing hint of something more. He kissed first one corner of her mouth and then the other. Her lips softened in anticipation of a real kiss, but it didn't come. His fingers tugged gently at her hair, tilting her head back so that he could feather a line of light kisses along the edge of her jaw, first one side and then the other.

Tessa had read books in which the author said that someone's bones were melting, but she'd never experienced the phenomenon herself—until this moment. Tessa's fingers curled into the fabric of his shirt as his teeth worried gently at her earlobe. His tongue traced the delicate whorls of her ear, and her breath escaped her on a sigh that teetered on the brink of a whimper.

Keefe continued his leisurely exploration, brushing kisses along the arch of each brow, the curve of her cheek, building the tension within her until, by the time he made his way back to her mouth, Tessa nearly moaned with relief. His teeth closed over her lower lip, nibbling and tasting as if her mouth were an exotic delicacy for him to savor.

She tried to deepen the kiss, but he wouldn't let her, pulling his mouth from hers and beginning his exploration of her face all over again. By the time he reached her mouth for the second time, Tessa was almost frantic. He'd said that sexy was soft, but there was nothing soft about the aching need that was building inside her. She'd never felt anything like it, never realized she could *want* so much.

His teeth closed gently over her lower lip, and her nails dug into his shoulders in sharp, unconscious demand. She felt Keefe's lips curve against hers—a smile of purely masculine satisfaction—and then he was crushing her mouth under his. Tessa arched into him, opening to him. His tongue took possession of her mouth, demanding a response she was only too eager to give.

Tessa had no idea how long the kiss lasted. It felt like forever and it seemed less than a heartbeat. It drained her, yet she felt more alive than she could ever remember feeling in her life. If it continued another second, she would surely die, yet when he lifted his head, she felt bereft.

"Are you trying to seduce me?" he asked huskily.

"I don't know." Her eyelids felt strangely heavy, and it was an effort to look at him. Was *she* seducing *him?* It seemed to her as if the shoe were on the other foot, but she wasn't going to argue. "Am I succeeding?"

"I think so." Keefe's laugh was ragged around the edges, and she felt a surge of satisfaction that she hadn't been the only one affected by that kiss.

She let her hands slide from his shoulders to his chest, and her fingers began working the buttons on the front of his shirt. Keefe watched her, his dark eyes hooded and unreadable. If she thought about it, Tessa knew, she would be shocked by her own actions. She wasn't the kind of woman who unbuttoned a man's shirt. In the early days of their marriage, Bobby had complained bitterly that she was too passive in bed, that she never initiated anything.

It hit her suddenly that she'd never *wanted* to initiate anything with her husband because she'd never really wanted him, not the way she wanted Keefe. Not the way it seemed she'd always wanted him.

Her teeth worried her lower lip as her fingers combed through a mat of crisp dark curls, her palm flattening over his heart. It thudded against her hand, the beat holding a ragged edge that sparked an unfamiliar feeling of feminine triumph in her.

"Do you mind being seduced?" she whispered.

"I should." He cupped his hands around her face, forcing her to look at him. "Tessa, are you sure this is what you want?"

She knew he was asking about much more than this moment. He was asking if she was sure about the future, about wanting to make their marriage real. Her answer came without hesitation.

"I'm sure. This is what I want."

It was a risk to believe her, Keefe thought. And even if he did believe her, they shouldn't jump into anything too quickly. They should take things slow and easy, build up to this moment. There was no reason to hurry this. No reason except the fact that he would probably go crazy if he didn't have her now. He ached with wanting her, hungered for the taste of her, the feel of her in his arms, in his bed.

His hand slid down her back, urging her closer, until she was pressed against him, his thighs braced on either side of her. He saw her eyes widen as she felt the rock-hard length of his erection pressed against her through the layers of their clothing. He waited, half expecting her to pull away, frightened by his blatant arousal. She was still for a moment, as if startled by the feel of him, and Keefe braced himself to let her go. But then her eyes seemed to darken, going from soft blue to smoky gray, and she leaned into him, pressing closer.

The movement dissolved the last remnants of his

control. If there were regrets in the future, so be it. This was worth the risk. *Tessa* was worth the risk.

He stood abruptly and bent to scoop her into his arms. Surprised, Tessa gasped and brought her arms up to circle his neck, clinging to him as he carried her from the living room, holding her as if she weighed next to nothing. He walked past her bedroom, where the baby lay asleep and pushed open the door to his room. Keefe set her on her feet beside the bed, tantalizing them both with the feel of her sliding down his body.

''Welcome to our wedding night,'' he said softly.

If asked, Tessa would have said that she knew all she cared to know about sex. After the first few months of her marriage to Bobby, she'd realized that, whatever problems they had in bed, they were as much his fault as hers, but that hadn't stopped her believing that she wasn't a particularly sexual person. No doubt there were those who enjoyed the sort of grappling encounters she endured, she'd thought, and she hadn't doubted that, with the right man, sex would certainly be more pleasant than it had been with Bobby. But she'd felt that, if she never had sex again, it wouldn't be any great loss.

It didn't take Keefe long to show her just how wrong she'd been.

He kissed her and touched her as if they had all the time in the world. There was nothing impatient or hurried about it. He undressed her as gently as if this were her first time, which, in a sense, it was. Certainly it was the first time she'd ever felt what she was feeling. As the last of her clothes whispered to the floor, she was suddenly aware that she hadn't lost all the weight she'd put on while carrying the baby.

"You're beautiful," Keefe murmured, interrupting her incoherent apology. He caught her hands and drew them gently away from her body. "Beautiful." He drifted a line of kisses along her collarbone.

"Exquisite." His tongue explored the ragged pulse that beat at the base of her throat.

"Lovely." His mouth trailed downward, and Tessa sucked in a startled breath as his tongue painted delicate patterns across her breast.

"Delicious," he whispered, and she forgot how to breathe when he drew her nipple into his mouth.

Sensation jolted through her, and her knees buckled. His arm like a steel band across her lower back, he supported her easily, taking his time with her breasts, feasting on her until Tessa thought she would surely die.

When he finally lifted his head, her breath was coming in shallow pants and her eyes held a shocked, dazed look that tore at the already ragged edges of Keefe's control. For the first time, he thought he understood why some men found virginity so appealing. There was something undeniably erotic about knowing that he was the first one to show Tessa the potential of her own body, that he was the first one to make her tremble with pleasure.

"Keefe?" She made his name a question, a plea.

"Ssshhh..." He eased her down on the bed and reached for his belt, tearing at it with impatient fingers. In less than a minute, his clothes were lying in a heap on the floor and he was lying over her, easing his legs between hers.

Tessa felt his arousal press against her and stiffened a little. No matter how much surprise she'd felt earlier, she knew what would happen now. *This* wasn't going to change, and she couldn't stop a quick rush of disappointment that all those wonderful sensations should end here.

But she soon realized that she'd been wrong again. Keefe sheathed himself in her body with one long, gliding thrust, filling her completely. Her eyes widened and she stared up at him, stunned by the sensation.

''Okay?'' he whispered, his voice strained.

''Y-yes.'' Her answer was hesitant. *Okay* didn't seem to be the word to describe what she was feeling, but she was in no condition to argue semantics. Fortunately, he didn't seem to need any other response.

Bracing his weight on his elbows, he began to move within her, and Tessa's mind went blank as she realized that she didn't know anything about sex. She had never known it could be like this, had never realized the potential for pleasure locked within her own body. If she'd had a moment to think about it, it might have frightened her, but she couldn't think. All she could do was feel.

Keefe felt her surrender herself completely to the pleasure and ground his teeth together against the need pounding in his veins. She was so sweetly responsive. There was no holding back. She gave herself without reservation. No coy games. No pretending. Just Tessa—all innocence and need.

He saw the startled wonder in her eyes as her climax took her, and then the feel of her body tightening around his dragged him headlong into the spinning whirlpool. Groaning, he gave himself over to the pleasure.

It was a long time before either of them spoke. Keefe used the last ounce of his energy to ease himself from Tessa's body and collapse on the bed next to her. Her murmur of protest ended when he slid one arm under her shoulders and dragged her against his body. They lay without speaking, listening to the ragged sound of each other's breathing slowly steadying.

"I guess I was wrong," Tessa said at last, her voice faint.

"About what?" Keefe turned his face into her hair, the crisp scent of her shampoo mingling with the earthy, musky smell of sex.

"About *this.*" One hand flapped limply in the air over their lax bodies. "Maybe I could learn to be good at it."

Keefe's big body shook with laughter. His arm tightened around her shoulders in a quick hug. "If you get any better at it, I'll be in a wheelchair before I'm forty."

She smiled against his chest. "I guess this means our marriage is real now."

"I guess it does," Keefe said, and waited for the doubts to surface. But all he felt was a deep sense of contentment.

"I'm glad," Tessa said simply, and he could only agree.

* * *

Tessa hummed to herself as she slid two loaf pans from the oven. The bread looked perfect. She turned one loaf out and rapped on the bottom with her knuckles, nodding with satisfaction at the slightly hollow sound. It sounded perfect, too. As she set the loaves on a wooden rack, her mouth curved in a secret smile. Actually, now that she thought about it, *life* seemed pretty close to perfect right now.

She stretched out one hand to look at the plain gold wedding band on her left hand. Keefe had placed it on her hand months ago, but until last night, its only purpose had been to support the lie they'd told Bobby's parents. Viewed in the light of a new day and a new future, it seemed to gleam a little brighter than it had before.

She thought suddenly of the expensive rings she'd left behind in the house she'd shared with Bobby, and her smile faded. Over the years, she'd come to view those rings as symbolic of everything that was wrong in her life. Rubbing her thumb across the simple gold band, Tessa promised herself that *this* ring would stand for something very different. Not that she had to worry about her marriage to Keefe being anything like her marriage to Bobby, she thought, remembering his tenderness the night before.

Keefe might not be in love with her, but he cared for her and, given time and the right kind of nurturing, that could grow into love. And she did want him to love her, she admitted to herself. Tessa sighed, her expression growing wistful. After last night, she couldn't pretend anymore. She loved him. Heart and soul, for better or worse, she loved him.

Once she'd admitted it, it seemed as if she'd felt that way forever. She thought back to that first summer after he and Dana were married. She'd loved him then with all the passion of a young girl. During the years since then, she'd thought about him often and smiled a little at that childish infatuation. But in retrospect, it was as if her feelings now had grown out of what she'd felt then. Once acknowledged, it seemed the most natural thing in the world, as if it simply had to be.

She would have given a great deal to know how Keefe felt about her, but she wasn't going to dwell on it. Not today, not when she was feeling good about life. Love was something that could grow with time. For now, what she had was enough. It was so much more than she'd imagined possible. A home, a healthy, happy baby—and Keefe. Life was too good for her to waste a minute of it worrying.

As if thinking about him had conjured him up, she heard the front door open and then Keefe's voice calling her name.

"Tessa?"

Her mouth widened in a smile. She hadn't expected to see him again until dinnertime, three hours from now. He was back early, and her heart took a quick leap upward at the thought that maybe he hadn't wanted to wait until evening to see her again.

"I'm in here," she called, wondering why he'd come in the front door rather than the kitchen door.

She heard the thud of his boots against the wooden floor and started forward to greet him. But his grim expression stopped her before she'd taken more than a step.

"We've got company," he said flatly, stepping aside to allow someone to walk past him.

Tessa stared blankly at the woman who entered her kitchen. Tall, slender, her light blond hair cut in a perfect—and very expensive—chin-length bob, with blue eyes that seemed to measure Tessa for a moment before her beautiful mouth curved in a smile that revealed a perfect set of sparkling teeth.

"Tessa! It's been ages."

Tessa felt the ground start to crumble beneath her feet.

"Dana?"

Chapter 15

"I know this is a surprise, but I hope it's not an entirely unwelcome one." Dana laughed softly, making a joke of the words, as if there could never be any question of her welcome anywhere.

"No, of course not."

When she was a girl, Tessa had been thrown from a horse, hitting the ground flat on her back, so hard that all the air was driven from her lungs. She remembered lying there, staring up at the sky and feeling quite calm as she waited for an angel to step off a cloud and take her away, because she was surely dead. She felt something very similar now. But there was no angel—then or now.

There was just Dana, standing there, looking at her expectantly.

"Of course you're welcome." Tessa didn't look at Keefe as she said it. She *couldn't* look at him, for fear of what she might see in his eyes. What was he thinking? Feeling? He and Dana had been married. He'd obviously loved her. Did he feel regret when he looked at her now? Was he thinking that he was married to the wrong sister? But if she couldn't bring herself to look at him, Dana didn't share her hesitation. She looked directly at him, her blue eyes sparkling with amusement, as if inviting him to share some private joke.

"I guess this is what Emily Post would probably have called 'a delicate social situation.' Ex-wife and ex-husband meeting for the first time since the divorce, and as in-laws, no less. I wonder what she would have suggested?"

"I doubt if it came up often enough for her to worry about it," Keefe said coolly. He didn't seem to share her amusement.

"Well, I'd say that we could just be good friends, but friendship never was our strong suit, was it?" Dana said, her tone adding intimacy to the words.

"No, we weren't ever friends," Keefe agreed flatly.

"Well, I'm sure, if we give it a little time, we'll get the hang of being in-laws. Although that sounds awfully stuffy and official, doesn't it?" Dana wrinkled her nose, and Tessa wondered despairingly how it was possible for her to look exquisite even with her nose scrunched up.

"Why are you here?" she heard herself asking, and then wished the words unsaid. Not that she didn't want an answer to the question, but she didn't want to sound too anxious, as if it bothered her to have her exquisitely beautiful, ridiculously slender, perfectly groomed older sister standing there looking at Keefe as if he were a menu item she was thinking about ordering.

Dana looked at her, her expression surprised, and perhaps just a little hurt. ''I know I should have called first but, well, to tell the truth, I wasn't sure you'd let me come.''

''Not let you—'' Tessa broke off, staring at her in surprise. She tried to remember the last time she'd seen Dana. It had probably been close to a year. She didn't remember the exact occasion, but she knew they hadn't exchanged any harsh words. In fact, she wouldn't be surprised if they hadn't exchanged any words at all. They had never had much to say to one another—good, bad or indifferent. ''Why would you think that I wouldn't let you come here?''

''Well, I haven't exactly been a model big sister,'' Dana admitted with a smile that was both rueful and apologetic. ''I didn't even come home from Europe for Bobby's funeral. I know I should have, but I've never been very good at things like that.'' She waved one hand in a vague gesture of dismissal.

''It's all right.'' Tessa had been so dazed that she barely remembered the funeral. She couldn't imagine that having Dana there would have made any difference at all.

''No, it's not all right,'' Dana said, sounding determined to shoulder the blame for past misdeeds. ''I should have been there. No matter how difficult it was for me, I should have been there.''

''It's all right,'' Tessa said again, biting back an unexpected jolt of amusement at the inadvertent implication that the funeral might have been harder on Dana than it had been on Bobby's widow. "There wasn't anything you could have done," she said truthfully.

"Maybe not, but I should have been there for you," Dana said.

Tessa tried to think of any time when Dana had been "there" for her. Nothing came to mind. But she seemed sincere in her regret.

"We're family," Dana was saying. "We may not always have been close, but family still means something. At least it should. I was hoping you wouldn't mind me hanging around for a little while—a few days, maybe. I think it would be nice if we took some time to, well, to get to know one another again."

Her smile was sweet and just a little self-deprecating. Despite past experience, Tessa felt herself softening. This was a side of Dana she'd never seen before. Of course, if they got to know one another, there wouldn't be any "again" about it, because they never *had* really known each other—a circumstance that had never seemed to bother her sister in the past. But people could change.

"How did you know where Tessa was?" Keefe asked abruptly.

"When I came home from Europe and found that Tessa had vanished without a trace, I called Aunt Molly," Dana said. "She told me all about your whirlwind courtship. I guess maybe *courtship* isn't exactly the right word to describe it, since she said you two already have a baby." She glanced across the kitchen to where David lay in his carrier, happily gumming a bright pink plastic ring. ''This must be my nephew.''

''That's David. My—our son,'' Tessa said, glancing at Keefe as she corrected herself. But he didn't seem to notice. He was watching Dana, his expression still unreadable.

''Isn't he adorable?'' Dana said, and this time her smile was patently false, but Tessa didn't hold it against her. She couldn't imagine anyone less likely than her sister to be captivated by a baby. What was surprising was that she'd even made the effort to comment. The Dana she knew wouldn't have bothered—unless she wanted something. And, of course, she did want something—she wanted to stay with them for a few days. Coming from Dana, it seemed such a strange request that Tessa couldn't help but think that maybe her older sister really had been seized by a wave of family feeling. What other possible reason could she have for coming here?

She glanced at Keefe, trying to read something of his thoughts, but whatever he was thinking, his expression revealed nothing. If he had any objection to having Dana as a houseguest, she couldn't tell. And if he was anxious to have his ex-wife stay, she couldn't read that, either.

''We aren't really set up for entertaining,'' she said slowly.

''I don't expect you to entertain me,'' Dana said lightly. ''I'm perfectly capable of entertaining myself.''

Tessa was doubtful. The Dana she remembered had not been particularly good at providing her own amusements. But then, that Dana wouldn't have expressed any interest in "family," either. People could change, she reminded herself again. The last thing she wanted was to have Keefe's ex-wife staying with them, especially now, when their relationship had just taken such an amazing new direction. But the fact that his ex-wife was also her sister complicated things. True, the relationship had never seemed to mean much to Dana before, but if she really *had* changed...

And why didn't Keefe give her some clue as to his preferences?

"If you're sure you want to stay," she said, letting the words trail off as she glanced at Keefe again. But his expression was closed, and his eyes were unreadable. Whatever he was thinking—or feeling—he was keeping it to himself.

"I knew I could count on you," Dana said with a dazzling smile.

Tessa smiled weakly in return and hoped she hadn't just made the worst mistake of her life.

"You want to run that by me again?" Jace asked. He'd been in the midst of unsaddling his horse, but he'd abandoned the task and turned to look at his partner, his expression one of disbelief.

"You heard me the first time." Keefe's tone bordered on surly, but he didn't try to soften it. For the first time in weeks, he wished he had a cigarette.

"Dana? Here?" Jace packed complete disbelief into the two words.

"She showed up midafternoon."

"What the hell for?" Jace's horse shifted restlessly,

and he turned to lift the saddle from the gelding's back.

"Says she wants to spend time with Tessa, get to know the baby."

"Bull! The day she takes an interest in anybody but herself is the day I grow sideburns, put on a spangled jumpsuit and become an Elvis impersonator."

Keefe smiled, but it was perfunctory. "That's all she says she wants."

"And you believe her?" Jace asked disbelievingly.

"If that isn't what she wants, then why is she here?"

"I don't know, but you can bet the ranch that there's another reason." Jace opened the corral gate and slapped the gelding on the rump to send him through it. He tilted his hat back on his head and looked at Keefe, his blue eyes holding a warning. "She's poison. Pure poison. You know it and I know it."

Keefe couldn't argue. "I'll keep an eye on her."

"You'd be better off throwing her skinny butt out," Jace said bluntly. "I don't know why you agreed to let her stay in the first place."

"It wasn't my decision." He reached for the cigarettes he no longer carried and then let his hand drop with a muttered curse. "She's my ex-wife, but she also happens to be Tessa's sister. I can't tell Tessa that she can't have her family here."

Jace shook his head as the corral gate thudded home and he swung the latch into place. "Family means something to the Walkers. Don't make the mistake of thinking it means something to everyone else.

Dana and Tessa may share blood, but that's all they share. Take my advice and get rid of her as soon as possible. Tell Tessa I'll be eating at my place tonight. I'm not in the mood to deal with your ex.''

Keefe's jaw was set tight with frustration as he watched the other man walk across the yard to the foreman's house. Jace was right about Dana. She was trouble. Four years of marriage had taught him just how *much* trouble. And he wasn't such a fool as to believe that all families shared the closeness that he and his family did. But that didn't change the facts. Dana was Tessa's sister, and Tessa had asked her to stay. As long as Tessa wanted her here, he couldn't ask her to leave. The only thing he could do was keep an eye on her and make sure that she didn't cause any trouble.

He just wished he knew what she was doing here. Still frowning, he took his hat off and ran his fingers through his hair. While he was at it, he might as well wish that, if she had to show up, she'd done it some other time. After last night... Keefe shook his head as he started up to the house. Hell, he still didn't know what to think about last night, but he knew he didn't want his sister-in-law around—especially not when she also happened to be his ex-wife.

''I hope it was okay to ask Dana to stay,'' Tessa said, her expression anxious.

''She's your sister,'' Keefe said.

He began unbuttoning his shirt, and she looked away. They were in his bedroom—her bedroom, now, she reminded herself. It was the first time they'd been alone together since Dana's arrival. She wasn't sure what bothered her more—talking about her sister, who happened to be his ex-wife, or watching him undress.

He shrugged out of his shirt and draped the garment over the back of a straight-backed chair. Tessa's heart bumped unevenly. His chest was solidly muscled, with the kind of long, ropy muscles that came from hard labor, rather than from hours in the gym. A mat of crisp black hair spread across the upper part of his chest, tapering down across his abdomen to disappear beneath the waist of his faded jeans. Just looking at him, she felt her breasts tighten and swell at the memory of those tight black curls rasping gently against her nipples.

His hands dropped to his belt buckle and she looked away, her mouth going dry. Despite what they'd shared last night, it seemed almost painfully intimate to watch him undress. Last night, everything had happened more or less on impulse and she'd let herself get swept along on the tide. Last night, she'd been so dazzled by the sensual response he stirred in her that she was hardly aware of him taking off his clothes. Events had simply flowed one into the other in a natural, inevitable progression.

Tonight, nothing seemed natural. Too much had happened, too quickly. Twenty-four hours ago, she hadn't known anything of what the future might hold. Then everything had seemed to fall into place with an ease that was little short of miraculous. For a few hours, she'd thought that maybe—just maybe—her life was finally on the right track.

And then Dana had shown up.

''Did David settle in all right?'' Keefe asked, his belt buckle jangling faintly as he pulled his belt free of his jeans.

''He seemed to.'' Tessa glanced at the partially open door on one side of the room. The baby had been sleeping in Tessa's room, but now that everything had changed—Tessa's moving into Keefe's room, and Dana's unexpected arrival—David's things had been moved into the small room next to Keefe's bedroom. The few things that had been stored there had been either moved out or shoved to one side to make room for his crib.

''I wonder if that room was intended to be a nursery,'' Tessa said chattily, trying not to hear the rasp of a zipper being lowered.

''Could be.'' Keefe sat down on the edge of the bed and reached for the bootjack.

''You're sure you don't mind Dana staying here?'' The subject was like a sore tooth—she just couldn't leave it alone.

''She's your sister,'' he said again. His boots thudded to the floor, first one and then the other. Tessa twisted her fingers together and wondered uneasily just how she should interpret that statement. Did he mean that Dana was only welcome because they were sisters? She wanted very much to believe that.

''I know it's awkward....'' she began. Keefe hooked his thumbs in the waistband of his jeans and shoved them down over his hips. She kept her eyes resolutely turned away and hoped he wouldn't notice the odd little catch in her voice. ''She's my sister, but she's also your ex-wife. I hadn't really given it much thought until now. I mean, I'd *thought* about it, but not really—about it being awkward, I mean. I guess, if we'd been closer—Dana and I—maybe I would have thought about it more, but we've never been particularly close, so it didn't seem…''

Keefe stood up. She knew he was moving toward her, because she could see his feet. She couldn't bring herself to raise her eyes any higher.

''…to matter,'' she continued, speaking a little more quickly. ''I was surprised that she'd want— But I can't think of any reason why she'd lie about it, so I guess she must really want to…''

Keefe's hand slid beneath the thick fall of dark gold hair to cup the back of her neck, and Tessa's words broke off in midsentence. She closed her eyes as a shiver of awareness spread outward from where he touched her until her whole body seemed to tingle with it.

''Dana is my ex-wife, and that's the end of my interest in her,'' he said softly. ''She's your sister, and that makes her welcome here for as long as you want her to stay.''

Tessa might have tried to explain that *want* wasn't exactly the word she'd have chosen, but he was loosening the belt of her robe with his free hand and she suddenly seemed to be having a difficult time putting together a coherent sentence.

''I don't want to talk about her anymore tonight, okay?''

''O-okay,'' she whispered, her voice catching in her throat as her robe fell open and he set his hand against her hip, where it seemed to burn through the thin cotton of her nightgown.

"Now, I've got a question for you," he murmured, his fingers shifting against her.

"What?"

"Are you ever going to look at me again?"

Tessa wouldn't have believed it was possible to put both amusement and desire in the same question. There seemed to be no end to the things she didn't know, she thought dazedly.

"I'm not sure," she said, answering his question in a voice thinned by nerves.

"I promise not to bite," he whispered, and then proved himself a liar by catching her lower lip between his teeth and worrying it gently.

Tessa's hands came up to grab hold of his shoulders as her knees threatened to give out under her. His skin was smooth and hot beneath her fingers. He smelled of soap and coffee and a faint, pleasantly musky smell that she could only define as "man." He took her mouth in a slow, deep kiss that left her drugged with hunger and clinging to him.

She offered not a word of protest when he bent to catch her under knees and shoulders and carried her to the bed. Her doubts were forgotten. Dana disappeared. Nothing existed but the two of them.

"I suppose I'm the last one up," Dana said as she entered the kitchen the next morning. "I have this vague idea that ranchers start their day before the sun comes up."

"More often than not," Tessa agreed. She glanced

up from the cookbook she was looking through, her welcoming smile wilting a little when she saw the other woman.

It didn't seem fair that her sister could look so beautiful first thing in the morning. Dana wore a pair of slim black jeans and a skinny little hot-pink rib-knit top that clung to her slender body in all the right places. Tessa was immediately conscious of the extra ten pounds she still carried from her pregnancy and the fact that her hair looked dishwater-blond in comparison to Dana's exquisite pale gold bob.

But it would take more than a haircut and clothes to close the gap between them, she admitted silently. Nature had simply been in an exceptionally generous mood when her older sister was born. She wanted to attribute Dana's flawless complexion and sapphire-blue eyes to a good foundation and colored contact lenses. But the truth, disgusting as it was, was that Dana was ridiculously beautiful, without the slightest need for cosmetic aids.

"Would you like some breakfast?" she asked, pushing fruitless comparisons to the back of her mind.

"I wouldn't mind a cup of coffee." Dana pulled out a chair and sat down, secure in the knowledge that someone else would provide what she'd requested.

"Cream or sugar?" Tessa asked as she got up and took a mug from the cupboard.

"A little of both, please. I don't suppose you have cappuccino?"

"Not even the instant kind," Tessa admitted, and then bit back a smile at her sister's slightly martyred sigh. She set the coffee down in front of Dana and then got a carton of cream from the refrigerator.

"Right from the carton," Dana commented, her thin brows arching in a silent comment. "It reminds me of the days when *I* was married to Keefe. He doesn't much care about the elegancies of life, does he?"

"Pouring the cream into a pitcher just makes for more work. The house and the baby take plenty of time, without me adding extra dishes to the picture." Tessa kept her tone light with an effort. She didn't care what Dana thought of the way she did—or didn't—set a table but the reference to Dana's marriage to Keefe cut like a knife. If only she could be sure he didn't still feel something for his first wife.

He couldn't have made love to me the way he did last night if he still loved her, she told herself. *Or could he?*

"I wasn't criticizing. Just commenting. I didn't mean to imply that I left Keefe over cream pitchers."

Dana's soft laugh grated on Tessa's nerves but she forced a smile. She wanted, more than anything, to ask just what *had* ended the marriage. David stirred, waving one tiny hand and cooing a demand for attention. Tessa turned to lift him from his carrier, grateful for the interruption. She wanted to know what had happened to Keefe's first marriage so badly that she was afraid the words might spill out against her will.

"He seems...healthy," Dana said, looking at the baby as if he were a member of an alien species.

"He's very healthy." Tessa looked down at the infant, her mouth softening in a smile. "And happy. Aren't you, sweetie?"

"Hmmm..." Dana took a sip of her coffee, her expression thoughtful. "From what I saw last night, Keefe seems very fond of him."

"I don't think *fond* is quite the right word," Tessa said, thinking of the light in Keefe's eyes when he held David.

Dana turned the coffee mug between her cupped hands. "I was surprised when Aunt Molly told me that you and Keefe were married." Her laugh was short and held little humor. "*Astonished* is a better description. I had no idea the two of you were so cozy."

"We always got along well." Tessa kept her gaze on David's face, afraid of what Dana might read in her expression.

Dana laughed again. "That must be something of an understatement! I didn't know you kept in touch after the divorce. I'm astonished that you did. Bobby Mallory struck me as the possessive sort."

Tessa barely controlled a flinch. *Possessive?* Yes, he'd certainly been that. She tugged David's T-shirt down over his tummy, aware that her hand was not completely steady. Time—and Keefe—had helped her to put most of the bad memories behind her, but there were moments when they swept back in through some little crack. This was one of them.

"Obviously, Bobby didn't know that Keefe and I were in touch," she said, pleased by the steadiness of her voice.

"'In touch,'" Dana repeated the phrase with an

ironic twist. "Now there's an interesting way of putting it."

Tessa glanced up in time to see her sister cast a pointed look at the baby in her arms. Of course. Dana thought that David was Keefe's child, conceived while Bobby was still alive. She felt the color creep up her throat and into her face.

"We—"

But Dana cut her off with a wave of one French-manicured hand. "I'm not passing judgment. It's none of my business. But I will admit that I was pretty surprised when I heard about it. I didn't think you had it in you. And Keefe, well, frankly, his strictly middle-class morality was one of his least attractive characteristics, as far as I was concerned. I certainly wouldn't have thought he'd mess around with a married woman. He must have changed quite a bit since the divorce."

Tessa sorted through several possible responses, abandoning each in turn. She finally settled for a vague murmur that her sister could interpret as agreement, embarrassment or indifference, whichever she pleased. Dana might be sincere in her desire for them to get to know each other better, but they were a long way away from being confidantes.

David's eyelids were starting to droop, and his mouth rounded in a perfect O as he yawned. Tessa rose and settled him gently back into his carrier, setting one hand on his stomach in a gentle rocking motion until he relaxed into drowsy contentment.

"Do you want anything to eat?" she asked, looking at her sister.

"Toast and orange juice, if you have it."

"It's not fresh-squeezed," Tessa warned as she slid two slices of bread into the toaster.

"I expected that," Dana said, sounding resigned. She didn't offer to help, and she didn't speak again until Tessa set the toast in front of her, along with butter, jelly and honey. "Thanks."

"Are you sure that's all you want?"

"This is more than I usually eat." Dana spread an infinitesimal layer of butter over one-quarter of a piece of toast. Tessa thought of the pancakes and bacon that she'd had for breakfast and sighed. She supposed she need look no farther for the reason she hadn't lost those last few pounds that stood between her and her prepregnancy weight. Looking at Dana's slender figure, she renewed her vow to watch what she ate.

Her mind suddenly flashed on a memory of Keefe saying she was beautiful as he undressed her, his hands on her body. She'd felt beautiful, she thought. The way he looked at her, the way he touched her—she'd *felt* beautiful.

Tessa looked across the table at her sister. *How many times had Keefe said those same words to Dana? And meant them?* The thought slipped in—unwanted and unwelcome. She'd been trying very hard not to think about Keefe's relationship with her sister, but there was no escaping the fact that they had been married, had loved, had made love. The image of Dana in Keefe's arms—in his bed—was painfully vivid. She wasn't sophisticated enough to ignore their past relationship. Her mouth twisted ruefully. No doubt another example of what Dana had so contemptuously referred to as ''middle-class morality.''

''I don't want you to feel uncomfortable about any of this,'' Dana said as she reached for a second piece of toast.

''Uncomfortable?'' Tessa made an effort to focus on the conversation.

''About my being here.'' Dana gestured gracefully with the knife. ''I know it's awkward—me being Keefe's ex-wife. But there's really nothing for you to worry about.''

''I'm not worried,'' Tessa lied.

''Good. Because what was between Keefe and I is gone and forgotten. I mean, we certainly did have *something*. Something rather amazing, actually.'' Her mouth curved in a slight, reminiscent smile that made Tessa's stomach knot. ''But it was a long time ago,'' Dana continued, more briskly. ''I just didn't want you to worry about…anything.''

''Thank you, but it wasn't really necessary to tell me that.'' Tessa forced her lips to curve in an unconcerned smile.

Had there ever been a less reassuring piece of reassurance? She wondered if it was possible that Dana's intention had been exactly the opposite of what it seemed—to plant doubts rather than to assuage them. But Dana's blue eyes were as clear and open as a child's, and Tessa pushed the suspicion aside.

But she couldn't push aside her words, or the doubts they'd planted.

Chapter 16

Wrist-deep in sudsy water, Tessa contemplated the Zen-like qualities of washing dishes. Like a domestic prayer wheel, it occupied the hands while leaving the mind free to contemplate the deeper meanings of life. Or to contemplate the not-so-deep questions of day-to-day living.

She liked this time of day, she thought as she rinsed a plate and set it in the drainer. Dinner was over, David was down for the night—or at least for a few hours. The darkness outside the window enfolded the house, cutting off the rest of the world as if it didn't exist. It was a peaceful, quiet time. A shrill burst of canned laughter from the television in the living room reminded her that it wasn't as quiet as it might have been. Frowning, she ran the dishcloth over a bowl.

Dana had been here nearly a week now, and Tessa was no closer to knowing why her sister was here than she had been the day she arrived. If it was because she wanted the two of them to get to know one another better, she had a peculiar way of going about it. It was true that they'd spent quite a bit of time together, but considering the ranch's relative isolation, there wasn't really any way for them to *avoid* each other. But spending time in the same house wasn't exactly getting to know one another, unless Dana thought it was all going to happen by osmosis.

Tessa fished a handful of flatware out of the water. She wiped each piece before dropping it into the rinse water. If she'd ever thought that blood was thicker than water, this past week had taught her differently. She and Dana had nothing in common beyond the fact that they'd been born to the same parents. There was no hidden bond of sisterly love just waiting to be uncovered, no dormant well of family feeling ready to spring free.

Closer acquaintance hadn't revealed any new and appealing aspects of her sister's personality. The fact was, Dana was astonishingly self-centered. As far as she was concerned, everything revolved around her. Not that she was entirely to blame for that attitude, Tessa thought. Considering the way she'd been raised, it would have been a miracle if she *didn't* think she was the center of the universe.

But understanding how she'd come to be the way she was didn't make her any better company. Tessa scooped the flatware out of the rinse water and dropped it into the basket hooked on the side of the drainer. She felt vaguely guilty for feeling the way she did. She couldn't shake the idea that she *should* love Dana, should feel some ties of blood and bone linking them together. But the feelings simply weren't there, and she wasn't going to pretend to herself that they were. With a sigh, she admitted to herself that she just didn't like her sister. And she didn't think Dana was any too fond of her, either. Which left the question of why Dana had made the effort to seek her out up in the air.

Or did it?

Tessa's fingers tightened around the edge of a plate, and she caught her lower lip between her teeth as she considered the probable answer to that question. Keefe. It was the only possible explanation. Dana hadn't come to see her, she'd come to see Keefe. The thought made Tessa's breath catch in her throat. She could never hope to compete with Dana. Not only was her older sister intimidatingly beautiful, but Keefe had once loved her. *Still* loved her? Tessa wondered, and felt her chest ache at the thought. She hadn't seen anything to suggest that Keefe was still in love with Dana, but that didn't necessarily mean anything. If he felt anything for his ex-wife, he wouldn't let it show.

If he still loved Dana, he wouldn't make love to you the way he does. The thought eased her fears, even if it didn't eliminate them. She knew better than to equate sex with love, but she couldn't believe that Keefe would make love to her so passionately if he was in love with another woman. Some men might be able to do that, but not Keefe. Still, it would have been nice to know just what he *did* feel—about her sister and about her.

Absorbed in her thoughts, her back to the door,

Tessa didn't realize that she was no longer alone until she felt someone right behind her. She sucked in a quick, startled breath and then released it on a sigh as a pair of masculine arms slid around her waist.

"You startled me." But she was smiling when Keefe pulled her back against his chest.

"Sorry."

"You don't sound it." She tilted her head to one side as he bent to nuzzle the sensitive skin under her ear.

"No, really, I'm terribly sorry." Since he was busy placing a biting series of kisses down the side of her neck, his apology was somewhat muffled. Tessa decided not to question his sincerity any further. Her hands were limp in the cooling dishwater as she leaned her head back against his shoulder and gave herself up to the shivers of pleasure racing through her.

This was a side of herself she'd never known existed, this warm, sensual creature who responded so easily to his touch. She'd never even imagined this person existed.

"Are you about done with the dishes?" he asked.

"Yes." The counters could have been stacked to the ceiling with dirty plates and she would still have answered in the affirmative. One of his hands slid from her waist to boldly cup her breast, and she forgot how to breathe. His touch burned through the layers of shirt and bra.

"It's getting late," he whispered against her throat. "Are you about ready to go to bed?"

His mouth closed over hers before she could say

anything, but her response was all the answer he needed. Her head tilted back against his shoulder, she met his kiss with all the passion in her—a passion he'd taught her. She could feel the hard strength of his big body against her back, feel the solid length of his arousal pressed against the soft fullness of her bottom. Her hands clenched around the edge of the sink as she felt the newly familiar sensation of bones and muscles dissolving.

He couldn't possibly love Dana and still kiss me like this, hold me like this. Even in her own mind, she didn't know whether the thought was statement or plea. Then Keefe's thumb brushed across her nipple and she stopped thinking at all.

"I don't know how you stand living out here. Even the TV reception is lousy." Dana's complaint preceded her entrance.

Her voice acted like a bucket of ice water on the couple by the sink. Keefe wrenched his mouth from Tessa's. For an instant—no more than a heartbeat—their eyes met, and she read pure frustration in his.

"What do people *do* for entertainment...?" Dana's voice trailed off as she walked into the kitchen and saw the two of them.

Keefe stepped away from Tessa. Picking up a dish towel, he took a plate from the drainer and began to dry it with more vigor than was strictly necessary. Still half turned from the sink, Tessa stared at her older sister blankly. There was a moment of dead silence, and she saw Dana look from her to Keefe. Her eyes narrowed into thin blue slits.

"Am I interrupting something?" she asked in a silky-soft tone.

"N-no." Tessa cleared her throat and managed a smile that probably looked as false as it felt. She shot a quick glance at Keefe, but he was drying a glass, focusing all his attention on the task. "We were just...ah...finishing up with the dishes."

"I don't remember you offering to help with the housework when we were married," Dana said, looking at Keefe. Her tone was light, but the look in her eyes was anything but.

"I don't remember you spending much time *doing* housework," he said without looking at her.

"I suppose not." She laughed, as if he'd just paid her a compliment. "I guess domesticity was never my strong suit."

"Not hardly." Keefe draped the towel across the top of the drainer and glanced at Tessa, his expression unreadable. "I've got something to talk over with Jace before I turn in."

"Okay."

She watched him walk out the door and then turned back to the sink, careful not to look at her sister. The water was cool. She pulled the plug and stood watching it drain out. She was acutely aware of Dana's eyes on her back.

"I don't know how you can stand having Jace Reno living here," Dana said.

"What?" The comment was so unexpected that Tessa turned to look at her.

"I couldn't stand him when Keefe and I were married,'' Dana said, coming farther into the room. ''He was always such a sanctimonious bastard.''

''Jace?'' The description was so far from the man she knew that Tessa shook her head in disbelief. She knew Dana and Jace were not on good terms—the icy politeness with which they treated one another made that unmistakably clear—but still... ''He's Keefe's best friend. And he's been a good friend to me since I came here.''

''I didn't mean to offend you,'' Dana said, pulling her mouth down in a pretty grimace of apology. ''It's just that...I've always thought Jace was at least partially to blame for the failure of my marriage to Keefe.''

''Jace?'' Tessa gaped at her in disbelief. ''I can't imagine that.''

''Perhaps you don't know him as well as you think,'' Dana said. She lifted one shoulder in a shrug.

''I think I know him well enough to know he'd never do anything to hurt a friend,'' Tessa said firmly. Whatever Dana was up to, she wasn't going to let her criticism of Jace go without comment. ''What did he do?''

Dana shrugged again, looking uncomfortable. ''Oh, it's a sordid little story, nothing you want to hear. Nothing I want to repeat, for that matter. Besides, it was a long time ago. No doubt he's changed a great deal since then. Just like the rest of us.'' She smiled faintly and wandered from the room.

Tessa watched her go and wished, not for the first time, that months ago she'd thought to ask her aunt Molly not to tell any of her family where she was.

* * *

Keefe scraped his knuckle on the edge of the manifold and muttered a curse. If there was one job he hated above all others, it was car repair of any kind. He avoided it when he could, but the fuel pump on his truck had breathed its last, leaving him no choice but to venture under the hood. But he didn't have to like it.

"How about something cold to drink?"

The voice came from the rear of the truck, soft and feminine. Keefe started to smile. Tessa.

"I'd just about kill for a cold beer," he said as he ducked out from under the hood and straightened. He set the wrench down on the fender and turned to face his visitor, his smile fading when he saw the woman who was approaching. "Dana."

"In the flesh," she said, apparently oblivious to the lack of welcome in his tone. She lifted one hand to display the amber-colored bottle that dangled between her fingers. "I come bringing gifts."

"Thanks." Keefe took the beer from her, though his enthusiasm for it wasn't what it had been a moment ago. He didn't like accepting any favors from his ex-wife, not even a beer from his own refrigerator.

"I saw you working out here and thought you might be thirsty."

"Thanks," he said again. He tilted his head back and took two deep swallows. The feel of her eyes on him made him uneasy. She was up to something. He didn't know what it was, but he was willing to bet that he wouldn't like it.

"It's awfully hot, isn't it?" Dana plucked at the thin fabric of her skinny little top in a move designed to draw attention to her body. She was braless, Keefe noticed, and the bright blue top clung to every curve. She was, what—thirty six now? But her body was still as tight and firm as it had been the day they met. Either she'd spent a lot of hours in a gym or she'd had a little surgical enhancement here and there. He wondered idly which it had been.

"I just took a shower, but I feel all sticky again." She laughed girlishly. "I feel like I might melt, just like a piece of candy left out in the sun."

"Or the Wicked Witch of the West standing under a sprinkler," Keefe said dryly.

Dana's smile seemed to freeze, and for just an instant he saw fury in her eyes, but it was gone instantly. She laughed again, a little ruefully. "You always did have an irritating sense of humor."

"Just one of my many charms." He took another swallow of beer and set the bottle on the workbench. He'd pulled the truck into the building that functioned as a sometime garage and full-time tool shed. It was a few degrees cooler than it would have been working in the full glare of the late-August sun. He waited, hoping Dana would leave, but she lingered.

"I hope it hasn't been too awkward—my being here, I mean." She widened her blue eyes in a way that he'd once thought revealed her vulnerability. "It's a strange situation, isn't it? Tessa being my sister, and now the two of you are married."

"Not all that strange." He shrugged. Dana's eyes dropped to his bare chest and he resisted the urge to reach for his shirt, which he'd tossed carelessly onto the truck's seat. He'd be damned if he was going to grab for his clothes like a terrified virgin in some Gothic novel!

"I was surprised to hear that you'd married Tessa," Dana said. She trailed one finger along the truck's battered fender. "And then, when I heard about the baby, it all made sense."

"Did it?" He watched her with the same caution he'd have felt toward a rattler. He knew from past experience that she could be just as dangerous.

"Of course." She laughed again, a soft sound of understanding. "I know your penchant for taking on lame dogs and birds with broken wings. When Tessa came to you, you would have felt you had to help her. She—"

"That's enough." Keefe spoke quietly, but there was a core of steel in the words. "My marriage is none of your business. You're here because Tessa asked you to stay, because you're her sister. You're a guest. Don't start thinking that the fact that we used to be married gives you any rights beyond that. Our marriage was over a long time ago."

Dana looked shaken by his flat tone, but she recovered quickly. "It may be over, but I don't think it's forgotten." She set one slim hand against his chest and lifted her eyes to his face. "Can you honestly say you've forgotten?"

"No, I can't. But then, I broke my leg when I was ten, and I haven't forgotten that, either."

Her fingers curled, exquisitely manicured nails digging into his skin. "That doesn't seem like a particularly apt comparison."

"It works for me."

He stepped back so that her hand dropped from him, but she followed, setting both hands on his chest and sliding her palms up to his shoulders, her fingers curving into the hard muscles there.

''You can't tell me you don't still feel something when you look at me,'' she murmured, crowding closer. ''What we had between us was too strong to just die.''

The tool bench pressed against his lower back, and Keefe chose not to slide away from Dana's grasping hands. They might as well have this out, here and now.

''Catching you in bed with another man didn't go a long way to making me feel good about our marriage,'' he pointed out.

''I made a terrible mistake!'' she cried. Quick tears filled her eyes, and her mouth trembled. ''It wouldn't ever have happened again. I told you I was sorry.''

''Sorry didn't really cut it. Especially since it wasn't the first time.''

''Who told you it wasn't the— Jace! I knew he was feeding you lies about me. Damn him!''

Keefe shook his head, cutting off her vicious tirade. ''Jace didn't say anything. He didn't have to.'' His laugh was short and held little humor. ''Man, you must have thought I was deaf, dumb and blind. Did you think I didn't know what you were doing? Hell, I saw you corner Jace and damn near rape him that last night we were in Santa Fe. The next day, when he said he'd decided to head for Houston instead of going on to Denver with us, I knew why he was doing it. Catching you with that two-bit bronc rider was just icing on the cake.''

''That's not what happened,'' Dana said desperately. ''Jace had been making passes at me. And you hadn't touched me in weeks.''

''You were sleeping with half the damned country,'' he snapped. Despite his determination not to let her get to him, the memory still stung.

''I wasn't! And if I was, it was only because I knew I was losing you and I...I just couldn't bear that!''

Before he realized what she intended, she had her arms wound around his neck and had put her mouth to his. There had been a time when the feel of Dana's lips on his, her slender body in his arms, had been enough to bring him to rock-hard arousal. But that had been a long time ago, before he realized that her beauty was nothing but a shell, before he kissed Tessa, held Tessa.

He jerked his head back, breaking off the one-sided kiss, and lifted his hands to pull her arms from around his neck. The move was only half completed when a small sound made him lift his head. Someone stood next to the tailgate, silhouetted against the bright sunlight outside, staring into the shed. Tessa. In the instant he realized she was there, she turned and disappeared.

''Damn!'' Keefe knew exactly how the scene must have looked to Tessa—him with his shirt off and Dana in his arms. As if he could read her mind, he knew what she'd be thinking. He wrenched Dana's arms loose, ignoring her faint gasp at his roughness.

''Keefe—''

"Shut up!" He sidestepped the hand she reached out to him. The need to see Tessa—to explain what had happened—beat in him with every breath he took, but he paused long enough to fix his ex-wife with a look of such burning contempt that she flinched back away from him. "You're not spending another night here. Pack your things and get out."

He turned and left the shed without waiting for a response, dismissing her from his thoughts the instant she was out of his sight. Dana was of no importance. Only Tessa mattered. He crossed the yard with long, ground-eating strides, barely restraining the urge to break into a sprint. His boots thudded against the porch floor, and then he was shoving open the screen door and stepping into the kitchen.

He paused just inside the doorway. After the bright sunshine outside, it took a moment for his eyes to adjust to the comparative dimness of the kitchen. But when they did, he saw that the room was empty, except for David, sound asleep in his carrier. Walking quietly, Keefe crossed the kitchen. He had to talk to Tessa.

She wasn't hard to find. She was standing in the middle of the living room, her hands held loosely at her sides, her expression almost blank. He had the sense that she wasn't quite sure what to do with herself, where to go. She seemed unaware of his approach.

"Tessa."

At the sound of his voice, she started and spun to face him. Keefe felt something twist painfully inside him at the look in her eyes. It was gone in an instant, but he knew he'd never forget the stark pain he'd seen there. He started to go to her, wanting to pull her into his arms and offer her comfort, but she shook her head and took a quick step back, one hand coming up, as if to keep him at a distance. And the ache in his chest grew tighter.

"I know what you saw." With an effort, he kept his voice low and calm. "But it wasn't what it looked like."

"Don't." She shook her head again, her eyes focusing somewhere near his collarbone, as if she couldn't bear to look at his face. "You don't have to explain anything to me."

"Tessa—"

"No, really. I'd rather you didn't." Her mouth twisted in a pathetic effort at a smile. "I know you haven't...that you wouldn't *sleep* with her. Not as long as we're married."

"I don't *want* to sleep with her!" But his forceful tone slid right past her.

"No one can control their feelings," she continued, as if he hadn't spoken. Her tone was quietly reminiscent. She might have been talking about something of little importance. Only the familiar way her fingers knotted together gave her away—that, and the hurt that left her eyes more gray than blue. "I knew, of course. I remembered the way you used to look at her. I used to think that I'd give anything in the world to have someone love me the way you loved Dana."

"It wasn't love," he said, realizing the full truth of that statement only now.

"I knew you didn't love me that way, and I thought

that was okay,'' she said, ignoring his protest. ''I thought it didn't really matter. You cared for me, and that would be enough. But, seeing you—the two of you—just now, I realized something.''

''Tessa, it wasn't—'' He took a step toward her, hands outstretched but she backed away, shaking her head with an abrupt movement that made her golden hair swing around her face.

''Don't!''

The sharp plea stopped him instantly. He let his hands drop to his sides, staring at her in helpless frustration. How could he make her understand what had happened, make her see that all he felt for Dana now was contempt and dislike and that what he felt for her years ago had been a tangled mix of lust, infatuation and a ridiculous belief that she needed him to take care of her?

''I won't be second-best,'' Tessa said slowly, as if working her thoughts out as she spoke. ''I thought it wouldn't matter. I thought I loved you enough that it wouldn't make a difference, that my love would be enough for both of us. But I just realized that I can't do it. I love you too much to be second-best in your life.''

Keefe felt as if all the air had been knocked from him. He stared at her, his thoughts scattered in a hundred different directions. She loved him? *She loved him?* The knowledge rolled over him in a slow, warm wave. Tessa loved him. Of course she did. It was as inevitable as...as him loving her. He didn't have to think about it or question it. It just *was.* As if it had always been and would always be.

He was distantly aware of hearing the squeak of the screen door opening and thought vaguely that it was probably Dana. He hoped she was on her way to pack her clothes. He hoped even more that she'd have the good sense to go straight to her room.

"Tessa, what you saw, it wasn't what it looked like." Keefe was surprised by how steady his voice was. Hell, considering the turmoil in his head, he was surprised he could put together a coherent sentence at all.

Her smile broke his heart. "I know. Your middle-class morality," she said, laughing a little, as if at some private joke. "You wouldn't have an affair, not even when our marriage isn't real."

"Our marriage *is* real," he said, raising his voice slightly, trying to get through to her.

"No, it isn't. You're in love with someone else."

"I am *not* in love with Dana." He didn't want to talk about his ex-wife, but maybe they had to get it out of the way before they could move on to other things. At the very least, he had to make Tessa see that his feelings for her sister were not an issue between them. He pushed his fingers through his hair as he sought the words to make her understand something he wasn't entirely sure he understood himself. "I don't think I was ever in love with her. I was in lust with her, maybe, but not in love."

"I saw the way you used to look at her," Tessa said, as if there were no arguing with that look. "You worshiped her."

"You were fourteen years old—too young to know the difference between love and lust." He shook his head, his mouth twisting in a rueful half smile. ''Besides, I'd convinced myself I was in love with her. Maybe, at the start, that's almost the same thing.''

She looked at him, her eyes searching, and Keefe dared to hope that he'd gotten through to her. He wanted to put his first marriage behind them, once and for all. But before she could say anything else, they were interrupted.

''Let go of me!'' Dana's demand was punctuated by a sharp crack as the kitchen screen door was jerked open with force enough to hit the side of the house.

''Just as soon as you provide some explanations,'' Jace said grimly. Overlying the sound of their footsteps was a thin, angry wail that galvanized both Tessa and Keefe.

''David!'' Tessa started forward, only to stop abruptly, her eyes widening in surprise.

Jace walked into the living room. The baby was tucked securely in the crook of his left arm and the fingers of his right hand were wrapped, just as securely, around Dana's upper arm. That she was with him unwillingly was obvious.

''I'll sue you for every miserable penny you've ever had.'' She spit the words at him, jerking futilely against his hold.

''She was getting into her car with the baby,'' he said, looking at Keefe and Tessa and ignoring Dana as if she didn't even exist.

''With David?'' Tessa hurried forward and took the baby from him. The infant's fussy wails subsided into annoyed mutterings when he felt his mother's arms.

''Is he okay?'' Keefe loomed over the two of them,

his big hand dwarfing the baby's head as he brushed a gentle finger down his cheek.

"I think so," Tessa said. Their earlier discussion was forgotten, pushed aside, their attention all for their son.

"Oh, for God's sake, I didn't hurt him," Dana said impatiently. She yanked against Jace's hold again, stumbling as he abruptly released her. She regained her balance and glared at him. "Bastard!"

He lifted his brows and placed himself directly—and obviously—between her and the door.

Assured that the baby was unharmed, Keefe lifted his head and looked at his ex-wife. "Where were you taking him?"

"Nowhere." Dana rubbed her hand over the marks Jace's fingers had left on her arm. "You had no right to manhandle me like that."

"Nowhere?" Jace ignored her complaint. "You were just going to sit in the car and commune with him?"

"I was just going to take him for a little ride," she said. She caught their looks of disbelief and flushed. "That's not a crime."

"Why?" Her baby secure in her arms, Tessa looked at her sister. "You've barely looked at him since you've been here."

"I..." Dana glanced from Tessa to Keefe, her expression uneasy. "He was fussing, and I thought a car ride might soothe him. I read that somewhere."

"He wasn't fussing," Tessa contradicted her flatly. "I would have heard him."

"Maybe you were busy with...other things," Dana

suggested, sliding a quick glance at Keefe and then looking away.

"I would have heard him," Tessa repeated, in a tone that left no room for argument.

"Where were you going?" Keefe asked.

"I already told you. I was taking him for a ride. Now, if you don't mind, I'd like to go." Chin in the air, she glanced at the doorway that Jace was blocking. He didn't move.

"Oh, for God's sake," she snapped, turning to glare at Keefe. "You told me to leave, didn't you? Well, I can't do it unless you let me out of this room."

"I want to know where you were going with my son."

"Only he's not your son, is he?" Dana snarled, anger stripping aside caution.

Taut silence followed her comment.

"Why would you say that?" Keefe's tone was softly threatening, and Tessa saw something that might have been fear flash across her sister's face. Dana's tongue came out to wet her lower lip, and she stared at him blankly for a moment.

"I... Molly told me," she said finally. Her voice took on new confidence as she continued. "She said I wasn't to mention it, and I wouldn't have, if you hadn't started this ridiculous inquisition."

"You're lying," Tessa said. "You haven't seen Aunt Molly in over a year."

"Of course I have. I saw her last week. Right before I came here. And I'm just now seeing what a mistake *that* was," Dana added, shaking her hair back from her face with a quick, easy movement. "I'm sorry if I brought up a painful subject, but really, you've all acted like a bunch of maniacs, so you really don't have anyone to blame but yourselves."

"Aunt Molly called a little while ago," Tessa said. She spoke slowly, working things out in her mind. With everything that had happened since, Molly Thorpe's call seemed as if it had been days ago. "She said she hadn't seen you in over a year. She was surprised when I told her you were here." She stopped and glanced at Keefe. It was the first time she'd looked at him since Jace dragged Dana into the room. "That's why I came looking for you. I thought it was so odd that Aunt Molly hadn't seen her, yet—"

"Yet she told us that Molly was the one who told her where you were," Keefe finished for her. He looked at his ex-wife. "So, if it wasn't Molly, just how did you know where Tessa was?" he asked softly. "There aren't that many people who know. My family and—"

"The good senator," Jace said grimly.

"Don't be ridiculous," Dana said, but she sounded more frightened than angry. "Of course it was Aunt Molly who told me. She probably just forgot. She's getting old, and—" Her eyes darted from one face to another, reading nothing but implacable determination to get at the truth. She must have realized that there was nothing she could say, no lie she could tell. Her hands clenched into fists at her sides, and her eyes blazed with a mixture of fury and fear.

"Damn you all," she shouted. "I wish I'd never

come here.'' Sinking down on the sofa, she burst into tears.

''Now there's a sentiment I think we can all share,'' Jace said dryly.

Once Dana stopped crying, she was willing to tell them the whole story.

''It isn't like you're going to have me prosecuted,'' she pointed out, with a return of her customary confidence.

''There are places around here where a body would never be found,'' Jace pointed out gently.

From the look in Dana's eyes, she wasn't entirely sure he was kidding. Neither was Tessa. She'd seen occasional glimpses of something very dangerous beneath Jace's easygoing facade.

Dana was still sitting on the sofa. Jace stood in the doorway, though it was obvious that Dana wasn't going to try and escape. She was not only resigned to telling her story, she seemed almost to be looking forward to it, which made Tessa a little uneasy. She'd put David down in his crib, lingering over him a moment, savoring the knowledge that he was safe, though she still couldn't quite believe that they'd almost lost him. And now, she was back in the living room, waiting to hear Dana's story.

It was really very simple. Dana had come back from Europe. She'd called her sister—probably on a slow day, Tessa thought cynically—and when she found the phone disconnected, she'd called the Mallorys. Dana had always gotten along better with Tessa's in-laws than Tessa had. The senator had been away from home, but Anne Mallory had invited her to lunch and, over three or four dry martinis, had told Dana the whole story.

Tessa had a hard time picturing her reserved mother-in-law sipping more than a glass of wine, let alone drinking enough to loosen her tongue. But then, Bobby's death had hit his mother hard, had changed her even more than Tessa had realized.

Apparently Anne had been blunt about wanting her grandson, at any price. Dana was vague about who had come up with the idea that she could come to the Flying Ace and find a way to take David from them. Tessa wanted to believe that it had been Anne Mallory. The last faint ties of family feeling made her reluctant to think that Dana had thought the plan up on her own.

"But why would you agree to something like that?" she asked when Dana paused.

"Why?" Dana laughed sharply. "Why do you think? Money." She laughed again when she saw the shock Tessa couldn't hide. "Your dear mother-in-law offered me a considerable sum to snatch her precious grandchild. My life-style is rather expensive to maintain. Besides, you never know when it might come in handy to have a senator—or a senator's wife—in your pocket."

Jace made a sound low in his throat, a sound that could only have been described as a growl. Beside her Tessa felt the tension in Keefe's body. She was too stunned to share their anger.

"Didn't it bother you?" she asked, bewildered by Dana's casual attitude.

"Didn't what bother me?"

"Taking David away from me—from us." Unconsciously she reached out, and Keefe's fingers wrapped around hers.

"Well, I wouldn't make baby-snatching a hobby," Dana said casually. "But I figured this was something of an exception. From what Bobby's mother told me, you can't have been very fond of him, so it didn't seem likely that you'd be too broken up over his kid, and since it isn't Keefe's child, I didn't see why he would care all that much." She laughed again, carelessly. "Not that I needed Anne Mallory to tell me it wasn't his baby."

She looked at Keefe, her blue eyes sparkling, as if at some private joke that the two of them shared. "I, of all people, know better than to believe you'd have an affair with another man's wife. Besides, even without that, I could never believe you'd sleep with Tessa." She glanced at Tessa, her eyes bright with malice. "No offense, little sister, but you're hardly his type. Not even in the running."

Tessa stared at her. She was too stunned to feel offended. Her sister didn't even seem to see anything really wrong with what she'd done—what she'd tried to do. She sought some response to Dana's words and found her mind had gone completely blank.

But, if she couldn't find any words, Keefe didn't have the same problem. "Tessa is twice the woman you could ever hope to be. If there's one thing in my life that I'm ashamed of, it's the fact that I was once so stupid that I actually thought I was in love with you. But I'm not sorry I did it. Because if I hadn't married you, I wouldn't have met Tessa, and having her is worth every minute of misery you put me through.''

Tessa caught her breath at the stark sincerity in his voice. She turned her head to look up at him and felt a sense of wonder at what was in his eyes. Dana spoke before she could decide just what it was she'd seen.

''I guess that puts me in my place,'' she said, but her laugh couldn't conceal how shaken she was by his contemptuous dismissal of her.

''I want you to leave now,'' Tessa told her with quiet dignity.

''I'd like nothing better,'' Dana said. She stood up, but hesitated a moment, looking at Keefe and Tessa. She seemed almost confused. ''You really love each other, don't you?''

''Yes.'' That was Keefe, and Tessa felt something melt inside her at the flat sureness of his response. ''And David is my child. You can tell Anne Mallory that, and you can also tell her that, if she ever comes near us again, we'll go to the press with everything we know and a few things we'll invent. By the time the media frenzy dies out, he'll have about as much chance of getting into the White House as Saddam Hussein.''

Dana didn't say anything, but she nodded before turning and walking out of the room. Jace stepped out of the doorway to let her pass and then looked at Keefe.

''I think I'll just follow along and keep an eye on her, make sure she gets her things packed and gets off the property with no problems.''

''Thanks.''

Jace lingered a moment longer, his eyes going from Keefe to Tessa and then back again. His smile held wicked humor. ''You're a little slow on the uptake sometimes, but I'm glad you finally figured things out.''

He was gone before Keefe could respond.

He left behind a deep silence. Tessa was acutely aware of the feel of Keefe's hand on hers, of the hard strength of his body next to her. She wanted to look at him, but she couldn't seem to raise her eyes to his face. What if the love she'd heard in his voice wasn't in his eyes?

''Jace is right—I am a little slow on the uptake sometimes,'' he said quietly. ''But I figure things out eventually.''

''What did you figure out?'' she asked, finding the courage to lift her eyes to his face.

''That I love you.'' He said it quietly, without flowery words or fanfare. Tessa had never heard anything more beautiful in her life. ''I thought that marrying you was the right thing to do. I kept telling myself that it was a practical arrangement, that we could make a good marriage because we suited each other.''

He brought his hand up to cup her cheek, and Tessa thought she might just drown in the warmth of his eyes. ''It took almost losing you for me to realize how much I love you.''

''I don't care what it took.'' She set her hand on his chest, just over his heart.

''About what you saw, earlier, with Dana...'' he began.

''No.'' She pressed her fingers over his mouth.

"Not another word about Dana. As far as I'm concerned, once she leaves this house, she's out of our lives forever. I no longer even have a sister."

"If that hurts you—"

"It doesn't." She shook her head. "Blood ties aren't what makes a family. It takes ties of the heart to do that."

"Ties of the heart," he repeated. His mouth curved in a smile. "We have plenty of those."

"Yes, we do," she whispered, just as his lips touched hers.

And Then

Rachel Walker's living room had never really been intended to hold nine adults, two children and two infants. It was Labor Day weekend, and the family had gathered at her house for a barbecue. But, in direct defiance of all laws governing southern California weather, it was pouring rain, with no sign of stopping. The barbecue had been scrapped in favor of take-out pizza, which was to be delivered at any minute.

Having everyone in the same room made things a little cramped, but no one seemed to mind being crowded. Certainly, Tessa had no objection to having Keefe's large figure looming over her as he perched on the arm of her chair. She looked around at the rest of the family and felt her mouth curve in a helpless, foolish smile of contentment.

Family. This was her family now. They had accepted her as one of their own, without question, without hesitation.

"He's growing like a weed," Keefe said, leaning over to brush David's cheek with the tip of his finger.

"I still can't believe how close we came to losing him." Tessa's voice trembled. It had been two weeks since Dana left the ranch, but the memory of what she'd almost done still sent chills up her spine.

"But we didn't." Keefe set his hand on her shoulder and pulled her close. "And I don't think we have to worry about the Mallorys anymore. After talking to Molly, I don't think he's got a snowball's chance in hell of making it into the White House."

Gage overheard his comment and gave a sharp bark of laughter. "With Molly Thorpe on his tail, I suspect he'll be lucky if he manages to hang onto his senate seat."

"I hope he loses that, too," Nikki said. "The last thing this country needs is someone like that holding an important office."

"Don't kid yourself, they're all like him," her husband said cynically.

"No politics," Rachel Walker decreed as she rose from her chair. "There isn't enough room in here for a free-for-all. The pizza should be here any minute. I'm going to go see what we have to drink. I don't need any help," she added, as various members of the family moved to get up. She paused in the doorway, turning back to look at them. Her eyes touched on each of her sons in turn, then moved on to their wives and children. Her mouth curved in a soft smile. "It's good to have the whole family here."

The room was silent for a moment after she left, as each of them considered her comment. For the four brothers, family was something they'd always been able to take for granted. No matter what else happened, they'd always had each other. For their wives, it was more akin to a miracle that never quite lost its shine. But Rachel's words had given them all pause. It *was* good to have the whole family together.

The melodic chime of the doorbell interrupted the moment.

"That must be the pizza," Sam said. "I'll get it."

Before he could get to his feet, his mother's voice called out from the kitchen, "Come in."

"She left the door unlocked again," Gage muttered in exasperation. "I've told her again and again that it's not safe."

"Los Olivos isn't exactly a crime center," his wife said comfortably.

"Maybe not, but she still ought to lock her door."

"Yeah, but think how handy it is not to have to get up to let in the pizza guy," Cole said, looking on the practical side of things.

But the woman who stepped into the living room wasn't delivering a pizza. Tall and slender, she wore a calf-length floral-print dress in soft shades of peach and ivory. Her strawberry-blond hair was drawn back and held against her nape by a plain gold clip. The gentle severity of the style might have looked harsh on another woman, but it suited her, highlighting the elegant sweep of her cheekbones and the delicate line of her jaw. The deep, clear sapphire of her eyes was emphasized by long, dark lashes.

She was, quite simply, the most beautiful woman Tessa had ever seen. She stood in the doorway and looked around the crowded room, her lovely eyes resting on first one person and then another, lingering on Sam a moment before drifting to Keefe, Gage and Cole in turn. Conversations ended abruptly as each of them became aware of her. Gage had been sitting on the sofa, holding his infant daughter, but when he saw the newcomer, he handed the baby to his wife and rose, his expression blank with shock. Tessa glanced up at Keefe, seeking an explanation, but he was staring at the woman, also. She felt his arm tense around her, and then he withdrew it and stood up.

Barely a minute before, the room had been filled with voices, conversations layered one on another, childish chatter blended with deeper adult tones. Now, the silence was so thick, it was almost visible. Even Danny and Mary were quiet, their wide eyes moving from their parents to the woman in the doorway.

Finding herself the focus of nearly a dozen pairs of eyes, Tessa would have broken and run. But the stranger stood her ground, her expression calm. Only the color that tinted her cheeks suggested she might not be as unaffected as she seemed.

"What does everyone want to drink?" Rachel's voice preceded her as she left the kitchen. "Pizza always seems to call for beer, but it's a little early in the day for that. Oh, hello." She smiled at the newcomer. "You don't look like you're delivering pizzas."

"No, I'm not." The woman's voice was low and a little husky. She half turned to look at Rachel, and the color slowly ebbed from her face, leaving her skin ivory-pale. ''I'm sorry to interrupt. It looks like you're having a party.''

''Not exactly,'' Rachel answered, absently. Her dark eyes were searching the woman's face. ''We were just...'' She let the words trail off. She lifted one hand and pressed her fingertips to her chest, as if to still the sudden acceleration of her heartbeat. When she spoke again, her voice was a whisper. ''Who are you?''

''Mom.'' Sam took a step forward, his expression tight and hard. ''Don't—''

''Who are you?'' Rachel asked again, louder this time.

For a moment, it seemed as if the woman weren't going to answer. She looked away from Rachel, her glance skating over the tense figures of Sam, Keefe, Gage and Cole. She looked back at Rachel, who was looking at her with a mixture of hope and fear that was painful to see.

''I shouldn't have come,'' she whispered, almost to herself. ''I didn't mean to—''

''Please.'' Rachel's hand came out, almost but not quite touching the woman's arm. ''Please, tell me. Who are you?''

''I... My name is Shannon. I think I'm your daughter.''

* * * * *

THE HOMECOMING

Maggie Shayne

To Eileen Fallon, my agent, mentor
and, most important, dear friend.

Chapter 1

Luke stood at the graveside of his best friend and mentor, the man he'd always wanted to emulate, and waited for the others to arrive—but they never did. The minister stood there, too. He was a small, skinny man with a road map of a face. He didn't wear flowing robes, though. The only things that marked him as a man of the cloth were the collar of his shirt and the Bible in his hand. It was a pretty day in Tennessee. Birds singing. Traffic rushing by. Flowers in bloom. Just like nothing had ever happened. Just like the greatest long-distance trucker in the business wasn't lying dead right now in a box about to be lowered into the cold womb of the earth.

The minister looked at his watch, then at Luke.

''Are you sure we're not early?'' Luke asked. He'd expected hundreds to be in attendance. Buck was a legend. A favorite of every truck-stop waitress and diesel mechanic in seven states. His rig had been the most recognizable one on the road, all decked out with chrome, and more lights than a Christmas tree. Oh, it had been a showpiece. Buck's pride and joy.

It twisted Luke's stomach to think of the way it had looked when he'd stopped by the wrecking yard to view the remains. Just a pile of twisted metal and shattered glass. Nothing left of its former glory.

And now it looked to Luke as though there was even less left of its owner-operator. It bothered him that no one had come to say goodbye to Buck.

The minister cleared his throat and met Luke's eyes. Luke sighed and gave him a nod. The preacher began to speak, but he didn't really have much to say. He read the Lord's Prayer, said how Buck had gone on to a better place. He talked about salvation. Luke listened until he couldn't listen anymore. Then he said, ''’Scuse me, Reverend, but um...do you think it would be all right if I, uh...''

The man smiled, new wrinkles appearing in his face. ''By all means, son. Say a few words. Lord knows, you knew this man better than I.''

Nodding, Luke cleared his throat. He held his hat, a duck-billed green one that had a bulldog and the word *Mack* on the front, in his hands in front of him. "Lord," he said, "this man was one of the good ones. I suppose you know that already, but I want to make sure it gets said. He never passed by a broken-down four-wheeler on the roadside without stopping to offer a hand. He never left a hitchhiker out in the rain. He never left less than a dollar tip for a waitress, even if all he ordered was a cup of coffee. And there was never a better driver. Not ever. Why, I've seen Buck Waters perform acrobatics with his rig when he lost his brakes on a three-mile downgrade, when any other driver would have wound up jackknifing and taking a lot of people with him. I've seen him pull out of a slide on roads so icy you couldn't walk on them. I've seen him avoid accidents that would have killed anyone else, when ignorant folks pulled out in front of him or cut him off. In fact, he never did have a wreck—not until this one. Now, I know it doesn't seem like much of a legacy to leave behind. But it's all he had. And I sure hope you won't hold that against him. Some men just aren't cut out for settling down, raising families and all that. And just because no one's here today, no kids or wife crying at the graveside...well, that doesn't mean Buck Waters wasn't loved. He was. And it doesn't mean he didn't touch lives. Because he touched mine."

Luke lowered his head as a flood of feeling rushed up into his throat and kept him from saying more.

A soft hand fell on his shoulder. ''That was very eloquent, son.''

He glanced up at the minister, pulled himself together and shook his head. ''It's not right that no one's here for him. There should have been lots of people here today.''

The older man's brows rose. ''Well, you're here.'' He paused a moment, deep in thought. ''From what you've said about your friend, it seems his life was as full as he wanted it to be. Maybe so is this service.''

''No,'' Luke said, shaking his head. ''Every man wants to think someone's going to miss him when he's gone. Every man wants to leave something of himself behind.''

Smiling very gently, the minister said, ''No, son. Not every man. But it's pretty obvious *you* want those things.''

''Me? No. No, not me.''

The minister looked at the shiny coffin and smiled sadly. ''Maybe this service is Buck's way of reminding you that you won't get those things in the end if you live the way he did. Family. Loved ones. Oh, I'm sure for him his life was perfect without those things. But maybe...yours isn't?'' He shrugged. ''It's something to think about, at any rate.''

Luke frowned but said nothing. A million disjointed thoughts were spinning in his head. Above them all was the voice of his mother, telling him he would never settle down, that he had been born with the wanderlust, just like his father.

The minister turned again to the open grave and held one hand, palm out, above it. ''Lord, we commend the soul of Buck Waters into thy tender care. May his soul fly on wings of angels into heaven. Amen.''

''Amen,'' Luke intoned. ''Hammer down, Buck.''

The minister patted Luke again as he left. Luke spent a few more moments in the cemetery. Then he headed into the parking lot, where his rig took up most of the spaces. It gleamed like a gem, that rig of his. A turquoise-blue Pete, with a sleeper the size of a condo. Had a fridge, a microwave, TV and VCR. He could live in it. Hell, he did, a lot of the time. The polished Aluminum Bud wheels all the way around shone in the sunlight. On the side, in silver lettering, was his name. Lucas Tyrel Mason Brand, Owner-Operator. The rig was running, flaps on top of the twin smokestacks clicking up and down as if talking to him. You didn't just shut a semi down for a brief stop and start it up again like you would with a car. You let her idle. Let her purr. It was good for her.

Luke climbed behind the wheel, closed his hands around its familiar shape. And he told himself he wasn't all that much like Buck. Sure, his life was on the road, hauling loads of goods from town to town, state to state. He didn't really have a home.

But, unlike Buck, he had family. Well…relatives, anyway. His daddy's wandering ways had seen to that. The man had been married to two women at the same time. Fathered two kids on the East Coast and five in Oklahoma before he died in a hail of gunfire twenty-some odd years ago. Luke had no real memory of John Brand. His own mother hadn't been a wife at all, legal or otherwise. She'd just been a fling. And Luke had been the result of it. Still, John Brand's name was listed on Luke's birth certificate. And the old bastard had sent money, even come to visit several times a year until he'd been killed, according to Luke's mother. Not that Luke had much memory of the man himself, but his mother had always been very honest about it all. And when she passed last year she'd made Luke promise to visit his seven half siblings and all those cousins in Texas—the children of John Brand's brother, Orrin.

Of course he hadn't done it. Hadn't seen any reason to. Until now.

He drew a deep breath, sighed heavily. He supposed having relatives didn't really mean a hell of a lot if you'd never met them. Still, it was a daunting prospect. What was he supposed to do? Just pull the big rig into some stranger's driveway and yell, "Hi there, I'm your illegitimate bastard half brother."

His mobile phone rang. He picked it up. "Lucas Brand Trucking," he said automatically.

"Hey, Luke, it's me. How was the funeral?" The voice on the other end belonged to Smitty, one of Luke's favorite brokers.

"Not too good, Smitty. But I suppose funerals aren't supposed to be."

"Guess not. Look, I know this is a bad time, but I've got a load bound for Texas, Luke. And it needs to go out today. Can you take it?"

Luke swallowed hard. Texas. Of all places. Odd coincidence, just when he'd been thinking about the relatives he'd never met. "Where in Texas?" he asked.

"Town called Quinn. It's in the neighborhood of El Paso," Smitty said.

The words fell on Luke like bricks. He just sat there a minute, blinking in shock.

"Luke?"

"You've gotta be kidding me," Luke finally managed to say. "Quinn? You said Quinn, Texas?"

"No, I'm not kidding. Why, what's wrong with Quinn? Look, the call just came in, Luke. I guess your friend Buck was slated to take this load today, but, uh…well, with the accident and all…"

"Buck? This was Buck's run?"

"Yeah. Is that too, you know, morbid for you, Luke?"

Luke closed his eyes. In his mind he heard the minister's words of only a few moments before. *Maybe this is Buck's way of reminding you that you won't get those things in the end if you live the way he did....*

Buck had never steered Luke wrong in his life. He'd been the father figure Luke had never had—had never even known he *wanted.* And crazy as it might seem, Luke had the feeling Buck was trying to guide him just one last time. It didn't make any sense to think that way. Hell, he wasn't even sure he believed in life after death. But...but he couldn't not do this. It was almost like Buck's last request.

"I'll take the load," he said finally.

"Great," Smitty said. "Luke, is there anywhere in particular you want to head from there? I can hook you up with an outgoing load if you want."

Luke licked his lips. "Let's leave this one open-ended. I might, um...I might be staying there a while."

He heard the surprise in the other man's voice when Smitty said, "Oh. Okay, sure, Luke, whatever you want. The load you're hauling out there is fertilizer. Pick it up at the Farm-Rite Depot on Eaton and Main. Can you find that?"

"Yeah," Luke said. "I can find it." He hung up the phone, glancing back toward the cemetery and the grave of his friend. "Hell, Buck, I suppose you're taking it easy on me. Cousins in Texas are going to be a lot easier to start off with than a pile of half sisters in Oklahoma."

Drawing a deep breath, he revved the engine, released the brake and slid the truck into gear.

Halfway there, Luke decided it might not be a bad idea to call these poor unsuspecting cousins in Quinn, Texas, and let them know he existed and would be in town for a visit soon. He had a momentary bout of panic when the operator told him there were five Brands listed in Quinn.

''Five?'' He downshifted, cradling the phone between his ear and shoulder.

He didn't have a clue.

''Do you know the address?'' the operator asked.

''No. Only that it's some kind of a ranch.''

''There's a dude ranch....''

''No, it's a regular ranch. Cattle, I think.'' He racked his brain to recall the name. His mom had mentioned it once, he was sure she had.

''I have two ranches. Sky Dancer Ranch, and The Texas Brand,'' the operator said.

''That's it. The Texas Brand.'' He swallowed hard. ''Can you connect me?''

Luke didn't know what to expect, really. The man on the phone, Garrett Brand, had been surprised but kind, and he'd seemed welcoming. He'd even given Luke directions to the ranch from the depot in town and asked him what time they could expect him. But Luke was still nervous. In his experience, in his entire life, the word *family* had almost no meaning. It was him and his mother. And sure, they'd been close, but in more of an ''us against the world'' kind of way. His mother had never let anyone else into their world. Friends, neighbors, they were held at arm's length. His mother had told him over and over again that they didn't need anyone else. That they would be fine all on their own. She'd been a strong, fiercely proud woman who couldn't seem to trust. And maybe that had a lot to do with his father, and maybe there was more to it. Luke didn't know and probably never would. But in his experience, family meant, ''hands off.'' It was a tight, closed relationship that did not welcome outsiders.

So when he pulled his rig into the dusty curving driveway, underneath the huge wooden arch that had ''Texas Brand'' carved into its face, Luke was totally unprepared for what awaited him.

It had only been four hours since he'd made that phone call. Yet a huge banner was draped from the wide front porch of the white ranch house. ''Welcome Luke'' was hand-painted in crooked letters across its face. Between that and the place where he brought his rig to a stop there must have been twenty people milling around amid picnic tables loaded with food.

His throat tightened up a little as he shut the rig down, opened his door and climbed out. When he looked up, a big man stood in front of him, wearing a ten-gallon hat and a warm smile. He reached out and clasped Luke's hand. ''I'm Garrett,'' he said. ''Welcome to the family, Luke.'' His grip was firm and dry, and he shook Luke's hand with enthusiasm.

Luke shook his head. "I didn't expect all this," he said. "You shouldn't have gone to all this fuss."

"Hey, it isn't every day we get a new member of the family," a dark-skinned man said. He grinned and nodded toward the woman on his arm, whose belly was swollen. "Although in a few months, we'll be getting a couple more, right, Elliot?"

Across the way another man, this one with reddish-brown hair, hugged his own woman to his side, and she, too, looked to be expecting. "Right you are, Wes. Three months, two weeks and three days, if Doc's accurate."

Wes shook Luke's hand, introducing his wife, Taylor, and then Elliot followed suit, along with his wife, Esmeralda. The next man to come up to him was as big as Garrett, but blond, and his wife was a bit of a thing named Penny, who cradled a baby boy in her arms. Then there were the handsome Adam and his wife Kirsten, who looked to Luke like they should be modeling western wear in a magazine. And then there was a fellow named Lash and his wife Jessi.

Finally yet another woman parted the crowd to bring two kids front and center. A strapping boy of six or so, and a little girl who couldn't have been more than three, stood right in front of Luke. The woman said, "I'm Chelsea, Garrett's wife. This is my son, Bubba, and Jessi's little girl, Maria-Michelle. And they have something for you.''

His head spinning, Luke hunkered down to more of a level with the kids. The little girl was just as pretty as a picture, and she held up a box to him. The little boy unfolded a piece of paper, and everyone around went silent as he cleared his throat.

''In our family, we have one rule
Bigger than all the rest,
Family comes first, and family is best!
So welcome to our family,
We're happy that you came.
But you need just one more thing
That goes with the family name.''

The little boy looked up shyly. ''I wrote it myself. Mom helped.''

''I don't know when I've heard a nicer poem, Bubba. Thanks.''

The little girl shoved the box at him and said, ''I helped whap it! I put on the bow!''

''And a beautiful bow it is,'' Luke said, taking the package. He opened it carefully, sticking the bow to his shirt pocket and seeing the little girl smile even wider. Then he took the lid off the box to find a soft brown Stetson hat inside.

He swallowed hard, taking it out of the box and turning it slowly, admiring its perfect shape and its hand-tooled leather band. "This is just…too much. You guys are…"

"Put it on!" Bubba said.

Luke looked at the men around him. Most of them wore hats like this one, the colors varied, of course. Slowly he took off his Mack hat and replaced it with the Stetson. Then he straightened.

A whoop went up, and then everyone was talking at once, slapping his back and tugging him toward the food. Someone turned on some country music. He smelled barbecue and smoke. And he felt…hell, he couldn't say just what he felt. It was as if his heart were swelling up in his chest. He hadn't known he could have this. He still couldn't believe it was for real. That these people wouldn't all just finish the show they were putting on for him and then send him on his way, and that would be the last he ever heard from them.

He was wrong about that, of course. Three months later he was still there, and for the first time in his life, he was part of a huge, open-armed, loving, real, honest-to-goodness family. And every night before he went to sleep, he whispered his thanks to his old friend Buck Waters for somehow leading Luke to what Buck himself had never had.

Chapter 2

Jasmine did not like having her son anywhere near the dive where she waited tables and occasionally danced on them. She didn't even like having Baxter in this part of Chicago. But once again, her low-life boss had forgotten to mail her paycheck, along with her roommate's, so she'd had no choice but to stop and pick them up. She pulled the car into the employee parking area in the back. There was not another vehicle in sight, and she considered that a good thing, given the kinds of people who tended to congregate at The Catwalk. Of course, most of them would be comatose at this time of the morning. Sighing, she turned to Baxter.

He sat in the passenger seat, looking up at her through the round lenses of his glasses. Seven years old, and already his teachers were suggesting he skip ahead a grade. He was fully smart enough to understand why he should do as she told him. He seldom did, however.

"Now listen to me," she said, and she made her voice as stern as it had ever been when speaking to her reason for being. "I have to get my paycheck so we can stop at the bank on the way to school and get you some cash for that end-of-the-year field trip today. All right?"

He nodded, pushing his glasses up on his nose with his forefinger. "And you have to get Aunt Rosebud's check, too."

"I know."

"And her bag, too, Mom. Don't forget her bag," he reminded her.

"I won't forget." She touseled her son's hair. "Your crazy Aunt Rosebud would forget her own head if it wasn't attached, wouldn't she?"

He giggled. "Nobody could forget their head," he said, though he was smiling. "But, yeah, she sure does forget things a lot."

Yes, she did. But last night, at least, she'd had reason for her customary absentmindedness. Jasmine's roommate had received a phone call last night from a lawyer, telling her that her mother had died shortly after she'd taken off. He'd been searching for Rosebud ever since. And even though Rosebud hadn't seen the woman in two years, the news had still hit her hard. Jasmine wanted to help, but she didn't know how. She and Rosebud were more like sisters than roommates. They worked together, lived together, shared their car, their expenses… even Baxter. Before Rosebud, Jasmine had never been willing to let any other human being into her world. It was just her and her son—no one else needed, wanted or welcome, thank you very much. But Rosebud had somehow worked her way into Jasmine's heart. It was good to have a friend. Someone you could trust. And it drove Jasmine crazy that she hadn't been able to ease the pain in Rosebud's eyes last night.

"Mom?"

Blinking, Jasmine brought her focus back to the matter at hand. Baxter. "Now, listen close, honey, it's only going to take me a minute to run into that building, grab the checks—"

"And Aunt Rosebud's bag."

"And Aunt Rosebud's bag, and run right back out again. I want you to *wait right here.* It's *very* important. Okay?"

Baxter nodded again. But already his attention was being pulled away from her, his big eyes straying as he scanned the parking area, the buildings, the pigeons on the roofs, the trash cans near Leo's office window, the rear entrance to the bar. "If there were an owl back here, there wouldn't be so many pigeons hanging around," Baxter said casually.

"That's good, Baxter. I'll be sure to tell my boss

that, but you need to pay attention to what I'm telling you now."

"No rats, either. Owls are their natural predators."

"Yes, that's true."

"We need more owls around here." He nodded thoughtfully, as if certain he'd just solved one of Chicago's biggest problems. Then he looked at her in all seriousness and said, "Can I drive the rest of the way to school?"

"You can't even reach the pedals!"

"Can so! Aunt Rosebud let me drive in the parkin' lot one day!" Then he clapped a hand over his mouth, and his eyes widened. Obviously he wasn't supposed to tell that little secret.

"Aunt Rosebud lets you do just about whatever you want," Jasmine said softly. "That doesn't mean I'm gonna let you do the same. Now, do you promise to stay in the car like I told you and be a good boy for a minute, so I can get those checks?"

"And Aunt Rosebud's bag," he gently reminded her. "Yes, I'll be good."

"Promise?"

He nodded solemnly. "Spit-swear!" he said, and he spat into his palm and offered it to her to shake.

"Where do you pick this stuff up, Bax? Look, a promise is a promise. I don't need a spit-swear, okay?"

He made a face. "Okay." Then he wiped his palm on his jeans.

Jasmine locked his door, then got out and locked her own before she closed it. She blew him a kiss and headed to the bar's back door, but when she tried to open it, it wouldn't give. Locked. Damn. She would have to go around to the front. A cold shiver danced up her spine the second her car and her son were out of her sight. ''It'll only be a minute,'' she told herself. ''He'll be fine.'' But she didn't like him being here. Not in this neighborhood, much less in this bar. She'd be damned before she would take him inside with her.

She walked through the front door, underneath the neon sign that read The Catwalk. On the walls were photos of mostly naked women in various poses. The round tables were clean, their chairs upside down on top of them. She waited tables here four nights a week. On weekends she danced. The stage was empty now except for the poles she and Rosebud and a couple of other girls twined themselves sensuously around on Friday and Saturday nights while music pounded and men howled. She never took *everything* off. And she never turned tricks, though several of the other dancers did, including Rosebud. She didn't like dancing for drunks for a living, but some nights she could bring home three hundred bucks just in tips. She couldn't make that kind of money anywhere else. And she needed that kind of money. She needed to keep Baxter in a good school, in a decent apartment, in a nice part of town. There was nothing she wouldn't do for her son. Nothing.

And she wouldn't do this forever. Just until something better came along. As far as she was concerned, it was a symptom of a sick society, though, when a classically trained dancer had to take her clothes off to make a living at her art.

She walked beyond the stage, into the back part of the building, which housed a communal dressing room for the dancers, the boss's office and the time clock, mounted on the wall in the hallway. Muffled voices came from Leo's office. If she wasn't quiet, he would be sure to come out and try to strong-arm her into working on her only night off. It never failed. So she walked softly up to the time clock in the hall. Sure enough, she spotted her check in the slot with her time card. Rosebud's was in her slot, as well. ''Damn Leo Hardison,'' she muttered under her breath. He couldn't be bothered to stick them into an envelope and mail them. She snatched both checks up, then tiptoed into the dressing room and spotted Rosebud's denim bag slung over the back of a chair near her makeup mirror. She'd half turned to go when something caught her eye, made her turn back. On Rosebud's dressing table a fat manilla envelope sat in front of the makeup mirror. The name Jenny Lee Walker was typed across the front.

Frowning, Jasmine picked it up and murmured, ''That's funny. I didn't think anybody but me knew

Rosebud's real name.'' It was addressed to her in care of The Catwalk; the return address was some law firm in Texas. Vaguely, Jasmine thought of the lawyer who'd contacted Rosebud with the news of her mother's death. Must be connected. Hell, maybe Rosebud had inherited a fortune or something. Jasmine stuffed the two checks and the big envelope inside Rosebud's oversize denim bag, hitched it over her shoulder and turned to leave.

She walked quietly into the hall and started down it, intending to go past Leo's office to the back door, which would save her a few steps. His office door was closed anyway, and the back door would open from the inside, even when the lock was engaged.

She was almost to the back exit when the gunshots rang out. Three explosions, equally spaced, each one making her heart slam against her chest and her entire body jerk in reaction as she stood there frozen. *Bang. Bang. Bang.*

Leo's office door flew open ahead of her, and she could see, for just an instant, very clearly inside. Leo stood there, holding the door open but still facing inside, muttering, ''What the hell did you do? Dammit, Petronella, what the hell did you do?''

Another man, familiar to her from the club, stood over the still body of a third, his back to Jasmine. ''Did what I had to.''

Jasmine's horrified gaze slid down to the man on the floor. He was bleeding from his head, a dark pool that spread itself slowly underneath him. Then something made her look past the body, up at the rear window. She saw the wide eyes and wire-rimmed glasses of her little boy looking right back at her.

"He was a cop!" Leo said. "You've murdered a freaking cop!"

Jasmine had to move, and she had to move fast, before either of those men looked up and saw Baxter there. She couldn't get out the back door without moving right past Leo's open office door, so she backed away instead, inching, as silently as her shaking knees would allow, back up the hall. If Leo or that other man so much as turned their heads, they would see Baxter.

"Why the hell didn't you know about this before now? Huh? What the hell am I paying you for, anyway?" Leo demanded, his voice loud, ringing, bouncing off the walls of the empty bar and off the insides of her head.

The other man swore. "I don't know everything that happens in the department, Leo. What do you think I am, the chief or something? Besides, this guy wasn't one of mine. He was a Fed."

A federal agent, her mind whispered, but only briefly. She didn't have time to listen or to try to analyze their words. She had to get to Baxter. Get him out of here before either Leo or his murdering cohort saw him...or realized she had ever been here. She eased back up the hall, the way she'd come, out into the front of the bar, toward the front door. She opened it carefully, started outside. And then she heard the clanging metal of those trash cans out back, underneath Leo's window.

"What the hell was that?" Leo asked suddenly.

Jasmine ran. She raced around the club, to the lot in the back. As she neared the lot, she saw Baxter running toward the car. The trash cans near the window he'd been peering through were lying on their sides. Then the bar's back door opened just as Baxter reached the car and yanked the passenger door open. Leo and the other man lunged out. The killer, Petronella, had a gun, and he lifted it, pointed it at Baxter, as the boy pulled the car door closed behind him. A shot rang out.

"Leave him alone!" Jasmine scooped up a broken piece of brick and hurled it at the man for all she was worth. It clocked him in the head, and he went to his knees. She heard her car start up and couldn't believe it. Leo was turning toward her now, squinting and shielding his eyes. He was looking right into the sun, and she was in the shadow of the building, she realized. But the other man was struggling to his feet again, pulling up the gun, pointing it at her. The next thing Jasmine knew, her car was lurching forward. She had to jump out of the way or get hit. Baxter's head was so low she didn't think he could possibly see where he was going. The car roared to a jerking, rocking stop right between her and the killer, and she yanked the door open and climbed in, shoving her baby aside, holding him down with one hand. She stomped the gas pedal and left rubber as she sped away.

"My God, baby. My God, baby, are you okay?" She kept her foot to the floor, veering in and out of lanes, as she ran her free hand over her son's head, his neck, his shoulders. "Are you hurt, Bax? Are you all right?" Her eyes were on him more than they were on the road, scanning him for injuries, fully expecting to see blood and bullet holes.

"I'm okay, Mom. I'm okay."

"You are?"

He nodded. Tears streaming, Jasmine let the relief course through her. It was true; he hadn't been hit. "Thank you, Jesus," she whispered, pulling him up onto the seat, into a one-armed hug. She kissed his face, felt the way he was trembling. She looked in the rearview mirror. No sign of anyone chasing them. She slowed down an iota. "Come on, baby, get your seat belt on now. We're gonna take you somewhere safe. Somewhere far, far away from those bad men. I promise you that. You're safe now, Baxter."

He nodded, but she didn't think he believed her.

Three things kept running through Jasmine's mind over and over again as she drove. Leo and that other man—the man she'd been seeing around The Catwalk for weeks lately—they'd seen her car. They'd seen Baxter. And they knew he had witnessed them murdering a federal agent. They'd tried to kill her little boy, and it would not be difficult for them to find her. She stroked Baxter's hair as she drove, while he refused to shed a single tear and yet shook all over. "It's gonna be okay, baby. I promise, it's gonna be okay."

He wasn't talking, wasn't asking questions, which was so unlike him that it scared her. His little arms were twined tight around his waist, his head down, his whole body shaking. Every few seconds Jasmine glanced into her rearview mirror again, but she didn't see them following her.

No, they wouldn't follow her. Why the hell should they? They knew where she lived.

Suddenly her heart seemed to freeze in her chest. Rosebud! God, she had to warn Rosebud! Looking around her, she spotted a pay phone. Dammit, she was so afraid to stop the car. But she had to.

She circled the block three times. The phone was on a corner, near a convenience store. It was broad daylight. It shouldn't feel so damn frightening. "Mama's gotta make a phone call, honey," she said softly, finally pulling the car to a stop with the driver's door right beside the pay phone. "Scootch right over here behind the wheel, baby. You can hold my hand the whole time, okay?"

Nodding, his huge dark eyes riveted to hers and wet with unshed tears, Baxter gripped her hand. She opened the car door, the quarter already in her hand. Getting out, she kept hold of Baxter with the other hand and dropped the coin into the slot. Carefully she punched the numbers. She noticed her nails. She and Rosebud had both had their nails freshly done just yesterday. Extra long and curving, and ruby-red. Rosebud had a white rose painted on every nail. Jasmine had opted for tiny sparkling bits of glass that looked like diamonds. They gleamed in the sunlight now as she punched the numbers on the keypad. Then she listened while the phone in her apartment rang and rang and rang. Why didn't she answer? Rosebud would have turned on the answering machine if she'd gone out.

What was she supposed to do, dammit? What the hell was she going to do?

She put the phone down, slid back into the car with Baxter, closed the door. *Think. Think, dammit!*

Rosebud might be out on the stoop. She did that sometimes, just sat on the stoop and watched the people go by. Said it helped her think. Jasmine could just drive by. Just drive by, not stop, not go inside, not risk her baby. Just drive by and see. If Rosebud was there, she could pick her up and they would be out of there. That would work. She could see it all plainly in her mind. She would just pick Rosebud up and they would speed away. And everything would be fine. They could go to some other city. It could work. She was forty-five minutes from the apartment by now. God, please let her get back in time.

She drove as fast as she dared. And when she got to her neighborhood, she put on her sunglasses and skirted the outermost streets, then dared to get in closer. "Lie down on the floor, baby," she told Baxter. "Stay down low for just a minute, okay, honey?"

He didn't argue, didn't ask why, for once. He just did what she said. She almost sobbed in a mix of relief and worry. It wasn't like her Bax to be so timid, so obedient, so quiet.

She turned and went closer, not turning onto her own street but passing by it and glancing down it as she did.

"Oh, no..."

Lights, flashing red and blue. Lots of them. She could see people standing in the street. She turned the wheel, went around the block, came back up to her street on the other side—her building was on the corner. She could see clearly from this end. She drove, almost holding her breath, until she reached the corner. And then she stopped and just sat there and looked.

Two men carried a stretcher out the front door onto the stoop, and started down the steps to the waiting ambulance. But the person on that stretcher didn't need any ambulance. Jasmine could see, even from here, the black vinyl that enveloped the victim on that stretcher. A body bag.

The men paused on the top step as a uniformed officer spoke to them. Leaning over, he unzipped the vinyl tomb. A hand fell free, slender and white, and Jasmine sucked in a breath. Long, freshly done nails adorned that hand. Bright red, with something tiny and white on every one.

She clapped a hand over her mouth to keep from crying out loud. But her tears rolled so thick and so fast she couldn't stop them.

Behind her, a horn blasted. She was holding up traffic.

The cop paused in zipping the body back up again and turned to look her way. Jasmine froze as she got a full view of his face. He was the same man who'd been with Leo this morning—the same man who'd killed a federal agent and done his best to kill her, too. He stood there with the sun winking off his shiny badge, and Jasmine whispered, ''Petronella.''

His eyes narrowed on her, and he lifted a hand to shield them from the sun, as if trying to see better. Jasmine stomped on the gas pedal, and the car lurched away.

Chapter 3

Luke kicked a chunk of moss off the wide stone steps of the old brick house and gnawed his lower lip. ''I've made up my mind, Garrett,'' he said to his cousin, a man who, in the past three months, had become almost a brother to him, something that still amazed Luke to no end. ''I'm staying.''

He looked up, saw the wide grin he'd known damn well he would see on the big man's Stetson-shaded face. Garrett slapped his shoulder. ''The family's gonna be glad to hear that, Luke. Chelsea's been nagging me every single night on this one. 'Can't you talk him into staying? Why don't you try harder?' And so on and on and on.''

Luke blew a long sigh. ''I didn't mean to leave everyone hanging so long. It's just that, well, it wasn't an easy decision.'' He looked at the gleaming machine parked in the long driveway. ''That rig's been my partner and pretty much my only friend for a long while now. But...well, hell, Garrett, I guess it took Buck's dying to make me realize it wasn't the only thing I wanted out of life.''

Garrett nodded. Luke had talked to him at length about Buck's life and death, and that moment when he'd made the decision to come out here. So he knew the story. ''Does that mean you've figured out what you do want, Luke?''

Luke smiled. ''What I've figured out is that my options are wide-open. I loved my mother dearly, Garrett, but she did me a little bit of a disservice in raising me the way she did. Refusing to share me with anyone else, or to let anyone else get close to her—to either of us. She raised me to believe it was better to be closed off, independent, solitary.'' He shook his head. ''I never in my wildest dreams imagined being a part of a huge, sprawling family like this one.''

Garrett nodded. ''I can't imagine not being a part of it. And it seems to just keep getting bigger!''

Luke laughed aloud, thinking of the two expectant daddies in the clan, Wes and Elliot, and how close Taylor and Esmeralda were to their due dates.

''But that's the beauty of it, Garrett. And that's what I want. I've spent a lot of time figuring that out. So much that I can see it in my mind just as clear as I can see you standing there. I want what you have, Garrett. I want a home that opens its arms up to me when I walk in the front door.'' He turned and looked back at the still sad looking brick house, seeing only its potential. ''I want a family that does the same. I want to find a woman who wants the same things out of life that I do. A good, clean, wholesome woman who can make biscuits and babies.''

Garrett laughed out loud, a deep booming sound. ''Well, we got the home part covered, at least. This place goes up for auction next week. And you're the only interested party in town.''

''How do you know that?'' Luke asked.

''My wholesome wife, my wholesome sister, my wholesome sisters-in-law—they're not beneath snooping. And it's a small town, so snooping ain't all that difficult. If anyone else were planning to bid on this old place at that tax auction, we'd know about it by now. They aren't.''

Sighing deeply, Luke looked at his rig, all shine and polish, in the dirt driveway. She gleamed under the bright Texas sunshine like a gem in a spotlight. ''Hell, I can't say I won't miss her,'' he said. ''But I got a hell of an offer on her.''

''You gonna take it?''

''Already did,'' Luke said. ''The buyer will be here this afternoon to pick her up. He's paying me enough to buy this place outright.''

''It'll take a lot of fixing up, you know.'' Garrett

gripped the old iron railing on the flagstone steps, gave it a shake. It wobbled loosely back and forth.

"Like I could have rented this place for three months and not figured that one out?"

Garrett shrugged. "It's solid, though, at the heart of it. Just needs some surface work done."

"Of course it's solid—it's made of brick. This is the one that even the Big Bad Wolf couldn't blow down." He slid his gaze over the faded red brick, the thick green vines twisting up the sides, with huge pink blossoms trumpeting every few inches. Both floors were lined with arched, stone-silled windows, the bricks around them turned lengthwise in fancy fan patterns. "They don't build them like this anymore."

"And don't forget the best part," Garrett said. "It's right next door to the Texas Brand."

"Key selling point," Luke said, and they both laughed.

Garrett's smile faded, and a sincere expression took its place. "I'm glad you came to us, Luke. And even more glad that you're staying."

Lowering his head, Luke shook it slowly. "You all made me feel like family right from the first. That's something I've never had. Never thought I could have."

"You *are* family. Don't forget that. In a family where family comes first, that means a whole lot." Garrett grinned. "Now I'm gonna head home before I wax any more sappy than I already have. See you for dinner, right?''

''Depends. Whose turn is it to cook?''

''Mine,'' Garrett said. ''I'm barbequing ribs. You don't want to miss that.''

''Trust me, I won't.''

Garrett smiled from ear to ear and turned to go, his long strides eating up the distance to his oversize pickup nearby.

Luke stood there a moment on the porch of his new home, the place where he'd come to find his roots, to start over, to make something of his own. He walked slowly to the rig, where she sat in the driveway. ''Well, old girl, I guess this is just about it. We've come to a fork in the road. You're goin' one way, and I'm goin' the other.'' He took off his duck-billed bulldog hat, opened the truck door and gently set it on the seat. Closing the door again, he headed back to the house, up the stone stairway, across the porch. He took another hat from the rack just inside the door. The Stetson of dark brown felt, with the leather hatband around it. He put it on.

He'd been switching hats for a while now. One day thinking of staying here and wearing the cowboy hat. The next day, aching for the open road and wearing his Mack hat. But today he knew he'd made a decision. He adjusted the Stetson on his head. And it felt right.

''This is it, baby,'' Jasmine said softly.

Baxter stirred beside her. He'd fallen asleep

miles and miles ago. For a while Jasmine hadn't been at all sure that she would ever find this place, tucked out here in the middle of nowhere. But now she knew she had. She looked at the photo that had been in the package addressed to Jenny Lee Walker. Her beautiful, gentle Rosebud. The big old brick house her headlights picked out of the dark Texas night was identical, right down to the vines clinging to one side. And the directions the lawyer had included in the package had been pretty close, too. She'd only gotten lost twice.

Rosebud's mother had left her this place. And Rosebud had no one else but Jasmine. She had been like a sister to Jasmine—like a second mom to Baxter, and Jasmine knew Rosebud had loved them as much as she could love anyone. She would have wanted it this way. And with the way things had happened—well, it almost seemed predestined. Rosebud was dead. Jasmine was on the run with Rosebud's bag—her ID, credit cards and driver's license—and that big envelope from the lawyer containing directions to the old house that belonged to Rosebud now, all in her back seat. Well, with all of that, it was easy to believe that maybe this was the way it was supposed to happen. It seemed way beyond the realm of coincidence.

At any rate, she was here now. At Rosebud's house. Jenny Lee's. She had to remember to call herself Jenny Lee. This wasn't Chicago. It wasn't a city, and the women here didn't use stage names. A Jenny Lee could blend in here, hide for a while in this haven while she decided what to do. A Rosebud would stand out.

She shut the car off in the driveway and removed the keys. The headlights went out, plunging the house into darkness. God, it was dark here. A thousand stars dotted the sky, but there was no moon tonight. Not a streetlight to be found. Jasmine opened the car door and heard the chirping, humming insects. She took a breath and smelled the sweetest smell on the wind. Flowers, maybe the ones on those vines that clung to the house.

Dark here, she mused, wasn't as scary as dark in Chicago. Dark here smelled good, and it had a musical backup that didn't include honking horns and screaming sirens. She was overcome suddenly with the feeling that she had done the right thing. Baxter would be safe here.

She shouldered Rosebud's bag—her bag now—scooped her sleepy son up into her arms and pushed the car door closed with her hip. ''Look, baby,'' she said softly. ''See this nice house? Hmm? It's far, far away from everything bad, Baxter. It's safe here. And it's just gonna be you and me from here on in. No one will ever hurt you, or scare you like that ever again. Okay?''

''But...but, Mom, whose house is this?'' He tugged his glasses from his shirt pocket and put them on.

She sniffed. "It's your Aunt Rosebud's, baby. She only found out about it the other day. She wants us to stay here, to be safe."

"So those bad men won't find us?" he asked.

"Yes."

He nodded, squirmed out of her arms and stood on his feet, holding her hand in one of his, rubbing his eyes with the other. Jasmine started forward. Baxter planted his feet.

"What is it, baby?" she asked, looking down at him.

"Are you sure they can't find us here?"

He looked up at her, so trusting, so frightened. "I'm sure, Baxter."

"They found Aunt Rosebud, didn't they, Mom?"

She closed her eyes.

"I saw," Baxter said softly. "You told me to stay down on the floor, but I didn't, Mom. I saw those men taking somebody away in an ambulance. It was Aunt Rosebud, wasn't it? That's why we didn't go pick her up and bring her with us...isn't it, Mom?"

Sniffling, Jasmine nodded. "Yeah, baby. But I don't want you to worry about your Aunt Rosebud anymore. She's with the angels now."

Baxter looked at the sky. A giant tear rolled down his face, from beneath his glasses, over his cheek. "I'm gonna miss you, Aunt Rosebud."

Closing her eyes to prevent her own tears from

spilling over, Jasmine scooped Bax up again, into her arms. He wrapped his legs around her waist and his arms around her neck like a little spider monkey, and she carried him across the worn driveway and up the wide flagstone steps to the porch. There had been a key in that packet from the lawyer. She held the key in her hand now. But when she braced the screen open with her hip and gripped the doorknob with a free hand, she found it turned freely. The place wasn't even locked.

That was odd.

She pushed the door open and stepped inside, into darkness. Her hands groped for a light switch. She really didn't expect much of a result when she snapped it on. But the room flooded with light anyway.

Blinking, she looked around, not understanding what she was seeing. The place was clean, neat, furnished. A brick fireplace faced her like a centerpiece, a few items resting on its stone hearth. A tacky red ceramic bull. A silver candle holder with no candles in it. A framed photograph of a semi truck. What the hell? To the left a huge archway led to another room, and a dark stairway led to the second floor. To the right were tall narrow windows, hung with dark green drapes. The furniture was mismatched. An overstuffed chair with a leafy green print. A dark brown corduroy recliner that listed a bit to the right. A blue floral camel back sofa with what looked like a wool horse blanket thrown over the back. The blanket was striped, brown, black, gray and white, with fringe on the ends. A big oval braided rug covered most of the floor, but she could see the hardwood underneath around the edges. There was an odd-shaped coffee table that looked like a slice straight out of a giant redwood, with legs attached. The thing gleamed under layers of shellac and still had bark around the outer edges. And on that table was a coffee cup. With a tiny bit of dark brew still in the bottom. She turned to look back at the door she'd just entered. A cowboy hat hung from a peg beside it.

Okay. Okay, so maybe she should have read all the papers in that envelope of Rosebud's before heading down here. But damn, she'd been driving for two days, almost nonstop. And there had been sheaves of documents in that envelope. There just hadn't been time. She'd wanted to get away, far away, from men who fired guns at innocent little boys.

She shouldn't have expected it to be easy.

"I'm so tired, Mom."

Sighing, she hugged Baxter tight, then laid him down on the sofa and pulled the striped blanket over him. "You go on to sleep now, Bax. Everything's gonna be just fine. You'll see. Just go to sleep."

He closed his eyes and rolled onto his side, snuggling under the covers. Jasmine pulled off his glasses and set them on the coffee table. She stayed beside Baxter, stroking his head gently, until he was sound asleep. Then, with a sigh, she got up, went to the door and turned the locks. She checked every window in the living room, making sure their locks were fastened, as well.

Someone was living here. No doubt about that. But whoever it was, they were obviously not home right now. The place was pitch-dark, and no vehicle had been in the driveway. Maybe by the time they got back she would have figured out exactly what Rosebud's legal rights were here.

She took the shoulder bag, her smaller handbag tucked deep inside it, and stepped through the archway. Finding a light switch, she flicked it on and stared into a giant of a room. A counter separated the dining room part from the kitchen part. She spotted the back door at the far end of the kitchen, made sure it was locked, and checked the windows in this portion of the house, as well. And then, finally feeling relatively safe, she hauled the big envelope out of Rosebud's bag and emptied its contents onto the table. She needed to figure out exactly what the situation was here. She'd expected to find an empty, abandoned house awaiting her, not one that was obviously being lived in. Rosebud's mother had been in a nursing home for the past two years, as far as Jasmine knew. So who'd been staying in her house? Thank goodness, she'd arrived while they were away. At least she'd caught one lucky break.

Her eyes felt dry and heavy as she sat at the dining room table and started reading through the documents in front of her. She wondered vaguely if whoever had been here had left any of that coffee around and decided to find out.

Luke heard something downstairs but dismissed it, rolled over and tried to go back to sleep. He still wasn't used to sleeping in a big bed in the middle of an even bigger bedroom. He'd thought his sleeper unit had plenty of room. But even with the double king-size model, it had been like a closet compared to this. So much space around him. Hell, he'd barely slept at all for the first few weeks. And he hadn't been used to the noise, either. Oh, he heard noises all night long when he slept in his rig off an exit or in a rest area. But not these kinds of noises. He was used to horns, traffic, slamming doors, radios blasting. The noises out here were different. Crickets singing nonstop. Night birds calling soft and sad. Coyotes crying like they'd lost their best friend. The wind moaning sometimes, as it moved on past. The house creaking.

It smelled different here, too. Instead of diesel fumes and the exhaust of truck-stop fryers, the scent of honeysuckle drifted through the open window on a breeze, mingling with the sweet smells of lush meadow grasses and wildflowers.

And fresh-brewed coffee.

Luke's eyes opened wide. Coffee? Wait a minute, that wasn't right.

He came more fully awake and sniffed the air. Yes, that was definitely a coffee aroma floating up the stairs to tickle his senses. Sitting up slowly, frowning, he glanced at the glowing green numbers on his bedside clock and wondered who the heck would have come creeping into his house at three in the morning to make coffee.

One of his cousins, he thought, flinging back the covers. Maybe someone was in some kind of trouble. Wait a minute! Maybe one of the babies was coming! Wes's wife, Taylor, was expecting her first baby any day now, as was Esmeralda, Elliot's strange young bride. Maybe one of the newest members of his long-lost family was in the process of arriving!

Luke got to his feet with a little surge of excitement building in his chest. He pulled on his jeans and thrust his arms into the long sleeves of a western shirt he didn't bother snapping up. Barefoot, he headed down the stairs of the home that would be his the second the formality of the auction was over, a week from now.

Light spilled from the dining room, so he stepped out there, then he blinked and rubbed his eyes and looked again.

A woman was standing at his counter, her back to him, pouring freshly brewed coffee into his favorite mug. She had big hair. Big black glossy hair that fell in riots of curls clear to the middle of her back. She wore skintight leggings that hugged her round butt so tightly that it looked as if she wore a thin coat of black paint instead of pants. They were just as tight down her thighs, and then down to the spike-heeled boots on her feet. There was an inch of toned flesh between where the pants ended and where the shirt began—if it could be called a shirt. It was made of metallic mesh so he could see right through to the bra or whatever she wore underneath. Right now it was merely a thin black strip across her back, beneath the silver mesh of the blouse.

''Excuse me?'' he said, when he could find his voice.

The woman whirled so fast her coffee sloshed over the sides of the cup and her big dangling earrings jangled like bells. Her eyes were as wide as saucers—huge dark eyes, lined in black, darkly shadowed lashes so thick they had to be fake. Lips so plump and red they looked like juicy ripe berries. He didn't think he'd ever seen so much makeup on one face before—'cept maybe on the dancing girls in Vegas. She didn't say anything, just took a step backward and reached for something. He heard rattling

''Didn't mean to startle you, ma'am.'' He held up both hands, starting toward her. ''I mean, I'm not gonna call the police or anything. Just curious as to what you're doing in my house in the middle of the night. Besides making coffee, I mean.'' He moved still closer.

She lifted a butcher knife. He saw it, went still and noticed her long, long nails, the bright red polish and the little glittery stones affixed to each one. ''You're, uh…not from around here, are you?'' he asked her.

''Who are you?'' she asked him. ''What do you want?''

''What do *I* want?'' He shook his head, his humor fading fast. ''Put the knife down.''

She only lifted it higher.

''Okay, fine, I'll start. And I'll talk over the knife.'' He glanced sideways at the phone. Wondered what his chances were of dialing Garrett's place before she could sink that blade into his back deep enough to kill him. Wondered why the hell she would want to. ''I'm Luke Brand. And this is my place.''

She shook her head fast. ''You're lying. Rosebu—my mother left me this house in her will. It's mine, not yours, and I want to know what you're doing trespassing.''

''Whoa, whoa, just a minute. Okay, it isn't my place…yet. But I do live here.'' He followed her gaze to the papers strewn all over the table. ''You see, this place is about to be auctioned for back taxes. You've made some kind of mistake. Now, I'm not gonna hold a grudge. You just put the knife down and gather up your papers and be on your way.''

''I'm not going anywhere.''

He took another step toward her, and she brandished the knife, slashing with it, though he was pretty sure she didn't have any intention of cutting him. Still, it pissed him off. ''Hell, that's about all of that I can take,'' he said. His hand shot out, capturing hers at the wrist. She punched him in the belly with her free hand, so he snapped his arm around her waist and pulled her hard against him, holding her empty arm pinned between his body and hers. Her knife-wielding hand was still in his grip.

She stared up at him, wide-eyed, panting. ''Let me go,'' she whispered.

He stared right back down at her. ''Drop the knife.''

''Never.''

Luke shrugged. ''Fine. I can hold you like this all night.'' But the words made him uncomfortably aware of her body there against his. Firm, tight little body, he thought. She felt like an athlete in his arms.

''Drop the knife,'' he said again.

''Go to hell,'' she replied.

Chapter 4

The man was long and tall and hard all over. Lean, and strong. Not soft and fleshy like the men she was used to fending off after hours at The Catwalk. She wouldn't be able to best him in a fight. But she wasn't going to surrender her only weapon, either, leaving Baxter defenseless in the next room.

The man held her for a long time. He was warm and clean. He smelled like the air here. Fresh and sweet, but with a subtle musky scent underlying all that—man scent. With his shirt open and his chest bare, it would be impossible not to notice. Especially since, at the moment, he was holding her pretty firmly against that bare chest. Her nose was almost touching it, her lips only a breath away.

Finally, with a sigh, he said, "I'm gonna be mad as hell if you slice me with my own knife, lady."

"I won't cut you unless you give me reason," she said.

"I won't give you reason. Hell, I *like* women."

She swallowed hard, certain he was up to something. "How stupid would I have to be to put the knife down?" she said. "I'm a woman, alone in the house with a man I don't know. So just let me go."

He seemed to think on that for a moment. "You know, you have a point there. Although it's a twisted one, being that you're the one who broke into *my* house—"

"I didn't break in. It was open. And if it hadn't been, I'd have used my key. Which I have—because it's *my* house."

He sighed, gnawed his lip. His heat was seeping through her clothes now, and this was way too close to be held to a man she'd never met. Way too close. And feeling way too little like a threat and too much like an embrace. Stupid, yes. But he wasn't hurting her. And she wasn't struggling to pull free.

"Okay, I'm gonna let you go now," he said at last. "I'll just take a step backward and let you go, and then you can explain to me what's going on here, okay?"

Her eyes affixed to his, she nodded slowly, every muscle coiled and ready for action. If he so much as looked like he might try anything…

He let go of her waist first, stepping back, away from her, before he released her wrist.

She lowered her arm, still clutching the knife to

her side. He drew a breath, watching her. It occurred to her that he seemed as wary and suspicious of her as she was of him. Never taking his eyes off the knife, he spoke, as carefully and softly as if he were speaking to a wild animal. "You say your mother left you this place in her will."

She nodded toward the table. "I got that package from her lawyer the day before yesterday. See for yourself."

He glanced quickly at the papers strewn on the table. "Do, um, you mind if I get a cup of that coffee first?"

She narrowed her eyes on him. "Sit. I'll get it."

He lifted his brows. "Either you're overcome with the irresistible urge to wait on me or you don't want me near the knife drawer," he said, but he kept his tone light, even attempted a shaky smile. She didn't respond, and his smile died. "Fine. I'll sit."

She kept the man in her peripheral vision as he went to the table, sat down and began to sort through the paperwork. But he was still nervous. He would look at the papers, then at her, back and forth, rapidly. He was probably afraid she would slip up behind him and slide her blade into his back. She was almost enjoying being the one in a position of power over him. It wasn't often she had the upper hand with a man. She poured him coffee, and picked up her own mug, carrying both in one hand, the knife in the other. She set his cup down, then took the seat opposite him.

"So, uh...you're Jenny Lee Walker?" he asked.

"Yes."

He held her gaze for a moment. Pursed his lips.

"What?"

"Nothing. You just...don't exactly look like a Jenny Lee to me."

Hell, neither had the real one, she thought. Aloud she said, "People change. I haven't used the name in years."

"No? What name have you been using?"

She could have said Rosebud. But sticking as close to the truth as possible had its benefits. It would only confuse Baxter to hear this man call her Rosebud. "Jasmine," she said finally.

He blinked. "Jasmine? Really?"

"What's wrong with Jasmine?" she asked, instantly defensive.

He shrugged. "Nothing. It...uh...it was my mother's favorite flower is all." He sighed and glanced at the papers again. "Well, Jasmine, your mother made this will over two years ago. According to the pages from the lawyer, Buzz Montana—he's local, by the way, so you can talk to him yourself if you want to—he's been renting the land out to defray the expenses of keeping it up and to cover his own fees. In fact, I know the ranchers who've been using the land to graze their cattle. Apparently things got bad enough that he decided to rent the house, as well. That was about the time I came along looking for a place. But it still wasn't enough to pay the taxes."

She blinked. "Taxes?"

"Property taxes. Look, this lawyer, he's been looking for you for two years. Where have you been?"

"That's none of your business," she said sharply. "I'm here now. And the place is mine."

"Not if you can't pay the back taxes, it's not. The state's going to auction the place off to get their money."

"Then it's mine until they do. It hasn't been sold yet, has it?"

"No. Not until a week from now. But—"

"Then for a week it's mine." And that, she told herself, would be long enough to figure out what the hell to do next.

He rose from his chair very slowly. "Look, lady, I don't even know if you *are* Jenny Lee Walker. For all I know you could have mugged her and stolen this envelope, along with her wallet."

She lifted her brows, getting to her feet, as well. "Oh, so I look like a mugger to you?"

"Or worse."

Her jaw dropped. She blinked in shock, because the slam was so unexpected. "What's that supposed to mean?"

"It means that I didn't fall off the turnip truck yesterday, honey. I've seen a lot of women like you in a lot of truck stops around this country. They come knocking on the sleeper in the middle of the night, asking if you want your *windows washed.*''

''You think I'm a whore?''

He shrugged. ''You sure as hell look like one.''

She smacked him. Hard, right across the face, and her long nails dragged over his cheek, leaving marks. Then they stood there, facing off across the table. She wasn't usually violent, but she'd been through hell the past two days. She'd seen a murder. She'd dodged bullets and seen them narrowly miss her little boy. She'd lost her best friend when she had been the real target. And she'd driven for hours and hours almost nonstop. She was tired, hungry and scared to death, and just when she had finally found what was supposed to be a haven, this redneck had to rise up and get in her way.

He stood there, not rocked in the least, it seemed, by the blow, even though tiny red beads were appearing now on his cheek.

''If you think you're gonna walk in here in the middle of the night,'' he said, ''and throw me out of my own house—''

''*My* own house,'' she corrected.

''Tell you what. You show me proof you're Jenny Lee Walker and I'll let you stay.''

''I don't have to prove anything to you. Who the hell do you think you are, anyway? I *own* this place. I don't have to answer to you. You're the one trespassing here.''

"I've paid my rent for the month," he snapped. "And I *can* prove that. You couldn't throw me out if you wanted to."

"Oh, trust me, I want to."

"Well, it ain't gonna happen. The only person being thrown out of here is you, lady. Now. Bag and baggage." He looked around. "Where is your baggage, anyway?"

"Still in the car," she lied. She couldn't very well tell him she'd arrived without much besides the clothes on her back, could she? He already suspected too much.

"Good. That should make this easier." He reached for her arm, closed his hand around it. "I don't want your kind hanging around here. So let's go. Come on."

"Mommy?"

The man's face changed. His smug, cynical sneer vanished. He looked as if he'd just been hit between the eyes with a sizable hammer.

Jasmine snapped her head to the left and saw Baxter standing in that big open archway, the blanket from the sofa wrapped around him and trailing behind. He'd gotten up and put his glasses on. She jerked her arm free of the stranger's grip and went to Baxter, knelt in front of him. "Oh, baby, I'm so sorry I woke you up with all that noise. It's okay, honey, I promise. It's okay." She hugged him.

He was looking past her, though, at the man. She sensed it the way mothers sense so many things about their sons. And she felt his fear, too. ''Is he one of the bad men, Mommy? Is he one of the—''

''Hush, baby. Hush, it's all right.'' She held her boy closer, praying he would say no more. She didn't need this stranger knowing her business.

She heard the stranger's voice as he muttered something under his breath. She thought he was cussing softly, but she couldn't really hear enough to be sure. Then his footsteps, soft and nearly soundless on the floor. And the next thing she heard was his voice again, coming from closer than before—and in a totally different tone.

''Hey there, kiddo,'' he said. ''My name's Luke Brand. What's yours?''

''B-Baxter.''

Jasmine straightened, picking Bax up, holding him tight to her and turning to put his back to the man, but Baxter twisted in her arms to face him anyway.

''Well, Baxter, I don't know what...what bad men you're talking about—'' he slanted a brief glance at Jasmine ''—but I promise, I'm not one of them. We don't allow bad men out here.''

''You don't?''

''Nope. Cross my heart. Your mom and I were just trying to straighten out some mix-ups, that's all.''

''Oh.'' Baxter looked at Jasmine. ''Do we really have to leave, Mom? It's still dark outside, and I'm scared. I don't want to go back out there. And we've been in the car for such a long time already, and—''

''Nobody has to go anywhere tonight,'' Luke Brand said softly. He met Jasmine's eyes, held them this time. ''And there's nothing to be afraid of. Not around here.'' He reached out and tousled Baxter's thick, dark blond hair. ''Okay, Baxter?''

Baxter smiled and laid his head on his mother's shoulder. ''Okay,'' he said.

Jasmine watched the man for signs of a con, but he seemed perfectly sincere, which was, of course, ridiculous. He was after something. He had an angle. She just hadn't spotted it yet. She would have expected him to be twice as eager to be rid of her once he realized she had a kid in tow. Most men were. Instead, he'd changed his attitude entirely. The hostility had vanished. And this Mr. Nice Guy routine had fallen into its place.

''Top of the stairs, Jasmine. First door on the left. That's the only bedroom made up for actual use at the moment. You and Baxter go on up there and get some rest. We can figure the rest of this out in the morning.''

His bed? He was giving her *his bed?*

She licked her lips, lowered her head, but didn't say thanks. She held Baxter a little tighter, snatched up her shoulder bag, turned and headed up the stairs without a backward glance.

Luke watched the woman go up the stairs and stood there for a long moment after she was out of sight. Hell. He felt as if he'd just been awakened by a hurricane that had only just blown itself out. Or maybe he was in the eye, because she would sure as hell be ripping and roaring in the morning.

The woman was a puzzle. Small and sexy as they made them. She had a centerfold's body and dressed to show it. Tight, tiny clothes. Too much makeup. Talons that would make a bald eagle jealous. Big, *big* hair. And she'd been packing so much heavy metal that she jingled and jangled with every move. Necklaces, bracelets, no less than a half-dozen pairs of little earrings to complement the big ones. No other piercings though. None visible, anyway. That didn't mean they weren't there.

He'd thought he had her pegged.

Then he'd heard that little voice calling her Mommy, and his theory got blown to hell. Oh, maybe it could have held its own if she'd reacted to that plea with a scowl, or by snapping at the kid. But no. Her face had gone all achy. Like that little voice calling her name was all it took to break her heart to bits. Her eyes even welled up. And then the way she picked the boy up and held him so protectively. She'd looked fierce then. Like she would claw Luke's eyes out if he so much as looked at the kid wrong.

That look was the one that got to him. Because *that* look was one he knew too well to ever mistake it. He'd seen it far too often—in his own mother's eyes. That fierce, single-minded devotion, the protectiveness that warned outsiders to stay clear. Luke's mother had loved him like that. Because he was all she'd had. Hell, she had almost ruined him with that fiercely protective love.

Jenny Lee—if that was her real name—loved her son utterly. That had been obvious to Luke in the few moments he'd seen them together. And any woman capable of loving a child that much, well...she rose a notch in his book. Hooker or no, she couldn't be all bad. Whether she loved him too much—enough to damage the kid—well, that remained to be seen.

The little boy, now there was another puzzle. Because that kid had been scared. No two ways about it. And who were these "bad men" he'd been afraid of?

Of course, no matter how devoted a mother Jasmine was or how frightened a child Baxter was, one truth remained that made them both Luke's enemies, in a manner of speaking. They had come to lay claim to the home he was in the process of making his own. They had come to derail his new start. They had come to take away the only thing he'd ever wanted badly enough to give up his rig for. He had sold his prize possession for this place. That couldn't be undone. There was no way he would give up without a hell of a fight.

Luke sat down, drank his coffee and pondered on the two wanderers for a while, giving them plenty of time to fall asleep as he continued to peruse the legal papers on the table. Then he slipped outside to the car. It was a ten-year-old station wagon, with plenty of rust. She'd locked it, of course, and the key was more than likely tucked into that oversize shoulder bag she'd taken to bed with her. But it was a car that had no trunk, so he figured if there was any luggage to be seen, he'd see it. Only he didn't. Because there wasn't any. It seemed to him that the woman had come here with nothing more than the clothes on her back and whatever she'd managed to cram into that shoulder bag of hers, which couldn't be much.

Illinois plates. She'd come a long way, then. He made a note of the number. Garrett could easily check it out. Having a cousin who was a small-town sheriff could, he realized, come in handy. He peered through the glass of the driver's door. He saw empty pop bottles and fast-food wrappers. Every one of them from some kind of "kid's meal." They'd eaten on the road. Or Baxter had, at least. Hadn't the woman eaten at all?

Sighing, he went back inside, settled himself down at the dining room table and proceeded to read every remaining scrap of paper in the large envelope she'd brought with her. He read until his head ached and his eyes watered, but he still couldn't find the truth she was hiding. And it was obvious there was one.

Hell.

He waited till six o'clock to call Garrett, knowing his cousin's house would be bustling with life by then. Garrett liked to get up before his wife and make a pot of coffee. He would pour her a cup when he heard her coming down the stairs. Claimed it was best to do this silently, give the caffeine a chance to kick in and then attempt human conversation. Of course, that was just a cover. Chelsea was head over heels for the big guy. Garrett probably just liked to have those few quiet minutes in the morning with his wife all to himself before little Bubba had to get up for school and the real world came crashing in.

Hell, Luke hated to interrupt that intimate few minutes for his cousin, but he wanted to catch Garrett before he headed out to check on the cattle, then went off to work at the sheriff's office in town.

Garrett answered on the second ring. And his greeting was, "This had better be good."

"Sorry, Garrett," Luke said. "But it is. Damn good. Or maybe damn bad would be more accurate."

"What's wrong, Luke?"

Luke could hear the concern in Garrett's tone, and he could also hear Chelsea in the background, asking if Luke was all right and what was going on. He smiled at the sweetness of having this big family suddenly all over every little problem.

"Tell your wife I'm fine. I just had an unexpected visitor drop by last night."

"He's fine, Chelsea. Give me a minute." Then Garrett sighed. "Ah, she's rushed upstairs to pick up the extension," he told Luke.

A second later the soft click told Luke that Chelsea was on the other phone.

"Go ahead, Luke," she said. "Tell us what's up."

He liked Chelsea. She was one of those rare, special women a man was lucky to stumble upon once in a lifetime. Garrett must have done something awfully good to have found her and made her his own.

"Okay," he said at last. "Last night a woman showed up here with a little boy. She says this place is hers, and that she's here to claim it."

Garrett said, "What's her name? Where's she from?"

Chelsea said, "What does she look like? Is she married?"

Luke withstood the bombardment of questions fairly well, he thought. "Her name, she says, is Jenny Lee Walker, but she goes by Jasmine. The car she's driving has Illinois plates on it."

"Number?" Garrett asked.

"DX7-381," Luke replied, rattling off the number he'd committed to memory. "She showed up with nothing at all, as far as I can see, besides her son and the clothes they're wearing, and this packet of papers from the law offices of Buzz Montana giving her ownership of this property. As for what she looks like, Chelsea, she looks like a high-priced lot lizard, and no, I don't think she's married. I didn't see a ring, anyway.''

''So that means you looked,'' Chelsea said. ''But what's a lot lizard?''

''It's trucker slang for a truck-stop prostitute,'' Garrett said, his tone decidedly darker. ''And it's not the kind of observation a Brand man makes about a lady.''

''She's no lady, Garrett. She broke in here, and when I came downstairs to see what was going on, she pulled a knife on me.''

Garrett waited, but Luke said no more. Garrett said, ''Why did she pull the knife, Luke?''

Luke thought on that. ''I don't know. I guess I scared her.''

''And?''

He shrugged. ''Well, she had her son with her. I suppose she thought I might be a threat to him.''

''Well damn, Luke,'' Chelsea said. ''Seems to me that shows courage, character and devotion. I mean, you're a pretty big fella for a woman to try to take on all alone, just to protect her son.'' Then her voice brightened. ''How old is the boy? Bubba's age?''

Luke sighed. ''Whose side are you guys on here, anyway?''

He could almost hear Garrett smile. ''Don't you worry, Luke. Family comes first with the Brands. Always has. But honor is right up there with it, and the Cowboy Code is our way of life.''

Luke made a face. ''Oh, come on. There's a code? Why is this the first I'm hearing of it?''

''It's the first time you've broken it, cousin,'' Garrett said. ''Being kind to women and children is at the top of the list.''

Luke groaned. ''I *was* kind.''

''Not if she heard that 'lot lizard' comment, you weren't.''

Luke thought about his comment last night about her clothes and her violent reaction. He still had the claw marks on his face. His cheek still stung. ''Well, the fact that she's still here—sleeping in my bed, I might add—ought to indicate my extreme kindness.'' He swallowed. ''So what's the penalty for breaking this code of yours, anyway?''

Garrett sighed. ''Well, when Ben, Wes and Elliot were kids, I'd just kick their backsides. But I suppose you're a bit too old for that. Then again…''

''Come on, Garrett!''

Garrett laughed softly, a deep rumbling sound. ''Relax, will you? We'll be over after breakfast, okay? We'll get this all sorted out.''

Breakfast. The mention of it made Luke's stomach growl. He was starved. It also made him think of the junk-food boxes and bags he'd seen in the woman's car last night. He bet the kid hadn't had an honest meal in at least a couple of days. And his mother might not have eaten much at all.

''Luke?''

''What? Oh, yeah, after breakfast. I'll see you then. And thanks, Garrett, Chelsea.''

''That's what family's for, Luke,'' Chelsea said.

Drawing a deep breath, Luke hung up the phone. Family. He was willing to bet that if the woman upstairs had any family at all besides her son, she wouldn't be here.

Hell. Looking at the poor little kid was like looking at a dim reflection of his own past.

Sighing, Luke went to the kitchen and opened the fridge to see what he could find for breakfast.

Chapter 5

She smelled something that tickled her senses and crept into her dreams. She was young again—eight or nine years old, at the most—and she was at her best friend Mary's house for a sleepover. First thing in the morning, Mary's mom made this huge breakfast. It was the smell of bacon cooking that woke young Jasmine that morning. And she lay there for a minute and thought how cool it must be to have a mom like Mary's. To wake up every morning to the smell of bacon cooking, or the sound of her humming softly in the kitchen.

At home, Jasmine woke to the smell of stale cigarette smoke and beer. Her own mom greeted her most mornings by groaning in hangover misery and telling her to get the hell out of her room. There was usually a strange man in her bed on those mornings. She didn't want to go home again after a sleepover with Mary. Or with Jeannette or with Valerie. She didn't want to wake up to overflowing ashtrays and half-filled beer glasses and spilled food and whatever man her mother had decided would be more important than her daughter this week. She didn't ever want to go home again. She lay there, at Mary's house, and she told herself that when she was a mom someday, she would be the kind of mom who made bacon in the mornings. She would never let anything ever be more important to her than her child. Especially not some strange man.

"Mommy?"

Jasmine opened her eyes slowly. She was lying on her back in a strange bed, and her little boy's smiling face hovered an inch above her own. "Smell that, Mommy? It smells just like home on Sundays!"

Jasmine blinked the haze from her brain, lifted her head and kissed Baxter's nose. "It does, doesn't it?" she asked, sniffing the air and smelling bacon and coffee and something sweet.

Baxter nodded hard, grinning, eyes wide. "Is it Sunday, Mom?"

"Nope. It's only Saturday."

He shrugged. "You think Mr. Brand is cooking us breakfast?"

"I don't know, honey."

"Can I go find out?"

"No, not just yet." She got out of the bed and looked down at herself. She'd slept in her clothes, minus the nylons and shoes, and they were wrinkled and messy. A glance in the mirror across the room almost made her jump. Her hair was wild and her makeup smeared. She looked like hell. She didn't want to face anyone like this.

The bedroom was nice, though. She'd come in here in the dark last night, and frankly, she'd been too tired to care to look around. She'd crawled into bed to snuggle with Bax until he fell asleep. The plan had been to get up and find a shower afterward, but she'd been out cold before she got around to it. She saw the bathroom now, as she looked around. It was just through a small door to the right, and a peek inside told her there were a tub and shower, towels and washcloths. Thank goodness.

She turned back to finish her inspection of the bedroom. The outmost wall was lined in tall narrow windows with sheer white curtains that let the sun beam through them like a golden spotlight. The bed was an old-looking four-poster, made of some dark, lustrous hardwood, and the large dresser matched. The bedside stand didn't. It was newer, and cheap looking, wood veneer, not the real stuff. And there was a small portable television set on top of the trunk at the foot of the bed. Not a picture on the wall. Not a rug on the floor. No trinkets or knick-nacks in sight. How long did that Luke character say he'd been living here? Three months? He sure didn't settle into a place fast, did he?

A tap on the bedroom door made her jump. "Who is it?" she asked, staring at the door, which had no lock, and praying it wouldn't open on her. And then she realized what an inane question she'd just asked and rolled her eyes.

"It's Luke. Breakfast will be ready in fifteen minutes, if you're hungry. And, um, if you need something to wear, you can snag a pair of sweats and a T-shirt out of my bottom drawer."

"What makes you think I don't have anything to wear?"

"You going to tell me you do?" he asked her. Or was he daring her?

"I'll be a half hour," she said, choosing to ignore his challenge. No human being could possibly get ready for anything in fifteen minutes.

Baxter tugged on her skirt. "Mom, can't I go down now? I'm starved. And I already washed up."

She glanced at her son, saw that he had indeed washed his face and tugged a comb through his hair. He was wearing the same clothes as yesterday, but that couldn't be helped. Still, she didn't want to let him out of her sight.

"Jasmine?" Luke's voice came through the door, deep and soft. "You're five hundred miles from whatever happened in Illinois. I'll watch him close, I promise. Why don't you let him come on down to breakfast?"

She glared at the door, almost let the words on the tip of her tongue spill out, but bit them back at the last possible moment. She swallowed hard, ignoring the redneck and turning to her son. "Bax, I'll hurry as fast as I can, okay, baby?" she said softly. "But please, don't go down to breakfast without me."

He pouted, sighed, hung his head. "Okay, Mom. I'll wait for you." Then he turned to the closed door. "We'll be down in a few minutes, Mr. Brand."

There was a hesitation. "Okay, Baxter. I'll keep it warm for you."

Jasmine hugged him close. "Thank you, hon." Then she glanced at the clock on the bedside stand and wondered if she could break the land speed record for shower, hair and makeup. She yanked open the bottom dresser drawer, and fished out a pair of gray sweatpants and a white T-shirt with some logo or other on the front. She didn't bother to look too closely, because it didn't really matter what the design was, it was still going to look like she was wearing a tent. She kissed Bax on the cheek and headed into the adjoining bathroom. "I'm gonna leave the door open a tiny bit, baby," she told Baxter. "So all you need to do is call me if you need me, okay?"

"Okay," he said, climbing onto the bed with a remote in his hand. He aimed it at the TV set, and she knew he would be okay for a few minutes.

* * *

Luke thought it odder than odd that the woman wouldn't let the kid out of her sight long enough to have breakfast when he was obviously hungry. What kind of a mother was she, anyway? Even his own overprotective, clinging mother hadn't been *that* bad. Hell, it didn't sit right with him. And he tried to wait, he really did, but fifteen minutes came and went, and he still didn't hear that boy coming down the stairs.

Fine. If she didn't want her son down here alone with the big bad Brand, he would just take matters into his own hands. He lifted the stoneware plate from the spot he'd set for Baxter at the table, heaped it full of food, filled a glass with milk and headed up the stairs. Once again he tapped on his own bedroom door, trying not to slop the milk as he did it.

"Who is it?" the little guy asked.

The sound of his voice brought a smile to Luke's face for some reason. Hell, the kid was cute. "It's Luke. I figured there was no sense making you wait for breakfast, so I brought you up a plateful, if that's okay."

The door whipped open so fast Luke almost dropped the plate. "You bet it's okay. Thanks, Mr. Brand."

Luke smiled, holding out the plate to the kid, looking nervously past him. Baxter grabbed his arm and tugged him right inside, though. He could hear the shower running, and the bathroom door was only half-closed. The woman wasn't shy, that was for sure. Then again, she probably hadn't expected him to come back. Much less come all the way inside this time. "Come on," Baxter said. "I'm watching *Star Rangers!*"

Luke glanced at the TV set, at the super heroes spin-kicking their way across the screen and the bad guys. "That's my little cousin Bubba's favorite show, too."

Baxter tugged Luke to the bed, and Luke sat down. The little guy did, too, but on the nearby chair, and he dug right into his food. In between bites, he said, "There are kids here?"

"Oh, a couple. Bubba's the closest to your age. You might get to meet him later on."

Baxter smiled, pushed his glasses up on his nose and kept on eating. "I knew there was bacon," he said. "At home, every Sunday morning, my mom gets up early, and she makes this big breakfast for all of us, with bacon."

"Oh yeah? For all of you?" Luke asked, sensing a shot at some information. And more than that. He hadn't exactly pegged Jasmine as a Sunday breakfast kind of a mother.

"Me and Aunt Rosebud and Mom," he explained.

"The three of you live together, then?"

The boy's face fell. He stopped eating, stared at

the floor. "We used to. But…not anymore. Aunt Rosebud's gone to live with the angels now."

Luke felt like a rat. His prying had ruined the kid's breakfast. What kind of a bully was he, anyway? "Hey, I have some friends up there, too," he said, forcing a smile. "I'll bet your Aunt Rosebud and my buddy Buck are having a heck of a good time with those angels."

Baxter lifted his head a little. "You think so?"

"Well, sure I do. Buck, he loved a good Sunday breakfast himself."

"And did he like to dance, too? Aunt Rosebud's a great dancer. Almost as good as my mom."

So his mother danced? Interesting. "He loved to dance, Baxter. Why, I'll bet they're gonna be best friends before long."

"Yeah," Baxter said. He smiled a little, and even started to pick at the food again. "Yeah, they will for sure." Then he paused and looked up. "Your friend Buck, he wasn't a bad guy, was he?"

"No, Bax. He was one of the best good guys I ever knew."

Baxter smiled more fully and devoted his attention to his food. Luke wanted to ask him about those bad guys he kept referring to, but he thought that just then it was more important for the child to eat than for Luke to have his curiosity satisfied. He could wait for his answers.

It occurred to him then that the shower had stopped running. And he turned to glance toward the bathroom door just as the woman stepped through it, wearing nothing but a towel and an expression of surprise.

''What are you doing in here?'' she blurted.

''I'm sorry.'' *Look away,* he told his eyes. They wouldn't budge. He couldn't make them budge. She was a totally different woman now. An incredibly beautiful woman. ''B-Baxter was hungry and I, um, I felt bad making him wait, so I brought his breakfast up.''

''And stayed to supervise while he ate it?''

He couldn't get over the difference in her with her face scrubbed so clean it glowed pink, and her hair wet and plastered to her head. He'd missed everything about her besides the thick coat of makeup. She had the face of a wood fairy. Tiny, elfin nose and a small, rounded chin. Sculpted cheekbones and full lips. And those eyes. Why on earth had she ever thought she needed to plaster coats of color over those eyes? They were huge and round and dark brown in color. He suddenly wished she would smile. He needed, suddenly, to see that face with a smile.

She didn't, but he kept looking anyway. His gaze skimmed down her neck and over her shoulders and arms. Toned. Firm. The woman was as fit as any he'd seen. She looked as if she worked out with weights or something. The towel hung loosely to the upper half of her thighs, and they, too, were shapely and toned. Her bare feet...she had the cutest little feet....

"You finished?" she asked.

He snapped his gaze up to her eyes and felt the skin under his collar get hot. "I, um...yeah. Yeah, I am." Unable to say anything remotely intelligent, he turned to leave. "Your breakfast is still warm, you know, if you want it. Although, maybe you don't. I didn't think...you probably don't eat that kind of..." As he spoke, he glanced over his shoulder and saw her munching a slice of bacon she'd snitched from her son's plate. "Or...maybe you do." He shrugged, more baffled than before, and opened the door to leave.

"Luke," she said.

He turned.

"That was nice, what you did. Bringing Baxter's breakfast up like that. Thank you."

He felt a smile tug at one side of his mouth. "That's okay."

"I really will only be a few more minutes," she said. And amazingly, incredibly, she smiled. Just a little bit. It was halfhearted, just a slight pulling of her lips upward at the corners. But even then it transformed her face. Made her eyes sparkle and dug dimples into her cheeks.

Oh, hell.

"Well, good. I'll be downstairs, then." Finally he got out of there, closing the door behind him and realizing he hadn't really been breathing in several minutes. Or it felt like it, anyway. He let the air out of him in a rush and headed for the kitchen. What was the matter with him, anyway? She doled out a grudging halfhearted thanks with an eyedropper, and he was reacting as if she'd kissed his feet in gratitude.

The man must be some kind of Neanderthal. It was obvious, because he didn't own a hair dryer. And his shampoo had been that practical kind with the conditioner already mixed in. He was definitely primitive. And big. His sweatpants and shirt positively hung on her.

But he'd been kind to Baxter, and that meant something. Even though she knew perfectly well it was more than likely all for show. An act to get what he wanted, win her trust and then stab her in the back, or get her into his bed and then stab her in the back, or whatever. They always wanted something.

Still, at least he made an effort to appear to be…kind of sweet. Maybe even a little shy. The way he'd stuttered and stammered when she'd walked out of the bathroom in a towel. It was far from the wolf whistles she'd come to expect from men when they saw her in various states of undress.

He'd seemed dumbstuck. Stood there with his soft brown hair and his baby-blue eyes and just stared at her.

So he was at least making an effort. It was a good job, too. She almost believed it was real.

She tugged a brush through her hair, wincing with every pull. And the whole time, her stomach was growling at the smell of the food Baxter was wolfing down in the bedroom.

Lifting her gaze to the bathroom mirror, she gave up on the hair, pulling it back into a ponytail. She did not have hair that was conducive to ponytails, she decided, as strand after curling strand escaped the confines of the pink hair tie she'd found in her purse.

Okay, fine. There was no hope for the hair, but at least she could do something about her face. She picked up Rosebud's big bag. She'd already taken her own smaller purse from inside it. Now she dumped the rest of the contents out onto the big countertop beside the bathroom sink…and stopped dead as the black revolver clunked heavily onto the tiny blue ceramic tiles.

Her throat went dry. She glanced toward the bedroom. Baxter was still engrossed in the TV program and the meal, so she pushed the door closed just a little more and carefully picked up the handgun. She wasn't familiar with guns or the way they worked, so it took her a moment to find the catch that released the round cylinder, allowing it to flip outward. There were bullets in each of the six small holes.

"Loaded," she whispered. "Damn you, Rosebud, how could you have kept a loaded gun so close to my baby?'' She quickly pulled the bullets out, one by one, holding the bunch of them in her palm. She didn't like guns. She was against them, thought they should be banned, for heaven's sake. But she wasn't about to give this one up. Not while Leo and his sleazy murdering friend, the dirty cop, might still be hunting her. Maybe if it were her alone they wanted—but it wasn't. They wanted Baxter. And she would fight to the death and burn every last principle she had for her little boy. Still, she would have to be very careful with this.

She found a small bottle of pain reliever among the articles that had spilled out of the bag and snatched it up, pouring the tablets into the toilet. Then she put the bullets into the bottle and capped it. Childproof cover. Good. She zipped the bottle into a small compartment in the big bag. Then she put the revolver into her own smaller purse.

''Mommy, can't we go downstairs yet?''

She glanced at the makeup scattered all over the counter and sighed in defeat. It just wasn't going to happen this morning. And it didn't matter, anyway. Hell, no one would recognize her looking the way she looked today. Like some fresh-faced farm girl in desperate need of her first trip to the salon. Maybe it was for the best. Holding Rosebud's bag at the edge, she scooped everything back into it and hung it on a peg in the wall. ''I'm coming, baby.''

She took her son's hand and led him out into the

hallway, then down the stairs. It was a nice house. It was a crying shame Rosebud hadn't lived to inherit it the way her mother had obviously intended. She would have loved it here. The staircase was old, too steep and too narrow, but the banister was heavy gleaming hardwood that had to be worth a fortune. She ran her hand over it slowly all the way to the bottom.

"It's all one piece," Luke Brand said.

Jasmine looked up, not expecting to see him standing just beyond the bottom step, staring up at her. "What?"

"The banister. It's cut from one continuous piece of hard maple, all the way up and along the landing."

"Oh."

He shrugged, shifted his feet. "It seemed really important to the assessors when they were out here last month. I guess they don't make them like that anymore. Just thought you'd be interested."

"It's...interesting all right."

"Well, anyway. Food's out here." Turning, he walked beneath the wide brick archway into the dining room. It was different now, with the morning sun slanting through the place. The big French doors on the far side of the room looked like a giant wall painting of lush green meadows that rolled endlessly. For a moment she just blinked at it.

"The...uh...drapes were closed last night, so

you maybe didn't notice the doors then. I put them in myself.''

Turning, she looked at him with brows raised. ''Did you?''

''It was just a back wall. Dark as a dungeon in here.'' He pulled out her chair. ''And I figured the place was as good as my own, so I didn't mind investing a little time and money in it.''

She looked at him, standing there, behind her chair. No one had ever pulled a chair out for her in her life that she could recall. She sat down and glimpsed the French doors again. Brass handled and hinged, the trim around them fit perfectly even at the corners. He'd done a good job. And there was a small, octagon-shaped deck beyond them. She would bet that hadn't been part of the original house, either.

Luke Brand was fetching plates from the oven now, setting one in front of her, heaped with enough food for three women, at least. Then he sat down across from her with his own.

''You didn't need to wait for me.''

He shrugged. ''I eat alone all the time. Decided company for breakfast might be nice for a change.''

She pressed her lips together, then turned to catch sight of Baxter. He was wandering the house, pausing at every window to look outside. He wanted to go out. She knew he did. It was killing her to keep him so cooped up.

''He can go outside and play, you know. The

road's a hundred feet from the house, and even if it weren't, there's no such thing as traffic out here."

She averted her eyes. "I'll take him out later on."

"Don't let him out of your sight much, do you?"

She looked at him quickly. "You have an opinion on my parenting skills, Mr. Brand?"

He shrugged. "Guess you'd know more about that than I would. I've never had a kid. Don't know much about 'em. Except that they need room to grow."

She shook her head. "You're right, you don't know much about kids."

He nodded at her plate. "You're not eating."

She shoveled a bite into her mouth without looking first. It turned out to be a portion of omelette that just about melted in her mouth. It was all she could do to keep from closing her eyes in ecstasy. And though she tried to keep her expression static, he saw right through it and smiled that charming smile of his. "Good, isn't it?"

She nodded, swallowing, and reached for the coffee. It was as heavenly as the omelette had been. "You're a chef or something, aren't you?"

"No. I'm a trucker. Or...was. I sold my rig to buy this place."

She lifted her brows, surprised by his answer. So he'd given up his livelihood to be here—and then she'd come along to claim the place. No wonder he'd been less than friendly last night. At least, until he'd met Baxter. "What are you going to do for a living now?"

He shrugged. "I've got time to figure it out. There seem to be enough odd jobs in town to keep me in demand until I decide."

"Odd jobs?"

He nodded. "Yeah, mostly courtesy of my cousins. Let's see, between them they have a cattle ranch, a horse ranch, a dude ranch, a veterinary clinic, a martial arts school—"

She held up a hand. "I get it. You've got a lot of family in town."

"You didn't even let me get to the P.I., the sheriff, the archaeologist and the shrink."

She tried to keep her face expressionless when he mentioned the sheriff. But she couldn't help but flash back to that cop, Petronella, standing over Rosebud's body, looking up at her. The same man she'd seen commit a murder—the man who'd taken a shot at her son.

"Actually, now that I think about it, you could probably find work with any of them, if you're looking."

She shook herself out of the disturbing memory and glanced into the next room to see that Baxter had settled down in front of the TV again. It wasn't good for him, all that television. "I would think you'd be pushing me to leave here, not giving me job tips that might keep me around even longer."

He shrugged. "This thing with the property will

get settled one way or another no matter what I do,'' he said. ''Frankly, I'm more concerned about your son right now than I am about who wins a fight over a house.''

She tipped her head to one side. He was trying to get to her by feigning concern for Baxter. It was low. She'd seen it before. Never done quite this well or convincingly, though.

''So what do you do for a living, Jasmine?''

She looked him dead in the eye. ''I'm a dancer.''

His brows rose. ''Really? What, ballet?''

Still watching him, she said, ''Exotic.''

His face stilled, mouth frozen into a thin line as he slowly digested that bit of information. ''You're a—'' Glancing toward Baxter, he lowered his voice to a whisper. ''You're a stripper?''

''That's right. So about that job you're going to help me find...''

''Mommy, Mommy, look! Horses! Real live horses! Just like on TV!''

Jasmine had to pull hard to yank her gaze away from Luke Brand's probing one, but she did, getting to her feet and going to the living room just as Baxter pulled the door open and ran outside.

There were people out there. Strangers on horseback, riding up to the house like something out of an old western. Jasmine sprinted after her son, her heart in her throat, and caught him just as he reached the dangerous hooves. She scooped him up, held him hard, her heart pounding as she turned and carried him back toward the house.

Luke stood there on the top step, looking at her, a deep frown etched between his brows. Then he looked past her, and his expression changed. He smiled, waved. ''Garrett, Chelsea, good to see you. Hey, Bubba! How's my best cowboy?''

''I rode all the way all by myself,'' a child's voice shouted.

Jasmine lifted her head, turning slowly to look more closely at the strangers from whom she'd just rescued her son. The man was so big he would have been frightening, except for the warm, easy smile he wore. He touched the brim of his hat and gave her a nod before dismounting and reaching up to help the woman down.

She was an attractive woman, probably in her thirties, with brown hair in a long ponytail. She put her hands on the man's shoulders as he helped her down. Then they both turned to look at the little boy, with his dark hair and striking blue eyes, sitting atop a pony, wearing a cowboy hat that was too big for him.

''These are some of my cousins, Garrett and Chelsea Brand, and their son, Bubba,'' Luke said to Jasmine. ''Folks, this is Jasmine, and her son, Baxter.''

Baxter had locked eyes on the little boy, riding that pony all by himself, and Jasmine knew she would never hear the end of this one. Even as she looked on, the boy called Bubba swung one leg over his saddle and leaped to the ground. It was all Jasmine could do not to shout a warning, certain he would hurt himself. But he didn't. He marched right up to Baxter instead.

"Hi."

"Hi," Baxter said, pushing his glasses up on his nose.

"You want to pet my pony?"

"Could I?"

"I don't think..." Jasmine began.

The woman spoke then. "The pony's gentle as a kitten," she said. "I wouldn't let Bubba anywhere near it if it were dangerous at all."

Bubba looked sturdy and strong compared to Baxter, though, Jasmine thought. He must be at least a couple of years older. And what might not be dangerous at all to him might very well be a threat to her own delicate little boy.

"Please, Mom?" Baxter asked.

"Oh, all right. But no riding on that thing."

"Okay!" Baxter and Bubba headed over to the pony. Meanwhile Garrett was tying the other two horses up to a rail that seemed to have been made for that very purpose.

"Shall we go inside to talk?" Garrett asked.

Talk...about what? Jasmine wondered.

"Oh, let's sit on the porch, so we can keep an eye on the boys, hmm?" Chelsea said with a glance at Jasmine.

"You probably think I'm an overprotective lunatic."

Chelsea shook her head. "Why should I think that? Luke says you're from Chicago. I'm from New York. I know full well that, in cities like those, letting your child out of your sight is practically courting disaster."

Oddly enough, it seemed the woman understood.

"It's different out here, but it takes time for a mom to get comfortable with that. So it's perfectly natural for you to want to keep a close watch on little Baxter. Heck, I'd be worried if you didn't!"

She *seemed* very kind...and genuine. That didn't mean she was. In Jasmine's experience, most people were not what they seemed. Still, she walked up onto the porch and sat in one of the white wicker chairs. Luke took the other one, while Chelsea and Garrett settled into the matching love seat. "So, um, I guess Luke has already told you about me."

"I called them this morning," Luke explained. "I thought they could help us get this mess straightened out."

She lifted her brows. "I don't understand how."

"Well, for one thing," Garrett said, "I knew your mother."

Jasmine's throat went dry as she stared at him. For just an instant she thought of her own drunken tramp of a mother who'd died young and left Jasmine on her own at fifteen. But then she realized these people all thought she was Rosebud. Jenny

Lee Walker. So the mother he was referring to was Rosebud's mother—the woman who'd left her this house.

''Oh,'' she said finally. ''How well did you know her?''

''Almost as well as I knew my own,'' Garrett said with a friendly smile, leaning back in his chair.

Jasmine braced herself. This was not a good sign.

Chapter 6

Luke saw Jasmine's reaction to Garrett's revelation that he'd known her mother. Fear. It was plain and easily read, even though she covered it fast. There had been a slight widening of those already huge dark eyes and the tiniest flare of her nostrils.

Why?

''It was before you were born, of course,'' Garrett said, comfortable in the chair, one arm slung casually around his wife's shoulders. ''Helena's husband had died young, left her widowed and alone, with this big house to care for and two hundred acres to farm. Of course, that's not a lot of land by Texas standards, but it's a lot to expect one woman to handle alone. She was lonely, I think.''

''Well, sure she was,'' Chelsea put in. ''Gosh, what did she do to make ends meet?''

''I was getting to that.'' Garrett smiled indulgently at his wife, tapped her nose with his forefinger.

The woman was way too relaxed, Jasmine thought vaguely. She sat there all calm and content watching the boys pet the pony, while Jasmine was nearly jumping out of her seat every time the beast moved. And the conversation had her nearly as jittery as the big hooves did.

''Helena needed some income to help keep the wolves at bay. Meanwhile, my own mother was struggling through with five young'uns and no help other than a husband who was raised to believe caring for the kids was women's work.'' He shrugged. ''So it was a match made in heaven. Helena came by almost every day and helped out around the house, for, oh, about a year. Then all of the sudden she up and moved away.''

''But she didn't sell the place,'' Luke said. ''I wonder why?''

''She might have considered it the last part of her husband she had to cling to,'' Chelsea said. ''Or maybe she intended to keep it for her daughter.''

''Well, that's what she did,'' Jasmine said softly.

Garrett took a breath and sighed. ''Luke, you've looked over this packet of paperwork Jasmine brought along?''

Luke nodded.

''And does it look to you like her claim is legit?''

Luke faced her squarely. She imagined he would

try to bluff his way through, make her out to be a fraud and then have his cousin the sheriff boot her out of here. Instead he said, "Yeah. It looks perfectly legit." He sighed then. "But that isn't gonna stop this place from being auctioned for back taxes next week—unless she can come up with fifty grand by then."

"Fifty..." She blinked her eyes in shock at the sheer size of the debt. Then she shook herself and sat up straighter. "Next week is next week. Right now, today, I am the rightful owner of this place, and I have every right to stay here."

Luke nodded slowly. "That's all well and good. But I've paid my rent to the lawyer your mother left in charge of things for the full month, in advance, and I have every right to stay here, too."

"Maybe you should go see the lawyer and let him decide," Chelsea suggested, her tone gentling, as if she were negotiating a truce between two squabbling children.

"That's a good start, but it won't happen until Monday. Buzz Montana's out of town for the weekend. Some case up north. And no judge is going to be willing to hear this on short notice without all the information in front of him. So even if you two decide to fight this out in court, you'd have to wait at least that long," Garrett said.

"I'm not leaving," Jasmine said.

"I'm not budging, either," Luke replied, crossing his arms over his chest. "Possession is nine-tenths of the law, isn't that right, Garrett? I mean, if I move out now, I might lose whatever meager claim I do have to this place.'' Garrett nodded, and Luke went on. ''Look, I'm not trying to be a hard case here, Jasmine. And the last thing I want is to see you and Baxter without a place to stay. But this place—it means more to me than you can know. I gave up my life's work for this—I can't just hand it over without a word.''

Jasmine frowned at him. God, he was good. He almost had her feeling sorry for him.

Chelsea got to her feet. ''Look, forgive me for being dense here, but I really fail to see the problem.''

All three of them looked at her as if she were insane.

She just waved a hand toward the house. ''Will you look at the size of this place? You telling me there's not room here for one man, one woman and a tiny little fella like Baxter over there? For one lousy weekend? Come on, people, this one's a no-brainer.''

Pursing his lips, rubbing his chin, Garrett nodded slowly. ''She does have a point.''

''Aw, come on, Garrett,'' Luke all but moaned.

Garrett lifted his eyebrows. Then, slowly, he got to his feet. ''Take a walk with me, cousin?''

Luke frowned but didn't argue. Garrett headed down the steps. Luke went with him.

Chelsea smiled at Jasmine. ''Don't you worry. Garrett will set him straight.''

''Will he?''

''Sure. Now let's talk about the clothing situation here. I'm assuming what you're wearing is not a fashion choice.''

Jasmine glanced down at the way-too-big sweats and T-shirt. ''They're not even mine.''

''No, I didn't really think you'd have chosen that particular T-shirt.''

She glanced down at her own chest, saw the bulldog logo, groaned. ''I pulled it on so fast I didn't even look to see what was on it.''

''The back's worse,'' Chelsea said. ''Built Like A Mack Truck, it says.''

Jasmine met Chelsea's eyes, saw the humor in them and heard herself laugh. She couldn't believe the sound was coming from her, not with all that had happened in the past few days. But somehow the woman had put her at ease and managed to make her laugh. Her smile lingered, and she said, ''Wait a minute, I think I've figured it out. You must be the shrink in the family. Luke mentioned there was one.''

Chelsea smiled. ''Guilty, I guess. I'm a psychologist. I mostly work with woman who've been victims of domestic violence.''

''Hell, you must have no shortage of patients, then.''

''Unfortunately, there always seem to be plenty.

Even out here.'' She sighed, rather sadly. ''But that's off the subject, isn't it?''

Jasmine shrugged, turning her attention toward her son again. ''I forgot what the subject was.''

''Your clothes. Or lack thereof. Seems like you left Chicago in a bit of a hurry.''

Jasmine sent her a sideways glance.

''Not that I'm prying. I'm not. I mean...unless you *want* to talk about it.''

''I don't.''

''Okay. At any rate, Luke mentioned the situation this morning.'' She got up as she spoke, stepped off the porch to her horse and tugged open a leather pouch strapped to the back of the saddle. She pulled a bag out of it and brought it back up the steps with her. ''I brought a few things for you. Just to tide you two over until you have a chance to do some shopping.''

Jasmine was so stunned she couldn't even speak. She pressed her fingertips to the front of her throat, where it felt like the air had frozen.

''It's no big deal,'' Chelsea assured her. ''A couple pairs of Bubba's jeans—hell, he grows out of them so fast I can barely keep up, anyway. A few shirts, and a handful of my stuff for you...although looking at you, I think you'll swim in my clothes.''

''Even if that were true, it wouldn't be for long. With Luke cooking the way he does, and me not having time to work out for three days running now...''

"You should come with me to the dojo this afternoon!" Chelsea said, as if it were the most exciting idea in history.

Jasmine lifted her brows. "The dojo?"

"The kids take karate lessons. Grown-ups, too, from time to time. Garrett's brother Ben owns the place. He'd be glad to let us use part of the gym. And then you can tell me how you stay looking like you do."

Jasmine lowered her head. Was it possible this woman really was as nice as she seemed to be? Just like Luke, she was either genuine, or a hell of an actress. "I guess I could. But I'm not sure about letting Bax do anything as violent as karate."

"It's not violent, Jasmine. Not when it's taught in keeping with its true principles. It's spiritual. Reserve judgment and see for yourself, okay?"

"Okay."

"Good."

Jasmine glanced over at Bax, saw him watching longingly as Bubba climbed up into the saddle and rode his pony in a small circle, demonstrating some technique, she supposed. A twinge of mother guilt tugged at her heart, but she held her ground. Baxter wasn't like this robust little Bubba. He was frail, delicate. He tended to bruise very easily.

"How old is he?" Chelsea asked, following her gaze.

"Seven. Just seven." Jasmine looked at the bigger, sturdier boy and asked, "How about Bubba?"

"His name is actually Ethan, you know. I fought the nickname from day one, but you just can't win against a town full of macho cowboy uncles. He's almost six."

Jasmine blinked. "Six? But he's so big!" She shook her head in disbelief. She would have pegged the child as at least eight or nine. "He must take after Garrett in size," she mused aloud. There must be some reason why he seemed so much bigger and more solid than her own precious son.

Chelsea said, "He's adopted, so that can't be it. I tend to think it's just all this fresh air and sunshine. Quinn's the best place in the world to raise children." She smiled warmly. "Your Baxter is just gonna love it here."

"We aren't gonna be here that long," Jasmine said, and then she wished she could take the words back, because she saw Chelsea's puzzled reaction. If this house were truly her inheritance, why wouldn't she be planning to live in it?

It probably sounded suspect to this woman. But then again, it was really none of her business.

Luke leaned against an elm tree in the backyard, where he had a clear view of the kids out front messing with the pony. "Look at the poor, scrawny little fella," he said. "He wants to ride Bubba's pony so bad he can hardly stand it, but his anal, overprotective mother is too afraid he'll get a bruise or a scratch to let him."

He turned his gaze to Garrett. ''So what did you want to talk to me about?''

''Uh, that.''

''What?''

''What you just said. About Jasmine.''

Luke shook his head slowly. ''She's a nut.''

''She's a woman, and she's on her own with that boy, and she's running scared,'' Garrett said, hunkering down and resting his elbows across his knees.

Luke lifted his brows. ''You got that feeling, too, huh?''

''It's pretty obvious she's in some kind of trouble.''

''Yeah.'' He drew a breath, not liking the tight, anxious feeling in his chest.

''Now, I know you haven't been a part of the family for all that long, but I thought you'd picked up on enough to know better than to act the way you are toward a woman in trouble, Luke.''

Luke frowned. ''What do you mean? I let her spend the night. I gave her my own bed. And I made her breakfast, for crying out loud.''

''And this morning you're ready to boot her out.''

''She's trying to take my house away from me!''

''Maybe she's got a legitimate claim,'' Garrett said, his tone deep and calm. ''But that's not why you want her out, and I think you know it.''

Luke sighed, averted his eyes, then peeked down

at Garrett again. "I don't think spending the weekend under the same roof with her is the smartest thing for me to do, is all."

"Why not?" Garrett asked.

"*Why not?* Hell, Garrett, have you taken a good look at that woman?"

Garrett pursed his lips. "So, you kind of like her."

"No. I don't. I don't like her at all. And I don't want to. She's not the kind of woman I want to get involved with, not in any way, shape or form. Besides, she's lying. I can tell."

"How?"

"She won't show me any ID, Garrett. We don't even know she *is* Jenny Lee Walker."

Garrett sighed. "Well, now, it wouldn't be too bright to come all the way out here and try to claim the place if she couldn't prove she was who she says she is, would it, Luke? Why would she lie about something that's so simple to check out?"

Luke lifted his brows. "Simple to check out?"

"Sure. We just check with the Illinois DMV, trace her plate number, get a copy of her driver's license down here and take a gander at the photo. What could be easier?"

Pursing his lips, Luke said, "Do it."

"Do it?"

"Please? I've got a feeling about her, Garrett. She's trouble with a capital *T.* Run the plates, too, while you're at it."

Garrett shrugged. ''Fine, I'll do it. Have to wait till Monday, though. The DMV won't be open on the weekend. Come Monday, I'll put in a call and they'll fax me the photo. Okay?''

He sighed. ''Okay.''

''Meanwhile, you need to straighten up and be a Brand. You got a woman and a kid in trouble, with nowhere to go. You keep her here. Put her up until we settle this thing. And try being nice to her.''

''Is that an order?''

Garrett smiled. ''Considering I'm the closest thing to a big brother you got, cousin, yep, consider it an order. But, uh…be careful.''

Luke straightened away from the tree. ''Careful? Why? Do you think she's dangerous?''

''Hoo-yeah,'' Garrett said. ''But not the way you think. See, there's this genetic defect that seems to run through the males in the Brand clan. Women who are trouble with a capital *T*—we tend to fall head over heels for 'em.''

''What, are you kidding me?''

''Nope.'' He shook his head. ''And seeing as how you're scared to death to be left alone with her—even while swearing up and down she's not the kind of woman you want to be involved with—well, that tells me one thing, cuz.''

''Oh yeah? What?''

Garrett got upright, adjusted his hat. ''You're probably already doomed.'' He slapped Luke on the shoulder with a sympathetic shake of his head and started back around to the house.

"What the hell is that supposed to mean? Garrett!"

But his big cousin was already vanishing from sight.

"I need to go into town for a few things. Do you want to ride along?"

She sensed the man was trying to make conversation, trying to be polite. But she also knew he wasn't doing it because he wanted to. His cousin must have told him to be nice to her. After he'd come back from his chat with the big guy, he'd told her she could stay here with him "until things were settled." Which, she assumed, meant until he could boot her out with the law firmly behind him.

At least he hadn't tried to get her into bed yet. Which was somehow both reassuring and insulting at the same time. Maybe he didn't like women.

Or maybe he just didn't like *her*.

"I want to, Mom!" Baxter said. "Can't we, please?"

She frowned, not wanting her son out in public—but then again, she reasoned, no one had shown up at the door with a gun yet. And if Leo or Petronella or any of their goons had been able to figure out where she'd gone, they would have. She had no doubt of that. So that probably meant she and Baxter were safe here. For the moment, at least.

"Please, Mom?"

She shrugged. "I do need to pick up a few things. All right, I guess so."

She glanced down at her attire. She'd put on a pair of the jeans Chelsea Brand had brought over and a white cotton button-down shirt. Her hair was still in a ponytail, her feet in her open-toed spiky-heeled boots and her face downright naked of makeup. "I'd better see what I can do about the way I look first."

"You're right," Luke said.

She looked up fast, ready to shoot back. "What?"

"You need some decent walking shoes, or sneakers, or something," he said. "Course, I can't help with that, being that everything I have is a hefty size eleven. But I *do* have a good rugged set of fingernail clippers if you want to use them."

She swung her gaze to his, her jaw gaping. "What the hell is that supposed to mean?" Holding up a hand, palm out, she studied her nails. They were gorgeous. Long and curving and airbrushed. "What's wrong with my nails?"

"Well, nothing—if you're a cougar. What are you plannin' to do with those things, shred cabbage?" He sent Baxter a grin and a wink, and Baxter laughed out loud, holding his belly.

"I suppose you could carve your initials in the elm tree out back, if you wanted," Luke went on.

"Or maybe in your forehead," she countered.

But it was tough to hold on to her anger when her son was laughing so hard. His little cheeks were turning red now, and his glasses had slid down his nose. "Oh, so you think it's funny, do you?" she said to her son. "I thought you liked my nails?"

He grinned so hard his dimples had dimples. "I think they're pretty, Mom." Giggle, chortle, chuckle. "Really."

"Yeah, sure you do." She scowled at him. "So am I allowed to go put on some makeup, or is that going to start another laugh riot down here?"

"You're pretty enough without it, Mom," Baxter said. "Isn't she, Luke?"

Luke looked like the kid had just kicked him in the belly. He stuttered, he stammered, he got red faced. "Well...I...er...um...just...uh..."

"I'll be down in ten minutes," she said, not even waiting for his verdict on her prettiness, or lack thereof. "You guys wait, or else."

"Okay," Baxter called, smiling all over. "But don't put on too much, okay, Mom?"

Luke was still stammering.

She met her time limit with two minutes to spare, heading back downstairs with her hair now loose and thoroughly brushed, and wearing minimal makeup—just enough to make her feel human.

"Okay, I'm ready," she said.

Luke was fidgeting near the doorway. He'd been looking outside at something and only turned to face her when she spoke. Then he offered a crooked smile. "You really do look just fine without all the goop on your face," he said.

Jasmine frowned. "Was that supposed to be an apology or a compliment?"

He shrugged, turning his attention back outside. She followed his gaze to see Baxter running through the tall summer grasses and wildflowers outside. "I figured it would be okay as long as I kept an eye on him," Luke said.

She lifted her brows. "He has allergies. He'll probably be up all night coughing. I'll have to pick up some antihistamine while we're out."

Luke started to say something nasty. She could tell by the look on his face and the quick beginning of a word that broke off so fast it came out sounding like a primal grunt. He bit his lip, drew a breath.

"What?" she asked, almost challenged.

"Nothing. I, um…I was going to say if you're short on cash, I could loan you enough to get you by for a while."

She blinked in surprise, then shook her head. "That cousin of yours really does have some influence with you, doesn't he?"

"Why do you say so?"

She shrugged. "Because I know perfectly well you'd sooner see me tarred and feathered and branded with a scarlet *S* for Stripper than holed up here in your precious house with you for a few days. And yet here you are, chivalrously offering me a loan."

He narrowed his eyes on her. ''Look, I was just trying to be nice.''

''Try being honest, instead. It's so much more satisfying.''

''Oh yeah?''

''Yeah.''

''Fine. I'll be honest. I think you're lying through your teeth about who you are, and I think you're running like hell from something or someone, and you're scared half out of your wits. And so's that boy out there. And maybe that's why you're hovering over the poor kid so close you're damn near smothering him, but I don't think so. From the looks of him, you've been doing that for a long time now. So maybe whatever happened to send you running out of Chicago has only turned it up a notch or two. But either way, the kid's the one suffering for it, and you need to ease up on him.''

She glared at him. ''You dare to criticize my parenting skills!''

''That's right. I do.''

''What do you know?'' she all but shouted. ''You've never been a parent!''

''No, but I've been a kid!''

''To hell with you. You don't know anything. That boy out there is my entire life. He's everything to me. Do you have any idea what it's like to love something that much? So much that if you lost it you'd just stop being? You'd just curl up and dry up and vanish? Do you have any idea how scary that is? I'd do anything for my son. And I have!''

He went quiet for a moment, staring at her as the high color in his face eased down a notch. Then he said, ''Like...the dancing?''

She lowered her eyes. ''I'm not ashamed of what I do. Dancing is art. The female body is beautiful. Women have been performing erotic dance for over five thousand years.''

He raised his eyebrows. ''But not for drunken perverts, for the most part.''

''Thanks. Jerk.''

He shrugged. ''I meant...it can't be fun.''

''Don't knock it till you've tried it.'' She was being sarcastic, but she didn't expect him to pick up on that.

''Come on, gimme a break, will you? I meant, it's a hell of a sacrifice to do what you do for a living. You must love him a lot.''

''I thought we'd already established that.''

He sighed, rolled his eyes. ''You ready to go, or what?''

She sent him a scowl and pushed past him out the door. Her feet tapped across the wood floor of the front porch, and she glanced out toward where Baxter had been playing.

He wasn't there.

''Bax?'' She tapped down the steps. ''Hon, where are you?''

''Up here, Mom! Look at me!''

She followed his voice and spotted him as the screen door banged closed and Luke stepped up beside her. Baxter was hanging upside down from a tree limb about fifteen feet in the air. To her, it looked more like a thousand feet, but her logical mind said fifteen. Even so, her blood ran icy cold. "Don't move!" she cried. "Don't you move, Baxter!" She ran down the steps and out toward the tree with Luke on her heels.

He said, "Will you stop panicking? You're scaring him."

"*I'm* scaring *him?*" She got to the tree trunk. Her shoes were long gone. She'd kicked them off on the way, and now she grabbed a low limb and pulled herself easily up onto it.

"Hey, wait a minute! What do you think you're— *Jasmine!*"

She wished he would shut up. "Stay still, Baxter," she called. "Mama's coming, baby. Just don't move."

She monkey-climbed her way up higher and higher. Her son was talking calmly, carrying on what sounded for all the world like a normal conversation with Luke, while she climbed like a wild woman. Finally, finally, she reached the limb where Baxter had been hanging. Only he wasn't there.

Her heart hammered so hard she thought it was coming through her chest, and she shot a glance toward the ground, half expecting to see his broken body lying there. Instead, she heard laughter and saw her son being held in the big arms of Luke Brand. Luke was grinning like a loon and ruffling Baxter's hair, and Bax was laughing out loud up at him.

Luke looked up. ''Hey, he's okay. You can come down now.''

She blew her hair out of her face. ''How did you get down there so fast, Baxter?''

He smiled. ''I just jumped. Luke catched me.''

''You jumped?'' She glared at Luke. ''He *jumped?*''

''Well, don't look at me, it wasn't my idea.'' He set Bax on his feet, brushed the twigs out of his hair, then looked up at her again. ''Well, are you coming or what? I swear, it takes more work to get you two going on a simple shopping trip than one man can bear to handle.''

Muttering under her breath, she started back along the limb. Only one of her footholds didn't hold so well. She heard the sharp crack of the small limb and, though she grabbed hold of another, her hands slipped over the smooth bark and she was plummeting earthward almost before she knew it.

She didn't even have time to shriek.

And then she was in those big arms, just as her son had been moments before. And Luke was looking down at her, his eyes surprised, then amused. His chest was supporting her, his arms under her shoulders and legs, holding her against him. So every time he breathed, she felt herself rise and fall with it. And his face was so close she could see the light shadow of stubble peeking out of his skin.

"You can put me down now."

"I can?" The words were muttered and not a real question. Then he caught himself, blinked and said, "Oh, right, sure," and set her on her feet.

Baxter was sitting there staring from one of them to the other. And Jasmine suddenly felt a rush of guilt rising up in her chest. She didn't know why. She hadn't done anything, and it wasn't as if she had any intention of changing that. But logical or not, the guilt was there, and in force. She'd nearly kissed this man, or maybe he had nearly kissed her. She couldn't be sure which, but there had definitely been a kiss lingering in the air between them, waiting to be claimed. She'd nearly kissed a man in front of her son. Her Baxter. As if he weren't even there. As if he didn't matter.

Chapter 7

Okay, Luke thought. So she was like a she-bear guarding a cub when it came to that boy of hers. Jasmine had clambered up the tree so all-fired fast that Luke hadn't even had time to offer to do it for her. Much less to suggest that might not be the safest course of action she could take. He had never seen anything like it. She hadn't even paused to think it over, just leaped onto the first branch she could reach and scuttled up so easily it would have made a mama chimp jealous of her skill.

Damn.

She loved the kid. Luke had already deduced that much. Hell, he *knew* she loved the kid. But in case there had been any room for doubt—in case he'd been thinking her overprotectiveness had some other cause, like anal-retentive disorder or something—he now knew better. She might be a lot of things, but chief among them was one: she was a devoted mother. And that was something he couldn't help but admire.

In all his life, as a kid like Baxter, with a mom like Jasmine, he had never ever once doubted that his mother loved him. That she would step in front of a speeding train for him without batting an eye. Even though she'd kept him from a lot of things—like close friends, extended family, a peer group—even though she'd smothered him to the point where he'd nearly grown up to be an isolated, cut-off loner of a man—he'd loved his mother. When he'd lost her, for a while he'd been lost himself. If he hadn't come here, found this big warm family...

Well, hell, it didn't pay much to think on what might have been.

Jasmine rode beside Baxter and Luke in the pickup that had been parked in back, out of sight, bouncing in her seat with every pothole they hit. She looked a bit more "Quinn" than she had when she'd first arrived. She'd gone lighter on the makeup by about a pound and a half, he guessed. And the hair wasn't quite so big now. Still full and fluffy, and soft as a dark silk cloud, but not as over the top as before. And the jeans and T-shirt looked good. Damn, they looked good, and he wasn't quite sure why. They weren't tight, but slightly loose. She just was one of those women he figured would look good in anything, including a feed sack. However, those ridiculous talons of hers, with their gemstones winking, were still in place. And those shoes! God, where did she shop, at some dominatrix supply store? The heels were like vampire stakes, sharpened up for business. How did a person *walk* in those things?

"You might miss a few of these Texas-sized potholes if you'd quit staring at me and keep your eyes on the road," she told him, her tone a little sharp.

He glanced from her feet to her face. No amount of makeup could hide those big brown eyes now that he'd noticed them. Doe eyes. He felt as if he might fall into them before he managed to jerk his gaze back to the road. "I was wondering how you manage to walk in those shoes," he said, to make conversation.

"One step at a time, cowboy. Just like everybody else."

He glanced sideways at her, saw her lips quirk in a slight smile and knew she was teasing him a little. He didn't say any more, but sent Baxter, who sat between them, a wink.

A short while later he pulled the pickup to a stop. "This looks like a good place to start," he said. "What do you think, Baxter?"

Bax glanced through the windshield, and his eyes lit up when he spotted the giant ice-cream cone on top of the small log building.

Jasmine rolled her eyes. ''Hell, you're just determined to make me fat, aren't you?''

Luke shrugged. ''I'm guessin' you could eat nonstop for about a week and still have a ways to go for that, woman.''

She smiled at him suddenly. Right out of the blue. ''Thank you.''

''Shoot, that was no compliment. Why do you city girls always take being malnourished as a good thing? You're downright scrawny.'' He looked at Baxter. ''I say we get her a triple scoop super mocha sundae with extra whipped cream.''

''Yeah!'' Baxter said, giggling.

Jasmine was glowering at Luke again. ''I'll have a soda,'' she said. ''Diet.''

''Darn. Looks like Bax will have to eat that sundae, then.''

Bax laughed as if he would bust a gut, and Jasmine's glower eased away. Maybe she was starting to understand that he was kidding here, trying to keep Baxter's mind off his troubles.

He thought so even more when Jasmine ordered a small cone with a chocolate dip. They ate at one of the umbrella shaded picnic tables outside. He got momentarily lost in watching Jasmine eat ice cream. It was suitable fodder for the Playboy Channel, he figured. Or maybe it was just him. When they finished, he hauled them all over to the Wal-Mart, found a parking spot and stopped the truck.

Jasmine looked at the store, then sent Luke a doubtful glance.

"Anything you could possibly want or need, this is the place you'll find it," Luke promised her. "Hair care, clothes, shoes, even groceries. Knock yourself out."

"If you say so." She drew a breath and reached for Baxter's hand.

"Jasmine?" Luke said, and she looked back at him. He made his eyes as sincere as he could. "Why don't you let Baxter hang with me while you get your shopping done? I just have a few errands in town. Heck, I take Bubba with me all the time. Sometimes for the whole weekend, and he hasn't once gone home with so much as a mosquito bite."

She bit her lower lip. Luke noticed it, then made himself stop noticing it. "I don't know..." she said. Which meant she was wavering.

"You said you had a lot to do. And you know it'll be easier without him in tow. I promise, I won't let him out of my sight, not even for a second."

"Please, Mom?" Baxter asked.

She met Luke's eyes again, and he saw her message clearly. Let anything happen to my boy and I will kill you slowly. But aloud she said, "Oh, all right."

Bax squealed with delight and clapped his hands together. But while he celebrated, Jasmine reached out, and her slender hand, with its deadly nails, locked around Luke's arm with surprising strength.

''It's important you keep that promise about not letting him out of your sight,'' she told him, her voice very low. ''Very important. And if you see any strangers paying him undue attention, get him out of there. Watch him, Luke.''

The way she said it, the intensity in her eyes and the pressure of her hand on his arm...all those things combined delivered a message he would have preferred not to have received. The kid was in danger. Or Jasmine believe him to be. So those ''bad guys'' Baxter had mentioned twice were not just unpleasant characters or casual enemies, were they?

What the hell was going on with these two?

Too late to ask. She released him, leaned down to kiss her son's face and got out of the truck. ''You be good, Baxter. You stay close to Luke, you hear?''

''I'll be good, Mom. Really.''

An hour later Jasmine emerged from the store, her arms loaded down with shopping bags. She'd cashed both her own paycheck and Rosebud's on her way out of Illinois, so cash wasn't a problem. Not yet, anyway. As she entered the store, she practically bumped into a woman she didn't know. The woman had a baby on her hip. Jasmine muttered an apology, but the woman only stepped back, looked at her closely, and then smiled and said, ''You must be Jasmine!''

Jasmine frowned, going on instant alert. ''How do you know who I am?''

She was a pretty thing, with a Lois Lane look about her, and her baby was utterly gorgeous. Fat cheeks, blond curls. A little boy, six or seven months old, by Jasmine's best guess, wearing a tiny baseball cap with his jumper. The woman went right on speaking. ''You're new in town. You're shopping right where my cousin said you'd be shopping. And of course, there are the nails. They clinched it.''

''Not the nails again,'' Jasmine muttered, relaxing a bit as it hit her this must be yet another Brand.

''They're gorgeous,'' the woman said. ''Let me take a few of those for you.'' She helped herself to three of Jasmine's bags, holding them in one hand and her baby in the other arm. ''I'm Penny. My husband Ben is Garrett's brother. And this is Zachary, our son.''

''He's adorable,'' Jasmine said, looking at the bright eyes that stared right back at her. The baby smiled and cooed. Then Jasmine said, ''Did Luke send you here, then?''

''Uh-huh. He said to pick you up. He and Baxter, your own adorable little fellow, will meet you at the dojo in a bit. Okay?''

Jasmine shrugged. ''Fine, I guess.'' She walked with Penny Brand out to her car, which turned out to be a hulking four-wheel-drive SUV in a pretty shade of forest-green. They stashed the bags in the back and the baby in the car seat, then got into the front.

As she fastened her seat belt, Penny said, "By the way, welcome to Quinn. I can't tell you how glad I am to meet you. It's like fate sent you along at the perfect time."

Jasmine frowned. "Why would you say that?"

Penny shrugged, turning the wheel, expertly pulling into the light traffic of town. "Baxter tells me you're a dancer."

"Um, yeah." She wondered if Luke had elaborated on that, if he'd told his cousin-in-law that she danced, all right—at a strip joint in the seedy part of Chicago.

"I think that is so incredible. God, I've always wished I could dance. I just seem to have two left feet. Were you formally trained or self-taught?"

So Luke hadn't told her the rest. Hell, he must be a throwback. You could only fake so much—she didn't think you could fake the kind of...chivalry, or whatever antiquated moral value prevented him from spilling her secrets to his family. And glancing at Penny, she saw yet another woman who seemed kind, friendly, genuinely interested in her, and not sporting any ulterior motives. She was beginning to think it didn't make a lot of sense to believe every single person she met was an incredibly talented actor, trying to snow her, up to no good.

My God, could these people genuinely be this nice?

"I, um…Chicago School of Dance," she said finally. "For three years. I worked two jobs to pay my tuition. But I had to drop out when Bax came along."

"Wow," Penny said, looking a little awed now. "You must be incredible. You're more than I could have hoped for." She seemed to be battling a full-blown face-splitting smile.

"Hoped for…for what?"

"Oh, just let me show you around the place first. We'll talk more after."

Jasmine studied the woman curiously as Penny drove into a parking lot and cut the engine. She glanced into the back. "Anything perishable back there?"

"No, nothing."

"Great. Let's go in then." She hopped out of the car, whipped open the back door and gathered up her baby. Then she headed toward the entrance of the large building.

It looked to Jasmine like a big old warehouse of some kind. Ribbed metal siding, a white metal roof. But the giant sign across the peak in front read The Dojo Spiritual Fitness Center, and underneath that, in slightly smaller script, Karate, Tae Kwon-Do, Tai Chi, Chi Gung, Yoga, Meditation.

As they walked toward the entrance, she wondered if Luke's cousin Ben looked anything like

David Carradine. Then she thought to glance around the parking lot. ''I don't see Luke's truck,'' she said. She opened the door, holding it for Penny.

''Oh, he'll be along,'' she said, coming inside with the baby.

Inside, thc place was even more impressive. Hardwood floors, stacks of mats, sliding walls that could divide the huge space into four separate rooms at will, and the walls...the walls had long, elegant dragons painted on them in brilliant reds, oranges and purples.

''Come on in, please,'' Penny said. ''It's just as well no one's here right now. Maybe I can convince you to indulge me just a little bit.''

''I don't follow.''

But Penny was already rushing through the place, pointing this way and that. ''That little room beyond the Plexiglas window is where the controls are for the sound system, the lighting, the divider walls, etc. It doubles as an office. The other doors over there are the rest rooms, and that final one leads upstairs. The entire second floor of the place is where we live.''

''Wow. Must be tons of room.''

''Oh, there is. I'll show you around up there later, if you like.'' She pulled a mat from the stack near the wall and set the baby down on it. Then she dipped into her purse for a handful of baby toys and put them down in front of him. Zachary grinned and gurgled and sat up by himself, then reached for his toys. ''That's a good baby,'' Penny said. She left him and walked the four steps into the control room and office, and a second later Jasmine heard strains of music wafting from unseen speakers.

Penny came back out again, smiling. ''Will you show me just a little?'' she asked.

Jasmine frowned, then she got it. ''You want me to dance?''

''I know it sounds silly, but, oh, please, I really do have a reason for asking. And I've loved dance all my life. And it's just you and me here, after all. Please?''

Jasmine shrugged. ''To tell you the truth, it's been killing me not to have time to dance in the past few days—or a gym to practice in.'' She glanced behind her toward the door. The music was seeping into her muscles, making them twitch with longing. ''Back in Chicago there was a gym right around the corner from the apartment. Rosebud and I used to go every day while Bax was at school. Kept us in shape, you know? I mean, it isn't like we had the chance to use our classical training much any other time....''

She found herself stretching as she spoke. Falling into her old patterns automatically, almost feeling as if Rosebud were with her, right now. In that old gym with the smelly locker room, their cheap boom box plugged into a wall socket, sitting on the floor. A handful of boys usually waiting for the room to free up so they could shoot hoops, heckling them.

She and Rosebud giving it right back. Then dancing until those mouthy punks were just gaping, awestruck.

And then she was dancing. It came to her as naturally as breathing. She let herself forget everything that had happened. For a brief time she was back there in that smelly gym around the corner. And Rosebud was with her, dancing in perfect synch. Closing her eyes, Jasmine gave herself over to the music, let it bend and move her body with its notes and rhythms. Moving her arms in graceful arcs. Dancing was her sweetest release—her haven where no hurt could get in. She lost herself completely to the music, to the dance, forgetting her audience of one woman and one baby. Forgetting the violence she had come here to escape. Forgetting everything, she danced.

Luke and Ben walked up to the front door of the dojo and heard music. ''Guess they got bored waiting for us,'' Ben said.

Luke smiled at him, glancing down at the boy attached to the small hand that had been nestled inside his larger one for most of the afternoon now. He liked that feeling a little bit too much. He knew he shouldn't let himself get as fond of Baxter as this, feel as protective of him as he did. He shouldn't get a little soft spot in his chest every time those round wire-rimmed glasses slid down the kid's nose. It was not a good idea to get this attached to a child like Bax, with a mother like Jasmine. She wouldn't like it. She would probably rebel violently against it. He knew that instinctively. Moms like Jasmine didn't like other people getting close to their sons.

But that thought—along with every other coherent thought he might have had—abandoned his brain when he stepped into the dojo and saw her. At first he didn't fully comprehend. Had Ben finally hired a professional dance instructor for that class Penny wanted to add to the selection here? But what would a dancer this good be doing in a backwater town like Quinn?

And then he realized what his gut had known from the first glance. That dancer was Jasmine. She swirled and dipped, and when her arms moved they were liquid. Her hair flew when she whirled, and she moved faster and faster until she was only a blur in his eyes. And finally she stopped, ending bent low, almost hugging herself, her breaths rushing in and out in short, shallow puffs and her skin damp and glowing.

For some reason, Garrett's words floated into his mind. "You're doomed, cuz." And he thought maybe he was. That was it for him—the moment when he walked in and saw her dancing. He didn't want it to be. But he saw now that he'd never had much choice in the matter. Otherwise, what was the heavy object that nailed him in the chest like a two-by-four just now?

Luke heard clapping. He blinked out of the stupor her dance had evoked in him and looked around. Ben was there, clapping slowly along with Penny. On the floor, wide-eyed, little Zachary grinned and copied them, smacking his tiny hands together repeatedly. Baxter clapped, too, louder and harder than anyone else.

Jasmine lifted her head, eyes wide in surprise. Her eyes seemed to find Luke's as if by radar, and then she lowered her gaze. Her face was already flushed with heat and exertion, but Luke thought it got even redder. Was she blushing? And how much sense did that make? She danced half-naked for men for a living. How could dancing this way, in front of him, fully clothed, make her blush?

"I told you my mom was the best dancer in the world!" Baxter said, his little chest puffing out.

"You sure did, Bax," Luke said.

"That was incredible," Penny said through her smile. "Incredible! Wasn't it, Ben?"

"Blew me away," Ben said. "Okay, Penny, you win."

Penny looked at him, brows rising high. "I get to have my dance class?"

He nodded. "Can't deprive the Quinn kids of learning something that powerful, now can we? And as for the teacher, well, we couldn't top what I've just seen here if we advertised for six months. If Jasmine wants the job, it's hers."

Penny clapped her hands together. Everyone was

smiling. Everyone, Luke noticed, except for Jasmine. She was still staring at him, and it hit him that maybe she was waiting for him to make some comment about what he'd seen just now. Everyone had raved about her dancing except for him, and, uh, little Zachary on the floor there. Although at least the little one had clapped and drooled. Anyway, before he could find words, Jasmine looked away from him, as if Ben's words had finally registered.

"What job?" she asked.

"I want to add dance classes to our schedule, for the local kids," Penny said. "I have almost fifty parents interested already. But I couldn't do it without a qualified teacher, and I just didn't know where to find one." She smiled. "Until now."

Jasmine sent a swift glance toward Luke yet again. It took a moment before it dawned on him what she was waiting for. She was expecting him to inform his cousins what kind of dancing she had been doing up until recently. To tell them that they wouldn't want a woman like her teaching ballet and the like to young impressionable kids.

"I really…don't think I'm…qualified," Jasmine said at last.

Luke swallowed hard. "You're right. You're not. What you're qualified for is dancing on some Paris stage while people throw roses at your feet."

Those big brown eyes went wider. Her lips

pulled slightly, and she lowered her head. "You know better than that Luke."

"No, I don't. I've never seen anything like that before, Jasmine. And I already know how wonderful you are with kids. So I'd say you're more than qualified to take this job on, if you want it. And...if you're planning to stay around Quinn awhile."

"Are you?" Penny asked.

"Are we, Mom?" Baxter echoed.

Luke looked at Baxter's hopeful expression and wondered how much his own mirrored it. He tried to school himself into a less obvious countenance, but he couldn't help hoping she would say yes.

Jasmine looked from one of them to the other and, sighing, closed her eyes. "I don't know. I'm sorry, I just...I don't know."

Being in Quinn, Texas, at night was as different from being in Chicago as being on another planet would be. It wasn't the sounds, or the lack of them. Or the smells, or the lack of *them.* It was the feeling. A safe, secure, utterly fictional feeling that all was right with the world. People who lived in small towns were seriously deluded. Lulled into believing in the spell places like this could cast.

Baxter was tucked safely in Luke Brand's big bed, sound asleep already. Jasmine sat outside on the porch swing, rocking slowly, breathing honeysuckle-laden night air and listening to the endless chorus of background music. Coyotes warbling their sad, lonely cries. Cicadas chirping madly. The distant moan of the wind. Above her, beyond the porch roof, were stars. She didn't think she had ever seen so many stars in the sky in her life. They spread like a twinkling blanket over the world.

The creak of the screen door and heavy footfalls spoke of Luke's approach even before he sat down beside her on the swing. He gave a push of his big boots and sent the thing into greater arcs than before. Then he crossed his arms behind his head and leaned back, stretching out his long legs.

"It's pretty here, isn't it?" he said. "Prettiest place I think I've ever seen. And I've seen a lot of places."

"It's pretty here," she agreed. "Can't argue with that."

"This place—it's part of what made me decide to stop running, put down some roots."

"I suppose it's as good a place as any to settle down."

"Nope," he said. "Better."

She lifted her brows. "Look, if you're trying to sell me on that job offer of Penny's—"

"Jasmine, I know something's wrong." He stopped the swing, sat up straighter and turned partway around to face her. "I know you're scared, but you've got to stop running sometime. Some*where.* Sooner or later, you have to turn around and fight this thing, whatever it is, or it'll dog you to the end of your days."

She averted her eyes. He was far more perceptive than she wanted him to be. ''What makes you think I'm running from anything?''

He looked at her, his expression telling her not to even bother with the denial. ''Sooner or later,'' he said again, ''you gotta stand and fight. For Baxter's sake, if not your own.''

She shook her head hard. ''It's for Baxter's sake I have to keep running.''

He paused a beat, maybe digesting that. Then he said, ''Tell me what it is.''

''I can't.''

Pursing his lips, he nodded. ''Okay, you can't. It doesn't matter what it is, anyway, because eventually it'll catch up to you. Here...*here* is where you have the best shot at beating it. Better than any other place where you might run out of time. Here, Jasmine. You can win here.''

Lifting her gaze slowly, she searched his eyes. ''What makes here so much different than anywhere else?''

He pinned her with a piercing stare. ''I'm here.''

She wished with everything in her that she could believe him. But she couldn't. She couldn't risk Baxter's life on the word of a man who was little more than a stranger to her. Sooner or later Petronella would track her down, and she needed to make sure she and Bax were gone before that happened. God, if he caught up to her here, Luke and his entire family would be at risk. That thought gave her pause. Since when did she worry about outsiders? It had been her and Baxter and, until recently, Rosebud, against the world.

And yet a part of her was beginning to care about these people. And a part of her longed to stay in a place like this. To take the job Ben and Penny had offered, teaching dance to children. God, it would be so much better than what she'd been doing for a living up to now. And living in a town like this one—with people like these, who, honest to God, seemed to care about others more than they did about themselves—would be heaven. For her, and especially for Baxter. Already Baxter's cheeks had a healthier glow to them than they'd ever had before. And he'd laughed out loud more in the time they'd spent here than he normally did in a whole week.

God, it would be perfect here.

If only it could be.

She stared back at Luke, unable to look away from that penetrating stare, and the next thing she knew, he was kissing her. His mouth pressed to hers, his arms slid gently around her. It wasn't the sloppy, groping sort of kiss men occasionally forced on her when they caught her alone in the parking lot after a show. This was different. Fleeting and tender. His hands gently cupped the back of her head, as his lips tasted hers lightly, softly.

Her breath sighed out slowly, and her body softened. And then he let her go.

She sat there reeling, wondering what the hell that meant or what he wanted or what she was supposed to do now.

But then a gut-wrenching scream shattered the night's song, chasing all those questions from her mind as she came to her feet in a single heartbeat. "Baxter!" she cried.

Chapter 8

"It's okay, baby. Hush, now, it's okay. Shh."

Her voice was like the wind, its soothing, healing song so gentle that it didn't matter what she said. It was the way she said it as she held little Baxter close to her, rocking him back and forth.

His nightmare had been a bad one. Luke could see that plainly in the boy's paler-than-normal face and sweat-damp hair. He'd rushed into the room on Jasmine's heels when the child had cried out, flicked on the light instantly, instinctively. Now he felt useless, standing there, watching Jasmine magically drive the fear away from her little boy with her embrace and her soft, calming voice. "It was only a dream, Bax. Only a dream. It wasn't real. Mama's right here. I won't let anything hurt you. You know that."

The child clung to her, trembling still, but nodding against her shoulder. Her hands moved over his small back in soothing circles, patting now and then but mostly rubbing. Where did mothers learn that? Luke wondered. Was there some kind of instruction manual that came with kids, or what? The woman was a master.

Sniffling, Baxter sat away from her a little, rubbed at his cheek with the back of his hand. ''Can I have some warm milk?''

''You can have anything you want, baby.''

Finally seeing something he could do, Luke came to attention. ''I'll get it.''

Jasmine turned as if she'd forgotten he was there. ''No, I have to do it.''

Luke lifted his brows. Baxter sniffled and said, ''No one else knows how to do it the way Mom does.''

''Oh. All right, then.''

Jasmine looked at him as she got to her feet, and he could see the worry in her eyes. The tension. And no wonder. His own heart was only just beginning to return to a normal rate. As she passed him, she reached up, closed her small hand on his arm. ''Would you stay with Bax while I get that milk?''

He glanced down at her, touching him like that. He wasn't sure she'd even thought about it first. He wasn't sure if it meant anything, or if it was just a reflexive action. For the first time since hearing the boy's scream, he let himself review what had happened just prior to it. That kiss on the porch swing, under the stars. What the hell had that been about? He hadn't meant to kiss her. Hadn't planned to kiss her. It just sort of…happened. And he didn't know what it meant to him, much less what she might be making of it in her mind. Did that touch have anything to do with the kiss? And if so, what?

Her hand was still on his arm. Experimentally he covered her hand with his own. "I'll be right here. Don't worry, Bax will be fine till you get back."

Lifting her gaze to his, she seemed a bit startled but more comforted. "You want me to bring you some warm milk, too?"

He shook his head left, then right. It was going to take a lot more than warm milk to help him get to sleep tonight, he thought vaguely. A hell of a lot more. For some reason he had a foolish image in his head—one of him sitting in a chair beside the bed, watching over the two of them while they slept. As if that would do any good. He couldn't very well keep their nightmares away.

He reached up in spite of himself and tucked her hair behind her ear. "Yell if you need any help with that milk."

She nodded and left the room.

Luke sighed as he watched her go. He *really* didn't want to be drawn to her the way he was. He'd tried to tell Garrett having her here with him wasn't a good idea. Damn his oversize meddling cowboy cousin, anyway. What the hell was he going to do with a woman like her? He'd barely survived the first overprotective woman in his life, why on earth would he want to take up with another one?

She was totally opposite from the kind of woman he thought he might want to settle down with someday. And besides, that someday was still a long way off. This whole "sell the truck, buy the ranch, put down roots" experiment was barely underway. He had no idea if he could be a settling-down kind of man. Suppose it turned out his mother had been right all along? Suppose he'd inherited his father's wanderlust? What then? This woman needed more than that. Hell, Baxter needed more than that. He didn't think he had enough love in him to heal the wounds he saw in these two wayfarers.

"Luke?"

He turned to look at Bax in the big bed, looking small and alone. "Yeah, pal?"

"I'm scared, Luke."

A tiny arrow slid right into his heart, and Luke went to the bed and sat down on the side. "It's okay to be scared. Just so you know you're not alone. I'm here, and your mom, too."

"But what if they find us?"

Luke drew his brows together. "What if who find you? Are you talking about your dream, Bax? 'Cause, you know, dreams aren't real."

"This one was. I dreamed of those men, back in

Chicago. The big one, he had a gun. And he shot that other man with it, and I saw! And then he tried to shoot me, and when Mommy made him stop, he tried to shoot her.'' He lowered his head, great big tears rolling down his face. ''And I think he got Aunt Rosebud. That's why she had to go live with the angels.''

He curled into Luke's arms, wrapped his small ones around Luke's neck and rested his face on his chest, while Luke sat there stunned right to his bones. ''I'm so afraid those men will find us. What if they hurt Mom the way they hurt Aunt Rosebud? What if I lose her, too?''

''Hey. You look at me, pal.'' Luke drew Baxter's chin up and stared right into his eyes. ''I promise you, I'm not gonna let anyone hurt you. Or your mom. You got that? Any bad guy tries to get near the two of you, he's gonna have to go through me and my whole family first. Now, you've only met a few of us. Bubba and Garrett and Chelsea, Ben and Penny and Zach. But there's a bunch more. There's Wes, Taylor, Adam, Kirsten, Elliot, Esmeralda, Lash and Jessi—oh, there's a pile of us Brands around here.''

''There are?'' The boy looked up, wide-eyed, trusting but doubtful.

''Wait…I have a picture,'' Luke said. ''We took one of the whole clan at the big family picnic a month ago.''

Luke got up, only to his surprise, the little fellow

clung like a burr—arms and legs wrapped tight. He carried Bax with him to the dresser, opened a drawer and reached in for the photo album he kept there. He was startled to feel soft, lacy, silky things brushing over his hands. Jasmine, it seemed, had commandeered some drawer space. And though his throat went dry as a bone, he ignored them and located the album.

Then he sat down on the bed with the boy on his lap and flipped pages until he found the photo. The eight-by-ten took up the entire page. "There now, see that?" Seventeen adults and three children were in that photo. The entire surviving Brand clan. Well, the legitimate branch of it, anyway. The Oklahoma wing of the family hadn't been present. "Most of the folks in this picture are within shouting distance, you know. This one here is Marcus. He's my half brother. And that cute one, there in the front, that's Sara, my half sister. You know I only met them a couple months ago?"

"Really?"

"Mmm-hmm. They live close by, down near El Paso. It's not far. And let me tell you what they told me when I first found all these relatives of mine. 'Luke,' they said. 'When one member of this family gets into trouble, every single Brand in Texas drops whatever they're doing and hightails it to them to help them out. Doesn't matter where they are, or what the trouble is. That's just the way this family works.'"

Baxter stared up at him, big brown eyes starting to look sleepy. ''But I'm not part of the family.''

''Well, heck, Baxter, you're livin' with me, aren't you?''

''Yeah....''

''Well, that makes you part of the family in my book. Besides, that's the other thing about this family. If they like you, they tend to want to make you an honorary Brand.''

''They do?''

''Oh, heck yeah. So you might as well consider yourself in. I doubt they'd listen even if you tried to tell 'em you didn't want to be. 'Specially Bubba. He's been itching for a cousin big enough for him to hang out with.''

Baxter smiled wider than Luke had ever seen him, hugged Luke tight and then crawled under the covers, taking the photo album with him. He curled up with it clasped to his chest and closed his eyes. ''Thanks, Luke,'' he said. ''I never had a real family before—'cept for Mom and Aunt Rosebud. I think I like having one this big.''

His throat so dry he could scarcely speak, Luke rasped, ''Me too.''

Jasmine stood in the doorway, the milk with a touch of honey and a bit of strong chamomile tea mixed in, warmed to just the right temperature, in her hands. The scene in the bedroom looked like the artwork from some sentimental Father's Day card. Luke sat on the edge of the bed, and Baxter lay in it, but he'd curled around Luke like a cat. And as he lay there sound asleep, Luke's oversize hand ran slowly over Baxter's dark blond hair, again and again.

The sight of her son with a man in such an affectionate way was totally foreign to Jasmine. And totally unexpected. She didn't think she liked it very much. A dark wave of something that felt a little bit like petty jealousy sloshed against her heart. She chased it away and told herself that was foolish, that her main concern had to be Baxter. And that for him to get attached to this cowboy, who could only be a temporary guest in their lives, would be a big mistake. Come to think of it, that might be a good thing for her to remember herself. She could easily get hurt. More importantly, Bax could get hurt.

From the looks of things, so might Luke. He was not, she finally admitted to herself, acting a part. He was genuine.

Jasmine sighed, lowering her gaze. "I think he's out cold, Luke," she whispered.

He turned toward her, then sent her a lopsided smile that told her she was too late to save him. Her Baxter had worked himself into the big guy's heart already. Carefully Luke eased himself off the bed and out of Baxter's clutches. Once on his feet, he bent to tuck the blankets around Baxter, and when he came toward the door, Jasmine reached for the light switch.

Luke's hand covered hers, closed around it and pulled it gently away. ''Why don't you leave it on for him?''

She frowned but left the light on. They stepped into the hall together, and Luke pulled the door closed, but not all the way closed. Then he tiptoed along the hall to the stairs and down them. Only when they were in the living room did he speak at something approaching a normal volume. Taking a seat on the sofa, he said, ''When I was a kid, I was scared to death of the dark. My mom thought it would make me weak to leave the light on for me. So she would just shut it off, close the door up tight and leave me there alone. Said it would cure me.''

Jasmine lifted her brows. ''Did it?''

He shook his head. ''I was still fighting it into my teens. And suffering from too little sleep all the while in between.'' He shrugged. ''Course, having that bright light on all night isn't the solution either. But I was thinking, we could maybe pick him up a night-light tomorrow. I mean—if it's okay with you. You're his mom, after all.''

She nodded slowly. ''Fine by me.'' Then she sighed. ''I'd never make him sleep in the dark if he was afraid. It's just...he's never been afraid before.''

Luke nodded, and she felt his eyes probing her

closely. ''Seems like something happened to make him afraid.''

She looked up sharply. What had Baxter told him?

''And you're afraid, too,'' he said. ''At first I thought you were just overprotective, and you are, to a point. But it's not just that.''

''I'm not overprotective.''

''Yeah, you are. I know. I had a mother just like you.''

She narrowed her eyes, opened her mouth to speak, but he held up a hand. ''Don't get defensive, Jasmine. You're a fine mother to that boy. Any fool could see that. I'm not arguing it. I got off the subject.''

''The subject being?'' she asked.

''What the hell happened in Chicago? I mean, damn, woman, I knew there was something dogging you. I thought it was a man, a bad relationship, a custody battle, something like that. But now...''

She went stiff. So Baxter had told him something after all.

''Jasmine, Baxter's troubles here are a damn sight bigger than fear of the dark or a scraped-up knee, and we both know it.''

She licked her lips, averting her eyes. She should go up to bed. She should walk away. ''What makes you think so?''

He sighed in exasperation, lifting his palms.

''Come on, Jasmine, will you quit with this? Baxter says someone tried to shoot him and you!''

''He just had a nightmare.''

''No wonder. Sounds like you've been living one lately.''

''Look, I can't talk about this.''

He said nothing for so long she had to lift her eyes and meet his steady gaze. Finally he just sighed. ''Sooner or later you're going to have to trust someone, Jasmine. If someone's after you, I can help. And I will. But I can't if you don't tell me what's going on.''

He waited. Jasmine stared at the floor, gnawed her lip and almost considered telling him the truth. But no, she couldn't do that, for so many reasons. First and foremost, because it would mean admitting she had no legal right to be staying in this house. She didn't really think he would toss her out if he knew that, but he could. And besides, one of the men after her was a cop. This man's cousin, Garrett, was a cop, too. How could she be sure they would believe her over that murdering bastard in Chicago? Sure, they might take her word for things at first—but when it came to her word against that of a police officer, that might change.

She squirmed inwardly. It was so ingrained in her not to trust, not to accept help from outsiders, not to let anyone in. And yet she'd never wanted to, felt driven to do just that, the way she did now. With this man. This family. But beyond all that lay one simple, dark truth that made the rest moot. Telling Luke and the Brands would add them to the list of targets to be silenced.

She didn't want to rain that kind of disaster down on this family. She'd stirred up enough of a whirlwind in their lives already.

Luke was still looking at her, still waiting. She lifted her gaze to his.

He saw her answer in her eyes, because he sighed and said, "Sooner or later, Jasmine, you're gonna trust me enough to open up to me." He offered her a small smile, one meant to be comforting, she was sure. "But for now...maybe you could just let me taste that special warm milk you make like no one else in the known universe?"

Her tense muscles uncoiled slowly, and if the breath rushed out of her in relief, well, she couldn't help that. She held up the glass, and he took it, sipped it, smacked his lips and wore a milk mustache. "Mmm. Bax was right."

"It's just milk and honey, with a little touch of chamomile."

He drank some more, then handed her the glass. "Finish it up, hon. You're gonna have trouble sleeping, too, after all this."

Hon. She didn't think anyone had called her that since Rosebud. It made her throat get tight and her eyes burn. He saw it, damn him. And though she sipped the milk to cover her pain, he didn't stop seeing it. She could feel him seeing it. When she set the glass down, he smiled, and reached up to brush her upper lip with his thumb. And then his eyes got darker, somehow. And he leaned closer and kissed her. It was soft, light, gentle. And when he lifted his head away, he licked his lips, tasting that milk and honey, she knew, because she'd tasted it on him, as well.

''I've been thinking about kissing you ever since I walked in and saw you dancing today.''

Her brows bent until they touched. ''Why?''

''Why?'' He shook his head. ''Because it was beautiful. You were…I've never known anyone who could move like that. It was like…music. Yeah. If music could move, that's what it would look like.''

She blinked. She didn't think she'd ever been given such a sincere compliment before. ''You thought all I could do was bump and grind?''

He checked her face quickly, as if looking to make sure she wasn't getting defensive on him. She couldn't blame him for that. She tended to get defensive where her work was concerned. She smiled a little. ''It's okay. Most people don't expect strippers to have a hell of a lot of talent. But I was classically trained. It's just not a very efficient way to earn a living, is all. I had a child to feed.''

He shook his head. ''You don't have to explain yourself to me.''

''I know.'' She looked at him, studied his blue eyes. ''But for some asinine reason, I want to. I've never felt ashamed of dancing for a living, Luke. Expressing emotions through dance, even emotions like passion or lust, is an art. Exotic dancing has a long history. Even a sacred one. I mean, the first striptease was The Dance of the Seven Veils, you know. And it was first performed by a goddess. It's not the dancers who should feel shame for what they do. Not if they do it well. It's the men who watch them. I mean, they have a choice, too. They can react with a stirring of desire, with appreciation and admiration and pleasure. Or they can shout obscenities and try to cop a feel at every opportunity. Either way, it doesn't change the quality of the dance.''

He tipped his head to one side, then averted his eyes. ''I never thought of it that way.''

''No. Most men don't.'' She looked at him, then looked again. His face was redder than before. His neck, too. ''It's embarrassing you, talking about this, isn't it?''

He lifted his gaze. ''No. That's not the word I would use.''

She looked closer. He looked away. ''Maybe you should go on up to bed,'' he suggested, his voice a little raspy.

Frowning, still not able to read him, she said, ''Oh. Well, okay.'' She got to her feet. Then she turned to look at him. ''Thanks,'' she said. ''For being so good to Baxter tonight.''

His face eased a bit, and he smiled. ''How could I not be? The kid's a charmer.''

''He is, isn't he?''

Luke nodded, but his eyes slid from hers to her lips, and then he lowered them to the floor again. ''Good night, Jasmine,'' he said, and he said it like a dismissal.

She shrugged, not getting him. She could almost think he wanted her...except if he did, he would have tried something more than just the innocent little kisses he'd stolen. He would have been all over her by now if that were the case. Or...the men she'd known up to now would have, anyway.

Then again, she reminded herself, Luke was nothing like the men she'd known up to now. She didn't know what to make of a man like him. How to read him. ''Good night, Luke.''

She felt his eyes on her all the way up the stairs, though. And when she turned at the top to look down at him, she saw him staring hard and met his eyes and swore there was desire there. He held her gaze for a long moment, and then he finally turned away.

Jasmine went into the bedroom and climbed carefully under the covers to snuggle up with her little boy. She held her son and vowed to keep his nightmares away.

When Jasmine went to bed, she left her bag on the table. Luke picked it up, struggling to resist the urge to go through it for some clue as to what she was hiding. He managed, though. He carried it to the hook on the wall and hung it up. It swung heavily, and when it hit the wall there was a clunk. A metallic clunk. One that made his breath hitch in his chest and drew his gaze back to the handbag.

Frowning, he told himself that wasn't what it sounded like, and that the shape now visible in the bottom of the bag wasn't what it looked like, and that the weight in the bag wasn't what it felt like. But he stopped resisting, and he took the bag down off the peg and reached inside to make sure.

A cold metal handgun lay in the bottom. His hand bumped against it, then closed around it, and he pulled it out. "Ah, hell." He checked it, saw that it was unloaded. At least she wasn't totally insane. Glancing guiltily toward the stairs, and feeling justified now, he carried the bag to the sofa with him and, sitting down, began pulling out its contents, item by item.

His Jasmine had two identities, it seemed. She had one driver's license with her own pretty face on it. The name it listed was Jasmine Delaney Jones. And she had a second driver's license, this one with another woman's face on it. Her name, it said, was Jenny Lee Walker.

He closed his eyes. Damn. Just how much trouble was Jasmine in?

His stomach clenched again, as it had when her words earlier had his mind conjuring images of her dancing just for him. And that made him wonder how much trouble *he* was in.

Baxter came down for breakfast just as Luke finished pouring orange juice and set the glass down on the table. The boy looked at the cereal bowl and the assortment of boxes on the table, then sent Luke a quizzical glance. ''But it's Sunday.''

''Oh, yeah, that's right,'' Luke said. He refilled his coffee cup and took a seat opposite the boy. ''And you usually have a big Sunday breakfast, don't you?''

Smiling, Baxter nodded.

''Well, to be honest, I always liked a big Sunday breakfast, too. But I learned pretty quick that it's a big mistake to fill up on Sunday morning around here.''

Baxter tipped his head sideways. ''Why?''

''Because every Sunday afternoon, the whole family heads over to the ranch for a giant barbeque.''

''They do?''

''Sure they do. So I tend to eat light on Sunday mornings, just to save room for all the goodies in the afternoon. There's usually pie and ice cream for dessert. I always make sure I leave room for that.''

''Wow.'' Baxter chose a box of cereal, poured, then paused and glanced at Luke. ''Is it just for real Brands, or can 'on'ry ones go, too?''

Reaching across the table, Luke ruffled the kid's hair. "Honorary ones are our favorites."

Baxter grinned wider and added milk to his cereal.

Luke felt eyes on him and looked up. Jasmine stood in the archway, and he had no idea how long she'd been there or how much she'd heard. She'd obviously been up for a while, though. Her hair was done. No ponytail necessary. It had been washed and spritzed and blow-dried so that its curls fell in bunches over her shoulders. Her makeup was done, too. Not to the same extremes as that first time he'd seen her. But more than the light touch of yesterday. Any flaws in her skin were hidden, and her high cheekbones were accentuated; her eyes were lined and shadowed, and her lashes were thickened. And her lips...her lips were shiny and moist and pink, and he thought they looked tastier than anything his cousins might have to offer this afternoon.

"Can I talk to you for a second, Luke?"

He realized he'd been staring at her, taking stock of every difference in her this morning and wondering why a woman as beautiful as she was would be so merciless as to try to make herself even more irresistible. She wore a pair of snug-fitting jeans she must have picked up in town on their shopping trip, and a ribbed tank top that showed off her figure and her tan.

Nodding, he got to his feet. "Be right back, pal," he said to Baxter, and then he joined Jasmine in the archway. She led him into the living room, then turned to face him. ''What are you doing, telling him he's an honorary Brand? Inviting him to family gatherings? What are you thinking?''

Her eyes were pained, her voice a harsh whisper.

''I…I just thought it would be fun for him, is all. He can play with Bubba and maybe ride a pony and—''

''He is *not* riding on any pony.''

''Aw, come on, Jasmine. I wouldn't let him get hurt. You know that.''

She stared into his eyes for so long he thought he could see her heartbeat, and then she finally turned away, sighing. ''Dammit, Luke, why do you have to be so damned good to him? Making him breakfast. Taking him for ice cream. Treating him like family.''

''What's so wrong with those things, Jasmine?''

She lifted her head fast. ''You're teaching him that it's okay to depend on other people. You're making him lose his edge, Luke.''

''Are we talking about Baxter now…or you?'' Luke asked.

''You're making him love you,'' she whispered.

''So I'll ask you again, are we talking about Baxter…or—''

''It's gonna break his heart when we have to leave,'' she said, interrupting him before he could finish the sentence. And yet, he thought, the question still applied.

Luke put a hand on her shoulder. Her silky, soft skin against his calluses. The friction made his stomach clench. "Who says you have to leave?"

Her eyes widened before she turned away. "I do. Life does. We can't stay, Luke."

He frowned, turning her to face him. "What do you mean, you can't stay? You're challenging me for the house, aren't you? What are you gonna do, sell it and move on?"

She stared at him hard and finally lowered her head. "I'm not challenging you for the house. I just needed someplace safe for a few days, until I could figure out what to do." She lifted her gaze to his again. "I'm sorry I made you think you might lose the place. You're not going to. We couldn't stay here, even if we wanted to."

"Why not?"

She started to turn away, but he held both shoulders now, and he wouldn't let her. "Why not, Jasmine?" he asked again.

"Because sooner or later our past is going to catch up with us, and when it does, we have to move on."

"You can't run forever," he said.

"You just watch me." Again she turned away from him. This time he let her. He stood there, wondering what the hell to do, how to get her to open up to him...knowing damn well that if he kept pushing, she would bolt. Finally he sighed and said, "At least come to the ranch with me today. At least let Baxter enjoy himself for a little while. He'll have so much fun at the Texas Brand. And you can be there to watch him every second.''

He saw her lower her head, shake it slowly. ''You're as good at wheedling as he is, you know that?''

Luke shrugged. ''So will you come?''

''Yeah. We'll come.'' She turned and waggled a finger at him. ''But no pony rides.''

''Yes, ma'am.''

Several hours later, Luke sat astride one of Wes's prize Appaloosas, with Baxter cradled in the saddle in front of him. Jasmine looked on, gnawing her lip and regretting that she'd ever let the two of them talk her into this insanity, praying Bax wouldn't fall and get trampled underneath those giant hooves. Of course, Luke had a firm hold on him. And Baxter was laughing and smiling as if he'd never had so much fun in his life.

''Luke's great with him, isn't he?'' Chelsea asked.

They were sitting across from one another at one of the picnic tables on the big front lawn, sipping coffee. Jasmine was surrounded by more women than she was used to seeing in one place. Women usually didn't like her too much. She'd always assumed that was because they saw her as a threat. These women, however, seemed as if that were the least of their worries. And to Jasmine's surprise, not one of their men had given her so much as a leering look when his wife's back was turned. Not one.

She didn't think they made men like these guys anymore. She was through doubting they were genuine, though.

Jessi, the Brand sister with the pixie short red hair, perched on the railing. Taylor, the stunning dark-skinned Comanche married to Wes Brand, sat sideways on the top step with her back against the railing and her belly looking like a beach ball in her lap. Esmeralda, the sloe-eyed, slightly otherworldly wife of Elliot, with her thick Spanish accent, was in a wicker rocker with her belly every bit as swollen. They were a fertile bunch, these Brands, Jasmine mused. Penny sat on a blanket in the grass and watched Jessi's gorgeous toddler, Maria-Michelle, play gently with her own infant, Zachary.

Jasmine listened to their conversation. They talked about their kids and their pets—Penny's family of bulldogs raced around with the kids like kids themselves, while Bubba's aging hound dog, Blue, observed with amused indulgence. They laughed and joked, and exchanged lighthearted gossip. One of the Loomis boys was getting married. The local bar was adding a dining room. Maria-Michelle had the sniffles.

The place spread out like some fairy-tale land peopled with characters straight out of a fantasy. Devoted husbands and loyal wives, happy families.

Horses and cattle and puppies racing to and fro. Big red barns and wide, rolling fields so green they hurt your eyes to look too long, underneath the biggest, bluest sky in all the world. For God's sake, there was even a tire swing in a tree out there in the distance! And a swimming hole ''down back'' she'd heard mentioned when the sun started beaming down hotter than before.

If someone had described this place, this scene, this family, to her before, she wouldn't have believed them. She would have called them a liar. She would have told them they'd been watching too much television. Damn, Rosebud would have loved this.

Of course, this family was sheltered here in this rural place. So far away from the touch of anything evil or dangerous. They wouldn't know what to do if they faced the kind of trouble haunting Jasmine and Baxter. They wouldn't have a clue.

Chelsea was getting up, waving now. ''Come on, kids. Come get changed and we'll take you out to the pond to cool off, okay?''

Luke got off the big horse, lifting Baxter easily and setting him on the ground. Baxter came running, eyes huge, face pink with the sun and exertion. He honestly looked happier than she'd ever seen him. ''Me too, Mom?''

Jasmine sent Luke a questioning look.

He gave her an imperceptible nod, and oddly, she found that was assurance enough for her. She was coming to trust the man, she realized with a start. If he said it was safe, she believed it. And that was just so odd it was like a *Twilight Zone* moment. She had to give her head a shake. This was all surreal. Was she dreaming this place? Was she dreaming *him?*

She didn't know. She would process all that later. For now, she took her son's hand and led him into the big farmhouse to help him change into the shorts Luke had insisted she bring along.

A short while later she was watching her son splash in a shallow frog pond with Bubba Brand, who seemed to have become his new best friend. And she realized it really was going to break Baxter's heart to leave here.

Why did life have to be so unfair?

Chapter 9

"So?" Garrett asked. He walked beside Luke, leading the horses the kids had been riding out to the stable.

"So, what?" Luke asked.

Behind him, the other men chuckled. And they were all there, too, following along for no good reason. Obviously this discussion was of interest to every macho Brand male in the county. Wes, the hot-tempered half Comanche. Elliot the redheaded jokester. Adam, the levelheaded *GQ* cover looka-like. And Lash, Garrett's deputy, even though he was a Brand by marriage, rather than blood. He'd married the baby sister of the family.

"So, has your houseguest told you anything about herself yet?"

Licking his lips, Luke stopped walking. The horse he'd been leading nickered and stomped a foot at him, impatient for the oats she knew awaited her in the stables, no doubt. Luke looked at the men. "I trust you guys like I've never trusted any man in my life except maybe for my old friend, Buck, whose death sort of led me to you all."

Wes lowered his head and reached up to clap Luke on the shoulder. Elliot grinned and shrugged, then said, "So what's not to trust?"

Luke shook his head. "I need to know you trust me the same way."

Ben bit his lower lip to hide a smile, and the other guys seemed to be battling the same. Garrett said, "You're falling for her already, huh?"

Luke swung his head around so fast he wrenched his neck. "What? No! I mean…not really. I…she…"

Garrett snorted, he was trying so hard not to laugh. Elliot reached up to smack Luke between the shoulder blades. "Just breathe, cuz. It's okay, it's happened to all of us."

Luke rolled his eyes. "There's nothing going on between the two of us."

"But you're attracted to her," Lash said, and it wasn't really even a question.

"Well, of course I'm attracted to her. I mean, have you *looked* at the woman? Who *wouldn't* be attracted to her? But that doesn't mean a damn thing. Hell, I'm not even sure I'm ready for a relationship with a woman. And even if I was, I'm not sure she'd be the one. She's sure as hell not what I had in mind."

"Nope. They never are," Elliot said, shaking his head slowly.

"Doesn't matter if he's ready or not, anyway," Lash said. "Jessi made up her mind a good hour ago. She pulled me aside after the meal, said she thought Jasmine was perfect for Luke."

"Yeah, Chelsea thinks Jasmine and little Baxter fit into this family like missing puzzle pieces," Garrett said.

Elliot grinned at Luke. "Well, hell, cousin, that just about seals your fate, then. If Jessi and Chelsea want her in, she'll be in, and you're the only single male left to marry off to *get* her in."

Luke felt the blood drain from his face. *"Marry?"*

Lash nodded. "Shoot, they're probably picking out flowers by now."

Luke just stood there, feeling his head spin and his stomach lurch. And then they all burst out laughing. It was one big masculine roar, and so many hands slapped his back and shoulders that he figured he'd be bruised the next day.

Then Garrett was in his face. "Hey, don't look like that. We were only teasing you, Luke. Come on, don't faint on us."

He shook himself, shot Garrett a scowl. "I don't *faint.*" Then he led the mare the rest of the way to the stable, talking as he went. ''Shoot, I wanted to talk to you guys about something important, and you all have to go off on me like a bunch of freak-ing....''

''Brothers?'' Garrett asked when they got to the stable door. He pulled it open and led the horse inside. All the others trooped past, and Luke stood there looking in at them, a horse at his side.

''Yeah,'' he said with a grudging smile. ''Yeah, that's exactly what you're acting like.'' He led the other horse inside, no longer angry. Then he held her while Wes rubbed her down.

''So what do you know about her?'' Garrett asked.

Luke sighed. ''That's what I wanted to talk about. She's in trouble, Garrett. And what I've found so far doesn't look good for her.''

Garrett lifted his brows. ''But you don't believe the evidence you're seeing?''

''No. And I don't want you all going against me on this. I want to give her the benefit of the doubt. I want to help her and Bax get past this trouble, whatever it is.''

The men looked at each other, then at Luke. Garrett said, ''You're the one who knows her best, Luke. We trust your judgment. If you say she's all right, then she's all right. If you take her side, we've got your back.''

''And if it turns out you were wrong,'' Wes said, ''then we'll all be wrong with you.''

Around him, the other men nodded in agreement. Luke lowered his head.

"Thanks. That means a lot."

"So? What have you found out? How can we help?"

The horse was dry now, and Wes opened the stall. Luke led her inside, and Elliot poured a scoop of grain for her. Garrett returned the other mount to its stall as well, and they all gathered in the middle of the stable in a semi-huddle.

"Baxter told me some men tried to shoot him and Jasmine, and he seems to think those men are still after them. Had a nightmare last night. Poor kid is terrified, and he's obviously been through something. Jasmine won't talk. But she's got two sets of ID in her purse. One belonging to Jenny Lee Walker and one to Jasmine Delaney Jones. And the photo on the Jenny Lee Walker license looks nothing like Jasmine. It's not the same woman."

"So Jasmine *isn't* a nickname. And she's not this Jenny Lee she claims to be," Adam said slowly. "So that means she has no real claim to your place."

"Right. And even if she did, I don't think she ever meant to stay long. She admitted as much. Said she just needed a safe place to figure things out. And she keeps insisting she and Baxter are gonna have to move on soon."

"Probably figures whoever's after her will catch up," Adam continued.

"Shoot, better they catch up to her here than anywhere else," Elliot said. "We can handle them if they show up here."

"That's what I've been trying to tell Jasmine," Luke said. "She's not buying it."

"What else?" Garrett asked. "There's obviously something else. What is it, Luke?"

Luke swallowed hard. "She's carrying a gun."

Garrett lowered his head, swore under his breath.

"I found it in her bag. A little .32 caliber revolver. Unloaded, and I didn't find any bullets. She must have them stashed somewhere else."

"At least she's using sense about it," Garrett said. He shook his head. "Look, I'm going into the office. I'll boot up the computers and see what I can find out on her, under either name. I can at least check wants and warrants."

"Garrett, I told you, she's not the one who's broken the law here," Luke said, instantly defensive. "I'm sure of that! All she's done is try to protect herself and her boy."

"Hey, take it easy. I believe you." Garrett's tone, his expression, were sincere. "But that doesn't mean she might not be in legal trouble. Innocent or otherwise. Or she might be wanted for questioning, as a material witness to something else. I have to check. It's just a starting point. If her name—either of her names—comes up anywhere, it gives us a place to begin trying to figure out how to help her."

''And how to protect her,'' Lash put in. ''Chicago's a rough town. Don't forget, I'm from there. And I still know folks there—that might be helpful in this.''

Drawing a breath, Luke sighed. ''Okay. All right, fine. But I'm coming with you, Garrett. I want to know what you find out.''

''It's gonna be all right,'' Garrett assured him. ''Lash, you'd best come along with us, too. Wes, Ben, Adam and Elliot, you get on out to the water hole and keep an eye on things. Don't let Jasmine or Baxter out of your sight until we get back, okay?''

They nodded and headed out. Garrett closed the stable doors behind himself, Luke and Lash, and the three of them piled into his pickup truck.

But what came up on the computer in Garrett's office in town was more than Luke wished he had seen.

''I really don't get it,'' Jasmine said. ''I could have driven Bax and me home all by myself. I mean, it isn't like Luke would have been upset or anything.''

''Oh, no, he wouldn't have cared in the least.'' Wes wheeled Luke's pickup into the driveway of the once-stately redbrick house and braked to a stop. Jasmine was crammed between him and his oversize brother Ben. Baxter was comfy on Ben's lap, apparently enjoying the ride.

"Then why did you two insist on coming with us?" Jasmine asked, looking from the dark chiseled one to the big blond one.

"Because we didn't want you coming home all alone," Wes said.

"Yeah," Ben added, opening his door and climbing out with Bax still attached to him at the waist. "After all, it's different out here than it is in the city. Quiet and isolated, and we didn't want you two to feel nervous or scared or…you know, anything like that."

She slid her gaze to the big guy's. He had the sweetest blue eyes she'd ever seen, and she wondered for a second just what genetic miracle had resulted in a family of such damn fine-looking men. "Luke told you to keep an eye on us, didn't he?"

Wes looked at Ben, gave a shrug. "He did seem to think it would be a good idea if we hung around until he got back."

She lowered her head. She would have liked to think that Luke had set his two cousins on her heels because he didn't trust her. Because he thought she might run off with the silver or something. But she knew full well that wasn't the case. He had sent them to protect her, because he knew she was in danger. And he didn't even *have* any silver.

And while all her history and all her conditioning wanted to tell these two to take a hike, that she could damn well take care of herself, her experience since arriving on Luke Brand's doorstep told her something else. Because she felt safe, and watched over, in a way she never had. And she knew Baxter felt it, too.

She tipped her head to one side. "Bax likes hot cocoa before bed," she said. "You guys want to have some with us?"

The two men smiled and nodded. A weakness for sweets seemed to be another genetic component common to all the Brand men, she thought vaguely, and led the way inside. "Where did you say Luke went again?"

"Just to help Garrett with a few things in town. Probably loading up feed or something."

She lifted her brows, wondering what kind of small-town feed store would be open this late on a Sunday night, but she didn't ask. It was odd. Luke had slipped away once earlier in the day while she and Bax had been occupied at the big Brand family gathering. He'd taken his cousin Jessi with him. But hell, it was none of her business. She went to the kitchen to brew cocoa, while Ben and Wes sat in the living room with Baxter. She could hear them well. Ben was kindling a fire in the fireplace as the night grew cooler, and Wes was speaking to Baxter.

"Do you know I'm half-Indian?" he asked.

"You are?" Jasmine could hear the fascination in her son's voice.

"Mmm-hmm. Comanche."

"Wow," Baxter said. "Do you know how to shoot a bow and arrow?"

Wes's deep chuckle was so warm Jasmine knew he wasn't the kind to be offended by the innocent questions of a child. "I'm learning," he said. "But I do know other things. Do you know what a shaman is, Baxter?"

"No," Bax said softly.

"Sure you do," Ben said from the fireplace. "It's like a medicine man."

"Ooh, yeah. I've seen them in the movies. They shake rattles and dance and do magic and stuff."

"Exactly," Ben said. "Wes is a genuine Indian shaman. He knows all about Comanche magic and animal totems and all that kind of stuff."

Jasmine turned the cocoa down to let it simmer and slipped to the archway, intrigued, and eager to see if Wes were kidding or sincere.

He was sitting on the sofa, facing Baxter, and looking dead serious. And with the flames of Ben's fire leaping up beyond him, and the smell of the burning wood, Jasmine found herself believing every word.

"Do you really?" Baxter asked.

"Yes, I really do. And I've got some Comanche magic for you, right here." Wes bent his head, and removed a thong with a large stone pendent on the end from around his neck. He showed the greenish stone to Baxter. Jasmine thought it was little more than a tumbled gemstone, like you could find in any nature store for a buck or two.

"It's got a paw print on it," Baxter said.

''That's a wolf paw. And on the back...'' He turned the stone over.

''Is that a wolf?'' Bax breathed, eyes wide behind his glasses.

Wes nodded. ''The spirit of the wolf is a friend of mine. My personal totem. And I've asked him to hang out with you for a while. He'll protect you from anything bad...nightmares or bad guys, or anything that comes along.''

Baxter seemed speechless as Wes put the thong around his neck. He took the stone in his hands and stared at it, turning it over and over. ''Is he real or pretend?''

''He's real. I met him once, in person. He came right up to me when I was camping out one night. I didn't know what to think. I thought he was just an ordinary wolf at first, and maybe I was gonna be his supper.''

''Were you scared?''

''Oh, yeah, you bet I was. But he didn't bite me. He just stood there and stared at me, and I sat where I was and stared back at him. He's been with me ever since. See, he wasn't an ordinary wolf at all. He was the spirit of the wolf. And that's a whole different thing.''

Baxter lowered his eyes. ''Then he's not real?''

Poking another log onto the burgeoning fire, Ben laughed. ''That's what I used to think about all Wes's mumbo jumbo, kid. But I've seen enough to know better by now.''

''He's real,'' Wes said. ''He'll come around if he's needed. Until then, he kind of hangs out in the shadows, just keeping an eye on things. You don't see him, but that doesn't mean he's not there. Now, it's not that I think you need extra protection, because you're probably the safest little guy in Texas, with Luke and your mom right here, and the rest of us just down the road a piece. But I heard you had a nightmare, so I thought this might help you feel even safer.''

Releasing the stone and letting it hang against his chest, Baxter said, ''Thanks, Mr. Brand.''

''You call me Uncle Wes, just like Bubba does, okay, Bax?''

Baxter smiled. ''Okay.''

Then Wes shook his hand, as if Baxter were an adult instead of a little boy. And Jasmine could see the way he sat up straighter in response to that.

She backed away as they continued talking. She poured the cocoa into mugs and carried them into the living room. The men sipped, and Baxter gulped. Then her son surprised her by saying he was going up to bed all by himself. He didn't seem the least bit afraid.

Ben volunteered to tuck him in and tell him a story, though, and Bax didn't argue. When they were alone, she looked at Wes. ''That was a special thing you did, giving him that stone. Thank you.''

He held up a hand as if fending off her thanks. ''He's a special kid. I just wish it was as easy to convince grown-ups that they're safe and protected.''

She averted her eyes.

''Now, I don't want to butt in, Jasmine. But I like you. My whole family likes you, and Luke...well, Luke needs to speak for himself, I guess. But we all know for a fact that no matter what it is that's chased you all the way from Chicago, it can't hurt you here.''

She sighed softly. ''I only wish that were true.''

Wes seemed to study her for a moment. Then he went on. ''Do you think you showed up here by accident?''

Jasmine tilted her head to one side. ''What do you mean?''

Wes shrugged. ''That packet of legal papers that led you here—I don't believe it just happened to show up at the exact moment when you needed a haven. You were led here, Jasmine, because there is nowhere else in the world where you and Baxter could be as safe as you are right here.''

She narrowed her eyes on him, tilting her head to one side. ''You really believe that?''

''I know it. We can help you. But only if you work up the courage to stop running. To turn and face it, and to stand and fight it, whatever it is. There's never gonna be a better time.''

She swallowed hard. She could almost believe him. But damn, she barely knew these people, this family. How could she put them at risk with her troubles? How could she put her son's life in their hands? How, when everything in her was screaming at her to take Baxter and run, and to keep on running?

A vehicle pulled in, and Jasmine tensed. Wes went to the window and looked out. "It's okay. Just Garrett dropping Luke off."

She took a breath, then got to her feet as she heard Ben clomping down the stairs. "Sounds like our ride home."

Jasmine nodded. "Thanks, you two. You really did take it above and beyond tonight."

Ben, much to her surprise, walked right up to her and gave her a hug. His big arms closed around her and squeezed. She tensed automatically, even now expecting a grope, a pinch, a bit of hip action. Something. There wasn't any. It was the kind of hug a brother would give to a sister. And there wasn't even a hint of anything else to it. He let her go and looked down at her. "We really, really hope you decide to stay, Jasmine. Penny and I want you to work with us at the dojo, teach those dance classes. And Bax is already like one of the family. You think about it, okay?"

For some reason she couldn't have hoped to name, her eyes were burning. She blinked, and muttered a response in a tight voice. Ben ruffled her hair the way he'd done to Baxter on occasion, and he and Wes turned to leave. When Jasmine turned to watch them go, she saw that Luke was standing in the doorway.

The men said their goodbyes. She heard Wes tell Luke to put him on speed-dial and call at the first sign of trouble. Luke nodded. But his face was drawn and tight when he came in.

At first she thought it was because of what he'd seen. Ben hugging her the way he did. ''That wasn't anything inappropriate, you know,'' she said. ''I've been groped by enough men to know when someone's up to no good, and your cousin wasn't.''

Luke blinked out of his distracted state and closed the door behind him as he came inside. ''I know,'' he said.

She blinked, frowned. ''You know? How do you know? You trust him that much?''

He smiled. ''Yes. But even if I didn't, there's the fact that Ben would burn out his own eyes before he'd look at another woman. He's completely devoted to Penny.''

She pursed her lips. ''Seems to be another Brand trait.''

''The one-woman-man bit?'' he asked. ''Yeah, it does, doesn't it? I don't know how the hell it missed my father.''

Jasmine tilted her head to one side. ''He cheated on your mother?''

''He never married my mother. He did marry two other women, though, both at the same time. Fathered kids by all three. And who the hell knows how many more?''

She shrugged. ''And his brother was the father of all those cousins of yours?'' she asked.

''Yeah. Maybe it skips a generation. Orrin cheated on his wife, too. Only once, but still, Wes is the result.''

''Oh. I wondered about that.''

He looked at her, and she thought he looked tired. Bags under his eyes, a weary look to his drawn mouth. ''Is Bax asleep?''

''Yeah. You want some cocoa or anything?''

He shook his head slowly from side to side. ''No, Jasmine. All I want is the truth. We need to talk.''

She met his eyes, swallowed hard and backed up a step. ''Where did you really go with your cousin the sheriff tonight?'' she asked him.

''To his office. To run your name—or should I say your names?—through the computer.''

She blinked rapidly. ''And what did you find?''

''I found that Jenny Lee Walker was murdered, and that there's a warrant out for your arrest for the crime. They're saying you killed her, Jasmine. And I know you have her wallet. Her credit cards. Her license. Her legal documents. And a gun in your bag. So now I want you to tell me what the hell is going on.''

She turned her back on him. ''How long before your cousin comes back to arrest me?'' she asked.

* * *

Luke could see in her eyes that she was going to run. The way she backed away so he couldn't touch her if he wanted to. The way she kept glancing past him toward the front door, and then over her shoulder toward the stairs. She was calculating how she could race up there, grab her son and flee into the night without letting him stop her. Her eyes were so wide and so damned pained that he ached just looking at her.

He didn't move toward her, because he was sure she would run like hell if he did. Instead, he held up both hands, palms facing her. "No one's going to arrest you. Garrett punched all the buttons and then left the room before anything came up on the screen. He didn't want to be put in a position of having to choose between upholding the law and keeping his word to me."

She rolled her eyes. "As if there would be any question of which he'd choose."

"You're right, there wouldn't have been. He'd choose breaking the law so he could keep his word to me. Risking his job, losing it most likely. It wouldn't even have been a contest. But since he prefers not to lose his job over this, he figured he'd turn his back. I think the political types call it plausible deniability."

She narrowed her eyes on him, doubting him, he knew.

"Look, Garrett was just here, wasn't he? If he were going to arrest you, he'd have done it. He trusts my judgment, and I don't think you're a killer. I'm willing to look the other way on the warrant until we figure this out. And Garrett...well, as far as he knows for sure, Jenny Lee Walker is alive and well and standing here in my living room.''

She blinked. He thought her stance eased just a little. She breathed, but it was a broken, stuttering breath. ''Why do you believe in me, Luke? You don't know anything about me except that I'm an unwed mother, a former stripper, a liar, a total screwup....'' Her body was shaking now, too, in time with her breaths, and her eyes were brimming.

He moved closer, slowly, put his hands on her shoulders. ''You wanna know what I know about you? Hmm?''

She lifted her wet eyes to his.

''You're the most devoted mother I've ever seen. You'd step in front of a speeding truck for Baxter, if it came to that. And I think maybe you have, a time or two. You're an incredibly talented dancer. You move like the wind, and watching you makes me get all choked up somehow. You're terrified, scared right to death of something right now, and you're afraid to trust me—probably because I'm a man and you've never yet met a man who did you anything but wrong. And everything you've done—no matter what it might have been or how bad it might seem—you did to protect Baxter. And that includes lying to me about who you are.''

She lowered her head. ''You don't need the kind

of trouble I'm in, Luke. You don't want it, trust me.''

He hooked a finger under her chin. Then he leaned down and pressed his mouth to hers. He tasted the same sweetness he'd tasted on her lips before. A little gloss, a little color, a little cocoa and the salt of her tears this time, too. But he tasted more of her this time, because she let him. She didn't go stiff, and she didn't pull away. She stood still and let him explore her mouth, and she moved hers beneath it. He didn't embrace her, he just kissed her. She didn't fall against his chest. She just stood there, trembling.

And finally he lifted his head away. He said, ''I need to be completely honest with you, Jasmine. I'm scared. I'm scared to death of wanting you as much as I do—because it isn't like any kind of one-night-stand wanting I've ever felt before. It's something more. My father was a bastard who could no more stay with one woman than fly to the moon. He was no kind of father to me at all, and I grew up my whole life with my mother telling me I was just like him. For a long time I believed it. Until I came out here, found this bunch of cowboys who turned out to be family, and saw that I wasn't just my father's blood. I was theirs, as well. And maybe I could be the kind of man my father never was. And maybe I could have the kind of life I never had. A solid home. A real family.

''But that's just a maybe. I don't know for sure.

I don't know if I can be what I plainly see you and Baxter need more than you need air. I don't know."

She frowned at him. "I didn't ask—"

"I do know that I can help you. Me and my family, we can help you get through this mess. And I know that I want you to stay and let us do that. After that…hell, Jasmine, we're just gonna have to wait and see."

She stared at him as if he'd grown a second head. "What did I ever say or do to make you think I was expecting you to take care of me or to become some kind of father figure to Baxter? Huh? Did I once suggest that I wanted to be some kind of small-town farm wife? Do I *look* to you like I belong out here in the middle of nowhere, chasing chickens with a broom? Do I? And as far as my sharing my son with you—with anyone—"

He was stunned. "I didn't mean…I was only trying…"

"You are so full of yourself, you know that? You are so freaking full of yourself. What, do you think I'm whiling away my hours fantasizing about you marrying me or something? You're insane!"

"Look, I insulted you, and I hurt you, and that wasn't what I meant to do. I was just trying to explain why I'm not on my knees groveling at your feet like any sane, rational man would be doing by now."

"It wouldn't matter if you were, Luke Brand. I grew up with a mother who cared more about whatever low-life man she was sleeping with at the moment than about her only child. I grew up waking to no breakfast, to empty bottles and overflowing ashtrays, and my mother hungover in bed with a stranger. I grew up to her brushing me off, sending me to my room, shooing me away so she could have her fun, and I vowed—I *vowed*—that I would never let any man come between my baby and me. He is the only person I need in my life. And I love him so much that I don't have any love left over to give to anyone else. So you can just take your stupid ideas and—''

''I'm sorry. Jasmine, please, I'm sorry. I did this wrong, and you're upset anyway, and this is way too soon for any of this, and we got way off the subject.''

She sniffed and kept her face averted. He thought maybe some of those tears had spilled over, but she wouldn't let him see, and he didn't want to force it. ''You're right, we did get off the subject, didn't we? You wanted me to tell you whether or not I murdered my best friend in the entire universe. The answer is no. I didn't kill Rosebud.''

''Rosebud? Jenny Lee Walker was Rosebud?''

She rushed right on, not hearing him or not wanting to. ''I'm just as guilty as if I did, though. It's my fault she's dead. The man who killed her was looking for me. She got in the way. Now, will you just leave me the hell alone?'' She started for the stairs.

He said, ‘‘No.’’

She stopped, went stiff, but didn’t face him. ‘‘What?’’

‘‘I said no. I’m not gonna leave you alone. You’ve been alone way too long already. You can be as mad at me as you want to, Jasmine, but I’m not gonna leave you alone, and my family’s not gonna leave you alone. We’re gonna be here, all of us, from now on. And I’ll tell you right now, if you go running off in the dead of night, I’m coming after you. I’m gonna make things okay for you and Baxter again somehow. But I’m definitely not gonna leave you alone. Not for a minute.’’

Chapter 10

The bedroom right next to Baxter's had a light on, glowing warm through the open door. She peeked inside when she passed and saw that the bed was all made up with a pretty comforter and fluffy pillows. There was a vase full of flowers, and a small clock on the bedside stand. She stood there for a minute, just looking. When had anyone had the time to…and who would bother…? Was this supposed to be for her? There was a small frame on that stand, too, with a snapshot inside. Glancing back down the stairs, she could only see Luke's back as he sat on the sofa, leaning on his knees and staring into the fire. Pensive. Silent. Lonely, she thought.

She turned back to the bedroom again, and this

time, stepped inside. An oval mirror that looked like an antique hung on one wall. A small dresser with four drawers, also very old looking, and with a knob missing, was just beneath it, wearing a lace dresser scarf. She moved closer to the little stand beside the bed, bent to pick up the framed snapshot for a closer look. It was Polaroid photo someone must have taken just today—of Baxter sitting proudly atop that pony of Bubba's. Her lips trembled, and Jasmine bit down to keep them still. Her finger touched the glass over the photo, tracing the brightest smile she'd ever seen her son wear as tears welled in her eyes. God, he loved it here. He was happier here than she had ever seen him. It had only been a couple of days, and already he had better color than he'd had before. His appetite was better. He was spending more time outdoors than he ever had, and loving every minute of it. Truth to tell, if she could stay, raise her son here in this child-friendly place, she would. But she couldn't. She just couldn't, because Leo and Petronella would catch up. She knew their kind. They were nothing like the Brand men. They didn't have a shred of honor or decency or care for anything besides themselves and the thickness of their wallets. And they would keep coming until they found her. The dream of settling down in a nice town like this, of taking a job giving dance classes for little girls, of raising her son where he could be happy and secure, would never be.

Unless...

She licked her lips as an idea formed in her mind. Maybe there was a way she could make those things happen. Maybe Wes Brand was right...that it was time for her to turn around and face the danger. To stand up and fight.

Luke sat up for hours, staring at the flames and wondering what he was feeling for Jasmine. If it was simple desire, then why did it twist him up in knots this way? And if it was more, then why was he so unsure? He'd undressed, tried to sleep, but the questions just wouldn't let him. What he felt for the boy, well, that was a different matter entirely. He loved the kid—almost fiercely. His heart swelled in his chest every time Bax looked up at him with those big intelligent eyes or shoved his glasses up on his nose with his forefinger. He wanted to fix everything that was wrong in the little guy's life and make sure nothing ever frightened him again. He wanted to watch those eyes light up when he brought home a puppy—or a pony. Or, hell, both. Why not?

He thought those feelings were a pretty good indication that he could stick with Baxter for the long haul. It was pretty obvious that he could never walk away from the kid, and it was even more obvious that it would rip Luke's heart out if Jasmine took Bax and walked away from *him.*

But what about Jasmine? What about her?

And as if thinking of her had conjured her somehow, he caught a whiff of her scent, so subtle it was barely there, but he never missed it when she was near. He heard the gentle brush of her feet on the stairs and sat up slowly, turning to look her way. It had been hours since she'd gone up to bed. And yet she didn't look as if she'd even undressed. She still wore the clothes she had earlier. Jeans that fit too good for a man's peace of mind, and a white button-down shirt that wouldn't have been sexy on anyone else.

"Can't sleep?" he asked her.

She swung her head toward him fast enough to let him know he'd startled her. "Uh, no. But I thought you'd have been out cold by now."

He shook his head. "Can't seem to shut my mind off."

Sighing, she shoved her hands in her jeans pockets and came toward him. "Bax and I have rained chaos down on your peaceful life out here, I guess."

"Hey, do I look like I mind?" He swung his legs off the couch, put his feet on the floor. Then, as her pretty eyes skimmed down him, he became acutely aware of his attire. A pair of boxers. Nothing else. Of course the blanket was still draped over his lap, but his knobby knees and hairy legs and bare feet were hers for the looking. Not to mention everything from the waist up. And she looked plenty. Then she looked at his face again, and she smiled.

"Are you blushing, Luke?"

He averted his gaze. "Just feeling a little exposed, is all." He tried to move the blanket to cover more of him.

"Hell, I've been seen by more eyes and in less clothes."

"Yeah, but I'll bet you looked a lot better." He was embarrassed right to his rapidly heating ears, and she, damn her, was coming closer. Her stockinged feet moved nearer, and she sat right down on the couch beside him.

She said, "Oh, I don't know. You aren't so bad, you know."

"No?" He managed to lift his head and meet her eyes. And he saw the teasing light in them.

"No. Well, except for those knobby knees."

He smiled with her. She had a way of putting him at ease, when she wanted to. "Knobby knees are one of the genetic traits the male members of the Brand clan try to keep secret."

"Guess I just found something to hold over you forever, then."

"Only if you plan to stick around that long."

Her smile died so suddenly that it was as if he'd slapped it away. And he was damned if he knew what insane urge had made him say the words he had. He must be losing his mind. But they were out there. There was no taking them back now.

Her voice very soft, she said, "The bedroom…is beautiful. Did you do that, Luke?"

''Yeah. Well, you know, I had some help from Chelsea and Jessi. We took turns slipping away during the day to add things. None of it's new or anything.''

She said, ''New or not, that's probably the nicest thing anyone's ever done for me.''

He shrugged. ''I just thought you ought to have some space of your own.''

She nodded at the couch. ''While you camp out on the sofa like a guest in your own home.''

''There are lots more rooms upstairs. I'll fix one up for me when I get around to it.''

She leaned back on his couch, pulled her legs up underneath her. ''It's good here. Bax loves it here. And I think he's starting to love you, too.''

''Don't think for a minute that it isn't mutual, Jasmine.''

That made her smile. ''You've done so much for us. You and your family. I can't believe I'm about to ask for even more.'' Her head lowered as she said the words, her hair falling like a curtain around her face.

He reached out, pushed her hair aside, gently tucking it behind her ear. ''Don't be sorry. Especially not if you're finally gonna let me help you out of this mess you're in.''

Lifting her head slowly, she smiled at him. ''I didn't think they made men like you anymore. All ready to charge in and save the day. You're like something out of a story, you know that? But no,

Luke, what I'm asking of you is a hell of a lot more than that."

"What, then?"

She drew a breath, a deep one, and lifted her chin. "I want you to take care of my son if…if anything happens to me."

Luke's brows came down hard. "Honey, nothing's gonna happen to you. Hey, come on, is that why you've been awake all night? You've been lying up there thinking about…about…"

"About dying. Because that's what will happen if they find me—*when* they find me. And it's driving me insane worrying about what's going to happen to my son if I'm not here to take care of him anymore."

He took both her shoulders and looked her firmly in the eye. "You aren't going to die. For crying out loud, Jasmine, you can't be thinking like this."

"Well, I am, and I will be until you tell me you'll take care of him."

He searched her face, wondering how she could survive any of this with such a grim attitude. "I can't believe there's any doubt in your mind that I would. Yes, Jasmine. I'd take care of Baxter if anything happened to you. I'd take care of him like he was my own. I promise you that. I'll swear it on the blood of every Brand who ever lived, if it'll make you feel better."

"It wouldn't be easy, you know. They might still come after him."

''I'm aware of that. Didn't you hear what I said? 'Like he was my own,' Jasmine.''

Her lips trembled, and her eyes welled. Her breath seemed to stutter out of her, and she seemed to go limp as she sank against him. Luke put his arms around her, held her gently, felt her shoulders tremble beneath his hands. ''Thank you,'' she whispered. ''You can't know how much it means to me, what you just said. Thank you, Luke.''

''Hell, Jasmine, don't cry. Please? You gotta stop thinking this way. Don't you know how safe you are here, with me? Hmm?''

She lifted her head from his chest and looked up at him.

''They'd have to go through me to get to you or Bax. And they'd better go through hard, because if there's a breath left in me, I'll spend it to keep you safe.''

She blinked, as if shocked right to the core by his words. And he was damned if he knew where they were coming from. They just spewed out without warning or planning, or even bothering to ask his brain for consent.

She was stunned. Frankly, so was he. If a year ago someone had told him he would be saying things like this to woman, he would have laughed in their face.

He didn't know how to shut himself up, or how he could possibly finish those words. But then he didn't have to, because she was kissing him. Her mouth closed over his. She suckled his lips and licked his tongue, and tears were streaming down her face the whole time. He kissed her back, just as eagerly. He held her hard, while her hands pushed his blanket away as if it were some unbearable annoyance. His hand cupped the back of her head, his fingers buried in her hair as he held her to him and tasted her, exploring her mouth the way he'd been wanting to do. This was what he'd dreamed of doing for hour after long, lonely hour. God, he didn't even know how badly he'd been wanting her until now. He was on fire just from this kiss.

She pushed him backward on the couch, and she bent over him, dragging her warm mouth away from his, and over his neck, to his chest. She used her tongue, even her teeth, to make him squirm and ache and burn. Every part of him was trembling. Every inch of him alive and aware and in horrible fiery need.

Then suddenly she got up, her hand clasping his, she tugged him to his feet. He rose. His boxer shorts bearing a tent pole, he followed her. She said, "I don't want us to wake Bax," and she led him through the dining room and kitchen, and out the back door. He closed it behind him, following her as if he were in some kind of hypnotic trance. She walked a little ways from the house, her bare feet in the dew-wet grass. He shivered in the cold. Then she let go of his hand and moved away from him.

And then, under the stars, in the moonlight, she began to dance.

So sensual, the way she moved, that it took his breath away, and he thought he would explode from desire. When she slid her hands up her thighs over her hips and around to the button of her jeans, popped it free and slid the zipper down, Luke lost the feeling in his legs. He landed in the wet grass on his backside, and the shorts were wet, and he was shivering and burning up at the same time. She wriggled the jeans slowly, slowly down over her hips and her legs, but the shirt fell, too, covering the delectable tanned skin a split second after she revealed it to him. Teasing glimpses were all he was given of the curve of her hips and the tops of her thighs. The rest of her legs, though, were given to him fully and slowly. She kicked the jeans off, and he reached for her, but she danced just out of reach. She went to work on the panties next, again giving him fleeting glimpses as she worked them slowly down. Her rounded buttocks were revealed at inch at a time, no more. The little crease where backside met thigh. God, he wanted to kiss her there.

Finally her fingers nimbly released the buttons of the pristine white button-down shirt. One by one. Top to bottom. She turned her back to him and slid the shirt off her shoulders, lower and lower, revealing the curve of her back. Then she turned fast as she lowered it all the way and pulled the loose shirt around in front of her. A flash of her backside made his heart palpitate. And now she danced in front of him, holding that shirt over her beautiful body.

She danced closer to him, and closer still. He reached out, caught the edge of the shirt in one hand. She smiled at him, and he yanked it away. And then he looked his fill as she danced still more. He got to his feet, reached out and caught her waist in his hands. And then he pulled her tight to him, and he kissed her long and deeply. His hands could touch every part of her now, and they did. Her back, her buttocks, her thighs. He rubbed and caressed her as he probed her mouth with his tongue. Her hands tugged on his shorts until they dropped to the ground and he stepped out of them, kicked them aside.

Luke scooped Jasmine up off her feet and carried her to a spot beneath the wide branches of an oak tree, and then he laid her down and kissed her from her head to her toes and back again. He nursed at her breasts until she pulled his hair, and then he lingered there longer. She arched against his hand when he slid it toward her center, and so he touched her there, and then more deeply. The way she moved in his arms, beneath his touch, it seemed to Luke as if she were dancing still. And finally he lowered his body over hers and slid himself inside her.

She closed her eyes, and she whispered his name. She was incredible. The scent of her hair, of her body—he was completely surrounded in her, drowning in her, and relishing every bit of it.

Luke took his time. He made love to Jasmine more tenderly and more thoroughly than he'd ever made love before. He made her tremble all over, made her cry his name out loud, made her contort her beautiful face in anguished ecstasy. And then he held her tenderly, and he kissed her face.

And she said, "Thank you, Luke."

He lifted his brows, holding her closer, wishing for a blanket as the heat of passion slowly cooled and he felt the chill of night's kiss raising goose bumps on his skin. "The pleasure was all mine, lady."

"Not for that," she said with a little laugh. "For all you've done for Bax and me. And for the promise you made." She rolled toward him and gently brushed a hand through his hair. "I hope you realize now how much it's all meant to me. I don't do this sort of thing very often."

Luke lay very still, staring hard at her. "What?"

She smiled softly, rolled onto her back and sat up, rubbing her arms. "It's getting cold. Let's go inside." Looking around, she spotted her white shirt and bounced easily to her feet to pick it up, pull it on.

"In a minute," he said. "First…tell me what you meant by that."

"By what?" She was fastening buttons now. One, then the next.

''By what you just said. That you were grateful to me—Jasmine, is that what this was all about? You showing gratitude? You thanking me for something?''

''Only partly.'' She blinked and stared at him. ''I wouldn't have made love to you just out of gratitude,'' she told him, coming closer. ''I wanted you. You wanted me. I like you. You like me. And I owed you…something special. Something as special as what you've done for me and Bax.'' She shrugged. ''It just…felt like the right thing to do.''

Luke lowered his head. He drew a breath, but for some reason his chest hurt. His throat was tight. He'd thought…he'd thought…hell, he didn't even want to think about what he'd thought. He was an idiot.

''Luke?'' She was right in front of him, now, wearing that shirt and nothing else, one hand on his cheek. ''Are you mad at me?''

''Of course I'm not mad at you.''

''Then what's wrong?''

He lifted his head and looked into her deep, wary eyes. She was like a wild thing. So untrusting, so afraid. Sex didn't mean love, because sex was a commodity and love was a weakness. She'd repaid him with sex. But she wasn't going to risk her heart on anything more.

And how could he blame her when, up until five minutes ago, he'd been more or less oblivious to his own feelings?

My God, he loved her. But if he said so, she would run like a doe from the archer. He licked his lips. ''Nothing's wrong, Jasmine. Just...next time you think you owe me something, tell me first, okay?''

''You telling me you didn't like my method of payback?'' She slid her hands up his chest and pressed a kiss to his mouth.

''Oh, I liked it fine,'' he whispered. Then he caught hold of himself, cleared his throat. ''But I'd have liked it better if it had been for other reasons.''

She frowned and stepped away from him. ''I never knew a man to give a damn about the motivations behind a woman offering him sex before, just so long as he got it.''

''Yeah, well, you've been hanging around with the wrong kind of men, then.''

She tilted her head to one side as if trying to puzzle him out. He shook his head, afraid he would say too much if he kept this conversation going. Instead, he slipped an arm around her shoulders and headed her toward the house, bending to scoop up discarded clothes along the way. ''Don't ever feel you have to repay me in any way for anything I do, okay, Jasmine?'' he asked softly. ''If I do something, it's because I want to do it. You don't owe me anything.''

She leaned her head on his shoulder. ''I don't understand you.''

''No,'' he said. ''I don't suppose you do.''

They went inside, where she kissed him goodnight and headed up to her bedroom. Luke went to the sofa and pulled his covers over him. And though he was bothered by her motivations, he didn't dwell on it long. His body was satisfied, and his soul drained. He was asleep moments after his head hit the pillow.

When Luke woke, the sun was streaming in through the eastern windows, the fire was long dead, and he was no closer to knowing all the answers. He only knew that he had somehow managed to fall in love with a woman who didn't seem to believe love existed. But he knew it did. Now, for the first time he could recall, he really knew it did.

Maybe he should tell her. No, no, maybe he should see to first things first here and stop thinking like a teenager with his first crush. Maybe he should take care of business—namely, eliminating the threat to Jasmine and her son. That had to come before anything else. How could he expect Jasmine to think about tender emotions and lifetime commitments when she had this threat hanging over her head?

That was it. That was exactly it. He had to go to Chicago. Simple. He didn't know why the hell he hadn't thought of it sooner. He was the man here. He was a Brand, for heaven's sake. He didn't need to wait for Jasmine's permission to get involved.

He needed to take this bull by the horns and twist until he broke its damned neck. Period.

He got up and ran upstairs, animated now that he had chosen a course of action, eager to get on with it. He tapped only once before opening the door to the bedroom he'd fixed up for Jasmine, with loads of help from his cousins-in-law. But she wasn't there, and the pretty comforter was undisturbed. The bed hadn't been slept in. Maybe she'd decided to sleep with her son. God, he hoped Bax hadn't had another bad dream. Luke had slept like a log last night—he could have slept right through it. He stepped into the hallway and turned to Baxter's room. But when he opened that door, he didn't like what he saw there at all. Bax, huddled on the bed with his knees drawn up to his chest, crying as if his little heart were broken in two. His glasses lay on the bed beside him, as if he'd had them on, but taken them off again.

Luke's own heart split open at the sight of the tears on the boy's face, and he quickly went to Bax, wrapped him in his arms and held him close. "Hey, now, come on. What's all this?" Bax hugged him back but didn't speak. If anything, his sobs got louder. "Baxter, come on, pal, tell me what's wrong. Did you have another nightmare? Hmm? Is that it?" The small head shook side to side very slightly, all without moving from Luke's shoulder. "No? Well, what then? Hmm? Come, on, Bax, you know whatever it is, I can make it better. You know that, right?''

Silence. The crying stopped, though a few spasmodic sobs kept on coming, like aftershocks, quaking Baxter's small body. He lifted his head, and he looked Luke right in the eyes, even though his were slightly unfocused without his glasses. ''You can? You really, really can make it better, Luke? You're not just saying that?''

''I'm not just saying that. Whatever is wrong right now, I promise you, I will fix it. I'll find a way. But I can't until you tell me what it is.'' He wanted to ask where Jasmine was. In the bathroom, maybe. He didn't hear the shower running, but that didn't mean much. But he would get to that later. First things first here.

Swiping his wet cheeks with the sleeves of his pajamas, Baxter lifted a hand and opened it to reveal a crumpled sheet of paper. Frowning, Luke took it and slowly smoothed it open. And then he read the lines with a sinking heart.

My sweet little boy,

Mommy has to go away for just a little while. But I know you will be safe and sound here with Luke and the Brands. They'll take very good care of you until I get back, and I promise that won't be very long. You are the most precious thing in all the world to me, and I could never stay away from you for very long.

You know that. Please don't be worried. Mommy's gonna make everything all right again. You be a good boy. I'll be with you again soon.
Love, Mommy

Chapter 11

Luke closed his eyes slowly, trying to digest what he was reading. But they popped open again when Baxter said, "She's gone back to Chicago. I know she has. She's going to try to get those men so they can't get me. Luke, they'll hurt her. I know they will! You have to do something."

Luke cupped the boy's face and said, "You bet I'll do something. Come on now, son. You need to get up and dressed. And you need to tell me everything that happened before you and your mom left Chicago, so that I can go fetch her back here safe and sound, all right?"

Baxter nodded.

"I won't let anything happen to her, Bax. I promise."

Baxter looked up into Luke's eyes, searching them, looking for something. Then, finally, he nodded. ''Okay,'' he said. ''I believe you.''

Twenty minutes later, Baxter and Luke stood on the porch of the ranch house at the Texas Brand, and Luke thumped on the door twice. It was Bubba who pulled the door open, and he grinned ear to ear when he saw Baxter standing there. ''Hey! I was gonna call you anyway this morning!'' Bubba said.

''Why's that?'' Baxter asked.

'''Cause I'm gonna go fishing in the water hole, and I was gonna ask you to come along. You want to?''

Baxter turned to look up at Luke, big eyes questioning. Luke hunkered down, clasped the boy's shoulders. ''I gave you my word, Bax. I don't ever go back on my word. I'll bring her home safe. You don't need to worry. You just have fun with Bubba and try not to think about anything other than the fact that your mom will be with you very, very soon. And all this trouble will be history. Okay?''

Bax nodded his head.

''You want to go fishing with Bubba?''

Again he nodded.

''Then you go ahead. Next time you see me, I'll have your mom with me. Okay?''

''Okay.'' Bax leaned in and hugged Luke's neck. ''Don't take too long, Luke.''

''I'll be as fast as I can, son.''

When Bax let go, Bubba grabbed his hand. ''Come on, I'll show you my new fishin' pole. I've got three now. Tell you what, you can use whichever one you want.'' He was still chattering as he led Bax outside and toward the shed beside the stable.

Luke watched the boys go, turning only when Garrett spoke. ''So what happened?''

Luke faced him, saw Chelsea at his side, worry in her eyes. ''She's gone. She left a note for Bax saying she was gonna make things right for him, and she'd be back soon.''

Chelsea closed her eyes slowly. ''She went after whoever's been dogging her.''

''What the hell is it with you women, anyway?'' Garrett muttered.

''She's protecting her son, Garrett. A mother would face down armies to protect her child,'' Chelsea said.

Luke sighed. ''Look, if you'll just keep Baxter for me, I'll head up there and take care of this. But I have to hurry. I don't know how much of a start she has and—''

''Hold on, hold on,'' Garrett said, holding up both hands. ''Luke, I know you're new to the clan here, but that's just not the way we do things.''

Luke tensed. He lifted his chin. ''I'm going after her, Garrett. There's nothing you can do to stop me, or to talk me out of it, and I don't have time to stand here while you try. She's in trouble, and I'm going after her.''

Garrett nodded impatiently. ''Yeah, yeah, of course you're going after her. You just aren't going after her alone.'' He turned to Chelsea.

She said, ''I'll throw a few things in a bag for you. You'd better call the boys. Luke, don't worry, we'll have you guys on the road in twenty minutes—fifteen maybe.'' Then she hurried up the stairs, while Garrett went to the phone.

Within ten minutes, the driveway was lined with pickups and SUVs, and Brands were everywhere. It was the damnedest thing Luke had ever seen. Garrett had said nothing on the phone other than ''Jasmine's in trouble. We're going to Chicago. Pronto.'' And from what Luke could see, no one asked what, why, when or where. They just hung up and headed over here. They made minutemen look slow.

Lash and Adam were elected to stay home and keep tabs on the family and the Quinn Sheriff's Department—Lash being the only deputy. Ben, Garrett, Wes and Elliot all began stowing their gear in Ben's big SUV. It had the most room, so it was, by default, the vehicle they would take. There was no discussion on this, it just seemed they all knew it. And the stuff they tossed into the back made Luke wonder if they were used to preparing for all out war. There were shotguns, boxes of ammo, a rope, even a bullwhip, along with a small overnight backpack for each of them. It made Luke's duffel bag with a change of clothes and a toothbrush crammed inside look damned insignificant.

"They aren't going to let you bring those weapons into the city," Luke said, nodding at the guns.

"That's okay, cuz. We weren't planning to ask," Wes said, slamming Luke on the shoulder. "Did someone call Marcus?"

"He'll be here in an hour to help keep an eye on things here," Garrett said. "Bax will be well protected while we're gone." Then Garrett turned to Chelsea, and kissed her long and hard. "Don't worry, hon. I'll be back soon."

"I'll be waiting."

Bubba ran up and leaped into Garrett's arms, hugging his neck. "Be careful, Dad."

"Always. You take good care of Baxter, okay? I'm trusting you to see to it he doesn't have any skinned-up knees or broken bones when his mom gets back here."

Bubba grinned. "We'll take it easy. Promise."

"Good." Garrett put the boy down.

Luke saw Baxter standing beside him. He'd watched the entire exchange between father and son like a hungry pup eyeing a T-bone. Luke hunkered down and held out his arms. Baxter's face lit up, and he ran into them, hugging Luke's neck, and Luke's throat closed up almost too much to let his words through. How had the little guy wrapped himself up so tight in Luke's heart so fast? "Now, if you're gonna stay here, you'll have to help Bubba with his chores—you know, he has that pony to take care of. You're gonna have to help with that."

"Sure will, Luke." As Luke expected, Bax's eyes lit up at the prospect. Good. Poor fellow needed something on his mind besides his mother and the trouble she was heading into.

"And try not to worry. Everything's gonna be fine. I always keep my promises."

Nodding, Baxter released his neck. But then, impulsively, he grabbed on again and leaned in close, and whispered, "I wish you were my dad." He hugged hard then let Luke go, and, turning, ran back to the house with Bubba at his side. They stopped at the porch to pick up the fishing poles they'd left leaning there. Luke glanced toward Chelsea, but not right at her. He didn't think he'd ever been so close to shedding tears in his life—definitely not since he'd been Baxter's age himself. "You'll keep an eye on them around the water, won't you? I mean, I don't know if Bax can swim, and..."

Chelsea smiled wide. "Gee, you're starting to sound like Jasmine. Don't you worry, Luke. They aren't getting out of my sight."

He nodded, and finally turned and got into the SUV. He had to, because his eyes were burning more every time anyone opened their mouth. And what Baxter had whispered so desperately into his ear just now had hit him like a freight train. Because the response that had leaped to his lips was, "Me too." And he realized that he meant it.

Ben drove, since it was his vehicle, and Luke sat beside him in the front. In the middle set of seats with Wes, Garrett manned a cell phone, using his authority as sheriff to check with the airlines to be sure Jasmine hadn't booked a flight to Chicago. If she had, they would have to follow suit to catch up to her. When he finished speaking, he said, "No tickets bought to anywhere in Jasmine's name or Jenny Lee's. She has to be driving."

"That's good news," Elliot said. He was in the third row of seats, the one farthest back, his arms braced on the back of the seat in front of him, and his head leaning forward, between Garrett and Wes. "We might be able to catch her."

"She couldn't have left much before dawn," Luke told them. "I was...um...awake till then. And she had to walk past me to get out of the house."

"Why don't you fill us in on what you know, Luke?" Garrett asked. "I assume you at least have an idea of where to look once we hit Chicago."

Luke nodded. "Jasmine worked at a club called The Catwalk," he said. "Bax says they stopped on the way to take him to his last day of school so she could pick up her paycheck. She told him to stay in the car, but he got out, climbed up on some trash cans and looked in through a window. He says he saw three men in a room. One of them pulled out a gun and shot another one in the head."

Wes whistled long and low.

"Oh, it gets worse. Bax was so scared he fell, knocking the trash cans down. It made a hell of a racket, and he ran for all he was worth back to the car. The two guys came out the back door of the building, and Bax says one of them shot at him."

"Heartless bastard," Elliot muttered.

"You can say that again. Anyway, Jasmine came running, threw a brick at the shooter, and only managed to piss him off more. He turned the gun on her then, which I imagine, knowing Jasmine, was her intention all along."

Ben nodded. "Yep. To take the shooter's attention off Bax. Damn, she's a hell of a woman, Luke."

Luke nodded. "You'll get no argument from me on that score. At any rate, Bax put the car into gear and it shot forward. Jasmine jumped in, pushed Bax down on the floor and hightailed it out of there. Bax said they were going to go home, pick up Jasmine's roommate—another dancer who went by the name of Rosebud—and take off. Rosebud, by the way, was really Jenny Lee Walker. But when they got there, there were police cars outside, and they were carrying a body out of the building with a sheet over it. Bax said her hand fell free, and he saw it and knew it was Rosebud, and that she was dead. He also saw the cop who seemed to be in charge of things—and he swears it was the same guy who tried to kill him back at the club. He says his mother saw the man, too, and he thought that was why she was so scared.''

Garrett nodded slowly, taking it all in. ''Was Bax able to explain how Jasmine got hold of Rosebud's ID, and that packet from her lawyer?''

Luke nodded. ''He said Rosebud asked his mom to pick up her bag from the club while she was there picking up her check. Said Rosebud was forgetful—was always leaving her purse everywhere and having to go back for it. I'm assuming the envelope from the lawyer was there with it. The address on it was in care of The Catwalk, and I wondered about that from the first time I saw it.''

''So the question is,'' Wes said slowly, ''why the hell did they murder the roommate?''

''I've been wondering that myself,'' Luke said. ''But it's possible they didn't see Jasmine up close enough to know for sure who she was. If they looked around the place to see who'd been there, they'd have found both women's checks gone, and Rosebud's bag, as well. It could have been either one of them.''

''So they decided to just murder them both, to be safe?'' Elliot asked.

''And the little boy, too,'' Luke said. ''But when Jasmine and Bax got away, they decided to frame Jasmine for her best friend's murder. That's what I found in the computer last night. A warrant for her arrest. God knows it couldn't have taken much. Not when Rosebud's wallet, her latest paycheck, her credit cards and her roommate all turned up missing at once. They had to know they'd find those things on Jasmine when she finally turned up, making her look even more guilty.''

''Sure,'' Garrett said. ''What better way to see to it they got their hands on her again than to put out a warrant on her? Especially on a murder charge. She'd be hunted down by law enforcement, brought back to Chicago as a prisoner and her son as a ward of the state. Easy prey at that point. For a man who calls himself a cop, anyway.''

Luke felt a darkness settle over his heart. ''And now she's decided to face these animals all on her own. If they hurt her, I swear…''

Garrett's hand closed on his shoulder from behind. ''We'll get there in time, Luke.''

''Yeah,'' Luke said softly. ''Yeah. We have to.''

She drove for nearly twenty-four hours straight through, stopping briefly at an all night convenience store before she hit the club. She used the store's rest room mirror and most of the makeup in her bag, and she changed clothes. She needed to look like the same Jasmine who'd run away from here. But she didn't feel the same. Something…something had changed.

The club was dim when she arrived. Chairs upside down atop tables, nothing but ghosts inside. And Leo. He came out from the back, onto the main floor, never looking up to see her standing there, just inside the door, waiting. Jasmine had taken her time, made sure he was alone, before she'd come inside. Leo moved behind the bar, started wiping glasses and lining them up one by one. One of his early-morning rituals that always took place hours and hours before opening time. She'd known exactly where to find him.

Her high heels clicked with purpose as she stepped toward him, and Leo looked up from his task, spotting her at last. He looked as surprised as if he'd spotted Elvis coming toward him.

"Hello, Leo."

He smiled slyly. "Welcome back, Jasmine." He set down the glass he'd been polishing and slung the towel over his shoulder. "Where you been?"

"Around."

He shrugged, and one hand slipped out of sight beneath the counter. Jasmine brought her gun around in front of her. "Uh-uh-uh. Keep your palms flat to the bar, boss. Where I can see them."

Leo swallowed hard, his gaze focused on her gun, his Adam's apple bulging. "Just take it easy," he said. His palms slid flat to the bar's gleaming surface. "I know you're probably upset about Rosebud. Hell, we all are. You know, they think you did it."

"Lucky for me you know I didn't."

"Well sure I do! I never believed it for a minute, Jasmine. I tried to tell the cops that, but—"

"Come out from behind the bar," she snapped,

using the gun's barrel to direct him as he moved. ''Right here. Take a couple chairs down so we can sit and have a talk.'' She reached behind her and turned the dead bolt lock on the front door. She knew the back one would be locked. It was almost always locked. Only opened from the inside. She stepped forward, waited for Leo to sit, and when he did, she sat down opposite him. Out of his reach, though.

''What do you want to talk about?''

''The dirty cop you're mixed up with, for starters. The one who shot the undercover Fed in your office last week. Petronella. What's his first name? Gianni?''

Leo's brows slammed down hard. ''So it *was* you out there in the alley.''

''It was me. You didn't see me?''

He shook his head. ''Just the kid.'' Then he looked up fast. ''It wasn't me takin' shots at your kid, Jasmine. It was him. I wouldn't hurt a kid. You know that.''

''I didn't see you trying to stop him.''

''He'd have *popped me* if I had.''

''Oh, hell, in that case, sure. Let him off a little boy. Who wouldn't? Besides anyone with a soul.''

Leo's eyes narrowed. ''Is that gun even loaded?''

''You wanna find out?''

He went silent.

''So that's why you killed Rosebud. We shared the car, and Bax was with her as often as with me.

You had no clue which one of us witnessed the murder.''

''I didn't have anything to do with...with what happened to Rosebud,'' Leo said.

''No?''

''No!''

''Then how did the bastard know where we lived?''

Leo lowered his head, averted his eyes. ''Look, I don't like the guy any better than you do. But I don't have any choice but to deal with him.''

''Why?''

He looked up slowly. ''He's a cop. He could shut me down if he wanted to. You know damn well some of the girls take customers upstairs after a show.''

''And you get a cut of the take.''

''It's my bar.''

Jasmine nodded. ''And then there's the gambling.''

''You know about that?''

She nodded once. ''Every Saturday night in the back room, midnight till dawn. Sure I know about it. Everybody knows about it.''

Sighing, Leo said, ''Yeah, everybody. Including Gianni Petronella. When he found out about that, he upped the payment plan. Started demanding more and more of a payoff to look the other way, and even started showing up some weekends to play cards with the customers. And then this new kid came along. Terry Peck. Became a regular before we knew it. And he turned out to be a Fed.''

''So you guys decided to kill him? Leo, do you have any idea how insane that is?''

''I didn't know Gianni was gonna pop the guy, I swear! He said we would meet with him in my office. Talk to him. When he pulled out that gun and put a bullet in him, I couldn't even believe it.''

Nodding slowly, Jasmine said, ''Looks like you're in over your head, Leo. So am I. But I'll tell you what. We're gonna help each other out of it.''

''Oh, no,'' Leo said. ''I'm not making a move against Petronella. You think I wanna end up like that Fed? No way, I won't do it.''

''Yes, you will, Leo. Because I've got sworn testimony sitting in a lawyer's office right now. I've written down everything I know, and I got friends to sign off on it, backing me up. If you don't do exactly what I tell you, it's going to the D.A. And you're going down. Not just for the gambling and the prostitution, Leo. But for killing a federal agent. I was there. I saw it. You understand?''

He shook his head. ''I should've let him kill you.''

''You didn't do a damn thing to stop him from killing me. My kid did that.''

''Yeah, there you go, what about your kid? You make a move like this, Gianni Petronella will take his revenge out on him. You know that, don't you? The guy's ruthless."

"My kid is in a place where a dozen guys like Gianni Petronella couldn't get at him. He's safe, Leo. But you aren't. Not unless you play this my way. We'll bring Petronella down. And we'll do it together. Or else. All right?"

Lowering his head, Leo swore a long streak. Then, finally, he lifted his head again, met her eyes and said, "What do you want me to do?"

"First," she said, stiffening her resolve, calling up all her courage, "I need my old job back."

It was a long, tense drive, with stops only when absolutely necessary. They hit Chicago with little more than the name of the strip club and the directions Lash had written out for them. It took a road map and a telephone book to get more precise about locale, and a short while later, they were there. They parked next to the curb, in front of the brick building with the red door and a neon silhouette of a nude woman in the window over the words The Catwalk. The window was dark. There wasn't another vehicle in sight.

"I'll check out back," Wes said, getting out of the car. Without a word, Elliot got out and went with him. Luke nodded vaguely at them, and went to the front entrance. But it was locked, and he couldn't see much at all through the windowpane.

Behind him, Garrett said, "We should have expected this, Luke. Places like this don't open till the sun goes down. Eight o'clock according to the sign there.''

Luke grated his teeth to keep from shouting obscenities. Dammit, where was Jasmine? What the hell was she doing? She could be hurt...or worse, and he would never know.

''Back's deserted. No cars, no lights, the place is locked up tight,'' Elliot said as he and Ben came back around the corner

''We're just gonna have to wait it out, Luke,'' Ben told him gently.

''There has to be a way we can find her. Let's check the apartment where she used to live. The neighborhood. We can drive around.'' He stopped there, knowing how useless it would be. They would never find Jasmine in a place this big, not unless she wanted to be found. At least, not until she came back to the club. And Luke was certain she would.

Garrett herded them all back into the car. They spent the longest day of Luke's life chasing shadows, and they didn't find Jasmine. Of course they didn't. He'd known they wouldn't. And still it damn near killed him to stop hunting, even to go back to the club.

But things got considerably worse when, as they finally headed back to the club in order to be there when it opened, the SUV blew a tire.

* * *

The club was full to capacity when Jasmine took the stage—but it wasn't the way it had been before. Before, she and Rosebud used to dance, then scoop up the money thrown at them and laugh to themselves that men were so stupid. Now…hell, now she just felt disgusted by those men. Because she'd learned that it wasn't some kind of genetic fault of the male sex that made them act that way. All men weren't like the grunting hogs in the club. There were good men out there. Honest ones, who cared about more than glimpsing a strange woman's body or copping a feel or getting laid. There were men like Luke Brand.

She wouldn't have believed it possible a month ago. Now, though, her tolerance level for these other men had reached an all-time low. They made her physically ill. But she had put the plan into motion now, and she had to play it out. So she danced, and the bass pounded in her temples, and she smelled the booze, sweat and smoke of the place and wondered how she'd borne it for so long.

But then she saw what she wanted to see out there in the crowd. At his table, with Leo. Gianni Petronella. And one of the girls, a seasoned pro named Grace, was giving him a little lap dance, exactly as planned. Petronella was so distracted by the wriggling on his lap and the flesh in his face that he hadn't even noticed Jasmine yet. But when

Grace got up, he looked, and his face went cold. Jasmine sent him a smile and saw his face tighten with impotent rage. Because what could he do? Blow her away right there on the stage? No, he would have to wait. And then she would have him.

She finished her number and left the stage, leaving the bills scattered on the floor for the next dancer to pick up. Backstage, she passed Grace. "Did you get it?" she asked.

Grace nodded and slapped the cold metal into Jasmine's hand. Jasmine glanced down at the clip from Petronella's handgun. "Thanks, Grace," she said.

"I loved Rosebud, too, you know," Grace told her. "You get the bastard, hon."

Chapter 12

It was after ten when the five tired, hungry, cranky Brand men strode through the front doors of the inner-city strip club. Luke needed a shower, a shave and a change of clothes. Though to tell the truth, he didn't much care how he looked to patrons of a place like this one. Not that any of them were looking at him, anyway.

No. Their focus was elsewhere, and he couldn't much blame them.

A small red-tinted spotlight cut through the smoke-veiled room to fall on the woman who was just now slinking her way onto the stage in time with a pounding backbeat. She wore shoes that consisted of little more than a foot-long spike heel and a toe strap. Her long, shapely legs played a game of peek-a-boo from behind their weblike stockings. She wore long black gloves, a body suit made mostly of black mesh, with leg openings that seemed waist high, a strategically placed black feather boa and a sequined face mask. All told, not a hell of a lot. Men hooted and whistled and howled like wolves, and the music blasted louder, and the woman twined the boa around herself as if it was about to become her next lover. Hands reached and groped, and lewd remarks were shouted.

''Hey, baby, lean down here, I have what you need!''

''Jasmine,'' Luke whispered, tensing.

A hand came down on his shoulder. ''Easy now,'' Garrett said.

The stage was only a small raised section of the floor, a platform about three feet higher than the rest of the room. The only thing between her curvaceous body gyrating on the stage and the groping, slavering drunks in the front row were a handful of sparsely placed bouncers.

One guy got between them and managed to plaster his palm to her backside before he got pushed back.

''Hold on now, Luke. Just take it easy!''

''I'll give them easy,'' Luke said, and he shook off Garrett's restraining hand and started shoving his way through bodies toward the stage.

''Ah, hell,'' Wes muttered. ''It's gonna be that dive down in Pueblo Bonito all over again.''

"Nah. We'll probably end up in an American jail this time," Elliot said, as he and the others began shoving their way through right behind Luke.

Luke paid little attention to whether or not they kept up. He plowed ahead until he reached the stage and, when a bouncer roughly the size and shape of a gorilla stepped up to block his path, he decked the guy. The bouncer went down hard. Luke used his chest as a step up to the stage. Someone yelled, and his masked beauty backed away as Luke strode up to her. Someone grabbed him from behind, and Luke spun around, swinging. His fist struck someone's jaw, and his attacker went down. But Luke wasn't the only one under attack at this point. In fact, the fight seemed to have spread from him to his cousins behind him, and even now was spreading further to uninvolved bystanders, who, upset at having their entertainment interrupted, were apparently amusing themselves by hauling off and popping the first guy who looked at them.

A chair flew past his head, and Luke grabbed his woman and pulled her low, out of its reach. Then he scooped her up, tossed her over his shoulder and strode across the stage, off the back of it and through the curtains there.

Petronella followed her into the back, just as Jasmine had intended. He came up behind her, gripped her arm and propelled her past the dressing room and into Leo's office. Good. That was exactly what she wanted.

"You don't need to manhandle me, Gianni," she told him. "I came back here to make a deal."

He closed the office door, threw the lock. "You got nothing I want," he said.

"How sure are you of that?" She walked to the desk, pulled out Leo's chair and sat down. "Look, if I were going to turn you in, don't you think I'd have done it by now? God knows I was mad enough to, after you murdered my roommate."

He narrowed his eyes. "You're coming with me," he said, pulling out his gun.

"And what if I don't? What are you gonna do? Shoot me right here, in a bar full of people?"

"Hell, sweetie, they won't even hear the shot with all the noise out front."

She frowned. It *was* noisier than hell out there.

"Come on. Let's keep this clean. Come on out to the car. I kill one more person in his office, Leo will have a heart attack."

She nodded slowly. "This isn't fair, you know. It wasn't my fault I walked into this damn bar when I did—just in time to see you put a bullet in that guy's head."

"Tough break," Petronella said. "But that's life."

"I heard he was some kind of cop," she asked.

"Fed. A damned nosy one."

She licked her lips. ''So that's it. You have to kill me then?''

''I got no choice, babe. It's nothing personal.''

Again she nodded. Then she glanced down at the telephone on Leo's desk. She said, ''Did you get all that?''

Petronella frowned hard. ''What? What are you—''

''Every word,'' a voice said from the other end of the phone. ''All of it on tape.''

Petronella yanked out his gun, brandishing it at her. ''What are you trying to pull?''

She shrugged. ''Hell, Gianni, I'm just admiring the wonders of speaker phone. Leaves the hands free to run the tape recorder, you know? If you shoot me now, we'll have that murder on tape live, rather than just a confession.''

Lunging forward, Petronella grabbed the phone's handset. ''Who is this?'' he demanded. ''Where are you?''

But there was click and then a dial tone. Before he could think it through, Jasmine drummed her fingers over the keypad, hitting random numbers before Petronella yanked the phone off the desk and threw it on the floor. Now redial would do him no good, either.

''Whoever it was, they're on their way here with the police right now.''

To her amazement, a distant siren punctuated the sentence.

Petronella backed away. ''You think this is gonna save you? Do you? I'll find you, you smug little bitch. And your kid, too.''

She shook her head. ''Not if you're in jail, you won't.''

He undid the lock, yanked open the door. A blast of sound rushed in, so much noise she thought a riot must have broken out in the bar. Petronella ran down the hall and out the back door. She stepped into the hall after him, but turned sharply at the sound of a familiar voice.

''That's it! I don't give a damn what your justification was, I don't want you dancing for men like that anymore. And maybe that sounds old-fashioned, and maybe you don't want any man telling you what to do.'' He was striding down the hall with a dancer flung over his shoulder. He stopped, set her down and softened his tone. ''Well, fine, then, I won't tell you. I'm begging you. Please, don't get up on that stage again. It twists me all up inside.''

The sounds of cracking bones and shattering glass came from the barroom. The sound of Petronella's car squealing away came from out back. Jasmine smiled crookedly, a little lump forming in her throat. The dancer wasn't so touched by Luke's emotional declaration, though. She hauled off and smacked him hard across the face.

Luke recoiled, blinking in shock. ''What the hell was that for?''

"Maybe she doesn't like being manhandled by strangers," Jasmine said.

It was Jasmine's voice he heard, and it wasn't coming from the half-naked woman he'd just carried off the stage. He turned his head slowly and saw her standing there, looking less like the woman he'd fallen head over heels for and more like the one who'd first shown up on his doorstep. Big hair, coats of makeup, skimpy clothes.

"You've got to be kidding me," Elliot said from behind him. Luke turned to see Elliot, Garrett, Ben and Wes stumbling through the curtains into the backstage area off to the right. Each of them rubbing a different body part, they hurried to the hall. The riot out front seemed content to go on without them.

Luke swallowed hard and looked at the girl in front of him. Reaching out, he tugged off her face mask. She was cute and young and angry as hell. He shrugged. "Sorry."

Jasmine crossed her arms over her chest and glared at him. "So just what the hell do you think you're doing, Luke?"

"I...I thought she was you," he said in defense.

"Oh, and if she had been, that would have been all right? Dammit, Luke, I had a plan!"

"What, to dance around up there half-naked so the bad guys would be sure to have a good clear shot at you?"

The young dancer was looking from one of them to the other, wide-eyed, and backing away. ''You're both crazy,'' she muttered.

''Yeah, well, you're too young to be stripping, so get your backside home before the sheriff here tosses you into jail,'' Luke muttered. He dragged his gaze away from Jasmine just long enough to send the girl a look that had her scurrying into the dressing room, slamming the door behind her, then he focused again on his reason for being here. His reason for being...period. He swore softly before he closed the distance between him and Jasmine in two long strides. Then he pulled her into his arms and hugged her hard to his chest. ''Damn, I'm glad to see you alive.''

She sighed in what sounded like exasperation. But she didn't pull away, and she even hugged him back. ''Come on,'' she said. ''Thanks to you, Petronella got away. But we have the goods on him now.''

Luke backed off, glanced at her.

''I'll explain later. I just need to grab something out of Leo's office first.''

She ducked back inside. Luke followed her, not knowing what the hell had transpired before he'd arrived. He watched as Jasmine went to a shelf in one corner, shoved some notebooks aside and pulled out a small camcorder. She pushed the stop button, then ejected a small tape. Then she went to the desk, opened the drawer and took out a mini-recorder, taking the microcassette from that, as well. Coming forward, she took his arm as sirens screamed outside.

"We'd better slip out the back," Jasmine said, leading Luke back into the hallway with his cousins. "Technically, I'm still wanted for murder."

"Wait up a sec," Elliot said. He tapped on the dressing room door. "Hey, come on, we'll give you a ride out of this hole."

"I'm not going anywhere with you lunatics," the dancer squeaked.

Elliot looked at Garret, brows raised. Garrett sighed. "Damn, I hate being the heavy. All right." He hauled his badge out of his pocket and walked into the dressing room. When he came out again, he had the girl by the arm. She looked scared half to death, but at least she was decently covered now in a long wrap, Luke saw with relief.

"Everyone, this is Misti," Jasmine said. "She's new here."

Luke pushed open the back door, and they all trooped out to Ben's SUV and piled in: Garrett in the front with Ben, Jasmine in the middle seat beside Luke, and in the back, Misti, Elliot and Wes. Police cars pulled up out front as they drove away. Their flashing red lights bathed the bar's open door and cast a strobe effect over the brawlers who'd spilled out into the street. Broken glass winked in the intermittent glow.

Jasmine shook her head. "What the hell did you guys *do* in there?"

"What, you don't know?" Elliot asked. "We *rescued* you!"

She rolled her eyes. "Leo will have to close down for a week just to fix the place up."

"That's gonna be a real drain on the moral fortitude of Chicago, I'll bet," Luke said.

She narrowed her eyes on him. "Some people depend on that place for their living."

"Yeah, well, some people depend on some pretty sleazy things in the name of money, Jasmine. That doesn't make them right."

"So now you're what, the Moral Majority?"

"Closest thing to it in this part of town."

"How dare you sit there and judge me?"

He blinked and stared at her. Somewhere, somehow, he'd gotten in over his head. "That's not what I was doing?"

"You damned well were!"

"No, I wasn't!"

"Were so," Misti put in with a huff. "And me, too."

"You don't need to be judged, you need to be grounded and sent to bed without supper."

"You wish," she snapped.

"I meant it literally, kid, not figuratively. And as for you," he said, and turned back to Jasmine.

"Stop this car and let me out," Jasmine said. "I've managed to get through my whole life without some half-baked male telling me how to run it. I don't intend to change now."

"Oh, and look where it's gotten you!" Luke said, his voice louder now.

Jasmine went utterly still, staring at him, stricken. "You mean the fact that I'm an unmarried mother who strips for a living?"

The pain in her voice, in her face, when she said those words to him shocked him into silence. He stammered, but nothing intelligible came out of his mouth, and then Jasmine opened her door and said, "Stop the car, Ben, or I'll jump out while it's moving."

Ben must have believed she meant it—Luke knew he sure as hell did—because he hit the brakes. Jasmine got out.

Garrett glared at Luke, and Wes shoved him. "Well, what are you waiting for? Go after her. We'll drive around the block till you've finished groveling, cuz."

Luke jumped out of the vehicle and took off after Jasmine. She moved fast for someone walking on five-inch railroad spikes, but he caught up in short order, gripped her shoulders and spun her around. "That's not what I meant, and you damned well know it," he managed to say. He'd been thinking up an appropriate apology for several yards and realized too late that wasn't it.

"Then just what *did* you mean? Hmm?" Hands

on her hips, she tapped one foot rapidly on the cracked sidewalk. "Well? I'm waiting?"

"I meant that making decisions on your own has gotten you into this situation that you're in right now. Running for your life, set up for murder, and too damned stubborn to let anyone help you."

"Oh, right. Like you?"

"Yeah. Like me."

"For your information, Luke, I had a plan back there. I gave Leo no choice but to cooperate, and it was working. I got Petronella admitting everything on tape. Audio *and* video! But you came along and distracted me, and he slipped away! I don't *need* your damned help!"

"I know you don't!" he shouted. Then, licking his lips, he lowered his head. "I know you don't. I came charging up here wanting to be your hero—like something out of a fairy tale, I guess. And here you were, doing just fine without me." He shrugged. "It's kind of deflating, you know?"

She seemed to soften just a little. "You...really? You came to rescue me? Like Elliot said?"

"Yeah. Really."

"Hey, mister," a voice said from behind him.

Luke waved a hand in the air without turning around to look. "Go away. I'm busy. Jasmine, I meant well, I really did. I was trying to save your life when I marched up on that stage the way I did."

She thought about that, then pouted, crossing her

arms over her chest. ''No way, Luke. If you're going to be honest here, let's do it all the way. You were all ticked off 'cuz you thought that was me up there shaking my tassels in front of strangers. Admit it. You didn't give a single thought to my safety at that moment. You were just plain jealous and possessive, like some kind of bossy, overbearing Neanderthal.''

''Mister!'' the voice behind him said again.

''Dammit, can't you see I'm in the middle of something here?'' Luke snapped. He turned partway around this time.

The kid stood behind him looking like yesterday's garbage. He had a blade in his hand, and he said, ''Just gimme your wallet and you won't get hurt.''

Jasmine sucked in a sharp breath. ''Give it to him, Luke,'' she whispered.

''Oh, for crying out loud,'' Luke said. ''Fine, here's my wallet.'' He punched the kid in the face so hard his nose crunched and his lip split. Blood spurted, and the kid went down. Luke bent long enough to snatch up the blade, whipped it over a nearby fence, then turned back to Jasmine again. ''Look, maybe you're right, maybe I was out of line, and maybe it did bug me to see you—or think I saw you—dancing for all those men.'' He lowered his head. ''If that makes me a closed-minded Neanderthal, then I guess I'm guilty.''

She was staring at him, wide-eyed, her gaze darting every now and then to the kid on the ground behind him. Luke kept his eyes on Jasmine. He heard Ben's SUV coming around the block, recognized the sound of the engine.

"Come on, please? Just come with me. Someplace where we can talk? Please?"

Blinking slowly, she nodded. The SUV stopped, and they stepped around the kid, who was pulling himself to his feet. Luke held Jasmine's arm in one hand and opened the door for her with the other.

Garrett nodded toward the kid, who'd taken off at an uneven run, clutching his bloodied nose. "Trouble?"

Luke followed his gaze. "Not so you'd notice."

"Well, if Luke is done picking on the locals, can we get something to eat somewhere before we head back home? My belly button's touching my backbone," Elliot said.

Jasmine sighed, lowered her eyes. "I can't go back with you guys. Not until I finish what I came here to do."

She lifted her head again and met Luke's eyes. "And don't you dare try to tell me I can't. That man is still on the loose. He's still a threat to my son, and I'm not going anywhere until I see to it that he's not."

Luke set his jaw, deciding it was better not to reply to that just now. Drawing a calming breath, he said, "Get us back on the highway, Ben. Best truck stop in the state is ten miles out. We'll get a good meal there and figure out what we're doing next."

Very softly, a throat cleared. All eyes turned to Misti, whom Luke had forgotten was still with them. "What about me?" she asked.

"*You* are going back home to your family," Garrett said.

"No way," she snapped.

Garrett eyed her. "They abuse you?"

Her brows came down fast. "No. I just don't get along with my mom. She doesn't understand me." And she averted her eyes.

"Hell, kid, a few years ago she *was* you. Trust me on this. Now, tell me where you live so I don't have to haul you into some juvey center somewhere."

Pouting, clearly ticked off, but maybe just a tiny bit relieved, she said, "Cedar Lake, Indiana."

Elliot was already unfolding the map in the back seat.

Chapter 13

Two hours later, they sat in a big booth at a truck stop, three on each side of the Formica table. Jasmine had made a point to squeeze into the side with Garrett and Elliot, rather than on the other padded seat with Luke. He was crammed over there between Ben and Wes and looking as if he thought he was the wronged party here.

She really was doing her best to stay angry with him for chasing her up here, for telling her what to do, for leaving Baxter when he'd promised to take care of him. And mostly for acting so damned judgmental about her former career. Hell, it hurt that he thought badly of her. It hurt a hell of a lot more than it should.

And yet...she was touched in spite of herself that

he had come here after her, that he had wanted to be her hero.

They'd dropped Misti off at her house. Jasmine had tried like hell not to be affected by that little scene. A middle-aged woman in a housecoat had come to the door to see who was outside. When she saw Misti get out of the hulking vehicle, she burst into tears and ran down the steps, wrapping her up tight and thanking Jesus out loud. When Jasmine had looked around her, she'd seen the big, rugged Brand men at their dopiest. Every last one of them choked up and trying to hide it. She glimpsed ten damp eyes and five crooked smiles in that SUV. And as much as she knew about men, she realized she was only just beginning to know these men.

She watched them smile kindly at the harried waitress as they ordered enough food for an entire football team and told her to keep the coffee coming, and she knew they weren't flirting. They were genuine. It was freaking eerie.

Jasmine had never liked men. Baxter's father had worked hard to gain her trust. He'd conned her all the way into his bed, then vanished the day she told him she was pregnant. She'd been young and, she thought, in love. He'd broken her heart. She hadn't trusted men since, and she hadn't ever thought that would change. These men, however, had given her no choice in the matter. In spite of herself, she felt safe with them. She felt cared for. As if she were something important to them, something worth protecting.

Sighing, leaning back in her bench seat crammed between two of the creatures she'd spent her life detesting, she said, "So where's my son, Luke? You promised me you'd take care of him, and yet here you are, and I don't see him anywhere."

Luke met her eyes across the table. "Baxter was fine once he got done crying himself into fits over waking up to find his mother gone."

She flinched. That blow hit home. "I left so I could make things right for him."

"He knows that. You think that made it any easier?"

She lowered her eyes. "I didn't want to hurt him. It was the only way I could see to—"

"It was the only way you could see because you have tunnel vision." She lifted her head, ready to snap back at him, but he shook his head and went on. "He's staying with Chelsea and Bubba until we get back."

"And you think Chelsea and Bubba will be able to protect him if Gianni Petronella finds out where he is?"

"No. I don't. That's why Lash and Jessi are there, too, along with Adam and Kirsten, and Taylor and Penny and Esmeralda...the whole family is closing ranks around Baxter," Luke said. "And not just the local ones, either."

Frowning, Jasmine averted her eyes. But he went

right on. ''By now I imagine Marcus and Casey have arrived, too—they only had a two-hour drive. Sara and Jake will make it in before the night's out. It's a longer haul from Gator's Bayou, Louisiana.''

She lifted her head slowly. ''I don't understand.''

''That's because you've never had a family around you. That's the way family works, Jasmine. They pull together, they take care of each other.''

She locked her gaze with his. ''Baxter isn't part of your family. He's mine. I'm his family.''

For a long, tense moment he stared back at her, and she knew her words had pissed him off on some level. Why, how, she wasn't sure. She didn't pretend to understand him, and she told herself she didn't want to try. But she knew that was a lie. Why, *why,* did she have to get so defensive where Bax was concerned? She knew Luke adored him.

''Shoot, don't try to tell Bubba that,'' Garrett said. His voice, lightened by his smile, broke the building tension. ''He sure does think of Baxter as family.''

''We all do,'' Wes said. ''Family doesn't have to be bound by blood, Jasmine. Love is the real bond.''

Ben nodded in agreement. ''Rosebud was family to you, wasn't she?''

Jasmine closed her eyes slowly. ''Rosebud was my best friend. She was like a sister to me, and she'd have given her right arm for Baxter.''

"News flash, Jasmine," Elliot said from beside her. "So would any of us."

She shot Elliot a glance, but he was already looking away from her, focused now on the waitress who was bearing down on them with a laden tray. "Ahh, here comes sustenance. And not a moment too soon, either!" Elliot got up and took the tray from the woman's hands, then stood quietly while she lifted the plates of food from it and deposited them on the table. The whole time she worked, she wore this look of amazed gratitude. When the tray was empty and she took it from him again, Elliot said, "Thank you, ma'am," as he slid back into his seat.

She smiled. "Thank *me?* You keep this up, it'll be *me* leaving *you* a tip." Giving him a friendly wink, she strolled away.

Jasmine watched. Some guy at another table was glaring at the waitress and tapping his empty coffee cup, while another party waved impatiently to get her attention. The Brand men were different. No doubt about it. It got very quiet as they dug into their meals. Jasmine gnawed on her burger and fries without really tasting them, and wondered how in the hell she was going to find Gianni Petronella.

Luke didn't eat with as much gusto as the other men did, she noticed. He picked at his food, ate a little, but didn't seem to take much pleasure in it. Mostly he drank coffee. Lots of coffee. He met her eyes every now and then, looking as if he had something to say, but he never said it. Just looked away again until, finally, he excused himself.

Ten minutes later he was back, and he slapped two keys on the table, each with numbered plastic ovals attached. ''I got us rooms for the night.''

Jasmine wiped her mouth with a napkin and glanced at her watch.

''That bar will be closed for the night within an hour, Jasmine. Besides, Petronella won't go back there. You've been up for...'' Luke looked at his watch. ''Hell, *I've* been up for over forty hours. You, for longer. We need to get some rest, figure out our next step. Just stay here. You're safe with us, you know you are.''

She lifted her brows, about to make some comment about how full of himself he was. But instead she recalled the punk on the street with the blade and the way Luke had reacted. She'd never seen anything like it. He was no more distracted by the kid than he would have been by a mosquito. Not even a little bit afraid. She did feel safe with him. And it was an odd sort of feeling. One she couldn't remember ever having before. It confused her on such a deep level that she couldn't even snap out a sarcastic reply. She just sat there, until finally she said, ''So you're cramming us all into two rooms?''

He shook his head and dangled a third key from his hands. ''Garrett and Ben get a room. Wes and Elliot get a room. You and I get a room.''

Her brows came down hard, and her reaction was

automatic. ''If you think for one minute that just because—''

''You've been under the same roof with me for long enough to know you can trust me, Jasmine. Twin beds, no ulterior motives except for the obvious one—I don't trust you not to run off the minute my back is turned. So I'm rooming with you. Period.''

Jasmine got to her feet and poked him in the chest with a long, shiny fingernail. ''No man tells me what to do. You room with your brothers. I'll room by myself.'' She snatched the key from his hand so fast he didn't have time to prevent it.

''Dammit, Jasmine—''

She strode out the diner's front door, underneath the jangling bells, and headed around to the rear, following the neon motel sign with the flickering arrow. She fully expected Luke would be right on her heels, and so she strode as purposefully as she could manage with her nose in the air and her heels clicking a no-nonsense cadence on the blacktop.

Three guys stood in a huddle, talking in the diesel-scented night air. Truckers, probably. Harmless, probably. But they looked at her as she passed, and she wondered what they thought they saw. Looking around, she saw where big rigs were parked in formation, an endless row of them. Here and there scantily clad women hopped up on the sides of them to rap on the doors and make their offers. ''Need your truck cleaned, baby? Twenty bucks.''

Jasmine's gaze slid back to the huddle of men. They were still eyeing her. Her short skirt and big hair and high heels probably made her look to them like one of the hookers who hung around places like this one. Then again, most of the patrons at The Catwalk made similar assumptions about her when she danced on that stage. They looked at her as if assessing a cut of meat, weighing its value against its price.

No one had looked at her that way in Quinn, Texas. Not even when she'd first arrived, in her short skirt and her high heels. Luke had never looked at her that way. Not even when she'd danced for him.

The men were coming closer now, smiling and speaking low to each other as they crossed the lot toward her. Where the hell was that pesky pain-in-the-ass cowboy, anyway? God, he followed her like a devoted hound when she didn't want him around, then vanished when she could actually use the help. He was *supposed* to follow her out of the diner. Damn him.

"Hey, honey," one said, but then he stopped walking, stopped talking, blinked twice and changed his attitude. "Um...I was just wondering which way to the rest rooms."

She frowned, wondering what the hell had changed his attitude. She glanced behind her but saw no one. Then she faced the men again, still some ten feet away from her. She lifted a hand, pointed the way, then continued her trek to the motel room. The men must have had a desperate need for that rest room because, when she glanced behind her to see where they were, they'd vanished. Long gone. Odd. Sighing, she searched for the door with the number that matched the one on the key she'd swiped from Luke, found it and let herself in.

Simple room. Twin beds, TV, bathroom, tacky framed prints on the walls with odd geometric patterns in primary colors. Jasmine closed the door behind her, turned the lock and sank onto the bed. It was late, after one in the morning, and she was tired. She'd driven a long way without sleep, and she'd come so close! Now she was just frustrated and cranky and exhausted. But she couldn't go to sleep. Not yet. She figured she would give the Brands an hour and then slip away. She would go to Leo's place and wake him, force him to tell her where this Gianni character lived, and then she would go to *his* house.

She reached into her handbag and touched the gun that was there. She'd taken the bullets out of hiding before she'd left the Brand place. The gun was loaded, and it was deadly. Gianni would either wait with her for the police to arrive and arrest him, or she would kill him. That simple. A shiver of unease worked up her spine when she thought of killing a man in cold blood. But then she thought about Rosebud, being shot down in her own apartment. She thought of that man turning and firing bullets at her own little boy. Shooting at a child with every intention of killing him. And when she thought about that, she really didn't think she would have any trouble at all pulling the trigger when the time came.

Besides, it was the only way. She needed him in prison or dead.

She took a cool shower to help wake herself up, and then she tugged more functional clothes out of the bottom of her deep bag. Jeans, flat shoes, a sleeveless denim button-down blouse. She scooped her heavy curls up into a ponytail, just to keep them out of the way. She didn't want her hair falling over her face or blocking her vision. She didn't want it providing a handhold for her enemy to latch on to, either. She'd thought about soaking off the long acrylic nails and decided against it. Pulling the trigger with them on would not be a problem. She'd tried it out on the way here. And the nails had the added benefit of being weapons in and of themselves. Every finger was as good as a small blade, with them in place.

Finally she was ready. She tucked the gun into the bag, stuffed the clothes she no longer wanted or needed into the trash—even the shoes. And went to the door of her room. Flicking the lock, she pulled the door open, looked both ways and stepped outside, only to trip over the big lump lying in front of the doorway. She nearly went headfirst onto the sidewalk, but the lump sat up and snagged her around the waist, pulling her down so she landed in his arms instead.

"Hey, Jasmine. Going out for a midnight stroll?" Luke asked, smiling innocently into her eyes.

She couldn't believe the nerve of the man! "What the hell are you doing camped outside my door?"

He shrugged. "You wouldn't let me share the room. It was the only way I could make sure you were safe."

"Safe from what!"

"From Leo, and this Gianni guy. I mean, suppose they followed us? Or got to Misti somehow and made her tell them where we were going? I don't plan to let them just walk in and shoot you the way they did your friend Rosebud, you know."

She started to speak, then stopped herself. There was a pillow behind him, and a blanket half over him. And she was on his lap, and his hands were anchored at her waist, and the way he looked at her was a way no one else had ever looked at her before. He looked at her eyes, then her lips, then her eyes again, over and over as he spoke. As if having trouble keeping focused. And her stomach did something funny, and instead of swearing at him, she heard herself say, "You've been sleeping out here on the sidewalk waiting for killers to show up?"

He said. "I wouldn't exactly call it sleeping."

She lowered her eyes.

"So where were you going, Jasmine?"

Inhaling deeply, she said, "To find Gianni."

"Yeah? And then what?"

Jasmine lifted her gaze to his. "Take him in or kill him, I guess."

"You do that, and even Garrett won't be able to keep you out of jail."

"Maybe not. But at least my son wouldn't have to be afraid anymore."

He stared into her eyes for a long time. "He'd be heartbroken instead. For the rest of his life, he'd hurt for the mother he lost."

She couldn't argue with that, so she didn't try. "At least he'd have a life."

"He has a life *now,* Jasmine. A good life. You made a fresh start in Texas. You have a good job waiting for you there, one you and Bax can both be proud of. You have friends there, people who care about you, and..." He let his voice trail off.

"And what?" she asked him. "And you? Are you going to say I have you? When we both know I'm the furthest thing from what you want. You told me yourself that you weren't ready for—"

"Dammit, Jasmine, will you just put the you and me part of this equation aside for a minute? I'm talking about you and Baxter and Quinn, Texas. I'm talking about you teaching dance at Ben's dojo. I'm talking about a place with enough fresh air and sunshine for Baxter to thrive on for years. Why do you want to turn the topic to you and me?''

She shrugged. ''You're the one camping on my doorstep and scooping me off stages and acting like you own me or something.''

He looked away. ''I didn't scoop you off any stage.''

''You thought it was me.''

''Hell, Jasmine, what do you want from me?''

She lifted her brows. ''I want you to walk away. Leave me alone. Just go back to Texas and forget all about me.'' She said it, but she knew that she was lying through her teeth.

He looked up at her slowly, held her gaze, and she was terrified for one brief moment that he would say ''All right'' and turn around and walk out of her life. She actually held her breath, and with every second that ticked by she expected him to say so long. But he didn't. Instead he said, ''I'm sorry, Jasmine, but I just can't do that.''

She almost sighed in relief. Did it show on her face? God, she hoped not. She hated feeling this way. No man had ever had her at this much of a disadvantage. If he knew, he would have the upper hand. She couldn't let on—dammit, she just couldn't.

So got herself upright, and she stepped back inside and held the door open, and said, ''I guess if you insist on being my shadow, you may as well come inside.''

He did, looking around, his eyes taking in every detail of the room, pausing on the wastebasket where the clothes she'd been wearing before draped over the edge and a single spiked heel stuck up like a potted plant. His lips pulled slightly at the corners, but other than that, there was no reaction, no comment.

He went casually to the bed on the left, flung back the covers and peeled off his jacket.

Jasmine managed to break the grip his eyes had on hers and turned away. ''Don't you want to take a shower before you turn in?''

''And give you time to take off on me? No way. I'll wait till morning, thanks.''

She shot him a glare. ''And what's to stop me from taking off in the…''

He was peeling off his shirt now. Draping it over the back of a chair, then pausing, turning to catch her staring at him. She couldn't help it, though. He looked better undressed than she'd ever imagined a man could look. Firm and smooth and dark. Her palms heated and dampened as she remembered the way his skin felt beneath them—and then against hers. It had never been that way for her with any other man—so intense, so deep. Like it wasn't just her body performing the sex act. It was as if her whole being had been making love to him. And the memory of it just wouldn't stop haunting her. Teasing her. Even now.

She looked away quickly. ''Never mind.''

‘‘What’s to stop you from taking off in the morning?’’ he said, finishing her question for her. ‘‘My cousins, of course.’’

Fabric brushed skin, and a quick darting peek from the corner of her eye told her he was sliding those jeans off. She jerked her gaze away fast, tried to focus on the room straight ahead of her instead. But there was a damned mirror on the dresser, projecting his boxer shorts–clad body sliding into the bed, pulling up the covers, settling his head on the pillow. Then he lifted his head briefly, met her eyes in the mirror and sent her a wink. ‘‘Night, Jasmine.’’

She released a burst of noisy air, clenched her fists and stomped to her own bed. Damn him. Damn him! He knew how she was feeling, and he just wanted to torture her. To make her squirm. He didn’t have to strip down to almost nothing. ‘‘This isn’t fair,’’ she snapped, yanking back the covers.

‘‘What isn’t?’’

‘‘You…showing up here and bossing me around. Keeping me from doing what I came here to do.’’

‘‘Jasmine, for crying out loud, I came here to keep you from getting yourself killed. And to fix this thing once and for all.’’

‘‘Oh, well, that’s much better than my plan, which was to *get* killed and *not* fix this thing. Thank goodness you arrived!’’ She stood on the far side of the bed with her back to him, undid her jeans and slid them off, leaving the shirt in place. And she couldn't help a quick glance at the mirror to see where his eyes were. They were glued to her legs, her thighs, and he looked like someone had hit him in the belly with a mallet. Good.

She got into her bed, pulled her covers up over her head, took off her shirt and bra, and then emerged again, keeping the blankets chin high. She flung the clothes toward the foot of the bed, where they hung haphazardly.

He was staring at her with pained eyes. She said, "What? I can't very well sleep in it! It's all I brought to wear tomorrow."

He nodded in short jerky motions. "So just what was your plan, anyway? I mean, besides the brilliant part about finding Gianni and killing him in cold blood. What were you planning on doing after that?"

She shrugged. "I hadn't thought that far ahead."

"You don't ever seem to think too far ahead, do you?"

She rolled to face him. "What's that supposed to mean?"

"Hell, Jasmine, think about it! First you run from this guy, then you turn around without so much as a so long and run right back to him again. What the hell happened to make you change directions on a dime like that?"

"I...I changed my mind."

"You changed your mind. First you're terrified and in hiding, and then you're hunting the man down, ready to blow him away. And you tell me you just changed your mind.''

She nodded hard. ''Why is that so hard to believe?''

He shook his head. ''Do you give any thought at all to these decisions of yours, or just act completely on impulse, doing whatever pops into your head at the time?''

''Of course I gave it thought! God, do you know how hard it was for me to leave Bax? To come back here to face a man I fully expected to do his best to kill me the minute he saw me?''

''Then why?''

She rolled away from him. ''For Baxter. He...he wants to stay in Quinn. I want him to have what he wants.''

He was silent for a long moment. ''And what about you, Jasmine? What do you want?''

''It's too late for what I want.'' She curled tighter around herself, closed her eyes. ''Just go to sleep now, Luke. It's late.''

He was silent. She kept her eyes closed, but his question lingered, whispered itself again and again in her mind. What did she want? It kept gnawing at her and eating at her until she couldn't keep the tears back anymore. And when they came, they came softly, quietly, and yet somehow, he knew.

A second later, his warm body curled around hers from behind. His arms came around her to hold her close. His breath came from close to her ear, and he said, "It's okay, Jasmine. Let it out. Talk to me. No one's here. No one ever needs to know. Just talk to me. Tell me what you want for you, what you think it's too late to have."

And it came out, all in a rush, with sobs and tears she hadn't meant to shed—especially not in front of a man. She wanted her mother—not the careless alcoholic who'd spent her nights in the arms of any man who would have her. The mother she'd dreamed about. One who loved her. Who held her and rocked her and brushed her hair and read her bedtime stories. She wanted her father. Not the one who'd knocked her mother up one night and left without a trace. But the one who would carry her around the house on his shoulders, and take her on camping trips and picnics. She wanted a childhood. Not the one she'd spent tiptoeing through the house in the mornings so as not to wake up her hungover mother and whatever stranger was in her bed. But a happy, loving one that only existed in her dreams.

Luke held her and stroked her hair and listened until the turmoil seemed to ease. And she relaxed against him. And she said, "More than anything else, I want those things for Baxter. All those things I never had. That happy, idyllic childhood. A home. A family." She bit her lip, closed her eyes. "And what have I given him? A mother who takes her clothes off for money. A front-row seat at a brutal murder. More fear and trauma than my lousy mother ever gave me, even at her worst. When I was so determined to be different. God, Luke, what have I done to my precious baby?''

''Jasmine, you've got it wrong. So wrong.'' Very gently, he rolled her over. She wore only her panties. Her chest was bare, and his arms were around her, holding her so close that their bodies touched all over. He tucked her head to his chest, and he rubbed his cheek over the top of her hair. ''There's a big difference, and you're missing it by a mile. Baxter knows you love him. He knows you'd die for him without batting an eye. He knew when you left that you had come up here to try to protect him. And he knows you are always there for him, no matter what, because you love him more than anything else in the world. He knows that, Jasmine.''

Her tears were wetting his chest. He didn't seem to mind. ''Do you think he does?''

''He told me how you threw something at the shooter the day of the murder. He told me you did it so the man would shoot at you instead of him. He's a bright kid, Jasmine. Too bright not to know what's happening here. He'd rather be with you, on the run or wherever, than in some perfect home with a picket fence without you.''

She tipped her head up, looked at his face. ''But I wanted to give him that. The home, the picket fence...''

''You will. You will. You'll see. You're almost there already. There's this one last problem we need to get past, and then you'll see it all fall into place.

Jasmine, don't you think maybe this all happened for a reason? Don't you think maybe you were led to Quinn because it was where you and Baxter belong?''

She lowered her eyes. ''I don't know. Your cousin Wes was saying something very similar. Maybe it's true.''

''It's true.'' He closed his eyes. ''It's true. The job, Ben and Penny deciding to hire a dance teacher just when you arrived...it's all fallen into place as if it were meant to be, Jasmine.''

She nodded. ''Maybe.''

''What are you afraid of?'' he asked her.

She closed her eyes. ''That it's all a dream. Just like the dreams I had as a little girl. They're golden bubbles that shimmer and gleam and float in front of your eyes, and they seem so real. So beautiful. So perfect. But the moment you reach out to touch them, they burst, and there's nothing left. Not even the illusion. It hurts when that happens, Luke. I don't want to hurt like that again. And I don't want Baxter to ever hurt like that.''

He held her closer, leaned in and kissed her forehead. ''Then don't look at the bubble. Look past the dream, Jasmine, look at what's real. Quinn is real. The Brands are real, and they adore you and Baxter. The job offer from Ben and Penny, that's real. You can make a fresh start in Quinn. That's real. That's not an illusion. So reach for that. And don't worry about the rest. Not now.''

She lifted her eyes to his, her hands at the back of his head, and she said, ''And what about you…and me?''

He closed his eyes slowly, bit his lip. ''I'm your friend, because that's what you need me to be right now.''

''I don't think I've ever had a man who was a friend before.''

''You do now.''

She thought he must be lying. Because she was all but naked, and he was holding her tight in his arms right now, and he was all but naked, too, and it wasn't difficult to tell that he wanted her. All the evidence was there. He leaned down and kissed her lips, long and slowly, and so tenderly she trembled inside. She knew he wanted to make love to her. And she didn't mind. He'd done so much for her already. And she liked making love to him. The last time had been like nothing she'd ever known.

But when he lifted his head, he rolled further onto his back, cradling her to his chest. His hand stroked her hair, and he said, ''Go to sleep, sweet Jasmine. I'm not gonna let any more bad dreams come near you tonight. You're safe now.''

He was so warm around her. So firm beneath her. She closed her eyes as his hand stroked her hair over and over again. ''I don't need any man to keep me safe,'' she whispered. ''Never have. Never will.'' And then she snuggled closer.

Chapter 14

It was heaven and hell all rolled into one warm, beautiful female form in his arms that night. He didn't sleep. He just held her. Looked at her. And he knew, as he'd never known before, that he would do whatever it took to get through to her, to reach her. She had built a brick wall around her heart. He had to tear it down brick by brick. He had to get to her. Letting her go was no longer an option he cared to consider.

She began to stir when the morning sun slanted in through the window blinds, making yellow slashes of light across her face. She opened her eyes, blinked him into focus and then looked confused. He smiled at her, kissed her forehead, then rolled out of bed and walked around the room picking up his clothes. ''I'm gonna get one of the guys over here to keep an eye on you while I shower,'' he said. ''Okay?''

She nodded confusedly and, holding the blankets to her chest, tugged her own clothes off the foot of the bed and pulled them to her. ''You didn't...I mean, you slept with me all night, and we didn't....''

''No,'' he said. ''We didn't.''

Tilting her head to one side, she said, ''Why?''

Luke grinned at her. ''Not because I wouldn't have liked to, believe me.'' But then he let the smile fade and went to sit on the edge of the bed. He stroked her hair, masses of it tangling around his fingers like coiled silk. ''God, you've got the most incredible hair, you know that?'' He drew a handful close to his face, inhaled its fragrance. Still fresh from her shower last night. But then he let it fall and looked her in the eyes. ''I want to make sure you know that I feel something for you. Something that has nothing to do with sex. I'd feel it even if I knew you were never, ever going to let me make love to you again. And I also want you to know that when we did make love—it meant something to me. I don't want us to do it again until it means something to you, too.''

She frowned very hard at him. ''Means something...? What are you saying?''

''Well, I can't be sure, because I've never been

through this before. But as near as I can figure, I'm in love with you, Jasmine."

She didn't react with a breathless sigh or a wavering smile. She didn't fall into his arms or cry or plaster his face with kisses. Instead, her eyes widened. She looked scared to death. "You...you love me? But...you *can't.*"

"Oh, I'm pretty sure I can." He drew a breath, examining her face, realizing he'd shaken her up with that declaration. "Look, I'm not expecting anything from you. This doesn't mean you have to say or do anything at all. Hell, I know you didn't need to hear this right now. To tell you the truth, I didn't intend to tell you until all this other stuff was behind us. But something made me go and let on anyway."

Jasmine blinked slowly. Then she ducked underneath the covers and wriggled around under there, and when she came out again, her bra was in place, and her arms were in the sleeves of the white button-down shirt. He loved that she hid from him to dress. It was such a contradiction. He'd seen her undressed. She'd stripped for strangers, and now she ducked under the covers to get dressed. It was a quirk. And it told him she valued him more than she did those strangers. And that meant something to him. Besides, he loved her quirks.

When she emerged, that confused, puzzled frown was still on her face. She slipped out the other side of the bed, stood up with her back to him and slowly buttoned the shirt. ''I don't get it,'' she said. ''I don't have any real claim to your house. You know that now, right? It's going to auction next Saturday, just as planned and there won't be anything stopping you from buying it.'' She finished buttoning the shirt and reached for the jeans, then turned her back to him again and sat on the edge of the bed to pull them over her legs. ''I don't have anything, you know. No money. Nothing of value. And I've got a kid, for crying out loud.'' She stood up, pulled the jeans over her hips and then snapped them, zipped them, faced him again. ''I just don't get what's in this for you. Why would you want to fall in love with someone like me?''

He probably should have been insulted. But he knew she quite simply had no frame of reference for what he was trying to say to her. He put his own jeans on but didn't bother yet with the shirt. ''I don't think people generally get a choice in the matter. You fall in love with someone for who they are, not what they have or what's in it for you. But maybe you can't really understand that until it happens to you. I mean, up until you came crashing into my life, I thought I was going to get to decide when, why, how and who I would love. But it doesn't happen that way, Jasmine.''

She lowered her head, totally confused, by the looks of her. He said, ''Will you stay put while I go next door and get one of the guys?''

''I'm not gonna run away, Luke. You don't have

to make one of your cousins guard me while you shower.''

He smiled. ''That's good to know.''

''What do you think we should do next?'' she asked.

Luke turned, and he couldn't help but feel it was good sign, her asking his opinion on this battle she'd been so determined to fight on her own up to now. ''I think we should take your tapes to the police, turn this whole mess over to them and go back to Texas where we belong.''

She shook her head slowly. ''I don't trust the police. Petronella's one of them.''

''Then we'll have Garrett contact the FBI. Hand the tapes over to them.''

''That's a little better.''

''Then that's what we'll do.'' He reached out, ran a finger down her cheek. He loved touching her. ''But until we're safely back home again, I'd still feel better if you weren't left alone too long.''

She sighed, but nodded. ''Fine. Go get the troops, then.''

Luke went to the door, opened it, and looked up and down the walk outside. The place was pretty silent this early in the morning. Nothing much stirred besides the light misty fog that had crept in overnight. He stepped outside, pulling the door closed behind him, and walked the few feet to the next door down, tapped on it. ''Ben? Garrett?''

He heard the door to Jasmine's room open and

glanced back down the sidewalk to see her there. She leaned out the door, her hair catching the breeze and dancing on it. "We should get coffee, Luke. Do you think the diner is open yet?"

Something moved in Luke's peripheral vision. A dark form swathed in the mists of the parking lot. Garrett opened the door and spoke, but Luke was turning away now, as that dark shape took the form of a man, and one arm rose slowly and pointed toward Jasmine. She couldn't see the man. There was no time to warn her.

Luke lunged as the distant arm came level. He threw himself between Jasmine and the gunman, and he never heard the bullets that hammered into his chest. But he felt them. They pounded and burned and tore, knocking him to the pavement as powerfully as if he'd been hit by a wrecking ball. Jasmine screamed. Garrett swore. The rest was a blur. What had been unfolding in slow motion suddenly jumped to fast forward. Jasmine fell to her knees at his side, leaning over him, crying. Her hands touched his chest and came away bloody. Her tears rained warm on his face. He didn't know where Garrett had gone. Ben was there, too, gently guiding Jasmine's hands back to Luke's chest, pressing them down on the wounds, instructing her to keep the pressure on. Luke didn't see the others. He heard footfalls in the parking lot, squealing tires. Everything had a distant, hollow sound to it—as if he were hearing it from the far end of a deep cave.

It occurred to him that there wasn't any pain now. That probably didn't bode well. Damn, he had things to do yet—for Jasmine, and for Baxter.

He forced his arm to move, lifted it, closed his hand on Ben's collar. "You're...my...witness."

"Don't try to talk, Luke. Take it easy, now. Help's on the way."

"God, what happened? What happened?" Jasmine was asking, choking on tears. "He's been shot. God, he's been shot."

"Ben..." Luke forced the words out, every one requiring tremendous effort. "Take the money. Buy the Walker place. For Jasmine."

"I understand, I got it, Luke, but please, stop talking now. I'm trying to keep you around long enough to see to all that yourself, so hush up."

Luke let his hand fall to the ground. He never felt it hit. He turned his gaze in search of Jasmine, whispered her name.

"I'm right here," she told him. And she moved so he could see her more clearly, but she still kept her hands pressed hard to his chest. "I'm right here, Luke."

He locked his eyes on her, held them there and knew she was unharmed. None of the bullets had reached her. Thank God, he thought. Thank God. "Go home," he told her. "Go home to Baxter." And then everything went dark. Her tears were the last thing he saw.

* * *

"Luke? Luke, come on? Don't fade on me now, come on! Luke?" Her entire body shook with tremors that seemed to come from down deep in her core. She leaned over Luke, her hands pressing hard to stop the blood pumping from his chest. He wasn't wearing a shirt, but his chest was slick with blood, and no matter how hard she pressed, it continued to seep out of him.

She understood what had happened. Luke had seen someone taking aim at her, out there in the misty parking lot somewhere. And he'd thrown himself into the line of fire. Like some kind of silver-screen hero. As if she were worth saving. He lay there on the concrete, blood all around him, under him, soaking through her jeans where she knelt beside him. Sirens wailed now, and all she could do was kneel beside Luke, her hands striving to keep the precious blood from flowing from his body. Her stomach heaved and clenched, and she felt dizzy. She had to battle the need to whirl away from him and throw up. He lay there, pale and still, his eyes closed now. Maybe he was dying. She didn't know. Maybe he was already dead. She couldn't stop trembling, sobbing. She hadn't felt this kind of panic hit her since that horrible day when she'd seen a man firing a gun at her own little boy. This sickening, gut-wrenching fear was the same. Except then, even as she'd sped away, she'd been able to see that Baxter was unharmed. This time, it was different. This time, the person she was so concerned for had holes torn through his body and blood streaming from the wounds.

"We got him!" someone called, and Ben looked up from what he was doing.

"Wes! Get over here and help me. We're gonna lose him if we can't stop this bleeding."

In a split second Wes Brand was kneeling opposite Ben. Jasmine had been paying little attention to what Ben was doing, but now she watched as his brother joined him. The two men moved their hands over Luke's body again and again. Wes muttered something in a low voice in a language that wasn't familiar to her. Comanche, she guessed. Jasmine wondered what earthly good they thought they were doing, but then the blood oozing from beneath her hands slowed. Her throat went dry. She thought she might be imagining things, but it slowed more. Maybe it only meant…no, no, Luke was still breathing. She lifted her gaze to the two brothers—their eyes were closed, their hands still moving. "Keep it up," she whispered. "Whatever you're doing, it's working. Keep it up."

The men didn't acknowledge her words. But she knew they heard. The blood flow eased more, and then it stopped—or she was pretty sure it stopped. She didn't dare take her hands away to check, but she couldn't see it flowing anymore, couldn't feel it pulsing against her hands, which were gloved now by the slick, glossy fluid.

Sirens screamed nearer. Men in white came with a gurney and cases full of supplies, and she was forced to move away from Luke. So were Wes and Ben. She got to her feet, staggering backward a few steps. For the first time she looked around her.

Dozens of people had gathered, forming a loose circle around the spot where Luke lay. Some were still in their nightclothes. They stared at her, shaking their heads, making sympathetic sounds as she scanned their faces. Dizziness, sickness, regret swamped her. Her world tilted, and her knees gave out. But a pair of arms closed around her waist before she could hit the pavement.

Wes held her easily upright. ''Come on, let's get you someplace where you can sit.''

''I have to go with Luke,'' she said. She lifted her gaze, blinking, not seeing anything clearly. Then Ben seemed to appear from nowhere a few feet away, clearing the crowd with a wave of his arms like Moses parting the Red Sea. Wes scooped her up and carried her back into motel room. Elliot appeared to open the door, so Wes could set her inside. Then Elliot handed her a bottle of water—she had no clue where he'd gotten it. But she sipped gratefully.

''Get her cleaned up and bring her on to the hospital,'' Elliot said. ''I'll ride with Luke.''

''No, I should go....'' She tried to get to her feet, but her legs buckled.

''We'll be two minutes behind the ambulance, if

that. I promise,'' Wes said. He nodded to Elliot, who ran out the door, back to the ambulance. A second later she heard its siren howl as it sped away.

Ben came out of the bathroom with an ice bucket full of water and a washcloth. He dipped her hands into the water and gently washed them. She tried not to look at the water as it changed to the color of Luke's blood. Ben took it away, dumped it, brought back more. Then he peeled off her white blouse, ruined now, while Wes brought a fresh shirt for her. It was Luke's shirt, she realized as they put it on her, dressing her as if she were a helpless child. She lowered her head to cry, but paused when she saw the police cars outside.

Near the nose of the first car, Garrett was talking to several police officers, who held a handcuffed tough between them. The guy was stocky, dark and thoroughly battered. His face looked as if someone had used it for a punching bag. ''Is that the man?'' she asked. ''Is he the one who shot Luke?''

''Yeah,'' Ben said. ''Garrett, Elliot and Wes chased him down.''

''He tossed the gun as he ran,'' Wes said. ''Had a silencer on it, which is why we didn't hear the shots. Is that the guy who's been after you and Baxter all this time?''

She shook her head slowly. ''No.''

She lowered her head. Ben raised it again. He was back with a fresh washcloth, and he wiped her face now. She tried not to think about what was on it. He washed her neck, buttoned up Luke's shirt for her. "There. Almost as good as new. You have a fresh pair of jeans in here?"

She nodded vaguely. "Yeah. I can...I can do the rest."

Jasmine got to her feet, only to have Ben's arm instantly link with hers to help her to the bathroom. Inside, she peeled of her blood-soaked jeans, then sat on the edge of the bathtub and cranked on the water, washing her legs as it ran. She had to close her eyes. God, she couldn't bear much more. Poor Luke.

Getting to her feet, she dried off, pulled on the fresh jeans and turned toward the mirror.

The woman who looked back at her was a stranger. Jasmine wasn't even sure she recognized her. This was not the loner who trusted no one and thought of men as a baby step up the evolutionary ladder from dogs. This was not the street-tough city girl who could coldly strip for money and never let it get to her. This was not the woman who didn't believe in love.

She didn't know who the hell this woman in the mirror was. And that scared her.

There was a tap on the door. "You okay in there, hon?"

Ben's voice, deep with concern. She turned and opened the door. "I'm ready."

Flanked by Ben and Wes, she moved out of the motel room. The minute she was in sight, two of the cops outside came toward her. Garrett was with them. The suspect, the shooter, was at the second police car with a third cop, some fifty feet away.

Garrett said, ''I know this is hard, hon, but we have to know. Do you know that man?'' He pointed at the suspect. ''Is this the guy you saw commit that murder at The Catwalk? The one who fired shots at you and your little boy?''

''No,'' she said. ''That's not him. Gianni probably hired him to…ohmyGod.'' She came to a halt, and all eyes were on her. She was the only one looking toward the cop in the distance, who had put the shooter into the back of the car and was getting into the front. ''That's him…that's the killer!''

''It is the same guy, after all?'' Garrett asked as the patrol car rolled around the diner, toward the highway.

''Not the shooter. The cop. That's him. That cop is the killer!''

All eyes turned toward the patrol car as it merged into traffic, picked up speed.

The two officers tensed, looking at each other in confusion, and one of them said, ''That's Officer Petronella, ma'am. Are you sure about this?''

''That is the man who tried to kill my son and shot at me. That's the man I saw murder the undercover agent at The Catwalk. I have his confession on audio and videotape, back in the motel room.'' Ben headed back to get them even as she went on. ''And if you get him behind a two-way mirror, I can promise you Leo, the bar's owner, will identify him, too.''

''Didn't I tell you he was dirty?'' one cop said to the other. ''We'd better get to this Leo fellow before Gianni does.'' He keyed a microphone clipped to his collar and started speaking into it as he headed for his car.

''I'm more worried about that suspect right now,'' the other cop said. ''If he worked for Petronella, he can testify to that in court. Hell, he'll never make it to the station.'' He looked at Garrett, then at Jasmine. ''There's still a warrant out for your arrest, ma'am.''

''I'll keep her and the evidence in my custody,'' Garrett said. ''When you're ready to take her statement and the tapes, we'll be at the hospital. But I promise you, once you do, that warrant will be dropped.''

The cop nodded. ''She's your responsibility, Sheriff Brand. Don't leave town until this is settled. Understand?''

Jasmine nodded. Then she and the others went to Ben's SUV and piled in. Garrett got behind the wheel, and as they sped toward the hospital, he said, ''I just hope to hell they catch that bastard.''

Jasmine hovered outside the doors of the room marked Trauma 1, trying to see beyond the mesh-lined safety glass and the sea-green lab coats that surrounded Luke. A pretty young nurse touched her shoulder and said, ''Come to the waiting room, miss. You'll be so much more comfortable there.''

''I'm *not* moving!'' She didn't speak the words so much as bark them. It was at least the fourth time the perky blonde had bothered her.

''Easy, Jazz. She's just trying to help.'' It was Wes's voice. He had a cup of coffee in one hand, and he sent the nurse an apologetic glance that told her it was all right, he would handle things. The nurse sighed and moved away. Wes came closer, pressed the cup into Jasmine's hand, looked past her at the windows, and saw no more than she'd been able to see before.

''You and Ben ought to be in there,'' Jasmine muttered. ''You could probably do as well as they are.''

He shook his head. ''They know what they're doing. This is Chicago. They know how to take care of gunshot wounds here.''

''It's been an hour.''

''It might be two. You sure you don't want to come sit with us?''

She shook her head, sighed, sipped the coffee. ''What was that, anyway? What you and Ben were doing back there to make the bleeding stop the way you did?''

Wes shrugged. ''I think Ben calls it reiki. He studied lots of Eastern mysticism along with martial arts a while back. Still keeps up with most of it. As for my part, I was just using an old Comanche healing technique. I think it's pretty much the same thing, either way.''

''It was amazing.''

Wes shrugged. ''Actually, stopping blood is fairly easy. I'll show you sometime.''

''I'd like that.'' She turned to peer through the window again.

''He's gonna be all right, Jasmine.''

She closed her eyes, lowered her head. ''Why did he do it, Wes? Why did he jump in front of me like that? What the hell could he possibly have been thinking?''

Wes frowned at her as if she were asking an inane question. ''He was trying to protect you.''

''By getting himself shot? God, Wes, I just don't get it. Who does something like that for someone else? And why, for God's sake?''

He just looked at her for a long moment. Then he said, ''You remember when you saw Petronella shooting at Baxter? What did you do?''

She paced away from the door, shaking her head. ''I threw something at him, yelled at him, waved my arms.''

''Why?''

''*Why?* To distract his attention away from my son, so he wouldn't shoot him.''

''And didn't it occur to you that the man would only shoot at you instead?'' Wes asked.

''I *knew* he would shoot at me instead. But it didn't matter. I mean, better me than Baxter.''

Wes came to where she stood, put a hand on her shoulder. ''And why would you be willing to risk your own life in order to save Baxter's?''

She blinked. ''Well...I'm his mother.''

''Oh. Well. If that's all it was... Would your mother have done that for you, do you think?''

''Shoot, my mother would have used me for a shield, given the chance.'' She licked her lips, lowered her head. ''But I'm not like her. I love my baby. I'd do anything for him. There's nothing in the world more important to me than that child, not even my own life. I'd die for him in a heartbeat and never once regret it. That's how much I love him.''

She finished speaking, lifted her head slowly. And Wes held her gaze and nodded slowly. ''And that's how much Luke loves you.''

It was like a flash of light in her eyes that was so bright it blinded her. The pain in her chest doubled, and for a second she couldn't breathe. She actually staggered backward as if Wes had delivered a physical blow. One hand pressed to her heart in a knee-jerk reaction, and she leaned against the wall behind her.

The double doors opened. People in green rushed out, wheeling Luke on the gurney amid them. One pushed an IV pole with bags swinging and tubes attached to Luke's arms.

''Are you family?'' a male doctor asked her. She

brushed him aside and tried to run along beside the gurney.

"I am," Wes told the doctor.

The gurney stopped at an elevator, and a nurse hit the button. Jasmine crowded her way between the people and leaned over Luke. God, he was so still, so very white. A sheet covered him from the hips down, and his chest was patched with bloody squares. Tubes in his nose. Tubes in his arms.

"Luke...?" Jasmine whispered.

The elevator doors opened. A nurse touched her arm. "We have to take him up to surgery now. Sixth floor. There's a waiting room up there. We're going to do everything we can, I promise you."

"Luke!"

They pushed him past her, into the elevator, as she stretched her hands out toward him, as if she could hold on to him somehow. Then the doors closed, and she stood there, staring. It wasn't possible that a man like Luke could love her the way Wes said he did. No one in her life had ever loved her like that. Well, no one except for Bax. But he had to love her. She was his mom. My God, the sheer magnitude of this was more than her mind could wrap itself around all at once. How could he love her that much? How could *anyone* love her that much? What the hell did she have that made her deserve it? And yet, it must be true. Because the man had dived in front of bullets for her. *He'd dived in front of bullets for her!* Shielded her with his own body. Knowing damn well he would be shot instead.

Who *did* things like that?

"Jasmine?"

She lifted her head, blinked at Wes.

"She looks shocky, Wes. Maybe we should get a doc to take a look at her," Elliot said.

"You all right, Jazz?"

She tipped her head to one side. When had Wes taken to calling her that? When had she decided she liked it? Why did it make her feel like part of his family? "They...have to operate on him," she said. "Sixth floor. We should go up."

Wes nodded. Garrett turned and punched the elevator button, and they stood there, waiting. "So what did they say to you, Wes?" Garrett asked.

"They needed the consent of a family member. That's all."

The doors opened; they all stepped inside. Jasmine watched Wes's face and saw his eyes. There was more. "That's not all," she said. "Tell us, Wes. I already know it's bad. That nurse told me they'd do everything they could. I know what that means as well as anyone. It means they're not sure they can save him."

Wes lowered his head. When he lifted it again, he glanced at Garrett, and Garrett nodded. "She's tougher than she looks. You might as well tell us the worst of it, Wes."

Swallowing hard, Wes said, "One bullet went

clear through, punctured a lung on the way. That's bad enough, but the second one is still inside him. It damaged his heart and lodged in his back—it's near his spine. They need to get it out, because if it shifts position it could kill him or cripple him. There's no telling yet how much damage it's already done. They need to repair the tear to his heart and get that bullet out of his spine. Then they'll work on the lung.''

The doors opened again. For a minute Jasmine couldn't even move. Garrett had to take her arm and push her along to get her going. Her feet came down then, one in front of the other, but she wasn't directing them.

Ben said, ''Has anyone called home?''

''Yeah,'' Garrett said. ''But it's time for an update.'' He pulled the cell phone out of his pocket.

''I want to talk to Baxter,'' Jasmine said softly.

''That's good, that'll help him feel better.''

''I don't know how. I can't tell him Luke will be okay. I can't tell him Petronella has been caught and locked up where he can't hurt us anymore. The only thing I can tell him is…that I'm sorry. I'm sorry I got the only man that boy has ever loved shot.'' She lifted her eyes, looking at each of the men in turn. ''And I need to tell you that, too. And your whole family. I'm sorry. I'm so damn sorry I ever darkened your door and brought all this trouble down on you. It's my fault Luke's lying in there fighting for his life. My fault. I wish I could take it back.''

Wes shook his head at her. ''Luke wouldn't have had it any other way, you know. If he had it to do over, he'd do it just the same.''

She closed her eyes and, finally, let Ben lead her to a chair.

Chapter 15

"I think he's coming around," a voice said. It was a gentle voice, a familiar one. Luke was struggling to stay afloat in a very deep, very dark sea, but waves kept pushing him under again. Then a hand closed around his, and he gripped it as if it were his lifeline.

"I'm right here, Luke. I'm right here."

Slowly he blinked his eyes open. "Jasmine...?"

"Right here," she said. He sought her out with his eyes, found her. She was a blur, but gradually she came into focus. She didn't look well. She was pale, and her hair was hanging in a limp ponytail with many strands dangling free. No makeup. She had red-rimmed, puffy eyes.

"You okay?" he asked weakly. God, why was it so much effort to put words together?

''Am *I* okay?'' She smiled, but sadly. ''I'm fine. You're the one who got himself shot.''

He frowned. Shot? It took moments of intense concentration to make sense of her words. Then, finally, he remembered. ''Did they get him?''

''Yeah. They got him.''

''And? What else?'' he asked her.

She said, ''It wasn't Petronella. Just one of his flunkies. Petronella took off with him before I could ID him. Bastard had the nerve to show up at the scene. But it's gonna be okay. The police tracked him down in short order. He'd already shot his flunky and dumped the body alongside the highway. He's in custody now. They have my tapes—but I made copies first, just in case. I'm in the clear, and there's plenty of evidence to send Petronella up for life. It's all going to be okay. Finally.''

He sighed his relief. Thank God the risk to Jasmine was ended. They'd gotten the bastard. He swallowed hard. Then Jasmine leaned over him, cupping his head with her soft hand and lifting his head just a little, holding a glass of water with a straw to his lips. He drank, then she lowered his head gently back against the pillows again. ''Damn, I'm weak. How bad off am I?''

''You're gonna be fine,'' she told him, setting the water down. But she wasn't facing him when she said it.

''Jasmine?''

She turned, sat on the edge of his bed, pressed

her hands to his cheeks and said, ''You're okay. We almost lost you, Luke, but you're okay now. They operated in Chicago. They said it went well, but they wanted to keep you out for a little while. There was some damage to your spine—nothing serious or permanent. One of the bullets came close, though. They didn't want you even trying to move until you'd had a couple days to let the healing process take hold.''

He blinked in shock, trying to take stock of his body, especially his legs and feet. They felt odd. Heavy and tingling, as if they'd gone to sleep. But he could feel them, at least. ''How long have I been unconscious?'' he asked.

''Two days. This morning they shipped you back here, to El Paso, and took you off sedation. You're back in Texas, Luke. We've been here a whole hour already.''

He closed his eyes, feeling an inexplicable surge of contentment wash through him like a warm tide. Hell, whatever happened, he could handle it here. Home. Texas. He really had sunk his roots into the Texas soil, then, hadn't he?

There was a tap on the door. Then it opened. ''Doc said he was coming around,'' Chelsea said, poking her head inside. ''I brought a visitor.''

The door opened wider, and Baxter came in, almost tiptoeing, his eyes wide and worried.

Jasmine gulped back a sob and ran to her son. She scooped him right up and held him tight, covering his little face with her kisses. ''Oh, Bax, honey, I missed you so much!''

''Me too, Mom,'' he said, hugging her neck.

In the bed, Luke's throat closed up tight, and his eyes burned.

''Thanks for bringing him, Chelsea. I couldn't wait, and I couldn't leave, and I just...thank you.''

''Hey, I'd have come whether you asked me to or not. Heck, the whole clan is out there waiting to see Luke. But I'll give the three of you some time first.'' She ducked back outside, and pulled the door closed behind her.

''Luke?'' Baxter asked softly. He squirmed out of his mother's arms, went to the chair and pulled it up close to the bed. Then he climbed up. ''You okay?''

''They tell me I'm gonna be just fine, kiddo. Nothing to worry about.''

Very gently, Bax reached out and hugged Luke's neck. ''You kept your promise,'' he said. ''Just like you said you would. You brought my mom back home.''

''Told you, kid. I never break a promise.'' Luke made the effort it took to put his arms around Bax and hug him in return, but damn, it was hard work.

''I love you, Luke,'' Baxter said.

Oh, hell, that did it. His eyes didn't just burn now, they welled to overflowing, despite Luke's rapid blinking. ''I love you, too, Bax.''

* * *

Jasmine stood there and watched the two embrace. She saw the tears in Luke's eyes and the adoration in Baxter's. And all of the sudden, she needed to be alone. She was so close to something. So close to finally understanding…it was nipping at her brain, and she just needed to grab hold of it and hold on.

She backed out of the room. The two were so involved with each other by then, she didn't think either of them would notice. She ran right past the crowd of Brands lingering in the hall, located the nearest rest room and ducked inside. She cranked on the cold water tap, splashed handfuls of it in her face, battled an attack of hyperventilation.

Both hands braced on the sink, she lifted her head and stared into the mirror. "My God," she whispered. "You love him. You love that man!"

Chelsea sat by the bedside. "Stop worrying, Luke. She only went to the rest room."

Luke frowned anyway, worried all the same. "She didn't look well, Chelsea." Baxter had curled up beside him on the bed, snuggled into a little ball in the crook of his arm, and fallen asleep.

"Well, *of course* she didn't. She's been holding a vigil at your bedside since you came out of surgery. They couldn't get her to leave. She flew home with you. The girl's got it bad, Luke."

He shook his head. "She feels responsible, I imagine. It's just guilt."

Chelsea smiled. "Ah, be dense if you want to. Why mess up a perfectly good Brand family tradition?"

He sent her a smirk. "How come Garrett's not with you?"

"The menfolk had to take off. Got a call from a neighbor. Seems the north pasture fence is down and we have cattle all over the place. They won't be long getting things squared away."

He nodded. There was yet another tap on the door, and a nurse came in. "We have to take Mr. Brand down to X-ray now. It won't take long."

Chelsea nodded, got to her feet and gathered Baxter up in her arms. "See you in a few minutes, Luke."

"Thanks, Chelsea. For taking such good care of Bax and...and, well, everything."

She nodded. "A fall wedding would be nice, don't you think?" She sent him a wink and carried Bax out into the waiting room.

Luke lay back, thinking his cousin-in-law had higher hopes than he did. Damn, a fall wedding sounded good to him, too, though. He smiled crookedly as the nurse wheeled him out of his room, into an elevator. Then she pulled a needle out of a deep white pocket.

"What's that?" he asked. "Not more sedatives, I hope. I'd like to stay awake for a while."

The nurse smiled down at him. "Just pain meds. Don't worry." She stuck the needle into his IV tube. A second ticked by, then two, and then his head was swimming.

"Whoa, those must be powerful...main peds...uh...I mean um..." He forgot what he'd been saying. The doors slid open, and she pushed him out. Ceiling lights flashed overhead, running past him as if they were attached to a conveyor belt. He found that incredibly funny and started to laugh, but it hurt when he laughed, and he wondered vaguely why his pain meds didn't prevent that.

Doors whooshed open. Fresh Texas air hit him in the face. Hey, he was outdoors. Since when did they put X-ray outdoors? Whoa, now his bed was being picked up. What the hell? He tried to lift his head, to make sense of what he was seeing before the ambulance doors slammed shut on him. A man, handing a wad of cash to the nurse. The nurse, yanking off her name tag and tossing it onto the ground, then hurrying away. Hell, she was no nurse at all.

Still not sure who this woman was she had become—or was in the process of becoming—Jasmine left the rest room and went back to the waiting area where the Brand women were gathered. Chelsea said, "They had to take Luke down for an X-ray. He'll be back in a minute."

"God, talk about padding the bill," Jasmine muttered. "They just X-rayed the poor man a few minutes before you all got here."

Jessi said, ''He'll be glowing in the dark if they keep this up.'' The others laughed. Kirsten and Penny. And the two women due to give birth at any moment, Taylor and Esmeralda.

Frowning, Jasmine said, ''Where'd all your husbands go?''

''Had a cattle emergency out at the ranch,'' Chelsea said. ''I'm sure they won't be long.''

''Oh.'' Jasmine sat down, drumming her fingers on the arm of the overstuffed chair and glancing down the hall toward X-ray.

Then Chelsea's cell phone rang. She answered it and said, ''No, Garrett's not available at the moment. This is his wife, can I take a message?'' She listened, and her gaze flew to Jasmine's. ''Oh, no.''

''What?'' Jasmine demanded.

Chelsea disconnected and eyed her. ''Petronella's escaped. And the tapes you gave the police have vanished from the evidence room.''

''Excuse me, ladies?'' a deep voice said. They turned to see the swarthy Mexican-American physician they all called Doc standing there by Luke's hospital room door. ''Can someone tell me where my patient has gone?''

''Oh, my God,'' Jasmine whispered. She whirled on Chelsea. ''Which way did that nurse take Luke?''

''To the elevator—I think it was going down. Why?''

''Because X-ray is down the hall.''

Chelsea frowned, looking from the doctor to Jasmine over and over. "You mean…you think…"

"I think Petronella somehow followed us here, and now he has Luke." Jasmine got to her feet, turned toward the elevator. "He probably even engineered that so-called emergency that got all the men out of the way."

"Wait!" Chelsea cried. "Jasmine, where the hell are you going?"

"I'm going after Luke!"

Chelsea caught her, gripped her shoulder, turned her around. "Not alone, you're not. That's not the way we do things in this family, Jasmine. You can't keep behaving like this loner you used to be, because that's not who you are anymore!"

"I'm not?" she asked, her tone impatient, even bordering on sarcastic.

"No. You're a Brand woman now. Maybe it's not official yet, but it's inevitable, and family means more than some legal documentation, anyway. You're one of us. So is Bax. And so is Luke. And Brands don't let family handle trouble alone."

For an instant, just an instant, she reeled at the power with which those words hit her. It was as if, suddenly, she knew it was utterly true. That was who she'd seen when she'd looked into the mirror. A woman who was part of a family. The family the child inside her had always longed for.

She was a Brand.

"Taylor and Esmeralda, you are far too pregnant

to be on this end of things. Take care of Baxter. Have Doc show you someplace safe to hole up, and insist some security people stay with you.'' She tossed the cell phone to Esmeralda, who caught it, frowned at it and handed it to Taylor. ''Try to contact the men and tell them what's happened.''

Doc was at the nurses' desk now, giving rapid orders. He turned and came toward Jasmine as she started for the elevator again. ''An ambulance just pulled out of the lot, without its crew. And someone left this note for you at the desk.''

He handed her a sealed envelope. She tore it open and read the note inside.

''Jasmine—If you want Luke Brand back alive, meet me when and where I say. Bring the original tapes, as I know full well those I stole were copies, and bring the boy. No one else, or your hero dies. Call this number in one hour for further instructions.'' It was signed GP.

She nodded. The elevator doors slid open, and she stepped inside. ''The note says I'm to come alone,'' she said.

''Right,'' Chelsea replied. Then she, Jessi, Penny and Kirsten joined her. As the door slid closed again, Jasmine saw Taylor and Esmeralda being led down a hall by Doc, who carried a still sleepy Baxter.

Five women got out of the elevator on the ground floor and into Chelsea's station wagon. After asking which way the stolen ambulance had gone, Jasmine drove, and Chelsea read the note aloud to the others as they sped down the highway out of El Paso.

Kirsten smiled. ‘‘That's the good thing about small towns, you know? Not that many phone numbers. Even fewer exchanges. That one in particular belongs to a little town between El Paso and Quinn, right on the Rio Grande. It's called Deadrock, and I don't imagine it has too many public telephones.’’

‘‘Chances are this Petronella character wouldn't be using a private one. He can't know anyone from around here, can he?’’

‘‘Doubtful,’’ Jasmine said. ‘‘But why wouldn't he have just used his cell phone?’’

‘‘In Deadrock?’’ Kirsten smiled slowly. ‘‘No reception whatsoever.’’

Chelsea nodded slowly. ‘‘If he's in a motel and we call, we might get the front desk first, then we'll know where he is. Either way, I don't like the idea of waiting an hour. Why don't we call him back right now?’’

‘‘'Cause you gave your cell phone to Taylor,’’ Jessi said.

Kirsten opened her designer handbag. ‘‘You think I leave home without one?’’ Then she frowned. ‘‘Should we call in the police on this?’’

‘‘And risk Luke's life?’’ Jasmine said, quickly and sharply. She schooled her tone before continuing. ‘‘No. We can call Garrett, tell him and the others where we're heading, but I don't think we should bring in any authorities. Not yet.'' She looked to Chelsea, a question in her eyes.

Chelsea nodded in agreement. ''We'll handle this the way we handle every other crisis—as a family. The men will be along as fast as they can get here. But we have a head start on catching up to this maniac. I have to believe we're the best chance Luke has right now.'' She looked around at the other women. ''So we go after him ourselves. Now. We don't wait. Agreed?''

One by one, the Brand women nodded.

Chapter 16

When Luke opened his eyes again, he was hurting big time. The pain was like a trail of fire, burning in his chest and his back. Hell, he couldn't even move without inducing more of it. And his legs tingled as if covered in fire ants. What the hell had happened? Where was he?

Warily he took in his surroundings, moving only his eyes, teeth grated. Paneled walls. A simple white globe of a light fixture in the ceiling. Cheesy art on the opposite walls. A window to the left—shade drawn, curtain closed so no light could stream in. He could only see the top of it without turning his head to see more. He was not in the hospital anymore.

And finally, a voice—from another room he

thought. The scent of tobacco smoke drifted on the air.

"I told you to call in an hour. Why are you early?" There was silence. Then, "If you can't obey simple instructions, maybe I should kill him and get the hell out of here."

Luke strained to lift his head. The spears of pain the act sent bolting through him were almost enough to make him scream aloud. But he forced it all the same and saw through the doorway into a second room, where a man sat at a table, smoking and speaking on the telephone.

"Fine. But this is your last chance, Jasmine. You bring the boy, and you bring the tapes, or your boyfriend here dies." He paused, flicked ashes onto the floor and nodded. "That's better. Now, there's a stretch of ground without much on it besides cactus and rock, twenty-one point five miles out of El Paso, heading west on 375. Only thing close is a billboard advertising the county fair. You know where I mean?" He nodded. "Good. That's where I'll be. Half hour. And, Jasmine? Don't bother trying to track me down through the phone number. I'll be long gone from here within minutes, and you'll only be wasting precious seconds of your boyfriend's life." He hung up the phone.

"You don't want those tapes, Petronella," Luke said, and it was a strain to say it. His voice came out gruff and hoarse. ‘‘You don’t have any need of them now. Everyone knows you’re guilty.’’

He shrugged. ‘‘Knowing it and proving it are two different things.’’

‘‘You killed the guy who shot me,’’ Luke went on.

‘‘That’s right, I did. Killed him with his own gun. For you, though, I’m gonna use mine. It hasn’t had a good workout since before I was arrested. I had to tuck it into hiding fast, to keep the cops from confiscating it.’’ He patted his side. His jacket hid the gun from view.

‘‘So you’ve got two murder raps, and the escape charge to boot. Don’t you see the tapes are of no use to you now?’’ Luke asked. ‘‘The only thing you can do now is run. You can never go back, even if you have the tapes.’’

Petronella got to his feet and walked slowly into the room where Luke was. He smoked slowly, thoughtfully. ‘‘You’re too smart for your own good, you know that?’’

‘‘You don’t want the tapes at all, do you?’’

Petronella thrust out a lower lip. ‘‘Nah. I want revenge. The bitch messed up my life, and she’s gonna pay. And there ain’t a thing you can do about it, being laid up like you are. You can’t even get out of that bed.’’

Luke wanted to leap out of the bed and nail the guy right then and there, but he could barely move. And then he thought maybe it was better to let Petronella go on believing he couldn't move at all. Even screaming pain was better than the numbness he'd felt before. But he would need every advantage.

"You're so close to the border, you know. You could walk out of here right now, cross the Rio Grande and be in Mexico. They'd never find you there. People get lost there all the time."

He nodded slowly. "That's the plan. Right after I off Jasmine and her scrawny kid, that's what I'll do. But first..." He reached into his jacket, pulled his gun level and aimed it at Luke. Luke tensed, preparing to lunge at the bastard with everything in him. But Petronella didn't fire. He frowned, looked at his gun, hefting it in his hand, his frown growing. "What the hell?" he asked, checking it, turning it over.

Luke almost went limp with relief when he saw that there was no clip in the gun's hollow handle. Petronella spewed a stream of obscenities. "Dammit, I don't have freaking time for this kind of—did you do this? Where the hell is my clip?" As he spoke, he worked the action of the gun. A single bullet popped out of the chamber and landed on the floor, rolling slowly.

One bullet.

Luke rolled out of the bed as Petronella reached for it. He landed hard, the bullet under him. Petronella gripped his shoulder, flung him onto his back.

Luke closed his hand around the bullet. ‘‘What’s the matter, Gianni? Is it your last one?’’

‘‘It’ll have to be enough. Gimme the bullet,’’ Petronella demanded.

Luke lay on his back on the floor. ‘‘No freaking way.’’

‘‘You think so, huh?’’ Petronella picked up a booted foot and stomped down hard on Luke’s chest, right over one of the bullet wounds.

Pain hit him so hard he howled with it, but he didn’t let go of the bullet. Arms crossed over his chest, he rolled onto his side, doubled in pain.

Petronella knelt in front of him. ‘‘Give it to me!’’

Luke decked him—just poked upward and outward with a fist and all the power he could put behind it. Which wasn’t a hell of a lot, he thought, but apparently it was enough to knock Petronella on his ass.

While the man was down, Luke rolled onto his belly, dragging himself, elbow over elbow, to the small room he’d spotted. He heard Petronella swear, heard him get up, and crawled faster. His upper body crossed the threshold. Petronella stepped down on the middle of Luke’s back.

‘‘Give me the effing bullet!’’

Luke’s back arched, chin coming off the floor in response to the weight on his injured back. The bastard would cripple him! He looked at the toilet ahead of him, lifted his arm, took careful aim despite the pain racking him—and let fly.

The small, shiny bullet flew in a perfect arc and hit the water with an anticlimactic little plop.

Petronella kicked him in the head, and Luke saw stars as the man walked over him to the toilet, and bent to thrust his hand into the water. Luke tried to move. And found he couldn't. Not at all. More interestingly than that, he couldn't feel much of anything anymore, either.

''Calling early didn't do a hell of a lot of good. I was hoping it was a pay phone or a motel, and someone else would answer. Someone who'd tell us where the phone was,'' Kirsten said after Jasmine's call to Petronella.

They'd stopped at a phone booth as they passed, just long enough for Chelsea to jump out, rip the telephone directory from its chain and jump back into the car again. Jessi was flipping through it now as they drove.

''I have it!'' she said. ''Shoot, it wasn't hard. Deadwood only takes up three pages. That number is for one of the rooms above the Deadwood Bar and Grill.''

''Which is dead opposite the direction we need to head to meet Petronella,'' Chelsea pointed out. ''If we go back, it'll make us late.''

Jasmine shook her head. ''And that could cost Luke his life. We have to make that meeting, Chelsea.''

''I agree.''

Jessi nodded hard. ''Me too.''

All the others in the car chimed in with agreement.

Jasmine thinned her lips. ''You know as well as I do that Petronella probably won't keep his side of the bargain. Even if we do everything he wants.''

''Fortunately,'' Chelsea said, reaching over to give Jasmine's hand a squeeze, ''we aren't going to leave that decision up to him.''

They reached the designated meeting place within minutes, since they were already nearly there. There was no significant cover around. Just a billboard, some cacti dotting the landscape, a tumbleweed here and there. ''We haven't got any weapons,'' Kirsten said as Chelsea pulled the car to a stop along the roadside in a cloud of dust.

''I do,'' Jasmine said. She tugged her gun out of her handbag.

''Hell, we all do,'' Jessi put in. She got out of the station wagon, crouched down, and when she rose again, she was tossing a decent-sized rock in her hand. The others got out, too, gathered around her, nodded. ''Best give one of us the gun, Jasmine,'' Jessi said. ''He'll probably search you, if he gets the chance. Besides, we're gonna need him alive, unless he brings Luke with him.''

Jasmine closed her eyes tight. ''God, Luke wasn't even supposed to be moving around much. And he missed his pain meds.'' It turned her stomach to think of the pain he must be in right now.

To think of what Petronella might have done to him.

"Luke's a Brand, Jasmine. He's tough as they come. He's gonna come through this all right," Jessi said.

"Come on, let's find cover and weapons. Set this up right under and around that billboard. Best spot possible."

"I don't see how we're supposed to find any cover out here," Jasmine said, squinting, shading her eyes with her hand. A cactus, a tumbleweed, the car, which he would surely search, and the billboard itself, were all she saw.

Jessi smiled and patted her on the back. "Yeah, but you're from out of town. Come on hon. Let us show you how we do things in Texas."

Kirsten pulled a pair of imitation calfskin gloves out of her designer bag, and slipped her hands into them. Then she walked right up to a cactus, broke off one of its arms and swung it a few times like a club, nodding in satisfaction. "Bastard's gonna wish he hadn't started up with us," she muttered.

The half hour ticked by slower than molasses on a midwinter day. But Jasmine was ready. Following Jessi's instructions, she'd snapped a handful of tangles off the tumbleweed and brushed away all the footprints that showed anywhere. Mostly the ground here was hard packed and barren. The desert wasn't all sand, the way she'd always thought.

Then she stood in plain sight underneath the billboard and waited.

Finally another car pulled to a stop alongside hers. Petronella sat still for a moment, looking around, listening. Then he got out, with his gun in hand. He strode right up to Chelsea's station wagon, opened its doors, searched inside it, then, satisfied, he looked up and down the road, and finally, walked off the pavement to where Jasmine waited, under the billboard, a hot, dry breeze raking her cheeks.

"I don't see the boy," he said.

"I didn't see any reason to bring him. You want the tapes. I want Luke. My son has nothing to do with it."

He shrugged. "Hell, I've only got one bullet on me anyway." He lifted the gun.

"Kill me and you won't get the tapes," she said, trying hard to hide the bolt of fear that jolted up her spine just then.

He smiled slowly. "Tapes aren't gonna do me any good anyway, sugar."

He smiled slowly, and his hand flexed on the gun so fast there was no time to do anything to prevent it. But only a dull click resulted when he pulled the trigger. Then Chelsea came hurtling down from the billboard where she'd been hiding—she'd had to stand on Jessi's shoulders to get hold of the sign's frame and had pulled herself up from there, clung to the back and waited for her moment. And it was perfect. She landed on top of Petronella, flattening him to the ground. He hit hard, but rolled over, flinging Chelsea off him. Kirsten leaped out from behind the one-armed cactus and smashed him in the face with her makeshift prickly club. He howled in agony, but already Jessi had shot out from where she'd been lying flat underneath the car and Penny rose up from under the tumbleweed. So when Petronella knocked Kirsten's club away and sat up with his hands to his face, it was only to get pegged by two cobble-sized stones, one from in front and one from behind.

He never stood a chance. His head was split open and bleeding in the back, swollen and purple on the front, and his face was extremely messed up, courtesy of the cactus. He never even got back on his feet again.

Jasmine yanked off her belt and tossed it to Jessi. Jessi knelt behind him and bound his hands. Then she tossed the gun back to Jasmine. "Your gun misfired," Jasmine said. "Mine won't. Where is Luke?"

He shook his head. "Damned wet powder," he muttered. "You can blow me away. I'll never tell you. You can just suffer for what you did. I can guarantee you he is—and the longer it takes you to find him, the better his chances of being dead before you do." He spat.

Jasmine pursed her lips. Jessi reached around the man from behind, grabbed his shirt by either side and tore it open, laying his chest and stomach bare. "Hey, Kirsten!" she called. "What'd you do with that cactus limb?"

"Oh, hell, Jessi, you don't want to beat the poor man with that thing," Chelsea said. "Not *there,* anyway." She nodded to Jasmine. "Let's yank off his pants. I mean, I think he'll talk faster."

Kirsten retrieved her limb and came forward, brushing it lightly over his chest, cactus spines raking his flesh. "Where did you leave Luke? Is he in that room you rented above the bar? Hmm?" She reached for his fly.

"Yes!" he shouted. Then, as she drew the club away, "How the hell did you know about the room?"

"City slicker," Jessi said. "You're clueless."

A huge pickup truck came skidding to a stop, sending up more dust clouds, and Brand men piled out of both doors and the back. They came running, then stopped and looked at the scene before them.

"You guys handle it from here," Jasmine said. "I'm going to find Luke."

"We'll send an ambulance, Jasmine," someone called.

She jumped in Chelsea's car and sped away.

She burst into the front part of the room, saw no one and raced through it, calling Luke's name. When she reached the bedroom she found him. He lay facedown on the floor, halfway into the small bathroom. His head was cut open, bleeding. His face was beaded with sweat and contorted in pain, and his eyes were squeezed shut tight.

She was beside him instantly. "Luke! It's all right. Hold on. Help is coming."

His eyes opened. He peered up at her. "You're alive...."

"Of course I'm alive. And Petronella's lucky to be. God, baby, what did he do to you?" She stroked his face, then dashed over him into the bathroom for a wet cool cloth. She wiped his face with it, then pressed it gently to the cut. "You have to be okay, Luke. Dammit, you have to be okay."

He smiled. "Doesn't matter. Just as long as you and Bax are."

She shook her head. "We won't be. Not if we don't have you."

His face changed. He looked surprised, but then something else. "Jasmine, even if I make it, I don't know...what I mean—I can't feel my legs, Jasmine. Not even a little."

"I love you, Luke," she whispered. "I finally understand what you were trying to tell me back there. I love you. Totally. I never thought I could feel this way for any man, but I do, and dammit, you promised me you'd help me start a new life. And I want that, Luke. I want to marry you. I want you to be a father to Baxter. I want that. Do you understand? So you just have to hang in there, Luke. You just have to. You *have to.*''

He managed to smile, even past all the pain. ''Well, hell, Jasmine, I couldn't die now if I wanted to. Not with an offer like that on the table.''

Epilogue

"Welcome Home, Luke" the banner read, when Garrett and Wes pulled up at the brick house that had been known as the old Walker place. It wasn't anymore. The title now read Luke and Jasmine Brand.

Everyone had gathered for the celebration of Luke's release from the hospital. God, it had been three entire weeks. The physical therapy had been brutal and was ongoing. But he was getting better.

Mostly because of Jasmine.

She stood on the porch now, little Baxter in front of her, her hands on his shoulders. They both smiled widely as he got out of the pickup and limped up the walk. He carried a canvas tote in his free hand and leaned heavily on the cane that looked as if it was going to be his walking partner for a long time to come. Maybe forever.

He didn't give a damn. He had what mattered. Jasmine had married him in the hospital room. She'd refused to wait. The legal matters had taken longer, but Luke had had a visit from his lawyer today, just before his release, and now that part, too, was official.

Beyond Jasmine, the house was alive. He could see his family peering out every window and door, their smiles as bright as the happy tears in their eyes. They loved him. They loved her, too.

He made it to the steps, glanced at Garrett and Wes, who'd flanked him all the way, the overprotective lugs. "Can you keep them all at bay for just a sec?" Luke asked.

The men nodded and ran up the steps, into the house, where the party was waiting. They closed the door.

"I'm so glad you're home now, Luke!" Baxter came off the porch and hurled himself into Luke's arms. Jasmine started forward, but Luke held up a hand, caught his balance and hugged the boy back.

"Not half as glad as I am, Bax," he said. "But here. I have a little surprise for you. Two, actually. Now, the first one just can't wait, so you'd better take it now. It's in here." He held up the canvas tote bag.

Frowning, Bax parted it on top to look inside. A small brown puppy poked his head out the top and licked Baxter's nose. The boy squealed and scooped it up, hugging it close. ''For me? Really, oh, really? Oh, Mom, can I keep him? Can I?''

Jasmine smiled damply, nodding her head hard, meeting Luke's eyes, love brimming from her own. He couldn't quite get used to that. A woman as special as this one, loving him the way she did.

Baxter sat on the steps, holding the squirming pup in his lap.

''I have one more surprise,'' Luke said. He pulled a document from his pocket, unfolded it. ''This.''

Baxter got up and handed the puppy to his mom so he could take a look.

''De...cree...of a...a...dop...adop...'' He blinked and his eyes widened. ''Adoption?'' he asked, looking up at Luke.

''Yep. It's a whole lot of big words and legal terms, Bax, but what it means is that from now on, I'm officially your father.''

Baxter's little lips quivered. Tears rose up and one fell over. He said, ''You...you...you're my dad?'' in a high, squeaky voice that wasn't like his own.

Luke nodded. He couldn't really talk just then. He leaned the cane against the porch, lowered himself onto the top step and folded his son into his arms. Baxter was hugging his neck so hard Luke almost couldn't breathe, and his tears were flowing so fast, Luke couldn't hold back his own.

''I've been wishing and wishing you could be my dad, Luke. And it came true. It really came true!'' Baxter said.

Jasmine came down the steps, sat down beside Luke and leaned her head on his shoulder.

''From now on, Bax, I'm gonna make all your wishes come true. And your mom's, too. I promise.''

He met Jasmine's eyes, saw that they were as wet as his own. She leaned in and kissed him on the lips, and she said, ''You've already granted all mine, Luke. Even the ones I never knew I had.''

The three of them embraced, and Luke knew he was home. They all were. Home.

* * * * *

DESTINY'S WOMAN

Lindsay McKenna

To KaraHand's Home in Lower Hutt, New Zealand, and the heart-centred women who care for those in need: Helen Henderson, RN, homoeopath, Deborah Mustard, RN, Reiki healer, and Cathy Garton, RN, homoeopath. I salute the 'Coyote Sisters,' who work with the disabled, the mentally handicapped, the children who require twenty-four-hour-a-day attention. Thank you for being there to help so that the parents of these children can have a day off from their labours of love. You are truly pioneers in this area of help for such families. I honour your compassion towards those in need. Truly, the three of you are Jaguar Clan members in the finest tradition of healers for our world. Thank you for being who you are—great role models for the rest of us to follow.

Chapter 1

"Maya, you can't ask me to go on a mission of this type with a male copilot in the back seat of my Apache helicopter," Akiva said as she sat tensely in the chair before her commanding officer. Her words were low and tortured. Pleading. Without realizing it, Akiva curled her fingers into fists on her tense thighs. Anxiously, she searched her C.O.'s narrowed, emerald eyes for her reaction.

Sighing, Maya sat back in her creaky chair, which had seen better days. Ordinarily, at the Black Jaguar Squadron headquarters, hidden deep in the Peruvian jungle about fifty miles from Machu Picchu, everyone got along with everyone else. Because of the importance of their mission, the U.S. Army had upgraded their facility from a base to squadron status. The change was good for morale, as well. Rarely was there an outburst of dissension such as the one Chief Warrant Officer Akiva Redtail was giving her right now. Propping her fingertips together, Maya leaned back and gave Akiva time to settle down.

"Look," Maya finally murmured in her husky voice, "the Perseus psychologist, Jenny Wright, came down here earlier this month and interviewed everyone who wanted to volunteer for these upcoming missions. Of all the applicants, she chose you to lead this clandestine jungle mission in Mexico. Jenny lobbied hard for you, Akiva, despite the fact that she's more than a little aware of your prejudice against Anglo men."

Akiva's nostrils flared and her eyes flashed with anger. "I've made no bones about my prejudice toward white men, Maya. I *never* have."

"Which is what got you in so much hot water when we were being trained to fly the Apache gunships at the army helicopter facility back in Fort Rucker."

"Yes," she said through gritted teeth, "I'm guilty as charged."

As Maya studied Akiva, who was one of her best combat helicopter pilots, she withheld the bulk of her comments, knowing they would only hurt or inflame Akiva at this point. She knew Akiva well from years of working with the stalwart woman pilot. Akiva was half Chiricahua Apache and half Lakota Sioux, and a warrior of her people. The red headband Akiva wore indicated she had passed all the brutal physical and mental trials the Apache people had challenged her with in order to reach warrior status. Not only that, Akiva proudly wore what was known as the third braid of the warrior, as well. Her waist-length, lustrous black hair was down today, the small braid, which began at the center part, hung down among the thick locks streaming across her proud shoulder. Only an Apache who had fulfilled specific demanding tasks could wear such a braid.

Because Maya wanted Akiva to embrace who she was, as she did every woman pilot at Black Jaguar Squadron, she allowed her to proudly wear the signs of her warrior status. After all, the prejudice against them as women combat pilots had been horrendous enough. Though the army was struggling mightily against old prejudices against women, Maya knew it was a wound that would be long in healing for most of the women pilots. Akiva certainly hadn't taken to being treated like a second-class citizen at Fort Rucker, where she and Maya and many of the other female pilots on the squadron had trained.

Leaning forward, Maya placed her elbows on her cluttered desk and slowly clasped her hands together. Akiva's face was filled with anger, hurt and confusion. Not surprising, since she was the most aggressive gunship pilot at the base—she'd bagged a Russian Kamov to prove it. Akiva was Maya's best pilot. Maybe it was her Apache blood, Maya thought, that gave her that natural aggression that was so needed in air combat. But being a pilot was one thing; being asked to command a small, hidden operation in Mexico was another matter entirely.

Akiva was in her element here at the squadron. She'd thrived as a combat pilot and more than earned her keep. But now she was being asked to step into a command situation, and that was a whole other story. Not every officer had the capability, intelligence, sensitivity or desire to manage a base operation. If Akiva took the assignment, she'd be sorely challenged to develop new skills. Could she? Would she?

Worst of all, Akiva's prejudice against white men would be the test. Could Akiva lay her prejudice aside and treat everyone fairly, including her second-in-command, Joe Calhoun? Though Joe was half Comanche, Maya knew Akiva thought he was white. However, Maya decided not to bring this point up because Akiva had to learn to deal with not only white men, but men in general. Joe would be a real challenge to Akiva. Maya already knew that Joe realized Akiva would be a challenge to him. He already knew Akiva didn't like him, but he didn't understand why. It wasn't Maya's job to fix this. It was up to Akiva and Joe to hammer out a truce for the higher goal of the mission.

"Let's look at this possible assignment another way," Maya said, purposely keeping her voice low and soothing. Ordinarily, she left the door to her office wide-open; it was one of her policies here at Black Jaguar—an open door to the C.O. so that everyone knew they counted and could walk in and speak to Maya whenever they had a problem. That plan had worked well, but today, Maya had closed the door. She knew about the explosion to come, and did not want Akiva embarrassed by her knee-jerk reaction to what would be asked of her.

Opening her hands, Maya continued, "I'm asking more of you, Akiva, than I've ever asked before. This assignment is not about a guy named Joe Calhoun who has been chosen as your copilot and executive officer at this new base ops. It's really a question of whether or not you want to take on a commanding officer's role or not. You must rise above your personal prejudice. That is what a good C.O. does. Everyone should be treated equally and with respect."

Nostrils flaring again, Akiva felt an internal trembling from her gut up to her throat. She was breathing chaotically because she was upset. Her fists tightened on the fabric of her black, body-hugging Nomex flight suit. "I would go to hell and back for you, Maya. Anything you've ever asked of me, I've tried to do to the best of my ability." Her voice broke. "If you gave me a woman copilot and X.O., I'd say without hesitation that yes, I'd try my best to be a leader. But you're throwing this white guy into the equation. Isn't it enough that it's going to be damn dangerous, with a lot of stress on the three-person ground crew and two pilots involved? Why throw in white bread?''

Mouth quirking, Maya said, ''We don't always get everything we want in life, Akiva. You know that better than most.''

''No kidding.'' Her voice grated as she exclaimed, ''I *want* this assignment, Maya. I *know* I can do it. I just don't what an anglo along for the ride and in my rear seat.''

''Joe Calhoun is our best night operations pilot. He taught night ops back at Fort Rucker for the last two years. He's here now, teaching all our pilots on the Apache Longbow upgrade. You even took training from him. You know how good he is at what he does. This little experiment in a bottle that the Pentagon wants us to undertake in Mexico in order to disrupt drug shipments across the Gulf to U.S. soil, is very important. The government is modeling this mission based on the success we've had down here in Peru, stopping cocaine shipments to Bolivia with our Apache gunships. Mexico is home to one of the big drug cartels. The Feds want to set up this base in the jungle—a place near what was once used by drug dealers as a touch-and-go ops to land and take on a lot of drugs. It's the perfect locale for us to hide.

''I want this black ops experiment to be successful, Akiva. I need you to rise above your own prejudice toward white men and look at the larger picture. Through our work here, we've halted fifty percent of the drugs flowing to Bolivia for shipment across the world. That's fifty percent less on the world market. The Pentagon is finally interested in the plan that I initiated here years ago. At long last they're willing to invest time, money and coordinated effort to see if they can apply what we've learned here elsewhere.''

Maya got up and jabbed her finger at her colleague. ''And you're the best pilot for this, Akiva. I need your aggression, your nose for combat, your fearlessness because we don't know what you're up against once we get that Apache helo, that three-woman ground crew and your copilot set up in the jungle. I don't want to see our years of hard work screwed up because you can't get a handle on your prejudice.''

Lips flattening, Akiva looked up at her C.O., who stood six feet tall in her black flight uniform. Maya's ebony hair shone with reddish highlights beneath the fluorescent lights. Maya wore no insignias on her uniform—standard operating procedure for a black ops covert operation, so as not to reveal any hint of who they were or where they came from. Still, Maya was a powerful woman, and Akiva's respect for her transcended her own anger and frustration.

''Listen,'' Akiva growled, ''I don't want to screw up your plans. I agree with them. I want to see what we've carved out here in the jungle put to use elsewhere, too. My gun sights are on the druggies. It does my heart good to turn them back or down 'em. Please…I don't mean to be a pain in the butt about this. I know I am.''

''Yes,'' Maya said mildly, ''you are definitely being a pain in the butt, Akiva.'' She came around her desk and sat on the edge of it, facing the pilot. Placing her hands beside her, Maya let the tension in the room build along with the silence. Akiva's jaw was set, her full mouth a slash as she struggled to suppress her emotions. One of the many things Maya appreciated about Akiva was that she was always a straight shooter and honest about her thoughts and feelings. That was okay as a pilot. But as a commanding officer, Akiva couldn't afford to use bald, undiplomatic words with the people on her team; it would cause immediate problems for everyone.

"You know, there's a big difference between being a gunship pilot and being an officer in command of a base."

"I know that." Her mouth puckered, her arched brows knitted, Akiva flashed her a frown as Maya regarded her thoughtfully. "And I feel I can do it."

Maya had her doubts. Pilots were a fraternity; and although they faced many stresses, not to mention outright danger, Maya knew from her own experience that it was easy to be a pilot than a manager of people.

"You know, when I hatched the plan for the Black Jaguar Base ops at Fort Rucker, I was mad as hell at the army establishment, at the prejudicial way they were treating our company of women training for Apache gunship flight."

"You took your anger and did something proactive with it," Akiva agreed in a low voice. She tried to relax. Sitting back, she folded her arms against her chest and crossed her legs. "And every one of us women were with you all the way on your concept for this base."

"Yes, that made it easy for me to get on with my plans." Maya saw the defensiveness in Akiva's body. The intent expression on her oval face and the predatory look in her flashing, gold-brown eyes told Maya that Akiva wasn't really listening to her; she was still wrestling with the fact that Chief Warrant Officer Joe Calhoun was to be her second-in-command.

"If you think that putting this ops into place was easy,

Akiva, you'd be wrong. It wasn't. I had never thought of myself as a C.O. All I wanted was to be allowed to fly combat and do what I loved most. I never entertained the idea of being here in this capacity, believe me.''

Akiva looked up at Maya, her eyes flat with confusion. ''Who else did you think would do it? You created this place, this idea, out of nothing. Sure, we all helped, but you were the guide. You're the one who had the vision.''

''Vision...hmm... Yes, that's the right word to use here, Akiva.'' Maya smiled slightly. ''Among your people, the Apache, do you have vision quests? A ceremony where you don't eat or drink for three to four days, and you pray to your spirits for guidance and help to reveal the future?''

''Yes, we do.''

''And you've gone on such vision quests?''

''Growing up on the res, I did. Why?'' Akiva was becoming uncomfortable. She saw that glint in Maya's emerald eyes and sensed she was up to something. That got Akiva's attention, for her superior was a woman of immense mystical powers. Oh, everyone in the BJS—Black Jaguar Squadron—talked about Maya's secretive background. It was whispered that she was one of the elite Black Jaguar Clan, a group of mysterious and powerful spiritual warriors who kept a very low profile, yet were out there on the leading edge, fighting the darkness. Akiva believed those stories about Maya, because among her own people, the jaguar was a living spirit. At one time, in the Southwestern U.S., jaguars had roamed freely—until miners had killed them all off and made coats out of their beautiful black-and-gold skins. Often Akiva had wanted to ask Maya about her background, for the rumors about her and her healer sister, Inca, were well known at the base.

"When was the last time you were on a quest?"

Shrugging, Akiva muttered, "Five years ago, I suppose. Why?"

"Aren't vision quests about deprivation? You don't drink water. You don't eat. You starve your physical body in order to make it a receptacle so that spirit can come to you and give you a dream…a vision that will help you grow and become an even better warrior than you are now, right?"

"Yes…" Akiva eyed Maya with growing distrust. She felt her C.O. heading toward some unknown goal with this unexpected maneuver in their conversation. She knew Maya's mystical training had taken place among her people in Brazil, where she was born. Oh, Maya never talked about it, mysticism was not a common topic of conversation on the Black Jaguar Base. Daily combat missions and the interdiction of drug shipments was what their lives revolved around. So it was a big surprise that threw Akiva off balance when Maya started talking to her in an intimate, knowing tone about her own background and belief system. Native Americans had vision quests; it was one of the sacred rites they chose to undertake, sometimes on a yearly basis.

It was a time of cleansing, a time to pray for healing of any bleeding wounds within them. And it was a brutal physical test, draining participants on the physical dimension in order to leave them open for spirit to speak to them—if they were fortunate enough to have that happen. An individual could go on a vision quest for four days and receive no vision, nothing. That was about the worst thing Akiva could imagine happening.

"Where are you going with this little analogy?" she demanded huskily, watching her superior like a hawk. Akiva could feel the energy shift, change and become very solid around Maya. Akiva was not clairvoyant, but she had a kind of all-terrain radar that she called "blind faith knowing." It had saved her butt many times out on gunship missions when deadly Black Shark Kamov helicopters, flown by Russian mercenary pilots paid by drug lords, had hunted her. She could sense the Kamovs before she ever saw them. Apache helicopters couldn't pick up the radar signature on the Kamov, so all the pilots in the Black Jaguar Squadron had to more or less rely on their well-honed intuition to be able to feel the enemy out before the drug runners shot them out of the sky.

Raising one eyebrow, Maya said quietly, "I want you to consider this new mission like a vision quest, Akiva. You will go in knowing there's likely to be physical deprivation and emotional demands placed upon you that you aren't sure you can deal with adequately or appropriately. In the process, there's going to be surrender to a higher power, just like on a quest. You have a hatred of white men. You're going into this vision quest with the opportunity to transcend your wounds by trying to rise above them." Maya's eyes glittered knowingly. "You're going to have to put your people and the mission before your own personal pain. In a vision quest, you are asked to put all your personal feelings aside and concentrate on praying to the Great Spirit for guidance, support and help. This black ops mission is well beyond you in some ways, and we both know it. I'm putting my money on you—that you'll transcend the fires, become better than you are presently, and grow into the job requirements. I'm not asking you to do anything more than you would in a vision quest, where the demands are just as brutal."

Akiva stared at Maya as her huskily spoken words went straight to her hurting heart. The truth behind them reverberated through her like an earthquake, and Akiva sensed the greater stage where this conflict was being played out, in the unseen worlds that surrounded them. She *felt* the importance of Maya's words.

"Joe Calhoun symbolizes your wound because he is a man," Maya continued softly. "He didn't cause your pain or your wounding, but because he's a man, he becomes that for you, Akiva. He's innocent in all of this. I'll be having a similar meeting with him in a little while, to tell him he's been selected for the black ops mission with you. Try to see him as an individual, not as the man or men who wounded you as a child growing up."

Akiva's gold eyes flared with surprise. She'd never spoken to Maya—indeed, not to anyone—about her childhood. As she looked into her C.O.'s deep green eyes, she felt heat flow through her and touch her aching heart. Yes, she was scarred, deeply wounded by white men. But how did Maya know?

Akiva thought better of asking. Maya was a medicine woman of her clan, and one simply did not go up and baldly ask how she knew a person's mind and heart. Medicine people often knew the unknowable, for they could pierce the veils of mystery and see a person's past as well as her present and future.

Akiva shifted uncomfortably in her chair now that she knew Maya had seen her ugly, sordid past. Shame flowed through her, for she didn't want anyone to know the torment and trauma she'd suffered and endured. The gentleness in Maya's tone ripped off some of the scabs over that festering wound that consumed her heart and spirit. Akiva could better keep her defense in place against someone who yelled at her, than she could against compassion and nurturance. Her life, thus far, had not included such things, so she didn't know how to deal with them.

"Your entire life, Akiva, has been a vision quest. I know you understand this."

Wincing, Akiva jerked her gaze from Maya's face to the tiled floor beneath her booted feet. She stared, unseeing, down at her highly polished combat boots, her black uniform blousing along the tops. Gulping, she gripped the arms of the chair. Red-hot pain gripped her heart. Her breathing deepened.

Maya reached out and placed her hand on Akiva's tense shoulder. "I know from my own experience that some people volunteer for such a life, Akiva. They are strong, old spirits who have gone through many, many lifetimes in human form, becoming spiritually strong under adverse circumstances that would normally destroy a person."

Her fingers tightened on Akiva's shoulder. "Much is asked of us when we volunteer for that kind of life mission, my sister. And I do know what I'm asking of you, Akiva. What I ask goes far beyond any military orders, or even this three-dimensional world. You came into this life like I did—to fight the darkness. To bring light back to the world. We are on the front lines of this war between dark and light. We were born and bred for it. We had to have a very tough beginning in order to shape and strengthen us for what lay ahead. I *need* you for this black ops, Akiva. I need your heart, your passionate spirit, your fearlessness and your focus. I know I'm asking a lot of you."

Maya's voice lowered. "But you must see this mission as a vision quest, one that will be brutal on you emotionally and mentally in ways you've never had to deal with before. I know you can handle it. You're courageous. Your bravery often leaves me breathless.'' Maya removed her hand and stood near Akiva, who had bent over in the chair, almost in a fetal position. Maya felt the depth of her pain and closed her eyes momentarily.

''Many are called, Akiva, but few can really answer the call. You're one who can. My bet is on you...that you'll pick up the reins of this mission and give it your heart and spirit. The light burns brightly in you, and your jaguar spirit guide from your great-great-grandmother is with you at all times. Jaguar people never flinch from what is racing toward them. We stand our ground, straight and tall, and we prepare ourselves for the assault coming our way. And deep inside us, Akiva, we know without a doubt that the light—the guardians on that other side of the veil—will protect us, work with us and help us to withstand the blows we're bound to suffer.''

Akiva forced herself to straighten. She felt Maya's warm, throbbing energy surrounding her, like a mother cradling her child lovingly to her breast. The sensation was so foreign to her that it left her a bit in shock—a good kind of shock. Though she'd hunted all her life, she'd never found such protection, such love and care until just now. Lifting her head, her eyes swimming with tears, she saw Maya's softened features waver before her as she looked down at her in those moments out of time.

Speechless, Akiva could only absorb what Maya was giving her. She saw the compassion in her superior's emerald eyes, and the gentle strength that had always emanated from her now filled Akiva. She was starved for such rich and caring emotions, absorbed them hungrily as they flowed through her, touching her wounded heart. Akiva had never talked to Maya of her own spiritual beliefs, or about her jaguar spirit guide, and she was stunned by the knowledge Maya possessed about her. Yet she felt no panic, because Maya had long ago proved that she could be trusted.

Gulping, Akiva forced back her tears as Maya smiled and then quietly moved away. As she stepped back, that warm, loving sensation began to ebb and dissolve, and Akiva grieved its loss. Maya had been energetically feeding her something she had looked for desperately all her life and believed never existed. But it did. Maya had given her hope. Hope that she would not always feel like a person left out on the hill, alone without help or support. For that was what vision quests were all about—facing nature and the spirit world alone, weaponless, vulnerable and open. Akiva never left herself vulnerable, never opened herself up to anyone. And yet, with her compassionate energy, Maya had just shown her that she, too, was deserving of nurturing, of care and protection.

Swallowing against the lump in her throat, Akiva sat there for a long time in silence. Maya walked around her desk, sat down and began to look for the set of orders in the piles of paper on her desk.

"A-all right, Maya. I'll take the mission. All I can say is I'll try." She drew in a ragged breath as Maya lifted her head. For a moment, Akiva swore she saw the face of a black jaguar staring back at her with sun-gold eyes and huge ebony pupils. But as swiftly as she'd seen it, the apparition was gone. So much was occurring that Akiva couldn't quite grasp it all. Something profound had just happened to her, and she knew it had to do with jaguar medicine and healing. Akiva's own jaguar spirit had been given to her long ago. At the time, she had been told that one day she would be properly trained to know how to work with and utilize the vast, transforming power of the jaguar spirit. Right now, all Akiva received from her jaguar guardian was a keen intuition that helped her sense Kamovs. She sometimes would see apparitions, just as she'd seen the jaguar transpose over Maya's face, but that was not often. And now, somehow, whatever energy Maya had transferred to her, was giving her the courage to take the mission—Joe Calhoun and all. A white man. Her enemy.

"Joe's a good person," Maya said, finally locating the orders. She reached for her pen in the pocket on the left arm of her uniform. "Try to see him as an individual, not as one of the men who hurt you. That is the vision quest you're taking on, Akiva." Maya scribbled her signature on the orders and handed them to Akiva. "Here, take these over to logistics, will you? They need to start getting this show on the road. You're now the commanding officer of Black Jaguar Base Alpha—the first base outside the hub we've set up here in Peru. I have every faith that you'll pull off this mission successfully."

Rising, Akiva took the papers. Her heart was beating painfully in her breast. She wondered if she could grow into the job as Maya seemed to think she could. "I don't want to disappoint you," she rasped unsteadily.

"I don't want you to disappoint yourself," Maya whispered, and then gave her a crooked smile. "Learn to trust outside yourself, Akiva. Joe Calhoun is a good person. He's no two-heart."

Again Akiva winced. She'd never realized her C.O. knew so much about her people until now. Two-hearts were people who lied, cheated, manipulated or deceived others for their own selfish ends.

"I'll try to hold that thought," she said, half joking as she moved to the door and opened it. Outside, women were moving quietly up and down the hall of the second floor of H.Q., where the offices were located.

"It's not going to be easy."

Akiva lifted her head and stood proudly in the doorway, as much of her old spirit and strength infused her once again. "Nothing in my life has *ever* been easy. Why should this be any different?"

Grinning like a jaguar, Maya said, "That's the spirit. That's what I want to hear from you. Get out of here. I need you down in logistics to initiate this mission at 1030 today. Start packing."

Akiva nodded, waving the orders in her hand. "I won't let you down, Maya. I promise...."

As she turned and moved down the hallway, Akiva felt her whole reality begin to slowly disintegrate around her. How was she going to make this work? How was she going to stop herself from ripping off Calhoun's head? How was she going to stop that violent, destructive anger she held toward all men?

Chapter 2

"Major Stevenson, I feel like a fox that's been given access to the henhouse," Joe Calhoun admitted, excitement in his deep Southern drawl as he sat in front of her desk. Joe had arrived promptly at 0930, unsure why the commanding officer wanted to see him. Now he knew: he was being offered a plum assignment to Black Jaguar Base Alpha. As executive officer, no less! For a U.S. Army chief warrant officer like him, this was an unheard of gift.

Warrant officers were in that gray area of army ranks—they were no longer enlisted, but weren't full-fledged officers, either. They played an important role in the army, but were outcasts of a sort, accepted neither above nor below them. No one really appreciated what they did militarily, and yet without them, the army helicopter program would die.

Maya smiled. "You Texas boys have a language all

your own, Chief Calhoun. But I'm glad you're willing to give this black ops a whirl."

He had a tough time sitting still in the dark green metal chair. "Yes, ma'am, I sure am." Joe felt like he was in a dream. As a half-breed Comanche who'd grown up in Texas, he'd long been an outcast. Joe had had a hard-scrabble life as a child, and been the victim of jeers and taunts throughout twelve years of school, where prejudice followed him mercilessly. He felt the army was giving him a chance to prove he was better than the names he'd been called, and he worked longer and harder than any-one else, trying to prove his self-worth.

All his life he'd been told he was worthless, except by his family, who loved him. That love had given him hope to cling to when things got bad at school. Joe worked hard at never making a mistake, because to make one, in his books, was the worst thing he could imagine. It would prove he was a "dumb redskin" who was too stupid to learn. He never told anyone of his heritage—ever. Now, as he sat there hearing words he'd never thought possible, it seemed as if all his hard work was going to pay off—he was going to be X.O. of a base! That was mind-blowing to Joe. He could barely sit still because of the happiness exploding through him. Finally, someone was going to give him a chance to prove himself!

"Now...can you tell me a little of how the night ops training went between you and Chief Redtail?"

Furrowing his brows, Joe avoided the C.O.'s penetrat-ing gaze. Clearing his throat, he opened his large, square hands. "Ma'am, she caught on the quickest of all the pilots when we trained her on the night scope we wear on our helmet to see in the dark."

Smiling to herself, Maya continued to hold his candid gaze. Just as she'd thought, Joe Calhoun—who had seemed from the start to be a throwback to a kinder, gentler time when women were put on pedestals and treated like ladies—was showing his warm, amicable nature. Maya had seen Calhoun's carefully written reports on the women pilots he'd trained. Oh, he'd been specific about weaknesses and strengths in night ops activities, but nary a word had been said about possible personal problems between himself and Akiva Redtail.

"Joe," Maya said, her voice ringing with authority, "it's very important for me to get the gist of the chemistry between you and Chief Redtail. After all, she's going to be your C.O. at this new base. I have more than a passing interest in how you two might get along." Maya's mouth twisted wryly. "There's a great Texas saying I heard from one of my pilots, who was born there—'you don't drop your gun to hug a grizzly bear.'"

Maya's meaning wasn't lost on Joe. Shifting uncomfortably in the chair, he rubbed his sweaty palms on his jungle-fatigue pants. "Yes, ma'am, I'm familiar with the phrase."

"Good." Maya pinned him with her narrowed gaze. "So, does it clarify the relationship between you and Chief Redtail?"

Joe pushed his long, thick fingers through his short black hair, as he did whenever he was nervous. There was a lock that always rebelled and dipped across his brow. Nervously, he pushed it back. "Ma'am, with all due respect, I *really* admire Chief Redtail. She's the best combat pilot you've got here at Black Jaguar Base, in my opinion."

Maya heard the respect and admiration in Calhoun's soft drawl, but she also saw his struggle to remain positive. Maya knew it was important to get all the cards laid out on the table, to have all the possible problems addressed now—not later, when they were in Mexico, fighting like two cats in a dogfight. Joe's easygoing Texas style made it hard for Maya to think that even Akiva's acidic temper could rile this good ole boy. Joe had, in her assessment, the patience of Job. He was infinitely tolerant, which would well work for him in this upcoming project, as Akiva was none of those things. Maya hoped Joe could provide the necessary balance to make this operation successful.

"I'm in agreement with you, Chief Calhoun, about Akiva's skills. She's the best we've got, which is one reason we're earmarking her for this mission. The other is that in your reports on the pilots, she scored consistently highest on night-scope trials with the Apache. We are in need of two pilots, the best two, because a lot of missions are going to be at night, out over the Gulf. You know as well as I do that flying over a large expanse of water poses potential problems with pilot disorientation. And flying at night, with the scope, is twice as tricky."

Nodding, Joe saw her expression remain hard. He could feel the C.O. casting around for something, and he knew what it was. Joe just didn't want to give it to her. He didn't want to paint Akiva in a bad light. It wasn't his nature to talk negatively of people; rather, he was always upbeat and positive about their strengths, never shooting them down for what they didn't do right, or what their weaknesses were.

God knew, he had his own set of problems to work on, and he wouldn't appreciate someone disemboweling him in public. His father, who was full-blood Comanche, had taught him to speak well of a person, that if he did so, energy would come back tenfold to him as a result. It was easy to eviscerate people, to tear them apart verbally, to shame or humiliate them. Joe had found that out early in his life. And he didn't ever want what had happened to him at school, to happen to others. The stubborn part of him, which was considerable when tapped, was rising to the surface as Major Stevenson continued to stare at him.

He felt like she was looking inside him and reading his mind. Lips pursed, he waited. What did she want? Why did she want to hear that Akiva Redtail practically hated the ground he walked on? Joe had never figured out why, exactly, Akiva disliked him so openly; he had chalked it up to a clash of personalities. Given his easy-going nature, he let her venomous comments and glares slide off him like water off a duck's back, and he didn't take it personally. At least, he tried not to....

"How do you feel toward Chief Redtail?" Maya asked in a low tone.

Brightening, Joe grinned. "She's an incredible combat pilot, ma'am. I really enjoyed teaching her the upgrade on the night optics. She was a pleasure to work with." Joe was, in fact, very drawn to Akiva, but she sure didn't like him, so he kept his desire for her to himself.

"So—" Maya fiddled with the pen in her fingertips and frowned down at it "—you have no problem going on this mission with her?"

"No, ma'am, I don't."

"Not *one* problem, Chief?"

Joe shook his head. "No, ma'am. She's all guts and glory, as we say in the trade. She's already bagged a Russian Kamov. And she's aggressive. That's what it takes out there—we both know that. I'm looking forward to being her back seat, to tell you the truth. I can learn plenty from her."

Smiling thinly, Maya raised her head and stopped thumping the pen against the desk. Joe's expression was so damned easy to read. The guy hid nothing in that square face of his. His gray eyes were wide and earnest. "I don't think it's telling any stories out of school, Chief, that Akiva rides roughshod on some people." Mainly white, Anglo men, but Maya swallowed those words.

Shrugging, Joe said, "I think most combat pilots are perfectionists, ma'am, and they get sour milk real fast when things aren't right. Their lives depend upon the equipment workin' constantly and the crew doin' their job like they're supposed to do. I don't fault her on that in the least. Do you?"

Maya smiled to herself, liking Joe's ability to stress the positive. "I agree with you, Chief." Still, Akiva would wear him down, and Maya wondered how thick Joe's hide really was. How long could he handle her acidic responses to him before he reared up on his hind legs and fought back? That was the fly in the ointment on this mission. It all hinged on Joe's patient, plodding personality, his ability to get along with her, no matter what.

"Ma'am, I feel you're like a huntin' dog sniffin' around for a bone of contention or somethin' here. Are you worried about me bein' able to get along with Chief Redtail?"

"I'm not concerned about you getting along with her," Maya said drolly. "It's the other way around. Akiva has a lot of knives in her drawer, and she's real good at pullin' them out and slicing and dicing, Chief. I just don't want *you* to be chopped up by her when she gets in one of those moods, is all. And I think you know what I'm talkin' about?"

Joe's mouth curved into a friendly smile. "My daddy always said that makin' it in life is like busting mustangs, ma'am. You're gonna get thrown a lot. You gotta expect it. But the key is you get back up, dust yourself off and get right back in the saddle again."

"Well," Maya said with a chuckle, "that about says it all when it comes to interfacing with Akiva. She's got some…weaknesses, Chief Calhoun. And it's my job to make damn sure you know them going into this black ops, so you're not surprised at the other end."

"Okay," Joe said, stymied. What problems? Akiva had a strong personality, one he admired, but he never considered her penchant for thoroughness and perfectionism to be a problem. It took a strong man or woman to be a combat pilot—that was part of the required package. And he had no problem with strong, confident women. So what was the major hinting at here? Granted, Joe had been at the base only a couple of months and didn't run into Akiva every day, although he wished, on a personal level, he did. Just getting to look at her tall, proud, powerful figure and those penetrating gold eyes of hers made his heart pound with silent need. But this was a busy place, and the training was grueling and ongoing. Joe had his hands full as an instructor pilot on the night optic upgrade training missions, so rarely saw Akiva.

"We have another sayin' in Texas, Major—'Never grumble, it makes you about as welcome as a rattlesnake in camp.'"

"Hmm, I see. Well, you need to know that Chief Redtail isn't all sweetness and light. She's going to need your help and I'm going to need you to roll with a lot of punches she's more than likely to throw your way. Don't take them personally, Chief Calhoun. If the heat in the kitchen gets to be a little much, sit her down with your diplomatic, good ole boy style and talk it out. Akiva can be reasoned with."

"I'll remember that, ma'am."

"Good." Maya looked at her watch. "Let's get down to logistics. Morgan Trayhern has just arrived with his second-in-command, Mike Houston, and Akiva should be in the planning room with them about now. We need to go over the assignment."

Leaping to his feet and coming to attention, Joe said, "Yes, ma'am. I'm more than ready for this. Thank you for the opportunity. I never expected this promotion."

As Maya got to her feet and grabbed the clipboard and pen from her desk, she gave the aviator a dark look. "Keep your positive attitude, Chief. You're gonna need it where you're goin'. And I feel you've more than earned this position."

Akiva sat on one side of the planning room and leaned back in the chair, her legs crossed. In the center of the room an overhead projector sat on a table, flashing the first diagram on the white wall in front of them. Two men—both civilians, although she knew they'd both been in the military at one time—stood talking in low tones to one another next to the projector. They'd introduced themselves to her earlier. Akiva had seen them on other occasions at the base, but had never been formally introduced until now. Though she'd arrived right on time for the planned meeting, now that she was here she found her heart beating in panic. Could she really command this mission? More than anything, Akiva didn't want to disappoint Maya. That one fear gave her the resolve to try and make the mission work.

Hearing the door open, Akiva turned to see who had come in. She saw Maya move briskly into the room, clipboard in her left hand. As Chief Warrant Officer Joe Calhoun followed, Akiva's brows knitted and her pulse accelerated. Akiva wanted to hate him. He was a white man. And right now, Calhoun represented all Anglo men to her. Working her mouth, she found a bitter taste in it. Reaching for a paper cup that sat next to her folding chair, Akiva took a quick gulp of the tepid water. When she looked up, she saw Joe Calhoun standing right in front of her, his large, square hand extended.

Akiva choked on the water that was halfway down her gullet. Coming up and out of the chair, she coughed deeply, her hand pressed against her throat. *Damn!* Moving away from him, she finished coughing and turned. Wiping her mouth with the back of her hand, she met his smiling gray eyes. His hand was still extended toward her.

''I just wanted to congratulate you, Chief Redtail.'' Joe saw her gold eyes narrow with fury. Her cheeks were red with embarrassment. He saw her gaze drop to his hand and then snap back up to his eyes.

''Thanks,'' Akiva mumbled. She ignored his hand and sat back down, crossing her arms belligerently. She wished mightily that Calhoun would go sit down in one of the chairs on the other side of the room. She didn't want to be anywhere near him.

Joe tempered his disappointment as Akiva refused to shake his hand. Okay, that was fine. He introduced himself to Morgan and Mike, who gripped his hand warmly with obvious welcome. Searching around, he saw a chair nearby and reached for it. As he sat down, he noticed Morgan Trayhern, Mike Houston and Major Stevenson studying them. Feeling heat crawl up his neck and into his face, he saw the quizzical look on the two men's faces, the worry banked in Major Stevenson's eyes. Everyone had seen Akiva snub him. Embarrassed, Joe felt as if he'd done something wrong, but there was nothing he could do to rectify it.

"Okay," Maya said crisply, "let's get this mission planning on the road. Chiefs Redtail and Calhoun, I think you already know Mr. Trayhern and Mr. Houston? Good. Morgan, do you want to start this briefing?"

Morgan Trayhern shrugged out of his dark green nylon jacket and placed it on the back of one of the chairs. Dressed in a pair of jeans, hiking boots and a dark blue polo shirt, he turned and opened up a briefing file. "Mike? You want to give Chiefs Redtail and Calhoun the dope, here?" He handed two sets of information packets to him to give to the warrant officers.

Houston, who was dressed similarly, nodded. He quickly handed out the twenty-page packets on the planned mission. Joe nodded and thanked him. Akiva's belligerent look faded and she actually softened the line of her mouth as he handed the papers to her.

Morgan stood at the projector. On the wall was a map of southern Mexico. "We were able to use satellite infrared to locate this little airport facility. It's hidden deep in the jungle and is completely surrounded by old-growth trees." Flashing his laser penlight, Morgan circled what appeared to be a small pinprick in the map. "This is the exit-entrance point. Many years ago druggies cleared this thousand-foot-long dirt runway for light, fixed-wing aircraft, as well as helicopters. They were using the aircraft to haul cocaine shipments."

Akiva sat up. "You said helicopters? What kind?"

Joe glanced at her. She was now in combat mode, tense and alert, her huge gold eyes narrowed on the map in front of them. Despite her prickliness, Joe couldn't help but admire Akiva. She was six feet tall, big boned, and her womanly body was firmly muscled beneath her tight-fitting black uniform. Joe would never admit it to anyone, because it would be considered sexist by the U.S. Army today, but by damn, she was a good-lookin' woman, with curves in all the right places. She was easy on the eyes, as his fellow Texans would say.

Joe's problem was that he wanted to stare like a slobbering fool at Akiva. She commanded everyone's attention whenever she strode into a room. He liked the fact she wore the bright red scarf of her Apache heritage around her head. Her high, sharp cheekbones and large, slightly tilted eyes gave her the look of a lone wolf on the hunt. That excited him. And yet she'd rebuffed his friendly overtures at every turn. Joe figured she didn't like him at all. Though disappointed, he still absorbed her intense beauty and dynamic energy as she sat up in the chair and pointed to the map.

Mike Houston, who stood next to Morgan, responded to her question. "All civilian types, Chief Redtail. No armed military rotorcraft that we can find."

"Good," Akiva muttered defiantly, "because if we're moving in, we need to know what's out there and around us."

"The closest town, San Cristobel," Morgan said, pointing to the north of their base of operations, "is here. It's a village of about a thousand people, all farmers. The jungle begins just outside their little community. Your base is fifty miles away, so there's no chance that they'll discover you. Few farmers penetrate the jungle, so it's your fortress of protection."

Houston grinned slightly and looked at Akiva and Joe. "I wouldn't bet that people in the village don't know this airport is here, however. So you need to keep on your guard in case someone wanders in someday while hunting for medicinal herbs or whatever."

Akiva nodded and, picking up the clipboard she'd leaned against her chair, she began to make notations on the mission. She respected Mike Houston. He was part Quechua Indian. And from what she had seen of him, his blood was decidedly more Indian than Anglo, which made her trust him more than she would most white men. Though Morgan Trayhern was Anglo through and through, Akiva gave him grudging respect as well. The man owned a black ops company known as Perseus, and he'd done a lot of good for people in trouble around the world. He was one of the few white men she'd seen who was truly good-hearted.

Most Anglos were bastards, in her experience. Sending Joe Calhoun a glance as she lifted her head, Akiva found her heart pounding briefly. Why did she feel so out of sorts around him? she wondered as she watched him write down information on a notepad he held in his large hands. His profile was strong, and for some reason reminded her of the White Mountains on the Apache reservation in Arizona where she'd grown up. The res was a craggy, windswept piece of land, baked by the brutal heat of the sun in summer and freezing cold in winter. Joe's face was craggy, too, with high cheekbones, a chiseled, full mouth, and strong chin.

He was six feet tall, like her, and medium boned, with more of a swimmer's body than a weight lifter's. Most Apache helo pilots were lean and mean looking. Joe was lean and tightly muscled, but he had a kind-looking face, not the face of an aggressor. He didn't fit the normal mold of a warrior, and that stymied Akiva. And yet the army had promoted him to instructor pilot, so he must have the goods or he wouldn't have made the grade to the Apache program. The old maxim of her grandmother—never judge a book by its cover—must apply to Joe, Akiva thought.

She remembered the warmth she had seen in his gray

eyes when she'd met him that first day of training in the Boeing Apache Longbow helicopter. Normally, combat pilots had predatory eyes, reminding Akiva of an eagle in search of its next quarry.

Not so Joe Calhoun. He'd completely thrown Akiva off guard with his friendly, good ole boy smile and demeanor. He was soft-spoken and gentle with her at all times. And unlike most pilots, Joe never cussed. That was a surprise to Akiva, because cursing in the heat and stress of battle was as common as breathing among combat people. And Joe had treated her like a lady, being solicitous and sensitive to her needs as a person, rather than a faceless soldier.

It hadn't taken Akiva long to realize Joe Calhoun was a man of the past, thrown into the present. In her mind he did not fit the combat or instructor pilot mode—at all. And because she couldn't pigeonhole him, he kept her off balance. Only when Akiva could label someone was she able to react in a way that protected her from that person. With Calhoun, there was no slot to place him in, and that unsettled Akiva completely. He'd always treated her with deference and respect. In fact, the admiration in his voice during training was wonderful—but Akiva tried to throw off his praise and warmth just as quickly as he dispensed it. Anglos were not to be trusted under any circumstance.

Yet the worst part was, she was drawn to him! Few men had stirred the flames within her as Joe did. Akiva tried to ignore her quickening heartbeat each time he gave her that gentle smile. Her yearning to know what it would be like to kiss his smiling mouth really shocked her. For all Joe's gentleness, which in itself was a powerful beacon that drew Akiva, he stirred her womanly nature, too. Akiva didn't like being drawn to an Anglo.

No matter how personable Joe appeared to be, somewhere within him was the darkness all Anglo men carried. She knew it lurked within him, even if she hadn't experienced it.

She glared at him for a moment. Why did he have to be so damned different? Was it because he was from Texas? She would feel a helluva lot less jumpy if she could only figure him out. Then she'd know what tact to take with him, her well-ordered world would once again fall into place and she could relax.

"And who's the drug lord in the area?" Akiva demanded in a dark tone.

Morgan's brows knitted. He replaced the map with a color photograph of an older man with silver hair. "Javier Rios. He's the kingpin of drugs in southern Mexico. His son, Luis, is a helicopter pilot, and they have four civilian helos that Luis and his mercenary pilots use to fly. The helos have a fixed fuel range and Luis takes his helos to dirt airstrips in various areas along Mexico's Gulf Coast, to fixed-wing planes that load it on board and fly it into the U.S. So Luis's job is as a middleman on these flights."

Akiva stared at the silver-haired gentleman, who stood against a background of whitewashed stucco arches overhung with hot-pink bougainvillea. It was a beautiful villa, the red-tiled patio behind him filled with several pottery urns holding blooming flowers.

Rios's heritage was clearly Castilian, Akiva noted. He was dressed like a patron of old in a wine-colored, short-waisted jacket embroidered with gold thread, a starched white shirt, and a maroon neckerchief held by a gold-and-amethyst clasp. The man's face was wide, and Akiva was sure that in his youth he'd been extremely good-looking. Now his silver hair was neatly cut and a small mustache lined his upper lip. But his eyes made Akiva shiver; a dark brown, they reminded her of the hooded look of a deadly viper getting ready to strike at its prey. Rios's thin lips were smiling, but the smile didn't reach his eyes. It was the lethal smile of someone who knew he had ultimate power over others. A chill worked its way through Akiva, though she tried to ignore it.

"Rios is well regarded in the archeological world," Morgan noted. "He's donated millions to a number of projects over in Italy and is on the board of a number of internationally famous museums. He has a penchant for Rome and loves all things Roman.

"The villa where this photo was taken is just outside San Cristobel. There is an airport near the town, and he routinely flies in and out.

"Javier Rios is a man of old world traditions. Those who know him say he's a throwback to the days of Queen Isabella, when Columbus was searching for the New World. He's highly educated, with a doctorate in history, and he sponsors worldwide workshops on Roman antiquity. His latest project is saving a number of mosaic walls and floors found in old Roman villas in northern Italy that are being threatened by rising waters from a nearby dam."

"What a nice guy he is," Akiva growled sarcastically. "The world probably looks up to him with admiration."

Joe grinned over at her. He liked Akiva's testy humor. Most combat pilots had a black sense of humor; it served to reduce stress during tense situations they often found themselves in. "My daddy always said that if it looks like manure, smells like manure, then it probably is manure."

A sour, unwilling grin pulled at Akiva's mouth. She met Joe's smiling gray eyes, and try as she might, she couldn't stop from grinning at his comment. "I like your daddy. He's a smart dude."

Nodding, Joe felt immediate warmth, soft and velvety, slip around his heart. It was the first time Akiva had actually been spontaneous with him. Maybe being a C.O. was going to change how she related to others. That possibility made him feel good inside.

"My daddy had a sayin' for every occasion," he assured her with a chuckle. Again, Joe saw a spark of warmth in her eyes. Joy deluged him unexpectedly. What would it be like to see that look in her eyes as he kissed her? The thought had heated promise. Joe carefully tucked that desire away in his heart, for now was not the time to pursue it—or her.

Morgan grinned over at Houston. "The world might see Javier Rios as an educated man of immense wealth who supports the arts, but beneath, he's a drug dealer, pure and simple. So, Joe, I think your assessment has cut to the core here. Manure is manure—even if you dress it up and hide it under expensive clothes."

Houston rubbed his chin and studied the two pilots who would be taking the mission. "Rios is a cultured man of letters and principles. He loves bullfighting, and supports the sport financially all over Mexico. At this villa he raises bulls that will be trained for the arena, not only in Mexico, but Spain as well."

Akiva shivered. "The bastard," she whispered tightly. "Treating those poor animals like that..."

"The bulls don't have a chance," Houston agreed. "If one is a little too frisky in the bullring, they drug it to slow it down, so the matador can plunge his sword into the animal's heart."

"And Rios does the same thing," Maya told them grimly. "This dude may look nice on the outside, but he's got a murderous heart. Morgan? Show them a picture of the son, Luis. He's a piece of work, just like his daddy.''

Akiva's eyes narrowed as a picture of Luis Rios flashed up on the screen. It was a color photo of him standing next to his civilian helicopter, decked out in a leather bombardier jacket, starched red shirt, a white silk scarf and tan chinos.

''Chip off the old block, I'd say,'' Akiva growled, and she gave Maya a knowing look. Luis Rios was drop-dead handsome, with black wavy hair, wide brown eyes, a long, angular face, patrician nose with flaring nostrils and a thin, smiling mouth. In Akiva's opinion he looked every inch the spoiled only child of a superwealthy family.

''This dog'll hunt,'' Joe muttered, more to himself than anyone else as they studied the photo.

Akiva turned and frowned. ''What?''

Joe tipped his head toward her. ''Texas sayin'. It means that the son is a sniffer-outer of the first degree.'' He punched his index finger toward the photo. ''I wouldn't trust this guy at all. He's a real predator. I see it in his eyes.''

Akiva agreed. ''And he's flying a helo. Weapons or not, it still makes him dangerous.''

''And,'' Houston warned them darkly, ''he's got three other helos in his little 'squadron.' We don't have any dope on him. The last person the Drug Enforcement Agency tried to put in the Rios camp was discovered. We never found his body. So we don't know that much about Luis or his helicopters and pilots. That's something you'll be finding out as you go along. The Pentagon wants Luis's movements charted. We need to know where he goes, where he sends these choppers along Mexico's Gulf

Coast and what kind of schedule he's got worked up for them."

"So he's usin' them to haul drugs out of the jungle," Joe drawled, "and then off-loading them to fixed-wing aircraft sitting on dirt strips near the Gulf Coast on the eastern side of Mexico? He's pretty sharp for a weasel."

Grimly, Houston nodded. "Yes, he is, Joe. But a helo, if equipped for a larger fuel load, could fly into the Texas border area. And he may be doing that. You're going to try and find this out."

"A helo can dip in and out of a jungle pretty easily," Akiva said. "Just chop trees in a fifty-foot radius and damn near any rotorcraft can drop down, pick up the cocaine and lift it out."

"That's what we think," Morgan said, giving Akiva a look filled with approval. "And that's part of your mission—find the holes chopped in the jungle. That means low-level reconnaissance."

Maya stood up and went over to the two pilots. "You're going to be given one Boeing Apache Longbow gunship and a Blackhawk. You'll use the Apache for interdiction efforts. Use the Blackhawk to start mapping, snooping and finding out what you can around the southern part of Mexico. We expect you to update your maps weekly, via satellite encryption code. You can send them by Satcom to us here, at the main base. The information you begin to accrue will be sent to the Pentagon, as well. With your efforts, we'll start building a picture of Rios's drug trade in southern Mexico."

"And every time he sends a shipment over the Gulf," Morgan said, "you'll be notified by an American submarine crew that's sitting on the bottom of the Gulf, on station, that there is an unidentified flight in process.

They will alert you on a special Satcom channel and give you the coordinates so you can intercept that bogey.''

Akiva's brows raised. ''Extreme, dude.''

''I thought you'd be impressed,'' Morgan murmured with a grin.

''I didn't know the U.S. Navy was involved like that,'' Joe said, amazed.

''Yes, they are. More than you know,'' Houston said. ''The navy sub lies on the bottom for three months at a time. We've been doing this for a couple of years and have a pretty accurate picture of who, what, where and when on every drug-initiated flight. If an American submarine picks up radio traffic or Satcom info, they'll notify you.''

''Is every flight a drug flight?'' Akiva inquired.

''No,'' Morgan answered. ''There are legitimate civilian flights into and out of Mexico over the Gulf.''

''But they file flight plans with the Federal Aviation Agency,'' Joe pointed out. ''And druggies don't.''

''Exactly,'' Mike said with a smile. ''Our submarine on station has an hourly updated FAA flight plan file on every aircraft coming out or going into that area of Mexico, so that when they make a call to you, you can be pretty damned sure it's a drug flight.''

''What do we do?'' Akiva asked. ''Shoot 'em down?''

Chuckling, Morgan shook his head. ''I wish, but no. First, you're going to follow the same operating procedure you do here—you must identify the aircraft or rotorcraft by the numbers on the fuselage. Your Apache has been downloaded with all the fixed-wing aircraft numbers for Mexico, the U.S.A. and nearby Central and South American countries. If none of them match, then you can assume it's a drug flight.''

''At that point,'' Houston said, removing the picture

of Luis Rios and putting in another photo that showed a single-engine aircraft dropping a load of what looked like plastic bags into the ocean hundreds of feet below, "you are going to scare the hell out of them and make them do one of a couple of things. First, most drug runners don't want to fight. They'll drop their drug shipment in the water and make a run back to Mexico if pressed. If that happens, a Coast Guard cruiser in the area will steam toward that area and pick up the evidence, if it hasn't sunk to the bottom by that time. Secondly, if the plane won't drop its drugs, then it's your responsibility to persuade it to turn back toward Mexico. Do *not* allow that plane to hightail it across the Gulf toward U.S. waters."

"And what do you specify as 'persuasion,' Mr. Houston?" Akiva stared at him.

"Your Apache is equipped with hellfire missiles, rockets and cannon fire. You persuade them to turn by firing in front of their nose."

"Under no circumstance are you to shoot them down," Maya warned. "Same SOP as we practice here, Akiva."

"And if they fire back at us?"

Maya grinned. "Well, then, the game plan changes. If you're fired upon, you are authorized to fire back."

"Good," Joe said with pleasure. "Just the kind of job I've always wanted—defensive countermeasures."

"I hope to hell they fire back."

Joe gave Akiva a knowing look. There was satisfaction in her husky voice when she spoke. He saw the predator's glint in her eyes and knew it well. She was a hunter of the first order, and he found himself more than a little excited at the chance to be in her back seat on these missions. With her three years of combat experience, she could teach him a lot. She was a master at combat tactics.

"That might happen once or twice," Morgan warned, "but they'll get the message real quick and *not* fire. There are no parachutes in those civilian planes, and Rios won't want to lose them and his pilots like that. No, they'll learn real fast not to fire on you."

"What we have to be careful of is Rios finding our base," Joe said. "Once he sees us interdicting his shipments and turnin' them back, he's gonna be one pissed-off dude."

"Yes," Maya warned, "Rios is a man of action. In all likelihood, he'll send his son, Luis, to do the dirty work. And with four helos, they can do a helluva job trying to locate your base. One thing in our favor is that they are civilian helos and don't have the equipment or instruments to easily follow or find you. From the air, your base will be tough to find, which is why we chose it. There is an opening in the trees, but it's about half a mile from your actual base, and you'll have to fly low, under the canopy, to get in and out. Even if Luis spots that hole, all he'll see from above is more jungle, not the base itself."

"But," Akiva said, "if it was an old drug-runner's base, why wouldn't he know about it?"

"Luis can't know everything," Mike said. "There are dirt airstrips all over southern Mexico, hundreds of 'em. Finding your base will be like trying to find the needle in the haystack."

"Still," Morgan cautioned, "you are going to have to stay alert. If Luis ever does find you, he'll come in and kill everyone."

"Worse," Akiva said, "he'll get his hands on the Apache. That could be disastrous."

"Right," Maya said. "So most of your flying is going to take place at night. Both helos are painted black, without insignias of any type. With the Blackhawk, you'll perform daylight combat missions. Combat with the Apache will be night activity only. You fly when the drug runners fly—in the dead of night.

"You don't want to fly near San Cristobel. You'll want to stay out of sight as much as possible. I've worked up a number of vectors that you will fly to and from your secret base, so that no one can get a fix on you and follow you home." Maya handed them each a manual. "Study it. Your lives, and the lives of your ground crew, depend upon it."

Akiva settled the manual in her lap. She felt the thrum of excitement, like a mighty ceremonial drum of her people, beating within her. The more she heard of this mission, the more she knew she was exactly fitted for it. She was the eagle stooping to dive, a sky predator, and with her flawless steed, an Apache Longbow, she knew she could wreak hell on earth in Javier Rios's neighborhood. She salivated at the opportunity. The only glitch in this mission was Joe Calhoun.

Risking a quick glance in the pilot's direction, she noticed that he sat relaxed and at ease in his chair. She saw no predatory excitement in his face or his eyes. He wasn't the kind of combat pilot Akiva wanted. No, she'd rather have had Wild Woman or Dallas or Snake; any of those women had the killer instincts that Akiva herself had honed to such a fine degree. And in their business, they stayed alive because of that steely combat readiness.

Joe Calhoun was an enigma to Akiva. He just couldn't be labeled, didn't easily fit anywhere in her world as she knew it. And yet he was going to be her back seat, the person she had to rely on to keep her safe on these missions. How was she going to trust an Anglo who looked more like he ought to be flying a cargo helicopter than a combat gunship?

Chapter 3

Joe felt like he'd stepped into a hill where rattlers lived, as far as Akiva was concerned. He'd seen the flash of irritation in her eyes when, after the two-hour briefing, Major Stevenson had ordered them to Akiva's office to work out the details of the base operation. Primarily, they were to choose the personnel who would be going with them, three enlisted people who would provide support for them in all respects.

As he followed Akiva into her tiny office on the second floor of the H.Q., he realized it was the first time he'd been in it.

"Close the door," she told him as she pushed several flight reports aside on her green metal desk, dropped her new manuals there and sat down. "Sit over there," she said, pointing to a green metal chair in the corner that had at least a dozen files stacked on it.

Closing the door quietly, Joe walked over to the chair, picked up the files and set them on the floor. He moved the chair to the opposite side of the desk from where she was sitting. Joe sensed her brittleness and distrust toward him. He could tell by her abruptness that she was stressed. But more than anything, he wanted this liaison to work between them.

Joe had to keep himself from staring at her. Akiva could have been a model in some chic Paris show, wearing designer clothes. Her face was angular and classic, with high cheekbones, wide intelligent eyes and a soft, full mouth.

Giving her a lopsided smile, he sat down and said, "You've been here at Black Jaguar Base for three years. I'm sure you've got some ideas of the personnel you'd like to have come with us?" Even as he asked the question, Joe wondered why he'd been chosen to be Akiva's X.O. She wasn't easy to work with—except in the cockpit, where she was all business.

He saw her gold eyes narrow speculatively on him. "Yes, I do have a list of people I want." Her nostrils flared as she waited for his reaction.

Joe sat there relaxed, his hands clasped on the desk in front of him. He was darkly tanned, the color emphasizing his large gray eyes. A lock of ebony hair dipped rebelliously across his wrinkled brow. She wished she could ignore him, but she'd promised Maya to try and make this work. "I'm new at this," she muttered defiantly.

"What? Being a C.O. instead of a pilot taking orders?"

She ignored his teasing demeanor. "Yes." The word came out like a trap snapping shut.

"When Major Stevenson told me I was going to be X.O., I wondered if I had the right stuff to do it." Opening his hands, Joe sat back and said, "It's one thing to be a pilot. Someone's always giving you orders and setting the tasks up for you. It's another to be figuring out the tasks and handin' them out.'' He gave her an understanding smile.

Joe had long dealt with his own fear of not living up to his assignments. He supposed that had had to do with his childhood. None of his peers had ever expected much of a half-breed. To this day, he lived in terror of someone finding out he'd made a mistake and marking it down in his military personnel jacket, where it would be counted against him later on.

Akiva grabbed a piece of paper and frowned down at it. Joe had a lot less pride than she did. She wasn't about to admit to him her reservations about being a C.O. His sincere humility was a powerful draw to her. He wasn't one of those testosterone-filled studs who snorted and stomped around, beating their chests and proclaiming they were the best pilots or leaders in the world. ''You were chosen because of your night optic background.''

The words were like an insult being hurled at him, but Joe allowed it to slide off him. ''You sit tall in the saddle,'' he drawled. When he saw her head snap up, and she gave him a confused look, he grinned a little. ''Another Texas saying. I guess now that we're gonna be workin' close, you'll get a gutful of 'em. It means that you're the right person to be chosen to head up this mission. It's a compliment.''

Why couldn't he be just as nasty and snarling as she was toward him? It would make Akiva's life a helluva lot easier. Anger, prejudice and hatred were things she knew how to battle. His laid-back nature in the face of her prickliness made her panicky inside.

Maya's advice about Akiva's need to leave her prejudice behind in order to make the transition to a C.O.

droned in her head. Damn, forgetting her past hurts was going to be the hardest thing in the world. As she searched Joe's friendly gray eyes and dropped her gaze to his full, mobile mouth, Akiva decided he must have led a rich and spoiled existence. No, he hadn't had life hurled at him like she had. Would he be able to handle this mission as her X.O.?

Wrestling with her anger and anxiety, she choked out, "Thanks…I think…for the compliment."

"You rode horses growin' up, didn't you?" Joe decided that maybe the best tact with Akiva was to get to know her on a more personal level. If he could disarm her prickly nature, it would serve all of them.

"Yes, I did." She scribbled some words at the top of the paper, trying to ignore his gaze.

"My daddy drives an eighteen-wheeler, a big rig, for a living. When I was a tadpole, he said I needed a horse. I remember he bought me this old fifteen-year-old quarter horse called Poncho. The horse had arthritis bad in the knees, but I was five years old and thought I'd died and gone to hog heaven."

Akiva's hand poised over the paper. Whether she liked to admit it or not, she enjoyed Joe's stories; she had since she'd first begun training with him. Even in the cockpit, while he was teaching the upgrade features of the optic night scope to her, he'd told her stories. They always served to relax her, and even now she could feel the tightness in her neck and shoulders beginning to dissolve at the sound of his soft Southern voice.

"Now, old Poncho, as my daddy called 'em, was an old ropin' horse of some repute. But for me, well, I was a greenhorn five-year-old who'd never thrown a leg over a horse before. Every self-respectin' Texan learns how to ride. Texas is a proud state with a long tradition of cowboys and cattle. My daddy was bound and determined to initiate me into Texas ways.'' Joe saw interest flicker in Akiva's shadowed eyes as she stared across the desk at him. She'd stopped writing to listen. Somehow, his storytelling was a connection with her that was good and healthy. It made his heart swell with unexpected happiness. Still, he knew Akiva would probably take that war ax she wore on her belt to his skull if he even breathed the possibility that he was drawn to her, man to woman.

''Apaches rode horses until they died under them,'' Akiva said. ''My great-great-grandmother rode with Geronimo and was one of his best warriors. I remember stories about her passed down through the women in our family. Apaches have endurance, Chief Calhoun. They would ride up to fifty miles a day, escaping the cavalry. Most of the time there were no horses around. If they found any, they'd steal them and ride them into exhaustion, then get off and keep trotting on foot in order to stay free of the white men chasing them.''

''Impressive,'' Joe murmured, leaning forward. He saw the pride reflected in her aloof face, in the way she held her chin at an arrogant angle. ''I don't know that much about your people, but I'd like to learn.'' And he would, only for other reasons—personal ones. Again he saw her eyes grow more golden for a moment. He was learning by reading her body language what impacted her positively. She was a woman who held her cards close to her chest, giving little away of how she might be feeling inside. Of course, Joe understood why. A combat helicopter pilot couldn't be hanging her emotional laundry out to dry in the middle of a dangerous flight mission.

''I come from very tough stock.'' Akiva said, then scowled and jabbed her finger at the paper in front of her. ''We need to get to work here, Chief.''

"Could you call me Joe when we're alone? I don't usually stand on protocol unless I need to."

Her mouth tightened. They were both the same rank. His request wasn't out of line. "Yeah...I guess..."

He was pushing her and he knew it. There was anger in her eyes now, and her mouth was a tight line, holding in a lot of unspoken words he was sure she wanted to fire off at him. "Thanks," he said genially, but with a serious look on his face.

Exhaling loudly, Akiva muttered, "These are the women I want coming with us," and she turned the paper around and shoved it in Joe's direction.

As he slowly read down through the list, Akiva sat stiffly, as if expecting him to fight her on the choices. Yet even as she did so, she realized there was nothing to dislike about the warrant officer; indeed, of the three men who had been assigned to their squadron to train the pilots on the Apache Longbow gunship, Akiva had felt most at ease around Joe.

"This is a mighty good list of people," he murmured, giving her an approving smile. "I've only been here a couple of months, but I'm familiar with all of them."

"Then...you approve?"

"Build the coop before you buy the chickens."

Akiva stared. And then she got it. A half smile threaded across her mouth as she took back the list of people she'd handed him. "It's a good thing I'm a country girl or I wouldn't have a clue as to your country sayings, Chief—er, I mean, Joe...." It disturbed Akiva to say his first name, made her feel too familiar with the kind of man she didn't want to be familiar with.

Akiva saw Joe's eyes lighten considerably as she tried to be somewhat pleasant—which wasn't her forte, certainly. Maya would be proud of her, she realized.

"I knew you were a country girl," he said. "I've seen you down at the mining side of this place, workin' in the garden with Jake Travers and his wife, Ana, whenever you get a chance. Only that kind of woman would be down on her hands and knees, fingers in the warm, black soil. Not a citified type."

"You don't miss much, do you?" The words came out sharp and nasty. Akiva mentally chastised herself. Maya never used such a voice or harsh words with anyone. Akiva had to struggle to learn how to be more like her, since she was a C.O. now and not just a pilot in the squadron.

With an easy, one-shoulder shrug, Joe said, "I like to think I keep my ear to the ground and my eyes peeled." He saw the confused expression in Akiva's face. She really didn't know what to do with him or how to respond to him. That was okay; at least she wasn't spitting bullets at him—yet. Somehow, he had to find the key to Akiva, a way to turn off the venom and nastiness and reach her as a human being.

Without a doubt, Joe knew she had a big heart, because he'd seen it in some situations. Like when she was with the children of the villages that lay around the base of the mountain where their operation was hidden. Akiva would hike down to the villages at least once a week to help the Angel of Death—aka their paramedic, Sergeant Angel Paredes—make her rounds to help the people. The villages were in the middle of the Peruvian jungle, and there was no medical help, no clinic or hospitals, available if someone fell sick. Joe had once gone with Sergeant Paredes, not knowing that Akiva would be joining them. Akiva almost didn't go because he'd tagged along, but he'd cajoled her into staying. He was glad he did, because he got to see the positive, healthy side of Akiva on that day.

She loved kids, big or small. When he had stood back, out of sight, he'd seen her open up to them in a way he'd never seen her do with the squadron. Joe had never seen Akiva smile, joke, gently tease or extend herself as she did with the many children who'd surrounded her the moment they walked into each village. She had hard candy in bright, colorful wrappers in her pockets, and she would hand a piece to each begging child.

Later, Joe had seen her hold babies and children whom Paredes had to work with medically. How gentle and tender Akiva had been with those little ones. Joe had mentally photographed that day into his heart. He was glad he'd seen Akiva let down her armored barriers; it served to remind him that beneath that warrior's facade was a vulnerable woman of immense ability to reach out and love others. And it also told him that her toughness was a protection. He had held back a lot of personal questions he wanted to ask her about her growing up years. Based upon his own struggles as a kid, he knew that events, good or bad, shaped each person during the formative years. His instincts told him that Akiva had had a hellacious childhood, probably one that would have shattered another child. He figured it was her tough Apache blood that had helped her to survive it.

"What are we going to do about medical emergencies?" Joe wondered aloud. He held her stare. "You got any ideas about that?"

"No...I haven't even thought about that...." she admitted. Akiva was proud of Joe for remembering such an important detail. At least he was thinking for the good of all, which Akiva knew wasn't typical of a white male.

"Do you want me to talk to the doc at the medical facility?" he offered.

"Yes, why don't you? We have Sergeant Paredes, but she's the only paramedic here. I don't think Major Stevenson wants to give her up to us."

Joe nodded. "Yeah, I understand why she wouldn't. If a crew member on one of the Apaches gets wounded, Paredes needs to be here to help the doctor do what she can for them."

Akiva sat back and felt herself relax. It had to be due to Joe's quiet demeanor, she decided. Of all the white men she'd ever met, he somehow helped her to let go of most of her protective armor. But Akiva would never let all that armor dissolve. Not ever. White men hurt women; it was that simple. "See what you can find out."

Nodding, Joe said, "Yes, I will, and then I'll let you know what the doc suggests."

"I hate the idea of being out there in the middle of that jungle with no medical resources. Any of us could get hurt. One of the ground crew could get sick.... This is something we need to plan an SOP for."

Joe raised his brows and gave her a hopeful look. "How about if I do the legwork on this problem? Can you trust me to come up with a game plan?" He knew from working with Akiva before that she did not trust him. Trust was something she didn't hand to a man under any circumstances, Joe knew. He watched her wrestle with his request. A good C.O. knew how to delegate. Would she allow him to tackle this one, small element without her micromanaging it?

"Yeah...okay. Do it. I've got my hands full with other stuff right now." Akiva felt a ribbon of heat flow through her when she saw his mouth pull into a smile. She didn't want to feel good because he smiled, but she did.

"What's the ETA—estimated time of arrival—on leaving for Alpha?"

"One week, if we get our stuff together on this."

"Good, I can hardly wait." He rubbed his hands together in anticipation.

Alpha Base was a terrible disappointment to Akiva. She'd flown the Apache Longbow down into the hole in the canopy, skimmed among the towering trees and landed on the overgrown, dirt airstrip near several buildings built out of corrugated tin and poles strung together haphazardly with nails and wire. Sergeant Mandy Cooper, the crew chief for the ground personnel, had flown the back seat with her.

Joe had flown the Blackhawk helicopter, setting it down two rotor lengths away from the Apache. The rest of the base personnel had flown in with him, along with a lot of supplies. He'd joined Akiva as they walked to their new home.

"Not much to it, is there?" Akiva said as she strode across the long, tangled grass, which grasped at her booted feet.

Joe eyed the main building, a hangar. "Bubble gum, paper clips and a lotta prayers, from the looks of it." He purposely walked at Akiva's speed, which was a fast stride. Today she wore that war ax on the belt around her waist, along with a leather scabbard on the other hip that contained a very old bowie knife. From Joe's understanding, Maya had allowed her to wear the weapons that had been passed down through her warrior family. Like him, Akiva wore a side arm in a black leather holster, along with a flak vest, known as a chicken plate, on the upper part of her body. As they crossed the grassy strip, he shrugged out of his own chicken plate and held it in his left hand as he surveyed their surroundings.

There were four buildings, the hangar being the largest. It could easily house both helos, effectively hiding them from prying eyes in the sky. The week before they'd flown to their new home, the Blackhawk had been the workhorse, bringing all the equipment and food that the crew would need to set up housekeeping.

Joe saw the three enlisted women hurrying to catch up with them. The looks of excitement and curiosity on their faces as they trotted across the thick green grass in their camouflage uniforms mirrored how he felt inside. As he glanced at Akiva's profile, he saw the same look on her face, too.

"I'm feelin' like a kid in a candy store," he said with a laugh.

Giving him a sidelong glance, Akiva tried not to allow Joe's laughter to affect her. But it did, in a good way. "We need to split up, take inventory, and then get back together later, wherever my office is going to be. We need to assess what's missing or what has to be done next." Akiva had been told they had a week to come online, ready to start interdiction missions. That wasn't long.

Nodding, Joe erased his smile and closeted his thrill over the assignment. Akiva was all business. He could see the cloak of command settling over her proud shoulders. It wasn't an easy cape to wear, he was discovering, even as X.O. His own job would be to handle the day-to-day workings of the three-woman crew, plus the scheduling of flights. As he saw it, he was to leave Akiva free to do planning and strategy for the missions. More than anything, he didn't want to be one more thing she needed to worry about. The past week, he'd seen the awareness in her eyes of just how much responsibility she was charged with on this mission. In one way, it was good, because that didn't leave her much time or energy to snap and snarl at him. She was too busy with planning.

Approaching the hangar, which was just three walls and a roof of corrugated tin, Joe stopped and looked at it more critically.

Akiva moved onto the hard-packed dirt floor of the building. Spotting several doors on one side, she went over and opened them. *Good.* Behind each, she found a small office. Each held a green, military-issue desk, paper, pens and the necessary things to make paperwork flow. The other crew members would each have an office to work from as well. She left Joe to look around, and continued her inspection of the new base by heading through another door into an alley between the hangar and the next largest building. It would serve as living quarters, mess hall and offices for the three enlisted women, Akiva realized. The sleeping quarters weren't much to rave about, she discovered as she opened a recently erected door in a plywood wall. There were three metal cots with green army blankets and a pillow on each, and that was it. A shower had been built at one end. *Spartan* was the word that came to mind. She noted her and Joe's quarters were at the front, a plyboard cubicle for each.

Moving out of that building, Akiva keyed her hearing to the excited voices of her crew. They were laughing, oohing and ahhing over the facilities. She felt a little of their excitement, but her mind was humming along, assessing, judging and planning. As she left the second building for the smaller one, across the alleyway, she laughed at herself. Maybe Maya was right; maybe she really did have what it took to lead a squadron. Her focus was on keeping her personnel safe, dry and fed.

In the third building, she found all their radio and satellite communications equipment, plus several computers, maps and boards on which to do planning for missions. This was where she would be spending much of her time. Stepping outside the rickety building again, Akiva spotted their electric generator. It had been put into a fairly well-built wooden structure that had a lot of padding to prevent the noise from being heard. An opening for the exhaust had been cut into the top of it. The gasoline needed to run it was in another tank near the edge of the jungle, which was slowly encroaching on the old airport facility. The tank had been painted camouflage colors so it blended in with their surroundings.

Turning, Akiva saw another, much larger storage tank, which held the fuel for the helicopters. Once a week, a Blackhawk would fly in with fuel bladders and refill it so they could keep flying their missions. That helicopter would come from a secret CIA base to the north of them. The CIA would become their main supplier for anything they needed to keep Alpha Base going.

"I'm happy as an armadillo diggin' for grub worms."

Akiva turned and couldn't help but grin. Joe ambled around the corner, his hands in the pockets of his camouflage pants, a pleased look on his face.

"Armadillos?"

"Yeah, those critters that live in Texas and are worse than prairie dogs, leavin' holes all around so folks can stumble into 'em and break a leg. And they're always diggin' for worms and grubs, their favorite dessert."

Joe halted about six feet from Akiva. She was happy; he could see it in the sunlight gold dancing in her eyes as she met and held his gaze. Her hands rested on her wide hips and she had long ago gotten rid of the uncomfortable chicken plate vest. In the black, body-fitting uniform, her womanly curves and stature were obvious. She was a woman of substance, of pride, strength and confidence. Best of all, her full mouth was no longer pursed like it usually was, he noted.

"You like our new home, then." Akiva turned, tearing her gaze from Joe's smiling face. The man's positive outlook on life was diametrically opposed to hers. He was always smiling and joking. She never did either.

"Shore 'nuff," he murmured. "I've got Sergeant Cooper whippin' the women into order over at that second building. I told her to set up housekeeping and unpack their duffel bags."

"Good." Akiva continued studying the way the jungle was hugging the base. She tried to stop her heart from opening up to Joe's sunny presence. Trying to avoid looking up again at his well-shaped mouth, Akiva wondered what it would be like to kiss him. Would Joe be as gentle as he seemed? Or hurtful like every other Anglo man she'd had the sorry misfortune to tangle with? Forcing her mind back to the present, Akiva was unhappy that she was evaluating Joe on such an intensely personal level.

Joe moved to where Akiva was standing with her back to him. He was getting used to how she tried to ignore him. Her thick black hair had been woven into one large braid, tied off with a piece of red yarn and then coiled at the back of her long neck so that it fit beneath her helmet when she flew. Now, as he approached her, she took out the pins holding her braid in place and let it roll down her long, strong spine. The urge to reach out and touch that frayed, silky rope was almost his undoing. He forced his hand to remain in his pants pocket, knowing she'd probably deck him if he tried to touch her. Frustrated, Joe wondered what made her so defensive.

"This is a good place, strategically speaking," he confided to her in a low voice. "The jungle is close enough to really hide us."

"Yes..." Akiva moved away from him. She didn't like Joe's intimacy with her. Giving him a hard look that said *Back off,* she announced, "I'll be in the tack and strat building," and she pointed behind them. "Ask Spec—Specialist—Bradford to get over here and get the computers and communications online."

Joe nodded. "Right away." He turned and headed back toward the hangar. Once again Akiva was all business. But the panicked look in her eyes told him she didn't want him getting that close to her in future. As he made his way with long, easy strides through the tangle of grass, Joe sighed inwardly. What was it about him that Akiva hated so much? She rarely tried to hide the fact she couldn't stand being in the same room with him.

As he stepped into the hangar to hunt down Iris Bradford, their radio communications specialist, Joe tried to stop the ache he felt in his chest. More than anything, he wanted others to like him, to think well of him. He wanted to make up for his youth, spent as an outcast because he had Comanche blood flowing through his veins. He felt a driving need to always look good to his superiors. As a result, he was a hard charger from a career point of view. He saw this X.O. opportunity as a possible gateway to becoming an officer in the U.S. Army someday soon, not just a warrant officer. However, his career was now in Akiva's hands. If she put a bad report in his personnel jacket, she could torpedo his career goals in a heartbeat.

And why? What was wrong with him? he wondered

as he poked his head into the first office, where he found blond-haired, blue-eyed Iris Bradford. She was twenty-three years old and a computer geek from the get-go. Five foot three inches tall, she was slightly chunky, big-boned and, he had learned, of Swedish background. She brightened when she saw him enter the office.

"Sir, I'm looking for the comms. You seen them?"

Joe nodded. "They're over in the last building, Bradford. Why don't you hightail it over there and get that stuff hummin'? Chief Redtail's over there, too."

Flushing with excitement, Iris said, "Yes, sir! This is *so* cool! I love this place! I'm so glad I was asked to be a part of the team." She flashed him a toothy smile, moved past him and then trotted out of the hangar toward the last building in the row.

Joe smiled and looked around the office. He saw a laptop computer on the desk, a printer, a telephone and a small gold plate on the front of the desk that said C.O. This was Akiva's office. Figuring his must be nearby, he left the office and closed the door. The next office over was indeed his. Standing there in front of his desk, where the small gold plate saying X.O. sat, he got chills. Excitement thrummed through him. Finally, the army was giving him a chance to show what he could do. Now his only problem was Akiva.

Chapter 4

Joe wondered where Akiva was. It was 2330, nearly midnight, of their first full day at Alpha. Everyone was in bed in the second building, each in her own plywood cubical containing a cot and metal locker. The C.O. and X.O. cubes were at the front, on either side of the aisle, the enlisted people's to the rear. The light had been doused a long time ago and thin filaments of moonlight threaded through the windows, which were covered with years of grime. As he walked quietly down the aisle toward the door, Joe mentally put cleaning the windows on his to-do list. Just because Navy Seabees had come in here and built them rough living quarters didn't mean the place was livable. From a cleanliness perspective it was a disaster.

Exhaustion pulled at him. Stuffing his hands into the pockets of his camouflage jacket, he headed out the door. Overhead, foglike clouds were gathering, due to the high humidity. The scream of monkeys and the hooting of owls drifted out of the darkened jungle as he walked across the flattened grass between the living quarters and the communications building. He had a hunch Akiva was still over there in the planning room, working out the myriad details of their upcoming flights, which would start as soon as they could get organized at the base.

Opening the rickety door as quietly as he could, he entered and stood just inside it. The Seabees had divided the room into three sections—the comms center, a meeting space where flight planning could be held, and a small cubicle with a desk in it. There were no doors on the partitioned-off areas, and he saw dim light flooding out of the smallest cube.

He moved to the office, stood in the doorway and felt his heart wrench. Akiva was sleeping over the flight maps, one arm beneath her cheek, the other spread across the table, a pencil hanging limply in her long, thin fingers. At some point she'd unraveled her braid, and her hair cloaked her shoulders like an ebony coverlet, the reddish highlights glowing in the light of the fluorescent lamp on the plywood table that served as a desk.

Hungrily his gaze swung back to her face. In sleep, Akiva looked incredibly vulnerable and beautiful. Joe was sure she had no idea how attractive she was to men. Although she never wore makeup, just the chiseled, patrician quality of her features would make any man look at her twice. Her full lips were soft now, and parted in sleep. Black strands of hair flowed down her temple, covering her ear and curving along her clean jawline. The bright red cotton scarf she wore across her brow highlighted her copper skin and black hair, presenting a dramatic picture.

Whether he wanted to or not, he needed to wake her up. Akiva had to get her sleep in order to keep going, and napping like this wasn't very restful. Gingerly, Joe slid his hand along her proud shoulder, the black uniform felt smooth beneath his fingers.

"Akiva?" he whispered. He squeezed her shoulder gently.

Akiva's brows moved slightly. Her mouth closed and then opened.

Heart speeding up, Joe found himself mesmerized by her soft, lush-looking mouth. What would it be like to lean down and caress those lips with his own? The thought was like a lightning bolt of fire and heat coursing through him and settling hotly in his lower body. Grinning to himself, Joe knew if Akiva had read his thoughts, she'd deck him. Rightfully so. Again he squeezed her shoulder, and deepened his voice.

"Akiva? Come on, time to wake up. You've got to get some good shut-eye, gal." The endearment slipped from his lips before he could stop it. Consarnit! Joe knew Akiva wouldn't take kindly to such familiarity. Had she heard him?

Groaning, Akiva heard a male voice somewhere in the folds of her fuzzy awareness. She also felt a hand—a man's hand—on her shoulder. Ordinarily, she wanted no one to touch her, for as an Apache woman, her body was sacred and not privy to idle touch by anyone without her permission. In her sluggish sleep state, however, her protective walls were no longer in place. The low, husky tone of the man's voice seemed like a warm stream flowing into the cold winter of her heart. He'd called her "gal," in a deep, intimate, caressing tone. The sensation was delicious—and surprising. Akiva had never felt such warmth flowing through her and she wanted badly to languish in the feeling. The man's touch was nurturing. Akiva had never experienced that with any man.

Again she heard her name called. This time she snapped awake out of habit. Sitting up, she blinked.

Joe released her shoulder and stepped back, knowing full well that Akiva would not like him touching her. Her eyes were slightly puffy with sleep, and half-open, with a drowsy look in their gold depths. Her black hair slid around her shoulders like a soft, silky shawl, and he ached to reach out and touch those vibrant strands to see what they felt like between his fingertips.

"What? What's wrong?"

"Whoa, nothing's wrong," Joe said, holding up his hands as she swung around. He could see the sleep leave her abruptly. Her eyes were narrowed and alert now, the gold depths penetrating. Inwardly he longed for the woman who had seemed so innocent and approachable while she slept. That woman was now hidden away once again beneath Akiva's massive armor plating.

Blinking rapidly, Akiva stared at Joe, who stood relaxed before her. His head was cocked to one side, his gray eyes hooded, with a look in them Akiva could not decipher. One corner of his mouth hitched upward.

She sat back in the creaky chair. "Everything okay?" she croaked, then cleared her throat. She tried desperately to shove the sleep away from her in order to think clearly.

"Everything's fine, Akiva. I just found you over here. I'm hitting the rack. I think you should, too." Joe gestured toward the table with maps spread across it. "This is no place to sleep. We need good, restful sleep. Come on, let's go."

Ordinarily, Akiva would have fought him. But Joe's voice was low and coaxing, like a hand caressing her in a very gentle and nonthreatening way. He was right: she needed a good night's sleep.

"Yeah, okay... Thanks..." She rose to her feet and rubbed her face tiredly.

Joe stepped aside and said, "I'll have Spec Dean wake us at 0600."

Feeling vulnerable because she was still wrapped in the last remnants of sleep, Akiva nodded. She watched Joe give her a slight smile, turn and leave. For a moment, as she stood there in the silent room, she missed his quiet strength and gentleness. Shaking her head, Akiva sternly told herself he was an Anglo and few of them ever had such attributes. Yet as she stood there alone, she realized that she hungered for Joe's nurturing nature, now that he was gone. Never had she felt such a driving urgency. At a loss to explain it, she sighed in frustration. How could she be so drawn to Joe? He was Anglo. Her enemy.

Turning, Akiva switched off the light, not wanting to waste electricity. Stumbling from the darkened room, she let her eyes adjust before walking to the door. The moonlight was like thin, diluted milk as it filtered through the glass panes of the grimy windows. As she sighed and rubbed her eyes, Akiva knew she had to get some decent sleep. Being a C.O. was hard work. Much harder than she'd ever anticipated. And tomorrow was another day with Joe...a man she did not want to work with or be around. Yet one she was beginning to need with the hunger of a lone wolf wanting a mate. It was a terrible cosmic joke—on her.

"Well," Joe said as he knocked lightly on the planning room door, a cup of coffee in hand, "what do you think?" It was late afternoon and Akiva was sitting at the planning table, several flight maps spread out in front of her. She was in her usual uniform, the bright red headband in place, her hair black and straight around her shoulders. Joe was glad she wore her hair down; it made her look incredibly beautiful.

Akiva turned. Her eyes narrowed. Joe was in his black flight uniform and was holding out a cup of coffee toward her.

"Dean got the coffeemaker going?" she asked, hope in her voice.

"Yeah. How about that? Would you like some?"

Akiva wanted coffee. But she didn't want to accept it from him. She saw the hope burning in his eyes. All day, in small, subtle ways, Joe had tried to be helpful, and yet stay out of her way. He wasn't dumb; he knew she really didn't want him around. Akiva eyed the coffee, wanting it desperately. But if she took it, Joe would think it was a sign of peace between them, and that's not how she felt.

"No...thanks. You go ahead and drink it." Again, that sense of incredible nurturing cloaked her. It was from Joe, Akiva realized, without a doubt. Her heart dropped with anguish. She desperately wanted that warmth from him, but wavered when she remembered her past experiences. She was torn, knowing that if she reached out for that warmth she craved, she'd be reaching out for him. Akiva could not have what he offered without accepting Joe's presence in her life. The realization was paralyzing to her. It filled her with a fear she could not sneer at, run from or face. At least not yet.

Joe shrugged and sipped the coffee. "Dean makes a mean cup of java."

"Smells good," Akiva admitted hoarsely. She turned her back on him and looked at the maps. Hearing him come closer, she tried to tell herself to stop soaking up his presence like a thirsty sponge. Was she so hungry for intimacy? So empty that even the remotest human warmth touched some dark, frightened part of her and made her feel almost out of control? Akiva had never experienced the overwhelming emotions she experienced now. It was as if Joe was creating a tidal wave of powerful, surging need in her—need that only he could fulfill. How was that possible? Akiva had always felt herself impervious to men and whatever crumbs they offered. Joe, however, was offering such a rich banquet, vital and nurturing energy that she wondered how she was going to stop herself from reaching out and consuming it like a starving wolf.

"How is the planning going? You're looking at potential flight routes from here, over the Gulf and back?"

Sighing, Akiva nodded and picked up the plastic protractor, tapping it against one of the colorful maps. "Yeah. Trying to figure out flight routes. We can never take the same one twice. Someone might be watching us. I'm trying to devise five different flight strategies, depending on where we meet up with a druggie, and how to fly that pattern back here to the base."

Joe stood quietly. "Mind if I take a look at what you've come up with so far?" His heart thumped hard in his chest. He knew Akiva was a hands-on manager, not one to give up territory or duties to others unless she absolutely had to. Oh, she'd been more than happy to have him, as X.O., handle all the things that needed to be reckoned with in setting up Alpha. But when it came to the serious stuff of planning interdiction, she'd made it clear she didn't want him nosing around.

Mouth thinning, Akiva scowled and put her hands over her notebook, where she'd been scribbling ideas. *Damn.* The last thing she wanted was Joe here. Why couldn't he just leave her alone? The more mature side of herself said, *Because he's the X.O. He has a right to be here.*

Besides, he might have some good ideas that you could use. The immature part of her, the wounded side, won out. Her voice became clipped. "I'll let you see them when I'm done. Don't you have other duties that need attending to?"

Wincing inwardly, Joe tried to tamp down his impatience and frustration. In an instant, he had seen Akiva put up her defensive guard; it was in her voice and in her stiffening body. Looking around, he saw that Iris Bradford had left the building. They were alone.

"Tell me something," Joe said in a low, soothing voice. "Am I green lookin', with scales and a set of horns on my head?"

Stunned, Akiva twisted around and stared at him, her mouth falling open. Joe was leaning languidly in the entranceway, his brows furrowed, his eyes dark and searching. "What?"

"Did I grow horns and a tail? Is that why you don't want me within ten feet of you at any time? Am I some virus you're afraid will infect you through casual contact?"

Akiva was shocked by his brazenness. Maybe she had misjudged him; she had thought Joe was a beta male, not an alpha one. She stared up at him, stunned speechless. The silence thickened between them. Gulping, she realized that if she spoke the truth, he could, by military regulations, have her strung up for dereliction of duty because of prejudice. And she wasn't about to let that occur. But if that was Joe's intent, she didn't sense it. There was nothing in his face or his voice that indicated he intended malice toward her. No, what she heard from him was hurt. Hurt that she was leaving him out of the loop, that she didn't need him around at all. And also, there was a gentle persistence in his tone clearly meant to create dialogue to get past the defensive anger on her part.

Her heart twinged with guilt...and another emotion that she refused to look at. Her gaze snapped away and then back to Joe.

"We're alone," he told her. "I would never bring this up within earshot of anyone, Akiva."

Lips pursed, she growled, "Look, I'm new at this...being a C.O. I don't know how to lead, I guess. And right now, all my attention is on our mission and flights."

"Understandable," Joe rasped. "And I haven't had any training to be an X.O., either, so maybe we're both floundering around, unsure and on shaky legs with our new assignments?" He saw her eyes fill with fear and uncertainty. "I know I'm feelin' that way." Well, that wasn't really true, but Joe decided the white lie might create some camaraderie between them—and perhaps create an opening with Akiva. There was no sense in accusing her. She'd only shut down and retreat inside that cool, icy tower. That was the last thing Joe wanted.

"Uh, yeah..." Akiva searched his hooded gray eyes. Her ability to read men was deadly accurate; she could smell them intuitively a mile away. And if her all-terrain radar was working correctly, she felt Joe trying to offer her an olive branch of peace. Her heart said to take it. Her mind screamed no. Torn, she shrugged.

"Let me... I'll be done with my preliminary flight paths probably by tonight. How about you look at them then?"

Nodding, Joe sipped the coffee, though he no longer tasted it. "That would be fine. Thanks. I gotta go. Spec Dean and Ferris have got the helos in the hangar, and they're going to begin working on the big rig for us. They have to go through normal pre-mission checks on it."

"Good. Fine...fine..."

Joe saw the indecision in Akiva's gold eyes. He saw her being pulled between her desire to be civil toward him and something else. What was that other thing? He sensed it more than saw it in her body language. It was as if she wanted to explain herself to him for some reason. "I'll see you later," he said, and turned on his heel.

"Better catch your sun rays today to keep that tan," Akiva called, trying to be friendly. "There's a lot less sun here, I think, than what we had back in Peru."

Stopping, Joe twisted around and gave her a quizzical look. She'd already turned her back to him and was bent over the maps once more. Confused by her words, he took a sip of coffee and then headed to the door. What had Akiva meant by that statement? Was she just trying to be pleasant? Maybe she was feeling bad about the way she was treating him and was trying to be social. Heartened, he took her off-the-wall comment as a white flag of truce—at least for now. His heart lightened with each stride, because Joe felt as if they'd taken a step together, in the same direction, for the first time.

Joe had asked the enlisted women to share the mess duties, taking turns being responsible for each day's meals. Spec Susan Dean, their ordnance person, had been given extra duty as chef today. She hailed from the Bronx, and had a distinct nasal twang to her voice. As they sat at the benches and tables in the dining area, she quickly served them their first dinner at Alpha. Dressed in her camos, her olive-green T-shirt damp with sweat, she zoomed around, passing out aluminum trays filled with the delicious smelling spaghetti she'd whipped up.

Joe sat on one side of the officers' table and Akiva sat opposite him. She was smiling at Susan, who was singing an Italian song in high falsetto as she served them their meals. It was 1800 hours, and Joe was glad to see everyone pulling together. This was going to be a tight team, and he was proud of the enlisted women, each of whom had pulled double duty today serving outside their trained area of expertise.

Susan set trays in front of Akiva and Joe. Her green eyes danced with pride. "There you go, Chiefs. My mama, who is a killer cook, gave me this recipe. Enjoy!" She turned and quickly went back to the makeshift kitchen for trays for the others.

Akiva grinned and picked up her fork. She risked a glance across the table at Joe. The black uniform he wore accentuated his black hair and darkly tanned features, making him look dangerous to her. Akiva couldn't pin down exactly what it was about Joe Calhoun that drew him to her, only that her silly heart was always thumping a little when he was in the vicinity. A rebellious lock of black hair dipped over his broad brow. She had the maddening urge to push it back into place. Stunned at her spontaneous feelings, Akiva scowled and forked the fragrant spaghetti into her mouth.

"Pretty good," Joe called to Susan, who was just sitting down to eat with her friends. "I almost feel like I'm back in New York City sittin' at an Italian café."

Susan glowed at the compliment as she dug into a huge pile of spaghetti. "Thanks, Chief."

"With this kind of food," Akiva said, turning toward the other table with a smile, "we'll survive. Nice job, Dean. Keep it up."

"Yes, ma'am, you bet I will."

"Hey," Spec Robin Ferris, the software expert, called,

"I'm next! It's my turn in mess tomorrow." She gave Susan a triumphant look. "I'm makin' chicken and dumplin's for dinner. How about *that?*"

Akiva grinned. "No food fights, ladies. We're all looking forward to your kitchen skills. Now, let's eat. We've got a night of work ahead of us."

The collective groan rose from the enlisted table. Akiva turned back and saw Joe watching her. He nodded and gave her an approving look, as if to say, *Well done.*

Glowing from the unvoiced compliment, Akiva turned her attention to eating. She was starved. Fortunately, Susan had made the most of their limited supplies, which consisted mainly of canned vegetables and meat.

"Things are lookin' good," Joe said in a low tone as they ate. "It's all comin' together around here. You can feel it. Good vibes, thanks to you."

Akiva's heart swelled at his sincere compliment. She nodded, but continued eating. Susan had somehow found flour and yeast and baked some homemade rolls. "Yes, it's looking good." She felt hopeful, despite her terror of being a bad C.O. She appreciated Joe's comment because it made her a bit more confident about being a leader. Even though there was only five people involved, to her it was a daunting task filled with land mines she could step on, and Akiva didn't want to do that.

Taking a roll, Joe sliced a pat of butter from the white dish before him and slathered it across the top. "Did you get those flight plans done?"

Nodding, Akiva wiped her mouth with her paper napkin. "Yes. I'll give them to you to study tonight. We'll go over them at the planning office tomorrow at 0800."

"Good. I'm anxious to see what you've come up with." And he was. Joe admired Akiva's intelligence and her combat experience. She didn't look real happy about him nosing around in her plans, however, even if she spoke the correct words any C.O. would say to an X.O.

"Yeah...well, don't knee-jerk on me, okay? I'm new at this."

Chuckling, Joe put his empty tray aside. After he wiped his own mouth, he wadded up his napkin and dropped it on the tray. "Like I'm going to jump down your throat or something? Scream and yell? Is that what you expect from me?"

"I'm just not used to working with...well...men. Women think a certain way. We see things differently than you. I'm used to working with my own gender, that's all."

"Three years down here with an all-woman crew would make a person get used to a certain way of thinking and seeing things," Joe agreed. "I guess I never thought of it from that perspective."

"You wouldn't. You're a man." *Oh, damn!* Akiva rolled her eyes as she saw Joe react to the insult. His eyes widened at first, and then she saw hurt in their gray depths. Guilt ate at her. "I didn't mean that like it came out," she muttered darkly so that only he could hear. It was the closest thing to an apology that he was going to get from her.

Joe settled his elbows on the table, his cup of coffee between his hands. "I'm looking forward to being taught how women think in strategic and tactical terms, Akiva. I know you can teach me a lot, and I'm willin' to learn. You ladies have forged a whole new concept about war and interdiction down here, and a lot of people need to learn from your experiences."

Oh, great. Now I really feel bitchy. Akiva didn't like herself at times, and this was one of them. Joe had been gentle and nonthreatening. He'd just given her a sincere compliment, and she'd jumped on him and bitten two big fang holes into him. Yet he was taking it in stride and turning a negative into a positive. Rubbing her furrowed brow, she growled, "Do me a favor and take the best that women offer, and not the worst...."

"You're under a lotta stress," he said confidentially as he sipped his coffee, his gaze on the table of enlisted women behind Akiva. The laughter and good-natured talk among them melted the tension. Yet Akiva was staring darkly down at her food, her brows furrowed. He also noticed there was a high, pink flush to her cheeks. Son of a gun, she was blushing! Joe sat there absorbing her response. Grinning a little to himself, he felt his spirits buoy. If she was blushing, it meant she felt badly over the acidic comment she'd just fired at him. That made him feel better. "Learning to be a leader is tough stuff," he added sympathetically.

"Yeah? Well, from the looks of things, Calhoun, you're doing a much better job as X.O. than I am as C.O." Blowing a breath of air in frustration, Akiva gave him a pleading look. "You're right, I am stressed out. I'm feelin' Maya breathing down my neck. I can hear her voice in the back of my head saying, 'Well, are you online yet? When's the first mission ready to roll?'"

Joe stopped himself from reaching out to touch Akiva's hand, which was resting near her tray. She'd bunched it into a fist. Right now, he knew she needed to be held, if only for a moment, to make the big, bad world go away temporarily, and give her some breathing room. "I don't think Major Stevenson would expect us to be gunnin' and runnin' so soon." He offered Akiva a skewed smile as he set his coffee cup down between his hands. "I just think you want to do a good job for her...for all of us. And I'd say that's the earmark of a good leader—the fact that you care."

Whether she wanted to or not, Akiva desperately needed someone to confide in. Back at the base, she had her tight circle of friends, her confidantes. Out here, she was cut off from everyone. She couldn't talk to the other women here; the gulf between enlisted and officers was like the Grand Canyon. As a fellow officer, Joe was someone she could confide in, but it was so hard. To open up meant to trust him, and she just couldn't do it. Yet when she gazed into his warm, lingering gray gaze, her heart expanded with such a powerful feeling of trust that it left Akiva momentarily breathless.

Opening and closing her fist convulsively, Akiva stared down at her tray. To look into Joe's dove-gray eyes was like spotting a shimmering rainbow after a hard rain. She simply wanted to lose herself in his gaze. That shook her deeply. No man in her life had ever affected her like this. Not ever.

She tried to stop herself from speaking, but the words slipped from between her pursed lips. "I—I really miss my friends back at the base...being able to talk to them...."

Joe saw the battle in Akiva's narrowed golden eyes. He saw her waver and almost trust him enough to open up to him. Sitting there, he realized he was holding his breath, hoping she'd do exactly that. When she didn't, he knew why: there wasn't a basis of trust between them.

"Maybe," he suggested gently, "over time I'll prove I have a good ear and can listen." He patted his shoulder and grinned a little. "And a shoulder to cry on, if you need one."

Chapter 5

"Bogey painted on radar five miles ahead," Joe warned Akiva, who was flying the Apache gunship toward their intended target. It was dusk; the horizon was darkening as they flew east over the calm waters of the Gulf. Tension sizzled through him. This was their first mission after taking a week to get Alpha online. The call had come in from the American sub sitting somewhere offshore, reporting a fixed-wing aircraft speeding over the water toward the U.S.

Akiva sat in the lower front cockpit of the Apache, the cannon directly beneath her flight boots as she flew. "Roger," she answered in a clipped tone. All her attention was on flying the swift gunship. Its shaking and trembling felt comforting to Akiva. She was relieved to get back up in the air and do something she knew she was very good at: hunting down drug aircraft.

What worried her as she kept gazing across her instrument panel was Joe Calhoun. She'd never flown a combat mission with him before. How good was he? Could he see trouble coming soon enough to warn her? Because she wasn't sure, Akiva watched her HUDs—heads-up-display screens—more than she would ordinarily. They were two square monitors in front of her, highlighted with colorful lines that told her in symbolic form what Joe was seeing from the rear cockpit, directly behind her.

Akiva moved the optic night scope into position over her right eye, flipped up the lid, then looked into it. The scope gave them a tremendous advantage, especially in combat, providing a huge amount of information. Akiva wasn't sure if there was any "enemy" around, but Luis Rios and his fleet of civilian helicopters was never far from her mind. The son of the drug lord was known to be aggressive and spontaneous. She sure didn't want Luis Rios to show up right now, even if his civilian helos weren't rigged with weapons. Besides, helos had only a certain fuel range, and their time would be spent intercepting fixed-wing aircraft over the Gulf. That didn't mean Luis couldn't wait on shore and attack them. That possibility nagged at Akiva. If Luis had his helo fleet retrofitted with larger fuel tanks, he could become a deadly threat to them over the land mass.

"Four miles," Joe said.

Akiva nodded. She saw the same blip on the screen. The HUD display shifted as Joe asked for a conformation of the type of aircraft it was. Instantly, it showed a profile of a twin-engine Beechcraft.

"Three miles..." Joe wiped at a dribble of sweat working its way down the side of his temple with a quick movement of his Nomex-gloved hand. His eyes were intent on the HUDs. At the same time, he was watching other equipment for any signs of trouble. Below them, at five thousand feet, the darkening waters of the Gulf looked peaceful. He sat in the upper cockpit, which rode piggyback style above the first one. His seat was closest to the rotor, and the familiar shaking as the blades whirled was something he enjoyed. The specially designed helmet he wore effectively cut out all the noise.

"Got a lot of cumulus up ahead," Joe warned. Over the Gulf, they had discovered, thunderstorms popped up suddenly and with a violence that he'd only seen in West Texas. Although the Apache was an all-weather helicopter, able to fly in fog and deteriorating IFR—instrument flight rules—conditions, a thunderstorm was something to be avoided if possible because of the massive up and down drafts of air that could literally toss an aircraft—any aircraft—around like a toy. The Apache was not a huge helicopter; sleek and streamlined, it was designed for combat. It would be like a wooden rowboat thrown on the mercy of a raging sea if it had to enter a thunderstorm to chase down the bogey ahead.

"I don't *like* storms," Akiva growled. Her gaze flicked to the thin green radar arm arcing across one of the HUDs. "That bogey doesn't, either."

"Yeah," Joe confirmed, "he's dropping elevation. He's going to try and go under it. Think he knows we got a fix on him? He's acting like he does."

"I don't know. This is our first mission. We got a big learning curve ahead of us. Just stay alert."

Grinning, he drawled, "Don't worry. I want something nice put in my personnel jacket when this is all over. Not 'Joe Calhoun sunk the Apache out in the Gulf.' Wouldn't look good, would it?"

His dry sense of humor during the tense moment got inside Akiva's normally unflappable facade. Chuckling outright, she muttered, "Calhoun, I've come to think that you will live and die for that personnel jacket report."

It felt good to hear Akiva laugh. It was the first time Joe had heard her laughter, and it warmed him immeasurably as he sat in the tight, narrow cockpit, the nylon harnesses biting deeply into his shoulders and across his thighs. ''Your laugh is like water runnin' over rocks at one of my favorite places on earth—Yosemite. Three miles...''

There was no time to absorb his huskily spoken words, though. Akiva was surprised at the unexpectedly intimate tone in his voice in that moment. Whether she wanted to or not, her heart accepted his compliment, for it was a beautiful one. She'd been to Yosemite National Park and had stood at the foot of the waterfall he was probably talking about. It was a grand waterfall, dropping a hundred feet, with rainbows shimmering through its spray as the sun moved across the sky. Enjoying the comparison of her laughter to the water singing on the rocks, she smiled a little.

''Two miles...you oughta be able to get a visual on him....''

Akiva lifted her head, her eyes moving to slits. She gripped the cyclic and collective, guiding the Apache smoothly in a descent toward the waters of the Gulf. The light was fading rapidly now, but she could see the dark, looming, cauliflower-shaped thunderheads directly ahead of them. Lightning flashed within the clouds, illuminating them momentarily as the bolt zigzagged through it.

''Yeah...'' She strained to look downward, searching for the plane. If it was a drug flight, the pilot probably wouldn't have his red and green flashing lights on, not wanting to be seen. Under FAA flight rules, all planes had to have lights on in order to be detected, so other aircraft wouldn't accidentally run into them. Of course, the Apache didn't have running lights on, either, but they were a military aircraft on a mission.

"I got 'em!" Joe said. "See 'em? Eleven o'clock, Akiva."

She cocked her head and peered through the cockpit Plexiglas.

"Roger. I see him."

"Hang on...gonna see if I can read the numbers on his fuselage." Joe picked up the pair of night-vision binoculars and aimed them down toward the fleeing plane. It was flying at a thousand feet, almost hugging the surface of the Gulf. In the dusky light, it was hard to read the numerals on the cream-colored fuselage of the twin-engine plane.

"I don't think he knows we're shadowing him," Joe murmured. He got the numbers and scribbled them down on the knee board strapped around his right thigh. Setting the binoculars aside, he quickly typed the numbers into his computer and sent the inquiry via satellite to deep within the Pentagon, where such aircraft numbers were stored.

"No, he doesn't—yet. Did you get the numbers?"

"Yes, ma'am. I've already inquired. Hold on...." Joe watched his right HUD light up with a response. He grinned savagely. "Wal, this good ole boy ain't on the FAA flight plans or register at all. How about that? I think we got a druggie on our hands, Chief Redtail."

Again she felt his warm, easygoing teasing dissolve some of the tension accumulating in her shoulders and neck as they chased the other aircraft. They were flying at fifteen hundred feet, directly behind its tail—a position called an aircraft's "six." There were no sideview mirrors on a plane, so the pilot wouldn't know they were there. Most civilian aircraft did not have the radar on board to alert them that another aircraft was shadowing them so closely.

''Good,'' Akiva said tightly. ''Let's rock 'n' roll.... You'd better strap those binoculars down so they aren't flying around the cabin. You could get a broken nose,'' she warned as she gripped the cyclic and collective a little tighter.

''Already done,'' Joe assured her. ''Ahm such a good-lookin' guy that I don't think a broken nose would hurt my looks, do you?''

Akiva couldn't help but laugh. ''Do you always joke in tense moments?''

''Jest my nature, Chief Redtail.''

Shaking her head, Akiva growled, ''You surprise me every day, Calhoun.''

''Good,'' he chortled, feeling her take the Apache to a higher speed, surging ahead of the fleeing Beechcraft. Joe enjoyed Akiva's flying ability; she was smooth as silk. The Apache was a living extension of her, shaking and trembling around him as she aimed the nose of the gunship a good half mile ahead of the drug plane.

The night was darkening. The water looked shiny and black below, except when a bolt of lightning flashed, reflecting across it.

''That dude is runnin' without lights. Shame on him. The FAA will fine him right and proper,'' Joe muttered.

''The least of his worries. Arm the cannon.''

''Online,'' he murmured, flipping a switch and watching his HUDs. ''You want to fire across his nose in warning?''

''Yes.'' Akiva smiled grimly. ''But first we're gonna scare him a little.''

Joe didn't have time to ask how. Akiva whipped the agile gunship around so that they were now facing the

Beechcraft racing toward them. She hovered the Apache at one thousand feet, directly in line with it.

"Flip on our running lights," she ordered tightly, her gaze locked on the aircraft barreling toward them. Akiva would bet the pilot wasn't that alert; he'd be more concerned about skirting the thunderhead to their right and staying out of any possible up or down drafts that would smash his aircraft, like a mosquito struck by a flyswatter, into the Gulf waters just below.

Her mouth twitched as she saw the plane.

"Half mile," Joe warned, tension in his voice.

"Sky chicken, Calhoun. Relax."

He'd automatically tensed. What if the pilot didn't see them? What if he was too busy dodging and ducking drafts and air turbulence? Would he see their green and red running lights? Joe's eyes widened. From where he sat above Akiva, he saw the Beechcraft come hurtling out of the surrounding darkness.

"Quarter mile..." he choked out. *Come on! See us!* Joe didn't want a midair collision. He'd heard the pilots at the base talk of playing "sky chicken." It was a game where a pilot would fly directly at another aircraft, never banking to the right or left. One of the pilots—the "chicken"—would have to give way at the last moment or there would be a head-on collision. Gulping, Joe sucked in a breath.

The Beechcraft loomed close. He could see the twin propellers spinning, the cream-and-orange design across the rounded nose. He braced himself and gasped.

At the last possible moment, the pilot of the plane saw them. Instantly, he banked sharply to the left and downward.

Akiva chuckled darkly. "Gotcha, you son of a

bitch..." Instantly she followed the plane down toward the water.

Joe's helmet banged the side of the cockpit as Akiva suddenly swung the gunship around. He was amazed at her swift response as she torqued the craft to its limits, twisting the helo like a hawk swooping in a dive after its scrambling prey.

Shaking his head, he hung on, feeling the immense press of gravity against him during the steep, tight turn. The Apache screamed in protest, shaking even harder. As Akiva pulled the helicopter out of the dive, she notched up the speed to match the Beechcraft's, which was now barely two hundred feet above the water's calm surface. Just the way the pilot was flying the plane indicated he was rattled. He'd lost his direction and was now flying due north, not east as before. Akiva brought the Apache up next to the Beechcraft, close to the pilot's side, so he could see that they were there.

"Call him on the radio," Akiva ordered tightly.

"Roger." Joe quickly placed the call, using at least ten different radio frequencies, one after another. It could be that the pilot had his radio off, as well as his lights. As Joe glanced out at the pilot leaning over his instruments, he shook his head. "No response, Akiva. I think he's got his radio turned off."

"Pity.... Hang on and warm up that cannon."

"Yes, ma'am."

For Akiva, this was old hat. She'd turned back many a helicopter and fixed-wing aircraft back in Peru. The only difference now was that instead of jungle below her, there was water. She kept herself on high alert, because water disorientation was nothing to fool with. She wasn't used to working over water and wanted to avoid the hazard.

Akiva felt the cannon beneath her feet shake the gunship. Joe had fired off a couple of rounds to make sure it was working properly.

"We're hot," he told her, satisfaction in his voice.

"Roger. Get ready to fire across his nose. I want this guy to realize we want him going *back* to Mexico."

"Right on..." Joe tensed as Akiva brought the gunship up and over the Beechcraft and then settled slightly ahead of it.

"Fire."

Finger on the trigger, Joe fired a short burst. He could see the red tracers arcing about twenty feet in front of the plane's nose.

Instantly, the Beechcraft turned and headed west—back toward Mexico.

"Whooee! That good ole boy must be ex-military! He got your message, Akiva. In big red letters." Joe whooped with glee once more.

A smile tugged at Akiva's mouth. "Yeah, he knew what firing across his bow meant. Let's just follow him to shore. Once he's there, we'll peel off and use corridor C to make our way back to Alpha."

"Roger that." Joe grinned. "Nice huntin', Akiva. I learned a thing or two from you tonight."

Akiva didn't answer. She was all business now. The plane was fleeing at top speed, gaining altitude to a thousand feet and heading back toward the land mass of Mexico, which she could see painted on the screen of her HUD.

"Just keep your eyes peeled for his friends. We don't know if he's making a call for help right now on his radio."

"Roger, gotcha. I'm on it." Joe frowned. He knew his business in the back seat. Why did Akiva have to remind him each time? Was it because she didn't trust him? Yes, he realized that was it. He watched the green radar hand sweep back and forth across the screen, but it remained blank, indicating no other aircraft were in the vicinity.

In another thirty minutes, the Beechcraft flew back over the Mexican coast. At that point, Akiva raised the Apache to ten thousand feet and flew back toward the base, using one of the five flight routes she'd worked out to get back to Alpha without being traced or followed. Joe relaxed a little in the cockpit. Looking at his watch, he saw that only an hour had passed since they'd sighted the bogey.

"Amazing how time flies when you're havin' fun," he noted. "One hour. It felt like ten minutes."

Akiva nodded and felt some of the tension draining out of her. "Yeah, it's an amazing thing. When you're in combat, time seems to speed up."

"Adrenaline," Joe agreed.

"Keep an eye out for more bogeys."

He frowned. Of course he was doing that. "Right," he murmured, "I'm always scanning the HUDs, Akiva. I'm not off in dreamland, believe me. It's my butt in this gunship, too. I don't want to be jumped or surprised any more than you do."

"I'm still the commander," she snapped. "And if anything happens, it will be my butt in the sling first." Frowning, Akiva locked the cyclic for a moment and moved her hand upward. With her fingers, she wiped the sweat away from her eyes. Tension was still thrumming through her and she knew the adrenaline in her bloodstream was making her feel this way. Unlocking the mechanism, she wrapped her fingers around the cyclic and continued to fly the gunship manually. Off to their left, thunderheads continued to billow and grow. Frowning, she glared at them. Thunderstorms were no good, and it looked like they would be playing tag around them quite often on these missions. That was one thing she hadn't counted on, and it left her uneasy.

"Do you want me to tell you I'm scanning once a minute?"

Her temper rose. The adrenaline was fraying it. Clamping her lips together, she counted to ten and hoped her voice wouldn't be charged with annoyance as she replied, "No, Mr. Calhoun, you don't have to give me minute-by-minute updates on the fact that your eyes are glued to those HUDs in front of you."

Joe felt her anger. He was angry, too. She didn't trust him at all. Well, once they got back to Alpha and on the ground, he was going to confront her.

It was another thirty minutes before they landed back at Alpha. Joe waited patiently outside the hangar as the three-woman ground crew pushed the Apache back into the hangar so it couldn't be seen. Akiva stood talking to the crew chief about a few software glitches, her Nomex gloves in her left hand and her helmet resting against her hip beneath her left arm.

The darkness was complete at Alpha, except for the dim light cast from the hangar, where the crew was putting the gunship to bed for the night. It would be refueled immediately, the ordnance replaced and checks run on the software, because no one knew when the next call from the American sub would come in.

The air was humid and unmoving as Joe waited. They would have to go to the planning shack to fill out their flight reports next. He'd talk to her about their problem in there, where they'd be alone and out of earshot of the busy ground crew.

Rubbing his jaw, he pulled off his helmet. The cool air felt good on his hot, sweaty head. Holding the helmet by the chin strap, he saw Akiva finally turn and walk toward him. Though her face was dark, he saw a gleam from her narrowed eyes. The way her mouth was set, he knew they were going to mix it up good once they were alone in the shack.

Joe opened the door for Akiva. It was just the way he was; he believed women should have doors opened for them. When he stepped aside to let her into the dimly lit room, she cut him an acidic look. Grimly, he followed her in and made sure the door was shut. The third room to the left, where there were two metal folding chairs and a makeshift desk of plywood set on wooden crates, was to be their report room.

Their booted feet echoed as they entered. Joe carefully set his helmet on the floor near his chair. Grabbing the white form that all crews had to fill out after a mission, he sat down opposite Akiva. The fluorescent overhead light made her copper skin look washed out.

Flicking her a glance as he pulled a pen from his left shoulder pocket, he saw fear in her eyes. Why fear? Over the coming talk they would have? He could feel the tension around her. Her long, thick braid, which lay across her proud shoulder and down the front of her black uniform, was frayed from the humidity. Tendrils of hair around her face softened her angular features, and Joe felt his heart lurch in his chest. More than anything, he wished Akiva wouldn't dislike him so much. Settling down, he scowled and filled out the report in precise, printed letters.

Quiet descended upon the room. Akiva wrote quickly, but neatly. She shot Joe a glance and saw his brow was furrowed. That lock of black hair dipped rebelliously over his perspiring brow, and she could feel his unhappiness. Their first confrontation was coming.

Akiva warred within herself. She was a C.O. How would Maya handle this? Akiva knew she'd been riding Joe when she shouldn't have. He was as well trained as she was, and she had no business bugging him constantly about his duties in the Apache. Licking her lower lip, she put the report aside.

Joe set his report aside, too. He slowly folded his hands in front of him and leveled a benign look at her across the table.

Akiva glared back. Her hands rested tensely on her long, curved thighs beneath the table. "Well?" she snapped. "Let's get this over with."

Joe's mouth crooked. Not exactly the way a good C.O. would start off a conversation. He searched her gold eyes, which were thundercloud dark with suspicion and distrust—toward him.

"Okay," he rasped, "let's." Opening his hands and keeping his voice low and nonthreatening, he said, "I know my duties in the Apache. What I need to know is why you don't trust me to be your back seat."

Stunned that he'd hit her point-blank with the real essence of their problem, Akiva froze momentarily. Rage moved through her like a rattler moving toward a prey. Trying to wrestle with her anger, she hissed, "I don't trust *any* man, so don't think you've been singled out!"

Joe absorbed her anger. It was like a slap in the face to him. "Whoa, just a minute. I don't buy that. You aren't like this around Mike Houston. You treat him with respect." Gazing into her angry eyes, he added, "That's all I need from you—respect."

"Mike Houston is different!" Akiva said as she suddenly stood up, her hands flat on the surface of the table.

She glared down at Joe, hoping to intimidate him into stopping his search for the real reason she didn't trust him.

Joe sat very still. Akiva's voice was grating. Her nostrils flared and she was breathing hard, as if he were physically attacking her. And through the anger, he still saw the fear in her eyes. Why fear? Mind spinning, he tried to figure it all out, but couldn't. Worse, they were still coming down off the adrenaline high of their combat mission, and he knew neither of them was particularly stable at this moment.

He stared up at her, her words echoing through his head. "Houston is different than me? How?"

"You don't get it, do you?" Akiva straightened and wrapped her arms tightly across her chest. She saw the confusion in his eyes. If she told him of her prejudice, he could put her on report and her career would be over. It was that simple.

"Okay," Joe muttered, "he was an *officer* in the army. I'm only a warrant officer. Is this what it's all about? Rank?" Joe knew it could well be that. He saw Akiva's face grow cold and stubborn-looking. Her full breasts rose and fell quickly beneath her black uniform. She stood there tensely, as if expecting him to throw a punch at her. Of course, he would never do that, but she looked like a boxer in a ring, ready to take a blow she expected was coming.

And then it struck him. "Wait a minute..." He rose out of his chair. "Wait..." And he quickly went over in his mind a conversation she'd had with him a week earlier. Holding out his hand toward her, his voice thunderstruck, he said, "Houston is part Quechua Indian, right?"

Shocked, Akiva stopped breathing for a moment. She avoided Joe's searching gaze. Right now, she hated his ability to stay in emotional control when she was out of control. Nostrils flaring again, she rasped, "Yes, he is. So what?"

"And you're Native American."

"Apache and Lakota Sioux. So what?" She saw his eyes turn pensive at the discovery and his mouth flex. He was putting it together, and that scared the hell out of Akiva.

"The other week," Joe said, softening his tone in hopes of defusing the tension between them, "you said something about me getting enough sun to keep my dark tan." He jerked back the sleeve on his uniform to show her his flesh.

Akiva glared at him. "I was just making conversation."

Joe stood there, his mind clicking over the entire scenario. "No...no, I don't think you were. I think I know what's at the heart of this problem between us." He lifted his head and squarely met her glare. Now the fear was real in her gold eyes. He watched as Akiva's mouth thinned, the corners pulling inward.

"You've got an ax to grind with white men, don't you? I never believed it when you said you had a problem with men in general." He wiped his mouth with the back of his hand and held her unsure gaze. "I see now...it's *white* men. And you're Native American." Joe saw her react as if his words had been bullets. Her eyes widened momentarily. And he understood the fear in their depths, because what he had just suggested was prejudice—one thing the army wouldn't tolerate. She wasn't about to admit it to him, though. He could see it in the jutting of her jaw and the way her mouth was set.

He laughed. It struck him as utter irony because, for

once in his life, not owning up to his Indian heritage had created a bias against him.

Akiva stared at him.

''This is too funny!'' Joe chortled. He yanked at the closure around his neck, the Velcro giving way, and pulled open his uniform so that Akiva could see his entire chest and torso. Beneath his uniform, he wore nothing.

''Look, will you?'' he entreated, gesturing to his exposed skin. ''If I was a *white* guy going after a suntan, would there be tan all over my body? You want me to strip completely out of my suit and prove to you that my color isn't just from the sun?''

Gawking and stunned, Akiva stared at his well-shaped chest, which was carpeted with thick black hair. He'd exposed himself down to his navel. Gulping, she watched as he shrugged out of the sleeves and exposed his full upper body.

''Look, will you? Do you see any tan lines on my shoulders? My neck or my chest? Don't you think there would be? And check out my back, too.'' Joe turned so that she could see all the way down to his hips, where his uniform hung.

Akiva saw the powerful muscles of his broad shoulders and the deep indentation of his spine. Again she gulped. As Joe turned around, jamming his arms back into the sleeves of his uniform and pressing the Velcro closed down the front, she felt shock flowing through her. And when he lifted his head to catch and capture her gaze, she saw a glint in his eyes she'd never seen before. He was no longer smiling. Now his mouth was pursed.

''Just for your information,'' he began in a low, emotional tone, ''this so-called suntan you think I have isn't one at all. The color you see on my hands—'' he held them out to her ''—is all *over* my body, Akiva. I'm half

Comanche and half white. What you mistook for a tan is from my daddy's side of the family. He's a full-blood Comanche.

"I think I've got it figured out now. Your prejudice is toward *white* men. Mike Houston is part Native American, so he's safe…someone you can trust because he has Indian blood in his veins just like you do."

The silence swirled thickly between them. Joe lowered his hands and moved his jaw, trying to stop the emotions from overwhelming him. "You don't trust Anglos. Okay, I can live with that," he continued. "And I know you're never going to admit that to me, because army regs aren't too nice about prejudice. They don't tolerate it."

He saw her drop her gaze to the table. The suffering he saw in Akiva's face nearly knocked him over. For an instant, Joe felt all her armor falling away. He kept his voice low because he didn't want to fight with her; he wanted to repair whatever the problem was.

"I'm Indian, too. Part Comanche," he repeated. "Maybe that's what you need to know in order to trust me in that cockpit with you, Akiva. And if it is, now you know the truth. I know my job in the Apache. My butt's on the line up there just like yours is. I don't want to get blown out of the sky, either. But you can't keep asking me every few minutes if I'm doing my job. I kept you well informed up there on that flight. I didn't screw up. I was on top of things."

The shock, like a lightning bolt, was still moving through Akiva. She stood there for a long minute, digesting his words. As she forced herself to look up at him, she saw that Joe wasn't angry with her. That surprised her. Instead, she saw him wrestling with finding a way to reach her.

Her heart hammered violently in her chest. She slowly

unwound her arms and let them drop to her sides. Closing her eyes, she took in a ragged breath and then exhaled it. Opening them, she saw the hurt in his face, and at the same time saw him struggling to connect with her. He was part Comanche! That revelation stunned her. What she'd thought was a dark tan was really due to his Indian genes. Joe carried the blood of Native Americans within him…just as she did. In her heart, that made him a friend, not a foe.

Rubbing her mouth with her fingers, she tried to find the right words to reply. "You've acted more like a C.O. in this little confrontation than I have," she admitted hoarsely.

"Akiva, I *care* about you." Joe opened his hands, his voice pleading. "I'm not interested in the army knowing anything about this conversation. I'm not your enemy. I never have been and never will be. I'm someone you can trust, if you'll just let me show you that. But if you don't let me, how can I? Trust is something we've got to have in that gunship cockpit, or it will kill us someday as we're battling one another instead of looking at our instruments or out the cockpit windows. We both know that."

Nodding, Akiva moved her fingertip around on the unpainted plywood in front of her. "You're right…." Her voice was choked. She swallowed against the lump forming in her throat. She had treated Joe without respect. He, on the other hand, had maintained respect throughout their confrontation. What did that say about *her?* Akiva was humiliated, and she had no one to blame but herself.

"I—owe you an apology…." she told him thickly, and raised her chin to meet his hooded gaze.

"I don't want your apology, Akiva," he pleaded hoarsely. "What I want is to earn your respect, your trust…."

Her heart filled with pain. Joe's pain. She'd treated him poorly. And yet, like a knight, he had treated her with gentlemanly respect and care. Oh, she felt his care, all right. She heard it in the quaver in his roughened tone. And she saw that mysterious look in his eyes that made her feel a little weak, a little shaky. It wasn't a bad feeling. No, it was a good one—so nurturing that she hungrily absorbed it.

Lifting her hands, she whispered, "As an Apache warrior, I've shamed myself before you. I haven't kept the warrior code—to protect all people, to care for them and be honorable at all times." Bitterly, she looked away. "I've failed you by behaving in a dishonorable way." Also, Akiva realized that the issue *wasn't* really Joe's heritage. Her *real* problem, her darkness, revolved around men in general, and her distrust of them. Worse, her fear of men glared fully in her face because of her growing feelings toward Joe, no matter how hard she tried to ignore her heart.

Joe saw the suffering in Akiva's face and knew she meant every word of what she said. She was more than contrite. "Listen, we're both tired. We're exhausted from this long runnin' battle of settin' Alpha up. Let's just bury the hatchet on this one, shall we?" He managed to lift one corner of his mouth as he saw her head snap up, her eyes flare with surprise at his suggestion.

Pointing to the leather-covered ax head she wore in the belt around her waist, he said in a teasing tone, "So long as you don't use that on me when you're pissed off, I think we got nowhere to go but up, gal. Fair 'nuff?"

Chapter 6

"Hey, Akiva..." Joe stuck his head into her open door along the hangar bay. She was sitting at her desk, doing the thing she hated most: paperwork. This morning, her black hair was long and free. In the past month, Joe had come to enjoy seeing her like that. The only time she wore her red scarf about her head was when she was going into battle. Otherwise, her hair was a beautiful black cloak about her squared shoulders. "You gotta see this. Come on...."

Akiva looked up to see Joe grinning idiotically, his hands on the doorjamb. He was dressed in his body-fitting, olive-green T-shirt and his camouflage pants. The look on his face sent a sheet of warmth through her.

Akiva put down her pencil and shoved the map aside. "What?"

"Ahh, come on.... If I told you, it wouldn't be a surprise." As he wiped from his brow the sweat he'd worked up in the hangar while helping with maintenance on the Apache with Spec Dean, he saw Akiva's gold eyes narrow. Since their confrontation a month ago, he'd seen Akiva lessen little by little the amount of armor she wore around him. She showed it in small ways, but he was grateful for anything other than the icy demeanor she'd maintained before. Every once in a while her delicious mouth would curve faintly in a slight smile when he teased or joked with her. And that was something Joe had discovered: humor got to Akiva. It was the only doorway that gave him entrance to her, and he used it often.

Looking at her wristwatch, Akiva saw it was 1130. It was Sunday, and the sky was a misty, milky-blue color with the usual low-hanging clouds hugging the jungle treetops around the base. "Almost lunchtime."

"Hoo doggies, it sure is," he muttered, straightening and looking at his watch. "Well, shucks, gal, let's grab a sandwich from the mess hall and take it with us, then."

"Where are we going?" Akiva asked, glad to be leaving her desk. Being C.O. meant being hounded by too much paperwork. She didn't know how Maya stood it. Akiva disliked the time it took. She would rather be flying. Coming around the desk, she met and held his dancing gray eyes. Ever since she'd realized Joe carried Native American blood in his veins, she had stopped being so hard on him. And to give him more than a little credit, he had graciously dropped the topic completely. He was more forgiving than she deserved, Akiva knew.

Joe moved away from the door as she stepped through it. Out in the hangar, all three women were working on the helos. The maintenance on them was constant, especially in this humid climate. Looking outside, Akiva could see sunlight beginning to pierce the canopy here and there. Joe stood with a smile on his face as he looked at her. Akiva swallowed. That smile always made her feel good. If she was honest, she'd have to admit that Joe was a wonderful addition to this group. The enlisted women doted upon him, loved his good-natured way with them. He was a good bridge between them and Akiva.

''You look like a man on a mission,'' she muttered in a low tone as she approached. Pushing thick strands of hair behind her shoulder, she saw his eyes widen momentarily, and the look in them changed. Her heart responded automatically. Akiva tried to ignore it, but Joe wasn't easy to ignore—not with his husky laughter floating through the hangar, or his Texas drawl reaching her office as she worked. Yes, Akiva liked his presence, but wasn't sure she wanted to admit that to herself.

''I am,'' he said wickedly. ''Come on, I got somethin' to show you.''

Hesitating, she said, ''What if we get a call?''

Joe pulled the cell phone from the clip on his web belt and held it up for her to see. ''Bradford's over at comms. She'll call us.'' Tucking the phone back on his belt, he led her outside the dark confines of the hangar. ''Actually, Dean found it yesterday and told me about it a little while ago. It's about a quarter mile from here. I thought you might like a break from all that paperwork that's choking you.''

Akiva gave him a grimace. ''You've got that right. Paperwork sucks. Give me a mission anytime.'' She walked in long strides past the group of buildings. In the distance, she could hear monkeys screeching, and parrots, well hidden in the dark jungle vegetation, calling to one another.

''Hold on a sec,'' Joe told her, and he trotted into the mess building.

Akiva smiled to herself. Joe seemed like such a little

boy sometimes, so exuberant about life in general. It didn't take much to get him excited and for that dancing laughter to shine like sunlight in his gray eyes. Pushing the toe of her flight boot into the red-colored soil, she shook her head.

Joe came out again with a sack. Holding it up, he said, "Lunch for two. Ferris has the duty. She's made some mean chicken sandwiches with pickle relish."

Akiva nodded and walked with him as he rounded the last building and headed off toward the jungle. "This isn't too far away, is it, Joe?"

"No...not far. I know, I know, you're worried about a mission call comin' in."

"Yes..." They'd been flying one or two flights a day, nearly every day. The flight patterns had been changing weekly as the drug-running pilots tried to find a way to get across the Gulf without the Apache interdicting them. So far, with the American sub's help, they'd turned back a total of fifty-five flights in the first month of actual air ops. Akiva was proud of their total. She could almost feel the building frustration of the drug lord as his flights were blockaded. No matter what plan the Rioses launched, she and Joe had stopped it. Satisfaction laced through her as they headed down a familiar path into the jungle.

"This is the way to our laundry stream," she said to Joe as she followed him closely down the trail, which was damp with fallen leaves. Akiva watched where she placed her feet; roots often popped up or were hidden by the leaves and could easily trip a person. As they moved deeper into the jungle, she spotted the small stream of clear water, a shallow creek about twenty feet wide. Dean, in her exploration of the place, had found it, and this was where everyone did their laundry.

More than once, Akiva had come down here with Joe, where, on her knees, she'd leaned over the stream and beaten her clothes with a rock to clean them. He'd often joked that they had the most modern gunships on the face of the earth and what were they doing? Going back to the Stone Age to wash their clothes. Of course, Alpha wasn't a fully functioning base. It was an experiment, and such social amenities as a clothes washer and dryer were not possible. Not until the crew proved that the base could work.

Here and there sunlight filtered through the thick trees and brush of the rain forest. This jungle was easy to walk through compared to the one Akiva knew in Peru, which was a nearly impenetrable green wall. As she followed Joe down the path, she heard him begin to hum a tune. He always hummed when he was happy, and he usually hummed some Texas ditty that was funny. Sometimes, to break up the tense atmosphere and the urgency that often hung over the base, he'd start singing in his deep Texas voice while working on one of the helicopters. It always lightened the atmosphere, and for that, Akiva was grateful.

"Joe? How much farther?" she asked, hurrying to keep up with him. They were past the laundry area. Here the path was covered with fresh grass that had not been tamped down by foot traffic. The path itself began to disappear as they moved along the stream, which widened considerably and deepened, too.

As she walked behind Joe, Akiva admired his broad back, appreciated his athletic build and the way he moved.

"Just a little farther," he called encouragingly over his shoulder. Akiva gave him a dark look of misgiving. He grinned at her. "Have faith, gal. Just keep followin' me."

When they were alone, Joe often called her "gal." It was a Texas endearment, although he didn't think Akiva realized that. Still, he cherished the moments of privacy they had—which were few and far between. She let him call her that, and the fact sent Joe's heart soaring. If they weren't flying a mission, they were usually at the base doing maintenance to keep the Apache flying, or they were trying to catch some sleep between flights, which could happen at any time. Most of them so far were at night, but now, that pattern was changing. That worried Joe, because it meant they could be detected a lot more easily by their enemy.

Swinging downhill, he skidded on the damp leaves along the stream. The terrain descended steeply for about a hundred feet, then smoothed out below. He turned and saw Akiva hesitate at the top of the leaf-covered hill strewn with bushes. She was looking at the waterfall tumbling into space to her left. Enjoying the expression of awe on her face as she perused the view, he called to her above the roar of the water. "Hey! Come on down! The view's even better from here." And he stretched his hand toward her.

Akiva skidded and slid down the steep hill. The soil had a clay base, and she felt like she was gliding on ice. Just as she made it to the bottom, both feet flew out from beneath her and she gave a cry of surprise. Joe was there to catch her. When his strong arms closed about her, Akiva gasped.

Joe buoyed her up and hooked his arms beneath her. She felt his hands, strong and warm, wrapping around her torso as she struggled to get her feet beneath her once again.

Gasping, she gripped his thick wrists to steady herself. Wildly aware of her back resting against his broad chest, his entire body like a bulwark steadying her own, she quickly pulled away. Everywhere his body had touched hers, she felt a burning sensation. It was a startling feeling, but not a bad one. As Akiva brushed herself off and avoided his gaze, she felt nervous and very shy. Straightening, she turned away from Joe altogether and looked at the waterfall plunging down the hill.

At the top was a huge black rock, cutting the stream into two distinct forks that merged again halfway down as the water tumbled downward. The mist rising from the round pool at the bottom floated upward like fog. Sunlight piercing the jungle canopy flashed through the mist, creating a beautiful, breathtaking rainbow. Akiva couldn't help but gasp with delight.

Joe inched closer to where she stood, her booted feet apart to keep her from falling on the slippery clay near the pool. "Purty, ain't it?"

She gave him a sideways glance. His Texas drawl always soothed her. "Yes...mind-blowing. I never expected this...." And she gestured to the beauty around them. The pool was circular and about the size of an Olympic swimming pool. All around it were trees of varying heights, with bromeliads and orchids hanging from their branches, or tucked into forks.

"Smell the orchids?" Joe asked with satisfaction. He savored the surprise and happiness in Akiva's face as she absorbed the peace and beauty of the spot. Setting down the sack that contained their lunch, he added, "As I said, Dean found this by accident the other day and she told me about it. I wanted to go check it out myself, and I figured, you bein' Indian, you'd like this place as much as I do."

Inhaling the faint, spicy fragrance that wafted around the pool, Akiva realized it was from the colorful orchids dotting the area. "This is incredible, Joe. Just fantastic!" She turned and smiled at him. He was regarding her through half-closed eyes, a thoughtful look on his face. "Thanks…I'm glad you hauled me away from my desk. This is worth it."

"Good." He reached out and briefly touched her upper arm. "Come on, let's eat and enjoy this little respite from our duties. I think we've earned it." He found a large black rock, worn flat with time, that would easily seat two people and keep them dry from the damp ground.

Joe had deliberately touched her. And when his fingers had met her firm arm, he'd seen Akiva's eyes flare with surprise…and then some other emotion. It was one he hadn't expected to see, and it took him by surprise.

Hope glowed brightly in Joe as he sat on the rock and opened the sack to hand Akiva her wrapped sandwich. She sat down, her back near his. The rock wasn't that big, and it forced them into a closeness he didn't mind at all. But did she? He watched like a starved dog as she pulled the wrap off her sandwich with her long and graceful fingers. Joe wondered what it would be like if Akiva touched him that way. Lately, since their truce, she was opening up to him, a little more each day. To Joe, it was like watching some rare, gorgeous flower begin to open, a petal at a time. Of course, he didn't share this thought with Akiva. She always seemed unsure of herself as a woman around him. Frowning, Joe decided to take a huge risk. As he bit into his sandwich and allowed the music of the waterfall to embrace them, he waited for an opportunity to spring his question.

Akiva munched her sandwich, but her attention was on the rugged beauty of the waterfall. She absorbed Joe's closeness and felt a camaraderie with him that she'd never experienced before with a man. Gesturing toward the water, she said, ''Has anyone made this the official bathtub for the group?'' It would surely beat the tepid and sometimes cold showers they took every morning back at their quarters.

''No, but as C.O., you can issue an order to make it such,'' he said. ''I think the ladies would like comin' here to take a bath.'' The water was clear, and the pool was about six to ten feet deep, as far as Joe could see. There was a sand and gravel bottom—much better than algae-covered rocks, which would make it slippery and hazardous.

''It will be a pleasure to write this order,'' Akiva chuckled.

Taking a deep breath, Joe decided to change topics. ''You know, when I was growin' up, my daddy never said much about his Comanche blood. You, on the other hand, got lucky and were raised in the ways of your people, weren't you?'' Joe twisted to look in her direction. This was the first time he'd tried to talk to her about such a personal topic. Would Akiva join in? Or would she shy away like the wild mustang he saw her as?

Her brows dipped and she looked down at her half-eaten sandwich. His heart raced a little with anticipation. Joe hungered for a more personal connection with Akiva. Would she allow it? He wasn't sure, but he had to try. His heart drove him to it.

''My people...'' Akiva began, her voice mirroring her bitterness. ''My father was Lakota, Joe. My mother was Apache.'' She snorted softly and took another small bite of her sandwich.

Joe waited. He'd heard the instant tension in her voice.

''I'm not one to profess great intuition or anything, gal, but I hear a lot of pain in your tone.'' How badly he wanted to turn and slide his arm around her drooping shoulders. Mention family to Akiva, and she seemed to shrink before his very eyes. It wasn't something Joe expected, so he felt like a man who had just discovered a claymore mine beneath his boot—if he moved, it would explode and kill him. Something drove him to take that chance, though. His heart thumped as he saw Akiva's profile soften. Ordinarily, she would draw up her armor and not allow him in. This time, something was different. He could feel it.

"Yeah...well, what is it my grandmother said once when I was a spindly kid of seven? She said my mother marrying a Lakota man was like throwing cold water on a hot fire. Apaches are known to be strong-willed, warrior people. And the Lakota are a Plains tribe who have lost their matriarchal way. They've become a nation of egotistical males who no longer respect their women as they did before."

"And so you were a child created out of the love of this water and fire?"

The huskiness of Joe's voice slid quietly into her heart, soothing the anger that she felt toward her family. Akiva heard the care in his tone. She was desperate to talk to someone, and since all her friends were back at the Black Jaguar Base, she felt overwhelmed with the need to share on a personal level. She'd had no one to confide in for the last six weeks. Since their confrontation, Joe had proved in so many ways that he could be trusted. Yet Akiva was afraid. It was a natural reaction, she supposed. Her distrust of men started when she was very young.

Finishing off the sandwich, she moved lithely to her feet, went over to the pool and knelt down on one knee. Sifting her hands through the tepid water, she washed them off. Then, standing, she wiped them on her thighs and turned to look at Joe. He was studying her, with a gentle expression on his face that she'd come to think must be pity for her. Akiva didn't like that, but her need to talk and share overrode her reaction.

"My mother said I was born into hell. A white man's hell. The Apaches don't believe in hell. We believe that when you die, your spirit moves on to a good place." She gestured around the area. "A place of beauty and serenity and goodness, like this place." She took a step closer to him and watched his face for any signs of disagreement or disinterest. Joe sat relaxed, one leg beneath him, his arms resting on his broad thigh. The warmth she saw in his eyes made her go on as she approached and then sat back down on the rock. This time, her hip just grazed his knee.

"She said that about you? That you were born into hell?"

Nodding, Akiva sighed. "My father had fetal alcohol syndrome—FAS. It's a well-known disease that's rampant among Indians. If a pregnant woman drinks liquor while carrying her baby, the baby is born with genetic defects, usually mental ones. My father had a real short fuse, was mentally unstable and would beat the hell out of me if I even breathed wrong sometimes...." Akiva glanced at Joe through her lashes to see what effect her admission had on him. What she saw she didn't expect. Anger instantly flickered in his darkening gray eyes. But she didn't feel it pointed toward her, but rather toward her father.

"That's a rough start," Joe said quietly, and he choked down the building rage he felt.

Giving a short, explosive laugh, Akiva tipped her head back and let the sound tumble out her mouth. It was absorbed by the roar of the waterfall. "I was born on the Red Rock Apache Reservation in the White Mountains of Arizona. My father wanted us to go north to live, to the Rosebud Reservation, where he came from. So two days after my birth, my mother packed us up and left with him.''

''You grew up on a Lakota reservation?'' Joe saw the play of emotions clearly across her proud copper features. He also saw the living hell in her eyes, and that shook him deeply. It was the first time Akiva was allowing him the privilege of seeing her simply as a human being—not a warrant officer, not as a gunship pilot or a C.O., but as a woman who was hurting deeply from her scarred past.

''I grew up in hell,'' she told him wryly. Sighing, Akiva crossed her legs and rested her elbows on her knees. Her voice sounded faraway even to her as she continued. ''I was the Apache brat on the res. I was different. I didn't belong. The Lakota kids teased me mercilessly—but that is the way of many Indians. They find out if you're weak or strong. If you're weak, they'll eat you alive and destroy you. But I wasn't going to let that happen. They could pull my braids all they wanted, taunt me that my mother was an Apache whore, and throw pebbles and sticks at me as they followed me around like a wolf pack at school, or on the way home.'' Her eyes flashed with anger. ''They were too cowardly to face me one-on-one like a warrior would. They always came after me in a group—both boys and girls. They thought there was strength in numbers....''

Akiva grinned slightly. ''What they didn't count on was my great-great-grandmother's warrior blood on my mother's side of the family. Na-u-kuzzi, Great Bear, was Geronimo's best warrior. She was my relative. I have her blood in my veins.'' Lifting her head proudly, Akiva held Joe's troubled gray gaze. ''One day, I'd had enough. One of the boys, Jerry Crow Boy, had thrown a pretty hefty stick at me. It hit me in the shoulder and hurt me. I felt a rage that day that just exploded—like a ten-ton nuclear bomb going off inside me, Joe. I picked the stick up, gave the Apache war cry, then turned and charged into that group of kids. I was swinging that stick as hard as I could.''

Chuckling darkly, Akiva laced her fingers together and said, ''They scattered like a pack of cowardly dogs in all directions. I went home that day feeling victorious. I held on to that stick—it became my war club. When I got home an hour later, some of the parents had already driven over to see my dad, and told him what I'd done. Of course, they left out the fact that Crow Boy had struck me first.''

Akiva tapped her right shoulder. ''Under my uniform here is a two-inch scar that stick had opened up. Of course, my father didn't care that I had blood all over my blouse from being hit by Crow Boy. My mother wasn't home at the time. She worked at the school as a secretary.''

Joe's stomach clenched. He knew from the look on Akiva's face, and the sound of her voice, that he wasn't going to like what she was going to tell him. ''So, what did your father do? Did he hear you out? Listen to both sides of the story first before acting?''

Snorting, Akiva flashed him a wicked look. ''Him? One thing you find out about Indian nations is that they're still fighting the battles they fought a hundred or more years ago between one another. I was the Apache whore's kid. I didn't count in Lakota eyes. I was the enemy. In my father's twisted reality, all Crow Boy had done was count coup on me. In his eyes, and with the urging of the other kids' parents, he saw Crow Boy's actions as honorable."

"What?" Joe couldn't keep the anger out of his voice.

"Yeah," Akiva murmured acidly. "Well, that was fine. I learned about counting coup the Plains Indian way. My father beat the tar out of me for attacking Crow Boy and his gang. He sent me to my room without dinner. I remember sitting in there, crying and wondering what I'd done wrong. I knew a lot about Lakota people, because he was always telling me stories of his people and downgrading anything Apache. He didn't like my Apache side. He saw it as a flaw, something to be ashamed of."

Keeping his mounting rage in check, Joe began to understand why Akiva always had her armor in place. "I can't imagine why he did that to you. You were a little girl, scared and alone.... You needed to be held, not hurt. You needed to be protected, cared for, not beaten...."

The wobble in Joe's voice opened up her heavily guarded heart as nothing else could have. Akiva sat there and felt the hot sting of tears at the back of her eyes. Lowering her lashes, she muttered off-key, "Indians are tough on their kids. It's the way it is."

"No," Joe rasped unsteadily, as he searched her suffering profile, "it's not. My dad never laid a hand on me. Oh, I got punished for what I did wrong, but he never killed my spirit or tried to break me the way your father tried to break you."

Lifting her chin, Akiva gazed at him through her lashes again. Joe's face was alive with emotions. She saw the anger, the sympathy and something else burning deep within his stormy gaze. Somehow, just sharing her past with him was helping to heal her, and Akiva didn't understand why. Suddenly, her pain oozed out of her, like pus from an infected wound. As she shared more with him, Akiva began to feel as if the pressure of her painful past was easing. She could feel herself being freed from it once and for all.

''My mother came home, saw what had happened, and the next day left my father. She took me back to the Red Rock Reservation, where we lived with my grandmother. But after the divorce, my mother fell for an alcoholic white man.'' Akiva's lips tightened. She picked at the flaking black stone they sat upon. ''He was a math teacher who taught on the res.''

''Sounds like you went from the frying pan into the fire?'' Joe guessed grimly as he saw the set of her mouth. Akiva dipped her head in answer, the silken coverlet of her black hair sliding across her shoulder and partially blocking his view of her haunted features.

''Yep,'' she sighed. ''Because he was a raging alcoholic, no school officials in their right mind would hire him. But things are desperate on a res, so he got hired even though he was drunk out of his gourd half the time at school. I was ashamed of him. I was angry at my mother. My only safe place was with my grandmother. When my mother remarried and we went to live in res housing, I tried to spend most of my time at my grandma's home instead.''

''And how did your stepfather get along with you?''

''Let's just say it wasn't pretty. I was eight by that time and I was a tough little kid. My grandmother let it be known that he was not to hit me. She was a pretty formidable warrior,'' Akiva told him. ''She had the blood of warriors in her veins, and she was the one who gave me back my spirit, my pride in who I was. She helped me to connect with the long line of honored Apache women warriors I came from.''

''And your mother?''

Shaking her head, Akiva whispered painfully, "She was beaten to a bloody pulp by that Anglo bastard once a week.... And when I was there, he beat me, too."

Wincing, Joe rapidly began to put the picture together as to why Akiva didn't trust men in general regardless of their skin color. Scowling, he picked up a damp leaf and methodically began to tear it into small pieces. Feeling her anguish, Joe looked up. Akiva was sitting there like a frozen statue, her eyes dark and distant. She wasn't here with him any longer, she was in the past, reliving that terrible nightmare of her childhood. Dropping the pieces of leaf, he rubbed his hands on his thighs. If he didn't, he was going to turn around and hold her, because that's what Akiva needed right now. To be held and to know that she was *safe.*

His mind clicked along at lightning speed over the incidents of the past six weeks with her: what she'd said, how she'd reacted to certain things he'd done or said. Her past was never far away from her. Not really. But was anyone's?

"Your grandmother gave you pride in being Apache?"

"Yes. She healed me with her jaguar spirit medicine. My stepfather kept beating me up until I was eleven." Akiva touched the leather-covered hatchet that hung from her web belt. "She threatened to use this war ax on him if he touched me again after that. She'd seen what my Lakota father had done to me—the scars on my body—and she swore to my mother and to him that if she saw one more scratch on me, she'd scalp him with the ax." Akiva's eyes glittered. "And she meant it, too. My grandmother was a warrior woman—the only living one on the res at the time."

"Jaguar medicine? My daddy vaguely mentioned this thing about animal medicine once or twice, but that's all

I know about it.'' Joe asked, puzzled. ''I've heard of wolf medicine, eagle...but jaguar?''

''Jaguars used to roam the Southwest.'' She noted his confused look. ''Did your father teach you about spirit guides?''

''No...he didn't. I'm afraid he wasn't tied to his people or the natural world. He never shared much of his beliefs with me. I do know that he comes from a long line of warriors, though.'' He shrugged. ''Maybe that's why I fly an Apache now. Instead of a horse, spear and bow, I have a helicopter with a cannon, rockets and missiles.''

''Each of us, whether we're Native American or not, has guides. These are spiritual beings who are much more evolved than we are. They love us unequivocally, no matter how bad we are, no matter how many mistakes we've made.'' Akiva shrugged. ''In the Christian faith, they are called angels, but to us, who are of an earth-based religion, they are spirit guides who come in many shapes and types. Jaguars were considered the most powerful spirit guide a person could have. An Indian with a jaguar guide is a great warrior who battles the dark side to bring light and harmony back into our third-dimensional world.''

''And you have such a guide?''

Akiva bowed her head. ''Yes, I do. I feel him around me at times of danger. I feel his thick, soft fur against my body, helping me, protecting me. I've never been trained how to use him, but I know he's there. I see his help strongly with regard to my intuition, in knowing when the enemy is near.''

''That must be a good feeling,'' Joe murmured, wishing that his father had taught him of his heritage. He liked the idea of such a spiritual protector being around in time of danger.

"It is." She tapped her head. "Sometimes I hear him whisper in my ear. It isn't in language—just a telepathic urge or emotion that is imprinted upon my mind. I always listen to his wise suggestions. He's helped me know when Kamovs are around. He's saved my life and the lives of other pilots with his warnings of danger to me." The corners of her mouth tipped wryly. "Only when I don't listen to him do I get into trouble."

Chuckling, Joe nodded. "I could sure use someone like that whispering to me. I'd probably avoid a lotta the potholes in life that I've stepped in with great regularity."

She smiled tentatively. "I know you have spirit guides. You just aren't in touch with them, is all. But you can be. All you need to do is desire it. Desire is intent, and intent draws the spirit guide closer to you. Just open up your heart and feel her."

"I'll try that the next time I'm in hot water," Joe promised seriously. He was glad to have this opening with Akiva. She was allowing him access to her as a person by sharing her private life with him. His heart ached for her.

Akiva eyed him for a long time, the silence strung gently between them. "You must have medicine people in your blood somewhere," she said finally.

"Why?"

"Because you're healing me. I never thought it was possible…until now…"

Chapter 7

"Luis, come, look at my latest acquisition." Don Javier Rios sat at his huge, carved mahogany desk, which was placed at one end of his den. His son, tall, dark and with looks that made the *señoritas* swoon with desire, stood looking out of the French windows, his hands in the pockets of his expensive tan pants.

"Come..." Javier pleaded. He picked up a three-foot-long sword from his collection, held it between his hands to show his son as Luis turned and walked toward him.

Luis knew what was coming. His stomach was in knots, his irritability and frustration barely in check. "What is it, *Patrón?*" For as long as he could remember, he had called his father *Patrón,* not Papa or Father. Because of the brilliance and wealth of his academically esteemed father, Luis had grown up in a movable household, on many continents.

"Look," Javier said, with deep pleasure resonating in his voice, "a Roman short sword. The one that was at auction in Europe. Is it not beautiful, my son?'' He held it up toward Luis as he came to a stop in front of the massive, carved desk.

Taking the sword with careless abandon, Luis looked at it more closely. ''This is authentic?'' Of course it would be. His father had great renown in archeological circles for his academic knowledge of the Roman era.

Chuckling, Javier, who was dressed in a starched white shirt and a black neckerchief, picked up a Cuban cigar from a nearby burgundy leather humidor. ''Of course it is. Britain, 30 A.D.'' He picked up the snippers and clipped off the end of the fragrant, thickly rolled cigar. There was nothing like a Cuban cigar anywhere in the world, and Javier cherished each one he smoked. His thick gray brows rose as he dug for a silver lighter in the pocket of his tan slacks. Lighting the cigar, he puffed on it contentedly, the thick white smoke curling upward around his head. He watched as his only son gingerly inspected the weapon. Oh, he knew that Luis, who was twenty-seven and still very young, didn't have his love of all things Roman. In fact, Luis cared little for antiquity at all. His son was in love with his helicopters. Flying was his passion. Javier watched his thin, dark brows bunch as he ran his fingers carefully and respectfully along the dull, aged blade.

''This one has seen some fighting,'' Luis said. ''A lot of nicks in it.'' Glancing up, he saw his father's light brown eyes settle on him, his mouth firm above his gray, meticulously shaped goatee and square chin. Luis knew what was coming. Inwardly, he tried to protect himself against it.

Javier rolled the Cuban cigar around in his mouth. ''I'm having Alejandro create replicas of it. Exact replicas, for the next spectacle. Just think, Luis—my Roman soldiers will be carrying a replica of the real thing.'' And he punched his square index finger toward the sword in his son's hands.

''Your soldiers will be well prepared in the arena,'' Luis teased lightly as he gently set the sword back on the desk in front of his father.

Gazing down at the ancient weapon, Javier studied the handle, which was made of brass and had once been wrapped, he was sure, in leather. In the heat of battle, a man sweated heavily. Without leather around the handle, the weapon would slip or fly out of a soldier's hand.

''I am thinking seriously of having my leather maker create a handle for this short sword. Do you think that wise?''

Luis moved his feet restlessly. ''Yes.''

''Why?'' He saw his son scowl and once again jam his hands into the pockets of his slacks.

''The sword would not be easy to hold without some kind of grip on it.''

''Very good!'' Javier exclaimed. He sat up and puffed once more on the cigar, then placed it in a crystal ashtray nearby. Running his large hand across the sword in a reverent gesture, he whispered, ''Think of who might have owned this sword, Luis. What did he look like? Was he a tribune, in charge of many soldiers? A centurion, responsible for his hundred-man phalanx? Perhaps a general? Why...even Caesar himself!'' His voice softened in excitement as he delicately touched each nick in the blade. ''How many battles was this sword in? Did the man who owned it die with it in his hand? What battles did this sword see? It was excavated at a Roman garrison site in England. Other objects were carbon dated for 30 A.D. That was a time when Julius Caesar was widening the Roman Empire, and he was pushing out the Celts and

Druids, slaughtering them, to bring Britannia beneath the yoke of Roman rule."

Sunlight poured through the French windows at that moment, and Luis lifted his head and watched the golden glow spill into the long, rectangular room. This was his father's Roman room, a place where he spent a good part of every day. At age sixty-five, Javier found his passion for all things Roman had pushed their other business aside. He'd given Luis free rein to begin to handle the other empire he'd built over the last fifty years: his cocaine trade. For the most part, he allowed Luis to manage it alone. However, Javier had a penchant for thoroughness and details, which was what had propelled him to the top of the trade in southern Mexico; he didn't overlook anything.

"You'll spend the next month wondering who owned that short sword," Luis told him genially.

"Ah, yes, my destiny, is it not?" Javier allowed his hands to rest on the million-dollar artifact.

With a slight smile, Luis nodded. "It is, *Patrón.*"

Sighing, Javier picked up the cigar and leaned back in his burgundy leather chair. He puffed on it, the white smoke swirling and reminding him of the wisps of clouds that always hung over the jungle surrounding his estate just outside San Cristobel.

"It has come to my attention, Luis, that in the last sixty days we've had fifty-five flights turned back from crossing the Gulf. I've talked to some of the pilots. We pay these men top money to fly the cocaine to the States."

Stomach tightening, Luis stood very still. His father's deep, rolling voice continued in a thoughtful manner. The *patrón* was not a man who gave in to his emotions. No, he saved his passion for his beloved Roman artifacts, which he'd collected nearly all his life.

"I asked Señor Bates, who has been in our employ the longest. He was in the U.S. Air Force at one time. I asked him *what* is turning you back. Why are you not completing your runs to the U.S.? He told me there is a black military helicopter, without any markings on it, that comes out of the night and fires across the nose of his aircraft. Señor Bates, having been in the military, knows that this is a warning to him. That if he does not turn back, he will be shot down with the next rounds being fired. So—" Javier shrugged "—he comes back here. Back to one of our dirt airstrips, our cocaine undelivered. Our people waiting for the shipment are very unhappy, Luis. Now, I know you have tried to reroute these flights up through Mexico and into the Southwestern U.S. to other dealers, but my son, this is an escalating problem. You need to solve it."

Taking another puff on the cigar, Javier placed it back in the ashtray. Weaving his fingers together, he placed them against his flat stomach. "Our main dealers along the Gulf Coast are angry. They're threatening to use our competitor in Colombia instead, if we can't get these shipments out to them in a timely manner."

"I know, *Patrón.*" Running his hand through his dark, long hair, Luis could not keep the frustration out of his voice. "I share your worry."

"What *is* this black helicopter?"

"Bates says it's a Boeing Apache gunship."

"U.S. Army?"

"Yes."

"But...no markings on it?"

"It's probably a spook gunship on a covert mission,"

Luis grumbled. He took the chair set off to one side of his father's desk and sat down dejectedly.

"So, we have the CIA in our backyard?"

Shrugging, Luis muttered, "It looks like it. I have men from San Cristobel looking around the jungle area. So far, they've come up with no leads. I've started sending my other three helicopters to follow the plane flying our Gulf Coast route, to see if we can spot or trace this Apache."

"I see...." Javier ran his fingers lightly over the sword. "Could this Apache be from another country other than the U.S.? What if one of the other drug lords bought it and is trying to hurt our business?"

"It's possible, *Patrón,* but doubtful. The U.S. is not going to let just anyone buy such a machine. It is state of the art, the best gunship in the world. They're very careful who has them."

"And what do you think?"

Grimacing, Luis shot his father an irritable look. "That it's spook-related. It's U.S."

"But the army...?"

"Why not?" Luis growled. "The Pentagon is financing a huge military buildup in Colombia right now, trying to destroy the drug trade there. They throw all kinds of money, equipment and military trainers at the Colombian government. Why not send this combat gunship to hunt us?"

"Do you think this Apache is part of that effort?"

"I don't know, *Patrón.* I lay awake at night trying to beat answers out of my brain, and I don't know—yet."

"So," Javier said softly, "you must have a plan to catch this Apache. Yes?"

"Yes." Luis sat up. "I've been working with Bates on the fifty-five incidents. I've tried changing the routes—where and when they leave Mexico and fly the Gulf. Every time, no matter what route I've chosen, that black helo shows up. I've changed times, places, and nothing works. They seem to know when we leave. It's uncanny.''

''Do we have a mole in our organization who is feeding them this information?''

Luis shook his head. ''No, because I'm the only one who tells which plane and pilot to leave, and from what airstrip, as well as what route to travel over the Gulf.'' He tapped his head. ''It's all up here, *Patrón.*''

Nodding, Javier stared down at the short sword. ''Yet they do not shoot our aircraft down. Do you think that odd?''

''Yes and no. Bates said if it's a U.S. gunship, they're probably under orders not to fire because if they make a mistake and shoot down a civilian plane, there will be an international incident. No, they want to keep their cover, keep their anonymity and keep nipping at our heels.'' Opening his hands, he added, ''I've routed fifty percent of these shipments north instead of over the Gulf. Our dealers are still getting the stuff, just not as quickly as they'd like.''

''Yes, but if we continue to swamp the Southwestern border of the U.S. with these FAA-unauthorized flights, then they will do something about it.'' Javier stroked his goatee in thought. ''Increased flights overland are going to net us a very swift response from border patrol and you know that.''

''Yes, *Patrón,* I do.''

''And trying to get the cocaine across the Gulf on boats is very hard,'' Javier sighed. ''The U.S. Coast Guard is too vigilant. They are waiting for us. No, we've got to get those flights across the Gulf going again, that is all there is to it."

Luis moved uncomfortably in the leather chair. The sunlight drifting into the room had disappeared. Outside, wispy white clouds over the jungle were moving languorously across the morning sky and blotting out the sun.

"I do have a plan, *Patrón.*"

"Ah. Yes?" Javier sat up, his brows arched expectantly. His mouth twitched. "You are such a good son, Luis. You are always thinking. I'm very proud of you."

Squirming inwardly, Luis said, "*Patrón,* it is a risk. A huge one."

"Yes? What is the plan?"

"I'm having the four helicopters armed with machine guns and rocket launchers."

Javier frowned. "If you arm them, then you'll be going after this Apache?"

"I *have* to, *Patrón.*"

Tapping his thick, square fingers on the polished surface of his mahogany desk, Javier thought for a moment before he spoke. He saw the anger and frustration in his son's face. Luis had always looked so much like his mother, God rest her soul—especially his eyes, and his long, narrow face. But those chocolate-colored eyes had an eagle's merciless glint in them. Javier knew Luis's square jaw and broad forehead came from him, as did his intense, aggressive personality. Marguerite, Luis's mother, had died in childbirth, leaving him to be raised solely by his father, so Javier's influence had dominated.

Don Rios still grieved for his lost wife. She had been ethereal and beautiful, more like the mists that formed and shifted above the humid jungle than flesh-and-blood human. She had been delicate and her health fragile.

When Luis was conceived, she had been joyous, and so had Javier. He had been totally unprepared to lose his wife, who held his heart so gently. It was the most bittersweet moment in his life when the doctor came out of the delivery room and told him sadly that his wife was dead, but that he was the proud father of a son who would carry on his name and empire.

Giving Luis a dark look now, Javier asked, "Do you not think that if you fire upon this gunship, it won't fire back at *you?*"

"Absolutely, *Patrón.* But our plan is to jump it—all four helicopters, from four different directions, all at once."

"It's my understanding the Apache has the most sophisticated radar system in the world. What makes you think the crew won't know you're coming?"

Shrugging, Luis got up and thrust his hands into the pockets of his slacks once again. "I know we're going up against one of the most deadly military helicopters in the world. But I'm doing my homework. I'm finding out more information. I have my lookouts posted in the jungle now, to alert me if they see or even *hear* a helicopter in their area. Somehow, we must find out where they are flying out of, where they're based."

"Yes," Javier agreed heavily, "if you want to kill a snake, you chop off its head." He picked up the short sword and made a swift, chopping motion to emphasize his point.

"I understand, *Patrón.*" Halting, Luis ran his fingers across his recently shaved jaw. "I'd give *anything* to know who the hell they are...."

"Well?" Akiva asked as she came over and stood by Joe and Spec Robin Ferris. Ferris, who was their software technician, had been working on a group of cables that snaked along the left side of the Apache. In the last five days, HUD screens had been blinking off and on, and she was trying to run down the problem.

It was very hot in the afternoon, with high humidity. Joe was in his camouflage pants, his olive-green T-shirt damp with sweat. Akiva was in her army uniform as well. They all stood looking at the opened panel.

Ferris sighed. "Ma'am, I'm not having any luck so far." She placed her short, slender fingers on the thick bunch of cables that were bound together and laid flat within the panel. "I've been doing checks all morning, and I'm finding nothing so far."

Akiva stared at the cables. Many panels on each side of the Apache fuselage housed white wire cables. Each cable was protected by waterproof sealing. "Humidity?" That was always a problem back at the Black Jaguar Base, which was also set in jungle terrain. Air vapor, over time, would condense into small droplets of water that could get into the wiring and potentially short out a system. The problem was finding out where it was occurring.

Ferris shrugged. "That would make sense, ma'am."

"We've been running diagnostics," Joe told her. Ordinarily, Akiva never came out to the hangar to check on maintenance. That was his area of responsibility. To keep the base running, she had her hands full with paperwork alone—paperwork he knew she hated. As Joe studied her profile, his heart speeded up. Ever since their talk down by the waterfall a month ago, their relationship had subtly but continuously changed—for the better, as far as he was concerned.

As Akiva reached forward and brushed her fingertips across the thick cables, Joe stepped back a little to give her room. He saw her brows knit as she continued to explore the two feet of exposed cables, which looked like bunches of spaghetti tied together.

"This is all damp," she muttered, rubbing her fingertips together.

"It's like that all the time," Ferris told her. "This is worse than back in Peru." Pointing out the hangar opening, she added, "We have ninety-percent humidity all the time, ma'am. It rains almost every afternoon, and maybe three nights a week. I dry off the cables regularly, particularly just before a mission. But there's nothing we can do about this high humidity."

Akiva nodded and glanced at Joe. Her pulse leaped when she found his gray eyes trained on her. Instantly, her heart opened to him. Trying to ignore her feelings, she muttered, "Okay, Ferris, keep following down the leads. It's probably humidity. That's the only thing that makes sense."

"Yes, ma'am...."

Akiva gave the young enlisted woman a slight smile. Ferris was twenty-two, with dark blond hair, green eyes and with a triangular shaped face. Akiva knew Ferris was their best software technician at the base, and if anyone could track down a problem, it was her. "I know you can find that gremlin for us."

"I will or else," Ferris promised fervently.

Joe turned and walked with Akiva as she left the area. "Hey," he said in a conspiratorial tone only she could hear as they headed back toward her office, "how about a spontaneous moment?"

She gave him a dark look. Joe was grinning. Her spirits lifted because of the intimate smile he shared with her. Halting at the door of her office, she said, "What's the matter, have I been working too hard? All work and not enough play, Calhoun?"

He liked her ability to tease him in return; that was a new facet of Akiva that she had started sharing with him since their gut-wrenching talk at the waterfall. "Something like that." Rather proudly he confided, "I got Dean, who has mess duty today, to make us a special dessert. I want to share it with you. Got ten minutes?"

"You're impossible," Akiva muttered. She turned and looked at her desk, which was strewn with paperwork that begged for attention. Between flying two missions a day, plus all the other demands on her time, Akiva had found that she was getting behind on the paperwork.

"Ten minutes," Joe pleaded. He saw her golden eyes become shadowed. Joe knew she was working eighteen hours a day nonstop, without proper rest or sleep. She was trying to learn to balance her C.O. duties against her mission duties. And right now, she needed a little time off.

Though he ached to reach out and touch her, he kept his hand at his side. Since their talk, the idea of kissing her, of pulling Akiva into his arms and holding her, to give her that sense of safety she'd never had with a man, was eating him alive. He knew he could open up a beautiful new world to her. More than anything, Joe wanted to be the one to share that discovery with Akiva.

"Oh, all right... I shouldn't..." Still she hesitated, looking at the papers that begged for her attention.

"Hoo doggies! Come on! You won't regret this...."

Chapter 8

"Ta-da!" Joe brought out his surprise from the mess kitchen. As he rounded the corner of the plywood wall that separated the kitchen from the dining area, the still-warm dessert in his hands, Akiva gave him a quizzical look.

"Sit down," Joe entreated. "We're gonna chow down like hawgs at the feedin' trough, sweetheart." With a flourish, he placed the dessert on the rough-hewn picnic table. "This is my mama's recipe for cheesecake," he informed her proudly. "Over the past few weeks, every time the spooks choppered in our supplies, I've been wranglin' with those good ole boys to get me the ingredients." He rubbed his hands, then headed back to the kitchen to retrieve paper napkins, flatware and an opened can of cherries in thick red sauce, which he set down next to the cheesecake.

Stunned, Akiva managed a slight smile as she sat down opposite him. The cheesecake was delicious looking. Her mouth watered. With another gleeful flourish and a boyish grin, he cut the cheesecake and placed two pieces on paper plates, then spooned several dollops of the cherries on top.

"Now, the only thing missing," he told her conspiratorially, sitting down opposite her, "is whipped cream. My mama would pile a ton of it on top." As he handed Akiva one of the plates, their fingers met and touched. Joe's hand tingled pleasantly from the contact. He saw that slight smile on Akiva's mouth. "You *do* like cheesecake, doncha?" He stopped, realizing he never thought to ask Akiva that question.

"Oh, yes, I love cheesecake," she murmured, and picked up her fork, hardly waiting for Joe to do the same. "This is a wonderful surprise, Joe." She cast him a dark look. "You're a first-class scrounger. Cheesecake isn't on our menu."

Grinning from ear to ear, Joe felt heat tunnel up his neck and into his face as relief rushed through him. Akiva slid the first bite into her mouth. He watched as she closed her eyes and chewed slowly, savoring it thoroughly. His heart speeded up again as he saw the expression on her face change to one of utter pleasure. Joy flowed through him. Anything he could do to make Akiva smile, to lift the weight of the world off her shoulders, if only for a moment, made him feel damn good. He was always looking for ways to give her a time-out, to play instead of work.

Digging into his own piece, he drawled, "This is heaven come to earth, gal. My mama's cheesecake is known throughout West Texas and the Panhandle. She's won all kinds of county and state prizes for it."

Opening her eyes, Akiva said, "I can see why! This is delicious, Joe. Really..."

Pleased, he murmured, "Consider it a gift from the heart. Mine to yours." He cut off another small chunk and popped it into his mouth, relishing it thoroughly.

A gift from the heart. Akiva bowed her head and tried not to think about his words, which had been spoken with husky sincerity. They were alone in the mess hall. It was midafternoon, with hazy sunlight shining through the clean windows of the building. For a moment, Akiva felt nothing but happiness, her heart soaring as she absorbed this unexpected moment with Joe. How many times had she wanted to just sit and talk to him, as they'd done that day at the waterfall? She was starved for conversation, but there was never time, and they were rarely alone. The base was small and there were people around them almost all the time.

Lifting her chin, she watched Joe as he ate voraciously. "One thing about you," she announced with irony in her voice. "There's no secret to how to get to you—through your stomach."

Chuckling, Joe said, "What's that old saying? A way to a man's heart is through his stomach?" He raised his right hand. "Guilty as charged, gal."

She laughed and continued to cut small chunks of the cheesecake, relishing every little bite. "You are going to share the rest of this with the women?"

"Shore 'nuff. But this came out of the oven two hours ago and I wanted you to have a piece when it was still slightly warm. That's when it's best—all the flavors are at their peak."

"Do you cook?" Akiva tilted her head and watched his gray eyes light up with pride.

"Sure do. When I was a whippersnapper, my mama shooed my little butt into the kitchen and told me I wasn't gonna be one of those Texas good ole boys who didn't know how to cook for hisself."

"She taught you well," Akiva murmured, laughter lurking in her eyes. She studied Joe closely. He was a good-looking man, and best of all, he had one hell of a sense of humor. Akiva truly appreciated that about him.

"My mama's a wise woman. My daddy was gone a lot on long hauls with his eighteen-wheel rig, drivin' back and forth across the U.S. almost weekly. I always looked forward to seein' him, when he drove in."

"That's not a life I'd like," Akiva murmured. She took her fork and stabbed a cherry that had fallen off the cheesecake, then slid it into her mouth.

"What?"

"One parent missing for most of the week. Didn't you miss him?"

"Oh, sure I did. But when he came home, he more than made up for his being gone."

"How?"

Joe finished off his cheesecake and put the plate and flatware aside. He got up and went to the coffee dispenser, which sat on a box near the wall of the kitchen. Pouring two cups, he said, "He made sure we had time together. Mama saved all my schoolwork in a pile on the coffee table near his chair. He'd sit with me and go over everything—the grades, the exercises, and any problems I had with stuff. I wasn't real good in English, so he used to spend time showing me how to diagram sentences." Coming back, he sat down and slid one of the thick white ceramic mugs over to Akiva.

"Thanks." She took the cup and sipped the coffee, her gaze never leaving his face. Just listening to Joe talk, hearing the stories he wove, always made her feel good. Akiva could feel the stress draining out of her neck and shoulders. She felt a sense of lightness when she shared these precious, stolen moments with Joe.

''One of the things his dad—my grandpappy—did was to make sure he was well schooled in English. Being Comanche and all, the old man had real problems getting and holding a job. So he taught my father English so he'd never have the same problems all his life.''

Nodding, Akiva said, ''Yes, it's a familiar situation. Was your grandfather's native tongue Comanche, with English as a second language?''

''Yep.''

''Do you speak Comanche?''

Shaking his head, Joe said, ''No...I don't. My dad said I needed to learn English, not our old language. Now, I'm regretful about that, after talking to you about your life as a Native American. I've missed a lot....'' He brightened. ''But Spanish was like a second language in our household, because we lived on the poor side of the tracks, with the Latinos. I was speaking Spanish more than any other language, except at school.''

''And I learned Spanish as a second language on the res,'' Akiva noted. ''Apache first, then Spanish, and finally English. And I still retain some of the Lakota, but I'm really rusty at it now.''

Joe gave her a searching look. ''What was it like growing up on the Red Rock Res? Was it better for you than the Lakota one? Did life settle down for you?''

Joe saw her gold eyes dim with memories. Her slender hands tightened momentarily around the cup. Knowing full well he was traipsing into her personal life once more, Joe held his breath. Akiva had no idea that he'd planned this whole thing to get a few minutes of quiet, uninterrupted time with her. She also didn't know that he'd ordered the three enlisted women to stay away from the mess for an hour so that they could talk. Of course, the women thought they were talking about business, but Joe wasn't going to tell them differently.

With a wave of her hand, Akiva said, "In one way it did. My mother was home with all our relatives who lived on the res. She felt better. But that lasted about six months. When I was nine, she married that Anglo teacher."

"Your grandmother, though," Joe said, "seems to have played a key role in your life. She did protect you from him and his bouts of drinking."

Grimly, Akiva sipped her coffee. "My grandmother saw what was going on and told my mother that I was going to come and live with her. She'd come over to my parents' house one evening and found me with a bloody nose and a black eye. My stepfather was roaring drunk, yelling and screaming at us. He was mean when he was drunk, Joe. All I could do—all I wanted to do—was run and hide." Her mouth quirked. "Only there was no safe place to do that. If I went to my room and closed the door, he'd smash it open with his foot and drag me out into the living room. My mother would try and protect me, and then he'd slap her around."

Joe shook his head. "I'm sorry, Akiva. I really am."

He reached over without thinking and laid his hand over her fist, which was resting on the table. Moving his fingers gently across hers, he worked her clenched fingers loose. Giving her cool, damp hand a tender squeeze, he looked into her face. The moment he'd touched her, he saw some of the darkness leave her wide, golden eyes. She was so beautiful to him. With her thick black hair hanging like a cloak around her shoulders, she made him ache to hold her and give her that sense of safety she so richly deserved.

Akiva froze inwardly as Joe picked up her hand and held it in his warm, dry one. Every time she talked about the past, she broke into a sweat. It was an automatic reaction, she knew; the past was never far away from her, emotionally. Yet his spontaneous gesture calmed her pounding heart, and she felt the adrenaline dissolving. His touch was magical. Healing. As she stared across the table at Joe, and saw his face alive with anger and pain—the pain she'd suffered as a child—something old and dark broke loose within her tightly armored heart.

Time slowed to a halt between them, like sunlight dancing on woven strands of gold. She felt her heart opening as his rough fingers caressed hers. The look in his stormy eyes made her feel a thread of happiness that was foreign to her. She *liked* Joe touching her. It made her feel safe. Protected. Hungering for more of that feeling, Akiva stared, confused, into his eyes.

''What's happening?'' she asked unsteadily as she looked down at their hands.

''Nothing that isn't good, gal,'' he whispered rawly. He lifted her hand in his larger one. Akiva's full attention was on the way his fingers grasped hers. ''You deserve some goodness in your life, Akiva. I'm sorry for what happened to you. I can't imagine you, a little girl goin' through that kind of hell... I wish—well, if I'd been there...''

Warmth and happiness suffused her unexpectedly. Akiva pulled her hand free, a bit frightened by what she was feeling. Wrestling with the happiness throbbing through her chest and warming her lower body, she sat there, hands in her lap beneath the table. The tender flame burning in Joe's gray eyes nearly unstrung her. There was nothing, absolutely nothing, to dislike about this man. And that scared her.

"My grandmother beat you to it," she managed to reply in a strained tone. "That night, she took me out of the house and told my parents they had shamed themselves, that no one should ever lift a hand to strike a child."

"Good for her," Joe rasped. Right now, Akiva's head was bowed and she was looking at her hands, buried beneath the table. Her high cheekbones were suffused with pink. The moment he'd touched her hand, he'd seen the corners of her drawn mouth ease, some of the pain she carried dissolve. And he'd seen something else—something so gossamer and fleeting, he wasn't sure if he'd made it up or not. Had he seen desire in Akiva's eyes? For him? Or was he imagining it because that's what he wanted—for her to like him…perhaps even to desire him? Oh, Joe knew that was a far-fetched dream of the young romantic still stuck inside him. He was an idealist at heart, and he held out hope for the hopeless.

Joe knew Akiva didn't trust men in general, and Anglo men in particular. The fact that he was part Indian was helping her accept him. And little by little, he'd felt the walls she held up to keep him out dissolving. Now, he sensed those walls were nearly gone, and it was a heady, scary moment for him. If he said the wrong thing, Akiva would shut him out once more, he knew. And that was the last thing he wanted. Somehow—Joe wasn't sure exactly how—he had to keep asking the right questions, keep the dialogue alive between them. This was one of many times when Joe felt inept as he floundered mentally and emotionally, casting around for the right words to keep that nurturing connection with Akiva strong.

"And so she brought you to her home?"

Nodding, Akiva lifted her hands. She pushed the last

of her cheesecake, uneaten, toward Joe. "Here, you finish it. I've lost my appetite."

Scowling, he whispered, "I'm sorry, gal. I didn't mean to upset you like this...."

"It's old news, Joe. Past history." She shrugged, as if ridding herself of that dark past. "I don't know what's going on, but every time I sit with you and talk about it, I feel like whatever I say or share with you is lightening a load from my shoulders." She gave him a confused look. "I can't explain why that's happening. It's never happened to me before."

He pulled the plate toward him. If the truth were known, he'd lost his appetite, too. Still, he picked up his fork and dug into the cheesecake, because if he didn't, he was going to reach over and pick up Akiva's hands, which were now clasped on the table in front of her.

"What we have," he said in a low tone, holding her uncertain gaze, "is somethin' special, gal. Somethin' that's being built over time. I like it...whatever it is...and I hope you do, too?" He held his breath as he saw Akiva's thin black brows gather. She looked up toward the ceiling, as if searching for words. Afraid, he felt a frisson of anxiety in his chest. His heart beat a little harder.

"Look," he counseled, "don't worry about us, or where this is goin'. We've got a mission and a base to run. That comes first. It's always first." Joe forced himself to eat the cheesecake, but he didn't taste it as he watched the play of emotions cross Akiva's face. Did she realize how devastatingly beautiful she was?

"Y-yes...the base. And our mission. It always comes first, Joe." Akiva didn't know what else to say. "I—well, frankly, my relationships with men haven't been anything to write home about."

"Based upon your early childhood, how could they be?"

"It's a trust issue," Akiva muttered.

"I know that."

She gave him a narrowed look. "I always feel like you know more than you're telling me. Sometimes I feel like you're reading my mind...." *Or my heart.* But Akiva didn't say that.

She saw Joe's mouth pull into that tender smile he sometimes gave her when they were alone. Akiva had come to cherish that special look. When she found herself wanting to slide her hands across the table to touch his, touch him as he'd just touched her, she was startled. What was going on here? What magic was at play? Stifling the urge, because Akiva was not one to brazenly go after a man or share her feelings with him, she sat quietly.

With a one-shouldered shrug, Joe finished the cheesecake and set the plate aside with the other one. "Maybe because I had a normal childhood and you didn't, and I can see the wounding it did to you?"

"I hate dragging my childhood around with me to this day. I try to get rid of it, but it's like an infection—it just stays with me."

"But your grandmother helped you in many ways, yes? That braid you always wear. I heard someone back at the Black Jaguar Base say once that only Apache men or women who passed all the tests of warrior training could wear it?"

Touching the slender braid hanging from the center part of her hair, Akiva said, "Yes, that's so."

"Your grandmother, it sounds like, gave you back your self-esteem, your confidence as a person."

His insight was always surprising, because Akiva never expected any man to have that ability to look into her heart and soul. Joe did on a regular basis. She was slowly getting used to it, but it still left her feeling slightly off balance. She knew so little of him in return. Yet she hungered for these rare moments of privacy with him.

"My grandmother held a ceremony with the local medicine woman. She brought the pieces of my shattered spirit back to me. Nowadays, it's called shamanism. She was able to help heal wounded souls who had lost pieces due to the trauma they'd endured.

"About a month after that ceremony, I began training to become a warrior like my great-great-grandmother. My grandmother gave me the war ax and the bowie knife I now carry on missions. She instilled in me the pride of our people—our toughness and endurance, and the fact that we never surrendered to the U.S. Army. We are the only nation who did not bow beneath the white man's heel. Oh, I know the Anglos' history books say different, but I believe the stories passed down to me."

"What kind of training did you go through?" Joe asked curiously.

"My grandmother had an old paint mustang that was probably well into his twenties. She taught me to ride. Not only to ride, but to do what we call a running mount and dismount." Gesturing with her hands, Akiva said, "I'd be at a full gallop, Joe, and with a signal, my grandmother would tell me to dismount. I'd grab the mustang's mane, swing my leg over his back, hit the ground running, then release his mane and keep running."

"Whew...that sounds tough."

"It was. I ate a lot of desert sand and rock before I got the hang of how to do it." She laughed, the memories flooding back to her. "Once I got that down, my grandmother had the mustang brought into a round enclosure made of brush and limbs tied together with ropes. It was probably as large as a small house. The horse would gallop around and around the edges of this enclosure and my grandma would stand in the middle, using a whip to keep the horse moving at high speed. She then told me to run toward the horse, grab his mane and fling myself up on his back."

Joe's eyes widened. "And you did?" That was an amazing feat of agility and physical strength. He saw Akiva smile broadly, with pride, for the first time. And when she smiled, her chin tilted at a confident angle, his heart pounded. How incredibly beautiful and soft she looked in that moment.

"Oh, yes. It took a lot of tries. I'd usually stumble and fall in the deep, soft sand of the enclosure. Or I'd grab the mane, but not grasp enough of it, and I'd go banging into the horse and be knocked off my feet, into the dirt. My grandmother would laugh, then tell me to get up, dust myself off and try again. Finally, after a lot of bumps and bruises, I got the hang of it." Akiva smiled in fond memory of those times. "Every day after school, after I got my homework done, I'd do running mounts and dismounts. The next test was to run five miles, then ten, fifteen and twenty, across the desert with a mouthful of water—and not swallow it as I ran." Her eyes glimmered as she saw her statement register. Joe's eyes widened considerably as he thought about what she'd just said.

"That sounds impossible," he muttered. "Hold water in your mouth and *run* twenty miles?"

"Yep." Pleased, Akiva added, "The last test—and there were fifteen of us who took this warrior test at the time—involved running twenty miles. Only that time we ran ten miles on the flat terrain of the desert, and the last ten climbing a mountain, where the medicine woman waited on top. We had to climb it, kneel down at a hole she'd dug and spit the water we'd carried into it. If we managed to do that, then we were awarded the third braid of a warrior.''

''Whew...'' Joe muttered, impressed. ''I never knew... I mean, that's *somethin'*.''

''There's more,'' she said. ''After that came training with the weapons of our people. I was taught how to throw a war ax and wield a bowie knife with deadly accuracy at both a still and a moving target. My grandmother then had me learn how to do it from the back of a galloping mustang.''

''Did you use a bow and arrow?''

''Oh, yes. And a spear, too. When Geronimo was running from the U.S. Army, dodging the brigades trying to capture him, his people were either riding or trotting on foot more than forty or fifty miles a day through the hot desert. If a horse died of exhaustion or lack of water, they got off and continued on foot at the same pace. Most horses were taught to eat cactus, which was peeled for them by my people, so they didn't get spines in their mouths. Those that wouldn't eat it died of dehydration.''

''And Geronimo and his people lived off the cactus as a source of water?''

Nodding, Akiva said in a low tone, ''My people are tough, Joe, with strong spirits. No matter how you beat us down, we will come back. We will stand and face you. And that is what my great-great-grandmother did. She was one of Geronimo's best warriors.''

''Before I met you, I didn't know Apaches had women warriors.''

''Of course they did. We're a matriarchal people. If a woman was good at something, she did it. If she took the tests of the warrior and passed them, then she wore the third braid. There was no gender difference to us.'' Akiva opened her hands, excitement in her low tone. ''My grandmother wore the third braid. My mother did not. But I brought pride back to our family once again, and I felt good about that.''

''And well you should,'' Joe declared, thoroughly impressed.

''At the ceremony when I became a warrior, all of my family was there, except for my stepfather. My grandmother made a speech to everyone. She held up her own war ax and bowie knife and announced that I would carry the family honor forward into this century, that I was now the warrior in the family.''

Akiva smiled softly and allowed her hands to drop back to the table. ''That was the greatest moment in my life, with everyone shouting, clapping and calling my name as my grandmother handed me those weapons. I wanted to cry for sheer joy, but I didn't. I stood there, tall and proud, though at twelve years old, I was pretty gangly. Five foot ten inches tall, I towered over all the other kids. My grandmother said that my great-great-grandmother had been six foot tall, an unheard of height among our people, especially back then. She predicted that I'd grow to six feet, too.

''The medicine woman who came forward to speak on my behalf, and who gave me the name Akiva, told me that I would carry on the family honor and make everyone proud. Not only my family, but the Apache nation.''

''Heavy-duty stuff,'' Joe murmured. He saw the glimmer of pride in Akiva's eyes. More than anything, he cherished the openness that now existed between them. She was talking to him as if he were her closest friend and confidant. Yes, he'd like to be that to her—and more. But for now, Joe was more than grateful for what existed between them. Another part of him hungered to connect with his own Comanche heritage. He was learning more every time Akiva shared her life on the res with him. It was a gift to him.

"Is that why you joined the army? To learn to fly?"

Akiva nodded. "I was a warrior, plain and simple. My grandmother told me that my horse would be an aircraft. That like my great-great-grandmother of old, I would be on the front lines battling darkness and making room for the light. The medicine woman told me that I now had my great-great-grandmother's spirit guide and guardian—a jaguar. That that was what had made Na-u-kuzzi so brave, heroic and powerful."

"Guides... Yes..." Joe recalled Akiva telling him about them earlier.

"Spirit guides come in various forms from Mother Earth and nature." She gestured to him. "You said you didn't know who your spirit guardian is?"

Shaking his head, he said, "No...I don't."

"Do you ever dream of a certain animal? Insect? Reptile?"

Rubbing his chin, he thought for a moment. "Well, yes..." He chuckled slightly. "I remember that, as a kid growing up in West Texas, from time to time I'd dream of a jaguar, too. Only this wasn't the gold kind with black spots. She was always black. She had huge gold eyes and a shiny black coat, and as she moved in my dreams, I could see a rainbow sheen on her coat. She was beautiful."

Akiva studied him in the silence. "I'm very impressed. Then you, too, have a jaguar guide." That confirmed to Akiva that Joe was truly a warrior for the light, just as she was.

From under her shirt, she pulled out a leather thong

that she wore around her neck at all times. On the end was a small leather pouch, stained and darkened over time from perspiration. With her fingers, Akiva opened up the dark leather bag and showed him what was inside.

"This is a jaguar claw that my great-great-grandmother was given by Geronimo. He, too, had a jaguar spirit guide. One time, when the U.S. Army nearly surrounded him and his people, my great-great-grandmother turned her mustang and rode back and attacked the entire column, scattering them in disarray. She then rode off into the mountains, so was never harmed or captured by the white men. Geronimo, when she caught up with them, rewarded her with this.

"He wore two claws. It is said that he had a black jaguar and a gold one as his guides. He was a medicine man of great powers."

Akiva held the claw up for Joe to look at. The obviously old, blackened claw had been pierced at the top, the hole threaded with a smaller leather thong.

"Wow," Joe whispered, "this is mighty special, Akiva."

"Do you know your guide's name?" Akiva demanded as she placed the claw back into the pouch and pulled the drawstrings closed.

Shaking his head, Joe said, "No. My daddy never exposed me to Comanche traditions like your grandmother did. I'm sorry he didn't. I'd like to know the history of his people as well as you know yours. Now I wished he had. I feel like I know only half of my family history." Before he'd met Akiva, Joe had shrugged off his Native American inheritance, seeing it only as something that caused prejudice against him; a blight on his youth. Now, seeing Akiva's strength and pride, he was hungry to connect with his past.

Nodding, Akiva slipped the medicine pouch beneath the green T-shirt she wore. She never wore a bra, so the pouch settled naturally between her breasts beneath the fabric. ''I don't think I'd have survived to adulthood without my grandmother, or the knowledge of my people.''

''I agree. Your grandmother must be a tough old buzzard.'' Joe grinned. ''She saved your life and gave you back your sense of selfhood. Who you were—and are.''

''And someday, you need to go to your father's people and find out more about who you are.'' Akiva gestured to his hand, which lay on the table. ''A part of you is Anglo, but the copper-skinned part of you, the Comanche, needs to be heard and embraced, as well. You need to know your family history, for it all counts. It makes you who you are now. And it's good to know what road you have traveled, and why you are where you are today.''

Joe grinned again. ''Well, this old dirt farmer Texas boy knows he's got miles to go compared to you. I'm *really* impressed, gal. You've always been a real special person in my eyes. And hearin' all this, well, I'm speechless. There aren't too many modern-day warriors around, but you have earned every bit of your status.''

Absorbing the respect and pride in Joe's voice, Akiva folded her hands. ''Among my people, warriors are in place to protect those who cannot defend themselves. We don't make war to make war. We defend the weak when they're attacked.''

''Much like what we're doin' right now on this mission,'' Joe observed.

''That's right,'' Akiva said, satisfaction in her tone. ''A true warrior is honor bound by history and tradition. We don't kill for the pleasure of it. We don't jump into fights just because we *can* fight. There has to be good reason for me to get involved. That's why I like the army, and flying the Apache. What we are doing is honorable and right. People's lives will be better because of what we do.''

''No disagreement there.'' He smiled, then saw Bradford coming to the mess door. Glancing down at his watch, he saw that their precious hour was over. ''Looks like it's time to start cookin' up dinner,'' he observed wryly. Giving Akiva a wink, he said, ''Let's do this again. More often? I like talkin' and sharin' with you. How about it?''

''Yes,'' Akiva said, turning as she heard the door opening, ''I'd like that.'' As she rose, she resumed her mask of C.O., though she cried silently at the loss of the openness she'd just enjoyed. Bradford entered and said hello to them, then hurried to the kitchen and her mess duties, and Akiva sighed inwardly. As she moved away from the table, she saw Joe picking up the plates and flatware. He could have left them for Bradford to clean up, but he didn't. Warmth stole through her heart. He was such a strong part of the team. He didn't see himself as something special. No, he worked daily, just as hard as everyone else.

As Akiva pushed open the door and stepped into the humid warmth of the late afternoon, she felt so much lighter. Happier. How long had it been since she'd felt like this? As she walked between the buildings back to the hangar, she could only recall two other times: when her grandmother had honored her in front of her nation, as she'd earned her warrior status, and again when she had her gold wings pinned on her uniform when graduating from flight school in the U.S. Army.

Slowing her stride, Akiva looked around at the wispy

clouds and the slanting light of day. The monkeys were screaming once more, their shrill voices carrying out of the shadowy jungle. The birds were quieting their calling as day began fading once again. The happiness she was feeling now was different. It was light, euphoric, and her heart felt as if it were an opening blossom within her chest.

Reaching up with her fingertips, she touched the area between her breasts. Joe's smile lingered in her heart. His deep Southern voice caressed her. And more than anything, where he'd touched her hand, her skin still tingled. In that moment, Akiva had never been happier. Or more afraid.

Chapter 9

"I've got a bad feelin'," Joe said over the intercom as they flew over the Gulf. The reassuring vibration of the Apache soothed him to a degree as he narrowed his gaze on the HUD, which showed two drug planes fifty miles offshore, heading on a direct track for Florida.

Tightening her lips, Akiva glared at the black night sky, which was crowded with thunderstorms on all sides. Lightning flashed almost constantly, causing them to lose their night vision, which was imperative in the use of their night optic scope, for precious minutes at a time. "I hate thunderstorms," she muttered defiantly. "I'm having trouble with my night vision. Are you?"

"Yeah," Joe said grimly. It was 0200, and they'd been torn out of a deep, badly needed sleep for this second mission. The first had occurred at 2100. On that mission, they'd turned a drug plane around and flown back to Alpha, arriving at 2300. They'd hit the sack, exhausted.

And then a second call came in from the American submarine, reporting two bogeys.

All around them, thunderheads were building rapidly. Akiva was flying the Apache between them because it would be a fool's undoing to fly through one. Besides the possibility of getting hit with fifty thousand watts of electricity from a bolt of lightning, the up and down drafts were violent enough to slam the Apache around and out of control.

Consequently, they were having to dodge and duck, flying around or under the storms. They had been told there was a front approaching—a mass of cold air hitting the highly humid warm air rising from the Gulf—making conditions unstable as hell. The Apache was bouncing around, sometimes lifting fifty to a hundred feet in seconds as it hit an invisible air pocket. Akiva was doing her best to keep the gunship stable, but Joe knew it was impossible under the circumstances. The harnesses bit deeply into his shoulders and thighs. He'd tightened them to a painful degree because if he left them loose he'd be bounced around in the cockpit. His job required that he keep his gaze steady and pinned on the HUDs for incoming radar information in order to give Akiva up-to-the-second briefings on where and how to fly.

"They're down on the deck, right over the water," Akiva muttered. "Both of 'em. This is new, Joe. The tactic is new. Two planes going out at once."

"Yeah." He chuckled darkly. "I think they've figured out there's only one of us, and if they throw two drug planes at us, we can chase only half the cargo. The other plane can escape and make it to the U.S. coast. They're not dumb boxes of rocks like I thought."

Grinning savagely, Akiva said, "No...they aren't." Her arm muscles were tight and her fingers gripped the collective and cyclic. The winds were chaotic, and the Apache was being buffeted constantly. Flying at ten thousand feet, they were racing to get ahead of the two planes in order to meet them and turn them back. Rain slashed and hammered at them relentlessly. Sometimes they ran into hail, which made Akiva very uneasy. The Plexiglas windshield at the front of the Apache was hard enough to withstand a direct hit from a 20mm cannon, but the sides weren't. Hail, if large enough, could potentially do a helluva lot of damage to her Apache, and that worried her. One huge ball of hail, about the size of a softball, hurtling at hundreds of miles an hour into their two-hundred-mile-an-hour Apache, could spell disaster if it hit the side of one of their cockpits, or worse, struck an engine and rendered it useless. She didn't want to think about such scenarios, but she had to, because any of them could happen. Worse, an engine could explode, and the fire might not be able to be put out by the built-in extinguishers. If that happened, the whole gunship could blow up, or fire would eat into their cabins, or the Apache could spin out of control. None of those possibilities were good. Her gut felt like it was weighted down with stones.

"These good ole boys drivin' these two planes are flyin' them like military pilots would—wingtips a hundred feet apart."

"They probably are ex-military," Akiva said.

"Russian? American?"

"Who knows? We're getting ahead of them. Tell me when I can drop altitude."

"Roger." He wrote down some numbers on his knee board, then punched a few figures into the computer and watched the info pop up on the right HUD. "Begin descent now to five thousand feet." A flash of lightning illuminated the cockpit, destroying his night vision.

"Damn..." He cursed softly, rubbing his eyes and blinking them rapidly.

Akiva heard Joe curse. That wasn't like him. He rarely uttered a nasty word. The tension was thick in the cockpit. The whine of the twin engines above them was comforting to Akiva. She glared at the bulbous cumulus clouds that rose in thick towers, probably up to forty thousand feet, on either side of them. Flying between two huge thunder cells like this was next to lunacy, but they had no choice.

Listening to Joe's quiet instructions, Akiva nosed the Apache downward on a glide path that would eventually bring them alongside the fleeing drug planes. First they had to get the fuselage numbers, check them against aircraft flight plans filed with the FAA, and then check another computer to see if they were known drug carriers. If they were indeed drug flights, as Akiva suspected, then she and Joe could fly ahead of them and try to fire to turn them back. But not until then.

The descent between the roiling, grumbling thunderheads increased in roughness. The cyclic between her legs wrenched from a sudden downdraft. The Apache groaned, and they dropped like a rock. Gasping, Akiva wrenched back and tried to steady the gunship. The engines whined loudly in protest.

"Heck of a roller-coaster ride," Joe muttered in a worried tone.

Perspiration dotted Akiva's bunched brow as she intently studied her flight instruments. In weather like this, especially over water, pilot disorientation was very real. A pilot had to believe her instruments and not what her eyes, or the sensations in her body, were telling her. The brain could easily receive mixed signals because of all the tossing around in the cockpit; while her inner ear was in a state of imbalance, it could send misinformation to her brain.

They finally reached the deck—pilots' jargon for right over the water—and hovered a hundred feet above the choppy surface. Akiva knew from experience that water directly beneath a thunderstorm was in turmoil, the waves often reaching five and six feet high, with the white spray thrown skyward. To her left were the two aircraft.

"You got them in sight?" she demanded tensely.

"Roger," Joe answered, binoculars raised to his eyes. Again, lightning flashed around them, and he jerked. "Damn, that was close!"

"No kidding." Akiva worriedly looked around. Rain slashed unrelentingly, making visibility almost impossible. Lightning was dancing all around them. They were now skirting the bottom of a monstrous thunderstorm. And the foolish pilots in the airplanes were heading directly beneath it. That was stupid. The chance of a massive downdraft slamming them into the grasping waves below was very real. Only a pilot running a drug flight would take such a chance. Unfortunately, Akiva and Joe would have to follow them.

Akiva waited impatiently for Joe to get the information they needed. It was tough, but he had night-vision binoculars and should be able to pick up the numbers off the fuselage no matter how dark it was.

The Apache hit another air pocket and surged upward. Hissing a curse, Akiva wrenched back the collective and steadied the craft. The whitish light of a nearby bolt of lightning exposed the two planes, which were less than five hundred feet from them. In this kind of weather, that was too close; the possibility of air collision was very real. But it couldn't be helped.

Sweat rolled down Akiva's temples. She pressed her

mouth into a thin line, her narrowed eyes focused on her instruments.

"Got 'em!" Joe crowed triumphantly when the information on the planes came back. "Both drug planes. These boys aren't even botherin' to change their numbers! They're getting brazen."

"Good," Akiva growled, and she powered up to take the Apache well ahead of them, intending to stop them.

Just then, a flash of light exploded around Akiva. She uttered a sharp cry. Blinded, she gripped the controls. The Apache shook violently. The engines dropped in power, then suddenly surged. Over her headset, she heard Joe give a shout of surprise.

It was over just as quickly as it had happened.

Stunned, Akiva looked around. Gasping, she said, "Joe! Where're our instruments? Where's—"

"Lightning hit us, Akiva."

The Apache was acting sluggish. Akiva looked at her blackened instrument panel. The software on board the Apache was backed up by a secondary system, but it clearly wasn't bridging the gap.

Her mind spun. The wind was slamming at them. Lightning had hit them! Right now, Akiva didn't care about the druggies. She looked around at the dark, malevolent sky. The rain was so bad she couldn't see below her to figure out how close she was to the Gulf waters.

"Hang on," Joe gasped, "lemme see what I can do to fire this software back up...."

"Hurry," Akiva ordered through clenched teeth. She stared at the dark instrument panel, mentally willing it to show her just the basics of her flight. Desperately needing the altitude indicator and several other major instruments that could get them safely out of here and back to base, she waited. Mouth dry, she licked her lower lip. Lightning was heavy now, dancing constantly around them. She could smell the burned wiring in the cockpit.

"Do we have a fire?" she demanded.

"No...not that I can see. I think the lightning struck and burned some of the wiring in the panels."

She dropped the Apache back to the deck. Below, maybe a hundred feet or less, she could see the white tops of the angry sea.

"I'm turning back, Joe. Screw the drug interdiction. We're in trouble."

"Roger that. Hold on...."

Suddenly, Akiva's main instrument panel flickered in front of her. Green light flashed, then disappeared. "No!"

"Hold on...." Joe repeated, his voice strained.

"Do whatever you did before," Akiva begged. "I need my instruments, Joe. We're flying blind." She could fly by the seat of her pants but over water and in a thunderstorm, with visibility almost nil, she knew her brain and inner ear could skew her perceptions and cause spatial flight disorientation. If that happened, they could be flying straight into the water and not even know it until it was too late. She desperately needed those instruments!

"Just...one more...sec..."

The instruments flared to life, the green lines much fainter than they should be, but visible. "Yes! Yes, they're on!" Instantly Akiva corrected their flight path. She had indeed been heading down toward the water, totally disoriented. Her heart was beating hard in her chest. Sweat was coursing down her rib cage beneath the uncomfortable chicken plate she wore. The Apache was getting slammed repeatedly by strong drafts as they tried to hurry out from beneath the massive thunderhead. Her teeth jarred. The harness bit savagely into her shoulders.

"We're blind, deaf and dumb," Joe informed her unhappily. "I can't get any of our weapons online. We have no radar...nothing. You're gonna have to fly on instruments to the base, Akiva."

"Great," she whispered angrily. "I hate thunderstorms."

"Yeah," Joe said sympathetically. He looked around. With the rain teeming down, it was impossible to see far. Only when lightning illuminated the sky could he hope to spot other aircraft.

"Keep your eyes peeled," Akiva warned. "You're our only radar now."

"I dunno who'd be out on a night like this," he joked. Wiping the sweat off his brow, he pushed the night scope back against his helmet and locked it in place. With the computer out of commission, the scope was of no use. And with lightning dancing around them, his night vision was destroyed.

"You okay?" he asked Akiva in a low, stressed tone.

"No. How about you?"

"No."

"At least we're honest with one another," she joked darkly, her lips lifting slightly.

"This isn't a time for heroics. Let's just muddle back to base ASAP."

"No argument from me."

As they flew out from beneath the thunderhead, the rain began to let up. The jarring was not as intense, and Akiva was able to steady the Apache's flight. They were less than ten miles from the shore.

Joe spread a map across his knees and took out a penlight. "You want to take corridor C back to Alpha?"

"Yes. It's the fastest. I don't trust these instruments to stay online. I just want to get back as soon as we can."

"Roger that." He scowled, wrote down the latitude and longitude and quickly scribbled out the math for her. Giving Akiva the flight direction, he kept a hand on the map.

They were flying the old-fashioned way—how planes were flown long before the advent of computers and automatic pilots. Joe looked around. Between the massive cumuli clouds hanging out over the Gulf, the night sky was dotted with stars. The rain had stopped, and so had most of the jarring.

They were flying at five thousand feet now, and he looked down out of the cockpit. There was the black expanse below them that he knew was the Gulf; it looked like slick black glass on this moonless night. As he looked up, he blinked. Was he seeing things? They were less than five miles from shore. Rubbing his eyes, he looked again.

"Akiva..." he said hesitantly, "I think I'm seein' something dead ahead of us...but I'm not sure. Damn, my night vision is shot. Do you see any black things above the jungle? In the night sky, about ten o'clock?"

Busy flying and watching her instruments, Akiva jerked her head up for a moment. She'd feel a helluva lot better being over land instead of water. If she had to set the Apache down, she could. On water, it would sink, and so would they. "What?" She peered, eyes squinting, toward the area Joe had mentioned.

"Am I seein' things, gal?"

Every time he called her that, his voice dropped to a caressing tone that made Akiva feel wonderfully safe and protected. She liked the endearment, and she was getting up her courage to tell Joe that. But to admit it meant admitting that he held emotional sway over her, and Akiva was afraid of that. She was a real coward, she had decided, on the emotional front. Oh, Joe was helping her climb a lot of walls she'd put up regarding men, and lately she had found herself desperately wanting to tell him that her heart took off with happiness every time she shared those rare private moments with him, or when he flashed that silly, tender smile of his and called her "gal."

Forcing her attention back to the present, Akiva peered through the darkness toward the coastline of Mexico. Compressing her lips, she studied the horizon, and then the darkened night sky pinpointed with blinking stars.

"I...yes...there's *something* out there, Joe. But I can't ID it. Can you?" Her hands automatically tightened around the controls. Whatever it was, it was *flying*. That wasn't a good sign. "There's no aircraft running lights on them."

"Roger," he told her grimly. "Let me see if I can get a fix on them with our night binoculars." He lifted them to his eyes. Everything appeared in various shades of grainy green, from very dark to very light.

"What?" Akiva demanded. She felt her heart begin to pound with dread. Something wasn't right. They never saw aircraft while coming back off a mission. This part of Mexico was nothing but wild, uninhabited jungle.

"Gal," he rasped tensely, "I'm looking at *four* helicopters comin' straight for us. And I see weapons on 'em. Rocket launchers on the skid mounts."

"Damn!"

Joe sucked in a slow, ragged breath, fear eating at him as he continued to watch them racing toward them. "And they know where we are, so that means they've got some kind of radar aboard those civilian helos."

"They're civilian?" Akiva's mind spun with possibilities. Right now, with their software fried, they had no weapons with which to protect themselves. They were, in essence, sitting ducks that could easily be shot out of the sky. Heart racing, she felt fear shoot through her, along with a rush of adrenaline that heightened all her senses.

"Roger that. All civilian. And," Joe growled unhappily, "they fit the ID of Luis Rios's four rotorcrafts, if I don't miss my guess."

"Okay, we're taking evasive action. I'm not sitting here letting them get a fix on us!" With that, Akiva sent the Apache skyward, its nose pointed straight up and clawing for air and altitude.

Joe hung on. "I'll try and keep you informed of their positioning," he told her. Oh, how he wished he had the software up and running! The Apache software was the most sophisticated in the world. Not only would it ID the four civilian helicopters, it would choose from an array of weapons and tell him which should be targeted first, second, third and fourth. Now, he had none of that information at hand.

"They're starting to spread out in a fan formation," he called to her, and gave her their positions. Right now, he was smashed back against the seat as the Apache continued its vertical climb.

"They don't know we aren't armed," Akiva told him.

"Yeah, but they're gonna find out real soon," he warned her.

Sweat trickled into Akiva's eyes, and she blinked rapidly. "I've got to get us over land." Wrenching the cyclic and pushing on the rudders with her booted feet, Akiva swung the Apache toward shore. Because the Apache could climb so rapidly, she knew she'd beat the other helos at their own game. Wrenching the power to redline, she heard the engines howl as she drove the Apache straight for the coast.

"Rockets fired! Eight o'clock!"

Joe's voice was tight with fear. Akiva snapped her head to the left. She saw two rockets heading up—directly at them.

Did the rockets have the ability to track them? Some did and some didn't. With a curse, she banked the Apache steeply, out of the target zone. "See if they follow us!" she gasped to Joe.

The gunship howled as the engines torqued, moving into a steep dive away from the approaching rockets.

Slammed around in the cockpit, Joe couldn't keep the binoculars up to his eyes. His helmet smashed into the Plexiglas. Cursing softly, he gripped the field glasses.

"No! No, they ain't bird-doggin' us!"

Relief shot through Akiva. Thank the Great Spirit! Mind racing, she saw the landfall coming up rapidly. Bringing the Apache out of the sharp bank, she leveled the helo out at two thousand feet. They were too low and too vulnerable to attack this way.

"Bogeys at six o'clock. They're gonna climb our tail rotor...."

"Roger." Akiva took a deep breath and again gunned the Apache to redline, hoping to climb up and out of the deadly situation.

"Two more rockets comin' in! Ten o'clock!" Joe barked.

Whipping the Apache around so that she could see them, Akiva hissed, her lips drawing away from her clenched teeth. The Apache surged valiantly beneath her hands and feet as she guided it up, up, up into the night sky. The engines screamed at every inch of air purchased.

The rockets hurtled toward them, their red-and-yellow trails glowing.

She heard Joe take in a breath of air. Her entire body jerked in spasm. Eyes widening, she watched the rockets come directly at them, closer and closer. Using every bit of combat knowledge she'd ever accrued, Akiva threw the Apache into another steep, banking dive. Only this time she headed straight for the helicopter that had just fired the rockets.

The rockets flew past, no more than twenty feet away from them. Joe let out a yell of triumph.

Akiva held the gunship in a tight turn and then straightened it out for level flight—aimed directly at the helo, which was less than a mile away from them. "I'm going to get this son of a bitch," she rasped between tight lips. "Hold on."

Joe braced himself, hands pressed against the narrow cockpit, legs spread on either side of the floor pedals. "What—" He didn't get to finish his question. Because he was sitting in the upper cockpit, he had a far better view of what was going on in the sky around them than Akiva did. She was hurtling the Apache directly at the helo. The pilot in that helo had to be scared out of his mind. Joe sucked in a gasp. Was Akiva going to hit him?

Within moments of collision, Joe gave a shout, thinking they were going to smash into the other chopper. At the last possible second, the civilian craft banked violently to the left. Akiva jerked the nose of the Apache up. The two helos passed within sixty feet of one another.

Jerking his head around, Joe pulled the binoculars to his eyes.

"Where's the rest of them?" Akiva yelled. "Dammit, tell me their positions!"

Joe knew she was, in effect, flying blind. Aircraft without wing and taillights were dark apparitions against the night sky. She could no more see them than he could without the help of the special binoculars. And worse, the other helos had radar on board, so they knew where the Apache was flying and could target it.

Akiva was jerking the Apache around, trying to make it a hard target to fire at. They were over land now. Joe was wrenched around repeatedly from side to side as he frantically searched the night sky around them.

"I don't see 'em!"

"I need an escape plan, Joe," Akiva rasped. "We can't lead these bastards back to Alpha. I'm low on fuel. Start thinking of where we can land. I'll be damned if we're leading them home!"

Joe gripped the map. He jammed the binoculars between his arm and body because if he set them down, they'd fly around his cockpit like a projectile and possibly knock him out or smash into the instrument panel, doing more damage. "Hold on…."

Suddenly, the *ping, ping, ping* walking up alongside the Apache caught Akiva's heightened attention. Cursing savagely, she saw bullets from a machine gun ripping into them, the sparks of the projectiles—red tracers—arcing behind. Out of the corner of her eye, she followed the tracers back and saw the dim silhouette of a helo no more than half a mile away. Cursing, she brought the Apache up into a high, swift climb to escape. The bullets continued to lace into the thin skin of the Apache.

Wrenching the gunship around, Akiva pulled it into an inside loop. This was a maneuver no other helicopter in the world but the Apache could do. Looping would get the gunship up and out of firing range, but would also afford her the chance of coming down on the bogey's six, where she could shoot at it. The only problem, she thought, as she pulled the shrieking Apache into the loop, was that they had ammunition, but couldn't fire it.

It didn't matter. Akiva had a plan.

Joe hung on. There was nothing else he could do as the Apache swung into a powerful inside loop. The rotors thumped and beat hard as the helo swung in a circle. As they came out of it, Joe could see Akiva maneuvering to get behind the helo that had fired at them. His lips parted, and he braced himself with his hands and feet.

Within seconds, Akiva situated the Apache behind the helo. Eyes slitted, she powered up the gunship. In moments the combat helicopter was within a hundred feet of the other helo's rotor blades. The other pilot didn't even know she was there. Good. "Hold on, Joe."

That was all the warning he got. His eyes bulged. He felt the Apache dropping—directly down upon the rotor assembly of the unsuspecting helo. Letting out a yell of surprise, he could do nothing but go along for the ride. What the hell was she doing? Joe watched as Akiva lowered the gunship quickly and precisely.

Within seconds, a shudder went through the Apache. Joe yelled again, feeling the impact. Sparks and fire erupted beneath the landing gear of the Apache. The gunship shuddered drunkenly.

Akiva gave an Apache war cry as she sank the cannon—the huge gun assembly that rested directly beneath her booted feet, between the landing gear—into the helicopters rotor blades. In seconds, the heavy metal smashed the thin rotors and cracked them.

Instantly, Akiva lifted the gunship upward and away. As she did, she saw the other helicopter floundering. Its rotors were chopped up, no longer able to keep it in the air. She grinned savagely. She had timed the attack so that the useless cannon would strike the bogey's blades and shatter them. Without blades, that chopper was going down. And indeed, as she watched with satisfaction, she saw fire break out on the rotor shaft.

"What the hell!" Joe yelped. There was a sudden explosion in the other craft, less than five hundred feet away. Flames, yellow and orange, lit up the night sky. He raised his gloved hand to protect his face.

As she moved the Apache away from the flame, a lethal smile curved Akiva's lips. "I used the cannon to tangle his blades."

Joe was breathing raggedly. "That was some kind of risk...."

Chortling, Akiva said, "Yeah, but what do you do if you don't have guns, Calhoun?"

Shakily, he put the binoculars to his eyes, searching for the other three helos. The Apache was screaming along at roughly two thousand feet, the jungle racing by below them. "I can't see 'em," he gasped, twisting frantically to the right and left.

"We're gonna get shot down if we don't set down," Akiva said raggedly. "We need a landing place, Joe. I'm going to try and outrun them, set the ship down, egress and then blow this helo up."

His mind raced as he considered her decision. "You want to land and try to make a run for it? Escape into the jungle? Work our way back to Alpha?"

"Yeah. You got a better plan? I'm all ears." Her heart was pounding wildly in her chest. The tremble of the helicopter heightened.

Joe rubbernecked constantly, trying to find the other three helos he knew were pursuing them. Unfortunately, without their sophisticated radar operational to show him what was out there waiting to kill them, their rear was just as vulnerable to attack. "No, it's a good plan. Let's try to get to within a hundred miles of Alpha. That's a long walk, but one we can make."

"That's what I figured." The Apache shook around Akiva. She didn't even have engine instruments online to tell how the helo had fared, but her hearing told her that the bullets had done damage. "I only have fifty pounds of fuel left. We're gonna have to sit down soon."

"I know." Then Joe spotted the helos. "All three of 'em are hanging back about four miles, on our six. I think you scared 'em off for now."

"For now," Akiva said grimly, relief sheeting through her. Below them, the canopy of the jungle raced by as she moved closer and closer. In an emergency combat situation, they could land and then rig the Apache to explode. Nothing would fall into the hands of an enemy. Akiva hated to lose a twenty-million-dollar gunship, but under the circumstances, there was no other choice open to them.

Joe spread the map across his knees, the penlight dancing across it as the gunship shook and shuddered. He could hear the port engine whining, and that meant something was wrong. "You'd better shut down the port," he warned.

"Yeah, roger. Was just going to do that. I don't want it to explode on us." And Akiva reached for the toggle switch that would shut it off. That meant they'd lose half their airspeed, and the civilian helos would catch up with them quickly.

"Find me a place to land, Calhoun. I'm getting jumpy. And we're running outta time in a helluva hurry up here...."

Joe peered intently down at the map, tracing their route with his Nomex-gloved index finger. Trying to hold the penlight steady enough with his other hand to read the fine print, he rasped, "Yeah, I'm workin' at it, gal...."

Akiva felt the Apache slow. The engine was shut down. She had to compensate immediately as they continued to limp along on one engine only. Sinking the gunship to treetop level, she licked her dry lips. Akiva could feel the helos hunting them. It was only a matter of a minute or more, and they'd jump them like buzzards on a half-dead carcass, shooting them out of the sky.

"Dammit, Joe!"

"I found one!"

Relief sheeted through Akiva. "Where? Tell me where!" Her hands were aching as she gripped the cyclic and collective. Her entire body was bathed in sweat.

Joe quickly gave her the coordinates. "It's a little meadow, near a stream," he told her quickly. "The jungle is real close."

"Good! Hold on!" Akiva swung the Apache to the north, toward their landing zone. Would they reach it in time? Would thcy get there before being in rocket range of the bogeys? She wasn't sure. "Get ready to egress!" she ordered Joe. Ordinarily, they would never get out of the cockpit with the rotors still spinning, but this time they'd have to.

"My harness is off," he told her. Joe stowed the optic scope into a side panel along with the binoculars. He gripped the map and, with shaking hands, quickly folded it up and jammed it inside his flight suit. They'd need a map to get back to Alpha.

In moments, Akiva had located the small patch of meadow. Without hesitation, she set the Apache down. Switching off the only engine, the rotors thumping overhead, she set the explosive device and timer that would incinerate the gunship. Luckily, the device did not rely on software.

"Okay, let's get outta here!" Akiva yelled. "We've got two minutes before detonation! Make a run for it, Joe!" And she fumbled with the handle that would open her cockpit.

Chapter 10

Joe knew he was the one in the most danger. If he completely raised the cockpit hood, it would smash into the whirling blades, or be ripped out of his hands by the powerful buffeting. The darkness was complete. Heart pounding, he saw Akiva egress successfully and leap down off the Apache. Jerking the handle, he opened the latch. Instantly, the covering was torn out of his hand. Plexiglas splintered. Metal and glass erupted, the spinning blades scattering all around him. Joe threw up his hands. Fortunately his helmet visor was down to protect his eyes as thousands of tiny projectiles exploded around him. It felt as if someone had shot two rounds from a shotgun directly at him.

Feeling the burning sensation of the glass striking his lower face and neck, he clambered quickly out of the cockpit. Ducking so that he wouldn't be cut in half by the whirling blades, Joe threw himself out of the cockpit, and aimed, headfirst, for the ground.

Striking the wet grass, he rolled over and over. Above him, he heard helicopters approaching low and fast. Hands—Akiva's hands—grabbed him. He stopped rolling.

"Get up!" she panted, jerking a look toward the sky. Now the helos had their running lights on. They were flashing red and green, approaching low and fast. Breathing harshly, Akiva helped Joe to his feet.

"Get outta here!" Joe yelled, leaping up. Then he followed her as she ran from the Apache, which sat there idling, its blades whirling slowly.

As she broke into a full run, Akiva lost her footing and fell in the thick tangle of slippery grass, her helmeted head striking a fallen log.

Joe raced toward Akiva. She lay unmoving, facedown, her arms spread out ahead of her. What the hell had happened? Gasping for breath, he knew they had less than two minutes to get away from the Apache before it blew. Bending down, he slipped his hands beneath her armpits, intending to turn her over. His shaking fingers made contact with the log. Instantly, he understood what had happened: she'd struck her head as she fell.

Glancing up, Joe saw that the jungle was less than a hundred feet away. They had to get there!

Rolling Akiva over, he pulled her into a fireman's hold across his broad shoulders. Grunting, he forced himself to his feet, moving unsteadily. Akiva was no lightweight. She was about his height and size, and probably weighed about twenty pounds less than he did. Groaning, he dug the toes of his boots into the damp grass and lunged toward the dark wall of jungle before them.

Just as Joe began to run, with Akiva flopping unconscious on his shoulders, he heard a noise that scared the living hell out of him. He'd recognize that sound anywhere: it was a rocket being fired! His brain spun. His eyes widened. Adrenaline surged through him as he took huge, leaping strides. The grass tangled dangerously around his lower legs and boots, for everything was wet and slippery.

And then the world collapsed in a thunderous explosion of heat and light. One moment Joe was running as hard as he could with Akiva, and the next, he felt himself being lifted and flung through the air like a rag doll. Just before his mind blanked out, he felt the heat of fire vomiting around him.

A cry tore from his contorted lips. Somewhere in his mind, he thought the helo was firing a rocket at the Apache. Then he realized he was wrong. They were firing at *them!* It was the last thing he remembered.

The bumpy motion of a vehicle revived Joe. He found himself lying on his side, on a rough surface of black nylon carpet. His hands and ankles were tied with thick ropes in front of him. Closing his eyes, his ears ringing badly, he thought he heard voices speaking in Spanish. There were some short barks of male laughter. He was in a vehicle…and it was bouncing along at a fairly high rate of speed over a dirt road.

He noted the metallic taste of blood in his mouth. The tightness alongside his right temple was warm—with blood leaking out of a head wound?

Akiva? Where was she? Biting back a groan, because his whole body felt bruised, he tried to turn onto his back, then stopped, looked up and blinked. It was then he realized he was in the rear of a sport utility vehicle. When he saw two men sitting above him in the seat, their backs to him, his heart pounded violently. Akiva lay unconscious against the rear door. Her hands and feet were bound as well, and the helmet she had worn was gone, revealing the bright red scarf around her head which kept the tangle of her long, black hair from covering her face.

Fear vomited through Joe. He inched toward Akiva. Reaching out, he settled his bound hands on her shoulder and shook her hard. Her face was bleached, her once glorious copper skin frighteningly pale. Not daring to speak, because he didn't want the men to hear him, Joe gripped her shoulder and gave her another sharp, short shake. Anxiously, he perused her face and head. Joe knew she had struck the log when she fell. Looking around, he realized it was daylight.

How long had he been unconscious? His memory was shorting out. And then he recalled with clarity the rocket being launched—at them. Had the Apache blown up? Worriedly, he searched Akiva's face. He saw a trickle of blood leaking from her hairline, down her left temple and onto her cheek, but that was all. Her lips were parted. Her thick black lashes were like ebony fans against her cheeks. She was achingly beautiful to him.

More fear stabbed at Joe. Behind him, he heard at least four voices, all men, talking in Spanish. Luckily, he knew the language.

Joe forced himself up on his left elbow. He inched over Akiva, his ear near her ear. "Akiva! Wake up! Wake up!" His voice was low and urgent. Turning, Joe waited to see if they'd heard him. No. The men were all talking animatedly, laughing, the air filled with the smoke of cigarettes.

Akiva groaned softly. She heard Joe's voice, very far away at first. Her head ached. The pain was drifting through her brain, which felt like a drum being pounded. Blinking slowly, she forced open her eyes. Joe was hunkered over her, his face tight with concern and anxiety.

For long moments, Akiva had no idea what had happened. Or where she was.

Joe's lips parted as Akiva slowly opened her eyes. Her once glorious gold gaze was murky; she was obviously disoriented. Giving her a wobbly grin, he leaned down, his head next to hers, and whispered, ''We're captured, Akiva. Just lie there and get your bearings. We're in an SUV going somewhere on a dirt road. There're four men in the front seats and they're all speaking Spanish. Just lie still. Don't talk. Get your bearings.'' He lifted his head, his mouth inches from her cheek. He wanted to protect Akiva as much as he could. Joe knew his back was to his captors, and he was sufficiently stretched out so that if one of them turned around to fire a gun at them, they'd hit him, not her. Above all, he wanted Akiva to live. To survive. His heart ached with a powerful, overwhelming emotion as he watched her fight off the semiconscious state. But Joe could do nothing but feel those emotions flowing like an unchecked river of heat and hope through him. In that moment, he realized he loved Akiva. And in the next moment, he was overwhelmed by that unexpected discovery.

His mind gyrated with a million questions and too few answers. They were captured. He knew they'd be interrogated. By whom? A drug lord? Yes, most probably. And their lives would be worthless. Joe knew that. As he held her dulled eyes, his mouth stretched into the semblance of a smile. ''Welcome back, gal. Somehow,'' he rasped, ''we'll get out of this—alive. You just have to trust me like you never have before. You hear me? Trust me, Akiva. Please...'' And his voice broke with the raw emotion he was helpless to control.

Mouth dry, and tasting blood, Akiva lay very still. She mentally checked her body, to see if anything was broken, or where she felt pain. With Joe hunkered near her, she felt a modicum of safety. Her heart pounded with dread. They were captured! Akiva knew what that meant. The thick hemp ropes binding her wrists together had cut off her circulation, and her fingertips were numb and looked strangely white. She slowly moved them, one at a time.

Gradually, during long minutes of bumping over the dirt road, Akiva's mind began to clear. Her head was pressed against Joe's lower arm. He kept his arm there purposely to give her a cushion to lean against so that her head wouldn't bang against the floor of the vehicle. For that, she was more than grateful. The pain in her head was like a throbbing drum, and she felt heat and pressure building to a blinding intensity behind her eyes.

"Okay?" Joe rasped near her ear.

She felt the warmth of his breath against her flesh. Absorbing his closeness, because she felt scared as never before, she nodded once.

"Anything broken?"

She shook her head slowly from side to side. Every time she moved it, dizziness washed over her. Leaning back against his proffered arm, she looked up into his stormy-looking gray eyes. She mouthed the word *concussion.*

Joe nodded. His lips became a grim line. "You slipped and hit your head on a log when we were running away from the gunship," he confided in a low tone.

Akiva closed her eyes and then opened them. Joe's face was dark and unshaven. It made his cheeks look hollow and his face narrower than usual. His hair was mussed, one black lock hanging over his bunched brow. Akiva had never seen the look that was in his eyes now, and it fed her hope when she knew, logically, there was none. Now she was getting a hint of a man she'd never seen: Joe Calhoun the warrior. Somewhere in her spinning head, Akiva realized she'd never fully trusted that Joe was truly a combat warrior. Oh, he flew a gunship, but he didn't have that kind of aggressive personality most Apache pilots showed off like a blazing sun. He was always quiet, steady and calm. Now, as she gazed up at him and held his darkening gaze, she realized with relief that Joe was a man who was up to handling this kind of situation. That made her feel safe despite their incredibly dangerous situation.

"W-where—" Her voice cracked. Her mouth was dry. Akiva was so thirsty she wanted to scream out for water.

Joe shook his head. He lifted his chin and looked around. The rear window was caked with yellow dust, and he could see a cloud billowing up behind the vehicle as it moved along. On either side of the thin, narrow dirt road, he saw fields of corn. Farther away, he saw jungle bordering the fields. Frowning, he leaned down again, close to Akiva's ear. Strands of her hair tickled his mouth as he whispered, "We're in an agricultural area. I see cornfields. I don't know where we are, but there're farmers out in the fields. The jungle is a long way off. This looks like an area I remember on the map. About twenty-five miles inland was a cleared strip of land that was flat and could be used for farming."

Akiva sighed. It helped if she kept her eyes open. When she closed them, dizziness swept over her until she felt like she was in a tornado, spinning continuously. Joe's voice, low and tense, soothed some of her anxiety. Akiva didn't look closely at what might happen. She was a woman. And if their enemies were ruthless drug soldiers capable of anything, she'd be at risk in more ways than Joe. Swallowing against her dry throat, Akiva tried to force her fear, her wildly galloping mind, to calm. Being with him soothed her somewhat.

"A-are you okay?" she managed to whisper. Akiva saw his eyes glimmer. A slight, one-cornered smile pulled at his thinned mouth.

"I'm fine, gal. Just bumps and bruises."

"A-and the Apache?"

Joe saw the fear in Akiva's eyes. There was no way she wanted that gunship to survive the blast and fall into enemy hands. Both the hardware and software aboard the Apache were found nowhere else in the world, and they knew drug dealers and foreign governments alike would pay millions to get their hands on it.

He shook his head. "I dunno. They shot a rocket at us. I was carryin' you away from the gunship when they fired. I thought they were aiming at the Apache." He gave her a rueful look. "I was wrong. They were shootin' at us."

Akiva moved her head closer and nuzzled her cheek against his chest. She felt sick to her stomach now. Joe's closeness made her symptoms go away, if only for a moment.

Surprised at Akiva's behavior, Joe lay there, stunned. He saw her lips part and go soft. And he saw the naked fear in her face. Knowing that she was thinking about the things that could happen now that they were prisoners, his heart ached with anxiety. He feared for Akiva, because she was a woman and the enemy was male, and he knew all too well what they might do to her. Bitterness coated his mouth. He leaned down and pressed a series of small, comforting kisses against her exposed neck, where her thick black hair had parted. A fierce love welled up in him. Sensing her fear, her uncertainty, Joe rubbed his cheek against hers gently.

"It's gonna be all right, gal. Somehow...we're gonna get out of this—alive. You hear me? Alive. Both of us. I won't let them hurt you. I'll die first. Just try and take it easy. Let's take this one minute at a time. We'll both be lookin' for a way to escape...so just hang in there. I'm with you all the way...."

Joe's words were like balm to the violent fear that was engulfing Akiva now. Cheek resting against his forearm, her face pressed against his damp uniform, she tried to stop a sob coming up in her throat. Hot tears pricked the backs of her tightly closed eyes. She felt Joe's mouth, strong and sure, caressing her nape. Each kiss he feathered along her neck, then against her temple, and finally, her cheek, was like a healing unguent to the fear that was eating her alive.

In those stolen, precious moments out of time, Akiva hungrily absorbed Joe's steadiness and believed the words he spoke roughly against her ear. Somehow, she told herself, she was going to have to get a handle on her fear and turn it into strength, as he had already done. Though she was surprised at her reactions, Akiva tried not to be too hard on herself. She was in shock, and shock did funny things to one's emotions.

As she lay there, being bumped and thrown from side to side in the speeding SUV, with Joe buttressing her and trying to keep her protected, Akiva felt the darkness claim her once again. She had no strength at the moment, and it was Joe's body, his spirit, that was feeding her and keeping her safe. As Akiva spiraled down into darkness once more, she saw a set of gold jaguar eyes with black pupils staring back at her.

The discomfort of her position, the jolting of the vehicle, all dissolved as Akiva stared, riveted, at the eyes, which stared back like brilliant suns. As she felt the spinning sensation deepen, her only anchor with any kind of reality was the black jaguar's face, which slowly congealed around those sun-gold eyes burning with raw power and energy.

Finally, the spinning stopped, and Akiva found herself standing on a grassy plain near a small, burbling creek. She was beneath the spreading arms of a massive old, white-barked sycamore tree, one that she recalled from the Red Rock Reservation. Oh, how many times had she gone to that Arizona sycamore, which was probably two hundred years old, and sat with her back against it, dreaming of a happy life instead of the one she had?

And it was during those times as a young girl as she closed her eyes and daydreamed, that she would see out of the swirling mists of rainbow-colored fog, a black jaguar striding lithely and silently toward her. Akiva remembered being scared out of her wits the first time she'd seen the jungle predator. Her eyes had flown open. She'd leaped to her feet and raced back to her grandmother's house, her heart slamming into her rib cage like a frightened rabbit's.

Now Akiva stood there and watched her spirit guide, the black jaguar, approach her, his tail twitching from side to side. She felt his incredible power, until it suffused her and fed her. The heat and light moved from her booted feet, up through her uniform-clad legs and into the center of her body. As the golden energy surged through her like a tidal wave, she felt it fill her aching head. In moments, she felt it begin to heal her, so that the dizziness dissolved. Standing with her legs slightly apart, Akiva knew this was a healing and that her spirit guide was helping her. Grateful, she opened her eyes once the huge wave of energy left her. She saw the black jaguar sitting there. To her surprise, there was an Apache warrior woman standing next to him.

Gasping, Akiva immediately understood it was her great-great-grandmother, Na-u-kuzzi. Her thick black hair hung almost to her waist and she had the third braid of an Apache warrior. Around her head was the red scarf proclaiming her the mighty warrior she was. She wore a long-sleeved white tunic over loose-fitting white pants pushed into leather boots that fitted snugly just below her knees. The tips of her boots were shaped in an upward spiral that reminded Akiva of Aladdin's shoes. The wise Apaches had purposely made their boots this way because with the curved leather tip they could quickly and effectively pick up and fling a rattlesnake or scorpion aside before it bit them.

In Na-u-kuzzi's left hand was her battle ax. Akiva saw the bowie knife hanging at her left side. The look on Na-u-kuzzi's face was one of quiet strength and pride. Akiva had never seen her before, for there were no pictures of her. She only knew, based on descriptions her grandmother had related to her as a child, that this was her ancestor. Now, standing in Na-u-kuzzi's powerful energy, Akiva was astounded and mesmerized by her not only as a woman, but as a warrior.

"Granddaughter, I have come to you for a reason," Na-u-kuzzi said.

Akiva realized the older woman's lips were not moving, that she was hearing her words inside her head telepathically. "Yes?"

"You will now take your final test to become a true warrior of The People." She reached out and slid her hand across the sleek black head of the jaguar that sat at her side, his eyes upon Akiva. "Use your fear to strengthen you. Trust the man who walks at your side, for he, too, has jaguar medicine. Only if you fight together, work together, will you have the possibility of surviving this test. Do you hear me, Granddaughter?''

Akiva nodded. ''Y-yes...I hear you. I'm afraid....''

''Of course you are. A true warrior is always afraid.'' Her ancestor laughed huskily. Raising her right hand with a flourish, she added, ''What separates a warrior from a coward is that you take the fear and transmute it into action to save your life instead of letting it paralyze you like a jaguar paralyzes its prey before leaping upon it.'' Her eyes sparkled with amusement. ''Call upon me by name. Call upon my spirit guide here, who is now with you, to infuse you with skill, strength and intelligence.''

Akiva nodded. Just being in Na-u-kuzzi's presence gave her an incredible burst of confidence and self-assuredness. ''I will, Great-great-grandmother. I promise....''

''Go then, my child. We are with you at all times, no matter how dark your world becomes. Call upon us. That is all you need to do. Remember who you are. Remember that my blood runs through your veins. That you have the heart of a warrior, as the man at your side does. Allow the love you've hidden to blossom from your heart to his. If you do this, you may survive...for your biggest test as a warrior will not be whether or not you can fight, but whether or not you can trust your fellow warrior and fight your enemies together.'' Her voice grew deep with warning. ''This is an opportunity, Akiva, for you to heal your wounds. Learn to trust...really *trust*....''

Chapter 11

Akiva tried to stop her teeth from chattering, but it was impossible. The hemp rope had been taken off their ankles and they'd been marched at gunpoint to a dank cell beneath what looked like a massive, yellow-stucco bullring. Arms wrapped around herself, Akiva stood in the center of the small rectangular cell, which had a small, barred window that allowed gray light to filter in.

His face set and determined, Joe tested the door again and again. It was made of thick, dark wood on massive iron hinges.

Dizziness washed over Akiva. She saw down in the fresh golden straw that had been spread across the hard-packed dirt floor of their cell, her back to the wall, her arms around herself, her knees drawn tightly against her body. Her head ached without respite because of the concussion.

"So what do we know?" she asked Joe. "That we're on a hornet's nest. That was Luis Rios, the son of Javier

Rios.'' Akiva frowned. ''We were briefed on them. Now here we are...''

They'd agreed to speak only English, though they both knew Spanish. After all, it was only a matter of time before their captors discovered they were American. The young leader, a man named Luis Rios, had their helmets. And inside the helmets, plainly marked, were the words *U.S. Army.* No, it wouldn't take much guesswork for him to figure out that they were a covert spook operation. Licking her dry lips, Akiva watched Joe, and her heart speeded up with an incredible avalanche of emotion. When the captors had pushed them out of the rear of the vehicle earlier, Joe had demanded food, water and medical attention for her. That had earned him the butt of a rifle in the middle of his back, a blow that had knocked him to his knees. Akiva had stood there, horrified by the vicious act. She'd seen the pleasure in Luis's handsome face. Obviously, he enjoyed seeing Joe in pain. If she hadn't been so dizzy, in so much pain herself, she'd have attacked him, but Akiva knew her concussion was slowing her down, to the point where she had trouble staying on her feet. She would never have been able to kick out with one foot and clip Luis's jaw like she wanted to do.

Ignoring the throbbing ache between his shoulder blades where the drug soldier had nailed him with the butt of his rifle earlier, Joe turned. In the grayish light of the damp, cold cell, he saw Akiva's pale, worried expression. He was worried, too: she needed medical attention. The look on her face—one of devastation and loss of hope—drew him over to her. Kneeling down on one knee, he placed his hands gently on her upper arms and stroked caressingly.

''I don't know what to do,'' he confided in a strained tone. ''How are *you* doing? You look like your head's killing you. Is it?'' He worried about the concussion. Somewhere in his spinning senses, Joe knew enough about medical conditions to know that a concussion could be dangerous, could cause bleeding in the brain. If that happened, a clot could form, and sooner or later kill the person. His fingers gripped her shoulders. Akiva's hair was in disarray. Earlier, the guards had taken her war ax and bowie knife, as well as both of their watches and their side arms.

''Yeah...this headache's a killer all right.'' She managed to lift one corner of her mouth as she gazed up into his dark, shadowed features. Joe looked different to her. Why? Was it because she was privy to his warrior side, had seen his protectiveness toward her? Or was his beard making his face look more chiseled and sharp? ''What I'd give for two aspirin right now,'' she joked wryly. Closing her eyes as Joe's hands ranged gently across her shoulders, then framed her face, Akiva wanted to sob. Struggling, she swallowed hard against the lump forming in her throat.

''Oh, Joe...I screwed up. I've lost a twenty-million-dollar gunship, put us in this position....'' Akiva felt his callused hands graze her cheeks tenderly. She opened her eyes, but tears blinded her.

''Shh, gal, you didn't do any of this.'' Joe leaned down and saw the glitter of tears making tracks down either side of her taut, pale face. ''You're gonna tell me you planned for that lightnin' bolt to hit us?'' he teased, and gave her a smile he didn't feel. Akiva was completely vulnerable to him for the first time. Relief surged through Joe as he realized why she was able to open up to him now. It was mostly because she was hurting from the injury to her head, and wrestling with the feeling that she hadn't performed up to par. But there was something else, and Joe saw it clearly: she was trusting him. With his thumbs, he brushed away the tears flooding from her anguished-looking eyes. His gaze moved down to her mouth, which was contorted with pain.

To hell with it. They were in a life and death situation. For all Joe knew, the drug dealers could come back and spray them with gunfire, killing them right then and there. Following his heart, which screamed out for him to kiss Akiva, he leaned down.

"I'm gonna kiss you, gal," he whispered, barely an inch from her mouth. "I've been wantin' to do this for a long, long time, and unless you say no..."

Sniffing unsteadily, Akiva whispered his name, her voice cracking. She reached up and slid her fingers around Joe's strong, thick neck. In the next instant, his mouth was settling tenderly against her trembling one.

Akiva couldn't stop shaking. She was so cold. So afraid. Mentally she tried to wrestle with her fears, but her body wasn't responding like she wanted it to. Maybe it was because of her injury, or shock from the combat. She just wasn't sure. Now, as Joe's warm, strong mouth moved gently across her lips in a slow, delicious exploration, Akiva drank in his heat and power, absorbing it into her shaking soul. He moved closer, his hands drifting from her face, down her slender neck, covering her shoulders and pulling her more surely against him.

Never had Akiva been kissed like this. His mouth was strong and cherishing. She lost herself in the splendor and heat created as they clung to one another. How could she have been so wrong about Joe? Right now, as his large, square hands caressed her shoulders and drew her against him, Akiva wanted more of him. Fear was overridden by something so incredibly beautiful and heart-stopping that Akiva surrendered to it...and to Joe. Right now, he was strong where she was weak. As he grazed her lips softly, worshipfully, Akiva realized in some dim recess of her mind and aching heart that it was all right for her to feel this way; that sometimes a man was stronger in a moment than a woman. And vice versa. All along, Akiva had thought that she had to be strong all the time, that no man could match her strength or her power. She was wrong. Moaning Joe's name against his searching mouth, Akiva deepened their kiss. His breath was chaotic and moist, flowing against her cheek.

Tunneling his fingers through her thick hair, he moved it aside like a curtain and eased back from her mouth. He trailed lingering kisses from her cheek down her jaw and neck as Akiva moaned.

Hands moving spasmodically against his shoulders, Akiva felt the icy coldness of fear dissolving beneath his tender ministrations. Her heart expanded and opened in a way she'd never known before. Euphoria flooded Akiva, left her breathless, left her staring up into Joe's stormy gray eyes, which burned with desire for her. In those precious seconds, Akiva realized that what she felt for Joe was love. Never in her life had she felt this way about a man before, and it left her frightened in new and different ways. Yet as she clung to Joe's tender, burning gaze, and he gently stroked her hair, Akiva knew somehow that she was safe with him. Protected. And most of all, loved. Yes, he loved her. Blinking through her tears, Akiva opened her mouth, but words failed her.

"Shh, gal, I know," Joe whispered unsteadily as he framed her face once more and gave her a tender smile. "We both feel it. And it's for real. It's ours...."

"I—I'm afraid, Joe...." There, the words were out. She blinked rapidly again and wiped away the last of her tears.

''So am I, gal.'' He eased back, his hands resting on her slumped shoulders. ''Militarily, we're not in a good position.'' His heart cried out with the unfairness of it all. Yet as Joe searched her anguished face, her soft, well-kissed mouth, he knew that Akiva would probably never have opened up to him this way under any other circumstances. Moving his fingers along the rip in her uniform near her left shoulder, he gazed at her tear-matted lashes and pained-filled eyes.

''We have one another,'' he told her in a low voice. Joe didn't want to risk anyone overhearing them. For all he knew, a guard was posted outside the door and could be eavesdropping. ''And we trust one another.''

Trust. There was that word. Joe released her. He sat down next to her, his back against the wall, their arms and legs touching.

''Come here,'' he rasped, and he opened his arms and drew Akiva into them. Joe situated her so that she lay on her left side against his body, facing him. He took her full weight, as he wanted to warm her up. At first he thought she might hesitate at such intimacy, but she surprised him by nestling in his arms without a fight. Joe began to understand how vulnerable Akiva really was. As she rested her head against his shoulder, her arm sliding up across his chest and around his neck, she sighed brokenly.

''It's gonna be all right, gal. Wait and see,'' he whispered against her ear, which was covered with the thick black silk of her hair. ''You bein' in my arms is a dream come true for me. I want you to know that.'' He smiled softly and closed his eyes, absorbing her softness. Akiva was a strong woman, a warrior without equal, and yet, in this moment, as their lives hung precariously by a thread, she trusted him. Trusted him! His heart soared like an eagle taking wing.

"I don't think so, Joe—"

"Shh, gal…just lie here with me. Lemme hold you. Lemme keep you warm and safe." He pressed a kiss against her hair. Little by little, Akiva was relaxing against him. He felt the roundness of her breasts against his chest, felt their rise and fall as she breathed. The warm moisture of her breath feathered across his neck. As he ran one hand slowly up and down the long indentation of her spine, he felt like a starving stray dog that had found not only shelter, but food as well. Akiva's nearness was food for his aching, pounding heart and spirit.

As he sat there with her in his arms, needing her as much as he needed to breathe, Joe wondered when it had all happened. When had he fallen in love with Akiva? Oh, he'd always been dazzled by her as a combat pilot—that reckless smile of hers, that gleam in her eye telling him she was a supreme hunter. But how long had he ached to discover this wonderful, soft, feminine side of her?

There were times when Joe sat alone at Alpha and wondered if Akiva would ever unveil her feminine side to him. When she'd told him of her childhood, he'd wanted to cry—for her, for what had been done to her. Joe understood that Akiva had had to be tough and defensive or she would not have survived. And more than anything, she was the consummate survivor. Only survivors paid one hell of a price for the hardscrabble life that had been thrust upon them as innocents. That natural innocence was something Joe had recognized in Akiva as he got to know her. She'd been a vulnerable little girl who had been thrown into a toxic, dysfunctional environment. It was no wonder she shielded herself from possible hurt. He didn't blame her at all.

As he lay there, the day dying, the grayness deepening until it was dark in the cell, Joe held Akiva as she slept in his arms. After a while, his backside became numb because of lack of circulation, but he didn't care. She was in his arms and his heart was soaring with a happiness he'd never experienced in his life.

Sitting there in the darkness, Joe heard the snort of what he thought were cattle and horses nearby. Sometimes he heard voices in Spanish, but the words were muted and he couldn't make out what the men said.

As he sat in the cell, holding the woman he loved more than life, Joe felt a kind of peace, despite their dire circumstances. In this moment that he'd never dreamed would happen, Akiva was all that mattered.

As she fell deeper into an exhausted sleep, he felt her body relax against the harder planes of his own. Her breathing slowed and deepened. Her arm slid off his shoulder and she tucked her hand against her breast, fingers softly curled. Before sleep finally claimed him, Joe wondered if Akiva had ever had a night, as a child, where she felt safe. Safe, embraced and well loved. Protected from the violence that had hounded her young life. Probably not. As exhaustion finally claimed him in the damp, chilly darkness of the cell, Joe knew that for at least this one night, Akiva slept knowing she was not only protected, but safe…and loved.

The rattling of the door pulled both of them from sleep. Joe jerked upward, instantly on guard. Akiva rolled away from him, sitting up and tensing. Both trained their gazes on the door.

Two guards dressed in camouflage fatigues and bearing military rifles stepped into the cell and stood on either side of the door.

Akiva glanced at Joe, who was slowly getting to his feet, his arms held tensely at his sides, his eyes narrowed. She saw a silver-haired man, dressed casually in a white shirt and tan slacks, a red neckerchief around his throat, enter their cell. It was Javier Rios himself. His dark brown eyes sparkled with humor. His face was narrow and he wore a silver goatee. As Akiva looked down at what he held in his hands, she gasped and leaped to her feet, her hair flying about her shoulders, her fists curling at her sides. He had her war ax and bowie knife!

One of the guards lowered his rifle barrel and pointed it at her. "Move again and you're dead," he snarled in Spanish.

Joe snapped a look at Akiva. All her attention was on the weapons the older man held in his hands. He saw her anger and her desire to have them back. Knowing how much they meant to her, Joe held his hand out to stop Akiva from moving forward. The dark looks on the guards' faces told him they'd shoot first and ask questions later.

"Ah," the visitor said, "so you are the owner of these archeological delights. Allow me to introduce myself." He bowed slightly to them. "I am Javier Rios." He looked with undisguised interest at Akiva. "Permit me to ask you some questions, *señorita,* for these weapons are very, very interesting to me. My son, Luis, took these off you out near the coast, after you were discovered by him."

Javier smiled slightly, a surge of excitement tunneling through him. This woman who stood before him dressed in black, a red scarf about her head, was a giant! He'd had no idea she was six feet tall. Luis had not said much about her, except that she was a woman. And Luis liked women for only one thing—keeping his bed warm. He'd neglected to mention that she was a warrior, no question about it.

Eagerness thrummed through Javier as he lifted the weapons for her to see more clearly. "Please, be at ease. I come to talk to you, *señorita,* about these magnificent, very old weapons they found on you." His voice lowered with excitement. "Tell me if I am correct or not, eh? I have pored over many, many archeological texts from my library, all day yesterday and long into the night. I have made many calls to museums in the U.S., even the Smithsonian, to verify what I think I hold in my hands. These are precious...." And his voice cracked.

Gathering himself, and trying to contain the thrill he felt, he looked up into Akiva's darkening face and narrowed eyes. Indeed, this woman was a true warrior! Even more excitement flowed through him. Moving his lips, he tried to steady his voice, but he always got emotionally overwhelmed when he held such treasures as these, with their history, in his hands.

"*Señorita,* I believe you are Chiricahua Apache." His eyes sparkled and he gestured with his chin. "You wear the third braid of the warrior. You have gone through arduous and dangerous trials to earn the right to wear that braid with honor. Further, you wear the red scarf of an Apache warrior. The Apaches had many women warriors in their bands. And these..." His voice trembled. "These...children of yours—why, they are priceless! I am holding a part of history...." He lifted his head and gazed at Akiva's wide eyes. His smile grew.

"According to my books, to my calls to people who are experts on Native American archeological treasures, this is a war ax that dates back roughly to 1860." He held the knife up, its leather scabbard stained from age and handling. "And this is a bowie knife! I simply cannot believe it! It is the real thing. Why, the blade has many nicks on it. The leather dates back to 1860, too, but the knife is much earlier, perhaps 1840...."

Gulping, Akiva eyed her weapons. How badly she wanted them back. The old man was positively salivating over them. He held them with such care that she was stunned.

"Tell me this is so?"

"Only when you give us water, food and medical help," Joe snarled. He cut a look to Akiva, who wanted desperately to reach out and claim her great-great-grandmother's weapons, he could tell.

"Ahh...yes, the male warrior at the side of this magnificent female." Javier's gaze settled on Joe. "I would guess, *señor,* that perhaps you, too, are part Native American? Perhaps not, eh? There were no weapons, other than a U.S. Army pistol, found on your person, so you may be Anglo after all."

"We demand to be treated according to the Geneva Convention of War," Joe said in a deep voice. When he lifted his hand, both guards went on alert. He let his arm drop back to his side.

"Yes, well..." Javier looked Akiva up and down with respect and obvious admiration. "I think we can do that, *señor.*" He smiled a little. "And then, *señorita,* will you kindly confirm what I hold in my hands?"

Akiva gulped. She knew they weren't in a military situation. Drug lords didn't follow Geneva accords any more than they followed the laws of the land. "You get us food, water and a medical doctor," she echoed huskily. "Then, maybe, I'll tell you more."

"Good enough," Javier said. He smiled at them and

again bowed slightly before stepping out into the poorly lit hall. The guards followed on his heels. One of them slammed the door shut and locked it.

Akiva felt shaky in the aftermath. She traded a silent look that spoke volumes with Joe as they waited several minutes before moving or speaking. If there was a guard outside the door, Akiva didn't want him to overhear them.

"Javier Rios," Joe finally said in a low voice. He went over to the door and tested it. It was locked. Turning, he saw Akiva sit down. She rubbed her face and pushed her hair back behind her shoulders.

"Yes," she whispered. She saw Joe looking down at her, that same tender flame burning in his eyes. The set of his mouth told her that he was ready to give his life for her, if necessary. Feeling eviscerated by Rios having her weapons, Akiva choked out, "Who is that man? How could he know so much about me?"

Shaking his head, Joe knelt down beside her, his arm going around her shoulders as he rasped, "I don't know. He's a historian, remember? From the briefing?"

"Oh, that's right," Akiva replied. "That would explain Javier's intense interest in my weapons. And it might also explain why we are being held here. From what I could see when they brought us in, there is an actual bullring built above these cells."

"Yeah, looks that way, as far as I could tell." Joe sat down next to her. His stomach was clenched with fear. With hunger. They'd had no water for nearly twenty-four hours, and he was dying for a cup right now. Running his fingers across Akiva's taut shoulders, the silk of her hair soothing to him, he whispered, "I hope like hell they give us the stuff we've asked for. You've got to be hungry and thirsty."

Nodding, Akiva looked up and almost drowned in his gray eyes. "I am, but to tell you the truth, Joe, having you here...holding me...has more than made up for everything else."

He met and held her golden eyes. This morning, in the gray light drifting in from the dirty window, he saw that she was looking more like her old self. Her skin was once again copper colored, her eyes much clearer. "Getting a good night's sleep helped, gal." His mouth hitched upward.

"No," Akiva whispered unsteadily, "it's because of you, Joe...it's you." She reached out, scared, and yet needing to touch him. Her hand settled over his. "You held me. You made me feel safe for the first time in my life. It's a miracle." Her voice quavered with unshed tears. "You're a miracle to me, to my heart. When you held me last night, my head was throbbing. I was in so much pain. Yet when you caressed my head, I felt the pain going away with each stroke of your hand. I felt it." Akiva gave him a puzzled look. "I don't know how you did it, but as I fell asleep, I was pain free. I felt so happy when you held me. Happier than I've ever been, and I don't know why. I've never trusted anyone like I trust you...."

Her words were like sunlight striking the rich, fertile earth of his heart. Akiva's voice was husky and off-key. He heard and felt her pain, her surprise, her yearning for him. Picking up her hand, he clasped it gently within his. She was so strong, and yet she was allowing him complete access to her as a woman. He struggled to speak, his emotions nearly overwhelming him.

"And I trust you, gal, with my life, my heart, my soul.... I always have and I always will." He lifted her long, slender fingers and saw small white scars that she'd probably gotten in childhood. Lifting her hand to his lips, he kissed the back of it tenderly. "What we have, Akiva, is good. It's solid." He turned and pulled her into his arms. She came without resistance, slipping her arms around him and holding him tightly. That gave Joe the courage to speak of what lay in his heart.

"I dunno how we're gonna get out of this trouble we're in, gal, but we will. I just feel it in my gut." Pressing a kiss to her hair, he whispered unsteadily, "I care so deeply for you, Akiva. I'd give my life for you in a heartbeat. I want what we have. We've earned this, gal. We've earned one another. I know we're in a god-awful mess, but I want to pursue what we have...once we get out of here...."

Akiva nuzzled Joe's hard jaw. His arms held her tightly, crushing the air out of her lungs. She felt his anxiety, his fear and his fierce love for her. All those chaotic emotions tumbled through her as she clung to him. "I do, too, Joe...." she rasped. Tears jammed into her tightly shut eyes. Fighting them back, Akiva opened her mouth, her lower lip trembling as she spoke in a haunted tone. "Your goodness, your kindness, Joe, comes from your heart and soul. I know that." Her hands tightened against his back as she held him tightly. "I—I trust you with my life...." She managed a short, nervous laugh. "I'm so afraid to say this, but life can be pretty short sometimes, and I want you to know something. I—my heart...you have my heart. I don't know when it happened...or how...I just know that I want more of what you share with me. You're unlike any man I've ever known or experienced...."

He nodded against her thick hair. "I hear you, gal," he whispered unsteadily. "When you have trust, you can build on it. And right now, that's what we've earned with one another. You're priceless to me. You hear that, Akiva? I respect you. I admire you. I want you in my life, always. In every way possible." Joe frowned and held her tightly. His voice roughened. "And we've got to get out of here. We've got to escape, because I want a life with you."

Chapter 12

"Now that you are fed, watered and medically taken care of," Javier said in an amused tone to his two guests, who were seated in front of the massive mahogany desk in his den, "I offer you a conciliatory olive branch of sorts." He pointed to the two weapons on his desk. "These belong to you, Warrant Officer Redtail? Yes?"

Akiva's head was still aching as she stared at the neatly dressed Javier Rios. Dr. Paulo Hernandez had put six stitches in a gash there less than half an hour ago. Joe sat next to her in a carved mahogany chair with a straight back and ornate arms. Two hours after Rios's initial visit to their cell, they'd been roughly taken out of their dungeon beneath what seemed to be, indeed, a bullring, and hustled toward the main house in the huge *estancia* complex. There they were put into separate rooms, told to strip out of their clothes, given a hot shower and fresh civilian clothes. Only the clothes weren't exactly modern looking to Akiva. Her attire consisted of a rough red woolen tunic that fell to just above her knees. A pair of white pants went with it, tied at the waist with a rope to keep them from falling down. Instead of being given her flight boots, she was told to put on a pair of high leather boots that tied just below her knees. A rough leather belt with beaten, thin brass disks around it pulled the tunic in at her waist. The guards had taken away her red scarf, which she wanted to tie around her head. That made her angry. She had just washed and towel dried her hair, but Akiva took the time to plait her third braid of a warrior before a guard shoved the point of his rifle into her ribs and told her to get up and leave the room. But then the guard had had second thoughts and had given her back her red scarf. She felt better wearing it in front of Rios.

She and Joe had been hustled out to another room—what looked like a kitchen in the basement of the main house—by guards. There, frightened looking women in black dresses with starched white aprons fed them. They sat side by side at the crimson-tiled table in the center of the hot, airless kitchen, where at least five cooks were working furiously nonstop, and ate voraciously of the salty beef-and-vegetable stew placed before them.

Afterward, they'd been escorted at gunpoint by their two scowling guards up to the second floor. The spacious den they entered looked more like a museum to Akiva. She traded a look with Joe, who had shaved as well as washed. He, too, was dressed in a red tunic and pants.

Already, they'd given Rios the standard military response to his questions: name, rank and serial number. That was what was required under the laws of the Geneva Convention. Javier's eyes sparkled and he seemed amused by their response to him.

"Well?" he said again, propping his long, square fingers together, his elbows resting on the thickly padded arms of his chair. ''Do I get something other than what you've told me already? Aren't you interested in the olive branch?''

Biting her lower lip, Akiva assessed the older man. In the back of the room, his sulking son, Luis, stood, arms across his chest. He'd argued heatedly with his father earlier. From what she had gathered, Luis wanted to simply put a gun to their temples and kill them. Heart thudding heavily, Akiva weighed the son's desire against what the father wanted. She knew, without a doubt, that the older man held their lives in his hands. Because of Joe's admission of his feelings for her, and her realization of how desperately she wanted to survive this unfolding nightmare to have a life with him, Akiva decided to talk.

''Okay,'' she said darkly, ''what's the olive branch?''

''Ahh, you are as intelligent as you look. A modern-day gladiatrix. Did you know that the Romans took prisoners, upstart warriors who fought against the greatest soldiers in the world, and brought them to Rome to fight in the Circus Maximus?'' Javier leaned forward, his voice becoming animated. ''And that there were women warriors, particularly among the Britons, who were gladiators? They fought just as valiantly and heroically as any male. Yes, they were a lost piece to my historical reenactments...until now.''

Confused, Akiva sat there. She saw Joe's expression go sour. What was Rios babbling about? Looking around, Akiva realized that all the weapons hanging along the scrubbed white walls of the long, rectangular room looked Roman or of that era. She was no expert, but she did recognize the short swords, the long, rectangular leather shield with brass embossing on it, the brass helmet with the red horsehair plume as a crest, and other pieces of armor a Roman soldier would wear.

"What olive branch?" Joe growled. He sat up. Instantly, the guard behind him stiffened, the muzzle of the rifle aimed at Joe's head.

Giving him a distraught look, Akiva raised her hand. She was afraid the guard, a big six-foot, heavily muscled Latino with a shaved head, would shoot Joe.

Chuckling indulgently, Javier raised his hand and flipped it toward the guard. "Chico, please...they are unarmed. They are not stupid enough to try and make an escape. They know better." His dark brown eyes settled back on Akiva. "My dear, I await with held breath for you to tell me of these wondrous weapons you carry."

"And if I do?"

With a one-shouldered shrug, Javier smiled, "Then I offer you the olive branch."

Moistening her lips, Akiva glanced at Joe. His brows were drawn down, and the look in his eyes shouted silently to her to be careful what she said. Nodding slightly, Akiva turned her attention back to the drug lord, who seemed, on the surface, like a doting old grandfather type. But she didn't fool herself; he was the one who had built this illegal empire. Choosing her words carefully, Akiva told him of the proud history and provenance of the weapons. With each piece of information, Javier became more riveted. Finally, he was leaning forward, his elbows on the desk, his eyes wide, like an excited child. In the back of her mind, she wondered if he was on drugs, demented or just plain loco. Akiva couldn't decide which as she finished explaining the historical significance of the weapons.

"Ahh, this is even better than I'd hoped." He patted the war ax and bowie knife. The thick, dark leather scabbard of the latter had many nicks and scrapes across its surface.

"Now, the olive branch," Joe muttered. "What are you offering us?"

Grinning slyly, Javier picked up the war ax. The head of it was encased in thick leather to protect it. The wooden handle, made of cottonwood, was stained to an umber color from being handled so much over the years.

"You are Native American, too? Yes?" Javier asked Joe.

Mouth tightening, Joe said nothing. He wasn't about to get chatty and friendly with the drug lord. The less Javier Rios knew about him, the less power and leverage the man held over him. Joe worried most about his family. He knew a powerful drug lord could easily locate his family and have them murdered. To protect himself and Akiva, Joe might have to give his name and rank, but he sure as hell wasn't going to give Javier any more ammo to harm those he loved.

Right now, he was desperately worried for Akiva. Rios was infatuated with her; it was as if he saw her as some exotic, rare bug to be studied intently beneath a microscope. It sickened Joe, and it made him anxious. He felt Javier was dangling them like helpless puppets, and their lives were forfeit. Joe was finding it hard to keep calm as he waited for a chance to escape.

"I see." Javier sighed, obviously disappointed. "You are not going to be friendly and open, as is your partner here." His mouth twitched. "Chico, put your rifle to Chief Warrant Officer Redtail's head, please?"

Joe nearly came out of the chair. Instantly, a thick, powerful hand gripped his shoulder and thrust him back. The other guard, at least six foot five inches tall, with shining obsidian eyes, grinned down at him. He had two front teeth missing, and there was a long scar from his cheekbone to his jaw on the left side of his pockmarked face.

"*Señor,*" Javier said smoothly, "if you do not answer me, I'm afraid we are going to lose your partner, here. I will have Chico take her out into our courtyard below, stand her against the wall and shoot her." He leaned forward, opened the top of his humidor and pulled out a thick Cuban cigar. "The choice is yours...."

Gulping unsteadily, Joe rasped, "Back off, dammit. I'll tell you."

Chico grinned lethally and looked to his master.

Javier barely nodded.

Chico removed the rifle point from Akiva's temple and took a step back behind her chair once more.

"Well, Chief Warrant Officer Calhoun?" Picking up the sterling silver snippers from the right side of his desk, Rios looked over the cigar in his fingers at Joe. "Are you Native American, too?"

"I'm part Comanche," Joe spat, his anger barely restrained. He gripped the arms of the chair, breathing hard. The look of terror in Akiva's eyes when the rifle had been jabbed against her left temple almost made him lose his perspective. Under no circumstances could he let Rios know he loved Akiva. No, the older man would hold it over his head for more information.

"And your accent? Hmm," he murmured, snipping off the end of the cigar. "Southern, possibly?"

"Texas," Joe said flatly.

"Ah...of course. The Comanches were a Southwest people who came down out of the Plains and did a lot of raiding in Arizona, New Mexico and Texas." Picking up his lighter, he smiled at Joe. "So, what is this all about? Luis and I have been trying to put this together. You fly a U.S. Army gunship called the Apache. She is

Apache. You are part Comanche. What is this? The Pentagon's latest ploy? To put Indians in the cockpit on a black ops mission to try and turn around my cocaine shipments to the U.S.? I'm *very* intrigued with this new plan of theirs."

Akiva sat very still. She and Joe still didn't know if their Apache had blown up or not. The rockets fired by Luis had rendered them unconscious before the gunship had had a chance to detonate. She tucked her lower lip between her teeth to keep herself from asking the burning question. Javier was playing them against one another. Feeling the sweat trickle down her rib cage as she sat there tensely Akiva recognized the meeting for what it was: an interrogation to find out more about them.

"We have better night vision."

Joe glared at Akiva. Damn her! She'd purposely pulled Javier's attention back to her. His mouth thinned. In that moment, he wanted to reach out and stop her from saying more. He watched as she sat up and leaned toward the old man, who was now lighting the cigar.

Puffing contentedly, Javier studied Akiva through the white, purling smoke. Putting the lighter aside, he pulled on the cigar before answering. "I see...well, yes, that does make sense...."

"What is the olive branch?" Akiva demanded. "You said if I told you the history of my weapons, you would offer us one."

Grinning again, Javier leaned back in the chair, puffed several more times and then said, "Ordinarily, we dispense with moles and those who would make war against us rather quickly. But over the years I've devised a different way to achieve our goals—and punish my enemies."

Pointing to the war ax, he lifted his finger and gestured

toward Akiva. ''Tomorrow, you will be given your ax back.'' Glancing over at Joe, he pointed to the knife on the desk. ''And you will be given the bowie.''

Frowning, Akiva stared at him. ''What are you talking about?''

Javier looked down the length of the room toward his son, who was now smiling. Glancing at the two pilots, he said, ''I am going to make you a deal that you cannot refuse. And here are my terms, which must be met. For the next three weeks, I'll be hosting a global gladiator tournament. My bullring, here at the edge of San Cristobel, becomes a combination of the Roman Colosseum and Circus Maximus. I'm sure you didn't know this, but I have set up a series of gladiator schools in Italy, the U.S., Canada, France, Germany, Peru and Mexico. People pay mucho bucks to pursue their fantasy of being a gladiator in combat.''

Akiva frowned, her mind spinning. ''To fight?''

''But of course,'' Javier chuckled. ''Only, down here where I am lord of all I survey, I do not have to worry about civility or legalities. Those who take my courses come to combat one another in the sands of my bullring. And—'' he smiled lethally ''—I offer them blood sport. When they are done pretending to be gladiators, I offer them modern-day gladiators as the ultimate reward and entertainment.''

A chill worked its way up Akiva's spine. She heard Joe move tensely beside her. Keeping her gaze on Javier, she asked in a low tone, ''And how does this involve us? Is this your olive branch?''

Puffing, the smoke curling lazily about his head, Javier showed his large, perfect teeth as he smiled. ''I train world-class gladiators here. You might say they are men who have refused to help me with cocaine. I give them a choice—they can become slaves who train and learn gladiatorial combat or they can die instantly, with a bullet in their brain by Chico. I'll offer you the same choice that I offer them, which is very Roman. You will fight in combat three times. If you happen to win each bout, then you will be awarded your freedom, just as the gladiators who survived fifty fights in the arena were given their freedom by the emperor of Rome."

Joe nearly choked on his rage. "You can't make us do this."

"Really?"

Akiva shot Joe a quick look. His face was set and a dull red. He was about to leap out of the chair again, his hands gripping the arms, his knuckles whitening.

"Wait!" Akiva begged him. She sat up and jerked a look at Javier, who studied them intently from beneath his gray brows. "You're saying if we go into combat, fight your gladiators or whoever they are...and if we win, you'll set us free?" Her heart was pounding. Wanting to believe Javier, but knowing better, Akiva found herself scrambling mentally for a plan. If they were loose in the bullring, there might be a way to escape at some point.

"Yes, my dear, you're correct."

"This is illegal!" Joe snarled. "You have no right to put her into such a situation. She's a woman."

"She's a warrior first," Javier said jovially. "And what's illegal about it? You're both warriors. You live to die. And that was the maxim of the gladiator—they lived and died to serve the emperor of Rome. This is no different, really. You live to die serving your country, the U.S.A. At least this way you have a chance. The other way—a bullet to the head—is no chance at all. Come, come, Warrant Officer Calhoun...you look like a sporting man. Are you going to sit there and tell me you want this beautiful woman warrior's brains splattered all over my wall? Frankly, I'm salivating over the idea of seeing both of you, as a team, coming up against my Roman soldiers in the ring. People are traveling from around the world to celebrate all things Roman for the next three weeks. They come in costume. We have parties. We have ceremonies to the old gods and goddesses.... It is as if a time machine has taken us back to the glory of Rome, in a most enjoyable way.''

Akiva sat back, trying to sort through all the information. ''People?''

''Yes, those who love Rome. Archeologists, both professional and amateur. Museum curators. And the thousands who are already here, camping outside my *estancia* in tents, waiting for the festivities to start tomorrow.'' Smiling happily, Javier said, ''Your capture couldn't have come at a better time. Now they will see real warriors in action—you. I will bill you as captured Celts, Briton warriors. You are dressed in their garb already, even if you don't realize it.'' He chuckled and waved his hand toward them.

Akiva looked down at the rough woolen clothing she wore, feeling stunned.

''No one but us will know the truth—that you are captured U.S. Army pilots. The thousands who will jam the seats of my magnificent bullring, all in Roman costume, will simply think you are part of the show. It will do you no good to try and shout for help, for Circus Maximus brings out the howling, primitive emotions all humans have. They are going to be looking for blood sport. So don't think that you can cry out for help, for it won't do you any good. I will have guards behind the many gates in and out of the bullring, keeping an eye on you at all times.''

"And if we refuse to fight?" Joe rasped, glaring at him.

Shrugging, Javier said, "Luis will be standing right behind my gilded throne, in his praetorian uniform, a pistol in his hand. If I give him the order to shoot you, he will. On the spot. Rest assured, Warrant Officer Calhoun, you'll fight for your life out there or you will be shot where you stand. It is your choice." Sitting up in his chair, his voice becoming enthusiastic again, Javier regarded Akiva. "My dear woman, you will be the hit of our event. Oh, we've had women who have trained to be gladiators, but never like this. No, you will become the star of our blood sport program. In all the years that I have been putting on this yearly event, it has always been men against men." He smiled savagely. "Now they will come up against a real woman warrior—a woman who has the blood of Apache warriors in her veins. They will get to see what it must have been like back in Rome when one of those Celtic women appeared in the arena.... Yes, this is going to be most exciting. I can hardly wait!"

Gulping, Akiva stared over at Joe. Then she looked back at Javier. "And we get the war ax and the bowie knife and that's it?"

"But of course," Javier exclaimed. "When captured enemy warriors were marched back from all points of the Roman empire, they were thrown into the arena with what they were accustomed to fighting with." His smile grew. "And I think, for your debut in the arena, you will come up against a band of Gaulish warriors, from Germania. I have five Mexican farmers who have refused to work in my cocaine factories. They have been training for six months in the art of the short sword and shield, the trident and net. Five against the two of you. That is good odds, eh?"

* * *

"I don't believe this," Joe said as he paced the length of their cold, damp cell. Night was falling. Akiva stood by the window, a pensive look on her face, her arms against her chest. "That old geezer is crazier than a loon."

"Maybe..." she murmured. She could barely see Joe, but could hear him walking back and forth in the straw that littered the hard dirt floor.

Turning to her, he said, "What are you thinking?"

"How we can turn this to our advantage and escape," Akiva said.

Sighing in frustration, Joe went over to her. He reached out and enclosed her hand in his. "He said there were a lot of doors into the bullring. Maybe we can make a run for one?"

"He mentioned that he'll have guards posted at every one," Akiva said, worried. "And every one of them will have weapons trained on us."

Joe gripped her hand. How he ached to have her fingers move across him, love him, as he wanted to love her. But now was not the time. "It sounds like Rios's blood sport features poor Mexican farmers who didn't want to be a part of his drug trade."

"Yeah," Akiva said sourly. She frowned. "I won't kill them, Joe. They're just as much pawns in this as we are. They're fighting at gunpoint, like us. They're not our enemy."

Nodding, he rasped, "We're not killing anyone. I just want to survive this with you." Worriedly, he looked down at her. The darkness was complete now; he couldn't really see her at all. But he felt the warmth of her body against his. "I'm scared. I'm scared for you. I don't want you hurt, gal...."

Snorting softly, Akiva said, "I've been thinking the same about you, Joe."

"Five to two. Bad odds."

"Yeah, but whose will to live will be the strongest? Ours. I'm not going to get hacked to death with whatever weapons they're carrying."

"All we have is your war ax and a knife."

She cut him a glance, even though she couldn't see him or his expression. "Do you know how to fight with a knife?"

"I took bayonet and rifle training in the army. Does that count?"

Chuckling at his dark humor, Akiva said, "No."

"You were taught?"

"Of course. Part of Apache warrior training."

"Ah, yes. Well, tell me all you know, because tomorrow I'm gonna have to use that knowledge to keep from bein' sliced and diced up like a beet."

Akiva couldn't help laughing softly. This was typical of Apache pilots—when things got really tense and life-threatening, their black humor surfaced. She heard Joe chuckling with her.

"My grandmother, if she were here, would be jumping up and down for joy," Akiva admitted, still smiling. "She'd tell us that the odds are even—that one good Apache warrior could take out ten white men in a heartbeat."

Raising his brows, Joe muttered, "Well, the odds are in our favor then, right?"

Mouth pursed, Akiva said, "Right." Tugging at his hand, she said, "Let's sit down. At least the old man gave us wool cloaks to go with the Celtic costumes we have to wear. If we sleep together, the cloaks around us, maybe we won't be so cold tonight."

Joe sat down in the thick, soft straw. The fragrance of it wafted upward and encircled them. They'd already laid their cloaks out. Tonight they would lie beside one another, their arms around each other, to stave off the chill and dampness. As he lay down next to Akiva Joe tried to keep desire for her out of his mind. When she'd settled next to him, facing him, he pulled one long, heavy cloak over them. He felt her head nestle in the crook of his shoulder and her hand slide across his torso. Adjusting the cloak across his shoulders, he eased it across Akiva's exposed back.

"There," he rasped against her hair. He felt the entire length of her body against his, the press of her breasts against his chest. She moved her long legs between his and they tangled comfortably beneath the cloak. Sliding his arm around her waist, he brought her fully against him.

"I'm warm already," Akiva murmured. Tiredness began to lap at her. Joe's masculine fragrance drifted into her nostrils. Closing her eyes, she smiled. "I feel like we're in a *heyoka* world, not the real world," she admitted to him in a whisper. Absorbing the sensation of Joe's strong hand stroking her back protectively, she sighed.

"Heyoka?"

"Yeah, that's a Lakota word for backward. It means chaos. Everything's turned upside down, the opposite of what you'd expect."

Akiva felt good and strong against him. Joe forced himself not to feel the burning ache in his lower body. Akiva was in his arms tonight because she trusted him, and he wasn't about to take advantage of that trust in a selfish desire to make love to her. No, right now he sensed she wanted, needed, his protection.

A feeling of deep satisfaction wove through him. It was one of the few things he could give Akiva right now—his warmth, a little solace. Because tomorrow they could die....

Chapter 13

The noise of a huge crowd rumbled through the bullring, above the cell where Akiva and Joe were being held. Akiva was sitting on the straw, tightly lacing up her knee-high leather boots, when the lock jangled and the door was pushed open. Joe was at the window and turned, his face grim. It was Luis Rios.

"Get up," Luis snarled.

Akiva looked at him and gawked. The son of the powerful drug lord was dressed in a splendid Roman uniform, replete with gold helmet topped with large ostrich plumes of bright red. Glancing over at Joe, she scrambled to her feet, her pulse skyrocketing. She had no idea what time it was, only that since dawn had filtered into their damp, cool cell, hundreds, maybe thousands of voices had begun to drift down to them.

Behind Luis were the two bald-headed guards. They, too, were in Roman uniform, except not quite as gaudy looking, and they wore AK-47s on their shoulders. So much for remaining true to history, Akiva thought sourly.

Luis adjusted the red woolen cloak that was pinned to the epaulets of his uniform. His gold metal breastplate was emblazoned with the wolf of Rome suckling the founders of the city. He wore a short sword in a leather scabbard at his side, and a dagger on the other. His eyes narrowed on them. ''You're up next.''

Akiva moved to Joe's side. Just his proximity made some of her fear ebb. ''Where are our weapons?'' she demanded hoarsely.

Grinning, Luis said, ''They'll be placed out in the center of the arena. You'll be marched at gunpoint to the entrance. A guard will open the door and you will walk out to the center and pick them up.'' His voice lowered in warning. ''If at any time you think of throwing that war ax or knife at my father or anyone in his entourage, think again.'' Hitching a thumb over his shoulder, he said, ''These two will have a bead drawn on you at all times. Any *hint* of you throwing any weapon toward my father, and these AK-47s, which have silencers on them, will kill you. Got it?''

Joe nodded. ''Yeah, we got it.'' His heart was pounding heavily in his chest. All morning long they'd been tense, irritable and jumpy. Who wouldn't be? This wasn't what Joe wanted at all. He wanted to tell Akiva how he felt about her, about the dreams he held for them, for their future.... But looking at the costumed enemy in front of him, and hearing the roar of the crowd, Joe felt a finality that he couldn't shake. This was real.

''The Gauls will come out. You will all turn and salute my father. Just follow along with what they say and do.''

''And then?'' Akiva demanded darkly.

Shrugging, Luis grinned. ''You fight—to the death.

Winner walks out of the arena to fight another day.'' His eyes glittered. ''And it won't be you, I'm sure. The Gauls are all trained Latino farmers who have worked with the weapons and other gladiators for six months now. They're good at what they do. Further, they know if they kill you, they get to live to fight another day, too.''

''And I suppose,'' Akiva said acidly, ''that means they get the lucky-three contract, too? If they survive three times in the ring, they go home?''

Luis bowed slightly to her. ''Yes, of course.''

''Somehow, I don't trust you or your father to be good at your word.''

A roar from the crowd rolled down the dimly lit corridor.

''I don't care what you think.'' Luis moved out of the cell and into the hallway. ''For your information, all the other events are not to the death. My father has this rule that if one gladiator gets wounded, pulls a muscle or is in some way incapacitated, the fighting stops. You, however, have been billed to the death. There is no stopping the fight after it begins. If you refuse to fight, you'll be shot. You either do the job right or you're dead—your choice. If the crowd sees some of you killed, we will announce that it was actors pretending. They will believe it. Now, get out there. Now!''

Joe moved out first. He wanted to put his fist into Luis's smirking face, but didn't dare. Akiva followed at his heels.

The corridor was dimly lit, wide and damp. A breeze blew through it. Up ahead, Joe saw a wooden gate, at least five feet tall. A guard in Roman costume stood at it, an AK-47 in hand. The ignorant crowd beyond, all lovers of Roman reenactments, would never know the truth, Joe realized. Wiping his mouth with the back of his hand, he tried to steady his emotions. His worry for Akiva was paramount. In the air, she had no equal; that was a fact. But on the ground? In a deadly fight like this?

Up ahead, shouting of the crowds dropped and a hush fell over the arena. The guard jerked his arm toward them.

"You're next!" he shouted, and he pulled open one of the two doors.

Sunlight struck Joe as he stepped into the arena, blinding him. Instantly, he put up his hand to shade his squinting eyes. He saw a chariot drawn by two black horses being driven out another gate across from them. Several other people, reenactors, he supposed, straggled after the chariot, shields and spears in hand. As he looked around, his mouth fell open. The bullring was huge, with at least six levels to it. There were probably three thousand people in Roman costumes in the stands!

Akiva moved to his side, her stride matching his. She looked back. As the guards closed the gate, she saw the AK-47s leveled at them. All her senses became acute as she began to feel adrenaline starting to pulse through her bloodstream.

"This is incredible," Joe rasped as he spotted their weapons lying in the center of the arena. The golden sand was deep and their footing was uncertain because of it.

Akiva looked around. "Yeah. Who would've thought? Look at the old man. He looks like Caesar himself up there."

Joe saw a white canopy over a dais on the first level of the bullring. Beneath it was Javier Rios. Dressed exactly like a Roman emperor, he was wearing a crisp white toga with a purple hem, with a wreath of olive branches around his head. A group of mean-looking guards in Roman costume surrounded his gold chair. There were women there, too—beautiful ones dressed in colorful gowns.

Looking around, Akiva said, "There're four entrance-exit points. Guards at each."

Joe nodded and slowed. He reached down, and picked up the war ax and handed it to Akiva. Taking the knife, he saw that the scabbard was missing. It was a huge knife, the blade long, nicked and made of steel. The handle had leather wrapped around it, making it easier to hold. Leather long ago darkened by sweat.

Amazed by all the cheering and screaming, Akiva turned slowly. People were shouting and calling to them. Some women waved scarves and others threw flowers toward them. Akiva's heart was pounding hard in her body. She turned and faced Joe, who had a look of awe in his eyes as he, too, surveyed the crowd.

"Listen, whatever happens, I'm *not* killing these guys. They're just farmers who have the fear of God put in them," Akiva reaffirmed. "I'm a warrior. I don't fight farmers."

Nodding, Joe said, "Gal, if they come at you, you're gonna have to defend yourself. And they're under the gun, too. If they don't kill us, they're going back to their farms in wooden coffins."

Nostrils flaring, Akiva looked around. "Here they come..."

Suddenly, a dozen horns blasted across the arena, and the crowd quieted instantly. Akiva saw five men coming toward them from another gate. She didn't know much about Roman history, but she vaguely recalled that Gaul, which was modern-day France, had some of the wildest, most determined warriors and had nearly thrown off the yoke of Rome. As she eyed the men struggling across the sand, Akiva's pulse bounded.

"Farmers, hell," she muttered, stepping close to Joe. "Look at those guys. They're all built like bulls!" They moved like trained fighters to Akiva, not unsure farmers.

Joe nodded. He knew what Latino farmers looked like: they were usually short, as well as lean and hard from all the physical work they did daily. But these men, all at least six feet tall, with rippling muscles, were not farmers. "They've lied to us," he growled angrily. "They purposely misled us."

Snorting, Akiva moved restlessly, her hand tightening on the handle of the war ax. "So what's new? Why should we believe *anything* Rios tells us? The bastard…"

Joe watched the men march toward them in a broken line, his mouth flattening. They wore bullet-shaped helmets on their heads, carried round shields made of wood, with brass crosses on each. Three had swords, and the other two had a rope net in one hand, a wicked looking trident in the other.

"I think Rios lied to lull us into thinking these five good ole boys were going to be easy to fight."

Taking a deep breath, Akiva studied them intently. "Well, I've changed my mind. Those dudes are out to take us down."

"Yeah…" And Joe moved between her and the five, who were now forming a line and facing the so-called Roman emperor.

Akiva glared up at Rios, who was a good three hundred feet away. She itched to throw the war ax at the old man and split his skull open. And she could do it. The risk wouldn't be worth it, however, because they'd be shot and killed. But did they have a chance otherwise? Glancing down the line that had formed, Akiva saw the Gauls looking at them with lethal regard. Glaring back, she saw them raise their right hands, fist closed, in a salute to Rios.

"We who are about to die salute you," the five boomed out in deep voices to their emperor.

Joe refused to raise his hand. He saw that Akiva, who stood nearby, didn't, either. Her chin jutted out in utter rebellion. Good for her.

His mind whirled. How could they take on five well-trained men, who were probably Rios's guards in disguise? They ranged in height from six to six foot five inches. And they were all built like powerhouses, their muscles heavy and well formed. That meant they worked out with heavy weights at a gym with great regularity. The clothes they wore were similar to his and Akiva's, except their leggings were crisscrossed with strips of white cotton material from their ankles to their thighs and they carried protective shields. Joe's anger began to simmer and push away some of his fear. They didn't stand a chance against these men.

Javier stood up and raised his hand. The crowd quieted.

"Friends, Romans, countrymen," he began, his voice echoing around the bullring. "Lend me your ears!"

A wild cheer went up, rippling through the reenactors.

"We have a woman gladiator! She is a Celt!"

Another roar went up and echoed wildly around the ring.

Javier smiled triumphantly. "Today, she and her companion go up against five Gauls, the best of Germania. It is a fight to the death! You will now see a *real* Circus Maximus or Colosseum event. When one of them falls, give a thumbs-up or thumbs-down. It is up to you as to who lives and dies in the sands this day! Let the fight begin!'' And he threw a red rose outward. It landed on the gold sands just inside the arena.

Akiva glanced at Joe. ''Did I tell you I was kick-box champion at Fort Rucker when I was going through flight training?''

He shook his head and watched as the five lowered their arms. ''No...you didn't. Did I tell you I'm a black belt in karate?''

She grinned tightly as she backed away, her eyes on the Gauls. ''No...you didn't.'' Gripping the war ax hard in her right hand, she said, ''Did I tell you that Apaches fight dirty?''

Joe's mouth twitched. ''No, but I'm all ears....''

''Watch me....'' And Akiva suddenly leaned down, scooped up a handful of sand and lunged forward. A war cry tore from her contorted lips. She launched herself at the biggest, closest Gaul, who had a sword in his right hand and a shield in his left. Within feet of him, she threw the sand into his face.

The Gaul shouted and lifted his sword hand to his eyes, unable to see.

In one smooth, unbroken motion, at great speed, Akiva leaped off the ground, both booted feet aimed directly at the Gaul, who was peddling backward, off balance.

Her boots smashed into the man's upper chest and neck.

Satisfaction burned through Akiva as she heard the man choke. She knew without a doubt she'd damaged his windpipe with the violent, well-aimed kick. Rolling to the side, she heard shouts of anger all around her.

The fight had begun.

Joe didn't waste a second as he saw Akiva attack the biggest Gaul. Following her lead, he scooped up sand and hurled it into the eyes of the second Gaul, who was shrieking and running at him, his sword raised high. Instantly, the man shouted and lost his balance on the slippery surface. With sand in his eyes, he couldn't see Joe coming.

Breathing hard, Joe jammed the heel of his boot into the man's chest. Instantly, there was a snapping, crunching sound. Joe had just broken the man's sternum, and probably some of his ribs. The Gaul groaned. The sword dropped from his hand. Joe grabbed it. Now he had a sword and a knife.

Turning, he saw another Gaul charging him, his trident extended. Out of the corner of his eye, he saw the other two going after Akiva, who was running away from them.

The Gaul threw the net at Joe. It snaked out.

Joe leaped aside, the net barely missing him. He saw the anger in the man's dark eyes. Without a net, the man had only his trident. Perspiration ran down Joe's face. His breath came in rasps. He heard the swelling roar of the crowd, but ignored it. Moving in a circle, he jerked to the right, then the left, as the Gaul jabbed outward with the forked spear.

Joe slashed downward with the short sword, each time the trident was thrust at him. The tines of the lethal weapon barely missed him. Abruptly, he jumped sideways and swung the sword forward. The blade bit savagely into the wooden handle, and with a loud *crack* the trident snapped in two.

Joe smiled lethally. The Gaul's eyes widened enormously—he knew he was in trouble. Backing off, he looked frantically around for a way to protect himself from Joe.

Joe dropped the short sword and lunged forward, delivering a series of karate strokes to the head and neck of the Gaul. The enemy went down like a felled bull, unconscious.

Jerking around, Joe looked for Akiva. There! She was running as fast as she could from the two Gauls, who pursued her at high speed.

Digging his feet into the sand, Joe sprinted toward the closest one. They were so intent on getting to Akiva that they didn't see him. *Too bad.* In a way, Joe thought, this was just like flying combat in an Apache gunship; he was coming up behind the Gaul, who had no idea he was there. Joe was the six position, the man's most vulnerable point. Joe heard the crowd screaming. It was a bloodcurdling sound.

Akiva tore forward, heading for the yellow stucco wall of the bullring. She could hear the Gaul gaining on her. He was bigger and longer legged than she. That was fine. Heading directly toward the wall as she was, she knew the Gaul would think she was trapping herself. Nothing could be further from the truth. Satisfaction soared through Akiva as she heard him breathing like a bull behind her. He was so close! Gripping the ax, she measured the distance left.

Now!

With a grunt, Akiva leaped upward. Feet first, she flew straight for the wall, her knees flexed. Behind her, she heard the Gaul gasp. As soon as she felt the solid impact of her boots meeting the wall, she doubled up, tucking her body tightly.

Joe had just felled the fourth Gaul and looked up to see something that made him gasp with surprise. As he stood over the unconscious man, he saw Akiva leap upward, her hair flying behind her. She hit the wall with her boots and then did a back flip high in the air. As she flipped, Akiva went up and over the head of the startled Gaul, landing heavily but solidly on her feet behind him.

The Gaul slammed into the wall. Grunting in pain, his head bloodied, he turned and lifted his shield and sword. Too late! The look of pure savagery and triumph on Akiva's face was very real. Her Apache war cry carried around the arena, where the people were jumping up and down, shouting with enthusiasm.

Joe stood breathing hard, hunkered over the Gaul as he watched Akiva finish off the last of their enemy. The instant she'd landed on her feet, she'd leaped up again, her boots aimed directly at the Gaul's head. In seconds, her powerful assault had smashed him back into the wall. The Gaul groaned. He sagged and slid to the ground, dropping his weapons.

Akiva turned, breathing hard. Wiping her mouth with the sleeve of her tunic, she saw Joe standing near the center, a wide grin on his face. Turning, she made sure all five Gauls were disabled and no longer a threat to them. When she saw that they lay unconscious, scattered around the arena, she walked slowly toward Joe, the shouts and cries of the crowd raining down upon her. She saw the triumph and pride in his eyes. Grinning tightly, Akiva looked toward the gate they'd come out. Luis was there, gesturing for them to come out. Javier was standing with his thumb up, indicating that all should live. The people's shouts confirmed it.

"You okay?" Akiva shouted over the roar.

Joe nodded. "Yeah. You?"

"Fine." She looked around. "Not bad for two Apache pilots, eh?"

Laughing deeply, Joe put his arm around Akiva's shoulders. The crowd's roar increased. Pulling her to him, he embraced her hard, once, and let her go. Sweat was running down her face. Her expression was taut and he saw the warrior in her now as never before.

"We'd better lay these weapons down or Luis will nail us," he told her.

Nodding, Akiva set the war ax at her feet. As she turned toward the gate, the roaring crowd kept cheering, waving scarves and throwing flowers into the arena. Joe walked at her side, his hand on her upper arm.

Her heart was pounding and the adrenaline was making her shaky. "We won...." she said, relief in her tone.

"Round one," Joe agreed. They approached the gate and it opened. Luis was standing just inside, a gold plated .45 pistol in his hand, aimed at them.

"Very good," he said smoothly. "Not exactly Roman tactics, but you did good. Now get back to your cell."

"I like how the winners are treated," Akiva said, eating wolfishly from the bowl of stew she'd been given. Sitting with Joe in a clean room at the main *estancia,* where they'd been moved from their cell once darkness had fallen, Akiva, who was starving, was glad for the meal. Javier Rios had also allowed them to take hot showers and don clean clothes. And although the clothes were the same warrior costume she'd worn earlier, Akiva luxuriated in the unexpected gift Javier Rios had bestowed upon them. They sat at a polished mahogany table. There was a tropical fruit salad available, along with fragrant black Colombian coffee and yeast rolls in a basket. To Akiva, it was a feast.

Joe ate like a starved wolf, also. He knew that food was fuel, and that they'd need it. Tomorrow, Luis had informed them as he'd brought them to the *estancia,* they would fight again. Round two.

Looking up at Akiva, who sat opposite him, her hair recently washed, Joe marveled at how beautiful she was. As he buttered a hot roll, he said, "I was impressed with your kick-boxing. You never told me you were a champion.''

''You never asked.''

Chuckling, he bit into the roll with a groan of satisfaction. ''At least he's feeding us right.''

''Yeah, no kidding.'' Akiva reached for another roll, tore it open and slathered it with butter. The room was small and well appointed. It was a drawing room of sorts, with French windows that looked out over the plaza below, where there was a huge, splashing fountain. She knew the room was probably bugged. Maybe it even had a camera or two hidden in it. Akiva wasn't about to talk to Joe about anything of importance. Knowing Javier Rios, he was probably watching them. The man was a voyeuristic lunatic.

They had just finished their meal when Javier entered with his two bald guards. He was still in his emperor's clothing, the circle of olive leaves crowning his head.

''Ahh, you have become the talk of the Circus Maximus,'' he said genially in greeting. Holding the white toga folds on his left arm, he raised his right hand with a flourish. ''This is your reward. Tonight, you will sleep in a special room reserved for gladiators who have won.''

Akiva scowled, but said nothing. She kept eating wolfishly, for she didn't trust Javier to continue to provide food for them. He could just as well starve them tomorrow.

''You said if we won three times in a row, you'd let us go,'' Joe reminded him.

''As emperor of Rome, my word is law,'' he assured them jovially. He gave Akiva a warm look. ''And you, my dear, surpass even my greatest expectations.''

Joe nudged her leg with his toes beneath the table. He saw anger in Akiva's eyes as she lifted her head, spoon in hand. Knowing her as he did, Joe figured she was going to deliver a nasty comment. Right now, they couldn't afford to antagonize Javier. Maybe this room where Javier would be putting them was one they could escape from. As Joe's toe grazed her leg, she looked up at him. He gave her a silent look of caution.

"I just want you to stick to your promise," she told Javier.

Chuckling, he neatly rearranged the folds of his toga that hung over his arm. "Oh, not to worry, my dear, I will. Well, I must go. We're having a Dionysus party tonight, filled with wine, women, song and who knows what else? Romans were so decadent. That's what I love about them. They worked hard, but they played hard, too." His eyes glimmered. "Enjoy yourselves tonight. Get a good night's sleep. At noon tomorrow, you will take on my charioteers...."

Frowning, Akiva waited until the entourage left and the door was closed and locked behind them. Taking another roll, she tore it open. "Charioteers?"

"Chariots drawn by horses," Joe said unhappily. He stopped eating, his appetite gone. "How will the two of us combat that?"

Snorting softly, Akiva gave him a narrow-eyed glance. "You said you rode when you were a kid?"

"Yeah. And was a member at the stables at Fort Rucker. I rode every day, when I got the chance." He smiled a little. "Until I came here—" He stopped abruptly, realizing that the room was probably bugged. Clearing his throat, he said, "Yeah, I can throw my leg over a horse and stay on, if that's what you're asking."

"Good. Tomorrow is more to my liking. Horses are something that can't always be controlled." And she smiled a jaguar smile.

Chapter 14

"Are you ready?" Joe asked Akiva in a low tone. They had been allowed to stay in the main *estancia* for a while after they'd eaten, much to their surprise. Then Chico, the guard, had led them to a basement room with bars on the only window. There were two beds, a toilet and two fresh costumes for them to wear the coming day.

Akiva sat on the edge of her bed as she finished lacing up her leather boots. Her hair was loose and free about her shoulders; the third braid hung from the center part, near her brow and she had faithfully tied her scarf about her head. Joe came and sat down next to her, his solid presence reassuring to her. She gave him what she hoped was a smile. Searching his gray eyes, she reached out and slid her hand into his.

"No. I'm scared."

"Makes two of us," he muttered, looking down at her long, strong fingers as they laced through his. With his other hand, he covered them in a caress. Though they were unable to find evidence last night, both felt they were being continually photographed by a hidden camera and recorded by a microphone. For that reason, they spoke in whispers.

"Listen," Joe said, his lips near her ear, "did you see that road leading out of the villa when they walked us from the bullring to the main hacienda?"

Nodding, Akiva said, "Yeah, I saw it. Right now, it's cluttered with cars of fans coming into the place. There are hundreds of tents on either side. Looks like a huge tent party."

"Right." Joe compressed his lips and then said, "We're near San Cristobel. Luis said as much. How close, I don't know. We haven't been let out to see much of anything."

"Are you thinking what I'm thinking? That if we can somehow escape the ring today, we can make it to that little town?"

"You got it, gal." He slid her a warm look. How beautiful Akiva looked, her dark hair flowing like black lava across her proud shoulders and cascading down around her breasts. The woolen tunic she wore today was black. He wondered if that was an omen. His body responded strongly as she met his gaze with her golden eyes. Automatically, her lips parted, and he wanted to kiss her breathless. Would he ever be able to?

"There's an airport at San Cristobel," Joe rasped softly near her ear. "That's where Luis keeps his helicopter fleet."

Nodding, Akiva turned, her lips brushing his cheek. Inhaling his male fragrance, she added, "We're on the same wavelength. If we can make it to the airport, we can steal one of his birds and get the hell out of Dodge."

Grinning, Joe nodded. "You got it, gal." He patted her hand and then released it.

"The question is how?"

Shrugging, he said, "I dunno. We're gonna have to wait for the opportunity."

Rolling her eyes, Akiva rasped, "Rios is putting us up against chariots."

Joe met and held her angry stare. "Just come out firing like you did yesterday, and we've got a chance." His smile was wolfish. "Kick-box champion. That's one helluva title."

"Yeah? Well, you weren't too shabby in the clutch yesterday, either." She tapped his large knuckles, which were thick and tough from his karate training. A black belt in the discipline wasn't easy to obtain, she knew.

"We're gonna need our wits about us today. We'll have to look for *any* break we can create. Rios's goons are gonna have their sights on us, for sure."

Rubbing her brow, Akiva agreed. There was a clock on the stand between the twin beds where they'd slept. It was almost noon. Scowling, she said, "Listen, if only one of us makes it, that's okay, too. If we make a break for it, Joe, and only one of us can get out, then do it."

Eyes glittering, Joe whispered harshly, "No way, gal. It's both of us or I'm sticking around." His mouth tightened as he held her stormy stare. "I'm not leavin' you behind. I'll die here first." And he would.

Shaken by the rough emotion in his tone, Akiva had no time to respond. The door was flung open. Chico stood there, the AK-47 pointed at them.

"Get up! It's show time."

Joe nailed her with a lethal look. As he rose from her side, he said harshly in a low voice, "It's together or nothing..." and he moved toward the door. Chico placed a pair of handcuffs on him, which became hidden by the tunic sleeves when Joe lowered his arms. To the reenactors lining the hillsides of the *estancia,* it would look like they were just going for a walk. The AK-47 was well hidden, hung on a shoulder strap beneath the red woolen cloak Chico wore over his centurion's uniform.

Akiva stood next to Joe and held out her hands to be cuffed. She saw two other Roman soldiers standing behind Chico, both just as big and goonish as he was. There was no way she and Joe could try and make an escape; they'd be gunned down in the hall before they ever reached the exit.

"Let's go," Chico growled, pushing her and then Joe ahead of him. "You got three thousand people salivating for your return performance. You're famous out there." And he chuckled darkly.

The roar of the crowd was deafening as Akiva and Joe walked slowly out to the center of the arena once again. Colorful scarves were raised and waved like flags. More flowers were tossed toward them. Neither responded as they walked grimly toward their meager weapons, which lay on the sand before them.

Akiva saw Javier Rios looking like a Roman emperor in his glorious gold chair, the praetorian guards surrounding him, grim and at attention, a bevy of young beauties dressed in revealing gowns nearby. She checked the exits in the arena; all four had Roman guards at them.

Joe scooped up their weapons and handed her the ax. His heart began a slow pounding as the horns sounded and echoed across the arena.

Akiva saw one massive gate, then a second, then a third open. Out of each came a red-and-gold chariot drawn by two horses. There was a driver in each, along with another Roman soldier who carried a spear or bow and arrow.

Turning, Akiva saw Joe's face. His expression was hard and assessing.

The chariots streamed into the arena, the drivers using whips to encourage the horses to gallop around the circumference. The crowd went wild, their enthusiastic screams deafening.

Akiva watched the chariots. Backing up against Joe's back, she shouted, "They aren't gonna be able to hit a damn thing riding in those chariots. Their aim will be off."

"Yeah," he shouted. "They're leaving one gate open. See it?"

Akiva turned. The west gate was standing open. The guard was about ten feet inside, holding the huge door open. "Yeah. I wonder why?"

Before Joe could speculate, he saw four mounted soldiers come galloping through the gate into the arena.

"Damn!"

Akiva nodded. She gripped the war ax. Sending a prayer to her great-great-grandmother, she pleaded for help, for strength as she watched the cadre of Roman cavalry, riding in pairs, speed past the slower moving chariots. Each rider had a heavy, rectangular leather shield, three feet long and two feet wide, to contend with. Each had a short sword, but it was sheathed. Akiva noted that trying to control the excited horses, which were decked out in bright red-and-gold blankets and saddles, was a major job. The riders had to use their right hands to control their fractious, jumpy mounts, which obviously weren't use to the high level of noise or the arena itself.

"The gate's stayin' open," Joe called as he slowly began to turn, the knife held low and close to his body.

Heart pounding, he watched the cavalry speed wildly around the arena. The crowd cheered long and lustily.

"Yeah!" Akiva shouted. Sweat wound down her rib cage. All her attention was focused on the lead Roman, riding a big, rangy black gelding about sixteen hands tall. The horse was raw-boned, fractious and wild-eyed, and the rider was having a hell of a time keeping him at a canter instead of an out-of-control gallop.

"If we can only get to that gate..." Joe shouted. The crowd went into a frenzy as the first chariot peeled off and came directly at them.

"Yes!" Akiva watched the team of white horses send up a spray of sand as the driver wrenched them toward the center, where they stood. "Joe?"

"Yeah?" He watched a second chariot peel off and follow the first toward them. It was like watching slow-moving aircraft lumbering toward them.

"Follow my lead. We need something to ride!" Akiva dug the toes of her boots into the sand and lunged toward the first chariot.

The crowd roared. The sound became rolling thunder.

Akiva headed at an angle toward the nearest white horse. She saw the driver's angry gaze pinned on her as she sprinted forward. The soldier with the spear was being bounced around so badly that he couldn't hope for an accurate strike.

Long hair flying behind her like an ebony banner, Akiva took a huge breath into her lungs. The horses were galloping wildly toward her. Fifteen feet. Ten...five...

Her Apache war cry split the air, drowned out by the lustily cheering crowds. The horses, however, heard the high-pitched scream. The nearest white gelding shied to the right, bumping into its teammate and throwing both horses off stride. The chariot lifted up on one wheel. The Roman with the spear tumbled out.

Reaching out, Akiva saw that neither horse had on blinders, so it was easy to make them shy when something jumped at them. Her fingers caught the leather of the nearest rein. In one smooth motion, she leaped upward.

Joe watched Akiva successfully leap upon the back of the white horse as he ran toward the second chariot. The crowd went wild. Now it was his turn. He wasn't at all sure he could do the same thing; he had never trained to mount a running horse, but he was going to try.

Akiva's legs wrapped around the horse's sweaty barrel. She heard the driver behind her curse. With her war ax, she twisted around and hacked at the traces. Leather flew in all directions as the blade bit deeply into it. If she could cut this horse away, then she had a mount.

The crowd was screaming and shouting.

The whip, wielded by the driver, came down again and again on her head and shoulders as she rode the charging, bucking horse. Her ax bit again and again into the leather. Gasping, Akiva saw the trace finally break. Twisting back around, she grabbed both reins to the horse's mouth and jerked him to the left, into two Roman cavalrymen coming straight for her.

The horse grunted as she dug her heels deeply into his sides. Behind her, she heard the charioteer shout. Glancing briefly over her shoulder, she saw the chariot flip, the driver thrown out. The other horse ran wildly, dragging the upside down chariot across the arena like a plow.

There was no time to celebrate. Akiva ran her wild-eyed mount directly into the two charging cavalry soldiers. Both were bearing down on her with abandon, their heavy, cumbersome shields throwing them off balance.

Smiling to herself, Akiva leaned low on the horse's neck, the white mane stinging her perspiring face. Her eyes narrowed as she guided the horse directly at them. This was ''sky chicken'' all over again—played on the ground and not in a helicopter. Bracing herself, she prepared to slam into the careening, charging Romans.

At the last second, the soldier on the bay horse peeled off to the left. Akiva hissed, and as the man on the rangy black gelding whipped by her, she lifted her booted foot and snapped it outward. The heel of her boot connected with the soldier's hip, and he yelped. In seconds, he'd tumbled off the horse. His shield flipped up into the air, turning over and over before it plunged into the sand, as he struck the ground face first, knocked out.

Good!

Akiva turned her horse around and jerked it to a halt. Joe? Where was Joe? Breathing hard, she rapidly scanned the arena. To her surprise, Joe was still on the ground. Two of the chariots were closing in on him. Akiva saw the other two Romans on their mounts turning to charge her.

''Hiyyaa!'' she shrieked at her jumpy, dancing mount.

The white gelding shot forward. Akiva raced across the arena toward Joe. Who would reach him first? She hunkered low on the animal's neck, urging every ounce of strength out of his pumping hindquarters.

Joe turned as he heard Akiva's voice. His eyes widened. She swung her horse at almost a ninety-degree angle around him, right in front of the oncoming chariot. As the horse turned and brushed past, she shot out her hand. In an instant, Joe realized what she was doing. Thrusting out his own hand, he gripped her fingers and held on. With a jerk, she pulled him up, up, and in a moment he was throwing his leg across her mount, settling behind her.

"Hold on!" Akiva shouted. Joe put his arms around her waist while she jammed her boots into the white gelding's flanks. The chariot was almost on top of them. A spear was thrown. It landed within inches of the fleeing white steed, which was now laboring mightily with two people on its back.

Joe clamped his legs around the heavily breathing animal. Jerking his head to the right and left, he saw the cavalry bearing down on them. Akiva was riding the horse for all it was worth. The roar and clamor echoed around the arena, making it impossible to talk. He saw her heading for the riderless black horse that was trotting near the wall.

"Behind!" he screamed at her. A Roman on a palomino was closing the distance between them. The soldier had dispensed with his shield and was guiding the horse with his left hand. In his right was a short sword—upraised.

Akiva jerked a look to the right. She saw the palomino approaching. "Hold on!"

Joe grunted and clung to Akiva. He felt the horse careen to the right—right in front of the charging palomino. Collision! Everything happened in split seconds. The white horse turned, clipping the shoulder of the charging palomino. The soldier's sword was coming down at them. Joe thrust his long, wicked looking bowie knife upward to stop it. Metal bit into metal. And then the palomino went down, the Roman soldier thrown over its head, screaming as he smashed into the wall.

"Whoa!" Akiva shrilled at the horse. The white horse practically skidded on its rear as she hauled back on the reins.

"Joe! Grab the palomino!"

He slid off and ran for the horse, which was standing there, dazed. Luckily for him, there was a saddle on it, unlike Akiva's steed. Grabbing the reins, he was quickly mounted.

The crowd's roar was now wild. He turned the horse around. Akiva had trotted over to the rangy black and literally leaped off the white horse, flush onto the stronger mount. Her face was savage looking, her eyes slitted with lethal ferocity. Grinning, Joe knew they had a chance to survive.

"Go after that chariot!" Akiva shouted, raising her war ax.

Joe saw the plan. He watched as the last Roman soldier, on a brown-and-white pinto, kept his distance from them. The man probably didn't want to end up like his comrades. Digging his heels into his mount, Joe followed Akiva as she sped across the sands of the arena toward the chariot, which was heading for the open gate. Her hair flew behind her as she forced the black to a wild ground-eating gallop in pursuit of it.

The other chariot was at the far end of the arena, along with the last cavalry soldier. Joe whipped his mount across the withers with the leather reins. Hunkering down, he closed the gap on Akiva.

The charioteer's eyes were huge as they bore down on him, and the man screamed at his partner to shoot at them. But the other man was fumbling badly with his bow and arrow. The sands of the arena had been dug up, creating deep ruts. Hitting bump after bump, the chariot was being tossed around like a bobbin on the surface of the ocean.

Akiva raced her horse up alongside the chariot. She was breathing hard, and sweat drenched her straining body, but she didn't hesitate for an instant. Giving a throaty war cry, she saw the driver's eyes bulge with terror. He held up his hand to try and avoid the oncoming ax as it slashed downward. As he released the reins, the horses, seeing the open gate, headed directly for it. The chariot lurched violently as the horses made the unexpected turn, throwing out both passengers.

Akiva followed the careening chariot now speeding down the wide tunnel. Jerking a look over her shoulder, she saw Joe riding in hot pursuit, no more than twenty feet behind her. She saw the gleam of triumph on his sweaty, hard features. In his hand, he held the bowie knife ready—just in case. Her war ax was now situated in her waist belt.

The chariot swayed drunkenly from side to side, scattering the few people in the tunnel. The horses were panicked. Every time the hub of a wheel struck the wall, sparks flew.

Akiva saw the opening at the other end. She restrained her charging horse and kept him just behind the chariot. There were no Roman guards there, only surprised fans. They, too, scattered like a flock of startled birds as the wild-eyed, runaway horses thundered at them.

Joe pulled alongside Akiva. She pointed to the opening. "Our freedom!"

"Let's get the hell outta here!" he shouted, his smile tight with triumph.

As the chariot and horses came charging out of the tunnel, Akiva saw the road—the only road that led in and out of Javier Rios's estate. Laying the leather to the black gelding's sweaty withers, she flattened herself on his back.

"Stay down!" she shouted to Joe, "and follow me!"

They galloped on, sending people flying in all directions. As Joe galloped past them, bringing up the rear, he twisted his head back toward the bullring. People thought this was an act, apparently. They were cheering and waving them on. He saw no guards...not yet.

They galloped down the dirt road, weaving around arriving cars, trucks and recreational vehicles. On either side was a huge tent city, spread out on the gentle green slopes around the bullring. Joe kept his attention on Akiva, who was pushing the huge black horse relentlessly. The animal was covered with sweat, flecks of foam flying from his neck and flanks. She was riding him hard, and he saw her objective. Down at the base of the hill, the road forked in a T.

Remembering the map, he whipped his horse alongside hers once more as they raced through the oncoming traffic. Drivers kept screeching to a halt when they saw them, gawking out their windows. Some waved. Others smiled. They all thought this was part of the reenactment excitement.

"Go to the left!" Joe shouted at her. He jabbed his hand in that direction. "San Cristobel is that way!"

Nodding, Akiva remained in perfect rhythm with her black gelding. The horse was powerful—a Thoroughbred with long, sturdy legs. Though he was wild-eyed, with foam streaming out his open mouth as Akiva sawed on the snaffle bit, he followed her directions flawlessly as she guided him down the last green hill and to the left.

There was a lot of traffic on the dirt road. Akiva wanted to reserve the horse's energy as much as she could, understanding that Rios would be after them shortly. The snarled traffic would hinder Rios's men from getting to them, however. No enemy could catch up with them in this kind of traffic—not in a car. So unless he had a helo at the *estancia,* they were going to get away, Akiva realized with soaring confidence.

Triumph swept through her as Joe pushed his mount abreast her own. They rode hard and close, their legs sometimes brushing. The country around them was flat and agricultural. Up ahead, Akiva could see the small town, which lay in a shallow valley.

"See it?" Joe shouted, jabbing his hand to the right.

"Yes! The airport!"

He grinned. It was a brief, tight grin.

Akiva rode the horse like she was part of the animal. Joe could see how all her warrior training as a child was paying off. The black was a big, stubborn animal, but he gave up all thought of battle under Akiva's knowledgeable hand. She pushed the animal to his limits, and his long stride ate up miles of the rutted road, the dust rising in clouds behind them.

Joe watched in awe as Akiva bent forward over the animal's neck. Her hair was flying across her shoulders, her body hunched and rhythmic as she squeezed every ounce of power from the black horse, and he couldn't help but marvel at her many natural abilities.

He had no idea how much time had elapsed as they galloped their winded mounts down the hill and into the bowl-shaped valley of San Cristobel. The sun was no longer above them. It might be around 1300, Joe thought, as he followed Akiva along the roadside. Cars would slow down or stop as they approached. That was good, because Joe didn't want to get hit. His legs were tiring, and he wasn't riding well. At least he could still hang on.

As they swept off the main road and over a green, grassy hillside toward the tiny airport, Joe could see four helicopters there. He was sure they belonged to the Rioses. Were there guards posted? Scanning the area, he saw only a farmer in a wide-brimmed straw hat near one of the two airport buildings.

Worried, Joe pulled alongside Akiva. "We gotta watch for guards!"

Nodding, she shouted, "You go around the buildings. I'll ride up to that first helo."

"Right."

Akiva dug her heels into her horse's heaving flanks as they galloped down the hill. Once on the hard dirt surface of the airport grounds, she slapped the reins against his wet sides and headed directly for a Bell helicopter. Though she scanned the area, she saw no guards. To her left, she saw Joe circling the buildings to make sure they were safe.

"Whoa!" she shouted, and pulled hard on the reins. The black skidded to a halt within three feet of the helicopter. Akiva leaped off. She slapped the animal on the rump, and, startled, the gelding trotted away.

Akiva ran forward, praying that the keys to the helo were there. As she jerked open the door, she saw them.

"Yes!" she shouted. Quickly, she untied the tether on the blades and threw the nylon rope to the ground. Climbing in, she settled herself in the seat. Instantly, the blades began to turn as she fired up the engines on the ship. Lifting her head, she saw Joe ride around a corner of one building. There was relief on his face. The horse leaped sideways as it saw the helicopter and Joe tumbled off. He quickly got to his feet and sprinted toward her.

Jerking the door open, he leaped in. He was covered with dust.

"Fuel?" he demanded, slamming it shut.

"Full tank. We're in business," Akiva growled triumphantly. She took the cyclic and collective in her hands. Giving him a tight grin, she said, "We're outta here, Calhoun. Hold on. We're makin' a run for the border!'' using the slang to indicate to him that they needed to get the hell out of there as fast as they could and head back to their covert base.

Chapter 15

"I think we should maintain radio silence," Joe told her over the helicopter intercom. They were twenty miles south of San Cristobel, and he was worriedly looking back toward the town to see if any other helicopters were taking off after them. So far, so good; there was no indication that Luis Rios and his henchmen were getting ready to chase them down.

Wiping his mouth, sweat still running off his face, Joe glanced over at Akiva. Her profile was set and serious, her mouth curved downward as she guided the helicopter swiftly at treetop level.

"No, we need to stay silent," she agreed.

Joe took a shaky breath and tightened the straps of his seat harness. "Heck of a day in the arena, wouldn't you say?" He cut her a quick glance. He saw Akiva's expression thaw momentarily.

"Yeah. It reminded me of my trials to get my third braid."

"Javier Rios is crazy."

"Maybe," Akiva muttered. "He's got the perfect setup there. He's seen as a philanthropist, he's got a global reenactors thing going on.... People don't have a clue what he really is underneath—a drug trafficker." She kept glancing at the instruments. The helicopter was shaking around her, and it felt good. Comforting. Being back in the air was where Akiva belonged. Still, her heart was pounding in her chest and fear was making her adrenaline run high. They weren't safe yet, not by a long shot.

"Isn't that the truth?" Joe drawled. He kept twisting around and checking the sky out behind them. Luis would get airborne as soon as he could make his way to the airport. Judging from the snarled traffic, Joe knew it would take a while.

"I'm heading back to Alpha," Akiva told him.

"Yes. But we don't know who'll be there. It's possible that Major Stevenson yanked the plug on the black ops when we didn't show up. I'm sure the women there contacted the main base to let them know we never came home."

"Yeah, and with Sat Intel," Akiva murmured, "they'd see what was left of that twenty-million-dollar Apache I blew up."

Reaching out, Joe pulled the heavy curtain of hair away from Akiva's drawn face. Instantly, her lips parted. An incredible love for her welled up through his chest, momentarily chasing away the fear tunneling through him. "If we make it home, I'm askin' Major Stevenson for some leave. You and I deserve some time alone... together."

Just the brush of his fingers along her hair sent prickles of pleasure across her cheek and neck. Akiva gave him a quick glance. She saw the smoky look in Joe's gray eyes. "You know what? You're the bravest person I've ever met. I was so glad you were with me.... We were a team. And we got out of there because of what we did—together."

Joe rested his hand on her shoulder, atop the ebony blanket of her thick, soft hair. "We're alive because we threw whatever prejudices we had aside, gal. And you trusted me. That's what really got us out of that fire. Trust."

Holding his warm gaze, Akiva managed a shaky smile. Every mile between them and Luis made her relax just a little more. "Trust? Yeah, a big hurdle for me. But you helped me overcome it, Joe. And yes, I'd sure like some time off. I'd like to spend it with you, somewhere quiet and peaceful...."

When they were within two miles of Alpha, Joe made a call to the base. He'd chosen a civilian channel that was least likely to be picked up or used. If Luis Rios's men were in the air, he and Akiva hadn't seen them. Joe acutely missed the Apache's wonderful radar equipment, which could spot aircraft thirty miles away.

As Akiva flew straight for the hole in the jungle, he called again.

"This is Alpha. Over," came a female voice over the line.

Joe smiled at Akiva. "Hey! That's Major Stevenson's voice! She must have flown in!"

Akiva grinned broadly. She brought the helo into a hover and then began to descend. "Our luck's changing!"

Joe radioed back and filled Major Stevenson in on their unexpected arrival. He didn't want to risk getting picked up over the airwaves by Rios. Sitting in the helo, Akiva smoothly guided the bird down under the canopy. Once there, she headed toward the dirt strip. On their final approach, Joe saw two black, unmarked Apache helicopters sitting just outside the hangar. His heart rose with joy. Gripping Akiva's shoulder, he rasped unsteadily, "We're home. Everything's gonna be okay now..."

A huge wave of emotion, mostly relief, broke through Akiva's intense focus as she sat the helicopter down two rotor lengths away from the familiar Apache. She nodded. "Yeah...home—" Her voice broke. Choking back a lump forming in her throat, she shut off the engine and waited.

Out the Plexiglas window, she saw both majors, Maya and Dane. Akiva knew she'd left the base in the hands of her X.O., Dallas Klein, so that she could be here. Wild Woman was there, too, the red streaks in her blond hair standing out like flames. So was Cam and Ana. Grinning, Akiva also saw Sergeant Paredes, the Angel of Death, beside them. She was waving her hand with joy. Akiva lifted hers in return.

"They look so good to me," she whispered, taking off the headset and putting it between the two seats. "I didn't realize how much I missed them until just now...."

Joe laughed. "Yeah, they're a sight for sore eyes, that's for sure. Come on, let's go meet them and fill them in on our wild ride."

Akiva hurriedly opened the door and got out once the rotors stopped spinning. In the late afternoon light, she saw all her friends, dressed in their black, body-fitting uniforms, move toward them in unison. The relief was evident on their smiling faces. As Joe dropped to the ground beside her, Akiva laughed. It was a laugh of sheer, unadulterated relief—of joy—that they were alive.

Wild Woman gave a screech and ran forward, her arms wide open. The smaller woman—she was only five foot four—threw herself at Akiva, wrapping her arms around her neck.

Laughing, Akiva caught Wild Woman and staggered back.

"Hey! You're alive!" Wild Woman whooped. She embraced Akiva, placed a big kiss on her cheek and then released her. She then went to Joe, threw her arms around him and did the same thing. Joe nearly toppled over as she spontaneously assaulted him with affection. Laughing, he hugged her and accepted her welcome-back kiss on his cheek.

Akiva came to attention and saluted Majors Stevenson and York. They returned her salutes, their faces filled with concern as well as happiness and undisguised welcome.

Joe released Wild Woman with a laugh, straightened up and saluted the officers in turn.

"At ease," Maya told them. Then she stepped forward and threw her arms around Akiva. "You had us worried," she muttered.

The simple fact of Maya's arms wrapping around her made Akiva sob involuntarily. Hugging Maya, she whispered, "Thanks for coming.... We were worried, too. We weren't sure we were going to make it back...."

Maya finally stepped away, tears in her eyes. "Thanks for showing up. We've been worried sick." Turning to Joe, she embraced him, too. "Joe? You okay?" she asked, releasing him.

A little shaken by Maya's uncharacteristic embrace, he grinned foolishly. "Yes, ma'am, I'm fine now that we've got the BJS here."

Dane York came forward, shook Akiva's hand and

welcomed her back. He did the same with Joe. "We're glad to see you two show up. Welcome home," he murmured, his voice filled with undisguised emotion.

Angel Paredes was next, grinning from ear to ear as she approached. She gave both Akiva and Joe welcome-home hugs. Looking at them critically, she said, "Well, I can see a few Band-Aids are in order here. Why don't you two come with me to your mess building? I've got my paramedic bag in there. And we got chow. Hot chow, ready to serve. You two look like starvin' jaguars to me."

"Sounds good!" Joe said, rubbing his hands together and grinning. "I'm starvin' for some good ole squadron chow."

Akiva kept looking skyward nervously.

Maya grew serious, understanding her concern. "We've got a third Apache on alert, just in case you're worried about Rios following you and strafing us where we stand."

Akiva nodded, relief dissolving some of her tension as she walked at Maya's side toward the building. "Good, because once that bastard gets airborne, he's got three civilian helos armed with rockets that will be looking for us."

"Because of the info on Rios's helos you fed into our computers," Dane told her with grim satisfaction as he walked between Joe and her, "we're expecting them. And if they show up, they're as good as dead."

Joe gawked at Major York, whose face held a look of grim satisfaction. "Sir? You mean..."

Maya gave him a predatory smile. "We've got permission to take 'em out, Joe. From the Pentagon itself. They didn't like the idea of having an Apache knocked out of the air. It's war now."

''Whew!'' he whispered. ''If Javier loses his only son, he'll be pissed off and in a get-even mode.''

''That's okay,'' Maya said. She reached the door of the mess hall and opened it for them. Gesturing for everyone to enter, she followed them in.

Akiva sat down at the table. The fragrant odor of spaghetti cooking made her mouth water. The enlisted women who had served at Alpha came over to them, and Akiva shook their hands. They were all crying. Maybe it wasn't a soldierly thing to do, but Akiva understood their tears. She wanted to cry herself, out of a sense of relief, more than anything.

''We never lost hope for you, ma'am,'' Iris Bradford sniffed, taking a tissue and wiping her nose and reddened eyes.

Akiva nodded. ''I'm glad.'' Angel was already pushing up the rough wool sleeve of her Roman tunic. Akiva's knuckles were red and oozing blood. Paredes quickly cleaned them up with a few expert swipes of an antiseptic damp cloth.

The other two enlisted women sat down at the table opposite them. Spec Robin Ferris said, ''When we lost radio contact with you, we called in the alarm to BJS.'' She smiled triumphantly. ''They came right away.''

''Yes, ma'am,'' Spec Susan Dean chimed in, ''they were here in a heartbeat. We've been working a search grid trying to find you. After the Sat Intel showed the Apache destroyed, we hoped that you might have survived.''

Maya stood near the table. It was clear that Akiva's stint as a C.O. had been successful. Her people doted upon her. Maya saw the eagerness in their young faces and heard the joy in their voices at the fact that Akiva was back, safe and sound. Maya felt good about her choice of leader for Alpha.

Joe looked up at Maya as Angel tended his many wounds and abrasions. "Major, did you realize we'd been kidnapped by Luis Rios?"

"We realized something happened," she admitted, her brows knitting. "We found the remains of the Apache, but no bodies with it. That's when we knew you'd escaped or were captured. We didn't know what had occurred."

"And then," Dane added, coming to his wife's side, "we found where someone had fired a rocket about two hundred feet away from the downed bird. There was a hole in the earth."

"Yeah," Joe said wryly, "I was carrying Akiva away from the Apache. She had been running with me and tripped over a root and hit her head on a log. It knocked her unconscious. I picked her up and started sprintin' for the jungle, but Rios got there and fired a rocket at us."

"It was the last thing Joe remembered," Akiva told them, and she filled them in on the rest of their extraordinary capture and escape.

Paredes had just finished her medical duties and closed her paramedic bag when Iris Bradford got up and called to her buddies to help her dish up the evening meal for everyone.

Maya shook her head and gave her husband a look of disbelief after hearing their story of capture and escape. "This is incredible. A modern-day Roman arena? Gladiator reenactors?"

Joe gave Akiva a look of respect. "Yes, ma'am, it was. I mean, I don't know if you're aware of this, but we got thousands of people in the U.S. who are Civil War reenactors. It's big business. And I guess in Mexico, Roman reenactors are 'in.' The biggest joke, though, was that the thousands of people comin' to the shindig didn't have a *clue* that we weren't there because we wanted to be." His voice deepened. "And I've gotta tell you all, Akiva here is an *incredible* gladiator. She gave the term woman warrior a whole new meaning out there in that arena. She bested the boys at their own games."

Eyes sparkling with pride, he saw Akiva lower her lashes, her cheeks turning a bright red at his enthusiastic and heartfelt praise. "She truly is a warrior in the finest sense of the word. If it hadn't been for her athletic ability—for her grabbin' that horse as it pulled that chariot—we wouldn't be sittin' here now." Joe looked up at Maya's dark features. "Ma'am, I strongly recommend that Akiva be put in for a medal of some kind. What she did was extraordinary. We owe our escape to her. There's no doubt about it."

"Ohh, Joe..." Akiva protested, embarrassed.

Maya smiled at her. "Ease off the throttles, Akiva. I'm *sure* both of you will be receiving commendations and medals."

"The episode serves to warn us about future secret installations that are not within BJS reach," Dane interjected in a worried voice. He scowled and settled his hands on his hips as he watched the three Alpha crew bring out steaming plates of spaghetti with huge meatballs.

"No kidding," Akiva said, her voice turning emotional. She thanked Iris, who brought over plates for her and Joe. "Let's eat, shall we? I'm starving to death!"

Turning around in the seat, Joe chuckled indulgently as he picked up his fork. "At least this time around, it doesn't feel like we're eating the Last Supper."

There were chuckles all around as everyone took

places at the tables and began to eat. Maya and Dane sat with Akiva and Joe, while the other pilots and personnel spread out at the other two tables. In moments, everyone was devoting all their attention to eating.

"This smells so good," Joe whispered. "Real American food..." And he dug into the spaghetti with unabashed relish.

Akiva chuckled and sprinkled some salt over hers. "This is the best gift I've had in a long time," she murmured. Still, worry threaded through her as she picked at the food. She looked across the table at Maya, who was eating with gusto.

"I'm sorry we had to blow up the Apache," she murmured. "I didn't want to...."

"You got struck by lightning," Maya offered gently. "You didn't have a choice, under the circumstances."

"Being a leader has made me respect tenfold what you do," Akiva told her in a low tone. She saw Maya lift her head, her emerald eyes widening with silent laughter.

"You'll get used to it, Akiva. Don't worry."

Staring at her, the fork halfway to her mouth, she said, "Get used to it? Don't we get to go home? Back to the base? I'd like to be just a pilot again."

Dane gave her a steady look. "Your operation here at Alpha has been very successful, Chief. According to the Pentagon and everyone concerned, Alpha is still on an operational footing."

Gulping, Akiva shot a look at Joe, who was frowning. "So, we're back in the frying pan here?" she asked. Right now she didn't feel as gung ho as she had before. She felt emotionally shredded, and she knew she was in shock over the last week, with the crash and loss of the Apache, and having their lives on the line day in and day out.

Maya cut up her spaghetti with her knife and fork. ''Slow down, Akiva. I know you're fried right now. Major York and I have been talking, and here's what we're going to do.'' She laid down the knife, placed her hands on the table and looked at Akiva. ''First, we're going to use that civilian helo you brought in. I'll have Wild Woman fly you to the nearest town in Mexico that has access to civilian airlines. You'll dress in civilian clothes, of course. She'll drop you off, you'll buy tickets and get to Cuzco, Peru, as soon as you can. From there, we'll pick you up and fly you back to the base.'' She picked some spaghetti up with her fork and popped it into her mouth.

''At the base, what I'll need ASAP are your reports. Akiva, because you're the C.O. of Alpha, I really need you to seriously evaluate what went right and wrong here. Joe, I'll need your input on how to fix what is weak about our black ops mission.''

Joe nodded. ''Yes, ma'am, I can do that.''

Maya stole a look at her husband, who was seated at her elbow. ''We felt that, because of the shock of your crash and subsequent capture, you both deserve about seven days R and R. We've got two suites at the Liberator Hotel in Cuzco lined up and waiting for you. The rooms even have hot tubs, and I'll bet you would like to soak away some of those bruises I see on your arms.''

Brightening, Joe glanced over at Akiva, who had a surprised look on her face.

''R and R. Hoo doggies, now that's somethin' I can handle just fine.''

Akiva smiled slightly at Joe. She saw the desire for her burning in his eyes. Yes, they needed—and deserved—that kind of time with onc another. She cut one of the huge meatballs with her fork. ''Thanks, Maya. We can use some downtime. I'm still in shock. I'm not feeling much emotionally—yet."

Nodding, Maya murmured, "I know. I can see it in your eyes."

Dane smiled congenially and finished off his plate of spaghetti. "In the meantime, we're putting Cam in command of Alpha until your return."

Akiva stared at Maya. "You want me back—here?" She sat up, her heart beating a little harder in her chest.

Maya lifted her head, her emerald eyes filled with amusement. "Why not? You were doing a good job."

"But...I lost an Apache...." Akiva knew that usually, if a helicopter was lost, the pilot's reputation suffered unless it was due to a mechanical problem. Getting struck by lightning wasn't exactly her fault, she knew, but it had cost her an expensive machine.

Waving her fork, Maya murmured, "We've been here since you went missing. I've had a chance to go through your paperwork and see the way you set up and were running Alpha." She gave both of them a warm look. "We saw nothing wrong with what you had laid out and were doing. Both Major York and I believe you two are best outfitted for this black ops."

"I don't know whether to be happy or sad about that," Akiva griped in a low voice.

Joe chortled. "Just say thank you, gal." And then he stopped, instantly aware of his mistake. Calling her the endearment in front of their commanding officers was a huge faux pas. Eyes widening, he shot a look at Maya. There was a slight hint of a smile on her lips as she continued to eat her meal. Dane glanced at his wife, at Akiva and then back at Joe, as if the feelings between Akiva and Joe had just become apparent to him. Watching Major York's face fill with surprise, Joe said nothing.

Mentally castigating himself for the slipup, he saw Akiva flush. She didn't look at him. Joe didn't blame her. Sitting there, he wondered if he'd screwed up but good. Although they were both of the same rank, romance wasn't exactly what the army had in mind between officers, and it was discouraged. Would Maya and Dane understand? Hands damp on his legs beneath the table, Joe felt angry at himself for not thinking first before he shot off his mouth. It was so easy to call Akiva "gal"...for she owned his heart, body and soul. Worriedly, Joe pushed his empty plate away and slowly put the flatware on top of it.

"I take it that we should have reserved only one suite, and not two, at the Liberator Hotel?" Maya asked wryly, her lips lifting and curving.

Akiva stared down at her plate. Yet as she heard not only the amusement in Maya's tone, but her acceptance that there was something serious between her and Joe, Akiva could hardly believe her ears. Although BJS was run by Maya, it was still a U.S. Army installation.

Lifting her chin, Akiva stared at Maya, who was grinning like a jaguar who had found her quarry. The merriment, the approval in Maya's eyes were obvious. Akiva felt an incredible warmth and acceptance from her C.O.

Heartened, she murmured, "Yes, one suite would be fine."

Chapter 16

"At ease," Maya murmured to Joe and Akiva as they entered her office at Black Jaguar Base. She gestured to two chairs in front of her desk. "Have a seat." Frowning, she looked at the two neatly typed reports she held in her hands.

Joe, who had been using an office down the hall, gave Akiva a wink. She smiled slightly as she sat down. He could hardly wait to get out of here and go to Cuzco. The idea of having Akiva all to himself was elating. Although she was once again dressed in her black uniform with the war ax and bowie knife once again tucked away beneath her belt, her hair tied back in a ponytail that fell to the middle of her back, he could see desire burning in her eyes—desire for him. It set his heart skittering with a happiness he'd never felt before.

Turning his attention to Maya, who was also in her black uniform, her hair cascading across her shoulders, he saw her brows draw downward as she flipped through their reports. Was something wrong? Joe sensed that Maya was juggling a lot of things; but then, as C.O., she was in a constant state of organized chaos. He waited, but not very patiently.

"Okay..." Maya murmured, looking up after they'd made themselves comfortable. She smiled a short, perfunctory smile. "Your reports are impeccable. Full of useful information for us and for the boys at the Pentagon to disseminate. I know it has taken nearly a day since your return to file these, and I want you to know how grateful I am. I know you'd rather be other places, and that's what I want to talk to you about."

Joe's heart fell. Wasn't Maya going to let them go to Cuzco? He had an uneasy feeling as he watched her tidy up the reports, put them to one side and fold her hands in front of her on the green metal desk. Trying to gird himself for disappointing news, he sat very still and waited.

"Akiva, you're Native American and aware that you each have a jaguar spirit guide?"

Taken aback, Akiva sat in silence, momentarily stunned by Maya's question. Ordinarily, they only talked military business, not about something like this. She saw the seriousness of Maya's emerald gaze. Opening her hands, she murmured, "Yes, ma'am..."

And then it dawned on Akiva that she'd never told anyone about it, except Joe. She glanced over at him. He had a nonplussed expression on his face. Feeling her gaze, he looked at her.

"I didn't say anything," he said, as if reading her mind.

Maya smiled thinly. "No, Akiva, Joe didn't talk to me."

"Oh...I see...." Well, she didn't, really, so she sat

quietly and waited, because she could see Maya had more to say.

"Joe, I know through my own mystic sources that you come from Comanche bloodlines. There has been a female jaguar spirit guide that has come down through your lineage to you, whether you're aware of it or not."

"...Okay, ma'am...." Unsure of where his C.O. was going with this unexpected conversation, Joe again traded looks with Akiva. She appeared just as confused as he was.

Maya stood up and rubbed her hands down the sides of her thighs. "You have heard, I'm sure, that I'm a member of a jaguar clan here in South America?"

Both nodded.

"It's like a black ops," Maya said wryly. She moved around the desk and quietly closed the door to her office so they could have absolute privacy. Walking slowly back to her seat, she sat down.

Akiva noted the door being shut. Maya rarely closed her office door; it was one of her hallmarks as a leader that her door was always open, so that anyone, officer or enlisted, could walk in and talk to her. Maya's openness as a C.O., her strong ties to her people at the BJS squadron, were legendary in the army. No C.O. did what she did. And for Maya to shut that door signaled something very serious to Akiva. Her heart pounded briefly with dread. Automatically, she clasped her hands in her lap, her gaze riveted on Maya, who sat looking somewhat amused as she picked up a pencil and tapped it against her desktop for a moment.

"Okay." Maya sighed, and giving them a quick smile to dispel the worry she saw etched in their faces, she continued, "What I'm going to say to you is absolutely confidential. Consider it a Q-clearance kind of thing, all right?''

Both nodded their heads.

Maya saw some relief in their expressions. They understood that Q-clearance represented the highest level of secrecy within the government. It was given on a need-to-know basis only.

''Originally, I intended to send you to Cuzco for your R and R. Well, that's changed,'' she murmured. ''I'm going to ask you to go somewhere else. Actually, it's even better, but you don't know that, and you're going to have to trust me on this.''

Frowning, Akiva stared bluntly at Maya. It wasn't like her C.O. to beat around the bush like this. Biting back questions, Akiva squelched her impatience. She saw Maya drop the pencil and fold her hands.

''I'm sending you to a place called the Village of the Clouds. It's a community up along the Peru-Brazil border—very hidden, very secret. Only special people go there…by invitation only. And your invitation is that you each have a jaguar spirit guide with you, whether you know it or not.'' Maya shot a look at Joe, whose brows were rising. She could see a lot of questions coming.

''This is a village that sits at the foot of the Andes, between the jungle and the mountains. It's a very unique agricultural village with a small community of…well, a certain type of people.'' Clearing her throat, she said, ''I got orders last night for you to go there, instead of going to Cuzco for your well deserved rest. Both of you are still in shock over what happened to you. This village is a place people go who are sick, or who are in training with the Jaguar Clan.''

Joe cocked his head. ''Which category do we fall into?''

Grinning, Maya said, ''Both.''

''This place...I've heard of it,'' Akiva murmured. ''It's a spiritual training center.''

''Correct. You may be more familiar with Spirit Lake, which the Eastern Cherokee have in North Carolina.'' With a shrug, Maya told them, ''Among the myths and legends of the Native Americans of North America, or Turtle Island, there is a sacred and secret place people can go for healing and help. The legend is that if people bathe in the waters of Spirit Lake, they will be healed.''

''Yes,'' Akiva murmured, ''I've heard of it.''

''The Eastern Cherokee nation was the largest on the East Coast,'' Maya murmured. ''Suffice to say, this lake does exist, but it doesn't unveil itself except to those who have earned the right to find it, and be healed by its special waters.''

Joe scratched his head. ''Ma'am? Is this village where you're sending us like that?''

''You got it, Joe.'' Maya smiled warmly. ''Again, you have to trust me on this. The Village of the Clouds is one of the most peaceful, healing and beautiful places on the face of Mother Earth. You go there by invitation only.'' She glanced at Akiva. ''Since Akiva is more steeped in her people's spiritual traditions, she understands better what I'm talking about. Joe, you've been away from your people's traditions, but this is an opportunity, if you choose, to reconnect with them. And if you don't, that's fine, too. No one is going to force you to do something you don't want to do. Just use your time there to soak up the peace and love that's so much a part of the place.''

Akiva stood up. ''I think I see what's happening.'' She looked down at Joe, who had a confused look on his face. ''This mission at Alpha was a test, wasn't it, Maya?''

She nodded gravely.

Joe frowned. ''A test?''

Akiva laughed sharply. ''Yes. My people believe that you are tested through life and death situations. If you pass, a new door—a better one, with more opportunities—is opened, granted to you because you not only passed the test, but lived to tell about it.'' Darkly, Akiva glanced over at Maya. ''This is a reward for surviving the mission, isn't it?''

''Yes,'' Maya murmured, ''it is.''

''Why didn't someone tell us earlier about this test?'' Joe demanded.

''Joe,'' Akiva said, ''the path we walk, because of our blood, is a spiritual one in the long run. From time to time we all get tested. You don't know going in that it's a test. Only afterward, if you survive it, do you figure it out.''

''Okay,'' Joe muttered, ''does this get us a brass ring?''

Maya chuckled. ''You could say that.''

Excitement began to thrum through Akiva. ''Joe, I think we just got the gold key to the city. Am I right, ma'am?'' She couldn't keep the sudden excitement out of her voice.

Pleased, Maya nodded. ''That's a roger. Okay, there's a helo warming up on the mining side to take us to Agua Caliente. We need to take the bus up the mountain to the temples of Machu Picchu. That is where one of two entrances to the Village of the Clouds is located.'' She stood up. ''Are you ready for your next adventure?''

Grinning broadly, Akiva whispered, ''Oh yes, ma'am!'' She turned to Joe, joy bursting through her. He stood, an unsure look on his face. Reaching out, she gripped his hand and squeezed it momentarily. ''Come on, Joe. Just trust me. This is going to be a mind-blowing and wonderful experience.''

''Will it help me understand my Comanche heritage?''

''Yes,'' Maya said. ''You're hungry to know about your Native American background and there you will start training to connect back to it.''

Joe grinned. ''That's a wish come true.''

''Open your eyes,'' Akiva told Joe softly.

Joe felt dizzy as he opened his eyes. Akiva was standing next to him, her hand gripping his. There was fog moving around them, thinning and thickening, as if whim to some breeze that he did not feel. Seconds earlier, they had been standing at the center of a place called the Temple of Balance. Maya had instructed them to stand in a particular spot, close their eyes, take a deep breath and relax. Joe had done that. When he'd closed his eyes, Akiva took his hand in a warm grip. He'd heard a popping sound, like a champagne bottle being opened, and felt a quick sense of movement, then nothing.

Looking through the cool, drifting fog, he saw the excitement on Akiva's face. Lifting her hand, he kissed the back of it. ''Okay, where we goin', gal? You seem to know a lot more about this than I do.''

''Keep trusting me,'' Akiva whispered, and she tugged on his hand and started walking through the fog. ''At one time, Maya told me about this village and how to get here. I always wanted to come but never thought I'd be given the invitation.''

They hadn't walked far when the fog began to rapidly thin. Joe saw that they were in the jungle, standing at the bottom of a small wooden bridge that arced across a small, burbling stream of clear water. Beyond it, the jungle disappeared and he saw a village of thatched huts.

People walking about—men, women and children—were dressed in pastel clothing, mostly long-sleeved cotton tops and pants that hung comfortably. Everyone wore sandals. A number of iron pots hanging from tripods over fires were being tended on the hard-packed ground at the center of the village. Joe could smell mouthwatering scents of food drifting through the air.

Excitedly, Akiva said, "Let's go!" and she leaped onto the bridge. Joe followed, grinning. He liked seeing Akiva in this childlike mood. They were now in civilian clothes, for they never left the base in their black uniforms. Akiva had on a pair of dark green nylon hiking pants, her hiking boots and a long-sleeved, pink cotton shirt. She wore her hair loose and free.

As they leaped off the bridge and onto a path that would lead them into the village, Joe saw an incredible sight to his left. In the distance, across a huge, flowered field, he saw the bluish slopes of the Andes. High above them the granite crags glistened with snow. Between the mountain and the village, a wall of white clouds billowed, rolling and shifting continually. He was sure they were due to the steamy heat of the jungle meeting the colder, drier air descending off the mighty Andes. It was a beautiful and awe-inspiring sight.

"Welcome," a male voice boomed.

Joe, who had been looking at the clouds, hadn't been watching where Akiva was leading him. He stopped abruptly. On the path in front of them was a very tall, regal looking old man with a beard. He wore a pair of dark blue pants, sandals on his feet and a pale blue cotton top that fell to midthigh.

"I'm Grandfather Adaire," he said with a welcoming smile. "And you're Akiva and Joe." He held out his thin hand toward them. "Welcome to our humble village. We're glad you could come."

As Joe slid his large, square hand into Adaire's, he felt a jolt of warmth move instantly up his arm and into his body. It was like getting a slight shock of electricity, but one that was pleasant. Adaire had long, silver hair that hung below his square, proud shoulders, and his aged skin looked paper thin, with deep lines and wrinkles. His eyes gleamed with warmth, however. Joe liked him immediately and enthusiastically pumped his hand.

"Hello, sir."

Chuckling, Adaire said, "Around here, we just go by first names. You may call me Adaire, or Grandfather, or Grandfather Adaire—whatever is comfortable for you."

Joe grinned.

As Adaire turned his attention to Akiva, her eyes widened with surprise—especially when Adaire stepped forward, opened his arms and wrapped them around her.

"Welcome home, Daughter," he rumbled.

Tears instantly flooded Akiva's eyes as she embraced the older man. The intense heat of his hands, as he slid them gently around her shoulders, permeated her like a bolt of unexpected lightning. Ordinarily, Akiva wanted no man to touch her...except for Joe, whom she loved and trusted with her life and her heart. But Grandfather Adaire melted all her usual barriers, and her heart burst open. Heat, soothing and healing, moved into her body. All Akiva could do was gasp softly, cling to his tall, bony frame and close her eyes.

Joe watched Akiva's face soften miraculously as Adaire eased back from their embrace. He was smiling down at her with such love that Joe swore he saw a gold color around the man's head and shoulders. Even more touching were the tears streaming down Akiva's cheeks as she gazed at the old man. Wanting to somehow help her, Joe stepped up and slid his hand into hers. She turned, her eyes wet with tears. He gavc her a tender look that told her he loved her. Akiva squeezed his hand in response and his heart soared.

"We want to welcome you to our village," Adaire told them with a slight smile. "Your hut is ready for you. If you'll follow me, we'll get you acclimated to your new home away from home."

Joe walked with Akiva, hand in hand. The path, hard packed by many who had walked it, was bordered on one side by jungle. He saw several red and yellow bromeliads in the limbs of the trees, as well as green and silver moss growing there.

As they walked around the central plaza, where many were helping with the cooking chores, Joe was amazed. He saw every color of skin on earth represented by the people who lived in the village. They lifted their hands and called to them in greeting as they passed by. The strange thing was their lips didn't move. And then it struck Joe that he was hearing their sincere greetings in his head and heart simultaneously. That was when he realized mental telepathy was being used, rather than spoken words. Shaken, he saw Akiva wipe the last of her tears from her cheeks.

At the end of the village was a small hut. The burbling stream wound behind it. Adaire led them inside, for there was no door. He turned and stood in the foyer.

"You will find everything you need here, children. You may wear the clothes you have on, or you may want to shed them for ours." He gestured to two sets of neatly folded clothes on a hand-hewn table. There was a bowl of fruit on it, as well. "Look around, explore and enjoy yourselves. Tonight, you'll have dinner at our hut. I'll have someone come and get you at that time. If you need anything, you may ask those who are living here. They will be eager to help, or to answer your questions."

Adaire smiled gently. "There is a path just outside your hut. It leads to a beautiful waterfall—very secluded and healing. If you feel like it, you might go there once you're settled in here."

"Thank you, Grandfather," Akiva said, her voice low and emotional. "This is...overwhelming...."

With a deep laugh, Adaire nodded and folded his hands inside the sleeves of his tunic. "I know it is, children. But you have time here to heal, and to open your hearts to one another. You have *earned* this privilege."

Joe watched Adaire leave. Turning, he gripped Akiva's hands. "This place... It's somethin' else, gal...." He looked around in awe.

"Yes, it is," Akiva sniffed. She self-consciously wiped the tears from her eyes. "What I couldn't say until now is that for as long as I can remember, I've seen Grandfather Adaire in my dreams, Joe. I remember, when I was so small and my father would beat me, and I'd cry myself asleep in my room afterward, I came to this place...and Grandfather would be here to greet me. He'd hold me and I always felt better afterward." Akiva's voice lowered. "He was the only male I ever trusted—" she smiled brokenly "—until you came along...." She reached out and slid her hand up Joe's arm.

Shaken by her admission, Joe rasped, "I don't pretend to understand all this. It reminds me of magic...." And he brought Akiva into his arms. She looked like she needed to be held, and he was just the man to do it. As her arms slid around his waist, Joe buried his face in her soft, clean hair and inhaled her special scent into his flaring nostrils.

"It is magic," she whispered unsteadily, nuzzling his neck with her cheek. When Joe held her, Akiva felt safe. Completely and utterly safe and loved in his strong, caring arms. She felt his lips press against her hair and she sighed brokenly and surrendered to him. "You're magic...." she whispered.

Rocking Akiva gently in his arms, Joe closed his eyes and simply held her. "My daddy always said truth was stranger than fiction, and I guess this village falls into that category," he chuckled against her ear. "But I don't care how strange it is, Akiva. All I want—all I need—is you, gal, and everything else, strange, magical or otherwise, will fall into place for me...for us...."

Nodding, her throat tightening with more tears, Akiva absorbed Joe's strength and quietness like a thirsty sponge. Finally, she said in a broken whisper, "Joe, Grandfather Adaire gave me a healing. When he held me back there, something beautiful...something wonderful happened." Closing her eyes, she murmured, "I felt so much of my anger and rage, my sense of injustice, dissolve. As he held me, he was filling me with this incredibly beautiful gold light. I saw it flowing out of his hands—I felt it! It was like warm, liquid sunlight, filling me and flushing out the darkness. My fears, my negativity, my rage toward men—I felt it oozing out of my feet, back into Mother Earth, who took it all away from me."

"You feel so soft and good to me," Joe murmured, kissing her hair once more. He felt her arms tighten around him. More than anything, he wanted to love Akiva. To fill her with his heart, his soul by touching her, kissing her and making her one with him.

"Why don't we change clothes," he rasped near her

ear, "and go find that waterfall? I don't know about you, but right now, all I want, Akiva, is you…the beauty of this place…the healing that's going on. I want to love you, gal…want to share my heart, my soul with you…."

Chapter 17

"I'm afraid," Akiva whispered. She sat facing Joe on the grassy bank of the pool beneath the waterfall. She had come and knelt between his thighs, resting her hands on his knees. They had decided to blend with the villagers and were wearing the soft cotton clothing that had been left for them.

Joe heard the waterfall in the background, the scream of monkeys and macaws in the jungle that surrounded this place of unearthly beauty. Although the music around him lifted his spirits, his heart beat hard in his chest as he searched Akiva's unsure eyes. Her hands were cool and damp as he grasped them with his own. The breeze was slight, and lifted some strands of her black hair, which shone with reddish highlights in a ray of noontime sunlight.

"Of what? Me?" he asked in a low tone. He watched as Akiva sat back on her heels. She had taken her shoes off earlier and wriggled her toes luxuriously in the short green grass that edged the bank of the large, shallow pool.

Bending her head, Akiva closed her eyes and concentrated on Joe's warm, strong hands enclosing hers. How much she needed his quiet strength right now! When she finally answered, the words came out low and halting. "...Yes and no... I'm mostly afraid of myself..."

Sliding his hands up her bare arms, he whispered, "Look at me, Akiva." When she lifted her head and opened those glorious golden eyes fraught with shadows, Joe felt hot tears behind his own. He fought them off, because right now, Akiva was completely vulnerable. It was a massive gift, one that touched his heart in a way he'd never felt before. Seeing her lower lip tremble as she gazed at him, he moved his hand caressingly across her proud shoulders. "Whatever it is," he told her in a rasp, "we'll handle it—together. We're a good team, you and I. We proved it in the arena. We trusted one another there with our lives. How can we not trust one another now?" He managed a slight, nervous smile, afraid of saying or doing the wrong thing right now. Afraid that he'd bumble and make an error that would cause her to retreat.

The feel of his strong hands on her shoulders, moving gently down her arms to where her hands were rigidly clasped in her lap, soothed Akiva. She gave a jerky nod in response to his searching question. Joe's gray eyes were wide, and she heard the incredible gentleness in his husky tone, felt him trying to engage and support her, even though he wasn't really aware of what she was afraid of—yet. Unable to hold his lambent gaze, though it made her heart lift with hope, she bowed her head and forced out the words gathering like a lump in her throat.

"Joe...I've never trusted men...white or red...not ever...."

"No wonder. Your father beat you. And then your stepfather.... You had no reason to trust men, Akiva. Anyone with an ounce of brains could understand where you're comin' from on this." He closed his hands around hers. They were so cold!

Seeing the suffering on her face now made Joe want to cry. Akiva was allowing him the privilege of seeing her without any defenses in place, allowing him access to her hurting heart and wounded soul. The love he felt for her was so deep and wide that it stunned even him as he responded emotionally to her needs. Akiva invited him to share a depth of love that Joe had never felt before, or was even aware could exist. But it did, here and now, with her....

"Well," she quavered uncertainly, "I guess you're right. I guess I've been blindly stumbling around all my life without understanding myself."

"Men wounded you and men weren't high on your list of people to trust."

Nodding, Akiva stole a glance at him through her damp lashes. Joe's face was strong and tender looking. His eyes burned with a fire that enveloped her, made her feel strong enough to go on. Joe deserved her honesty. He, more than anyone, did. He'd earned it the hard way: he'd fought in life-and-death circumstances at her side. He'd shown her that he had earned her trust in a way only a warrior could know and honor.

"I have been so angry all my life...angry at men. I hated them for a long time. When I got to Fort Rucker for Apache training, and Major York was breaking us down—or trying to, because we were women and he wanted to see us fail—I just saw red." She blinked and lifted her head, looking over at the waterfall. It was so clean and clear, and she felt so raw inside right now. As the mist from the falling water collected above the pool, a shaft of sunlight struck the myriad droplets and created a rainbow. A rainbow meant much to Akiva. To the Apache nation, it was a sign of grace, of blessing, from the Great Spirit. The shimmering bands of color gave her hope that she could share with Joe what was eating her up alive inside.

"Lucky for me, I had kick-boxing as a positive activity to take the edge off my rage and hatred of men. The way York was pushing us, trying to get us to fail, well, I was ready to lash back. Fortunately, Maya saw the steam building in me and she got me into kick-boxing as an outlet. I took my fear, anger and sense of injustice about what was occurring to all of us there, out on my poor opponents." She managed a clipped smile and pulled her hand from his. Pushing several strands of hair from her face, she placed her fingers across Joe's hand. "I beat the living daylights out of the men who challenged me in the kick-box ring. I *wanted* to hurt them."

Nodding, Joe said quietly, "What Major York did was wrong. He's admitted that now, and he's made amends. So much so that he's given his heart, his life, to Maya. But it didn't help any of you women going through flight school then. I'm glad you went into kick-boxing."

With a ragged sigh, Akiva looked up at him. "It was all a mask, Joe. I was really afraid of men, of what they could do to me if I trusted them. I just couldn't—" Her voice broke. "Oh, I had a few guys, off and on through my life, who wanted a relationship with me, but I froze. I wouldn't let them into my life. I couldn't—I just... couldn't...."

"And with good reason," Joe whispered. He saw the

tears beading on her thick, black lashes. Her lips were parted, and he felt her suffering so acutely that he felt overwhelmed by it, by the sheer torture of what she had carried all her life within her. "I don't know how you managed to reach out to me, gal...." He lifted his hand and grazed her cheek.

Closing her eyes, Akiva absorbed the wonderful pressure of his fingertips upon her flesh. "Every time...every time you touch me, Joe, I feel my heart opening up more and more to you. I feel like you're the sunlight to my dark, dark soul, which has been left freezing in the winter of my wounded heart."

Cocking his head, he studied her closely. Her lower lip was wet with tears that fell silently down her face. "Maybe because we share Indian blood?" he suggested softly. It was hell to sit here with her and not pull her into his arms, for he knew that was what Akiva needed right now. Not raw sex, but love. He wanted to show her his love by holding her, giving her a sense of protection from the world around her. More and more, Joe was realizing the many colors and depths and shades and tones of love. Before, he'd been pretty much like any other guy—he'd equated it with sex. But he was finding out, in the past months with Akiva, that love was like the rainbow shimmering over the pool beside them. It was colorful bands and striations of rich and fragile emotions all combined. And he knew from loving Akiva that he had the emotional capacity to respond to every one of them.

The realization filled him with a stunning awareness. Just as she had the courage to open up to him, share her vulnerability, her fears, her secrets and darkness, he recognized that he had a similar capacity to absorb them all. It left Joe stunned, left him feeling humbled by love itself, for it was so profound and deep that he knew he'd only scratched the surface of it before with other women. Akiva was opening up a whole new, wondrous world to him emotionally.

Akiva sat there wrestling with her fears and the rocketing emotions that were battering her inside. "Yes... your being Indian helps...because we're aware that we're part of spirit, too, Joe. I know you haven't been steeped in our traditions, but I've seen you, time after time at Alpha, use your heart, your intuition with our team...with me...and it helped me begin to open up and trust you. I realized after our confrontation that my real problem was distrust of men, no matter what color their skin was. I know you didn't realize it at the time. You may not now, but you have such goodness and strength within you. For me, it was easy to turn to you. You are like sunlight and I couldn't help but open up to you."

"I think," Joe told her in a husky tone, "that all people are fragile, delicate flowers deep inside. That sometimes we get stomped on by life and nearly destroyed, gal." He reached out and stroked his fingers caressingly along the side of her face, tucking a few strands of hair behind her ear. "I know I don't have the training in Native American traditions you had, and I can see how they've helped you, how they've sustained you in the dark night of your soul. I came from a pretty happy family. My problems were I saw myself comin' from the wrong side of the tracks, and worried that no one would see my abilities, my talents. That they'd put me in a box and never let me prove my worth." He shared a sad smile with her. "I didn't want people to think I was a dumb box of rocks, just because my daddy was poor and a truck driver."

She managed a partial smile and moved her fingers gently across his dark, hairy hand. ''I understand, Joe. I really do. I guess I never saw myself as being a poor, underprivileged Indian kid from the res.''

''You were too busy surviving your father and stepfather,'' Joe rasped, his brow dipping. He saw her try to smile. As she lifted her head, the path of her tears gleamed against her copper skin. How beautiful she looked in that moment! ''Listen, I'm here for you, Akiva. In any way I can,'' he murmured. ''The gift of yourself, your trust, is all I want or will ever need.'' He gestured to the rainbow shimmering above the pool. ''You're my rainbow. Did you know that? You make me feel like a rainbow inside. Every time I see you, my heart races. And when you smile—'' he touched the corners of her mouth with his thumbs ''—I feel like bursting out in song.''

Just the touch sent a shiver of yearning through to the core of her heart and body. Catching his hands in hers, Akiva tilted her head and gazed into his dove-gray eyes. Joe was so open, so accessible, that it gave her the courage to speak of her worst fears and secrets. ''I love the idea of being your rainbow...but I never felt that way inside myself. Joe, I need to tell you the rest of what burdens me.''

''I'm listenin','' he whispered rawly. ''We'll handle it—together.''

Taking a deep breath, Akiva said in a broken tone, ''I was so afraid of men, I never slept with one. I didn't want to. I didn't want to put myself under their control. I couldn't trust my feelings with them, and if I couldn't do that, I wasn't going to sleep with one.''

Gulping, Joe absorbed her halting words laced with so much tortured pain. ''And that's your big secret?'' he asked, meeting her tear-damp eyes. "That you're a virgin?"

Wryly, she said, "Yeah, at twenty-four..."

"There's no shame in that. How can there be? With what happened to you, Akiva, I don't blame you." Joe opened his hands and placed them over hers, adding, "I don't even see how you can open yourself up to me. I'm sitting here stunned by how much I love you, want you, and I'm riding on a wave of happiness just having you here...."

Frowning, Akiva gazed into his eyes. "You mean...it doesn't bother you that I'm not...well, experienced?"

Shrugging, Joe whispered, "A woman's body is sacred, Akiva. It's too bad more boys who masquerade as men don't honor that, or get it." Slipping his fingers through hers, he added in a low voice, "No, it doesn't bother me at all. It scares me a little, because I don't profess to be the world's greatest expert on makin' love. I've got some experience, yes...but I worry I'll hurt you, or do something to make you retreat from me. I worry that I'll blunder, or cause you pain—and that's the *last* thing I want to do, gal. You're so precious to me, as special as that rainbow out there over the water. I worry about *me,* not you." And the corners of his mouth lifted with sad irony.

"Joe, you would never hurt me. Not ever." Akiva's voice grew raspy with tears. "You never realized it, but the three months at Alpha were some of the best and happiest I've ever experienced. I really looked forward to seeing you every morning...sharing coffee with you at the mess. Having those stolen moments when we were completely alone..." Sniffing, Akiva raised her hands and tried to wipe away her tears. "I was worried that I wouldn't be good enough...that I couldn't please you. Or I wouldn't know how to do it..."

Laughing gently, he opened his arms. "Come here, gal," he murmured huskily.

Akiva moved into his arms. She snuggled against him and rested her head on his shoulder as he held her tightly. A ragged sigh tore from her lips.

"*This* is what I need, Joe. You..."

His heart ached with such love for Akiva, for her brutal honesty and her simplicity, that Joe could do nothing but hold and rock her for a long, long time. They sat there on the bank, the roar of the waterfall behind them and the rainbow glinting in an arc of pale pink, gold, green and lavender colors. All Joe wanted was to share his spirit, his heart with Akiva as he sat there with her in his arms.

In some ways, she was still a hurt little, eight-year-old-girl who had sobbed out her heart in her room after her father had beaten her. Joe couldn't understand how any parent could do that to a child. It was beyond him. Now he was getting a raw taste of what it had done to this magnificent woman whose heart was that of a jaguar, who never quit, who had fought back and survived even when the odds were against her. As he slowly rocked Akiva in his arms, to an ancient rhythm known only to the beating heart of Mother Earth, many awarenesses avalanched upon Joe.

In that time out of time, as the earth seemed to hold her breath, the sun stopped moving and the rainbow—the symbol of their love for one another—became stronger and more colorful, Joe felt his fears of hurting Akiva dissolve. In their wake was the driving, raw need to connect with her heart and share what he felt with her.

As Joe eased Akiva to the ground, the grass soft and

fragrant, like a living blanket beneath them, he smiled tenderly into her face. He saw the gold in her eyes, saw that the darkness was gone. Her lips parted as he eased her onto her back. Her hair cascaded like silk around her, becoming a dark halo about her head as he leaned down to find her mouth.

The moment Joe's mouth brushed hers, Akiva felt some of her fear dissolve. As his tongue tenderly laved her lower lip, she felt more at ease. She concentrated on the sensations, the tingling, the delicious heat moving like a flowing stream from her lips, toward the center of her body, to her swiftly beating heart. As his mouth cherished hers, she became lost in the splendor of golden stars beginning to explode deep within her lower body. It was then that Akiva felt, for the first time, the stirrings of her as a woman who needed her man. Sliding her arms across Joe's broad shoulders, she leaned up and boldly returned his kiss.

Akiva felt Joe's smile across her mouth. His hand moved to her cheek and pushed the curtain of her hair aside. Fingers grazing Akiva's neck and moving slowly down the soft cotton of her shirt, he cupped her small breast. The sensations that sparked as he moved his thumb languidly across the tightening peak of her breast caught her by surprise. It was a delicious feeling, and she moaned and pressed closer, wanting more of the pleasure that he was creating within her.

Heartened by her moan of rapture, Joe lost a little more of his anxiety. Akiva's mouth was soft and bold beneath his. Her breath was becoming chaotic, and she was twisting and turning, obviously enjoying what he was doing to pleasure her. The elation in his heart grew and he became bolder because of his need to show her how much he loved her.

In minutes, Akiva was divested of her top and slacks. She lay on the grass, warmed by the afternoon sunlight, and watched through half-closed eyes as Joe undressed. He was powerfully built, his shoulders broad, his chest deep and darkly haired. Her gaze drifted to his lower body, and she felt her heart quicken. But it wasn't out of fear, it was out of anticipation and a driving need to couple with him, to make them complete and whole.

As he settled beside her, his length against hers, she turned toward him and smiled softly. Easing her fingers upward across his hair-roughened cheek, she whispered, "Why was I so afraid?" and she smiled softly into his stormy eyes.

"I love you, Akiva," Joe rasped against her smiling mouth. "Love never hurts. It can only heal...." And he leaned down and brushed the peak of her hardened nipple with his tongue. Instantly, she responded. Her hands gripped his shoulders, and she gasped in surprise. Taking the nipple into his mouth, Joe suckled her gently. With one arm he brought her strong, writhing body against his. She was moaning with incredible pleasure as he followed his heart's voice and turned off the fear in his head. In that moment, Joe transcended his own dread of hurting Akiva instead of giving her happiness and elation. For the first time, he gave himself free rein, letting his sense of smell, taste and touch tell him what Akiva would enjoy.

The rainbow colors deepened. The sun glowed more strongly in the sky, its rays warm upon them. The music of the water tumbling into the emerald green pool below became part of the rhythmic music and magic as Joe eased her long, curved thighs apart with his knee. As he moved over Akiva, he placed his arm beneath her head. She was smiling up at him, wonder in her eyes, sunlight dancing in their depths, plus a love so clean and clear it went straight to his pounding heart and heated body. Everything was perfect. So perfect. As he smiled down at Akiva, he brought his other hand beneath her wide hips, lifting her just enough to move into her hot slick depths. Moving slowly, he allowed her body to accommodate his entrance. Akiva's eyes widened with surprise, and then her lashes fell. As he gently continued the slow rhythm just within the gates of her moist, feminine core, Joe began to see desire replace her surprise. And when her arms slid around his shoulders, he smiled down at her.

"It feels good, doesn't it?"

Akiva nodded, but couldn't talk now. Her body was beginning to burn, and a hungry desire, like that of a starving jaguar, began to gnaw at her. She was no longer satisfied with Joe's slow entry. Primal knowing took over, and Akiva slid her long legs around his. She arched and pulled him more deeply into her singing body. The world tilted, and she closed her eyes. A soft, ragged sigh issued from her lips as she felt Joe's weight more surely upon her, a warm, safe blanket.

Like the rainbow that shimmered and undulated behind them, Joe established the rhythm Akiva wanted. The burning knot in his lower body quickly magnified, a volcano ready to explode. He heard her soft cries of pleasure, saw the sensuous look on her face. They were linked to one another—one heart beating hard, one body moving and flowing, like the restless beauty of the waterfall plummeting into the emerald waters below. All of nature was embracing them, and all of nature was inside them—connected, heated, throbbing with new, pulsing life.

When the sunlit explosion occurred deep within Akiva's wildly writhing body, it took her by utter surprise.

She gave a sharp cry. Instantly, she arched and froze in Joe's protective arms, her hands opening and closing spasmodically against his back. He seemed to understand what was happening. Cradling her face into his shoulder, he continued to move strongly within her, prolonging the savage pleasure and heat fanning out through her like raw sunlight spilling across the surface of wildly frothing water. Like a million dappling, glistening lights dancing—that was how Akiva felt as she gave Joe the ultimate gift of her body, heart and soul.

Within moments, she felt him tense. His arms became strong bands about her, crushing the breath from her lungs. He groaned like a jaguar claiming his mate. Understanding on a deep, primal level that Joe had just given the gift of himself to her, Akiva clung to him. She tasted the salt of his perspiration on his shoulder as she pressed small kiss after another across his tense flesh. As they lay locked in that timeless moment of heat, passion, love and life, Akiva had never felt so fulfilled, so satiated and at peace with herself, or the world that now hazily intruded upon them in the aftermath.

Joe groaned and rolled off her. He brought Akiva into his arms and they lay on their sides, facing one another. Her skin was slick with perspiration, and he eased the dark hair that clung to her cheek away from her face. Akiva's eyes were half-open, the glorious gold color of dancing sunlight.

"You are my rainbow woman," he told her in a roughened tone. "I love you like I've never loved anyone." Continuing to smooth her mussed hair away from her face, he saw the joy and pleasure in her expression. There was wonderment in Akiva's eyes. And the happiness that exploded through Joe was like a volcano flowing outward, spewing wave after wave of hot lava.

"I...can't talk...only feel," she whispered as she caressed Joe's face. "I love you so much...." And she did, with all the brightness and strength of her heart and soul.

Joe understood. Lying back on the grass, he pulled Akiva close to him. Her long, strong body flowed against him like water flowed against a rock. In many ways, he realized, he was a rock to Akiva—stable and steady, someone she could rely on, someone who would be there to cushion her moments of anger and hurt, but also to share her joy and laughter.

Inwardly, Joe knew that their relationship would be fraught with highs and lows as Akiva worked on healing that old wound deep within her. He'd already experienced it at Alpha: one day she would reach out to him, tentative and unsure, and the next showed him that freezing glare of anger that bubbled so close to the surface. In many ways, he'd been her whipping post, but he hadn't taken her mood shifts and swings negatively. Because he loved her, he could tolerate them, and now, understanding where they had come from, he had no problem at all absorbing her darker moments. In the end, that wound would be cleansed by his love for her, and would one day cease to exist. As he leaned down and pressed soft kisses to the top of her head, which was resting against his chest, Joe smiled to himself.

Yes, he knew he could give Akiva what she needed in order to heal. And she, without knowing it, was healing him of his past, too. Joe was realizing he had nothing to prove to anyone. Over the months of working with Akiva, he had lost the drive to impress her. His past habits had dissolved, freeing him up as never before.

He sighed euphorically. The sunlight warmed him, the breeze softly touched his damp body to dry him. The grass was springy and embracing beneath his naked flesh. And best of all, Akiva's long, sinuous form lay like a warm blanket against his. Life didn't get any better than this, and Joe absorbed it all.

Akiva smiled softly as she sat between Joe's thighs. He was leaning on an old log on the bank, overlooking the waterfall. As Joe's hands came to rest on her shoulders, she tipped her head back against his strong body and sighed. The sun had shifted, although she wasn't aware of time passing. The rainbow was still there, but faintly, because the sun's rays now slanted at a different angle. It didn't matter; the rainbow burning brightly within her body more than made up the difference.

The songs of birds, the music of the water splashing into the green depths of the pool made her heart mushroom with such joy that Akiva opened her eyes and looked up at Joe. His hair was ruffled, that one precocious lock falling over his broad, smooth forehead. He smiled down at her wordlessly, his gray eyes burning with love—for her. Lips parting, Akiva whispered, "You are my sun. The Apache people worship the sun, for it gives not only light, but life, my darling. You have brought light into the darkness of my heart and soul. Your warmth, your love, has allowed me to let go of the past and believe there is a better way to live." Akiva's fingers slipped upward over Joe's strongly corded neck to his cheek. "You've given me my life back, beloved. You gave it with your love. You had such patience with me...."

Capturing her long, artistic fingers, Joe kissed them gently, then brought her hand down to her breast and held it there. "I'll be your sun," he said in a husky tone, "if you'll be my rainbow. Fair enough?"

Laughing softly, Akiva leaned down and kissed his hand. "Fair enough."

As she lifted her head and stared out across the pool, she was suffused with a joy she'd never known before. Words were inadequate. The late afternoon mirrored that feeling in all respects, for she knew Mother Earth loved her children and would talk to them in symbolic ways. Right now, Akiva and Joe were one with her, and one with each other. The moment of integration was magical and made Akiva feel like a wondrous child, wide-eyed and as open as that fragile flower Joe had compared her to earlier.

Brushing her cheek against his hand, Akiva could only smile and feel the continuous joy that ran through her like a wild, tumultuous river. She was free. Really free, for the first time in her life. And Joe's love for her had been the key. He'd taken her edginess, her hardened rage, and transformed it patiently simply by loving her and seeing who she was beneath all that armor she wore.

"I might be a warrior," she told Joe quietly, "but I'm a woman first. And I want to share and explore that part of me with you. Always...."

Reaching down, Joe slipped his arms around Akiva. She sighed and tipped her head back to rest on his proffered shoulder. Brushing her cheek with kisses, he murmured, "You're the bravest, gutsiest woman I've ever known, gal. You have the heart of a jaguar, the soul of a rainbow. I just hope and pray I can always do right by you...."

Opening her eyes, Akiva drowned in Joe's burning gray ones. "You will, because you love me...and I will become more the rainbow for you over time, and less the warrior."

Smiling gently, Joe kissed her brow. "You'll always be a warrior for those who need you to be that, Akiva. In the quiet moments, alone, you'll share the rainbow with me. It doesn't get any better than that. Not ever..."

Epilogue

Akiva sat down with Joe in the planning room at the Black Jaguar Base. With them were Maya and Dane, Cam Anderson, Morgan Trayhern and his assistant, Mike Houston. An aide shut the door to the small but well lit room and quietly left them alone. The table was oval and made out of highly polished mahogany with a golden grain.

Maya sat at one end, Dane at the other. Akiva was glad Joe was at her side, as she noted the seriousness in everyone's faces. She and Joe had returned just a week ago from the beautiful Village of the Clouds. And now they were preparing to return to Alpha and run it. Joe cocked his head and gave her a wink. She smiled slightly.

''I'm glad everyone could make it,'' Maya said, opening a file folder marked Top Secret. ''We're here to initiate the second thrust of a three-pronged assault on the Mexican drug trade. Thus far, our insurgence into southern Mexico, into Javier Rios's area, has been an unqualified success.'' Maya gave Akiva a warm look and then shifted her gaze to Joe.

''Akiva and Joe are doing an admirable job at Alpha. We're sending them back with two Boeing Apache Longbows, plus the Blackhawk they presently have. They will also have a civilian helicopter that they'll use at their discretion, to fly to the spook base west of them for any supplies they might need. Things will continue as before there.''

Maya smiled a jaguar smile. ''The Pentagon is constantly eavesdropping on Rios's communications. He sends a lot of satellite transmissions, and the Pentagon is taping them all. To say he's upset about Akiva and Joe dodging his clutches and leaving his arena is putting it mildly. Good job, gang. I'm proud of you. We've got him unsettled. The helicopter you stole has never been reported to the police or anyone else. They're writing it off. His son, Luis, is buying a new one, only this time it's a Russian Kamov Black Shark.''

Akiva scowled. ''Great. We're back to square one. The Apache won't be able to pick up the radar signature on it.''

''Don't be griping too much,'' Maya teased darkly. ''We just found out on a Sat Intel that the two new drug lords moving into Peru to take over after the last one I dusted off are buying four new Kamovs to replace the ones we blew out of the sky that day.''

''Ouch,'' Joe muttered. ''Looks like everyone is gonna have their hands full.''

''Yep,'' Maya sighed, ''business as usual.''

''Druggies keep it interesting,'' Dane said in a dry, humorless voice.

''At least,'' Mike Houston put in on an upbeat note,

"you are now getting replacements here at BJS to give your original women pilots some downtime and rest."

Nodding, Maya said, "Yes, that's true. We have ten new Apache pilots, male and female, coming on temporary duty to us. But the pressure on my original pilots to train them under combat conditions provides *more* stress, not less right now, Mike. About three months after the initial training period, the pressure will start to ease. But not until then."

Morgan brightened and folded his large hands on the table, his own copy of the top secret file beneath them. "I've authorized the army to send down six of their best instructor pilots to work with you, Maya."

Her brows raised. "Oh?"

"Yes." He smiled slightly, his hair black and silver beneath the washed-out light of the fluorescent fixture above the table. "I talked the army chief of staff into seeing it my way. You need to train in a group of instructors who will know the lay of the land down here and what these Apache pilots are getting into. They're coming down here to look, gauge and then set up another program at Fort Rucker that will mimic what is being done here. I see this plan as an interim step. Right now, you're on combat footing. You don't need to be stretched even further training these pilots. You need something in between, and I think we've got a fix on it."

"Good," Maya murmured. "We need all the help we can get."

Dane leaned forward and said, "This is good news, Morgan. Thanks. Maybe, if Maya approves it, I can work with that IP team. I'm pretty good at making up charts, blueprints and templates."

"Say no more," Maya muttered with a grin, "it's all

yours, Major York. I've got enough to do, thank you very much.''

Akiva nodded. Because she'd had a taste of being a C.O., she understood as never before the strain, the demands and stresses on the major. And her admiration for Maya skyrocketed even more. Akiva only hoped that she could juggle her tasks half as well as Maya could.

She felt Joe's hand sneak beneath the table where they were sitting. His fingers moved over hers, which were resting on her thigh. Giving him a glance, she saw him smile slightly, his gray eyes warm with love for her. It was as if he was reading her mind and feeling her worry about her job as C.O. at Alpha. With him at her side, she knew she could do it.

Dane rubbed his hands together, flashing everyone a triumphant grin. ''Excellent. Thank you, Major.''

''You're welcome, Major. You're a real glutton for punishment, if you ask me. But—'' Maya sighed and looked down the table at her husband ''—better you than me. Thank you.''

Dane nodded and gave her a slight, gallant nod of his head. ''My pleasure, Major.''

Maya snorted and gave him a narrowed look that was filled with playfulness. Everyone at the table tittered. And then they grew solemn once again as she flipped to the next order of business on her agenda.

''Okay, let's move on to Chief Cam Anderson's mission.'' Maya looked down the table at Cam, whose copper-colored hair hung in heavy curls around her proud shoulders as she smiled tentatively back.

Pages were shuffled as Maya made sure she had all Cam's orders in front of her before she continued. ''Now, I've talked to the new president of Mexico, Alejandro Feliz. He basically got elected on a reform platform, promising to wipe out the connection between the major drug families in his country, clean up the police department, which is being paid off big time by the drug families, and generally scrub house. I talked to his secretary of defense, and they both said they want our help.''

''*How* do they want our help?'' Morgan demanded in a heavy voice. ''Payoffs from druggies are legendary in their country. We've tried working with them before, but it puts our people at too high a risk. You can't trust anyone. The drug families have moles in every local, regional and federal police agency.''

Shrugging, Maya said, ''That's true. But President Feliz says he's going to make a clean sweep. At first I was skeptical, but after two phone conversations with him, I'm convinced he means business. He knows he's got a dysfunctional country that's run by the shadow legacy of the drug families. And he knows the only way to clean it up is from the inside out.'' Maya shot a glance at Cam, who was dressed in her black flight uniform. ''The president asked for our help. He wants to know how to create a black ops situation with his elite air force helicopter units so that they can fly into areas where drugs such as marijuana are being grown, and drop the troops off and let them destroy the fields. This is a big deal,'' Maya told them.

Houston nodded. ''It is. Mexico has a lot of mountainous agricultural areas where marijuana is being grown alongside other legal crops. Many farmers in northern Mexico, especially along the Baja coast, are trading in their traditional crops for marijuana. It pays them a hell of a lot more than potatoes, yams or corn can.''

''That's right,'' Dane murmured. ''The economy in Mexico sucks, and people are struggling to survive. Raising and selling marijuana is an easy way to make a buck.

The U.S. border at San Diego is less than an hour away, so it's a real easy proposition for them.''

''Well,'' Maya growled, ''I'm not wasting one of my key pilots by sending her after some dirt-poor farmers in Mexico. The president is gonna have to deal with that particular problem. Cam is going on temporary duty to Tijuana, Mexico, where she's going to be training an elite helicopter squadron to go in and begin to interdict drug flights that are heading north over the U.S. border. It doesn't matter if it's cocaine, marijuana or whatever. Her job is to teach these Mexican pilots interdiction routines we've learned and perfected here in Peru.''

''Do they have Apaches?'' Akiva asked.

Maya shook her head. ''No, but the U.S. Army, thanks to Morgan's work, is going to 'loan' four original Apache models to the Mexican pilots. Right now, eight pilots are going to be graduating in about another week from Fort Rucker. This is a top secret operation. The drug families haven't got wind of any of this yet...but they will.''

''And my job,'' Cam said in a clear, firm voice, ''is to teach these guys the ins and outs of air interdiction? How to turn these flights back into Mexican airspace?''

''Correct.'' Maya's eyes glittered. ''Just like here, you won't be authorized to fire upon any civilian fixed-wing or rotor aircraft. I don't want those boys getting trigger happy. The moment one of them fires a cannon or rocket at some civilian aircraft, whether it's carrying drugs or not, all hell will break loose. You're going to teach the fine art of sky chicken and other wonderful assault tools that we've created down here at BJS over the last three years.''

Cam smiled grimly. ''It will be a pleasure.''

Morgan scowled. ''I've been running into a lot of prejudice against women by the Mexicans. Their country is very backward about women being equals,'' he warned. Looking at Cam, he added, ''The eight pilots now going through Fort Rucker are being given a quick shakedown on women being equals in the cockpit, but I can't guarantee that it's going to be a picnic for you, Cam.''

''No,'' Houston warned in a gravelly tone as he stared at Cam. ''You need to know going into this that you're going to be locking horns with all of 'em. They aren't going to want to take you seriously. If you were a man, no problem. But you're a woman, and unfortunately, in their country, women stay home as housewives and mothers. They don't fly combat helicopters.''

''So,'' Maya summed up, ''Cam, you're going into a highly charged prejudicial situation and you're going to have to get firm, put up strong boundaries and make them do it your way or no way.''

Cam smiled slightly. ''I'd like to think I'm a steel hand in a velvet glove, Major.''

''I know you are,'' Maya said. ''That's why you got chosen for this backbreaking TAD.'' She slid Akiva a look. ''If I sent Akiva, she'd have these guys running and screaming in eight different directions because she doesn't put up with any kind of male prejudice toward a woman.''

Akiva had the good grace to flush. ''That's true,'' she murmured, her mouth drawing upward.

Maya laughed briefly. ''Akiva doesn't suffer second-class citizenship at all. Nor should any of us,'' she said, losing her smile. Her emerald eyes narrowed on Cam. ''You have a lot of diplomacy, and even though you're strong, you can bend without breaking. Your main job is interdiction. We've got to start cutting down on the hundreds of drug flights a week, originating from all over

Mexico. We've got to stop them from crossing the U.S. border.''

Nodding, Cam said, ''I feel strongly I can do this, Major. And I'm appreciative that you're letting me.''

Joe grinned across the table at Cam. ''Just kick butt and take names like you do down here,'' he chuckled.

''Humph,'' Akiva groused, ''if those eight didn't square away pronto, I'd hang their hides off the Apache's blades.''

''Precisely my point,'' Maya said, as she looked at Akiva and then over at Cam, who was smiling. ''I need a woman pilot who doesn't want to do that first. But as a last resort...''

Everyone chuckled.

Leaning back in her chair, Maya gave Joe and Akiva a thoughtful look. ''And I have a happy announcement to make—one you can spread like gossip around the squadron.'' Maya knew that any news flew around the BJS like wildfire, so it was an inside joke. ''Joe?''

Akiva frowned and looked at Joe. He smiled nervously and stood up after releasing her hand beneath the table. Smoothing down his black uniform, he dug into his left pocket.

''I thought this was a good place to share something happy with ya'll,'' he told them. Digging deeper into his pocket, he found and pulled out a small gold box. His heart speeded up with anticipation. Akiva gave him a quizzical look. Grinning uncertainly down at her, he said, ''This is a surprise, gal...''

''I guess so,'' Akiva murmured.

Everyone at the table chuckled indulgently again.

''There,'' Joe said with relief. He was so nervous that he was fumbling with the small box. Finally, he got it open. ''This is for you, Akiva...an engagement ring.''

He placed the open box on the table in front of her. "The major helped me pick it out in Cuzco last week, after we got back. It's gold topaz, pink tourmaline, purple amethyst and green emerald put into a channel setting, so it's flush with the gold of the ring. That way, you can wear it...if you want...and it won't catch on your clothes or anything." Mouth dry, he sat down and pushed the box a little closer to the edge of the table where Akiva was sitting. Placing his hand behind her chair, his arm around her shoulders, he swallowed hard and began.

"I'm askin' you to be my wife, Akiva. When the time's right, gal, I'd like to tie the knot with you. Major Stevenson has already given us the green light to fly north, to our families, to have the wedding." Searching her eyes, he saw shock and then such warmth in them. "Well? I know this is a little surprisin' to you and all...but I thought this was the right place to ask you...with all your other family bein' here...." His heart raced as Akiva stared down in shock at the proffered set of rings.

Joe watched with trepidation and anxiety as Akiva lifted her hands and touched the set. One was a plain gold wedding band; the other, similar band was set with seven small squares of expensive gemstones.

"I chose the design because it reminded me of you, gal," he admitted in a strangled tone. Shrugging, Joe looked around at the people in the room. They were all grinning, expectation and happiness clearly written in their expressions. Heartened, he added, "I know you had a dark, stormy beginning in your life, your childhood."

Akiva looked at him. Hot tears filled her eyes as she took out the engagement ring and held it gently between her fingers.

"And I just wanted you to know how much of a rainbow you are to me,'' he added thickly, his voice turning emotional. ''You color my life with such beauty. The way you see the world through those sunlit eyes of yours makes me feel like I'm flyin', gal.'' He lifted his hand and enclosed hers as she held the ring. ''Would you do me the honor of being my partner? My best friend? My wife?''

Choking back tears, Akiva melted beneath his pleading tone, which was raw with feeling. No one had ever loved her as Joe did. Akiva was constantly amazed by his thoughtfulness, his sensitivity toward her and her needs. It was as if he could read her mind and her healing heart. ''Y-yes, you know I will....''

Reaching over, she threw her arms around his shoulders and embraced him. Burying her face against his neck, she started to sob. Akiva couldn't help herself. Joe brought out everything good and kind within her. As his arms wrapped around her, she heard the room burst into shouts, laughter and clapping. The joy that swirled around her and Joe in that moment made Akiva feel giddy. She was overflowing with so much happiness that she didn't know what to do except feel his goodness and love overwhelm her.

Maya rose, a smile lingering on her mouth. ''Congratulations, Akiva and Joe. We couldn't be happier for you. You *deserve* one another.''

Sniffing, Akiva lifted her head as Joe raised her left hand and slid the engagement ring onto her finger. Even in the fluorescent lights it sparkled and scintillated as she moved her hand slightly. A rainbow...she was *his* rainbow in life. What a wonderful thing to be for another person. Leaning over, Akiva placed a quick kiss on his mouth.

''Thank you,'' she murmured softly, tears drifting

down her cheeks. "I'll try to be more a rainbow than a thunderstorm in your life, Joe."

"But it's the rain from the thunderstorm that creates the rainbow," Joe reminded her softly.

Everyone laughed. Akiva turned and looked at her friends. Their eyes were warm and she knew in her heart they were truly happy for her and Joe. Cam, who sat across from her, was self-consciously wiping the tears from her forest-green eyes. The way her lips were pulled into a smile made Akiva wince inwardly. She knew of Cam's own unhappy past. And more than anything, she wished happiness for her, for not much good had followed Cam through her twenty-five years of hardscrabble life.

Joe rose to his feet and pulled Akiva's chair back so that she could stand. Everyone came around the table, shook hands and congratulated them. Maya stood back, her fists resting languidly on her hips, her smile wide.

As Morgan joined Maya, she looked up at him. "Well, let's see," she said conspiratorially, "Jenny Wright is marrying Matt Davis, the mercenary who came down here with her. Ana has married Jake and they work here with us. Now, Joe and Akiva. Looks like we're on a roll, eh?"

Grinning, Morgan said, "Marriages forged in the fires of hell always grow into heaven. I know. It happened to me. I guess my people at Perseus are going to follow my lead," he agreed in a low tone, a smile playing across his mouth as he watched Akiva with Joe.

"Hmm, like our own," Maya murmured as Dane came to stand with them at the end of the table. She watched as Mike opened the door and everyone else began to file out of the room. Soon the four of them were alone.

"I'm your heaven," Dane reminded her archly, his

grin confident and cocky as he dropped his arm across her shoulder and gave her a quick embrace.

"Oh? So I'm your hell?"

"Ouch...no! I didn't mean it that way...."

Morgan chuckled. "Considering you two were arch enemies when he came down here, I'd say whatever hell you had between you is long gone, and you're both in heaven, from the looks of it." His eyes glinted knowingly as he surveyed them.

"Love takes working on a day at a time," Maya murmured.

Dane kissed his wife's hair and then whispered, "Yes, and I love every second of it with you."

"You're such a romantic, York." She jabbed him playfully in the ribs. "And so full of it."

Houston chuckled and joined them. "I think all of us have pretty good marriage partners." His eyes brightened. "Did I tell you Ann is pregnant again? We've got number two coming along in about six months."

Stunned, Morgan looked at him. "Congratulations. Does my wife know?"

"Oh, yeah," Mike chortled. "Laura was the *first* to know. Your wife may not work at Perseus, but she knows *everything.*"

"That's true," Morgan said, his brows dipping, "and I'm always the last to know."

Dane gave his wife a warm look and kept his arm around her. In this room, away from prying eyes, he could show his affection for Maya. Out there on the base, he couldn't, due to military regulations. "So, you're going to be a father two times over. Congratulations, Mike." He offered his hand to the man.

Grinning proudly, Mike shook it. "Thanks, Dane."

"Is Ann happy about it?" Morgan asked.

"Oh, yeah! She wants a bunch of 'em. The more the merrier. She's been a flight surgeon so long that she really missed her mothering years, so she's makin' up for it now." He smiled softly. "And I like being a dad to these kids we're having. Nothing is more satisfying."

"Humph," Morgan groused good-naturedly, "wait until they hit their terrible twos and then the hormone strike in their teen years. That's when you want to give them away."

Laughing, Maya said, "Oh, Morgan, you love your four kids through all their ups and downs! I think you and Laura both have broad enough shoulders to ride through those little tempests in a teapot."

"True," Morgan murmured, offering his hand to Mike. "Got a name picked out yet?"

Houston shook his head. "Naw, we're workin' on that right now. Anne's got about fifty baby name books spread all over the house. She's makin' lists, and I'm sure I'll have a ton of 'em to look at when I get home."

"Somehow," Maya said wryly, "you get through it and love every moment of it with her."

Having the good grace to flush, Houston stuck his hands in the pockets of his dark blue chinos. "Guilty as charged. I like having a life partner." He threw a look over his shoulder toward the open door. "Joe and Akiva are gonna have the same kind of marriage we have. A working partnership based on mutual respect and love. It doesn't get any better than that."

Maya slid her arm around her husband's waist and gave him a look of open affection, something she had to be careful not to do among the squadron personnel. "Akiva needed someone like Joe. He's going to take good care of her. She's very wounded in some ways, but I can already see the changes he's helped her to make."

''Yeah,'' Houston said, impressed, ''she's lost a lot of that tough armor she was wearin' like a good friend. I think you're right—Joe is going to be her safe place where she can let down, just be, and find out that some men are trustworthy, after all.'' He grinned, pleased with himself. ''Like us. We're great role models for men.''

Snorting, Maya said, ''Isn't *that* the truth? Frankly, I'd like to shoot all the rest and put them out of their misery and clone you guys. Women would be a lot better off.''

The room was filled with a raucous round of laughter.

Morgan shook his head. ''Getting serious for a moment, Maya, how do you think Chief Anderson is going to get along on this mission?''

Leaning languidly against Dane's tall, strong frame, Maya murmured, ''Cam has some problems. She's still emotionally wounded from the time we were shot down.''

''Yes,'' Dane agreed, worried. ''Cam thinks she abandoned Maya to the drug lord. She didn't. She made the correct tactical decision. Maya was unconscious and there was no way Cam could have carried her into that jungle. They'd both have been captured if she hadn't made a run for it on her own. But Cam isn't convinced of that, even now. I see it every day, in small ways around here.''

''Yeah,'' Maya sighed. ''She's developed into a mother hen, smothering her chicks. I've had a couple of talks with her about this, but it's like she's trying to make sure no one on her watch or under her wing gets hurt.''

''Well,'' Morgan said, ''that's pure folly. If she's in command, things can happen out there.''

''I know, I know. But that's a cross she bears and takes with her on this mission.'' Maya frowned. ''I just hope that she doesn't get in trouble with it. Mexican men aren't exactly thrilled about equal rights for women. They aren't going to take kindly to a woman being their boss."

"Yeah," Mike said, "I can see there's going to be hell to pay on that front. But you wouldn't have chosen Cam if she didn't have what it takes to make this a successful mission."

Maya nodded and glanced around at the men. "Sometimes you put an officer in charge who doesn't have all the job skills in place, and hope that the mission will train and teach them. This is the case with Cam. She has the abilities. It's just a question of whether or not she'll pull out these tools and use them or knee-jerk back because of this wound."

"All we can hope for," Dane told Morgan, "is that she'll grow into the mission. Cam has that potential."

"Well, with those Mexican pilots," Maya growled, "she's gonna have her hands full. I just hope one of them is a little less Neanderthal and a little more forward looking and thinking. If there's one out of the eight, then Cam has a chance. If not, then her mission objective is doomed to fail."

As Akiva and Joe walked across the roughened black lava surface within the hollow echo of the cave, they shared a smile with one another. Joe saw her lift her left hand once again, to look at her sparkling engagement ring.

"You like it, gal?"

"You know I do." Sighing, Akiva tossed her head and gave him a soft smile. "It was a beautiful surprise, Joe."

Wriggling his thick brows, he gave her an elfin grin. "I like surprising you. You deserve nice surprises. You had enough of the other kind."

Losing her smile, she gave him a warm, longing look.

"You're the nicest surprise I've ever had, Joe Calhoun. I always thought life was going to treat me rough, like it always had, but you walked into my life and turned me upside down and inside out."

"Give yourself credit," he said as they slowed to allow an electric car carrying supplies pass by them. "You took me in stride. That took a lotta courage." Around them, the cave was like a hive of busy bees, the activity nonstop. Voices echoed mutely throughout the hollow area.

Trailing her fingers through black strands of hair that had wafted across her lower face, Akiva said, "I realized my problem was distrust of men, not just Anglos, and you helped bring that awareness to me. Once I realized that, I started growing because somewhere in my soul, I knew I could trust you."

"You trusted on blind faith knowing," Joe whispered, giving her a tender smile. How he ached to touch Akiva as they continued their walk back into the cave recesses. But he couldn't. Not now, at least.

"Yes...yes, I did." Akiva walked closely enough so that her arm brushed against his momentarily. "And I'm going to keep on trusting you, Joe—with my life and my heart."

At her words, Joe reached out and gripped her long fingers and gave them a gentle squeeze.

"Forever, gal. Forever."

* * * * *

Look out for Lindsay McKenna's next
brand-new MORGAN'S MERCENARIES story—
The Heart Beneath
will be on the shelves in September 2003
from Silhouette Special Edition.

Turn the page for a sneak preview…

The Heart Beneath

by

Lindsay McKenna

Lieutenant Wes James studied the stranger as he came to a stop before him and Lieutenant Callie Evans. The man was tall and carried himself like an ex-military officer. Wes would recognize that bearing in anyone, whether in uniform or not.

''Yes, sir?'' Wes began. ''How can I help you?''

''I'm Morgan Trayhern,'' he said, his voice deep and shaken. ''Are you two part of the earthquake rescue team?''

''Yes, sir, we are,'' Wes said, and quickly introduced himself and Callie.

''My wife, Laura, is somewhere in that collapsed hotel,'' he began, his voice breaking. Battling back tears, he rasped, ''I'd left her five minutes earlier, to go down to the hotel bar and meet an old friend for drinks.'' Rubbing his dirty, unshaved face, Morgan closed his eyes for a moment. When he opened them again, he looked directly at Callie. ''When the quake hit, everything just exploded around us. I made it out the front door before...before it collapsed.'' Morgan turned and looked at the fourteen-story heap of concrete and steel that was stacked like broken gray pancakes.

''You were lucky, Mr. Trayhern,'' Callie said soothingly.

Wes frowned. ''Wait a minute...you're *the* Morgan Trayhern? You were in the Marine Corps?''

''Yes, that's right, Lieutenant James.''

Eyes widening, Wes glanced over at Callie. ''You remember him, don't you?'' Morgan Trayhern was a part of Corps history, because of his role in the Vietnam War. ''He's a living legend among us....'' Wes felt his heart contract for the man, who had obviously been digging and hunting for his missing wife since the earthquake occurred. He pulled a canteen from his web belt. ''Here, sir. You must be thirsty. Have some.''

Gratefully, Morgan took the canteen and drank deeply, then returned it.

''What floor was your wife on, Mr. Trayhern?'' Callie asked, her heart filled with anguish for the man she felt she knew well, after learning about him in Corps history.

''The fourteenth floor, Lieutenant Evans. Why? Does it make a difference?''

Nodding, Callie said, ''Yes, sir, it often can. As these floors pancake on top of one another, most survivors are found on the upper floors, because the crushing weight lower down is so intense.'' She saw hope ignite in his murky gray eyes. Holding up her hand, she added, ''I can't guarantee you she's alive, sir, but it's hopeful. Okay?''

''It sounds good to me, Lieutenant. I've been digging through that rubble all night, calling out for her. So far I haven't heard her....'' He choked on a sob.

''Voices don't carry well through the rubble, sir, so don't take that as a good or bad sign,'' Callie said softly. She patted his shoulder gently. ''Why don't you rest for a while here with Lieutenant James? Let me and my dog start the first grid search that Lieutenant James has prepared.''

Morgan shook his head. ''Rest? When my wife might be alive?'' He wiped his reddened eyes. ''No...I'll keep hunting till I know...for sure...one way or another. I won't leave her up there alone. I need her. I love her and I won't desert her now....''

Callie gave him a sympathetic look that she hoped spoke volumes to his torn spirit. Giving Wes a heartfelt glance, she pulled on her thick, protective gloves and said, ''I'll see you after I'm done with the first grid.''

''Be careful up there,'' Wes warned in a low tone. ''The aftershocks are almost as bad as the original trembler.'' Suddenly Wes was afraid for her. His heart ached, knowing he could lose her just as he had lost a loved one in the past. He wanted to protect Callie. He wanted to reach out, grip her shoulder before she went off to climb the dangerous rubble, but he couldn't...not under the circumstances.

Their first priority was finding Laura Trayhern. And Wes believed they *would* find her. He only hoped it wouldn't be too late—for Morgan and Laura. Or for him and Callie....

* * * *

Don't forget The Heart Beneath
will be on sale in September 2003.

Dad by Choice by Marie Ferrarella
20th June 2003

Cassidy's Kids by Tara Taylor Quinn
18th July 2003

Married to the Boss by Lori Foster
18th July 2003

For the Sake of a Child by Stella Bagwell
15th August 2003

Prescription: Baby by Jule McBride
15th August 2003

The Detective's Dilemma by Arlene James
19th September 2003

Formula: Father by Karen Hughes
19th September 2003

Billion Dollar Bride by Muriel Jensen
17th October 2003

Her Best Friend's Baby by Vicki Lewis Thompson
17th October 2003

Guarding Camille by Judy Christenberry
21st November 2003

The Toddler's Tale by Rebecca Winters
21st November 2003

A Dad at Last by Marie Ferrarella
19th December 2003

Maitland Maternity

MAITLAND/GEN/bV2

THE COLTONS ARE BACK!

The Coltons—
When this most talked about dynasty is threatened, only family, privilege and the power of love can protect them!

Look out for these wonderful spin-off stories:

WHITE DOVE'S PROMISE by Stella Bagwell
August 2003 - Silhouette Special Edition

THE COYOTE'S CRY by Jackie Merritt
September 2003 - Silhouette Special Edition

WILLOW IN BLOOM by Victoria Pade
October 2003 - Silhouette Special Edition

A COLTON FAMILY CHRISTMAS
by Judy Christenberry, Linda Turner
and Carolyn Zane
November 2003 - Silhouette Books 3 in1